Don't point th

Do not trouble to worry whodunnit – almost everyone dunnit, including two or three governments, a picture-restorer, an almost-royal personage, a blind car-bodymaker, Charlie's manservant, who (unlike Jeeves) carries brass knuckles and a Luger, and especially that Mrs Spon.

All seven deadly sins – and a few of more recent invention – take place first in a London flat, then on a Texas millionaire's rancho, and wind up down a certain hole in North West Lancashire. If you could breed a P.G. Wodehouse novel to a James Bond thriller, you might expect something comparable to *Don't Point That Thing at Me*.

Winner of the John Creasey Memorial Award, 1974. Sunday Telegraph 'Crime Book of the Year'.

Ian Fleming and Dostoevsky have nothing interesting in common. Dostoevsky and Dashiell Hammett have: the understanding that conscience is integral to the crime story proper as against the mere thriller. This is the factor that makes Kyril Bonfiglioli's first novel of special interest.

Times Literary Supplement

Although the style of Kyril Bonfiglioli's debut may not appeal to every thriller addict, harsh as it is at times, the plot and action more than hold their own . . . Murders, and much more, abound to make a normal life so boring when one reaches the last page. *Financial Times*

Among the many promising newcomers to murder and mayhem my most enjoyable find is Kyril Bonfiglioli. His picturesque tale of a rich and wicked art dealer who steals a Goya for a richer and wickeder Texan is exciting, moving and very, very funny. *Sunday Telegraph*

Kyril Bonfiglioli has written a superb, zany thriller which cheered me up after 'flu. The style is a homage to and a slight imitation of P.G. Wodehouse – and a very good imitation. Art-dealer, villain-about-Piccadilly, plays Wooster, and a thug called Jock Strapp is Jeeves, always ready with just the right brand of tea, whisky and fisticuffs . . . A fast-moving, hilarious, sarcastic thriller with a marvellous drive in a white Rolls down to Texas. *Susan Hill, The Listener*

After you with the pistol

Aided by his most trusty thug, the one-fanged, monocular, knuckle-dustered Jock, Charlie is coerced into a plot to assassinate a Very Important Person Indeed, undergoes an intensive course at a college whose syllabus is quite unlike that of Vassar, entangled in a conspiracy which threatens to split a large chink in the Bamboo Curtain, and becomes the terrified owner of the costliest baby powder in the world.

As if this were not enough, Charlie gives his reluctant benison to a Giorgione painting, sticks a Rembrandt etching in a safe place, acquires a Rouault gouache without actually stealing it, sees something horrid in a Chinese dentist's office and performs Actual Bodily Harm on a Stipendiary Magistrate.

Behind the shifting back-cloth lurks the dread shadow of Colonel Blucher and the frightful threat to Charlie of betrayal not only by his wife but also by his hypochondriac canary.

Something nasty in the woodshed

A witty irreverent gem of a book which mustn't be missed.

Daily Telegraph

Nice and Nasty . . . (There's a delightful ear-nailing episode).

New Statesman

A cast of eccentrics ranging from a depraved old peer who offers a lesson in seduction to a giggling don strong on Satanist revivals. The result is hilarious.

The Guardian

Kyril Bonfiglioli

'By an odd coincidence' Charlie Mortdecai affords us more than a glimpse of his creator, Kyril Bonfiglioli. Writing in the 1970's, Bonfiglioli described himself as 'about the same height and weight as Charlie Mortdecai . . . with similar tastes and talents'. They also shared the same profession, art dealing; yet Bonfiglioli assured us that 'there the resemblance ends, for he . . . never killed anyone in his life'.

Bonfiglioli was born in 1928 of an English mother and Italo-Slovene father. Spending his early days in Eastbourne and later five years in the army, Bonfiglioli was a Balliol man and proud of it. Although he claimed to share the late W.C. Fields 'fondness' of children, he was twice married and had several of his own. Latterly he lived in Ireland, 'where they are tolerant of idiots', and then Jersey, where the third of these novels is set.

Bonfiglioli claimed to be 'abstemious in all things except drink, food, tobacco and talking' and to be 'loved and respected by all who know him slightly'. He died in Jersey in 1985.

Bonfiglioli's historical novel *All the Tea in China*, featuring the escapades of one of Charlie Mortdecai's early-Victorian ancestors, is also available from Black Spring Press, as is the previously unpublished *The Great Mortdecai Moustache Mystery*, which has been completed by Craig Brown. Soon to follow will be *The Mortdecai ABC, A Kyril Bonfiglioli Reader*, edited by his widow Margaret Bonfiglioli, including letters, short stories, editorials, illustrations and anecdotes.

Don't point that thing at me

After you with the pistol

Something nasty in the woodshed

Kyril Bonfiglioli

The Mortdecai Trilogy

Black Spring Press

The Mortdecai Trilogy first published in 1991 by Black Spring Press
Reprinted 1991, 1992, 1995, 1997, 1999

Black Spring Press Ltd
126 Cornwall Road
LONDON SE1 8TQ

British Library Cataloguing in Publication data
Bonfiglioli, Kyril
    The Mortdecai Trilogy
    I. Title
    823.914 [F]

    ISBN 0 948238 11 9

Designed by Phil Baines
Phototypeset by Selectmove Limited
Printed by The Guernsey Press Company Limited

Contents

Don't point that thing at me

The epigraphs are all by Robert Browning, except one, which is a palpable forgery.

This is not an autobiographical novel: it is about some *other* portly, dissolute, immoral and middle-aged art dealer. The rest of the characters are quite imaginary too, especially that Mrs. Spon, but most of the places are real.

I

> So old a story, and tell it no better?
>
> *Pippa Passes*

When you burn an old carved and gilt picture frame it makes a muted hissing noise in the grate – a sort of genteel *fooh* – and the gold leaf tints the flames a wonderful peacock blue-green. I was watching this effect smugly on Wednesday evening when Martland came to see me. He rang the bell three times very fast, an imperious man in a hurry. I was more or less expecting him, so when my thug Jock put his head around the door, eyebrows elaborately raised, I was able to put a certain aplomb into my 'Wheel him in.'

Somewhere in the trash he reads Martland has read that heavy men walk with surprising lightness and grace; as a result he trips about like a portly elf hoping to be picked up by a leprechaun. In he pranced, all silent and catlike and absurd, buttocks swaying noiselessly.

'Don't get up,' he sneered, when he saw that I had no intention of doing so. 'I'll help myself, shall I?'

Ignoring the more inviting bottles on the drinks tray, he unerringly snared the great Rodney decanter from underneath and poured himself a gross amount of what he thought would be my Taylor '31. A score to me already, for I had filled it with Invalid Port of an unbelievable nastiness. He didn't notice: score two to me. Of course, he is only a policeman. Perhaps 'was' by now.

He lowered his massive bum into my little *Régence fauteuil* and smacked his lips courteously over the crimson garbage in his glass. I could almost hear him scrabbling about in his brain for a deft, light opening. His Oscar Wilde touch. Martland has only two personalities – Wilde and Eeyore. Nevertheless, he is a very cruel and dangerous policeman. Or perhaps 'was' – or have I said that?

'My dear boy,' he said finally, 'such ostentation. Even your firewood is gilded now.'

'An old frame,' I said, playing it straight. 'Thought I'd burn it.'

'But such a waste. A nice Louis Seize carved frame . . .'

'You know bloody well it isn't a nice Louis anything frame,' I snarled. 'It's a repro Chippendale trailing-vine pattern made about last week by one of those firms in the Greyhound Road. Came off a picture I bought the other day.'

You never know what Martland knows or doesn't know, but I felt fairly safe on the subject of antique frames: even Martland couldn't have taken a course on them, I thought.

'Would have been interesting if it had been a Louis Seize one though, you must admit; say about 50 by 110 centimetres,' he mumbled, gazing meditatively at the last of it glowing in the grate.

At that point my thug came in and deposited about twenty pounds of coal onto it and retired after giving Martland a civil smile. Jock's idea of a civil smile is rolling back part of his upper lip from a long, yellow dogtooth. It frightens *me*.

'Listen, Martland,' I said evenly. 'If I had lifted that Goya, or fenced it, you can't really think that I'd bring it here in its frame, for God's sake? And then burn the frame in my own grate? I mean, I'm not a *dullard*, am I?'

He made embarrassed, protesting noises as though nothing was further from his thoughts than the princely Goya whose theft from Madrid had filled the newspapers for the past five days. He helped out the noises by flapping his hands a bit, slopping some of the alleged wine onto a nearby rug.

'That,' I said crisply, 'is a valuable Savonnerie rug. Port is bad for it. Moreover, there is probably a priceless Old Master cunningly concealed beneath it. Port would be very bad for that.'

He leered at me nastily, knowing that I was quite possibly telling the truth. I leered back coyly, knowing that I was telling the truth. From the shadows beyond the doorway my thug Jock was smiling his civilest smile. We were all happy to the casual eye, had there been such an eye on the premises.

At this stage, before anyone starts to think that Martland is, or was, an ineffectual neddy, I had better fill in a bit of background. You doubtless know that, except under very extraordinary circumstances, English policemen never carry any weapon but the old Punch-and-Judy wooden truncheon. You know too that they never, never resort to physical unkindness – they dare not even spank the bottoms of little boys caught scrumping apples nowadays, for fear of assault charges and official inquiries and Amnesty International.

You know all this for certain, because you have never heard of the Special Powers Group – SPG – which is a peculiar kind of outsider-police squad conjured up by the Home Office during a fit of fact-facing in the weeks following the Great Train Robbery. The SPG was engendered by an Order in Council and has something called a Sealed Mandate from the Home Secretary and one of his more permanent civil servants. It is said to cover five sheets of brief-paper and has to be signed afresh every three months. The burden of its song is that only the nicest and most balanced chaps are to be recruited into the SPG, but that, once in, they are to be allowed to get away with murder – to say the least – so long as they get results. There are to be no more Great Train jobs, even if this entails – perish the thought – bashing a few baddies without first standing them expensive trials. (It's saved a fortune in dock-briefs already.) All the newspapers, even the Australian-owned sort, have made a deal with the Home Office whereby they get the stories hot from the septic tank in exchange for sieving out the firearms-and-torture bit. Charming.

The SPG – or SOGPU as I've heard it called – needs have no further truck with the Civil Service except for one horrified little man in the Treasury; and its Mandate instructs – if you please *instructs* – Commissioners of Police to afford them 'all administrative facilities without disciplinary obligations or clerical formalities'. The regular police love that bit, naturally. The SPG is answerable only to the Queen's First Minister through its Procurator, who is a belted Earl and a Privy Councillor and hangs about public lavatories late at night.

Its actual, executive head is a former colonel of paratroops who was at school with me and has the curious rank of Extra Chief

Superintendent. Very able chap, name of Martland. Likes hurting people, a lot.

He would clearly have liked to hurt me a bit there and then, in an inquiring sort of way, but Jock was hovering outside the door, belching demurely now and then to remind me that he was on call if required. Jock is a sort of anti-Jeeves: silent, resourceful, respectful even, when the mood takes him, but sort of drunk all the time, really, and fond of smashing people's faces in. You can't run a fine-arts business these days without a thug and Jock is one of the best in the trade. Well, you know, *was*.

Having introduced Jock – his surname escapes me, I should think it would be his mother's – I suppose I had better give a few facts about myself. I am Charlie Mortdecai. I mean, I was actually christened Charlie; I think my mother was perhaps getting at my father in some obscure way. The Mortdecai tag I am very happy with: a touch of ancientry, a hint of Jewry, a whiff of corruption – no collector can resist crossing swords with a dealer called Mortdecai, for God's sake. I am in the prime of life, if that tells you anything, of barely average height, of sadly over-average weight and am possessed of the intriguing remains of rather flashy good looks. (Sometimes, in a subdued light, and with my tummy tucked in, I could almost fancy me myself.) I like art and money and dirty jokes and drink. I am very successful. I discovered at my goodish second-rate Public School that almost anyone can win a fight if he is prepared to put his thumb into the other fellow's eye. Most people cannot bring themselves to do it, did you know that?

Moreover, I'm a Hon., for my daddy was Bernard, First Baron Mortdecai of Silverdale in the County Palatine of Lancaster. He was the second greatest art dealer of the century: he poisoned his life trying to overprice Duveen out of the field. He got his barony ostensibly for giving the nation a third of a million pounds' worth of good but unsaleable art, but actually for forgetting something embarrassing he knew about someone. His memoirs are to be published after my brother's death, say about next April, with any luck. I recommend them.

Meanwhile, back at the Mortdecai bunkhouse, old straw boss Martland was fretting, or pretending to. He is a terrible actor, but then he is pretty terrible when he's not acting, so it's often difficult to tell, if you follow me.

'Oh, come on, Charlie,' he said petulantly. I gave just enough flicker of the eyebrow to indicate that we had not been at school together all that recently.

'How do you mean, "Come on"?' I asked.

'I mean, let's stop playing silly buggers.'

I considered three clever retorts to that one but found that I couldn't really be bothered. There are times when I am prepared to bandy words with Martland, but this was one of the other times.

'Just what,' I asked reasonably, 'do you think I might give you that you think you might want?'

'Any sort of a lead on the Goya job,' he said in his defeated Eeyore voice. I raised an icy eyebrow or two. He squirmed a bit.

'There are diplomatic considerations, you know,' he moaned faintly.

'Yes,' I said with some satisfaction, 'I see how there might be.'

'Just a name or an address, Charlie. Or anything, really. You must have heard something.'

'And where would the old *cui bono* enter in?' I asked. 'Where is the well-known carrot? Or are you leaning on the old school spirit again?'

'It could buy you a lot of peace and quiet, Charlie. Unless, of course, you happened to be in the Goya trade yourself, as a principal.'

I pondered ostentatiously awhile, careful not to seem too eager, thoughtfully guzzling the real Taylor '31 which was inhabiting my glass.

'All right,' I said at last. 'Middle-aged, rough-spoken chap in the National Gallery, name of Jim Turner.'

The Martland ballpoint skittered happily over the regulation notebook.

'Full name?' he asked briskly.

'James Mallord William.'

He started to write it down, then froze, glaring at me evilly.

'1775 to 1851,' I quipped. 'Stole from Goya all the time. But then old Goya was a bit of a tea leaf himself, wasn't he?'

I have never been so near to getting a knuckle-sandwich in my life. Luckily for what's left of my patrician profile, Jock aptly entered, bearing the television set before him like an unabashed unmarried mum. Martland let prudence rule.

'Har har,' he said politely, putting the notebook away.

'Tonight is Wednesday, you see,' I explained.

'?'

'Professional wrestling. On the telly. Jock and I never miss it; so many of his friends play. Won't you stay and watch?'

'Good night,' said Martland.

For nearly an hour Jock and I regaled ourselves – and the SPG tape recorders – with the grunts and brays of the catchweight kings and the astonishingly lucid commentary of Mr Kent Walton, the only man I can think of who is wholly good at his job.

'That man is astonishingly lucid, etc.,' I said to Jock.

'Yeah. For a minute back there I thought he'd have had the other bugger's ear off.'

'No, Jock, not Pallo. Kent Walton.'

'Well, it looks like Pallo to me.'

'Never mind, Jock.'

'O.K., Mr Charlie.'

It was a splendid programme: all the baddies cheated shamefully, the referee never quite caught them at it, but the good guys always won by a folding press at the last minute. Except in the Pallo bout, naturally. So satisfactory. It was satisfactory, too, to think of all the clever young career bobbies who would, even then, be checking every Turner in the National Gallery. There are a great many Turners in the National Gallery. Martland was smart enough to know that I wouldn't have made a feeble joke just to tease him: every Turner would be checked. Tucked behind one of them, no doubt, his men would find an envelope. Inside – again, no doubt – would be one of those photographs.

When the last bout had ended – with a dramatic Boston Crab this time – Jock and I drank some whisky together, as is our custom on wrestling nights. Red Hackle de Luxe for me and Johnny Walker for Jock. He prefers it; also, he knows his station in life. We had by then, of course, unstuck the little microphone that Martland had carelessly left behind under the seat of the *fauteuil*. (Jock had been sitting there, so the recorder had doubtless picked up rude noises as well as the wrestling.) Jock, with rare imagination, dropped the little bug into a tumbler, adding water and an Alka-Seltzer tablet. Then he got the giggles, a horrid sight and sound.

'Calm yourself, Jock,' I said, 'for there is work to be done. *Que hodie non est, eras erit*, which means that tomorrow, at about noon, I expect to be arrested. This must take place in the Park if possible, so that I can make a scene if I think fit. Immediately afterwards this flat will be searched. You must not be here, nor must you-know-what. Put it in the headcloth of the hardtop as before, put the hardtop on the MGB and take it to Spinoza's for service. Make sure that you see Mr Spinoza himself. Be there at eight sharp. Got that?'

'Yes, Mr Charlie.'

With that he toddled off to his bedroom down the hall, where I could hear him still giggling and farting happily. His bedroom is neat, simply furnished, full of fresh air: just what you would wish your Rover Scout son's room to be. On the wall hangs a chart of the Badges and Ranks of the British Army; on the bedside table is a framed photograph of Shirley Temple; on the chest of drawers stands a model galleon, not quite finished, and a tidy pile of *Motor Cycle* magazines. I think he used to use pine disinfectant as an after-shave lotion.

My own bedroom is a pretty faithful reconstruction of the business premises of an expensive whore of the Directoire period. For me it is full of charming memories but it would probably make you – manly British reader – vomit. But there.

I sank into a happy, dream-free sleep, for there is nothing like your catchweight wrestling for purging the mind with pity and terror; it is the only mental catharsis worth the name. Nor is there any sleep so sweet as that of the unjust.

That was Wednesday night and nobody woke me up.

2

I am the man you see here plain enough:
Grant I'm a beast, why, beasts must lead beasts' lives!
Suppose I own at once to tail and claws;
The tailless man exceeds me: but being tailed
I'll lash out lion-fashion, and leave apes
To dock their stump and dress their haunches up,
My business is not to remake myself,
But make the absolute best of what God made. . . .

And as this cabin gets upholstery,
That hutch should rustle with sufficient straw.

Bishop Blougram's Apology

Nobody woke me up until ten o'clock of a beautiful summer's morning, when Jock came in with my tea and the canary, which was singing its little heart out, as ever. I bade them both good morning: Jock *prefers* me to greet the canary and it costs nothing to accommodate him in so small a matter.

'Ah' I added, 'the good old soothing Oolong or Lapsang!'

'Eh?'

'Bring me my whangee, my yellowest shoes, and the old green Homburg,' I quoted on. 'I am going into the Park to do pastoral dances.'

'Eh?'

'Oh, never mind, Jock. Bertram Wooster speaking, not I.'

'O.K., Mr Charlie.'

I often think that Jock should take up squash. He'd have made a splendid wall.

'Did you take the MGB in, Jock?'

'Yeah.'

'Good. Everything O.K.?' A silly question, of course, and of course I paid for it.

'Yeah. Well, uh, the you-know-what was a bit too big to go under the headcloth so I had to cut a bit off the edge, *you* know.'

'You cut a you what you didn't Jock . . .'

'All right Mr Charlie, just having my joke.'

'Yes, all right Jock. Jolly good. Did Mr Spinoza say anything?'

'Yeah, he said a *dirty* word.'

'Yes, he would, I suppose.'

'Yeah.'

I embarked on the quotidian *schrecklichkeit* of getting up. With occasional help from Jock I weaned myself gingerly from shower to razor, from dexedrine to intolerable decision about necktie; arriving safely, forty minutes later, at the bourne of breakfast, the only breakfast worth the name, the *cheminot*'s breakfast, the great bowl of coffee laced and gadrooned and filigreed with rum. I was up. I had not been sick. The snail was on the thorn, to name but one.

'I don't think we've *got* a green Homburg, Mr Charlie.'

'It's all right, Jock.'

'I could send the porter's little girl over to Lock's if you like?'

'No, it's all right, Jock.'

'She'd go for half a crown.'

'No, it's all *right*, Jock.'

'O.K., Mr Charlie.'

'You must be out of the flat in ten minutes, Jock. No guns or anything like that left here, of course. All alarms turned on and interlocked. Foto-Rekorda loaded with film and cocked – you know.'

'Yeah, I know.'

'Yeah,' I said, draping an extra set of inverted commas around the word, like the verbal snob I am.

Picture, then, this portly lecher swishing down Upper Brook Street, W.I, all sails set for St. James's Park and high adventure. A tiny muscle twitching in the cheek – perhaps in the best tradition

– but otherwise outwardly urbane, poised, ready to buy a bunch of violets from the first drab and toss her a golden sov.; Captain Hugh Drummond-Mortdecai MC, with a music-hall song on his whistling lips and a fold of silk underpants trapped between his well-powdered buttocks, bless him.

They were after me from the moment I emerged, of course – well, not actually *after* me because it was a 'front tail' and very prettily done too: the SPG boys have a year's training, for God's sake – but they didn't pick me up at noon as predicted. Back and forth I went past the pond (saying unforgivable things to my friend the pelican) but all they did was pretend to examine the insides of their absurd hats (bursting with two-way radios, no doubt) and make furtive signals to each other with their red, knobbly hands. I was really beginning to think that I had overrated Martland and was just about to beat up to the Reform Club and make someone give me luncheon – their cold table is the best in the world you know – when:

There they were. One on each side of me. Enormous, righteous, capable, deadly, stupid, unscrupulous, grave, watchful, hating me gently.

One of them laid a restraining hand on my wrist.

'Be off with you,' I quavered. 'Where do you think you are – *Hyde* Park?'

'Mr Mortdecai?' he grumbled capably.

'Stop grumbling capably at me,' I protested, 'this is, as you well know, I.'

'Then I must ask you to come along with me, Sir.'

I gazed at the man. I had no idea that people still said that. Is 'dumbfounded' the word I want?

'Eh?' I said, quoting freely from Jock.

'You must come along o'me, Sir.' He was working well now, really settling in to the part.

'Where are you taking me?'

'Where would you like to go, Sir?'

'Well, er . . . *home?*'

'I'm afraid that wouldn't do, Sir. We wouldn't have our equipment there, you see.'

'Equipment? Oh, yes. I quite see. Goodness.' I counted my pulse, my corpuscles and a few other necessary parts. *Equipment*. Dammit,

Martland and I had been at school together. They were trying to frighten me, clearly.

'You are trying to frighten me, clearly,' I said.

'No, Sir. Not yet we aren't, Sir.'

Can you think of a really smart answer to that one? Neither could I.

'Oh well then. Off to Scotland Yard, I suppose?' I said brightly, not really hoping much.

'No, really, Sir, that wouldn't do, you know that. They're dead narrow-minded there. We thought perhaps our Cottage Hospital, out Esher way.'

Martland had once, in an expansive moment, told me about the 'Cottage Hospital' – it had given me horrid dreams for days afterward.

'No no no no, no no no,' I cried jovially, 'I couldn't dream of taking you lads so far out of your way.'

'Well then,' said Plug Ugly II, giving tongue for the first time, 'what about your little place in the country, down by Stoke Poges?'

I must admit that here I may have blenched a trifle. My private life is an open book for all to read but I did think that 'Possets' was a retreat known only to a few intimate friends. There was nothing that you could call illegal there but I do have a few bits of equipment myself which other folk might think a bit frivolous. A bit Mr Norris – you know.

'Country cottage?' I riposted, quick as a flash. 'Countrycottage countrycottage countrycottage?'

'Yes, Sir,' said Plug Ugly II.

'Nice and private,' quipped his straight man.

After a few false starts I suggested (unruffled now, suave, cool) that what would be nicest of all would be to go and call on old Martland; delightful chap, was at school with me. They seemed happy to fall in with any suggestion I made so long as it was that one, and next thing all three of us were bundling into a chance cruising taxi and P.U.II was mumbling an address into the cabby's ear, as though I didn't know Martland's address as well as my own tax code.

'Northampton Park, *Canonbury?*' I tittered, 'since when has old Martland been calling it Canonbury?'

They both smiled at me, kindly. It was almost as bad as Jock's civil smile. My body temperature dropped quite two degrees, I could feel it. Fahrenheit of course: I have no wish to exaggerate.

'I mean, it's hardly even Islington,' I babbled on, *diminuendo*, 'more Newington Green if you ask me; I mean, what a ridiculous . . .'

I had just noticed that the interior of the chance cruising taxi was short of a few of the usual fitments, like notices about fares, advertisements, *door handles*. What it did have was a radio-telephone and a single handcuff attached to a ring-bolt in the floor. I sort of fell silent.

They didn't seem to think they needed the handcuff; they sat and looked at me thoughtfully, almost kindly, as though they were aunts wondering what I would like for tea.

We drew up in front of Martland's house just as his basket-work Mini trundled in from the Balls Pond Road end. It parked itself rather badly and disgorged Martland, cross and drenched.

This was both good and bad.

Good, because it meant that Martland couldn't have stayed very long at the siege of my flat: Jock had evidently interlocked all the alarms as instructed and Martland, as he masterfully celluloided his way through my front door, would have been met by a Bull-O-Bashan Mk IV siren and a mightly deluge from the automatic fire sprinklers. Moreover, a piercingly strident bell, inaccessibly high on the street-front wall, would have joined in the fun and lights would have flashed in Half Moon Street Police Station and in the Bruton Street depot of an internationally known security organization which I always call Set-a-Thief. A dinky little Japanese frame-a-second robot camera would have been snapping away from its eyrie in the chandelier and, worst of all, the termagant *concierge* would have come raging up the stairs, her malignant tongue cracking like a Boer's stock whip.

Long before I made friends with Mr Spinoza he had asked some of his friends to 'do my pad' as they say, so I knew the general form. The noise of bells and sirens indescribable, the water ineluctable, the conflict of burly Z-car chaps, hairy-assed Security chaps and ordinary villains quite dreadful and, riding clear and hideous over all, the intolerable scourging of the *concierge's* tongue, not to be borne. Poor Martland, I thought happily.

Perhaps I should explain that –

(a) The SPG people obviously carry no identification and take care not to be known to the ordinary police, for some of their work consists in sorting out naughty coppers

(b) Certain rats of the underworld have recently, with singular providence, done some deliberately clumsy and nasty 'jobs' while posing as SPG

(c) The ordinary police are not particularly keen even on *real* SPG men and

(d) The mindless bullies in my Security firm always release their pepper guns, two-way radios, aniline dye sprays, Dobermann Pinscher dogs and rubber coshes long before they ask any questions.

Goodness, what a mess it must have been. And thanks to the little camera I would certainly get the whole flat handsomely redecorated by Mrs. Spon – long overdue, I must say – at someone else's expense.

Goodness, too, how cross Martland must be.

Yes, that was the bad bit, of course. He snapped me one pale glare as he bounded noiselessly (fat men move with surprising grace etc.) up the steps, dropped his keys, dropped his hat, stood on it, and finally preceded us into the house. No good for C. Mortdecai was what I reckoned all that boded. Plug Ugly II, as he stood aside to let me pass, looked at me so kindly that I felt my breakfast frothing in the small intestine. Clenching my buttocks bravely I sauntered in and with a tolerant snigger surveyed what he probably called The Lounge. I had not seen curtains of that pattern since I seduced the House Mother in my Approved School; the carpet was a refugee from a provincial cinema foyer and the wallpaper had little silver-grey flock *fleurs-de-lis*. Yes, truly. All spotlessly clean, of course. You could have eaten your dinner off them, if you kept your eyes closed.

They said I could sit down, in fact they urged me to. I could feel my liver, heavy and sullen, crowding my heart. I no longer wanted any luncheon.

Martland, reappearing reclothed, dry, was quite himself again and full of fun.

'Well well well,' he cried, rubbing his hands, 'well, well.'

'I must be off now,' I said firmly.

'No no no,' he cried, 'why, you've only just come. What would you like to drink?'

'Some whisky, please.'

'Jolly good.' He poured himself a big one but me none. 'Har, har,' I thought.

'Har, har,' I said, out loud, brave.

'Ho, ho,' he riposted archly.

We sat in silence then for quite five minutes, they obviously waiting for me to start to babble protestingly, me determined to do nothing of the kind, but just worrying a little about making Martland any crosser. The minutes wagged on. I could hear a large, cheap watch ticking in the waistcoat of one of the Plug Uglies, that's how old-fashioned they were. A little immigrant child ran past on the pavement outside shrieking 'M'Gawa! M'Gawa!' or words to that effect. Martland's face had relaxed into the complacent smirk of the master of a lordly house, surrounded by friends and loved ones, sated with port and good talk. The hot, itchy, distant-traffic-buzzing silence fretted on. I wanted to go to the lavatory. They kept on looking at me, politely, attentively. Capably.

Martland at last lumbered to his feet with surprising grace etc. and put a record on the turntable, fastidiously balancing the output to the big Quad stereo speakers. It was that lovely record of trains going by, the one we all bought when we could first afford stereo. I never tire of it.

'Maurice,' he said politely to one of his hooligans, 'would you kindly fetch the twelve-volt high-tension motor-car battery from the charging bench in the basement?'

'And Alan,' he went on, 'would you please draw the curtains and take Mr Mortdecai's trousers down?'

Now just what can one do when this sort of thing happens? Struggle? What expression can one wear on the well-bred face? Contempt? Outrage? Dignified unconcern? While I was selecting an expression I was deftly divested of the small clothes and all I registered was funky panic. Martland tactfully turned his back and busied himself coaxing a few more decibels out of the stereo equipment. Maurice – I shall always think of him as Maurice – had tucked the first terminal cosily into place half a minute before Martland signalled lewdly for the second to be clipped on. Beautifully timed, the Flying Scotsman whooped stereophonically for a level crossing. I competed in mono.

And so the long day wore on. Not for many minutes, I must

admit. I can stand anything but pain; moreover, the thought that someone is deliberately hurting me, and not minding, upsets me badly. They seemed to know instinctively the point at which I had decided to cry *capivi* for when I came round after that time they had put my trousers back on and there was a great glass of whisky three inches from my nose, with beaded bubbles winking at the brim. I drank it while their faces swam swooningly into focus; they looked kind, pleased with me, proud of me. I was a credit to them, I felt.

'Are you all right, Charlie?' asked Martland, anxiously.

'I must go to the lavatory now,' I said.

'So you shall, dear boy, so you shall. Maurice, help Mr M.'

Maurice took me down to the children's loo; they wouldn't be back from school for another hour, he told me. I found the Margaret Tarrant squirrels and bunnies soothing. I needed soothing.

When we got back to the Lounge the gramophone was dispensing Swan Lake, if you please. Martland has a very simple mind: he probably puts Ravel's Bolero on the turntable when seducing shopgirls.

'Tell me all about it,' he said gently, almost caressingly, his impression of a Harley Street abortionist.

'My bottom hurts,' I whined.

'Yes, yes,' he said. 'But the photograph.'

'Ah,' I said sagely, wagging my head, 'the phokodarts. You have given me too much whisky on an umpty stemach. You *know* I haven't had any lunch.' And with that I gave them some of the whisky back rather dramatically. Martland looked vexed but I thought the effect on his sofa cover was something of an improvement. We got through the next two or three minutes without too much damaging the new-found amenities. Martland explained that they had indeed found a photograph behind a Turner in the National Gallery at 5.15 that morning. It was tucked behind *Ulysses Deriding Polyphemus* (No. 508). He went on in his court-room voice –

'The photograph depicts, ah, two consenting adult males, ah, consenting.'

'Having congress, you mean?'

'Just so.'

'And one of the faces had been cut out?'

'Both of the faces.'

I got up and went over to where my hat was. The two louts did not move but looked sort of alert. I was not really in any shape to dive out of windows. I pulled down the sweatband of the hat, tore back some of the buckram and offered Martland the tiny oval of photograph. He looked at it blankly.

'Well, dear boy,' he said softly, 'you mustn't keep us in suspense. Who is the gentleman?'

It was my turn to look blank.

'Don't you really know?'

He looked at it again.

'Much hairier in the face nowadays,' I prompted.

He shook his head.

'Chap called Gloag,' I told him. 'Known to his friends as "Hockbottle" for some obscene reason. He took the photograph himself. At Cambridge.'

Martland, suddenly, inexplicably, looked very worried indeed. So did his mates, who clustered around, passing the tiny picture from hand to grubby hand. Then they all started nodding, tentatively at first and then positively. They looked rather funny but I was feeling too tired to enjoy it really.

Martland wheeled on me, his face evil now.

'Come on, Mortdecai,' he said, all urbanity gone, 'tell me it all this time. Fast, before I lose my temper.'

'Sandwich?' I asked diffidently. 'Bottle of beer?'

'Later.'

'Oh. All right. Hockbottle Gloag came to see me three weeks ago. He gave me the cut-out of his face and said to keep it very safe, it was a free pardon for him and money in the bank for me. He wouldn't explain but I knew he wouldn't be trying to con me, he's terrified of Jock. He said he'd ring me up every day from then on and if he missed a day it would mean he was in trouble and I was to tell you to ask Turner in the National Gallery. That's all. It has nothing to do with the Goya so far as I know – I just seized that opportunity to slip you the word. *Is* Hockbottle in trouble? Have you got him in that bloody Cottage Hospital of yours?'

Martland didn't answer. He just stood looking at me, rubbing the side of his face, making a nasty soft rasping sound. I could almost hear him wondering whether the battery would coax a little more truth out of me. I hoped not: the truth had to be delivered in carefully spaced rations, so as to give him a healthy appetite for later lies.

Perhaps he decided that I was telling the truth, as far as it went; perhaps he simply decided that he already had enough to worry about.

He had, in fact, no idea how much he had to worry about.

'Go away,' he said, finally.

I collected my hat, tidied it, made for the door.

'Don't leave town?' I prompted in the doorway.

'Don't leave town,' he agreed, absently. I didn't like to remind him about the sandwich.

I had to walk miles before I found a taxi. It had all its door handles. I fell soundly asleep, the sleep of a good, successful liar. Goodness, the flat was in a mess. I telephoned Mrs. Spon and told her that I was at last ready to redecorate. She came round before dinner and helped us tidy the place up – success has not spoiled her – and afterward we spent a happy hour in front of the fire choosing chintzes and wallpapers and things and then we all three sat round the kitchen table and tore into an enormous fry-up such as very few people can make today.

After Mrs. Spon had left I said to Jock, 'Do you know what, Jock?' and he said, 'No, what?'

'I think Mr Gloag is dead.'

'Greedy, I expect,' said Jock, elliptically. 'Who d'you reckon killed him, then?'

'Mr Martland, I fancy. But I think that for once he rather wishes he hadn't.'

'Eh?'

'Yes. Well, good night, Jock.'

'Good night, Mr Charlie.'

I undressed and put a little more Pomade Divine on my wounds. Suddenly I felt shatteringly tired – I always do after torture. Jock had put a hotty in my bed, bless him. He knows.

3

Yet half I seemed to recognize some trick
Of mischief happened to me, God knows when –
In a bad dream perhaps. Here ended, then,
Progress this way. When, in the very nick
Of giving up, one time more, came a click
As when a trap shuts – you're inside the den!

Childe Roland

Dawn broke for me, at ten o'clock sharp, with one of the finest cups of tea I have ever been privileged to toy with. The canary was in splendid voice. The snail, once again, was on the thorn and showed no signs of dismounting. I hardly winced as the blisters from Martland's battery made themselves felt, although I did, at one stage, find myself longing for Pantagruel's goose's neck.

I had a long chat on the telephone with my insurance brokers and explained to them how they could put the bite on Martland's ear for the damage to my decorations and promised them the photographs of the intruders as soon as Jock had developed them.

Then I put on a dashing little tropical-weight worsted, a curly-brimmed coker and a pair of buckskins created by Lobb in a moment of genius. (My tie, if I recall correctly, was a *foulard*, predominantly *merde d'oie* in colour, though why you should be interested I cannot imagine.) Thus clad – and with my blisters well Vaselined – I sauntered to the Park to inspect the pelican and other feathered friends. They were in great shape. 'This weather,' they seemed to be saying, 'is capital.' I gave them my benison.

Then I went a-slumming through the art-dealing district, carefully keeping my face straight as I looked in the shop windows – sorry, *gallery* windows – at the tatty Shayers and reach-me-down Koekkoeks. Heigh-ho. After a while I was sure that I had no tail (remember that bit, it matters) neither in front nor behind, and popped into Mason's Yard. There are galleries there too, of course, but I was bent on seeing Mr Spinoza, who is only an art dealer in one very specialized sort of way.

Moishe Spinoza Barzilai is, as a matter of fact, Basil Wayne & Co., the great coach builders of whom even you, ignorant readers, must have heard, although not point one per cent of you will ever afford his lovely panel beating, still less his princely upholstery. Unless, of course, you are reading below your station in life and happen to be an Indian Maharajah or a Texan oil-field proprietor.

Mr Spinoza creates very special one-off bodies for the great cars of the world. He has heard of Hooper and Mulliner and speaks kindly, if a little vaguely, of them. He will restore or re-create the occasional vintage Rolls, Infanta or Mercedes if he feels like it. Bugattis, Cords, Hirondelles and Leyland Straight-Eights will be considered. So will about three other *marques*. But ask him to tart up a Mini with basketwork and silver condom dispensers or to build flip-back fornication benches into a Jaguar and he will spit right into your eye. I mean *really!* What he most loves is a Hispano-Suiza – an 'Izzer-Swizzer.' Can't understand it myself, but there.

He also dabbles in crime. It's a sort of hobby with him. He can't need the money.

Currently, he was rebuilding for my best customer a latish Silver Ghost Rolls Royce, which was what I had come to inspect, in a way. My customer, Milton Krampf (yes, truly), had bought it from a right villain who had found it in a farmyard chocked up and running a chaff cutter and turnip slicer after a long career as stock truck, hearse, station wagon, shooting brake, baronial wedding present and mobile shagging station; in the reverse order, of course. Mr. Spinoza had found six perfectly right artillery wheels for it at one hundred pounds apiece, had built a scrupulously exact *Roi des Belges* open tourer body and painted it with sixteen coats of Queen Anne white, each one rubbed down wet-and-dry, and was now finishing the olive-green crushed Levant Morocco upholstery and free-handing with the fitch the lovely arabesques of the *carrosserie* lines. He wasn't doing the work himself, of course; he's blind. Was, rather.

I walked round the car, admiring it Platonically. There was no point in desiring it – it was a rich man's car. Would do about seven miles to the gallon, which is all right if you own an oil field. Milton Krampf owns a lot of oil fields. First to last, the car would stand him in at about £24,000. Paying that would hurt him about as much as picking his nose. (They say a man who knows how rich he is ain't rich – well, Krampf knows. A man telephones him every morning, one hour after the New York Stock Exchange opens, and tells him exactly how rich he is. It makes his day.)

A naughty apprentice told me that Mr Spinoza was in his office and I picked my way thither.

'Hullo, Mr Spinoza,' I cried cheerily, 'here's a fine morning to be alive in!'

He peered malevolently at a spot three inches above my left shoulder.

'Oo hucking hastard,' he spat. (No roof to his mouth, you know. Poor chap.) 'Oo other hucking hiss-hot. How air oo hoe your hace here, oo hurd-murgling hod?'

The rest was a bit rude so I shan't quote him too verbatim, if you don't mind. What he was vexed about was my sending the MGB in with the little special matter in the headcloth at such an early hour the day before. 'At sparrow-fart,' as he neatly put it. Moreover, he was afraid that people would think he was working on it and he had evolved a dreadful mental image of queues of chaps in cloth caps insisting that he respray their MG's.

When he had drawn to a provisional close, I spoke to him sternly.

'Mr Spinoza,' I said, 'I did not come here to discuss with you my relationship with my mummy, which is a matter for me and my psychiatrist alone. I came to remonstrate with you about using Dirty Words to Jock, who is, as you know, sensitive.'

Mr S used a lot more *very* dirty words and some which I couldn't make out but which were probably vile. When the air had thinned a little he bitterly offered to walk over to the Rolls with me and discuss headlamps. I was surprised and saddened to see a great vulgar Duesenburg – if that's how you spell it – in the workshop, and said so, which rather started him off again. I have never had any daughters but this did not stop Mr Spinoza sketching out their careers from the nursery to the street corner, so to speak. I leaned on the side of the Silver Ghost, admiring his command of language. 'A feast of reason and a flow of soul' is how Alexander Pope (1688–1744) would have summed it up.

While we were thus civilly biffing the ball of conversation to and fro, a sound which I can best describe as a DONK came in from the South side of Mason's Yard. More or less simultaneously a sort of *WANG* occurred about three feet north of my belly button and a large pimple appeared in the door-panel of the Silver Ghost. Slapping two and two together in the twinkling of an eye, I lay down, without a thought for my valuable suit. Look, I'm an experienced coward. Mr Spinoza, whose hand had been on the door, realized that someone was getting at his panel work. He straightened up and cried 'Oi!' or it might have been 'Oy!'

There was another DONK outside, followed, this time, not by a *WANG* but by a sort of crisp, mushy noise and a lot of the back of Mr Spinoza's head distributed itself freely over the wall behind us. None of it got on to my suit, I'm happy to say. Mr Spinoza, too, lay down then, but too late by now, of course. There was a blue-black hole in his upper lip and a piece of his false teeth arrangements was protruding from the corner of his mouth. He looked quite beastly.

I wish I could say that I had liked him, but I never really did, you know.

Gentlemen of my age and full habit (as the tailors say) almost never scuttle on all fours over oily garage floors, particularly when they are wearing expensive and rather new tropical-weight worsted suitings. This was clearly a day for breaking rules, however, so I put my nose down and scuttled, successfully. I must have looked absurd but I got out into the yard and across it into the doorway of the O'Flaherty Gallery. Mr O'Flaherty, who knew my father well, is an elderly Jew called Groenblatter or something like that and is swart as an Ethiop. He put his hands to his cheeks when he saw me and rocked his head to and fro, keening something that sounded like *Mmm-Mmm-Mmmm* on the note of G above high C.

'How's business today?' I asked bravely but in a voice that wobbled a bit.

'Don't ask it, don't ask it,' he replied automatically, then –

'Who attacked you so, Charlie boy, somebody's husband? Or somebody's wife, God forbid?'

'Look, Mr G, nobody attacked me, there's some sort of trouble at Mr Spinoza's and I'm getting away fast – who wants to be involved – when I trip and fall, is all. Now like a good friend you should ask Perce to get me a taxi arreddy, I don't feel so good.' I always find myself talking like that with Mr G.

Perce, Mr G's rat-faced little thug – he can't afford a good, big one – got the taxi and I promised to send Mr G a good customer, which I knew would keep him from gossiping.

Arrived home, I collapsed into a chair, suddenly quaking with delayed horror. Jock made me a cup of wonderfully refreshing mint tea which made me feel a great deal better, especially after I had followed it with four fluid ozs of whisky.

Jock pointed out that if I said I'd been knocked down by a motor car the Insurance would buy me a new suit. This completed the cure and I got on to the brokers straight away, for my no-claims bonus is just a dream of childhood now. There's nothing like a little insurance to smooth the troubled brow, take my word for it. Meanwhile, Jock sent the porter's little girl to Prunier in a taxi for a box of luncheon *à porter*. There was a dear little turbot *soufflé*, a *Varieté Prunier* (six oysters, each cooked a different way) and two of their *petits pots de crème de chocolat*.

I had a nap and awoke much mollified and spent a useful afternoon with my ultra-violet machine and a grease crayon, mapping the passages of repaint ('strengthening' as we call it in the trade) on a gorgeous panel by – well, more or *less* by – the Allunno di Amico di Sandro. (God bless Berenson, I say.) Then I wrote a few paragraphs of my paper for *Burlington Magazine* in which I shall prove, once and for all, that the Tallard Madonna in the Ashmolean is by Giorgione after all, and despite that awful man Berenson.

Dinner was pork chops with the kidneys in and chips and beer. I always send Jock out for the beer in a jug and make him wear a cloth cap. It seems to taste better and he doesn't mind a bit. They won't serve the porter's little girl, you see.

After dinner Mrs Spon arrived with lots of samples of gimp and bobbles and crétonnes for cushion covers and things and pink mosquito netting for the standing drapes round my bed. I had to be firm about the netting, I must admit it was rather lovely but I insisted that it should be blue-for-a-boy. I mean, I have my little ways but I'm not a deviate, for God's sake, am I, I asked her.

She was already just a little cross when Martland arrived and loomed in the doorway like a pollution problem. Diffidently, for him, but definitely doomlike.

They admitted, grudgingly, that they knew each other by sight. Mrs Spon flounced over to the window. I know lots of men who can flounce but Mrs Spon is the last woman who can do it. There was a sticky sort of silence of the sort which I relish. Finally Martland whispered, 'Perhaps you should ask the old doxy to leave' in just too loud a whisper.

Mrs Spon rounded on him and Told Him Off. I had heard of her talents in that direction but had never before been privileged to hear her unlock the word bag. It was a literary and emotional feast: Martland withered visibly. There is no one like your gently nurtured triple-divorcee for really putting the verbal leather in. 'Wart on the tax-payer's arse,' 'traffic-warden's catamite,' and 'poor man's Colonel Wigg' are just a few of the good things she served up but there was more – much more. She swept out at last, in a cloud of '*Ragazza*' and lovely epithets. She was wearing a suede knickerbocker suit but you'd have sworn she twitched a twelve-foot train of brocade away from Martland as she passed him.

'Golly,' he said when she'd gone.

'Yes,' I said, happily.

'Well. Well, look, Charlie, what I really came to say was how sick and sorry I am about all this.'

I gave him my cold look. The big, economy size.

'I mean,' he went on, 'you've had a filthy rotten time and I think you're owed an explanation. I want to put you in the picture – which will give you a bit of a whip-hand, I don't mind telling you – and er ask your er help.'

'Gor blimey,' I thought.

'Sit down,' I said, frigidly. 'I myself prefer to stand, for reasons which will occur to you. I shall certainly listen to your explanations and apologies; beyond that I can make no promises.'

'Yes,' he said. He fidgeted a little, like a man who is expecting to be offered a drink and thinks you've forgotten to do the honours.

When he realized that it was definitely Temperance Night for him he resumed.

'Do you know why Spinoza was shot this morning?'

'Haven't the faintest,' I said boredly, although a multiplicity of ideas about it had been running through my head all afternoon. Wrong ones.

'It was meant for you, Charlie.'

My heart started rattling about irresponsibly in my rib cage. My armpits became cold and wet. I wanted to go to the lavatory.

I mean, electric batteries and so forth are one thing, within reason of course, but that someone actually means to kill you, forever, is a thought that the mind cannot accept, it wants to vomit it out; ordinary people just don't have the mental or emotional clichés to deal with news like that.

'How can you possibly be sure of that?' I asked after a moment.

'Well, to be perfectly frank, Maurice thought it *was* you he shot. It was certainly you he meant to shoot.'

'Maurice?' I said. '*Maurice*? You mean *your* Maurice? Whatever would he want to do that for?'

'Well, I sort of told him to, really.'

I sat down after all.

Jock's craggy form disengaged itself smoothly from the shadows just outside the door and came to rest behind my chair. He was breathing through his nose for once, making a plaintive, whistling noise on the exhaust stroke.

'Did you ring, Sir?'

Jock really is marvellous. I mean, imagine saying that. What tact, what *savoir faire*, what a boost for the young master in time of stress. I felt so much better.

'Jock,' I said, 'have you a pair of brass knuckles about you? I may ask you to hit Mr Martland in a moment or two.'

Jock didn't actually answer, he knows a rhetorical question when he hears one. But I sensed him pat his hip pocket – 'me bin' he calls it – where six ounces of cunningly fashioned brass have lived a snug and smelly life since he was the youngest juvenile delinquent in Hoxton.

Martland was shaking his head vigorously, impatiently. 'No need for that at all, none at all. Try and understand, Charlie.'

'Try and make me understand,' I said. Grim, sore-arsed.

He heaved what I took to be a sigh. '*Tout comprendre, c'est tout pardonner,*' he said.

'I say, that's neat!'

'Look, Charlie, I was up half the night with that bloodthirsty little old maniac at the Home Office, telling him about our chat yesterday.'

'Chat' was good.

'When I told him how much you knew about this file,' Martland went on, 'nothing would do but he must have you done permanently. "Terminated with extreme prejudice" was how he put it, silly little sod. Been reading too many thrillers in between the cups of tea.'

'No,' I said kindly, 'that one hasn't got into the thrillers yet, except the *Sunday Times*. That's CIA jargon. He's probably been reading the Green Berets file.'

'Be that as it may,' he went on, 'be that as it may' – he obviously fancied that snappy little phrase – 'be that as it may, I tried to make him see that as yet we really didn't know what you knew nor where you got it, which was more important; and that it would be madness to liquidate you at this stage. Er, or at any stage of course, but I couldn't say that, could I? Well, I tried to get him to refer it to the Minister but he said the Minister would be drunk by then and he himself wasn't permanent enough to disturb him with impunity at that time of night and anyway . . . anyway I had to come into line and so this morning I thought the best thing was to put Maurice on the assignment, being an impulsive boy, and so give you a fair chance of survival, you see. And Charlie, I'm really so glad that he got the wrong chap.'

'Yes,' I said. But I wondered how he had known that I would be at Mr Spinoza's that morning.

'How did you know that I would be at Mr Spinoza's this morning?' I asked, casually.

'Maurice followed you, Charlie.' Wide-eyed, offhand.

'Bloody liar,' I thought.

'I see,' I said.

I excused myself on the pretext of slipping into something more comfortable, as the tarts say. Something more comfortable was a wonderfully vulgar blue velvet smoking jacket into which Mrs Spon had once sewn, with her own hands, a lot of cunningly designed webbing which supported a rather shaky old gold-plated riverboat gambler's revolver, calibre something like .28. I had only eleven of the ancient pinfire cartridges for it and had grave doubts of their usefulness, not to speak of their safety. But this wasn't for killing anyone, it was for making me feel young and tough and capable. People who have pistols for killing people keep them in boxes or drawers; wearing them is only for making you ride tall in the saddle. I used some mouthwash, renewed the Vaseline on my blisters and cantered back into the drawing room, tall as can be in my high-cantled saddle.

I paused behind Martland's chair and reflected on how much I disliked the back of his head. It wasn't that there were rolls of Teuton fat sprouting hog bristles or anything like that; just a neat and hateful smugness, an unjustified but invincible cockiness. Like a female journalist, really. I decided that I could afford the luxury of losing my temper: it would fit into the picture I wanted to create. I took out the little pistol and ground the muzzle into his right ear hole. He sat very still indeed – nothing really wrong with his nerves – and spoke plaintively.

'For Christ's sake be careful with that thing, Charlie, those pinfire cartridges are highly unstable.'

I ground some more; it was making my blisters feel better. It was just like him to have been looking at my firearm permit.

'Jock,' I said crisply, 'we are going to defenestrate Mr Martland.'

Jock's eyes lit up.

'I'll get a razor blade, Mr Charlie.'

'No no, Jock, wrong word. I mean we're going to push him out of a window. Your bedroom window, I think. Yes, and we'll undress him first and say that he was making advances to you and jumped out of the window in a frenzy of thwarted love.'

'I say, Charlie, really, what a filthy rotten idea; I mean, think of my wife.'

'I never think of policeman's wives, their beauty maddens me like wine. Anyway, the sodomy bit will make your Minister slap a D-Notice on the whole thing, which is good for both of us.'

Jock was already leading him from the room by means of the 'Quiet Come-Along' which painfully involves the victim's little finger. Jock had learned that one from a mental nurse. Capable lads, those.

Jock's bedroom, as ever, was bursting with what passes for fresh air in W.I, the stuff was streaming in from the wide-open window. (Why do people build houses to keep the climate out, then cut holes in the walls to let it in again? I shall never understand.)

'Show Mr Martland the spiky railings in the area, Jock,' I said nastily. (You've no idea how nasty my voice can be when I try. I was an adjutant once, in your actual Guards.) Jock held him out so that he could see the railings then started to undress him. He just stood there, unresisting, a shaky smile trembling at one corner of his mouth, until Jock began to unbuckle his belt. Then he started to talk, rapidly.

The burden of his song was that if I could only be dissuaded from my course he would arrange for me to receive

(i) the untold riches of the Orient

(ii) his undying respect and esteem and

(iii) legal immunity for me and mine, yea, even unto the third and fourth generations. At this point I cocked an ear. (How I wish I could really move my ears, don't you? The Bursar of my College could.)

'You interest me strangely,' I said. 'Put him down a moment, Jock, for he is going to Tell All.'

We didn't lay another finger on him, he went on and on of his own accord. You don't have to be a coward to dislike dropping thirty feet on to spiky railings, especially in the nude. I'm sure that in his place I'd have blubbered.

The story so far turned out to be as follows, to wit: Hockbottle Gloag, with an extraordinary lack of finesse, had put the bite directly onto the ear of his old College Chum – the other part of the 'consenting males' sketch – sending him a 35-mm contact print of the naughty photograph. (This was by no means part of the agreed plan and was very vexing. I suppose he needed spending money, poor chap; I wish he'd asked me.) The now very august chum, living in dread of his wife's Sister and other Relations, had decided to cough up the reasonable sum involved but had also asked an Assistant Commissioner of Police to dinner and had put out dainty feelers over the port, such as, 'What do you fellows do about blackmailers nowadays, eh, Freddy?' and so forth. The Assistant Commissioner, who had seen certain unpublished material about the Chum in a newspaper editor's safe, shied like a startled stallion. Decided that it wasn't anything he could afford to know about and – perhaps spitefully – gave Chum the name and number of old Martland. 'Just in case anyone you know ever gets pestered, Sir, ha ha.'

Chummy then asks Martland to dinner and gives him all the news that's fit to print. Martland says, 'Leave it to us, Sir, we're used to dealing with dastards of that kidney,' and swings into action.

Next day, some sort of equerry, snorting genteelly into his Squadron-Leading moustaches, calls on Hockbottle and hands him over an attaché case full of great coarse ten-pound notes. Five minutes later, Martland and his gauleiters canter in and whisk poor Hockbottle off to the Cottage Hospital of evil fame. He gets a touch of the car battery just to soften him up and comes out of his faint with the regulation glass of Scotch under his nose. But he is made of sterner stuff than me: your actual boofter often is.

'Faugh,' he says, or it might have been 'Pooh!' petulantly; 'take the nasty stuff away. Have you no Chartreuse? And you needn't think you're frightening me: I *adore* being roughed up by great big hairy dears like you.' He proves it, shows them. They are revolted.

Now Martland's brief is only to put the fear of God into Hockbottle and to make it clear that this photograph nuisance must now cease. He has been specifically ordered not to pry and has been told nothing embarrassing, but by nature and long habit he is nosy and has, moreover, a quite unwholesome horror of pooves. He decides to get to the bottom of the mystery (an unfortunate expression perhaps) and to make Hockbottle Tell All.

'Very well,' he says grimly, 'this one will really hurt you.'

'Promises, promises,' simpers Hockbottle.

So now they give him a treatment which hurts you at the base of the septum and this is one which even Hockbottle is unlikely to relish. When he regains consciousness this time, he is very angry and also scared of losing his good looks, and he tells Martland that he has some very powerful insurance c/o the Hon. Charlie Mortdecai and they'd better look out, so there. He then shuts up firmly and Martland, now enraged, gives him yet another treatment, hitherto reserved solely for Chinese double agents.

Hockbottle, to everyone's dismay, drops dead. Dicky ticker, d'you see.

Well, worse things happen in war, as they say, and no one ever really liked Hockbottle of course, except perhaps a few Guardsmen from Chelsea Barracks, but Martland is not a man who appreciates uncovenanted mercies. The whole thing strikes him as thoroughly unsatisfactory, especially since he still has not found out what it is all about.

Judge of his chagrin then, when Chum telephones in a serious tizzy and asks him to call round immediately, bringing the wretched Hockers with him. Martland says yes, certainly, he'll be there in a few minutes but it's a little er difficult to bring Mr er Gloag just at present. When he arrives he is shown, distraughtly, a most distressing letter. Even Martland, whose taste has a few little blemishes in it, boggles at the paper it is written on: imitation parchment with edges both deckled and gilt, richly embossed bogus coat of arms at the top and a polychrome view of a desert sunset at the foot of the page. The address, inscribed in Olde Englysshe lettering, is '*Rancho de los Siete Dolores de la Virgen*,' New Mexico. In short, it is from my very good customer Milton Krampf.

The letter says – mind you, I never saw it, so I'm paraphrasing Martland's account – that Mr Krampf admires the eminent Chum very much and wants to start a fan club (!) to distribute little known biographical material about said Chum to Senators, Congressmen, British MP's and *Paris Match*. (Terrifying, that last bit, you will admit.) He further says that a Mr Hogwattle Gloat has been in touch with him and is prepared to kick in with some illustrated reminiscences of 'your mutual schooldays in Cambridge'. He also says how about the three of them meeting someplace and seeing if they can't work out something to their mutual advantages. In other words, it is the bite. Coy and clumsy perhaps, but unmistakably the bite. (That made, so far, two members of the cast who'd gone off their chumps, leaving only me sane and responsible. I think.)

Martland paused in his narrative and I did not urge him on, for this was very bad news, for when millionaires go mad poorer people get hurt. I was so disturbed that I unthinkingly gave Martland a drink. A bad mistake that, I needed him to stay on edge. As he filled with the old familiar juice you could see his confidence returning, his head reassuming the habitual, maddeningly pompous poise.

How he must have been loathed by his brother officers as they watched him bully and arsehole-creep his way up the service. But one had to remember, all the time, that he was dangerous and far cleverer than he looked or talked.

'Martland,' I said after a time, 'did you say that your hirelings followed me to Spinoza's this morning?'

'That's right.' Crisply, much too crisply. He was definitely feeling his oats again.

'Jock, Mr Martland is telling me *fibs*. Smack him, please.'

Jock drifted out of the shadows, gently relieved Martland of his glass and bent down to stare benignly into his face. Martland stared back, wide-eyed, his mouth opening a little. A mistake that, the open mouth. Jock's great hand swung round in a half circle and struck Martland's cheek with a loud report.

Martland sailed over the arm of the sofa and fetched up against the wainscot. He sat there a while; his little eyes dripping tears of hatred and funk. His mouth, closed now, writhed – he was counting his teeth, I expect.

'I think that perhaps that was silly of me,' I said. 'I mean, killing you is safe enough, it sort of ties things up for good, doesn't it, but just hurting you will only make you vengeful.' I let him think about that for a time, to get the nasty implications. He thought about it. He got them.

At last he cranked a sickly smirk on to his face – beastly sight, that – and came and sat down again.

'I shan't bear a grudge, Charlie. I dare say you feel I deserve a bit of a bashing after this morning. Not yourself yet, I mean to say.'

'There is something in what you say,' I said, truthfully, for there was something in what he said. 'I have had a long day, full of mopery and mayhem. If I stay up any longer I am likely to make a serious error of judgment. Goodnight.' With this I swept out of the room. Martland's mouth was open again as I closed the door.

A brief, delicious session under the warm shower, a whisk of costly dentifrice around the old ivory castles, a puff of Johnson's Baby Powder here and there, a dive between the sheets and I was my own man again. Krampf's idiotic departure from his script worried me, perhaps more than the attempt on my own life now, but I felt that there was nothing which could not more profitably be worried about on the morrow which is, as is well known, another day.

I rinsed the cares from my mind with a few pages of Firbank and swam gently and tenderly down into sleep. Sleep is not, with me, a mere switching off: it is a very positive pleasure to be supped and savoured with expertise. It was a good night; sleep pampered me like a familiar, salty mistress who yet always has a new delight with which to surprise her jaded lover.

My blisters, too, were much better.

4

Morning's at seven,
The hill-side's dew-pearled,

Pippa Passes

I carolled at Jock as he aroused me, but my heart wasn't really in the statement. Morning was in fact at ten, as usual, and Upper Brook Street was merely wet. It was a gritty, drizzling, clammy day and the sky was the colour of mouse dirt. Pippa would have stayed in bed and no snail in his senses would have climbed a thorn. My cup of tea, which usually droppeth like the gentle rain from heaven, tasted like a vulture's crutch. The canary looked constipated and gave me a surly glance instead of the customary stave or two of song.

'Mr Martland's downstairs, Mr Charlie. Bin waiting half an hour.'

I snarled and drew a fold of silk sheet over my head, burrowing down back into the womby warmth where no one can hurt you.

'You ought to see his moosh, where I hit him, it's a treat, honest. *All* colours.'

That fetched me. The day had at least one treat to offer. Against my better judgment I got up.

A mouth wash, half a dexedrine, a morsel of anchovy toast and a Charvet dressing-gown – all in the order named – and I was ready to deal with any number of Martlands.

'Lead me to this Martland,' I ordered.

I must say he did look lovely; it wasn't just the rich autumnal tints on his swollen moosh, it was the play of expressions over it which enchanted me. You may compile your own list of these; I have no heart for it just now. The one which matters for this narrative was the last: a kind of sheepish false bonhomie with a careful dash of wryness, like two drops of Worcester sauce in a plate of gravy soup.

He bounced up and strode toward me, face first, hand out-stretched for a manly grip.

'Friends again, Charlie?' he mumbled.

It was my turn to drop the lower jaw – I broke out in a sweat of embarrassment and shame for the man. Well, I *mean*. I made a sort of gruff, gargling noise which seemed to satisfy him for he dropped my hand and settled back cosily on to the sofa. To hide my nonplussedness I ordered Jock to make coffee for us.

We waited for the coffee in silence, more or less. Martland tried a weather gambit – he's one of those people who always know when the latest V-shaped depression is likely to emerge from its roost over Iceland. I explained kindly that until I had drunk coffee of a morning I was a poor judge of meteorology.

(What is the origin of this strange British preoccupation with the weather? How can adult male Empire-builders gravely discuss whether or no it is raining, has rained or is likely to rain? Can you imagine the most barren-minded Parisian, Viennese or Berliner demeaning himself by talking such piffle? '*Ils sont fous ces Bretons,*' says Obelix, rightly. I suppose it is really just another manifestation of the Englishman's fantasy about the soil. The most urbane cit is, in his inner heart, a yeoman farmer and yearns for leather gaiters and a shotgun.)

The coffee having arrived (how hard it is to write without the ablative absolute!) we guzzled genteelly for a while, passing each other sugar and cream and things and beaming falsely from time to time. Then I lowered the boom.

'You were going to tell me how you knew I was at Spinoza's,' I said.

'Charlie, why ever are you so fascinated by that particular detail?'

It was a very good question indeed, but one which I had no intention of answering. I stared at him blankly.

'Oh, well, it's quite simple really. We happen to know that old Spinoza has – had, rather – about a quarter of a million grubby pound notes from the Great Train job. He paid for them in clean fivers and got a hundred and seventy-five pounds per cent. Bloody old crook. Well, we knew he would be having to unload soon so we hired a little yob who works for one of the galleries in Mason's Yard to watch the place for us. Anyone, well, interesting, goes to see Spinoza, we get the word on our yob's little walkie-talkie.'

'Really,' I said. 'Now I do call that riveting. What about callers before gallery hours?'

'Ah, yes, well, there we have to take a chance, of course. I mean, there just aren't funds to run shifts on all these jobs. Cost a fortune.'

I made a mental 'whew' of relief, believing him. A thought struck me.

'Martland, is your nark a little tit called Perce, works for the O'Flaherty Gallery?'

'Well, yes, I think that is his name, as a matter of fact.'

'Just so,' I said.

I cocked an ear; Jock was outside the door, breathing through his nose, making mental notes, if you can properly call them that. There's no doubt that I was much relieved to learn that only Perce was suborned; had Mr Spinoza been playing the strumpet with me all would have been lost. In spades. I must have allowed my expression to relax for I realized that Martland was looking at me curiously. This would not do. Change the subject.

'Well now,' I cried heartily, 'what's the deal? Where are these riches of the Orient you were pressing upon me last night? "Nay, even unto half your kingdom" was the sum mentioned, I believe?'

'Oh, really, come now Charlie, last night was last night, wasn't it? I mean, we were both a bit overwrought, weren't we? You're surely not holding me to that . . .?'

'The window is still there,' I said simply, 'and so is Jock. And I may say that I am still overwrought; no one has ever tried to murder me in cold blood before.'

'But obviously I've taken precautions this time, haven't I?' he said, and he patted a hip pocket. This told me that his pistol, if anywhere, was under his armpit, of course.

'Let us play a game, Martland. If you can get that thing out before Jock hits you on the head, you win the coconut.'

'Oh come on, Charlie, let's stop sodding about. I'm quite prepared to offer you substantial ah benefits and ah concessions if you'll play along with our side over this business. You know damn well I'm in the shit and if I can't recruit you that awful old man in the Home Office will be baying for your blood again. What will you settle for? I'm sure you aren't interested in the sort of money my department can offer.'

'I think I'd like a Bonzo dog.'

'Oh God, Charlie, can't you be serious?'

'No, really, a greyhound; you know, a silver one.'

'You can't mean you want to be a Queen's Messenger? What in God's name for? And what makes you think I could swing that?'

I said, 'First, yes, I do; second, mind your own business; third, you can swing it if you have to. I also want the diplomatic passport that goes with it and the privilege of taking a diplomatic bag to the Embassy in Washington.'

He leaned back in his chair, all knowing and relaxed now. 'And what is likely to be in the bag, or is that not my business either?'

'A Rolls Royce, as a matter of fact. Well, it won't actually be in a bag, of course, but it will be smothered in diplomatic seals. Same thing.'

He looked grave, worried; his under-engined brain revving furiously as its *deux chevaux* tried to cope with this gradient.

'Charlie, if it's going to be full of drugs the answer is no repeat no. If it's grubby pound notes in a reasonable quantity I might see my way, but I don't think I could protect you afterwards.'

'It is neither,' I said firmly. 'On my word of honour.' I looked him squarely and frankly in the eye as I said it, so that he would be sure that I was lying. (Those notes from the Train will have to be changed soon, won't they?) He eyed me back like a trusting comrade, then carefully placed all ten fingertips together, eyeing them with modest pride as though he'd done something clever. He was thinking hard and didn't care who knew it.

'Well, I suppose something on those lines could be worked out,' he said at last. 'You realize, of course, that the degree of co-operation expected from you would have to be proportionate to the difficulty of getting you what you ask?'

'Oh yes,' I replied brightly, 'you will want me to kill Mr Krampf, won't you?'

'Yes, that's right. How did you guess?'

'Well, clearly, now that Hockbottle has been, er, terminated, you can't possibly leave Krampf alive, knowing what he does, can you? And I may say it's a bit rough on me because he happens to be a rather good customer of mine.'

'Yes, I know.'

'Yes, I thought you would know by now. Otherwise I probably wouldn't have mentioned it, ha ha.'

'Ha ha.'

'Anyway, it's clear that you can't put any pressure on a chap as rich as Krampf except by killing him. It's also clear that I can get close to him and that getting me to do it will save your estimates a fortune. Moreover, no one could possibly be as expendable as me from your point of view – and I can scarcely be traced to any official agency. Lastly, if I do it clumsily and get myself into an electric chair you've killed both Krampf and me with one gallstone.'

'Well, some of that's more or less true,' he said.

'Yes,' I said.

Then I sat at my silly little French desk – the one the witty dealer called a *malheur-du-jour* because he paid too much for it – and wrote a list of all the things I wanted Martland to do. It was quite long. His face darkened as he read but he bore it like a little man and tucked the paper carefully in his wallet. I noticed that he was not wearing a shoulder holster after all, but that had not been my first mistake that day by any means.

The coffee was by now cold and horrid, so I courteously gave him what was left of it. I daresay he didn't notice. Then he left after a chummy commonplace or two; for a moment I feared he was going to shake my hand again.

'Jock,' I said, 'I am going back to bed. Be so kind as to bring me all the London telephone books, a shakerful of cocktails – any sort, let it be a surprise – and several watercress sandwiches made of soft white bread.'

Bed is the only place for protracted telephoning. It is also excellently suited to reading, sleeping and listening to canaries. It is not at all a good place for sex: sex should take place in armchairs, or in bathrooms, or on lawns which have been brushed but not too recently mown, or on sandy beaches if you happen to have been circumcised. If you are too tired to have intercourse except in bed you are probably too tired anyway and should be husbanding your strength. Women are the great advocates of sex in bed because they have bad figures to hide (usually) and cold feet to warm (always). Boys are different, of course. But you probably knew that. I must try not to be didactic.

After an hour I arose, draped the person in whipcord and hopsack and descended to the kitchen to give the canary one more chance to be civil to me. It was more than civil, almost busting its tiny gut with song, vowing that all would yet be well. I accepted its assurances guardedly.

Calling for coat and hat I tripped downstairs – I never use the lift on Saturdays, it's my day for exercise. (Well, I use it going *up*, naturally.)

The concierge emerged from her lair and gibbered at me: I silenced her with a finger to my lips and significantly raised eyebrows. Never fails. She slunk back, mopping and mowing.

I walked all the way to Sotheby's, holding my tummy in nearly the whole time, terribly good for one. There was a picture belonging to me in the sale, a tiny canvas of a Venetian nobleman's barge with liveried gondoliers and a wonderfully blue sky. I had bought it months before, hoping to persuade myself that it was by Longhi, but my efforts had been in vain so I had put it into Sotheby's, who had austerely called it 'Venetian School, XVIII Century.' I ran it up to the figure I had paid for it, then left it to its own devices. To my delight it ran for another three hundred and fifty before being knocked down to a man I detest. It is probably in a Duke Street window this moment, labelled Marieschi or some such nonsense. I stayed another ten minutes and spent my profit on a doubtful but splendidly naughty Bartolomaeus Spränger showing Mars diddling Venus with his helmet on – such *manners*! On my way out of the Rooms I telephoned a rich turkey farmer in Suffolk and sold him the Spränger, sight unseen, for what is known as an undisclosed sum, and toddled righteously away towards Piccadilly. There's nothing like a little dealing to buck one up.

Across Piccadilly without so much as a bad fright, through Fortnum's for the sake of the lovely smells, a step along Jermyn Street and I was snug in Jules's Bar, ordering luncheon and blotting up my fifth White Lady. (I forgot to tell you what Jock's surprise had been; sorry.) As a serious gastronome I deplore cocktails of course, but then I also deplore dishonesty, promiscuity, inebriety and many another goody.

If anyone had been following me hitherto they were welcome, I'm sure. For the afternoon, however, I needed privacy from the SPG boys so I scanned the room carefully from time to time as I ate. By closing time the whole population of the bar had changed except for one or two permanent fixtures whom I knew by sight: if there had been a tail he must be outside and by now probably very cross.

He was both outside and cross.

He was also Martland's man Maurice. (I suppose I hadn't really expected Martland to play it straight: the school we were at together wasn't a particularly good one. Long on sodomy and things but a bit short on the straight bat, honour and other expensive extras, although they talked a lot about them in Chapel. Cold baths a-plenty, of course, but you, who have never taken one, may be surprised to learn that your actual cold bath is your great begetter of your animal passions. Rotten bad for the heart, too, they tell me.)

Maurice had a newspaper in front of his face and was peering at me through a hole in it, just like they do in the storybooks. I took a couple of rapid paces to the left: the paper swung around after me. Then three to the right and again the paper swung, like the fire shield of a field gun. He did look silly. I walked over to him and poked my finger through the hole in his paper.

'Booh!' I said and waited for his devastating retort.

'Please take your finger out of my newspaper,' he retorted devastatingly.

I wiggled the finger, resting my nose on the top of the newspaper.

'Piss off!' he snarled, scarlet-faced. Better, that.

I pissed off, well pleased with myself. Round the corner of St James's Street clumped a policeman, one of those young, pink, indignant policemen you meet so often nowadays. Ambitious, virtuous and hell on evil-doers.

'Officer!' I gobbled angrily, 'I have just been obscenely accosted by that wretched fellow with the newspaper.' I pointed a shaking finger at Maurice who paused guiltily in midstride. The policeman went white about the lips and bore down on Maurice who was still on one foot, newspaper outstretched, looking extraordinarily like a cruel parody of Gilbert's 'Eros' at Piccadilly Circus. (Did you know that Eros is made of aluminium? I'm sure there's a moral there somewhere. Or a joke.)

'I'll be at your Station in forty minutes,' I cried after the policeman, and nipped into a passing taxi. It had all its handles.

Now, as I've already told you, Martland's men have a year's training. Ergo, spotting Maurice so easily had to mean that Maurice was there to be spotted. It took me a long time but I spotted her in the end: a burly, clean-shaven, auntlike woman in a Triumph Herald: an excellent car for tailing people in, unremarkable, easily parked and with a tighter turning circle than a London taxi. It was unfair on her not to have had a companion though. I simply hopped out at Piccadilly Circus, went in one Underground entrance and out of another. Triumph Heralds are not all that easily parkable.

My second taxi took me to Bethnal Green Road, Shoreditch, a wonderful place where all sorts of recondite crafts are plied. Over-tipping the driver, as is my foolish wont, he 'gave' me 'Nostalgia for the fourth at Kempton Park.' Still wondering what on earth he could mean, I climbed the stairs to my liner's studio.

Here I'd better explain what a liner is. Most old paintings need a new support before they can be cleaned. In its simplest form, this involves soaking the old canvas with glue, 'compo' or wax, then bonding it, so to speak, to a new canvas by means of a hot table and pressure. Sometimes the old canvas is too far gone; sometimes during the work the paint comes adrift (the picture 'blows up' as they say). In either of these cases a 'transfer' is called for. This means that the painting is fastened face downwards and every shred of canvas is removed from the paint. The new canvas is then stuck on to the back of the paint and your picture is sound again. If it is painted on panel (wood) which has gone rotten or wormy, a really top reliner can plane all the wood off, leaving only the crust of paint, to which he then sticks a canvas. All very, very tricky work and highly paid. A good liner has a pretty shrewd idea of the value of the painting he is treating and usually charges accordingly. He makes more money than many of the dealers he works for. He is indispensable. Any idiot can clean a painting – and many of them do – and most competent artists can strengthen (touch up) or replace missing bits of paint; indeed many famous painters have made a good thing out of this as a secret sideline. (Very delicate work, like the rigging of ships, was often painted with a varnish medium for easy handling: this is hell to clean because, of course, it comes off with the dirty varnish. Consequently, many cleaners simply photograph the rigging or whatever, ruthlessly clean it off, then repaint it from the photograph. Well, why not?) But a good liner, as I was saying, is a pearl beyond price.

Pete does not look like a pearl. He looks like a dirty and sinister little Welshman, but he has the curiously beautiful manners which even the basest Celt displays in his own home. He opened the ceremonial tin of Spam and brewed a huge metal pot of lovely strong Brooke Bond PG Tips. I hastily volunteered to make the bread and butter – his nails were *filthy* – and to slice the Spam. It was a lovely tea party, I adore Spam, and the tea had condensed milk in it and came out a rich orange colour. (How different, how very different, from the home life of our own dear queen.)

I told him the Spränger would be arriving from Sotheby's and that I thought the drapery over Venus's oh-be-joyful was later work and probably concealed a very fair example of the nun's wink.

'Scrub,' I told him, 'but scrub with care.'

We then repaired to his studio under the roof so that I could inspect work in progress. All very satisfactory. He was having great trouble with my little Sienese tryptich (*is* that how you spell it?) but then he'd been having trouble with it for eighteen months. I never got the bill for it and now I probably never shall.

Then I told him about Mr Spinoza and explained certain new arrangements. He didn't like them a bit but soon stopped shrieking when I filled his mouth with gold, as it were. He keeps his money in the tea caddy, if you want to know. There was one more ordeal to be undergone before I could get away from his carious, onion-laden breath.

'Just got time for a tune, then, ain't I?' he cried with the coy, treat-giving air of a Quartermaster dishing out prophylactics.

'Capital, capital,' I responded, rubbing hypocritical hands. He sat down at his little electric organ (it cost him £400) and treated me to 'Turn back, oh man, Forswear thy foolish ways' which moved me deeply. There is something curiously wrong about most Welsh voices, a kind of cardboard quality under the slick of gold, which irks me greatly. Pete's singing can reduce a public bar full of people to tears of sheer pleasure – I've seen it – but it always makes me feel that I've eaten too many Spam sandwiches.

I applauded loudly and, since he was particularly indispensable at that juncture, begged humbly for another. He gave me 'There is a Fountain Filled with Blood,' which never fails to please. I tottered downstairs and into the street, my bowels heavy with strong tea and foreboding.

The Bethnal Green Road at half past six on a Saturday night is not a *locus classicus* for taxis. In the end I took a bus; the conductor wore a turban and hated me on sight. I could see him memorizing me so that he could go on hating me after I'd got off.

Much depressed, I entered the flat and stood limply while Jock took my hat and coat away from me. He steered me to my favourite chair and brought me a glass of whisky calculated to stun a Clydesdale stallion. I revived enough to play a record of Amelita Galli-Curci singing 'Un Di Felice' with Tito Schipa; that reassured me in the *bel canto* department and the rest of the album dissipated most of the foreboding. Bathed and dinner-jacketed, I was in the mood for Wilton's lovely *art-nouveau* décor and even more in the mood for their Oysters Mornay. I also had a baked custard, a thing I wouldn't dream of eating anywhere else.

Home again, I was in time for a rattling John Wayne Western on the television, which I let Jock watch with me. We drank a great deal of whisky, for this was Saturday night.

I suppose I went to bed at some stage.

5

For he 'gins to guess the purpose of the garden,
With the sly mute thing beside, there, for a warden.

What's the leopard-dog-thing, constant at his side,
A leer and lie in every eye of its obsequious hide?

You must have noticed from time to time, self-indulgent reader, that brandy, unless you positively stupefy yourself with it, tends to drive sleep away, rather than induce it. I am told, by those who have drunk it, that with cheap brandy the effect is even more marked. It is otherwise with Scotch whisky; a benign fluid. All credit, I say, to the man who first invented it, be his skin of whatever hue. Indeed, my only quarrel with him is that sixteen fluid ozs of his brainchild, taken orally *per diem* for ten years or so, lessens one's zest for the primal act. I used to think that my flagging powers were the result of advancing age combining with the ennui natural to an experienced *coureur*, but Jock disabused me. He calls it 'brewer's droop'.

Be that as it may, I find that drinking a sound twelve-year-old Scotch in good quantity gives me six hours of flawless slumber, followed by a compulsion to get up in the morning and bustle about. Accordingly, I got up, without the sweet coercion of Bohea, and stamped downstairs, intending to roust Jock out and point out to him the benefits of early rising. To my mild chagrin he was already up and out of the flat, so I made my own breakfast: a bottle of Bass. I can heartily recommend it. I shall not pretend that I would not have liked a cup of tea, but the truth is that I am a little afraid of these new electric kettles: in my experience they eject their plugs savagely at you while you stand beside them waiting for them to boil.

There is only one thing to do early on a Sunday morning in London and that is to visit Club Row. I tiptoed downstairs so as not to disturb my Madame Defarge and made my way to the mews. All three cars were there but Jock's huge motorbike, which generates enough power to light a small town, was absent. I gave a whimsical Gallic wink and shrug to a passing cat: Jock was probably in love again, I thought. When chaps like him are in rut they'll travel miles, you know, escaping from prison first if needs be.

Club Row used to be just a row of shifty chaps selling stolen dogs: nowadays it is an enormous open-air mart. I roved about for an hour but the old magic didn't work. I bought a disgusting plastic object to tease Jock with – it was called 'Drat That Dog' – and drove home, too distraught even to lose my way. I thought of dropping in at Farm Street to catch one of those rattling Jesuit sermons but felt that might be too dangerous in my present mood. The sweet logic and lucidity of high-powered Jesuits works on me like a siren-song and I have a dread that one day I shall be Saved – like a menopausal woman – *how* Mrs Spon would laugh! Do they really wash you in the blood of the lamb or is that only the Salvation Army?

Jock was at home, elaborately unsurprised at my early rising. We did not question each other. While he cooked my breakfast I slipped the 'Drat That Dog' into the canary's cage.

Then I had a little zizz until Martland telephoned.

'Look, Charlie,' he quacked, 'it just isn't on. I can't organize all that Diplomatic bit, the Foreign Office told me to go and piss up my kilt.'

I was in no mood to be trifled with by the Martlands of this world.

'Very well,' I rapped out crisply, 'let us forget the whole thing.' And I hung up. Then I changed my clothes and laid a course for the Café Royal and luncheon.

'Jock,' I said as I left, 'Mr Martland will be telephoning again shortly to say that everything is all right after all. Tell him "all right," would you. All right?'

'All right, Mr Charlie.'

The Café Royal was full of people pretending they went there often. I liked my lunch but I forget what it was.

When I got back to the flat Jock told me that Martland had called in person, all the way from what he calls Canonbury, to wrangle with me, but that Jock had turned him away.

'He bloody near spit on the mat' was how Jock summed up his parting mood.

I went to bed and read a naughty book until I fell asleep, which was soon. You can't get good naughty books any more, there aren't the craftsmen nowadays, you see. Those Swedish ones with coloured photographs are the worst, don't you think? Like illustrations to a handbook of gynaecology.

Mrs Spon woke me up, charging into my bedroom in a red, wet-look trouser suit; she looked like a washable Scarlet Woman. I hid under the bedclothes until she promised she was only here to play Gin Rummy. She plays a lovely game of Gin but has terrible luck, poor dear; I usually win six or seven pounds off her but then she's had a *fortune* from me at interior decorating. (It is my invariable practice, when playing Gin Rummy, to leave one card accidentally in the box: it is amazing how much edge you can get from the knowledge that there is, for example, no nine of spades in the pack.)

After a while she complained of the cold as she always does – I will not have central heating, it ruins one's antique furniture and dries up one's tubes. So she got into bed beside me, as she always does (look, she must be *sixty* for God's sake), and we played 'gotcha' for a while between hands. Then she rang for Jock who brought a naked sword to put between us and a lot of hot pastrami sandwiches on garlicky bread. We were drinking Valpolicella, hell on the bowels but delicious and so cheap. I won six or seven pounds from her; it was such a lovely evening; tears start to my eyes as I recall it. It is no use treasuring these moments as they occur, it spoils them; they are only for remembering.

When she had gone, after one last 'gotcha', Jock brought me my bedtime rations: whisky, milk, chicken sandwiches and aluminium hydroxide for the ulcer.

'Jock,' I said, after thanking him civilly, 'we must do something about nasty Perce, Mr O'Flaherty's little git.'

'I already done it, Mr Charlie. 'Smorning, before you was up.'

'Did you really, Jock? My word, you think of everything. Did you hurt him very much?'

'Yes, Mr Charlie.'

'Oh dear. Not . . .?'

'Nah. Nuffing that a good dentist couldn't put right in a coupla munce. And, uh, I don't reckon he'll feel like doing any *courting* for a bit, either, see what I mean.'

'Poor little chap,' I said.

'Yeah,' said Jock. 'Goodnight, Mr Charlie.'

'One other thing,' I said crisply. 'I am disturbed at the state of hygiene in the canary's cage. Could you see that it's cleaned out soon, please?'

'I already done it, Mr Charlie. While you was out at lunch.'

'Oh. Everything all right?'

'Yeah. 'Course.'

'Oh, well, thanks, Jock. Goodnight.'

I didn't sleep very well that night.

If either Krampf *or* Gloag had departed from the agreed plan I could have borne it with fortitude, but two idiots in a team of three seemed excessive. I had told Hockbottle Gloag when he first approached me that I had no intention of helping him to blackmail his august Chum – introducing Hockers to Krampf was as far as I was prepared to go. Later, when Krampf had suggested to me that the photograph could be used, not for coarse money squeezing, but for facilitating the export, to him, of hot works of art, I had let him wring from me my slow consent, but only on condition that I should write the script, and play both the lead and the comic relief. But, as Schnozzle Durante never tired of saying, 'Everybody wants to get in on the act.' Gloag had already paid the price for this foot-light fever and it looked as though Krampf was at least getting a pro forma invoice.

6

Still, what if I approach the august sphere
Named now with only one name, disentwine
That under-current soft and argentine
From its fierce mate . . .?

Sordello

The telephone woke me at a most *inconvenient* hour on Monday. A honeyed American voice asked if it could speak to Mr Mortdecai's secretary.

'One moooment please,' I crooned, 'I'll put you throooo.' I stuffed the telephone under my pillow and lit a cigarette, musing the while. Finally I rang for Jock, briefed him and gave him the telephone. Holding it between hairy thumb and forefinger, pinky delicately crooked, he fluted, 'Mr Mortdecai's seckritry 'ere.' Then he got the giggles – disastrous after yesterday's feast of beans – and so did I and the telephone got dropped; the Honeyed American Voice must have thought it all *most* peculiar. It turned out that it – the H.A.V. – was a Colonel Blucher's secretary at the American Embassy, and that Colonel Blucher would like to see Mr Mortdecai at ten o'clock. Jock, properly shocked, said that there was no chance of Mr Mortdecai being out of bed at that hour and that he never received gentlemen in bed. (More giggles.) The voice, no whit less honeyed, said that, well, Colonel Blucher had in fact envisaged Mr. Mortdecai calling on *him* and would ten thirty be more convenient. Jock fought a stout rearguard action – in a curious way he's rather proud to work for anyone as slothful as me – and finally they struck a bargain for noon.

As soon as Jock put the instrument down I lifted it again and dialed the Embassy (499 9000, if you want to know). One of the most beautiful voices I have ever heard answered – a furry, milky contralto which made my coccyx curl into ringlets. It quite distinctly said:

'Care to embrace me?'

'Eh?' I gobbled, 'what's that what's that?'

'American Embassy' – this time in rather more sanitary tones.

'Oh. Yes. Of course. Silly of me. Ah, what I wanted to know was whether you have a Colonel Blucher working there.'

There was a click or two, a muted electric 'grrr' and before I could do anything about it I was once more in communication with the original Honeyed (honied?) Voice. She didn't say she was Colonel anyone's secretary this time, she said she was the War Room, CumQuicJac or SecSatSix or some such mumbo-jumbo. What *children* these warriors are.

I couldn't very well say that I was just checking to see whether Col. Blucher was real or just a Heartless Practical Joke, could I? In the end, after a bit of spluttering, I said that I had an appointment with her guv'nor, d'ye see, at sort of noon really, and what number in Grosvenor Square was the Embassy. This should have been a heavy score to me – lovely footwork you must admit – but she was a fast, damaging counterpuncher.

'Number twenty-four,' she warbled unhesitatingly, 'that's two, four.'

I rang off after a mumbled civility or two. Rolled up, horse, foot and guns. I mean, fancy a bloody great place like that *having* a street number, for God's sake.

Jock averted his gaze: he knows when the young master has taken a bit of stick.

I pushed my breakfast moodily round the plate for a while then told Jock to give it to the deserving poor and bring me in its stead a large glass of gin with both sorts of vermouth in it and some fizzy lemonade. A quick actor, that drink, gets you to where you live in no time.

Sucking a perfumed cachou, I walked to Grosvenor Square, soberly clad and musing madly. The musing was to no avail; my mind was as blank as the new, soft fallen mask of snow upon the mountains and the moors. The cachou lasted as far as the portals of the Embassy, within which stood a capable-looking military man, standing at what is laughingly called ease. The jut of his craggy jaw made it clear to the trained eye that he was there to keep out Commie bastards and anyone else who might be plotting to overthrow the Constitution of the United States. I met his eye fearlessly and asked him if this was number twenty-four and he didn't know, which made me feel better.

A succession of well-designed young ladies took charge of me, wafting me ever deeper into the building. Each one of them was tall, slim, hygienic, graceful and endowed with amazingly large tits: I'm afraid I probably stared rather. I fetched up all standing (nautical term) at the outer office of Col. Blucher, where sat the Voice itself. She, as was fitting, had the finest endowment of all. I should think she had to type at arm's length. In the twinkling of an eye – and I mean that most sincerely – I was shunted into the inner office, where a lean, wholesome, uniformed youth gave me a chair.

I recognized the chair as soon as I applied my bottom to it. It was covered with shiny leather and the front legs were half an inch shorter than the back legs. This gives the sitter a vague feeling of unease, impermanence, inferiority. I have one myself, for seating chaps on who are trying to sell paintings to me. On no account was I going to take crap of this kind; I arose and made for the sofa.

'Forgive me,' I said sheepishly, 'I have these piles, you know? Haemorrhoids?'

He knew. Judging from the smile he cranked on to his face, I should say he had just developed them. He sat down behind the desk. I raised an eyebrow.

'I have an appointment with Colonel Blucher,' I said.

'I am Colonel Blucher, sir,' replied the youth.

I'd lost that rally, anyway, but I was still ahead on the chair-to-sofa move, he had to twist his neck and raise his voice when he spoke to me. He looked extraordinarily young to be a colonel and, curiously, his uniform didn't fit. Have you ever seen an American officer – nay, an American *private* even – with an ill-fitting uniform?

Tucking this thought away into a mental ticket pocket, I addressed the man.

'Oh, ah,' was the phrase I selected.

Perhaps I could have done better, given more time.

He picked up a pen and teased a folder which lay on his shining, empty desk. The folder had all sorts of coloured signals stuck on to it, including a big orange-coloured one with an exclamation mark in black. I had a nasty feeling that perhaps the file was labelled 'Hon C Mortdecai' but on second thoughts I decided that it was just there to frighten me.

'Mr Mortdecai,' he said at last, 'we have been asked by your Foreign Office to honour a diplomatic *laissez-passer* in your name and on a temporary basis. There seems to be no intention to accredit you to the British Embassy in Washington or to any Legation or Consulate, and our *vis-à-vis* in your Foreign Office seems to know nothing about you. I may say we have received the impression that he cares less. Would you perhaps like to comment on this situation?'

'Nope,' I replied.

This seemed to please him. He changed to another pen and stirred the folder about a bit more.

'Mr Mortdecai, you will appreciate that I have to enter in my report the purpose of your visit to the United States.'

'I am to deliver a valuable antique motor car under diplomatic seal,' I said, 'and I hope to do a little sightseeing in the South and West. I am very interested in the Old West,' I added defiantly, smugly conscious of a card up my sleeve.

'Yes, indeed,' he said politely, 'I read your article on "Nineteenth Century British Travellers to the American Frontier." It was very very fascinating.'

There was a distinct draft up my sleeve where the card had been, and a nasty feeling that someone had been doing a little research into C. Mortdecai.

'We are puzzled,' he went on, 'that anyone should want to seal diplomatically an empty automobile. I take it that it will, in fact, be empty, Mr Mortdecai?'

'It will contain my personal effects; viz., one case of gents' natty suitings, one ditto of costly haberdashery, a canvas bag of books to suit every mood – none of them very obscene – and a supply of cigarettes and old Scotch whisky. I shall be happy to pay duty on the last if you prefer.'

'Mr Mortdecai, if we accept your diplomatic status' – did he linger a moment at that point? – 'we shall of course respect it fully. But we have, as you know, this theoretical right to declare you *persona non grata*; although we exercise it very rarely toward representatives of your country.'

'Yes,' I babbled, 'old Guy slipped through all right, didn't he?'

He pricked his ears; I bit my tongue.

'Did you know Mr Burgess well?' he asked, inspecting his pen closely for defects in its manufacture.

'No no no,' I cried, 'no no no no no. Hardly ever met the feller. Probably had a jar of sherbet with him once in a while: I mean, you couldn't live in the same city with Guy Burgess and not find yourself in the same bar sometimes, could you? Matter of statistics, I mean.'

He opened the folder and read a few lines, raising one eyebrow in a disturbing way.

'Have you ever been a member of the Communist or Anarchist parties, Mr Mortdecai?'

'Good Lord no!' I cried gaily, 'filthy capitalist, me. Grind the workers' faces, I say.'

'When you were at school?' he prompted gently.

'Oh. Well, yes, I think I did take the Red side in the debating society at school once or twice. But in the Lower Sixth we all got either religion or Communism – it goes with acne you know. Vanishes as soon as you have proper sexual intercourse.'

'Yes,' he said quietly. I suddenly saw that he had acne. Strike two, as I believe they say over there. And how on earth had they dredged up all this dirt about me in a couple of days? A more unnerving thought: *had* it only been dredged in the last couple of days? The folder looked fat and well-handled as a Welsh barmaid. I wanted to go to the lavatory.

The silence went on and on. I lit a cigarette to show how unperturbed I was but he was ready for that one, too. He pressed a button and told his secretary to ask the janitor for an ashtray. When she brought it she turned the air conditioner up as well. Strike three. My turn to pitch.

'Colonel,' I said crisply, 'suppose I give you my word of honour as a nobleman' – *that* was a spitball – 'that I am totally uninterested in politics and that my mission has nothing to do with drugs, contraband, currency, white slavery, perversion or the Mafia, but that it does concern the interests of some of the Highest in the Land?'

To my amazement it seemed to work. He nodded slowly, initialled the front of the file and sat back in his chair. Americans have some curious pockets of old-fashionedness. One could feel the atmosphere of the room relaxing; even the air conditioner seemed to have changed its note. I cocked an ear.

'Forgive me,' I said, 'but I think that your wire recorder has run out of wire.'

'Why, thank you,' he said and pressed another button. The mammiferous secretary slithered in, changed the spool and slithered out again, giving me a small, hygienic smile en route. An English secretary would have sniffed.

'Do you know Milton Krampf well?' Blucher asked suddenly. Clearly, the ball game was still on.

'Krampf?' I said. 'Krampf? Yes, to be sure, very good customer of mine. Hope to spend a few days with him. Very nice old sausage. Bit potty of course but he can afford to be, can't he, ha ha.'

'Well, no, Mr Mortdecai, I in fact was referring to Dr Milton Krampf III, Mr Milton Krampf Junior's son.'

'Ah, there you have me,' I said truthfully, 'never met any of the family.'

'Really, Mr Mortdecai? Yet Dr Krampf is a well-known art historian, is he not?'

'News to me. What's his field supposed to be?' The Colonel flipped through the file – perhaps it was the *Krampf* file after all.

'He seems to have published numerous papers in American and Canadian journals,' he said, 'including "The Non-Image in Dérain's Middle Period," "Chromato-Spacial Relationships in Dufy," "Léger and Counter-Symbolism" . . . '

'Stop!' I cried, squirming. 'Enough. I could make up the rest of the titles myself. I know this sort of thing well, it has nothing to do with art history as I know it; my work lies with the Old Masters and I publish in the *Burlington Magazine* – I am quite a different sort of snob from this Krampf, our scholarly paths would never cross.'

'I see.'

He didn't see at all but he would have died rather than admit it. We parted in the usual flurry of insincerities. He still looked young, but not quite as young as when I had come in. I walked home, musing again.

Jock had a sauté of chicken livers ready for me but I had no stomach for the feast. Instead I chewed a banana and about a third of a bottle of gin. Then I had a little zizz, a little slumber, a little folding of the hands in sleep. A zizz, you know, is a very present help in trouble. With me, it takes the place of the kind, wise, tobacco-smelling, tweed-clad *English* father that other boys had when I was a schoolboy; the sort of father you could talk things over with during long tramps over the hills; who would gruffly tell you that 'a chap can only do his best' and that you 'must play the man' and then teach you to cast a trout-fly.

My father wasn't like that.

Sleep has often taken the place of this mythical man for me: often I have woken up comforted and advised, my worries resolved, my duty clear.

But this time I awoke unrefreshed and with no good news teeming in my brain. There was no comfortable feeling that a warm, tweedy arm had been about my shoulder, only the old gin-ache at the base of the skull and a vague taste of dog dung in the mouth.

'Heigh-ho,' I remember saying as I listened to the Alka-Seltzer fussing in its glass. I tried the effect of a clean shirt and a washed face; there was some slight improvement but various small nit-sized worries were still there. I have a dislike for coincidences and I *detest* clever young American colonels, especially when their uniforms do not quite fit them.

I was rather a cheery, carefree chap in those days, always ready to welcome a little adversity just for the pleasure of dealing with it deftly. So I was worried at feeling worried, if you see what I mean. One should only have a sense of impending doom when one is constipated and I was not, as it happened.

Jock handed me a stiff envelope when I emerged: it had been delivered, while I slept, by what he described as a long streak of pee in a bowler hat. Jock, with unerring aim, had offered him a pint of beer in the kitchen, which had been refused with some brusqueness.

The writer, who seemed to be assistant private secretary to someone else's permanent under-secretary or something, said that he was instructed to request me (or was it the other way about? – I forget) to present myself at Room 504 in one of the uglier new Government office blocks at 10.30 a.m. the following day, there to meet a Mr L.J. Crouch.

Now, I have only two basic rules for the conduct of my life, to wit:

Rule A My time and services are at the complete disposal of the customer at any time of the day or night and no trouble is too great when the interests of others can be served.

Rule B On the other hand, I'm buggered if I'm going to be buggered about.

I handed the note to Jock.

'This clearly falls under Rule B, does it not, Jock?'

'Dead right it does, Mr Charlie.'

'Ten thirty is the time stated?'

'Yeah.'

'Then call me at eleven in the morning.'

'O.K., Mr Charlie.'

Happier after that expression of poco-curantism, I strolled down to Veeraswamy's and thoughtfully gorged myself with curried lamb and buttered chapatis. The splendidly dressed doorman gave me his usual splendidly military salute in exchange for the shiniest half crown I could find in my pocket. Cheap at the price. When depressed, go and find someone to salute you.

Curry, in my small experience, makes women want to go to bed and make love; it just makes me want to go to bed and get the weight off my stomach. Curiously ponderous stuff, curry.

I carried my freight distressfully to bed and Jock brought me whisky and soda to cool the blood. I read Karl Popper's *Poverty of Historicism* for a while then fell asleep to dream guilty, furtive dreams about Punjabi colonels in deerstalker hats.

The burglar alarm went off at 3 a.m. When we are at home this only takes the form of a low, whining noise, pitched at a menacing frequency, which sounds in both bedrooms, both bathrooms, the drawing room and Jock's bog. It stops as soon as each of us has pressed a switch, so that we know we are both alert. I pressed my switch and it stopped immediately. I went to my post, which is an armchair in the darkest corner of my bedroom, after I had stuffed my bolster under the covers to simulate a sleeping Mortdecai. Above the armchair is a trophy of antique firearms, one of which is an 8-bore shotgun by Joe Manton, loaded with dust shot in the right-hand barrel, BB in the other. An old-fashioned bell pull below it releases the clamps which hold it to the wall. My job was to lurk there motionless, watching the door and the windows. Jock, meantime, would have checked the bellboard to ascertain where the alarm had been triggered from, then stationed himself by the tradesmen's door whence he could cut off retreats and, if necessary, follow an intruder upstairs to my room. I lurked, in a deadly silence broken only by my load of curry, which was churning about inside me like socks in a washing machine. It is very difficult to be frightened when you are gripping a loaded 8-bore shotgun but I managed it. This should not have been *happening*, you see.

After an eon or two the alarm made one brief peep, which was my signal to go downstairs. Sodden with funk, I crept down to the kitchen, where Jock stood naked and shadowy by the door, balancing an old 9-mm Luger in his hand. On the bellboard a violet light marked FRONT DOOR was still flickering frantically. With a couple of jerks of the head Jock outlined our tactics: I slid into the drawing room where I could cover lobby and front door, Jock silently drew the bolts of the tradesmen's door. I heard him wrench it open and bound into the corridor – then he called me low and urgently. I ran through the dining room, into the kitchen, out of the door. Only Jock was in the corridor. I followed his stare to the lift indicator: it said '5' – my floor. At that moment the lift motor growled and the '5' flicked out and Jock hurtled to the stairhead and vanished downwards with scarcely a sound. You should have seen Jock in action – an intimidating sight, especially when naked, as then. I ran down half a flight until I could see into the well of the staircase: Jock had taken up a position on the ground floor, covering the lift doors. After a second or two he jumped up and vanished into the back regions; puzzled for a moment, I suddenly realized that the lift must have gone down into the basement. I galloped down, humpetty-dump, all fright forgotten now, and had reached the third floor when a glance at the indicator showed me that the lift was again rising. Up I fled again, arriving at the fifth floor sadly blown. The indicator had stopped at '3'. I slammed into the flat, stumbled through into the drawing room and knelt down beside the record-player console. A button inside it communicated with the 'Set-A-Thief' duty room – I yearned for those thugs. I didn't press the button, for someone hit me at the base of the skull, just where my gin-ache still lingered. My chin hooked on to the edge of the console and there I hung awhile, feeling very silly. Then he hit me again and I sank effortlessly through the floor, miles and miles and miles.

About a lifetime later I awoke, with great reluctance. Jock's huge face hung moonlike over me, making worried noises. When I spoke, shattering echoes boomed and rattled through my poor head. I was filled with hatred and misery.

'Did you kill him?' I asked hungrily.

'No, Mr Charlie. I waited at the bottom for a bit and the lift stopped at "3" and I waited a bit more then I tried the button and it came down empty so I went up in it to here and you weren't outside so I went to the top of the stairs to see if I could see you and then I heard the lift going down again and I thought this could go on all bleeding night and I came in here looking for you and here you were and so I thought . . .' I raised a hand feebly.

'Stop,' I said. 'I cannot possibly follow all this at the moment. It makes my head hurt. Search the flat, lock the doors, get me to bed and find me the largest sleeping pill ever made. And get some clothes on, you idiot, you'll catch your death.'

At this point I switched off C. Mortdecai as an individual and let the poor chap swim through the floor again, down to a sunless sea.

If anyone cut my throat after that, they were welcome.

7

Who'd stoop to blame
This sort of trifling? Even had you skill
In speech – (which I have not) – to make your will
Quite clear to such an one, and say, 'Just this
Or that in you disgusts me; here you miss,
Or there exceed the mark' – . . .
– E'en then would be some stooping; and I choose
Never to stoop.

My Last Duchess

I very carefully levered up an eyelid and shut it again fast. A merciless sunbeam had squirted straight in, making my brain bleed.

Much later I tried again.

The sunshine had been smothered and Jock was hovering at the foot of my bed, wringing his hands. He was also carrying a tea tray, but I have the distinct impression that he was wringing the hands, too.

'Go away,' I whimpered. He set the tray down and poured a cup for me; it sounded, inside my poor head, like someone flushing a lavatory in an echo chamber. I whimpered a little more and turned away but Jock gently waggled my shoulder, murmuring, 'Now now' or 'There there' or words to that effect. I sat up to remonstrate with him – the action seemed to leave half my skull behind on the pillow. I felt the afflicted area gingerly: it was sort of spongy and squashy to the touch but to my surprise was not caked with blood. I decided that had my skull been fractured I would not have woken up at all. Not that it seemed to matter that morning.

The tea was not my customary Lapsang or Oolong but Twining's robuster Queen Mary's Blend: shrewd Jock, he knew that a morning like this called for sterner stuff. I got the first cupful down, then Jock fed me two Alka-Seltzers (the *noise!*), two Beecham's Powders and two dexedrines, in the order named, washing the whole collection down with a second cup of Queen Mary's best and brightest. I shall never say another harsh word about that sainted woman.

Soon I became capable once more of rational thought, and rational thought urged me to go back to sleep at once. I sank down in the general direction of the pillows but Jock firmly scooped me up and balanced cups of tea all over me so that I dared not move.

'There's this tart been ringing up all day,' he said, 'says she's that deputy secretary bloke's secretary and it's about your travel papers and you ought to get around there if you can stand and her gaffer'll see you any time up to half past four. It's three now, nearly.'

Creaking and grunting I hoisted myself to the surface.

'Who do you think it was then last night, Mr Charlie?'

'Not one of Martland's lot, anyway,' I answered. 'They would have expected the full treatment like last time. Anything missing?'

'Not that I can see.'

'Well, they didn't go to all that trouble just to sock me on the back of the head, that's for certain.'

'Could have just been an ordinary villain: hadn't cased us proper, didn't reckon on two of us, lost his head and buggered off a bit sharpish. He left this stuck in the front door lock, that's why the alarm light kept on.'

'This' was a pocket calendar made of stiff celluloid, the size and shape of a playing card, bearing on the reverse an impassioned plea for the reader to drink someone's Milk Stout. It would diddle open almost any sort of spring cylinder lock. It would be useless against my Chubb dead-lock with the phosphor-bronze rollers in the wards, and anyone who had spent even a week's remedial training in Borstal would have known that. I didn't like it. Raw novices do not try their prentice hands on fifth floor penthouse flats in Upper Brook Street.

I started to think about it for the first time and liked it less and less.

'Jock,' I said, 'if we disturbed him while he was trying to celly the lock, why wasn't he *there* when we disturbed him? And since he wasn't there, how could he discover there were two of us? And if he'd given it up *before* you popped out, why did he leave a useful celly behind and why did he linger in the lift instead of, ah, buggering off a bit sharpish?'

Jock opened his mouth a bit to help him think. I could see that it hurt him.

'Never mind,' I said, kindly, 'I know how you feel. Mine hurts too. It seems to me that the villain poked his celly into the lock just to trigger the alarm, then lay in wait in the lift. When you popped out, he popped down, to draw you away. Then up again to the third, knowing you would wait for him downstairs like a sensible chap; out of the lift and up to the fifth on foot, knowing that he could handle me alone. Having done so, he hears you arrive, hides behind a door and exits quietly while you are succouring the young master. The whole idea was to get me alone with the door open and you safely out of the way for a few minutes. What we need to wonder is not how, or even who, but why.'

'Taking something . . .'

'If so, it must have been something portable, easily found – because he can't have expected much time – and something very important to make the risk worthwhile. Something recently arrived, too, probably, because there is a sort of impromptu aroma about the whole thing.'

'. . . or leaving something,' Jock continued with remorseless logic.

I jumped, making my headache rear up and smite me. It was a nasty thought, that one.

'What on earth would anyone want to leave here?' I squeaked, dreading the answer.

'Well, like a bug,' said Jock. 'Or a couple of ounces of heroin, enough to put you inside for twelve munce. Or say arf a pound of plastic explosive . . .'

'I am going back to bed,' I said firmly. 'I want no part of any of this. Nobody ordered bombs.'

'No, Mr Charlie, you got to go to this assistant secretary geezer. I'll nip round to the garage and fetch the big jam jar.'

'What, and leave me alone in a flat *sown* with Teller mines?' I wailed.

But he was gone. Grumbling bitterly I climbed into a random assortment of gents' wear and crept through the flat and downstairs. Nothing exploded under my feet.

Jock was awaiting me at street level in the Rolls and as a special treat for me he was wearing his chauffeur's cap. When we arrived at the Ministry he even jumped out and opened the door for me; he knew it would cheer me up, bless him.

Do you know, I honestly can't remember which Ministry it was; this was soon after the Wilson administration, you see, and you remember how he muddled them all up and changed all the names. They say that there are still a few lorn civil servants haunting the pavements of Whitehall like ghosts, plucking at strangers' sleeves and begging to be told the way to the Ministry of Technological Integration. Their salaries keep on coming, of course, because of Giro, but what really hurts them most is that their Ministries haven't *missed* them yet.

Be that as it may, Jock left me at this Ministry and various super young men passed me through door after door – each young man more beautifully dressed, each door heavier and silenter than the last – until I was alone with L.J. Crouch. I had fortified myself against a sort of English Colonel Blucher but nothing could have been further from the facts. A great, jolly, big-boned, straw-haired chap lowered his boots from a well-chewed desk and lumbered to meet me, beaming merrily.

'Ha!' he roared, 'Capital! Glad to see you on your feet, young feller! Best thing after a crunch – get up and charge about. *Nil illegitimis carborundum*, eh? Don't let the bastards wear you down!'

I tittered feebly and sank into the fat leather armchair he indicated. Cigars, whisky and soda were conjured into my listless hands while I gazed around me. The furniture, unmistakably, came from a better class vicarage: all well made but sort of trodden on. In front of me, above his chair, sixty rat-faced boys squinted and goggled at me from a prep school group photograph; above them hung a piece of an Eights oar, splintered and charred and bearing the colours of St. Edmund Hall. In a corner sat an old brass naval shell-case, crammed with stout sticks and fencing foils of the old butterfly-hilted *fleuret* pattern. Two walls were hung with early English watercolours of the good, drab, bluish kind. Nothing is more tedious, as Sir Karl Parker used to say, than an early English watercolour – unless it be a *faded* early English watercolour. But I cut my business teeth on them and always hold them in respect.

'Know about watercolours?' asked Crouch, following my gaze.

'A bit,' I said, looking him straight in the eye. 'You have a J. M. W. Turner of the Loire which can't be right because the original is in the Ashmolean; a magnificent Callow of about 1840; a Farington which needs cleaning; a polychrome James Bourne – rare, those; a Peter de Wint hayfield with a repainted sky; an excellent John Sell Cotman; a pair of rather flashy Varleys from his last period; a Payne which was reproduced in *Connoisseur* before the war; a Rowlandson which Sabine had for sale in about 1940; a Francis Nicholson of Scarborough all faded pink – he *would* use indigo; a valuable Cozens and the finest Edridge I have ever seen.'

'My word,' he said. 'Full marks, Mortdecai. I see you know about watercolours.'

'Can't resist showing off,' I said sheepishly. 'Just a knack, really.'

'Mind you, the Edridge was sold me as a Girtin.'

'They always are,' I said simply.

'Well, come on, what'll you give me for the lot?'

A dealer has to get used to this sort of thing. I used to take offence once upon a time, before I learned the value of money.

'Two thousand, two hundred and fifty,' I said, still looking him straight in the eye. He was startled.

'*Pounds?*'

'Guineas,' I replied. 'Naturally.'

'God bless my soul. I stopped buying years ago, when the dear old Walker Galleries closed. I knew prices had gone up but . . .'

'The prices of these will be going down unless you get them out of this sunny room. They've taken about as much fading as they'll stand.'

Ten minutes later he took my cheque with trembling fingers. I let him keep the Nicholson in exchange for an Albert Goodwin which had been hanging in the cloakroom. His outer door opened a fraction and closed again with a respectful click. He started like a guilty thing and looked at the clock. It was 4.30: he was going to miss his train. So were his beautiful young men, if he didn't look sharp.

'Repeat after me,' he said briskly, pulling a grubby piece of card from a desk drawer, 'I, Charlie Strafford Van Cleef Mortdecai, a true and loyal servant of Her Britannic Majesty, do solemnly swear . . .'

I gaped at the man. Was he doubting my cheque?

'Come on,' he said, 'cough it up, old chap.'

I coughed it up, line by line, swearing to be a faithful carrier of Her Majesty's messages within and without her realms notwithstanding, heretofore, whatsoever and so help me God. Then he gave me a little jeweller's box with a rummy-looking silver dog inside, a document starting 'We, Barbara Castle, request and require' and a thin, red leather folder stamped in gold with the words 'Court of St. James's.' I signed things until my hand ached.

'Don't know what it's all about and don't want to,' he kept saying as I signed. I respected his wishes.

The young men shunted me out, glaring at me for making them miss their trains. Creatures of habit, of course. Couldn't stand the life myself.

Martland was parked on a double yellow line outside, pulling rank on a brace of traffic wardens; in another moment he would have been telling them to get their hair cut. He waved me crossly into his awful basketwork Mini and took me to the American Embassy, where a mild, bored man spattered my new papers with State Department seals and wished me a vurry, vurry happy visit to the US of A. Then back to the flat, where I gave Martland a drink and he gave me a wallet-load of airline tickets, freight vouchers and the like, also a typed list of timetables, names and procedures. (Codswallop, all of it, that last lot.) He was silent, sulky preoccupied. He said it wasn't he that had had me turned over the night before, and he didn't much care who had. On the other hand he didn't seem particularly surprised: more vexed, really. I suspected that he was beginning to suspect, with me, that the tangled web we weave was starting to get our knickers in a twist. Like me, he may have been wondering who, after all, was manipulating whom.

'Charlie,' he said ponderously, his hand on the door knob, 'if you are by any chance conning me over that Goya picture, or if you let me down over this Krampf matter, I shall have to have you done, you realize that, don't you? In fact I may have to do it anyway.'

I invited him to feel the back of my head, which felt like a goitre which had lost its sense of direction, but he refused in an offensive way. He slammed the door when he went out and my cosh-ache reverberated.

8

. . . Bearing aloft another Ganymede
On pinions imped, as 't were, but not past bearing,
Nor unfit yet for the fowler's purposes;
Feathered, in short, as a prince o' th'air – no moorgame.
If Paracelsus weighs that jot, this tittle,
God knows your atomy were ponderable –
(Love weighing t'other pan down!) . . .
. . . in a word,
In half a word's space, – let's say, ere you flinched,
Or Paracelsus wove one of those thoughts,
Lighter than lad's-love, delicate as death,
I'd draft you thither.

Paracelsus

I was off to the Americas – it was the first day of the hols. I sprang out of bed, calling for my bucket and spade, my sandshoes and my sun hat. Without the aid of stimulants I gambolled downstairs, carolling –

'This time tomorrow I shall be
Far from this Academee,'

disturbing Jock who was moodily packing my lightweights for the American adventure.

'You all right, Mr Charlie?' he asked nastily.

'Jock, I cannot tell you how all right I am –

"No more Latin, no more French,
No more sitting on the hard school bench,"'

I went on.

It was a fine morning which would have earned a *proxime accessit* from Pippa herself. The sun was shining, the canary bellowing with joy. Breakfast was cold kedgeree of which I ate great store – nothing nicer – washed down with bottled beer. Jock was sulking a little at being left behind but was really looking forward to having the flat to himself; he has his friends in to play dominoes when I'm away, I believe.

Then I opened about a week's accumulated mail, made out a paying-in slip, wrote a few cheques for the more importunate creditors, telephoned Dial-A-Dolly and dictated a dozen letters, had lunch.

Before setting out on a lengthy expedition I always have the same lunch which Ratty made for the Sea Rat and which they ate on the grass by the roadside. Ratty, you will remember, *literate* reader, '. . . packed a simple meal in which . . . he took care to include a yard of long French bread, a sausage out of which the garlic sang, some cheese which lay down and cried, and a long-necked straw-covered flask containing bottled sunshine and garnered on far Southern slopes.'

I pity anyone whose saliva does not flow in sympathy with those beautiful lines. How many men of my age have tastes and appetites distantly governed by these – not even half-remembered – words?

Jock drove me to Mr Spinoza's where we loaded the Silver Ghost with my suitcases (one pigskin, one canvas), and the book bag. Spinoza's foreman, with almost Japanese good taste, had not hammered out the bullet dimple in the door but had drilled it out and inlaid a disc of burnished brass, neatly engraved with Spinoza's initials and the date on which he had gone to meet his jealous god – 'the Maker of the makers of all makes' as Kipling has so deftly put it.

Spinoza and I had had some difficulty in dissuading Krampf from having a synchro-mesh gear-box fitted to the Ghost; now every sprocket and shaft in it was a perfect replica of the original contents of the box, with thirty thousand miles of simulated wear lovingly buffed in by the naughty apprentice. The gears engaged in a way which reminded me of a warm spoon going in to a great deal of caviar. The foreman's metaphor was perhaps more *general* than caviar – he likened it to having hasty congress with a lady of easy virtue whom he was in the habit of patronizing. I stared at the fellow: he was nearly twice my age.

'I admire you,' I cried, admiringly. 'However do you manage to keep so virile in the evening of your days?'

'Ah, well, Sir,' he replied modestly, 'your verality is a matter of your actual birth and breeding. My farver was a terrible man for rumpy-pumpy; he had hair thick as a yard-brush all down his old back to the day of his death.' He dashed a manly tear away. 'Not but what I don't always feel quite up to the demands my lady friends make on me. Sometimes, Sir, it's like trying to shove a marshmallow into a money-box.'

'I know just what you mean,' I replied. We shook hands with emotion, he received a furtive tenner with dignity, Jock and I drove away. Everyone in the workshop was waving except the naughty apprentice who was wetting himself with recondite laughter. I think he used to think I *fancied* him, for God's sake.

Our progress to London Airport was almost royal; I found myself doing that wonderfully elliptical, downward-curving, quite inimitable wave that Her Majesty Queen Elizabeth the Queen Mother so excels at. One expected, naturally, a certain amount of *empressement* to be derived from hurrying noiselessly through London and its purlieus in £25,000 worth of pure white antique Rolls Royce, but I confess the merry laughter – the *holiday* mood – which our passage caused surprised me. It was not until we arrived at the Airport that I found the three inflated french letters, big as balloons, which the naughty apprentice had tied to our hood-stays.

At the Airport we found two surly, rat-faced men who denied that there ever was any such car, any such flight, any such *airline* even. Jock finally lumbered out of the driving seat and said two short and dirty words to them, whereupon the relevant documents were found in the twinkling of a bloodshot eye. I gave them a 'nicker' on Jock's advice and you'd have been surprised how smoothly the machinery rolled into motion. They drained the petrol out of the Rolls and disconnected the batteries. A beautiful young man with *huge* eyelashes emerged from some fastness and produced a pair of nippers from a leather case. He clipped little lead seals on to every openable aperture of the Ghost (which was already mounted on a pallet), then winked at Jock, sneered at me and flounced back to his embroidery. A customs man who had been watching this came forward and took away all the bits of paper the F.O. man had given me. A dear little tractor hooked itself on to the pallet and chugged away with it. I've never seen a Rolls look so silly. That seemed to be that. Jock walked me to the Passenger Building and I let him buy me a drink, because he likes to keep his end up in public, then we bade each other gruff farewells.

My flight was announced by Donald Duck noises from a loudspeaker; I arose and shuffled off towards the statistical improbability of dying in an airplane crash. Personally, the thought of such a death appalls me little – what civilized man would not rather die like Icarus than be mangled to death on a Motorway by a Ford Popular?

When they let us undo our belts again a nice American sitting next to me offered me a huge and beautiful cigar. He was so diffident and called me 'Sir' so nicely that I had to take it. (It really was a lovely one, from the *atelier* of Henry Upmann.) He told me confidentially and impressively that meeting one's death in an airplane accident is a statistical improbability.

'Well, that's good news,' I tittered.

'Statistically,' he explained, 'you are in far greater hazard driving a three-year-old auto for eleven miles on a Freeway, according to the best actuaries.'

'Really,' I said – a word I only use when being told statistics by nice Americans.

'You can bet on it,' he said warmly. 'Personally, I fly many, many thousands of miles every year.'

'Well, there you are,' I said politely. 'Or rather, here you are, to prove the figures are right. What?'

'Exactly,' he said, drawing the word out.

We lapsed into a friendly silence, content with the rightness of our thinking, our cigars, teatlike, comforting our fears as our great gray dray horse of metal sped across St. George's Channel on its bright and battering sandals. After a while he leaned towards me.

'But just before take-off,' he murmured, 'don't your ass-hole pucker just a leetle?'

I thought about it carefully.

'More on landing, really,' I said at last, 'which is all wrong when you come to think about it.'

He thought about it for several minutes.

'You mean, like in an elevator?'

'Exactly.'

He guffawed happily, his own man again now, reassured that all men are sphincters at bottom, if I may coin a phrase.

Having settled the amenities, we got out our *work*, like two old women at a quilting-bee. Mine took the shape of a dreary German paperback on the Settecento in Naples (it takes a German *kunst-kenner* to make that epoch dull) while he unzipped a document case full of computer paper, infinitely incomprehensible. I battled for a while with Professor Aschloch's tulgey prose – only German poets have ever written lucid German prose – then closed my eyes, wondering bitterly which of my enemies the nice American worked for.

He had made one mistake in an otherwise flawless performance: he hadn't told me his name. Have you ever exchanged three words with an American without being told his name?

I seemed to have made a great many enemies since Wednesday. The likeliest and nastiest possibility, the one which caused most *puckering*, was Colonel Blucher's lot, whoever they were. Martland was a horrible bastard in his own insular way but he could never shake off that blessed British sense of perspective. The grim, unbelievably rich US Government Agencies were another matter. Too serious, too dedicated; they believe it's all *real*.

Acid digestive juices, triggered by *angst*, started to slosh about in my stomach and uneasy gurgles came from the small intestine. I positively welcomed the stewardess with her tray of pallid garbage; I shovelled the stuff down like a starving man while my nice American waved his away, all jaded and travelled and statistically improbable.

Ulcer appeased for the nonce by plastic smoked salmon, rubber chop in vitreous aspic, chicken turd wrapped in polystyrene bacon and weeping half-thawed strawberry on dollop of shaving soap, I felt able to examine the possibility that I might be mistaken and that the man was, after all, just a wholesome American dolt. (Like a British dolt, really, only with better manners.)

Why, after all, should anyone want to plant such a man on me? What could I get *up* to on the journey? What, if it came to that, could *he* get up to on the journey? Extract a confession from me? Prevent me seizing command of the aircraft or overthrowing the Constitution of the United States? Surely, too, it would be a waste of an agent, for after several hours of propinquity I could scarcely fail to recognize him in the future. No; clearly, he must be what he seemed, an indifferent-honest executive, perhaps one of that super research firm which sells the State Department advice on where to start its next minor war. I turned to him, warm and relaxed, with new confidence. A man who smokes Upmanns cannot be all bad.

'I say, forgive me, but what are you doing?' I asked, in as British a way as I could muster. Gladly, he folded up the concertina of computer paper he had been grappling with (easy, though, for anyone who can handle an American Sunday newspaper) and turned amiably toward me.

'Why, I've been uh correlating and uh collating and uh evaluating this very, very complete printout of costs-sales data on a retail multiplex in uh Great Britain, Sir,' he explained candidly.

I continued to look at him, eyebrows hoisted a little, tiny, polite British question-marks shimmering from my hairline.

'Fish and chips,' he explained. I dropped the lower jaw a bit, achieving, I felt, an even more British effect.

'Fish and chips?'

'Right. I'm thinking of buying it.'

'Oh. Really. Er, much of it?'

'Well, yeah, kind of, all of it.' I made interested, interrogatory faces and he went on, and on. It appeared that fish and chips represent the last £100M industry in Britain still unclobbered and that he was about to clobber it. Seventeen thousand friers, almost all independent and many of them only marginally profitable, using half a million tons of fish, a million tons of potatoes and 100 thousand tons of fat and oil. They use, he told me, whatever fish their 'sender' chooses to sell them and pay whatever they have to; frying the stuff, for the most part, in oil which a Hottentot would spurn as a sexual lubricant. He painted a grisly picture of the present and a rosy one of the future, when he would have bought all the shops and franchised them back on his terms.

It all seemed to make very good sense and I decided, as he droned usefully on, that I would provisionally believe him to be genuine at least until we landed. In fact we rather chummed up, to the point where he asked me to come and stay at his apartment. Well, of course, I didn't believe in him *that* much, so I'm afraid I told him that I would be staying at the British Embassy. He looked at me thoughtfully, then told me about his dream of getting a duke to be chairman of his English company.

'Capital idea!' I said heartily, 'Can't have too many of them. Wonderful little workers, every one. Mind you, there's pretty stiff competition for your actual dukes today; even the merchant banks can't seem to hold them any more, they're all going into the menagerie trade as fast as they can. They may creep out into the open again now that Wilson's gone, of course, but if I were you I'd settle for a marquess or a brace of earls: far more of them about and they're much less uppity.'

'Earls?' he said. 'Say, do you by any chance know the Earl of Snowdon?' His eyes shone with innocence but I started like a guilty thing upon a fearful summons.

'Certainly not,' I twittered, 'no no no. He's something quite different again; anyway he's got a job, at the Design Centre I think, terrible lot there, except him of course, designs elephant aviaries for the Zoo, jolly good ones I'm sure. Very capable. Capital fellow. Happily married; dear little wife. Yes.' I subsided. He ground on implacably.

'Parm me, but are you an aristocrat?'

'No no no,' I said again, wriggling with embarrassment, 'nothing of the sort. Rotten shot. I'm only a nobleman and my brother bagged the only title: my father sort of dropped me a courtesy, ha ha.' He looked puzzled and distressed so I tried to explain.

'England isn't like the Continent, you see, nor even like Scotland in this respect. The *seize quartiers* "noble in all his branches" thing is something we don't like to talk about and there aren't half a dozen families with straight descent from a knight of the Conquest, I should think – and they aren't titled. Anyway,' I rambled on, 'no one in his senses would want to be descended from one of that lot: the Conquest was something between a joint-stock company and a Yukon gold-rush; William the Conk himself was a sort of primitive Cecil Roberts and his followers were bums, chancers, queers and comic singers.'

He was boggling beautifully now, so I couldn't resist going on.

'Broadly speaking, practically none of the aristocracy are peers today and very few of the peers are aristocrats by any standard which would be taken seriously on the Continent: most of them are lucky if they can trace their family back to some hard-faced oick who did well out of the Dissolution of the Monasteries.'

This really upset him; one end of his concertina of printouts escaped from his lap and cascaded on to the floor between our feet. We both stooped for it but I, being thinner than he by an inch or two, stooped lower, so that our heads did not actually ring together; but my nose (Norman, with Roman remains) found itself half inside his jacket and practically nuzzling the black butt of an automatic pistol in a shoulder clip.

'Ooops!' I squeaked, quite unnerved. He chuckled kindly, fatly.

'Don't you give that iron no never-mind, son; why, we Texans feel kind of undressed without one of them things.'

We chattered on in a desultory way but I found it hard to concentrate on the prettier points of fish-frying. Texas businessmen doubtless often carry pistols but I found it hard to believe that they would favour the inconvenient length of a Colt's Woodsman, which is a small calibre, long-barrelled automatic used only for target shooting and, more rarely, by professional killers who know they can plant its small bullet in just the right place. As a handy weapon of self-defence for the ordinary citizen it simply doesn't exist. Moreover, Texas businessmen, I felt sure, would be unlikely to house their pistols in Bryson rapid-release spring-clips.

The journey seemed to get longer all the time, if you follow me. The United States seemed distant and undesirable. As we landed the nice American finally told me his name – Brown, spelt b.r.a.u.n, pronounced Brawn. 'A likely story,' I thought. We farewelled and, a moment after we left the plane, he vanished. Once his warm and portly presence was gone I found I liked him less and less.

Martland had fulfilled my list of instructions faithfully – he would make someone a lovely wife. There was a big sad chap to meet me who guided me to an echoing bay where the Rolls stood and shimmered on its pallet, surrounded by other chaps with dear little petrol tankers, exotic licence plates, books of travellers' cheques and I don't know what-all. Oh yes, and a grave chap who struck my passport savagely with a rubber stamp. I accepted all their offerings with a weary courtesy, like a Crowned Head receiving specimens of native handicraft. There was also a furious little mannikin from the British Embassy but he was on the other side of a sort of pig-wire barrier – he had neglected to get the right sort of pass or something and the big, impassive Americans ignored his squeakings and gibberings completely, as did I. The chap with the petrol tanker wrenched the necessary lead seals off with pliers and tossed them through the wire to the squeaking chap as one throws peanuts to a zoo-bound ape, making vulgar clicking noises with his tongue and pretending to scratch his armpits. I began to fear for his health – the squeaking chap I mean, not the petrol chap.

I mounted the Rolls, sucking my lungs full of that unparalleled smell of new coachwork, new hide upholstery. The big sad chap, knowing his place, stood on the running-board to guide me out. The Rolls started up gently, gladly, like a well-goosed widow, and we drifted out of the Goods Area making about as much noise as a goldfish in a bowl. I could tell by the looks on their rough, untutored American faces that, had they been brought up in another culture, they would have been knuckling their foreheads. As a mark of respect, d'you see.

At the exit we were met by the chap from the Embassy, still squeaking and now well-nigh self-strangled with rage and chagrin. Had he been brought up in another culture he would probably have knuckled *my* forehead to some purpose. I reasoned with him, begging him to be a credit to the Corps Diplomatique, and he at last rallied. What it all boiled down to was that the Ambassador was at some Xanadu-like golf links far away, playing golf or rounders or something with one of their Presidents or Congressmen or whatever they are, but that he would be back in the morning, when I must report to him, shit or bust and cap in hand, to receive his admonitions and surrender my Greyhound and that he, the squeaker, demanded to know the name of the *bloody* man who had dared to tamper with the leaden Foreign Office seals on the Rolls. I told him that the chap's name was McMurdo (for the spur of the moment not bad, you must agree) and promised to try to find time to call on the Ambassador perhaps during the next few days.

He started getting incoherent again and kept beginning sentences with the words 'Do you realize . . .' and not finishing them, so I set my face against him.

'Pull yourself together,' I told him sternly, pressing a pound note into his hand. As I drove away I caught a glimpse of him in the driving mirror; he was jumping up and down on something. Too emotional by half, some of these diplomatic chaps. He'd be no good in Moscow, they'd have him compromised in a trice.

I found my hotel and handed over the Rolls to an able-looking brownish chap in the garage: he had a witty twinkle in his eye, I took to him instantly. We agreed that he could use only the duster on the coachwork and nothing else: Mr Spinoza would have *haunted* me if I'd let his Special Secret Wax be scoured with detergents or ossified with silicones. Then I rode the elevator – as they say over there, did you know? – up to the reception desk (my bags with me) and so by easy stages to a well-appointed suite with a lavatory worthy of the goddess Cloaca herself. Like a true-born Englishman I turned the ridiculous air conditioning off and threw open the windows.

Fifteen minutes later I turned the air conditioning back on and had to telephone the desk to send someone up to close the windows for me, oh the shame of it.

Later on they sent me up some sandwiches which I didn't much like.

Later still I read myself to sleep with one half-comprehended paragraph.

9

Does he stand stock-still henceforth? Or proceed
Dizzily, yet with course straightforward still,
Down-trampling vulgar hindrance? – as the reed
Is crushed beneath its tramp when that blind will
Hatched in some old-world beast's brain bids it speed
Where the sun wants brute-presence to fulfil
Life's purpose in a new far zone, ere ice
Enwomb the pasture-track its fortalice.

The Two Poets of Croisic

Do you know, they brought me a cup of tea in the morning – and jolly good tea it was too. If I could remember the name of the hotel I'd tell you.

Then they gave me one of those delicious elaborate American breakfasts, all sweet bacon and hotcakes and syrup and I didn't like it really.

I rode the elevator (!) down to the garage to inquire after the Rolls which had, it seemed, passed a comfortable night. The brownish chap hadn't been able to resist washing the windows but only with soap and water, he swore, so I pardoned him and gave him of my plenty. Ten minutes later I was in an enormous taxi-cab, an air-conditioned one, hired for the day for fifty dollars; it seems an awful lot, I know, but money's worth awfully little over there, you'd be surprised. It's because there's so much of it, you see.

The driver's name seemed to be Bud and somehow he'd got the notion that mine was Mac. I explained amicably that it was, in fact, Charlie, but he replied:

'Yeah? Well, that's very nice, Mac.'

I didn't mind after a while – I mean, when in *Rome*, eh? – and soon he was driving me round the sights of Washington, sparing nothing. It is a surprisingly splendid and graceful city, although built largely of a grotty kind of limestone; I loved every minute. The great heat was tempered by an agreeable little breeze which whipped the girls' cotton frocks about in the most pleasing way. How is it that American girls all contrive to have such appetizing legs; round, smooth, sturdily slender? If it comes to that, how is it that they all have such amazing tits? Bigger, perhaps, than you and I like them, but nonetheless delicious. When we stopped for a traffic light, a particularly well-nourished young person crossed in front of us, her stupendous mammaries jouncing up and down quite four inches at each step.

'My word, Bud,' I said to Bud, 'what an entrancing creature, to be sure!'

'Ya mean de dame wit de big knockers? Nah. In bed, they'd kinda spread out like a coupla fried eggs, king-size.'

The thought made me feel quite faint. He went on to give me a summary of his personal tastes in these matters, which I found fascinating but *bizarre* to a degree.

It has been suggested, with some truth, that Van Dyck's work when he was at Genoa constitutes the best group of portraits in the world. I came round to this point of view myself in the National Gallery at Washington: until you have seen their *Clelia Cattaneo* you can scarcely claim to have seen anything. I stayed an hour only in the Gallery: you can't absorb much art of that richness at one sitting, and I'd really only intended to look at one particular Giorgione. Had I but time as this fell sergeant Death is swift in his arrest, I could have unfolded a tale or two about it, but that shot is no longer on the board.

Emerging, already half drunk on injudiciously mixed art, I directed Bud to drive me to a typical lower-middle-class saloon for a cold beer and a bite of luncheon.

At the entrance Bud looked at me dubiously, up and down, and suggested that we try somewhere 'classier'.

'Nonsense, my dear Bud,' I cried staunchly, 'this is the normal, sober garb or kit of an English gentleman of fashion about to pay a call on his country's Envoy *in partibus* and I am sure it is well-known to these honest Washington folk. In Sir Toby's valiant words: "These clothes are good enough to drink in, and so be these boots, too." Lead on.'

He shrugged, in the expressive way these chaps have, and led duly on. He was very big and strong-looking but people nevertheless stared a little – he was dressed a bit informally perhaps, as cabbies often are, while I, as I have said, was correctly clothed as for interviewing ambassadors, merchant bankers and other grandees. In England no one would have remarked the contrast between us but they have no idea of democracy in America. Odd, that.

We ate in a sort of stall or booth, rather like the old-fashioned London chop house but flimsier. My steak was quite lovely but embarrassingly large: it seemed to be a cross-section through an ox. I had a salad with mine but Bud ordered a potato – *such* a potato; a prodigious tuber bred, he told me, on the plains of Idaho. I suppose I left about ten ounces of my steak and Bud quite coolly told the waiter (*his* name was Mac, too) to wrap it up for his dog and the waiter didn't even flicker although they both knew quite well that it would constitute Mrs Bud's supper that night. Steak is fearfully dear in Washington, as I daresay you know.

Bud may have licked me at the steak eating but I had him whipped at the liquor drinking. They have something there called, obscurely, High Balls, which we moved on to after our beer; he was no match for me at that game, quite outclassed. He eyed me, in fact, with a new respect. I believe I asked him to come and stay with me in London at one stage; at least I know I meant to.

As we left the bar a rather droll-looking citizen swayed across my path and asked, 'Whaddaya, some kinova nut or sumpn?' to which I replied in a matey phrase which I had heard Bud use to a fellow cabbie earlier in the day, as follows:

'Ah, go blow it out your ass!' (*A man hath joy by the answer of his mouth; and a word spoken in due season, how good it is!* Prov. XV: 23.)

To my dismay and puzzlement, the drunk chap took exception, for he hit me very hard in the face, making my nose bleed freely down my shirt. Vexed at this, I fear I retaliated.

When I was in one of those joke-and-dagger units in the war – yes, the *Second* World War, chicks – I went on one of those unarmed combat courses and, do you know, I was frightfully good at it, though you wouldn't think it to look at me.

I popped the heel of my hand under his nose – *so* much better than a punch – then toed him hard in the cobblers and, as he quite understandably doubled up, drove my knee into what was left of his poor face. He sort of fell down, not unnaturally in the circumstances, and as a precaution I stamped on each of his hands as I stepped over him. Well, he did hit me first, you know, as I'm sure he'd be the first to admit. Bud, *enormously* impressed, hustled me outside while the saloon behind us applauded – pit, circle and gallery. An unpopular bloke, no doubt. I had very little trouble getting into the cab, although the driver's seat had changed sides again.

All the beautiful young men at the Embassy hated me on sight, nasty little cupcakes, but they passed me through to the Ambassador with no more delay than was necessary to make them feel important. The Ambassador received me in his shirt sleeves, if you'll believe it, and he, too, didn't seem to fancy me much. He accepted my courtly, old-world salutations with what I can only describe as a honk.

Now, for most practical purposes the ordinary consumer can divide Ambassadors up into two classes: the thin ones who tend to be suave, well-bred, affable; and the fleshier chaps who are none of these things. His present Excellency definitely fell into the latter grade: his ample mush was pleated with fat, wormed with the great pox and so besprent with whelks, bubukles and burst capillaries that it seemed like a contour map of the Trossachs. His great plum-coloured gobbler hung slack and he sprayed one when he spoke. I couldn't find it in my heart to love him but, poor chap, he was probably a Labour appointment: his corridors of power led only to the Gents.

'I won't beat about the bush, Mortdecai,' he honked, 'you are clearly an awful man. Here we are, trying to establish an image of a white-hot technological Britain, ready to compete on modern terms with any jet-age country in the world and here *you* are, walking about Washington in a sort of Bertie Wooster outfit as though you were something the Tourist Board had dreamed up to advertise Ye Olde Brytysshe Raylewayes.'

'I say,' I said, 'you pronounced that last bit marvellously.'

'Moreover,' he ground on, 'your ridiculous bowler is dented, your absurd umbrella bent, your shirt covered with blood and you have a black eye.'

'You should see the other feller?' I chirrupped brightly, but it didn't go down a bit well. He was in his stride now.

'The fact that you are quite evidently as drunk as a fiddler's bitch in no way excuses a man of your age' – a nasty one, that – 'looking and behaving like a fugitive from a home for alcoholic music-hall artistes. I know little of why you are here and I wish to know nothing. I have been asked to assist you if possible, but I have not been instructed to do so: you may assume that I shall not. The only advice I offer is that you do not apply to this Embassy for help if and when you outrage the laws of the United States, for I shall unhesitatingly disown you and recommend imprisonment and deportation. If you turn right when you leave this room you will see the Chancery, where you will be given a receipt for your Silver Greyhound and a temporary civil passport in exchange for your Diplomatic one, which should never have been issued. Good day, Mr Mortdecai.'

With that, he started grimly signing letters or whatever it is that Ambassadors grimly sign when they want you to leave. I considered being horribly sick on his desk but feared that he might declare me a Distressed British Subject there and then, so I simply left the room in a marked manner and stayed not upon the order of my going. But I turned *left* as I went out of the room, which took me into a typists' pool, through which I strolled debonairly, twirling my brolly and whistling a few staves of 'Show Us Your Knickers, Elsie.'

I found Bud asleep in the parking lot and he drove me to a nearby saloon, in fact to more than one. I remember one particular place where a portly young woman took off her clothes to music, while dancing on the bar counter within reach of my hand. I had never seen an ecdysiast before; toward the end she was wearing nothing but seven beads, four of them sweat. I think that was the place we were chucked out of.

I know I went to bed but I must admit the details are a bit fuzzy: I'm not sure I even brushed my teeth.

IO

Then we began to ride. My soul
Smoothed itself out, a long-cramped scroll
Freshening and fluttering in the wind.
Past hopes already lay behind.

The Last Ride Together

I awoke feeling positively chipper but the feeling didn't last. By the time I had dressed and packed I was being shaken with hangover like a rat in the grip of a keen but inexperienced terrier. I made it down to the hotel bar by easy stages (take the *slow* lift, never the express one) and the barman had me diagnosed and treated in no time at all. Your actual hangover, he explained, is no more than a withdrawal syndrome; halt the withdrawal by injecting more of what is withdrawing and the syndrome vanishes with a rustle of black wings. It seemed to make good sense. His prescription was simply Scotch and branch water – he swore a great oath that the branch water was freighted in fresh and fresh each morning from the Appalachian mountains, would you believe it? I tipped him with no niggardly hand.

Well medicated, but by no means potted, I paid my bill at the desk, collected a spotless Silver Ghost from a reluctant brownish chap and drove carefully away in the general direction of New Mexico. Posterity will want to know that I was wearing my Complete American Disguise: a cream tussore suit, sunglasses and a cocoa-coloured straw hat with a burnt-orange ribbon. The effect was pretty sexy, I don't mind telling you. Mr Abercrombie would have *bitten* Mr Fitch if he'd seen it and the *Tailor and Cutter* would have been moved to tears.

Curiously, I was afraid again. I felt obscurely that this land – 'where law and custom alike are based on the dreams of spinsters' – was nevertheless a land where I might well get hurt if I were not careful – or even if I *were* careful.

By the time that I was quite clear of the city's unlovely faubourgs and purlieus I needed petrol: the Silver Ghost is a lovely car but its best friend would have to admit that its m.'s per g. are few. I selected a petrol station that looked as though it could use the business and drew up. This was near a place called Charlottesville on the edge of the Shenandoah National Park. The attendant was standing with his back to me, arms akimbo, saying, 'Howd'ya like that guy?' and staring after a large powder-blue car which was vanishing at great speed down the road. He didn't realize my presence until I switched off the engine, then he double-took the Rolls in the most gratifying way, whispering 'shee-*it!*' again and again. (I was to hear enough admiring 'shee-its' in the next few days to refertilize the entire Oklahoma dust bowl.) He giggled like a virgin as he dipped the nozzle into the petrol tank and sped me on my way with one last dungy praise spattering my ears. I wondered vaguely what the powder-blue car had done to earn his disapproval.

I got a little lost after that, but an hour later I hit Interstate Highway 8I at Lexington and made excellent time down through Virginia. Once over the State line into Tennessee I called it quits for the day and booked in at a Genuine Log Kabins Motel. The yellow-haired, slack-mouthed, fat-arsed landlady wiggled her surplus flesh at me in the most revolting way: she looked about as hard to get as a haircut and at about the same price. Everything in my Kabin was screwed to the floor: the landlady told me that newlyweds often furnish their entire apartments with stuff they steal from motels, they spend the whole night unscrewing things, she told me with a coy giggle, indicating that she could think of better ways of passing the time. Like being screwed to the floor, I dare say.

The sheets were bright red. 'By golly,' I told them, 'I'd blush too, if I were you.'

For supper I had some Old Fashioned Mountain Boys' Corned Beef Hash; you'd think it would be delicious in Tennessee but it wasn't, you know; not a patch on Jock's. I drank some of my store of Red Hackle De Luxe and went to sleep instantly – you'd never have unscrewed *me*.

You can't get an early morning cup of tea in an American motel, not even for ready money; I wished I had brought a portable apparatus along. You've no idea how hard it is to get dressed without a cheering cup inside you. I hobbled to the restaurant and drank a whole pot of their coffee, which was excellent and nerved me to try the sweet Canadian bacon and hot cakes. Not at all bad, really. I noticed that the owner of the powder-blue car – or one very like it – had selected the same motel, but I didn't see him, or her. I idly wondered whether they'd done much unscrewing. For my part, I checked out with a clear conscience, I hadn't stolen anything for days.

I hardly got lost at all that morning. I was on US 40 in not much more than an hour and sailed clear across Tennessee on it, wonderful scenery. I had lunch in Nashville: spareribs and spoon bread and the finest jukebox I ever saw: it was a privilege to sit in front of it. Dazed with hot pork and decibels I nearly stepped under the wheels of a powder-blue car as I stepped off the sidewalk (pavement). Now, at the last count I'm sure there were probably half a million powder-blue cars in the United States, but when pedestrians walk under their wheels American drivers usually turn a bit powder-blue themselves and lean out and curse you roundly, calling you 'Buster' if you happen to be at all portly. This one did not: he looked through me and drove on, a thick-set, jowly chap rather like my Mr Braun, the crown prince of fish and chips, but hatted and sunglassed to the point of anonymity.

I dismissed the incident from my mind until I reached the outskirts of Memphis late that evening, when I was overtaken by just such a car driven by just such a chap.

They brought me coffee in my hotel room that night and a bottle of branch water for my Scotch; I locked the door and put in a call to Mr Krampf. American telephonists are wonderful, you just tell them the name and address of the chap you want to talk to and they do the rest. Krampf sounded a bit tight but very friendly; there was a lot of noise in the background which suggested that he had guests with him who were also a bit tight. I told him that

I was on schedule, making no reference to his departure from our original plan.

'Well, that's just dandy,' he bellowed. 'Just dandy.' He said it a few times more, he's like that.

'Mr Krampf,' I went on guardedly, 'I seem to have a sort of companion on the road, if you know what I mean. A late model, powder-blue Buick convertible with New York plates. Do you have any idea . . .?'

There was a long pause, then he chuckled fruitily.

'That's awright, son, that's your kind of escort. Wouldn't want anyone hijacking that old Rolls and Royce of mine.'

I made relieved noises and he went on: 'Hey, let's don't let him know we tumbled him, just make like he wasn't there and when he gets here and tells me you never made him I'll chew his nuts off, huh?'

'All right, Mr Krampf,' I said, 'but don't be too hard on him, will you. I mean, I was rather on the *qui vive*, you know.'

He delivered another fruity chuckle – or perhaps it was a belch – and rang off. Then somebody else rang off. Perhaps it was just the hotel telephonist, but the noises weren't quite right for that. Then I rang off and treated myself to a belch, too, and went to bed.

Nothing else happened that night, except that I worried a lot. Krampf hadn't made his millions by being a drunken old fart; to be a millionaire you need brains, ruthlessness and a certain little maggot in your brain. Krampf had all these and he was cleverer than me and much more evil. This was all wrong. My bowels whined and grumbled, they wanted to go home. Above all, they wanted no part in assassinating clever millionaires in their own homes. I finally nagged myself to sleep.

I I

> Yet now I wake in such decrepitude
> As I had slidden down and fallen afar,
> Past even the presence of my former self,
> Grasping the while for stay at facts which snap,
> Till I am found away from my own world,
> Feeling for foot-hold through a blank profound,
> Along with unborn people in strange lands . . .
>
> *A Death in the Desert*

It was Sunday but you'd never have thought so by what was going on when I got to Little Rock, Arkansas. Some sort of protest was going on and, as usual, short-haired chaps in dark blue were boredly biffing longhaired chaps in pale blue jeans, who were calling them pigs and throwing stones and things. All very sad. As a Russian said a hundred years ago, these people believe that they are the doctors of society, whereas in fact they are only the disease. Traffic was at a standstill and, several cars ahead of me, I could see the blue Buick, bogged down in a sea of long hair and flourishing riot sticks.

I killed the engine and mused. Why the devil would Krampf go to the expense and trouble of escorting across half a continent a motor car which no one in his senses would attempt to steal – and escorting it in so curiously oblique a way? Setting aside the strong possibility that he was barmy, I decided that he must have told someone about the extra piece of canvas which ought to be secreted about the car – *that* made him pretty barmy of course – and was now regretting it. Worse, he might be playing some deeper and more convoluted game, which would be consistent with his unscripted letter to the almost royal Chum. He could scarcely have guessed at the little murder job which Martland had entrusted to me but he might well have come to consider me, for other reasons, as sort of redundant and a threat to his security. 'The heart is deceitful about all things, and desperately corrupt; who can understand it?' cries Jeremiah XVII:9 and as you know, Jeremiah XVII:9 was a chap with great insight into these matters, as well as being a little barmy himself.

My little private store of worries and ass puckerings was much augmented by all this; I found myself pining for Jock's strong right arm and brass-garnished bunch of fives. The plot was thickening in a marked manner; if I could not soon lay hold of a spoon with which to stir it, there was a distinct danger that it might stick to the bottom. *My* bottom, probably. And then where would the Hon. C. Mortdecai be? There was a dusty answer to that one.

The traffic moved on after everyone concerned had been thoroughly biffed and bashed and screamed at and I didn't spot the Buick again until just after the Shawnee crossing of the North Canadian River, where I glimpsed it lurking down a side road. I stopped at the next petrol station (they call it *gas* there, I wonder why?) hoping to give the driver a good eyeballing as he passed.

What I saw made me gape and gibber like a housewife choosing Daz on the television; two or three seconds later I was twenty miles down the road, sitting on a motel bed and sucking in whisky until I could think straight. It was the same car – at least it bore the same number plates – but overnight it had lost a deep dent in a fender and acquired a suit of whitewall tires and another radio antenna. The driver had lost a few stones and become a thin, dyspeptic cove with a mouth like the slot in a piggy-bank. In short, it was not the same car at all. The implications were unclear but one thing stood out like Priapus: there was no way in which this could be a change for the better. Someone was devoting a good deal of time and trouble and expense to the affairs of C. Mortdecai and it certainly wasn't the Distressed Gentlefolk's Aid Society. A stupid man might not have been too frightened but I was not stupid enough for that. A really bright chap, on the other hand, would have dumped everything and run for home with all speed, but I was not really bright, either.

What I did was leave the motel, telling them that I would be back after dinner (I'd already paid, naturally) and drive circuitously to the heart of Oklahoma City, arriving tired and grim.

Not too near the centre I found a solid, sober sort of hotel which looked as though it would not knowingly harbour the more obvious kind of *barbouze* or assassin. I drove into the underground garage and waited until the night attendant had exhausted his stock of admiring 'shee-*its*', then I told him that the Rolls was entered in an RR *Concours d'Elégance* in Los Angeles the following week and that a hated rival would stop at nothing to impede my progress or the car's chances of success.

'What would you do,' I asked him hypothetically 'if a stranger offered you money to let him sit in the car for five minutes while you went away and sat in your office?'

'Well, Sir,' he said, 'I guess I'd jest wave this little old wrench at him and tell him to haul his ass out of here, then I'd ring the desk upstairs and then in the morning I'd kind of tell you how much money he'd offered me, see what I mean, Sir.'

'I do indeed. You are clearly a capital fellow. Even if nothing happens I shall assume, in the morning, that you refused let us say five, ah, *bucks*, what?'

'Thank you, Sir.'

I went up in the lift or elevator and started work on the desk clerk. He was a well-scrubbed, snotty little chap in one of those suits only desk clerks can buy – or would want – and his breath smelled of something unwholesome and probably illegal. He studied my luggage like a pawnbroker before he peevishly admitted that he did have a vacant room with bath, but he thawed fast when he saw my diplomatic passport and the five-dollar bill I had carelessly left inside it. He was just sliding the money towards him when I trapped it with a well-shaped forefinger. I leaned over the counter and lowered my voice.

'No one but you and I knows that I am here tonight. Do you follow me?'

He nodded, both our fingers still on the money.

'Consequently, anyone telephoning me will be trying to *locate* me. Are you still following?'

He still was.

'Now, none of my *friends* could possibly be trying to get in touch with me here and my enemies are members of a political party which is dedicated to the overthrow of the United States. So what will you do if somebody calls me?'

'Call the cops?'

I winced with unfeigned chagrin.

'No no NO,' I said. 'By no means the cops. Why do you think I'm *in* Oklahoma City?'

That really fetched him. Awe stole into his juicy eyes and his lips parted with a tiny plop.

'You mean, just call you? Sir?' he said at last.

'Right,' I said, and released the five dollars. He stared at me until I was inside the lift. I felt reasonably secure – desk clerks all over the world have two talents: selling information and knowing when not to sell information. These simple skills spell survival to them.

My room was large, well-proportioned and pleasant but the air conditioning made tiresome noises at random intervals. I asked room service for a selection of their best sandwiches, a bottle of branch water, a good drinking glass and the house detective. They all arrived together. I took pains to befriend the detective, who was an awkward, seven-foot youth with a shoulder holster which creaked noisily when he sat down. I gave him Scotch whisky and a load of old moody similar to that which the desk clerk had gobbled. He was a serious boy and asked for my credentials; they impressed him considerably and he promised to keep a special eye on my floor that night.

When he had gone, five dollars later, I inspected my sandwiches with moody pleasure; there was great store of them, on two sorts of bread and filled with all manner of good things: I did my best with them, drank some more Scotch and got into bed, feeling that I had secured myself as best I could.

I shut my eyes and the air conditioner rushed into my head, carrying with it all manner of dread and speculation, a thousand horrid fancies and a mounting panic. I dared not take a sleeping pill. After an interminable half hour I gave up the fight for sleep and put the light on. There was only one thing for it – I lifted the telephone and put in a call to Mrs Spon in London. London, England, that is.

She came through in a mere twenty minutes, shrieking and honking with rage at being awakened and swearing by strange gods. I could hear her vile little poodle Pisse-Partout in the background, adding his soprano yelps to the din; it made me quite homesick.

I soothed her with a few well chosen words and she soon got it into her head that this was a matter of some seriousness. I told her that, at all costs, Jock must be at the *Rancho de los Siete Dolores* by Tuesday and that she must see to it. She promised. The problem of getting an American visa in a few hours is nothing to a woman like her: she once got a private audience of the Pope just by knocking on the door and saying she was expected; they say he very nearly gave her a contract to redo the Sistine Chapel.

Knowing that Jock would be there to meet me eased my worst fears; it only remained now to get there without leaving any bloodstains in my spoor.

I sank into an uneasy slumber interspersed, curiously, with erotic dreams.

12

There was no tea to be had in the morning but I was on the very threshold of the old West and knew that I had to learn to rough it. 'Pioneers! Oh, Pioneers!' as Walt Whitman never tired of exclaiming.

Neither the desk nor the garage had anything to report, so I toddled out to take the air and see if the neighbourhood was blue-Buick-infested. What I found was a sort of bar advertising in its window something called the Old Oklahoma Cattleman's Breakfast Special. Who could resist it? Not I.

The O.O.C.B.S. proved to be a thick steak, almost raw, a hunk of salt bacon the size and shape of my fist, a pile of hot sourdough biscuits, a tin pot of ferocious coffee and half a gill of rye whisky. Now I am a man of iron, as you will by now have realized, but I confess I belched. I was trapped, for the barman and the short-order cook were both leaning on the bar, watching my future career with considerable interest as it were, their faces grave and courteous but sort of expectant. Britain's honour lay in pawn to my knife and fork. I weakened some of the coffee with some of the whisky and drank it, suppressing a gagging shudder. I found strength after this to try a hot biscuit, then some more coffee, then a corner of the bacon and so on. Appetite grew on what it fed upon and soon, to the amazement of myself and all beholders, the very steak itself fell to my bow and spear. 'Tis from scenes like this that Britain's greatness springs. I accepted a free drink from the barman, shook hands gravely and made a good exit. Not all Ambassadors sit in Embassies, you know.

Much fortified, I collected the Rolls and turned my face toward the Golden West, the Lyonesse of our times, the nursery of the great American fairy tale. At noon I crossed the State line into the panhandle of Texas, a solemn moment for any man who rode with the Lone Ranger each Saturday morning as a child.

Mindful of the Buick-mounted rustler on my trail, I started to buy a few gallons of petrol at almost every petrol station, taking care to inquire at each one for the road to Amarillo – which lay due West on that very road. Sure enough, the blue car swept by me somewhere between the townships of McLean and Groom, the driver looking neither to right nor left. Clearly, he was satisfied of my destination and intended to front-tail me to Amarillo. I let him have a few reassuring glimpses of me in his driving mirror, lying a mile behind him, then chose a useful left hand turning and sped south to Claude then southeast through Clarendon to the Prairie Dog Town fork of the Red River – there's a place name to stir the blood – which I crossed at Estelline. I felt no need of luncheon but kept up my strength with a little rye whisky here and there and an occasional egg to give it something to bite on. Following the least probable roads I worked my way West again and by mid-afternoon I was satisfied that I must have lost the Buick for good. Needless to say I had lost myself too, but that was of secondary importance. I found a sleepy motel staffed by one thirteen-year-old boy who hired me a cabin without raising his eyes from his comic book.

'Hail Columbia! Happy land!' I told him, borrowing freely from R.H. Horne, 'Hail, ye heroes! Heaven-born band!'

He almost looked up, but decided in favour of The Teenage Werewolf From Ten Thousand Fathoms – I couldn't find it in my heart to blame him.

I zizzed away the worst of the afternoon, awakening some three hours later with a mighty thirst. When I had seen to that I strolled outside to stretch my legs and scare up some ham and eggs. A furlong down the dusty road, under the shade of a valley cottonwood, stood a powder-blue Buick.

That settled it: the Rolls was bugged. No human agency could have tracked me through that mazey day unaided. Quite calm, I ate the bacon and shirred eggs along with great manly cups of coffee, then sauntered back to the Rolls with the air of a man quite unencumbered with powder-blue Buicks. It took me almost ten minutes to find the tiny transistorized tracer beacon: it was magnetized fiercely to the underside of my right hand front mudguard.

I started the Ghost and drifted away in the wrong direction; after a few miles I hailed, frantically, a State Trooper mounted on an unbelievable motor bike and proclaimed myself lost.

When a native son is unwise enough to ask the way of an American policeman he is either jailed for vagrancy or, if the policeman is a kindly one, told to buy a map. This one, I swear, would have *struck* me for flagging him down had I not been wearing an English accent and a Rolls Royce of great beauty, but these beguiled him into a *pro hac vice* civility. I got out of the car and, as he pointed things out to me on the map, leaned lightly against his great Harley Davidson machine, letting the grumble of the idling engine drown the smart click of the mini-transmitter's magnet as it clamped itself under his rear mudguard. He roared away northwards at a dashing pace; I lurked down a dirt road until the Buick dawdled by in confident pursuit, then off I went like the clappers, south and west.

A vast, theatrical moon rose over Texas and I drove on spellbound for hours through forests of Spanish Bayonet and fields of amaranthine sagebrush. At last, on the edge of the Llano Estacado, the Staked Plains themselves, I edged the Rolls into a friendly canyon and settled down to sleep behind the wheel, a bottle of whisky within easy reach in case of mountain lions.

Prompt on cue, a coyote curdled the thin distances of the night air with his whooping love song and, as I drifted into sleep, I thought I heard the muted thunder of far away, unshod hooves.

13

I met him thus:
I crossed a ridge of short broken hills
Like an old lion's cheek-teeth . . .

An Epistle

I was awakened by a shot.

Not thrilled? Then I venture to guess that you have never been awakened in that way yourself. For my part I found myself down among the accelerator and brake pedals before I was properly awake, whimpering with terror and groping frantically for the Banker's Special pistol in its hidey-hole under the seat.

Nothing happened.

I thumbed back the hammer and peeped, wincing, over the edge of the window.

Nothing went on happening.

I looked through the other windows – nothing – and decided that I had dreamed the shot, for my sleep had been illustrated with the dread exploits of Comancheros, Apaches, Quantrill's guerrillas and other fiends in human shape. I treated myself to another O.O.C.B.S. breakfast, only this time without the steak, ham, hot biscuits or coffee. There were one or two bad moments but I was not sick and the old rapture was soon recaptured and I felt emboldened to step out for *un petit promenade hygiénique*. As I opened the car door another shot rang out, followed one fifth of a second later by the bang of the car door closing again. There is still nothing wrong with the Mortdecai reaction time.

I listened carefully to my audile memory, recalling the exact noise of the shot.

1. It had not been the unmistakable, explicit BANG of a shotgun
2. Not the vicious CRACK of a small calibre rifle
3. Not the BOOM of a .45 pistol
4. Not the ear-stinging WHAM of a heavy calibre standard rifle, or a magnum pistol fired in your direction
5. Not the terrifying whip-crack WHANG-UP of a high velocity sporting rifle fired towards you, but something of the same nature
6. A sporting rifle, then, but
7. Not fired in the canyon because no echoes and surely
8. *Not fired at me* – dammit, a Girl *Guide* couldn't miss a Rolls Royce with two slowly aimed shots.

My intellect was satisfied that it was some honest rancher smartening up the local coyotes: my body took longer to pacify. I crept back on to the seat and twitched gently for fifteen minutes, nibbling at the rye from time to time. After about a hundred years I heard an old car start up miles away across the desert and chug even further away. I sneered at my craven self.

'You craven wretch,' I sneered. Inexplicably, I then fell asleep for another hour. Nature knows, you know.

It was still only nine o'clock when I set off on the last leg of my journey, feeling old and dirty and incapable. You probably know the feeling if you are over eighteen.

It is hard to drive in a cringing position but nevertheless I got the Rolls into its stride and strode across the Staked Plains at a good mile-munching pace. The Staked Plains are not really very exciting, when you've seen one Staked Plain you've seen them all. I particularly don't want to tell you where Krampf's rancho is – perhaps *was* now – but I don't mind admitting that it lay two hundred straightish miles from my overnight bivouac and between the Sacramento Mountains and the Rio Hondo. Just names on a map that morning, the poetry all gone. There's nothing like gunfire to drive the glamour from words. I soon became tired of the creosote bushes, desert willows and screwbeams, not to mention the eternal, giant cacti, so different from the ones Mrs Spon grows in her conservatoilette.

I entered New Mexico at noon, still unmolested, still feeling old and dirty. At Lovington (named after old Oliver Loving who blazed the fearful Goodnight-Loving trail in '66 and died along it of arrow wounds the following year) I had a bath, a shave, a change of raiment and a dish of *Huevos 'Ojos de Comanchero,'* which sounded lovely. In reality it was the most terrifying sight I had seen to date: two fried eggs decorated with ketchup, Tabasco and chopped chillis in the semblance of a pair of bloodshot eyes – I would as soon have eaten my own leg. I waved the grimly thing away; Old Oklahoma Cattlemen are one thing but these were merely tetrous. I tried, instead, 'Chilli 'n' Franks' which proved to be rather good, just like chilli con carne but with dear little salty bangers instead of the ground meat. While I ate, various admiring *peons* were handwashing the Rolls, with soap 'n' water only, of course.

With a bare hundred miles to go, clean, dapper and now only middle-aged again, I pointed the Rolls' nose toward the Ranch of the Seven Sorrows of the Virgin, where I would lay down my pilgrim's scrip of care, my cockle-hat of fear and my staff of illegality; where, moreover, I would take delivery of a great deal of money and perhaps kill a Krampf. Or perhaps not. I had left England prepared to keep my part of the bargain with Martland, but I had thought a great deal during those hundreds of remorseless American miles and had evolved certain arguments against keeping faith with him. (We had never been *friends* at school after all, for he was the house tart, and known to one and all as 'Shagnasty': not for nothing does a boy acquire such a name.)

I had also bought a denser pair of sunglasses; my old ones were calculated for the lemonade-like rays of the English sun and were no proof against the brutal onslaught of the desert light. Even the shadows, razor edged, purple and green, were painful to look at. I drove with all windows shut and the side blinds drawn across: the inside of the Rolls was like an ill-regulated sauna bath but this was better than letting in the dry, scorching fury of the air outside. I was soon sitting in a distressful swamp of sweat and my old wound started to trouble me; chilli 'n' trepidation were playing the devil with my small intestines and my borborigmus was often louder than the engine of the Rolls, which loped on undeterred, quietly guzzling its pint of petrol per statute mile.

By mid-afternoon I was alarmed to notice that I had stopped sweating and had started talking to myself – and *was listening*. It was becoming difficult to distinguish the road amongst the writhing pools of heat-haze and I could not tell whether the scraggy-feathered road-runners were under my wheels or a furlong ahead of me.

Half an hour later I was on a dirt road under a spur of the Sacramento range, lost. I stopped to consult the map and found myself listening to the enormous silence – 'that silence where the birds are dead yet something singeth like a bird'.

From somewhere above me a shot was fired, but there was no sound of a bullet passing and I had no intention of cringing twice in one day. Moreover, there was no mistaking the nature of the firearm, it was the wholesome bark, flattened by the heavy air, of a large calibre pistol loaded with black powder. High on the ridge above me was a horseman waving a broad brimmed hat and already starting to descend with casual mastery of – and disregard for – his mount. *Her* mount, as it turned out, and what a mount. *¡Que caballo!* I knew what it was immediately, although I had never before seen the true *bayo naranjado* – the vivid orange dun with a pure white mane and tail. It was entire – no one, surely, could geld a horse like that – and came down the ragged rock slope as though it were Newmarket Heath. The low-horned, double-girthed Texas saddle was enriched with silver *conchos* over intricately tooled and inlaid leathers and the girl herself was dressed like a museum exhibit of Old Texas: low-crowned black Stetson with rattler band and woven-hair storm-strap, bandana with the ends falling almost to the waist, brown Levi's tucked into unbelievable Justin boots which were themselves tucked into antique silver Spanish stirrups and garnished with Kelly spurs fashioned, apparently, of gold.

She arrived at the foot of the slope in a small avalanche, reins slack, welded to her saddle with fierce thighs, and the stallion took the storm ditch as though it was not there, landing dramatically beside the Rolls in a spatter of stones.

I wound a window down and peered out with a polite expression. I was met with a spray of cheesy foam from the horse's mouth; it showed me some of its huge yellow teeth and offered to bite my face off, so I wound the window up again. The girl was inspecting the Rolls; as her horse moved forward past the window I found myself staring at a beautiful gunbelt of Mexican work with *buscadero* holsters, containing a pair of pristine Dragoon-pattern Colts, the paper-cartridge model of the 1840s, with grips by Louis Comfort

Tiffany – unmistakable – dating from perhaps twenty years later. She wore them correctly for the Southwest – butts forward, as though for the flashy Border cross-draw or the cavalry twist (much more sensible), and they were not tied down, of course – this was no Hollywood mock-up but a perfect historical reconstruction. (Try mounting or even trotting with pistols in open holsters tied down to your thighs.) From the saddle scabbard protruded, as was only fitting, the butt of a One-in-One-Thousand Winchester repeater.

From hat to horseshoes she must have been worth a fortune as she sat – it gave me a new vision of the uses of wealth – and that was not counting her splendid person, which looked even more valuable. I am not, as you may have guessed, especially keen on commonplace sex, especially with women, but this vision unequivocally stirred my soggy flesh. The silk shirt was pasted to her perfect form with delicate sweat, the Levi's made no bones about her pelvic delights. She had the perfect round hard bottom of the horsewoman but not the beamy breadth of the girl who started to ride too young.

I emerged from the other side of the car and addressed her across the bonnet – I am just enough of a horseman never to try to make friends with tired stallions on hot days.

'Good afternoon,' I said, by way of a talking point.

She looked me up and down. I sucked in my tummy. My face was as blank as I could make it but she knew, she knew. They know, you know.

'Hi,' she said. It left me gasping for air.

'Can you by any chance direct me to the *Rancho de los Siete Dolores?*' I asked.

Her bee-stung lips parted, the little white teeth opened a fraction; perhaps it was a sort of smile.

'What is the old auto worth?' she asked.

'I'm afraid it's not for sale, really.'

'You are stupid. Also overweight. But cute.' There was a hint of a foreign accent in her voice, but it was not Mexican. Vienna perhaps, perhaps Buda. I asked the way again. She raised the handle of her beautiful quirt to her eyes and scanned the Western horizon. It was one of those quirts with a bit of pierced horn let into the handle: more useful than a telescope in that climate. I began, for the first time, to understand Sacher-Masoch.

'Go that way right across lots,' she pointed, 'the desert is no worse than the road. Follow the bones when you come to them.'

I tried to think of another talking point but something told me she was not much of a chatterbox – indeed, even as I searched for a way to detain her she had flicked the thong of her quirt under the stallion's belly and was away into the shimmering jumble of baking rock. Well, you can't win them all. 'Lucky old saddle,' I thought.

In twenty minutes I came upon the first of the bones she had spoken of: the bleached skeleton of a Texas Longhorn artistically disposed beside a faint track. Then another and another, until I reached a huge ranch gateway in the middle of nowhere. Its sunbleached crossbar supported a great polychromed Mexican carving of an agonized Madonna and a board hung below into which had been burned the rancho's brand – two Spanish bits. I wondered whether there was a joke implied and decided that, if there was, it was not of Mr Krampf's making.

Past the gate the trail was well-defined; the buffalo grass became richer with every furlong and I began to get glimpses of groups of horseflesh crowded under the cottonwoods – Morgans, Palominos, Appaloosas and I don't know what-all. Occasional riders began to fall in casually behind and beside me: by the time I reached the huge, rambling *hacienda* itself I was escorted by quite a dozen *charro*-clad desperadoes, all pretending that I wasn't there.

The house was astonishingly beautiful, all white columns and porticoes, the outside a maze of green lawns, fountains, patios, flowering agaves and yuccas. The door of a carport rolled itself up unbidden and I gentled the Rolls in, between a Bugatti and a Cord. When I emerged, bags in hand, my escort of bandits had vanished upon some unheard summons and only a small, impertinent boy was visible. He fluted something in Spanish, whisked my luggage away from me and indicated a shady patio, to which I made my way in as elegant a fashion as my tortured trousers would allow.

I sat down on a marble bench, stretched luxuriously and rested my grateful eyes on the statuary half-hidden in the green shade. One statue, more weather-worn than the others, proved to be an ancient and immobile old lady, hands folded in lap, gazing at me incuriously. I leaped to my feet and bowed – she was the kind of woman to whom people would always accord bows. She inclined her head a little. I fidgeted. Clearly, this must be Krampf's mother.

'Have I the honour of addressing Mrs Krampf?' I asked at length.

'No, Sir,' she replied in the careful English of the well-taught foreigner, 'you address the Countess Grettheim.'

'Forgive me,' I said, sincerely, for which of us, not being a Krampf, would care to be mistaken for one?

'Are Mr and Mrs Krampf at home?' I asked.

'I could not say,' she replied serenely. The subject was evidently closed. The silence stretched out beyond the point where I dared do anything about it. If the old lady's mission in life was to prevent me feeling cosy, she was certainly in fine midseason form – '*si extraordinairement distinguée*' as Mallarmé used to say, '*quand je lui dis bonjour, je me fais toujours l'effet de lui dire "merde"*'.

I looked at the statues again. There was an excellent copy of the Venus Callipygea, on whose cool marble buttocks my eyes lingered gratefully. Determined not to be flustered, I succeeded so well that my sun-sore eyelids began to droop.

'Are you not thirsty?' the old lady suddenly asked.

'Eh? Oh, well, er –'

'Then why do you not ring for a servant?'

She knew bloody well why I did not ring for a servant, the old bitch. I did ring for one then, though, and a strapping hussy appeared wearing one of those blouses – you know, the ones with a sort of drawstring or rip-cord – bearing a tall glass full of something delicious.

I inclined politely toward the Countess before taking the first sip. This, too, proved a mistake, for she gave me a basilisk stare as though I'd said, 'Cheers, dears.'

It occurred to me that I should tell her my name, so I did and a certain limited thaw set in; clearly, I should have done this before.

'I am Mr Krampf's mother-in-law,' she said suddenly and her toneless voice and impassive face somehow carried words of contempt for people named Krampf. And for people named Mortdecai, too, for that matter.

'Indeed,' I said, with just a hint of polite incredulity in my voice.

Nothing happened for some time except that I finished my drink and summoned the courage to ring for another. She already had me summed up as a low-life; I felt she might as well know me for a toper as well.

Later, a barefoot peon crept in and mumbled to her in thick Spanish, then crept out again. After a while she said, 'My daughter is now in and wishes to see you,' then closed her parchment eyelids with finality. I was dismissed. As I left the patio I distinctly heard her say, 'You will have time to couple with her once before dinner, if you are quick.' I stopped as though I had been shot in the back. C. Mortdecai is not often at a loss for words but a loss is what he was at then. Without opening her eyes she went on – 'Her husband will not mind, he does not care to do it himself.'

There was still nothing in this for me. I let the words hang reverberating in the still air while I slunk away. A servant fielded me neatly as I entered the house and led me to a small tapestry-hung chamber on the first floor. I sank into the most sumptuous sofa you can imagine and tried to decide whether I was sunstruck or whether the old lady was the family loony.

You will not be surprised, percipient reader, to learn that when the tapestries parted the girl who entered the room was the girl I had seen on the stallion. I, however, was very surprised, for when I had last met Mrs Krampf – in London, two years before – she had been a villainous old boot wearing a ginger wig and weighing in at some sixteen stones. No one had told me that there was a later model.

Retrieving my eyes, which had been sticking out like chapel hat pegs, I started to scramble to my feet, making rather a nonsense of it what with my short legs and the unreasonably deep sofa. Upright at last, and rather cross, I saw that she was wearing what I suppose I shall have to describe as a Mocking Smile. Almost, one could imagine a red, red rose between her Pearly Teeth.

'If you call me "amigo,"' I snapped, 'I shall scream.' She raised an eyebrow shaped like a seagull's wing and the smile left her face.

'But I had no intention of being so, ah, *fresh*, Mr Mortdecai, nor do I care to ape the speech of these Mexican savages. The *pistolero valiente* disguise is a whim of my kooky husband' – she had a wonderfully fastidious way of using Americanisms – 'and the pistols are something to do with castration complexes: I do not care to understand, I have no interest in Dr Freud and his dirty mind.'

I had her placed now: Viennese Jewess, the loveliest women in the world and the cleverest. I pulled myself together.

'Forgive me,' I said. 'Please let us start again. My name is Mortdecai.' I put my heels together and bowed over her hand; she had the long and lovely fingers of her race and they were as hard as nails.

'Mine is Johanna. You know my married name.' I got the impression that she pronounced it as infrequently as possible. She motioned me back into the sofa – all her gestures were beautiful – and stood there, legs astride. Looking up at her from the depths of that bloody sofa was awkward; lowering my gaze I found myself staring at her jean-gripped crotch, fourteen inches from my nose. (I use fourteen in the Borgesian sense of course.)

'Those are beautiful pistols,' I said, desperately. She did something astonishingly swift and complicated with her right hand and, simultaneously it seemed, a Tiffany butt was six inches from my face. I took it from her respectfully – look, the Dragoon Colt is over a foot long and weighs more than four pounds: unless you've handled one you can't begin to understand the strength and skill you need to flip it about casually. This was an intimidating young woman.

It was indeed a very beautiful pistol. I spun the cylinder – it was loaded in all chambers but, correctly, one nipple was uncapped for the hammer to ride on. There was much splendid engraving and I was startled to see the initials J.S.M.

'Surely these did not belong to John Singleton Mosby?' I asked, awestruck.

'I think that was his name. A cavalry raider or something of that sort. My husband never tires of telling how much he paid for them – for myself, I forget, but it seemed an excessive amount.'

'Yes,' I said, cupidity stabbing me like a knife. 'But are these not rather big weapons for a lady? I mean, you handle them beautifully but I should have thought something like a Colt Lightning or the Wells Fargo model perhaps . . .?'

She took the pistol, checked the position of the hammer and prestidigitated it back into the holster.

'My husband insists on these big ones,' she said, boredly. 'It is something to do with the castration complex or the organ inferiority or some such nastiness. But you must be thirsty, my husband tells me you are *often* thirsty, I shall bring you some drink.' With that she left me. I began to feel a bit castrated myself.

She was back in about two minutes, having changed into a minimal cotton frock and followed by a drinks-laden peon. Her manner, too, had changed and she sank down beside me with a friendly smile. *Close* beside me. I sort of inched away a bit. Cringed away would be better. She looked at me curiously for a moment, then giggled.

'I see. My mother has been talking to you. Ever since she caught me when I was seventeen wearing nothing under my dress she has been convinced that I am a mare in heat. It is not true.' She was making me a large, strong drink – the peon had been dismissed. 'On the other hand,' she continued, handing me the glass with a dazzling smile, 'I have an unaccountable passion for men of your age and build.' I simpered a little, making it clear that I recognized a joke and perhaps a mild *tease*.

'Tee hee,' I said. Then 'Aren't you having a drink?'

'I never drink alcohol. I do not like to blunt my senses.'

'Goodness,' I babbled, 'but how awful for you. Not drinking, I mean. I mean, imagine getting up in the morning knowing that you're not going to feel any better all day.'

'But I feel lovely all day, every day. Feel me.' I spilled quite a lot of my drink.

'No, really,' she said, '*feel.*'

I gingerly prodded a golden, rounded forearm.

'Not there, stupid: here!' She flipped a button open and two of the most beautiful breasts in the world sprang out, quite bare, hard and richly nippled. In all civility I could not decline to grasp one, indeed, my hand made the decision for me. My castration complex had vanished like an evil dream. She pulled my head down to her.

Much as I enjoy kissing girls' nipples, I must say I usually feel a bit sheepish about it, don't you? I'm reminded of fat old men sucking juicily at their teat-like cigars. However, the extravagance of Johanna's response to my first tentative grazing on her lovely pastures was such as to dispel all embarrassment from my mind, replacing it with fears for my own health. She reared up like a tortured cat and wrapped herself around me as though she were in the last extremities of drowning. Her slim, calloused fingers grasped me with delicious ferocity and I soon ascertained that her policy on underwear had not changed since she was seventeen.

'Wait,' I said urgently, 'shouldn't I take a shower first? I'm filthy.'

'I know,' she snarled, 'I love it. You smell like a horse. You *are* a horse.'

Obediently, I broke into a canter, urged by her drumming heels. I was glad she had taken her spurs off.

Descriptions of middle-aged art dealers being ravished are neither instructive nor edifying, so I shall draw a row of '*frissons*' like a shower curtain across the extraordinary scene which followed. Here they are:

. . . .

I was shown to my room by the barefooted hussy in the drawstring blouse. She smiled at me blandly, pointing her lavish bosom like a pair of pistols.

'I am at your service while you stay at the Rancho, señor,' she said guilelessly. 'My name is Josefina – that is, like Josephine.'

'How apt,' I murmured, 'in the circumstances.'

She didn't get it.

As the Countess had predicted, I was just in time for dinner. Changed and bathed, I sat down feeling more like the C. Mortdecai we know and love but I admit to having felt a little chary, a little *coy*, about meeting the old lady's eye. As it happened, she avoided catching mine; she was a dedicated food eater, it was a pleasure to sit in front of her.

'Tell me,' I said to Johanna as the second course appeared, 'where is your husband?'

'He is in his bedroom. Next to the little dressing room where I, ah, received you.'

I stared at her in panic – no sensate human being could have slept through the zoo-like racket of our coupling. Seeing my consternation she laughed merrily.

'Please do not worry about it. He did not hear a thing, he has been dead several hours.'

I don't really remember what we had for dinner. I'm sure it was delicious but I seemed to have difficulty swallowing and I kept on dropping knives, forks and things. 'Quaking' is the only word for what I was doing. All I remember is the old Countess opposite me, cramming the groceries into her frail body like one who provisions a yacht for a long voyage. '*Cur quis non prandeat hoc est?*' seemed to be her attitude.

We had reached the port and walnuts stage before I recovered enough aplomb to venture another question.

'Oh yes,' Johanna replied indifferently, 'it will have been his heart, I suppose. The doctor lives thirty miles away and is drunk; he will come in the morning. Why do you eat so little? You should take more exercise. I will lend you a mare in the morning, a gallop will do you good.'

I became scarlet and silent.

The old lady rang a silver bell which stood by her place and a whey-faced priest stole in and said a long Latin grace to which both the women listened with bent heads. Then the Countess rose and made her way with fragile dignity to the door, where she let out a fart of such frightening power and timbre that I feared she had done herself a mischief. The priest sat down at the end of the table and began gobbling nuts and guzzling wine as though his life depended on it. Johanna sat smiling dreamily into space, presumably envisaging a blissfully Krampf-free future. I certainly hoped she was not envisaging any bliss which would involve my participation in the near future: all I wanted was some Scotch and a big fat sleeping pill.

It was not to be. Johanna took me by the hand and led me off to see the corpse, much as one might be taken to see the ornamental waterfowl in an English house. Krampf lay naked and nasty and very dead indeed, displaying all the signs of a massive coronary occlusion, as the thriller writers say. (There are *no* outward signs of death by massive coronary occlusion.) On the carpet beside his bed lay a little silver box which I remembered; it always held his heart pills. Krampf had gone to join Hockbottle: dicky tickers, both of them. To name but a few.

His death solved a few problems and created a few more. There was something about the situation which I could not, at that stage of the evening, quite define, but I knew that the word 'trouble' figured in it somewhere. Feeling sure that Johanna would not mind, I drew back the sheet which covered him: there was no mark of violence on his lardy body. She came and stood on the other side of the bed and we looked down at him dispassionately. I had lost a rich customer; she had lost a rich husband; there was little quantitative difference between our sorrows and the qualitative difference was that she, presumably, stood to gain a lot of money and I stood to lose some. Had Krampf been alive he would have felt like Jesus Christ between the two thieves, and indeed, death had lent him a certain spirituality, a certain waxy saintliness.

'He was a dirty ape,' she said at last. 'Also base and greedy.'

'I am all those things,' I answered quietly, 'yet I do not think I am like Krampf was.'

'No,' she said. 'He was mean in a shabby, tight-fisted way. I do not think you are mean like that, or at all. Why should rich men be mean?'

'I think it is because they would like to stay rich.'

She thought about that and didn't like it.

'No,' she said again. 'His greed was not of that sort. It was other people's lives he was greedy for: he collected his fellow men like postage stamps. He did not really want the stolen picture which you have in the cover of the Rolls Royce: it was you he was buying. You would never have got free from him after this deal. You would have been kissing his pimply behind for the rest of your life.'

This upset me very much. First, even Krampf could not have known – should not have known – just where the Goya was supposed to be hidden; second, here was yet another person apparently manipulating me instead of *vice versa*; third, this was a woman, for God's sake, deep into the conspiracy and bubbling over with dangerous facts. Krampf had always been rash but he knew the basic rules of villainy. How on earth had he sunk to the point of telling things to a woman?

The whole complexion of Krampf's death changed; before, it had been an extreme awkwardness, now it was a peril. With all this dangerous knowledge surging about so freely there were dozens of motives for killing him when previously there had only been one: Martland's.

Moreover, I had decided only that morning not to carry out my part of the contract I had made with Martland for the terminating of Krampf. I have no patience with the absurd respect in which human life is held these days – indeed, our chief trouble is that there is far too *much* human life around – but as I grow older I find myself less and less keen on actually topping people myself. Particularly when they happen to be my best customers. Nevertheless, I should probably have kept faith with Martland as per contract had it not occurred to me that morning that I was already on the butcher's bill myself and that once I had killed Krampf I would be there redoubled, in spades, for a variety of reasons which you can surely work out for yourself.

'When did he go mad, child?' I asked gently.

'In the womb, I think. Badly, when he started to make plots with a man called Gloag.'

I winced.

'Yes,' I said, 'that figures.'

Despite appearances I was now certain that Krampf had been murdered: there were far too many motives. There are also far too many ways of simulating death by heart disease – and even more of inducing it in someone already prone to it.

I was piggy-in-the-middle and it felt horrid. Only Martland's word as a prefect stood between me and the ultimate in whackings from that fell school sergeant Death. Martland's word was as good as his bond, but his bond was mere Monopoly money. I pulled myself together.

'Well, Johanna,' I said brightly, 'I must be off to bed.'

'Yes,' she said, taking me firmly by the hand, 'we must.'

'Look, my dear, I'm really awfully tired, you know. And I'm not a young man any more . . .'

'Ah, but I have a way of curing both those things – come and see.'

I'm not really weak, you know, just bad and easily led. I shambled after her, my manhood cringing. The night was intolerably hot.

Her room greeted us with steamy heat like a buffet in the face – I panicked as she drew me in and bolted the door.

'The windows are sealed,' she explained, 'the drapes are closed, the central heating turned up high. Look, I am sweating already!'

I looked. She was.

'This is the best way of all to do it,' she went on, peeling off my drenched shirt, 'and you will find yourself young and vigorous, I promise you, it never fails, we shall be like animals in a tropical swamp.'

I tried a tentative bellow of lust but without much conviction. She was anointing me copiously from a bottle of baby oil, handing me the bottle, stepping out of the last of her clothes and offering the

astonishing landscape of her steaming body to the oil. I oiled. From
some undreamed-of reservoir my body summoned up a gravity tank
of incalescent libido.

'There, you see?' she said, gaily, pointing at me, and led me
to one of those terrifying water-filled plastic beds – eclipsing me
with her deliquescent body, coaxing succulent sounds from the
contiguity of our bellies, shaming forth a long dead, steel hard,
adolescent Mortdecai demented with furtive lust: Mortdecai Minor,
the likeliest candidate for wanker's doom.

'Tonight, because you are tired, I am no longer the mare. You
are the lazy circus horse and I shall school you in the *haute école*.
Lie back, you will like this very much, I promise.'

I liked it.

14

> Ottima: Then, Venus' body, had we come upon
>   My husband Luca Gaddi's murdered corpse
>   Within there, at his couch-foot, covered close –
>   Would you have pored upon it? Why persist
>   In poring now upon it? . . .
>
> Sebald: Off, off; take your hands off mine!
>   'Tis the hot evening – off! Oh, morning, is it?

Pippa Passes

Slowly, painfully, I ungummed my eyes. The room was still in utter blackness and smelled of goat. A clock had been chiming somewhere but what hour, of what day even, I knew not. I suppose you could say that I had slept fitfully but I cannot pretend that I awoke refreshed. More knackered, really. I squirmed out of the steaming bed and dragged myself wetly to where the window had to be. I was one hundred years old and knew that my prostate gland could never be the same again. What I panted for, as the hart for cooling springs, was fresh air – not a commodity I often pant for. I found the heavy drapes, drew them apart with an effort and reeled back aghast. Outside, a carnival was in full swing – I thought I had taken leave of my senses, despite prep school assurances that you go *blind* first.

The windows on this side of the house gave on to the desert and there, a couple of furlongs from the house, the darkness was splashed with crisscross rows of coloured lights, blazing for half a mile in each direction. As I gaped uncomprehendingly Johanna slithered up behind me and pasted her viscous form lovingly against my back.

'They have lit up the airstrip, little stallion,' she murmured soothingly between my shoulder blades, 'a plane must be arriving. I wonder who?' What she was really wondering, evidently, was whether spavined old Mortdecai had one more gallop left in his thoroughbred loins but the sheepish answer was plain to see. Her loving moo became a *moue* but she did not reproach me. She was a *lady* – I know it sounds silly – still is for all I know.

Effete or not, I have strong feelings about aircraft landing unexpectedly in the early hours of the morning at country houses where I am staying in equivocal circumstances. It is my invariable practice in such cases to greet the occupants of these machines fully dressed, showered and with a pistol or similar device in my waistband, lest they (the aviators) should prove to be inimical to my best interests.

Accordingly, I showered, dressed, tucked the Banker's Special into its cosy nest and made for the great downstairs, where I found something astonishingly nasty to drink called *tequila*. It tasted of fine old vintage battery acid but I drank quite a lot of it, thirstily, before Johanna came down. She looked courteous, friendly but aloof; no hint of our late chumminess apparent on her lovely face.

A peon fluttered in and harangued her in the vile *argot* which passes for Spanish in those parts. She turned to me, well-bred surprise civilly concealed.

'A Señor Strapp has arrived,' she said wonderingly, 'and says that he must see you at once. He says that you expect him . . .?'

I boggled a moment, about to deny all knowledge of any Strapps, before the penny dropped and the mental W.C. door flew open.

'Ah, yes, of course,' I cried, 'that's old Jock! Quite forgotten. Silly of me. My servant, sort of. Should have told you he was meeting me here. He'll really be no trouble, just a heap of bedding and a bone to gnaw. Should have warned you. Sorry.'

Even as I babbled, Jock's massy frame filled the doorway, his ill-hewn ashlar head weaving from side to side, eyes blinking at the light. I gave a glad cry and he returned a one-fang grin.

'Jock!' I cried, 'I am so glad you could come.' (Johanna,

inexplicably, giggled.) 'I trust you are well, Jock and, er, *fit?*'
He caught my drift and blinked affirmatively. 'Go and get washed
and fed, Jock, then meet me here, please, in half an hour. We are
leaving.'

He shambled off, led by a she-peon, and Johanna rounded on me.

'How can you be leaving? Do you not love me? What have I done?
Are we not to be married?' This was my day for gaping – I did it
again. While I gaped she continued her amazing tirade.

'Do you think I give myself like an animal to every man I meet?
Did you not realize last night that you are my first and only passion,
that I belong to you, that I am your woman?'

Huckleberry Finn's words sprang to my mind: 'The statements
was interesting but tough,' but this was no time for breezy quoting –
she looked as though one wrong answer would send her galloping up
to the boudoir for her Dragoon Colts. My jaws unlocked themselves
and I began to drivel fast, as though drivelling for my life.

'Never dreamed . . . didn't dare hope . . . plaything of an idle
hour . . . too old . . . too fat . . . burned out . . . bemused . . .
haven't had my tea . . . in terrible danger here . . .' That last bit
seemed to interest her: I had to give a clumsily edited version of my
grounds for fear; such as Martlands, Buicks, Bluchers and Brauns,
to name but a few.

'I see,' she said at last. 'Yes, in the circumstances perhaps you had
better leave for the moment. When you are safe, get in touch with
me and I will come to you and we shall be happy ever after. Take
the Rolls Royce – and anything in it – it is my engagement present
to you.'

'Good God,' I quavered, aghast, 'you can't give me that, I mean,
worth a fortune, quite ridiculous.'

'I already have a fortune,' she said, simply. 'Also, I love you.
Please not to insult me by refusing. Try to understand that I am
yours and so, naturally, everything I have is yours too.'

'Gaw Blimey,' I thought. Clearly, I was being ridiculed in some
complicated way – and for unguessed-at reasons – or was I? The
glint in her eye was dangerous, genuinely.

'Ah, well, in that case,' I said, 'there is one thing I really have
to have for my own safety – it's a sort of photographic negative, I
fancy, and perhaps some prints of – well –'

'Of two deviates playing at bulldozers? I know it. The faces have been cut out of the print but my husband says that one of them is the nasty Mr Gloag and the other the brother-in-law of your –'

'Yes, yes,' I broke in. 'That's it. The very thing. No use to you, you know. Your husband was only going to use it to get diplomatic bag facilities for stolen pictures and even that was too dangerous. Even for him. I mean, look at him.'

She looked at *me* curiously for a while then led the way to Krampf's study, which was a riot of undigested wealth, a cinema usherette's nightmare of Tsarskoe Selo. When I tell you that the central attraction – the Main Feature, so to speak – was an enormous, nude, hairy trollop by Henner which hung against Louis XIV *boiseries* and was lit by two of the most awful Tiffany lamps I have ever seen, then I think I have said all. Mrs Spon would have *catted* right there, on the Aubusson.

'*Merde,*' I said, awestruck.

She nodded gravely. 'It is beautiful, is it not. I designed it for him when we were first married, when I still thought I loved him.'

She led the way through to Krampf's private bog, where a fine Bouguereau – if you like Bouguereau – twinkled saucy titties and bums down into the still waters of a porcelain *bidet* which might have been designed for Catherine the Great in one of her more salty moods. The picture, cunningly, did not conceal a safe, but a carved panel just beside it did. Johanna had to diddle it in all sorts of complicated ways before it swung open to reveal groaning shelves of great coarse currency notes – I've never seen such a vulgar sight – as well as passbooks from the banks of all the world and a number of leather-covered suitcase handles. (I did not have to heft these to know that they were made of platinum, for I had given Krampf the notion myself. It's a good wheeze, the customs haven't got on to it yet. You're welcome, I shan't need it again.) She opened a drawer concealed in the side wall of the safe and tossed a parcel of envelopes to me.

'What you want should be in there,' she said indifferently and went to perch delicately on the edge of the bidet. I riffled through the package reverently. One envelope contained insurance policies beyond the dreams of avarice, another a mass of wills and codicils, another held simply a list of names with coded references against each. (Knowing Krampf's predilections, there was probably a fortune in that list alone, if one spent a little time on it, but I am not a brave man.) The next envelope was full of smaller envelopes, each one bearing a rare foreign stamp in the top right-hand corner: rich and devious readers will recognize the dodge – you simply stick an ordinary new postage stamp over the rarity and post it to yourself or your agent in some foreign capital. It is the easiest way of moving heavy spending money about the world without losing too much in commission.

The last envelope was the one I wanted – needed – and it seemed to be in order. There was the magnum print with the faces cut out and a strip of 35-mm negatives on British film stock. A length of amateurish contact prints mostly showed the Backs at Cambridge but the centre frame showed the fronts all right: Hockbottle seemed to have been in charge that day and it had been Chummy's turn in the barrel. His familiar grin, straight into the camera, showed that he didn't mind a bit. I burned it without compunction and threw the ashes into the naughty *bidet*. It represented a lot of money but, as I just said, I am not a brave man – even money can come too dear.

I was not troubled about the possible existence of other prints: Krampf may have been imprudent but he had not, I thought, been wholly potty and, in any case, prints are too easily faked these days; people want to see the negative – and the original negative at that, negatives prepared from a positive print are easily detectable.

She twisted round and stared at the smear of ashes in the *bidet*.

'Are you happy now, Charlie? Is that really all you wanted?'

'Yes. Thank you. It makes me a little safer, I think. Not much, but a little. Thank you very much.'

She rose and went to the safe, selected a couple of chunks of currency and closed the panel negligently.

'Here is some journey money, please take it. You will perhaps need *des fonds sérieux* to help you get safely away.'

They were two fat bricks of bank notes, still in their wrappers, one English, one American. The total amount had to be something quite indecent.

'Oh, but I couldn't possibly take this,' I squeaked, 'it's a terrible lot of money.'

'But I keep telling you, I *have* a terrible lot of money now – this in the safe is nothing, a cash reserve he kept for small bribes to

Senators and for unexpected trips. You are please to take it; I shall not be happy unless I know that you have proper funds while you are avoiding these unpleasant men.'

My further protestations were cut short by frightful shrieks from downstairs, superimposed on a bass of snarling roars. We raced for the stairhead and looked down into the hall on a scene of gladiatorial horror: Jock had a peon in each hand and was methodically beating them together like a pair of cymbals, while others, of both sexes, milled around him, tore at his hair, hung on his arms and were hurled off spinning across the tiled floor.

'¡Bravo toro!' cried Johanna piercingly and the *mêlée* became a tableau.

'Put those people down, Jock,' I said severely, 'you don't know *where* they've been.'

'I was only trying to find out what they'd done with you, Mr Charlie – you said half an hour, didn't you?'

I apologized all round; the peons couldn't understand my polished Castilian but they knew what it was all right; there was a good deal of bowing and scraping and forelock-tugging and polite murmurs of '*de nada*' and they accepted a dollar apiece with every mark of pleasure. One went so far as to intimate courteously that, since his nose was squashed to a pulp, he merited a little extra honorarium but Johanna would not let me give him any more.

'With one dollar he will get beautifully drunk,' she explained, 'but with two he would do something foolish, perhaps go off and get married.'

She explained this to the peon, too, who followed her reasoning carefully and gravely concurred at the end. They are a logical lot.

'A logical lot, Jock, don't you think?' I asked later.

'Nah,' he said. 'Lot of bloody Pakis if you ask me.'

We got away before the sun was very high. I had breakfasted lightly on a little more *tequila* – it's beastly but it sort of grows on you – and had contrived to avoid a farewell exhibition-bout with my doting Johanna. She was most convincingly tearful and distrait, saying that she would live only for my message that she might join me and live happily ever after.

'Where we going, then, Mr Charlie?'

'I'll think about that as we go, Jock. In the meantime, there's only this road. Let's move.'

But as we drove – as Jock drove, to be exact, for he had slept on the plane – I mused about Johanna. What earthly purpose could all that incredible codswallop of hers be serving? Did she really think that I was swallowing it? Did she think I could believe her bowled over by the faded allure of portly, past-it Mortdecai? 'Garn' was the word which kept springing to mind. And yet; and yet . . . Karl Popper urges us to be constantly on our guard against the fashionable disease of our time: the assumption that things cannot be taken at their face value, that an apparent syllogism must be the *rationale* of an irrational motive, that a human avowal must conceal some self-seeking baseness. (Freud assures us that Leonardo's John the Baptist is a homosexual symbol, his upward-pointing index finger seeking to penetrate the fundament of the universe; art historians know that it is a centuries-old cliché of Christian iconography.)

Perhaps, then, all was as it seemed, all to the gravy; indeed, as we soared up winding roads into the high country stretching its strong limbs in the young sunshine, it was hard to credit my fears and suspicions.

Perhaps Krampf had indeed died of heart disease after excess at table: statistically he was a sitter for just that. Perhaps Johanna had indeed fallen violently in love with me: my friends have sometimes been kind enough to say that I have a certain appeal, perhaps an adroitness in these little matters. Perhaps the second powder-blue Buick and its driver were merely a relief shift ordered by Krampf: I had had no opportunity to put this to him. Perhaps, last of all, I would indeed send for Johanna and live the life of Riley with her and her millions until my glands gave out.

The more I thought about this view of things the more sensible it became and the sweeter shone the sun on the unjust. I leaned back luxuriously into the rich-smelling leather of the Rolls – *my* Rolls! – and quietly whistled a happy stave or two.

Martland, surely, would never believe that Krampf's infarct was natural; he would assume that I had murdered him as per invoice and had been devilish clever about it.

Only Johanna knew that I had burned the negative and if I dropped the merest hint to Martland that I might just have forgotten to do so he would never dare unleash his death dogs on me but would be forced to respect his word and protect me from all annoyances; such as, for instance, death.

I liked it; I liked it all, it fitted together, it made nonsense of my fears, I felt positively young again. For two pins, I'd have turned back and given Johanna a little farewell token of my esteem after all, that's how young I felt. The lark was on the wing and flying strongly, while the snail was positively striding up its favourite thorn.

Admittedly, there was one fly trampling about in the ointment of my content: I was now the proud but shy owner of about half a million pounds' worth of hot Goya – the hottest piece of property in the world. Despite what you read in the Sunday papers, America is not seething with mad millionaires panting to buy stolen masterpieces and gloat over them in their underground aviaries. As a matter of fact, the late Krampf had been the only one I knew of and I did not much want another like him. A superb spender, but hard on the nervous system.

Destroying the painting was out of the question: my soul is all stained and shagged with sin like a cigarette smoker's moustache but I am quite incapable of destroyin orks of art. Steal them, yes, cheerfully, it is a mark of respect an love, but destroy them, never. Why, even the Woosters had a code, as we are told on the highest authority.

Probably the best thing was to take it back to England – it was, after all, as well hidden now as it ever could be – and get in touch with a specialist friend who knows how to do discreet deals with insurance companies.

You know, all those dreary pink Renoirs which are incessantly getting pinched in the South of France are either sold back to the insurers at a straight 20 per cent of the sum insured – the companies won't pay a franc more, it's a matter of professional ethics – or they are pinched at the express request of the owners and immediately destroyed. The French *arriviste*, you see, lives in such a continual agony of snobbism that he dares not put his Renoir, bought three years ago, into a public auction and so admit that he is short of a little change – still less dare he take the risk that it might fetch less than he has told all his awful friends it is worth. He would rather die; or, in practical terms, he would rather assassinate the painting and collect the *nouveaux francs*. In England the police tend to purse their lips and wag their fingers at insurance co's who buy back stolen things from the thieves: they feel that this is not a way to discourage villainy – in fact the whole process is strictly against the law.

Nevertheless, if a certain young man, not unknown at Lloyd's, murmurs in the proper ear that a bundle of currency posted to an accommodation address in Streatham will bring about a change of heart in certain thieves and cause them to panic and dump the swag in a left-luggage office – well, insurance co's are only human you know (or didn't you know?) and a thousand pounds is a great deal less than, say, five thousand ditto. The certain young man not unknown at Lloyd's was also not unknown to me and although he didn't like murmuring in that sort of ear more than once or twice a year he had, I knew, a heart of gold and owed me a trifling kindness. Moreover, he was terrified of Jock. Don't think I'm recommending this particular caper, though: the police are professionals and we laymen are only gifted amateurs, at the best. If you must sin, find an obscure, unexplored branch of crime that the Yard hasn't any experts in and work it gently, don't milk it dry, and vary your *modus operandi* continually. They'll get on to you in the end, of course, but if you're not greedy you may have a few good years first.

As I was saying, before the above gnomic utterances, I was by now wholly reconciled to a Panglossian view of things: all was explicable, the tangled web made, after all, a comprehensible pattern when looked at in sunlight and also, after all, one Mortdecai was worth a whole barrelful of Martlands, Bluchers, Krampfs and other dullards. ('One of the most remarkable phenomena connected with the practice of mendacity is the vast number of deliberate lies we tell ourselves, whom, of all persons, we can least expect to deceive.' J.S. Lefanu.)

To complete my skimpy breakfast, and to celebrate the victory of virtue over dullness, I opened a bottle of the twelve-year-old Scotch and was just raising it to my lips when I saw the powder-blue Buick. It was coming out of an *arroyo* ahead of us, coming fast, engine howling in a low gear, coming straight for our nearside. Our offside was barely a yard from a sheer drop of hundreds of feet – it was a fair cop. I'd had my life. Jock – I've told you how fast he could be when necessary – wrenched the wheel over to the left, stood on the brakes, snatched first gear before the Rolls stalled and was turning right as the Buick hit us. The Buick man had known nothing of the strength of a vintage Rolls Royce, nor of Jock's fighting brain; our radiator gutted his car's side with a ghastly shriek of metal and the Buick span like a top, ending up poised on the shoulder of the road, its rear end impossibly extended over the precipice. The driver, face contorted with who knows what emotion, was fighting frantically with the door handle, his features a mask of nasty blood. Jock got out, ponderously strolled over to him and stared, looked up and down the road, went to the front of the mangled Buick, found a handhold and heaved enormously. The Buick tilted, started to go very slowly: Jock had time to get to the window again and give the driver a friendly grin before the nose went up and slid out of sight, slowly still. The driver showed us all his teeth in a silent scream before he went; we heard the Buick bounce three times, amazingly loudly, but never a thread of the driver's scream – those Buicks must be better soundproofed than you'd think. I believe, but I am not sure even now, that it was friendly Mr Braun – who was once again proving to me the statistical improbability of death in an aircraft accident.

I was surprised – and pardonably proud – to find that throughout the episode I had not lost my grip on the Scotch bottle: I had my drink and, since the circumstances were exceptional, offered the bottle to Jock.

'That was a bit vindictive, Jock,' I said reprovingly.

'Lost my temper,' he admitted. 'Bloody road hog.'

'He might easily have done us a mischief,' I agreed. Then I told him about things, especially like powder-blue Buicks and the dreadful – is that word really so worn out? – the dreadful danger I was – we were – in, despite my recent brief and lovely courtship with the phantasms of success, safety and happy-ever-after. (It seemed hard to believe that I could have been dallying, so few minutes before, with so patently tinsel a mental mistress as safety.) My eloquence ran to such heights of bitter self-mockery that I heard myself, aghast, telling Jock to leave me, to get out from under before the great axe fell.

'Bollocks,' I'm happy to say, was his response to that suggestion. (But 'happy to say' is not true either: his loyalty served me but briefly and him but shabbily – you might say that his 'bollocks' were the death of him.)

When the whisky had somewhat soothed our nerves we corked the bottle and got out of the car to examine its wounds. An Anglia driver would have done this first, of course, raging at fate, but we Rolls owners are made of sterner stuff. The radiator was scarred, weeping a little on to the baking road; a headlamp and sidelamp were quite ruined; the offside mudguard was heavily crumpled but still not quite so much that it would flay the tire. The show was, if necessary, on the road. I went back into the car and thought, while Jock fussed over the damage. I may have sipped a little at the whisky bottle and who shall blame me?

No one passed along the road, in either direction. A grasshopper stridulated endlessly; I minded this at first but soon learned to live with it. Having thought, I checked my thinking both ways from the ace. The result came out the same again and again. I didn't like it, but there you are, aren't you?

We sent the Rolls over the precipice. I am not ashamed to say that I wept a little to see all that beauty, that power and grace and history, being tossed into an arid canyon like a cigar end chucked down a lavatory pan. Even in death the car was elegant; it described great majestic curves as it rebounded in an almost leisurely way from boulder to boulder and came to rest, far below us, wedged upside-down in the throat of a deep crevasse, its lovely underparts bared to the sex of sunshine for a few seconds before a hundred tons of scree, dislodged by its passage, roared down and covered it.

The death of the Buick driver had been nothing compared with this: human death in reality seems poor stuff to a devoted television watcher, but who amongst you, seasoned readers, has seen a Rolls Royce Silver Ghost die on its back? I was inexpressibly moved. Jock seemed to sense this in his rough way for he moved closer to me and uttered words of comfort.

'It was insured full comprehensive, Mr Charlie,' he said.

'Yes, Jock,' I answered gruffly, 'you read my thoughts, as usual. But what is more to the point, just now, is how easily could the Rolls be salvaged?'

He brooded down into the shimmering, rock-strewn haze.

'How are you getting down there?' he began. 'This side's all avalanches and the other side's a cliff. Very dodgy.'

'Right.'

'Then you got to get it out of that crack, haven't you?'

'Right again.'

'*Dead* dodgy.'

'Yes.'

'And then you got to get it back up here, right?'

'Right.'

'Have to close this road a couple of days while the tackle's working, I reckon.'

'That's what I thought.'

'Mind you, if it was some stupid mountaineering twit stuck down there, or some old tart's puppy dog, they'd have him up before you could cough, wouldn't they, but this is only an old jam jar, isn't it? You'd have to want it real bad – or want something in it real bad – before you'd go slummocking down there.' He nudged me and winked enormously. He was never very good at winking, it contorted his face horribly. I nudged him back. We smirked.

Then we trudged up the road, Jock carrying our one suitcase now holding essentials for both of us, which he was supposed to have salvaged with wonderful presence of mind as the Rolls teetered on the very brink of the precipice.

'Whither Mortdecai?' about summed up my thought on that baking, dusty road. It is hard to think constructively once the fine, white grit of New Mexico has crept up your trouser legs and joined the sweat of your crotch. All I could decide was that the stars in their courses were hotly anti-Mortdecai and that, noble sentiments aside, I was well rid of what was probably the most conspicuous motor car on the North American subcontinent.

On the other hand, pedestrians are more conspicuous in New Mexico than most motor cars: a fact I realized when a car swept past us going in the direction we had come from; all its occupants goggled at us as though we were Teenage Things from Outer Space. It was an official car of some sort, a black and white Olds-mobile Super 88, and it did not stop – why should it? To be on foot in the United States is only immoral, not illegal. Unless you're a bum, of course. It's just like in England, really: you can wander abroad and lodge in the open air so long as you've a home to go to; it's only an offence if you *haven't* one – on the same principle that ensures you cannot borrow money from a bank unless you don't need any.

After what seemed a great many hours we found a patch of shade afforded by some nameless starveling trees and without a word spoken we sank down in their ungenerous umbrage.

'When a car passes going in our direction, Jock, we shall leap to our feet and hail it.'

'All right, Mr Charlie.'

With that we both fell asleep instantly.

15

John of the Temple, whose fame so bragged,
Is burning alive in Paris square!
How can he curse, if his mouth is gagged?
Or wriggle his neck, with a collar there?
Or heave his chest, while a band goes round?
Or threat with his fist, since his arms are spliced?
Or kick with his feet, now his legs are bound?
– Thinks John, I will call upon Jesus Christ.

The Heretic's Tragedy

A couple of hours later we were rudely awakened when a car travelling in our direction screeched to a halt beside us. It was the official looking car which had passed earlier and four huge rough men poured out of it, waving pistols and handcuffs and other symbols of Law 'n' Order. In a trice, before we were properly awake, we were sitting manacled in the car, surrounded by deputy sheriffs. Jock, when he had sized up the situation, started to make a deep growling noise and to tense his muscles. The deputy beside him, with a deft backhanded flip, laid a leather-covered blackjack smartly against Jock's upper lip and nostrils. It is exquisitely painful: tears sprang to Jock's eyes and he fell silent.

'Now look here!' I cried angrily.

'Shaddap.'

I too fell silent.

They hit Jock again when we arrived at the sheriff's office in the single broad dusty street of an empty little town; he had shrugged off the deputy's officious hands and made snarling noises, so one of them casually bent down and coshed him hard behind the knee. That is pretty painful too; we all had to wait a while before he could walk into the office – he was much too big to carry. They didn't hit me; I was *demure*.

What they do to you in this particular sheriff's office is as follows: they hang you up on a door by your handcuffs then they hit you quite gently but insistently on the kidneys, for quite a long time. It makes you cry, if you want to know. It would make anybody cry after a time. They don't ask you any questions and they don't leave any marks on you, except where the handcuffs bit in, and you did that yourself, struggling, didn't you?

'I shut my eyes and turned them on my heart, I asked one draught of earlier, happier sights . . .'

After a certain time the sheriff himself came into the room. He was a slight and studious man with an intelligent look and a disapproving scowl. The deputies stopped hitting our kidneys and pocketed their blackjacks.

'Why have these men not been charged?' he asked coldly. 'How many times do I have to tell you that suspects are not to be questioned before they have been properly booked?'

'We weren't questioning them, sheriff,' said one in an insubordinate tone. 'If we was questioning them they'd be hanging the other way around and we'd be beating on their balls, you know that, sheriff. We was just kind of getting their minds right for being questioned by *you*, sheriff.'

He stroked his face all down one side, quite thoroughly, making a gentle, half-audible sound like an old lady caressing a pet toad.

'Bring them in to me,' he said and turned on his heel.

'Bring' was right – we couldn't have made our own way to his office. He let us sit on chairs, but only because we couldn't stand up. Now, suddenly, I was very angry indeed, a rare emotion for me and one which I have schooled myself to avoid since my disastrous childhood.

When I could speak properly through the choking and the sobs I gave him the full business, especially the diplomatic passport bit. It worked, he started to look angry himself and perhaps a little frightened. Our gyves were removed and our possessions returned to us, except for my Banker's Special. Jock's Luger was in the suitcase which, I was relieved to notice, had not been opened: Jock had prudently swallowed the key and, in the excitement of spoiling our personal plumbing, the deputies had not taken time out to force the lock. It was a very *good* lock and a very strong case.

'Now you will have the goodness, perhaps, to explain this extraordinary treatment, Sir,' I said, giving him my dirtiest glare, 'and suggest reasons why I should not request my Ambassador to arrange to have you and your ruffians broken.'

He looked at me long and thoughtfully, his clever eyes flickering as his brain raced. I was a lot of trouble for him whichever way the cat jumped; a lot of paperwork at the best, a lot of grief at the worst. I could see him reach a decision and I trembled inwardly. Before he could speak I attacked again.

'If you choose not to answer, of course, I can simply call the Embassy and give them the bald facts as they stand.'

'Don't push too hard, Mr Mortdecai. I am about to book you both on suspicion of murder and your diplomatic status isn't worth a pile of rat dirt in that league.'

I spluttered in a British sort of way to hide my consternation. Surely no one could have seen Jock's little momentary squib of ill-temper with the Buick – and anyway, at a distance it would surely have seemed that he was trying to *save* the poor fellow . . .?

'Just who am I – are we – supposed to have murdered?'

'Milton Quintus Desiré Krampf.'

'*Desiré?*'

'That's how I have it.'

'Gawblimey. You're sure it wasn't '*Voulu*?'

'No,' he said, in a literate sort of way and with half a smile. '"Desiré" is how I have it here.' One got the impression that if he'd been an Englishman he'd have seconded my 'Gawblimey' but one had, too, the impression that he was quite content *not* to be an Englishman, perhaps particularly not the portly Englishman now cowering manfully in front of him.

'Go on,' I said. 'Frighten me.'

'I never try to. Some people I hurt; it's part of the job. Some I kill: that too. Who needs to frighten? I'm not that kind of a policeman.'

'I bet you frighten your psychiatrist,' I quipped and straightaway wished I hadn't. He did not give me a cold, blank stare, he didn't look at me at all. He looked at the desk top where the scratches and the fly shit were, then he opened a drawer and took out one of those thin, black, gnarled cheroots and lit it. He didn't even blow the rank smoke in my face – he wasn't that kind of a policeman.

But he had, somehow, succeeded in frightening me. My kidneys started to hurt terribly.

'My kidneys are hurting me terribly,' I said, 'and I have to go to the lavatory.'

He gestured economically toward a door and I got there without actually screaming out loud. It was a very *nice* little lavatory. I rested my head against the cool, tiled wall and piddled wearily. There was no actual blood, which mildly surprised me. At eye level someone had scratched 'MOTHER F' into the wall before they had been interrupted. I speculated – '– ATHER'? – then collected myself, remembering Jock's plight; adjusted clothing before leaving.

'Your turn, Jock,' I said firmly as I re-entered the room, 'should have thought of you first.' Jock shambled out; the sheriff didn't look impatient, he didn't really look anything – I wished he would. I cleared my throat.

'Sheriff,' I said, 'I saw Mr Krampf's body yesterday – goodness, was it only yesterday – and he had quite clearly died of a coronary in the ordinary way of business. What gives with the murder bit?'

'You may speak English, Mr Mortdecai; I am an uneducated man but I read a great deal. Mr Krampf died of a deep puncture wound in the heart. Someone – you, I must suppose – introduced a long and very thin instrument into his side between the fifth and sixth ribs and carefully wiped off the very slight surface bleeding which would have ensued.

'It is not a rare *modus operandi* on our West Coast: the Chinese Tongs used to favour a six-inch nail, the Japanese use a sharpened umbrella rib. It's all-same Sicilian stiletto, I suppose, except that the Sicilians usually strike upwards through the diaphragm. Had Mr Krampf's heart been young and sound he might well have survived so small a puncture – the muscle could have kind of clenched itself around the hole – but Mr Krampf's heart was by no means healthy. Had he been a poor man his history of heart disease might have caused the manner of his death to escape notice, but he was not a man at all, he was a hundred million dollars. That means a great deal of insurance pressure in this country, Mr Mortdecai, and our insurance investigators make the Chicago riot police look like Girl Scouts. Even the drunkest doctor takes a veddy, veddy careful look at a hundred million dollars' worth of dead meat.'

I pondered a bit. Dawn broke.

'The old lady!' I cried. 'The Countess! A hatpin! She was a leading Krampf-hater and a hatpin owner if ever I saw one!'

He shook his head slowly. 'Not a chance, Mr Mortdecai. I'm surprised to hear you trying to pin your slaying on the sweetest and innocentest little old lady you ever saw. Besides, we already checked. She covers her head with a shawl in church and doesn't have a hat or a hatpin in her possession. We *looked*. Anyway, one of the servants has sworn a statement that you were seen entering Krampf's personal suite, drunk, at about the time of death and that your servant Strapp acted like a homicidal maniac during your visit to the rancho, breaking the same servant's nose and beating up everyone. Moreover, you are known to be Mrs Krampf's lover – we have a really fascinating statement from the woman who makes her bed – so there's a double motive of sex and money as well as opportunity. I'd say you should tell it all now, starting with where you hid the murder weapon, so I don't have to have you interrogated.'

He repeated the word 'interrogated' as though he liked the sound of it. To say that my blood ran cold would be idle: it was already as cold as a tart's kiss. Had I been guilty I would have 'spilled my guts' – may I use dialect? – there and then, rather than meet those deputies again, especially *frontally*. If Winter comes, can Spring be far behind? A still, small voice whispered 'stall' in my ear.

'Do you mean to say that you have arrested Johanna Krampf?' I cried.

'Mr Mortdecai, you cannot be as simple as you pretend. Mrs Krampf is now many millions of dollars herself; a poor sheriff does not arrest millions of dollars, they have not a stain on their character. Should I call in a stenographer now, so that you can make the statement?'

What had I to lose? In any case, no one could hurt me too obscenely in front of a sweet little bosomy stenographer.

So he pressed a buzzer and in clunked the nastier of the two deputies, a pencil engulfed in one meaty fist, a shorthand pad in the other.

I may have squeaked – I don't remember and it is not important. There is no doubt that I was distressed.

'Are you unwell, Mr Mortdecai?' asked the sheriff pleasantly.

'Not really,' I said. 'Just a touch of proctalgia.' He didn't ask what it meant; just as well, really.

'Statement by C. Mortdecai,' he said crisply to the stenographic ruffian, 'given at so and so on such and such a date before me, so and so, and witnessed by such and such another.' With that he shot a finger out at me, like one of those capable television chaps. I did not hesitate: it was time to put on a bit of dog.

'I did not kill Krampf,' I said, 'and I have no idea who did. I am a British diplomat and protest strongly against this disgraceful treatment. I suggest you either release me at once or allow me to telephone the nearest British Consul before you ruin your career irretrievably. Can you spell "irretrievably"?' I asked over my shoulder at the stenographer. But he was no longer taking down my words, he was advancing toward me with the blackjack in his hairy paw. Before I could even cringe the door opened and two almost identical men entered.

This final Kafkaesque touch was too much for me: I succumbed to hysterical giggles. No one looked at me; the deputy was slinking out, the sheriff was looking at the two men's credentials, the two men were looking through the sheriff. Then the sheriff slunk out. I pulled myself together.

'What is the meaning of this intrusion?' I asked, still giggling like a little mad thing. They were very polite, pretended not to hear me, sat down side by side behind the sheriff's desk. They were astonishingly alike; the same suits, the same haircuts, the same neat briefcases and the same slight bulges under the nattily tailored left armpits. They looked like Colonel Blucher's younger brothers. They were probably rather alarming people in their quiet way. I pulled myself together and stopped giggling. I could tell Jock didn't like them, he had started breathing through his nose, a sure sign.

One of them pulled out a little wire recorder, tested it briefly, switched it off and sat back, folding his arms. The other pulled out a slim manila file, read the contents with mild interest and sat back, folding his arms. They didn't look at each other once, they didn't look at Jock. First they looked at the ceiling for a while, as though it was something of a novelty, then they looked at me as though I was nothing of the kind. They looked at me as though they saw a great many of me every day and felt none the richer for it. One of them, on some unseen cue, at last uttered,

'Mr Mortdecai, we are members of a small Federal Agency of which you have never heard. We report directly to the Vice-President. We are in a position to help you. We have formed the opinion that you are in urgent need of help and we may say that this opinion has been formed after some extensive study of your recent activities, which seem to have been dumb.'

'Oh, ah,' I said feebly.

'I should make it very clear that we are not interested in law enforcement as such; indeed, such an interest would often conflict with our specific duties.'

'Yes,' I said. 'Do you know a chap called Colonel Blucher? Or, if it comes to that, another chap named Martland?'

'Mr Mortdecai, we feel we can best help you at this juncture by encouraging you to answer our questions rather than ask any of your own. A few right answers could get you out of here in ten minutes; wrong answers, or a whole lot of questions, would make us lose interest in you and we'd just kind of hand you back to the sheriff. Personally, and off the record, I would not, myself, care to be held for murder in this county, would you, Smith?'

Smith shook his head emphatically, lips tightened.

'Ask away,' I quavered, 'I have nothing to hide.'

'Well, that's already being a little less than candid, Sir, but we'll let it pass this time. Would you tell us first, please, what you did with the negative and prints of a certain photograph, formerly in the possession of Milton Krampf?'

(Did you know that in the olden days when a sailor died at sea and the sailmaker was sewing him up in his tarpaulin jacket, along with an anchor shackle, prior to committing him to the deep, that the last stitch was always ritually passed through the corpse's nose? It was to give him his last chance to come to life and cry out. I felt like just such a sailor at that moment. I came to life and cried out. This last stitch had finally awakened me from the cataleptic trance I must have been in for days. Far, far too many people knew far, far too much about my little affairs: the game was up, all was known, God was not in his heaven, the snail was unthorned and C. Mortdecai was *dans la purée noire*. He had been *dumb*.)

'What negative?' I asked brightly.

They looked at each other wearily and began to gather their things together. I was still being dumb.

'Wait!' I cried. 'Silly of me. The negative. Yes, of course. The *photographic* negative. Yes. Oh, yes, yes, yes. As a matter of fact I burned it, much too dangerous to have about one.'

'We are glad you said that, Sir, for we have reason to believe it is true. Indeed, we found traces of ash in a, uh, curious footbath in Mr Krampf's private bathroom.'

You will agree, I'm sure, that this was no time to expatiate on the niceties of French plumbing.

'Well, there you are, you see,' I said.

'How many prints, Mr Mortdecai?'

'I burned the two with the negative; I only know of one other, in London, and the faces have been cut out of that – I daresay you know all about it.'

'Thank you. We feared you might pretend to know of others and attempt to use this as a means of protecting yourself. It would not have protected you but it would have given us a fair amount of embarrassment.'

'Oh, good.'

'Mr Mortdecai, have you asked yourself how we happen to be here so soon after the killing?'

'Look, I said I'd answer your questions and I will: if I have guts I'm prepared to spill them now – I'm quite unmanned. But if you want me to ask *myself* questions, you must get me something to eat and drink. Anything will do to eat; my drink is in the outer office if King Kong and Godzilla out there haven't stolen it all. Oh, and my servant needs something too, of course.'

One of them put his head out of the door and muttered; my whisky, not too depleted, appeared and I sucked hungrily at it, then passed it to Jock. The boys in the Brooks Bros suits didn't want any – they probably lived on iced water and tin tacks.

'No,' I resumed, 'I have not asked myself that. If I really started to ask myself about the events of the last thirty-six hours

I should probably be forced to conclude that there is a world-wide anti-Mortdecai conspiracy. But tell me, if it will cheer you up.'

'We don't much want to tell you, Mr Mortdecai. We just wanted to hear what you would say. So far we like your answers. Now tell us about the way you lost the Rolls Royce.' At this point they switched the wire recorder on.

I told them frankly about the collision but altered the subsequent events a little, telling them lovely stories about Jock's gallant bid to save the Buick as it teetered on the brink; then how we had tried to back the Rolls on to the road, how the wheels had spun, the shoulder crumbled and the car gone to join the Buick.

'And your suitcase, Mr Mortdecai?'

'Brilliant presence of mind on the part of Jock – snatched it at the last moment.'

They switched off the recorder.

'We do not necessarily believe all or any of this, Mr Mortdecai, but again it happens to be the story we wanted. Now, have you anything else in your possession which you intended to deliver to Mr Krampf?'

'No. Honour bright. *Search* us.'

They started studying the ceiling again, they had all the time in the world.

Later, the door knocked and a deputy brought in a paper sack of food; I almost fainted away at the wonderful fragrance of hamburgers and coffee. Jock and I ate two hamburgers each; our interrogators didn't like the look of theirs. They pushed them away delicately with the backs of their fingers, in unison, as though they'd rehearsed it. There was a little carton of chilli to spread on the hamburgers. I had lots of it but it spoils the taste of whisky, you know.

I cannot remember much about the rest of the questions, except that they went on for a long time and some of them were surprisingly vague and general. Sometimes the wire recorder was on, sometimes not. Probably another was on all the time, inside one of the briefcases. I got the impression that they were becoming very bored with the whole thing, but I was by then so sleepy with food and liquor and exhaustion that I could only concentrate with difficulty. Much of the time I simply told them the truth – a course Sir Henry Wotton (another man who went abroad to lie) recommended as a way of baffling your adversaries. Another chap once said, 'If you wish to preserve your secret, wrap it up in frankness.' I wrapped, profusely. But you know, playing a sort of fugue with truth and mendacity makes one lose, after a while, one's grip on reality. My father always warned me against lying where the truth would do; he had early realized that my memory – essential equipment of the liar – was faulty. 'Moreover,' he used to say, 'a lie is a work of art. We *sell* works of art, we don't give them away. Eschew falsehood, my son.' That is why I never lie when selling works of art. Buying them is another matter, of course.

As I was saying, they asked a lot of rather vague questions, few of them apparently germane to the issue. Mind you, I wasn't so terribly sure what the point at issue was, so perhaps I wasn't the best judge. They wanted to know about Hockbottle although they seemed to know more about him than I did. On the other hand, they seemed not to have heard that he was dead; funny, that. I brought Colonel Blucher's name into the conversation several times – I even tried pronouncing it 'Blootcher' – but they didn't react at all.

At last, they started stuffing their gear away into the matching briefcases with an air of finality, which warned me that the big question was about to be asked in an offhand, casual way as they rose to go.

'Tell me, Mr Mortdecai,' said one of them in an offhand, casual way as they rose to go, 'what did you think of Mrs Krampf?'

'Her heart,' I said bitterly, 'is like spittle on the palm that the Tartar slaps – no telling which way it will pitch.'

'That's very nice, Mr Mortdecai,' said one, nodding appreciatively, 'that's M.P. Shiel, isn't it? Do I understand that you consider her as being in some way responsible for your present predicament?'

'Of course I do, I'm not a complete bloody idiot. "Patsy" is the word over here, I believe.'

'You could just be mistaken there,' the other agent said gently. 'You have no cogent reason for supposing that Mrs Krampf is other than sincere in her feelings toward you; certainly none for supposing that she has set you up.'

I snarled.

'Mr. Mortdecai, I don't wish to be impertinent, but may I ask whether you have had a wide experience of women?'

'Some of my best friends are women,' I snapped, 'though I certainly wouldn't want my daughter to marry one of them.'

'I see. Well, I think we need not keep you from your journey any longer, Sir. The sheriff will be told that you did not kill Mr Krampf and since you no longer seem to be a possible embarrassment to Washington we have no further interest in you just now. If we turn out to be wrong we shall, uh, be able to find you, of course.'

'Of course,' I agreed.

As they crossed the room I rummaged desperately in my poor jumbled brain and picked out the big, knobbly question that hadn't been asked.

'Who did kill Krampf?' I asked.

They paused and looked back at me blankly.

'We don't have the faintest idea. We came down here to do it ourselves so it doesn't matter too much.'

It was a lovely exit line, you must admit.

'Could I have a drop more whisky, Mr Charlie?'

'Yes, of course, Jock, do; it'll bring the roses back into your cheeks.'

'Ta. Glug, suck. Aarhh. Well, that's all right then, isn't it, Mr Charlie?'

I rounded on him savagely.

'Of course it's not all right, you sodding idiot, those two goons have every intention of stamping on both of us as soon as we're well away from here. Look, you think those deputies out there are pigs? Well, they're bloody suffragettes beside those two mealy-mouthed murderers – these are genuine Presidential trouble-shooters and the trouble is us.'

'I don't get it. Why di'n't they shoot us then?'

'Oh Christ Jock, look, would Mr Martland shoot us if he thought it was a good idea?'

'Yeah, 'course.'

'But would he do it in Half Moon Street Police Station in front of all the regular coppers?'

'No, 'course not. Oh, I get it. Ooh.'

'I'm sorry I called you a sodding idiot, Jock.'

'That's all right, Mr Charlie, you was a bit worked up, I expect.'

'Yes, Jock.'

The sheriff came in and gave us back the contents of our pockets, including my Banker's Special. The cartridges were in a separate envelope. He was no longer urbane, he hated us now very much.

'I have been instructed,' he said, like a man spitting out fish-bones, 'not to book you for the murder you committed yesterday. There is a cab outside and I would like for you to get into it and get out of this county and never come back.' He shut his eyes very tightly and kept them shut as though hoping to wake up in a different time stream, one in which C. Mortdecai and J. Strapp had never been born.

We tiptoed out.

The deputies were in the outer office, standing tall, wearing the mindless sneers of their kind. I walked up close to the larger and nastier of the two.

'Your mother and father only met once,' I said carefully, 'and money changed hands. Probably a dime.'

As we pushed the street door open Jock said, 'What's a dime in English money, Mr Charlie?'

A huge, dishevelled car was quaking and farting at the curb outside. The driver, an evident alcoholic, told us that it was a fine evening and I could not find it in my heart to contradict him. He explained, as we climbed in, that he had another passenger to pick up en route and there she was on the next corner, as sweet and saucy a little wench as you could wish for.

She sat between us, smoothing her minimal print skirt over her naughty dimpled thighs and smiling up at us like a fallen angel. There's nothing like a pretty little girl to take a fellow's mind off his troubles, is there, especially when she looks as though she can be had. She told us that her name was Cinderella Gottschalk and we believed her – I mean, she couldn't have made it up, could she – and Jock gave her the last drink in the bottle. She said that she declared it was real crazy drinking liquor or words to that effect. She wore her cute little breasts high up under her chin, the way they used to in the 'fifties, *you* remember. In short, we had become firm friends and were ten miles out of town before a car behind us hit its siren and pulled out alongside. Our driver was giggling as he pulled over to the side and stopped. The official car shrieked to a rocking halt across our bows and out leaped the same two deputies, wearing the same sneers and pointing the same pistols.

'Oh my Gawd,' said Jock – a phrase I have repeatedly asked him not to use – 'what now?'

'They probably forgot to ask me where I get my hair done,' I said bravely. But it wasn't that. They yanked the door open and addressed our little Southern Belle.

'Parm me, Miss, how old are you?'

'Why, Jed Tuttle,' she sniggered, 'you know mah age jest as well as . . .'

'The age, Cindy,' he snapped.

'Rising fourteen,' she simpered, with a coy pout.

My heart sank.

'All right, you filthy deviates – out!' said the deputy.

They didn't hit us when they got us back to the office, they were going off duty and had no time to spare. They simply bunged us into the Tank.

'See you in the morning,' they told us, cosily.

'I demand to make a phone call.'

'In the morning, maybe, when you're sober.'

They left us there without even saying goodnight.

The Tank was a cube composed entirely of bars, except for the tiled floor which was covered with a thin crust of old vomit. The only furniture was an open plastic bucket which had not been emptied lately. Several kilowatts of fluorescent lighting poured pitilessly down from the ceiling high above. I could find no adequate words, but Jock rose to the occasion.

'Well, fuck this for a game of darts,' he said.

'Just so.'

We went to the corner furthest from the slop pail and propped our weary bodies against the bars. Much later, the night duty deputy appeared – an enormous, elderly fatty with a huge face like a bishop's bottom, rosy and round and hot. He stood by the Tank and sniffed with a pained expression on his nose.

'Youse stink like a coupla pigs or sompn,' he said, wagging his great head. 'Never could figure out how growed-up men could get theirselves in sich a state. I get drunk myself, times, but I don't get myself all shitten up like pigs or sompn.'

'It isn't us stinking,' I said politely, 'it's mostly this bucket. Do you think you could take it away?'

'Nope. We got a cleaning lady for them chores and she's to home by now. Anyways, say I take the bucket away, what you gonna spew into?'

'We don't *want* to be sick. We're not drunk. We're British diplomats and we protest strongly at this treatment, there's going to be a big scandal when we get out of here, why don't you let us make a phone call and do yourself a bit of good?'

He stroked his great face carefully, all over; it took quite a while.

'Nope,' he said at last. 'Have to ask the sheriff and he's to home by now. He don't admire to be disturbed at home, 'cept for homicide of white Caucasians.'

'Well, at least give us something to sit on, couldn't you: I mean, *look* at the floor – and this suit cost me, ah, four hundred dollars.'

That fetched him, it was something he could understand. He came closer and studied my apparel carefully. Desperate for his sympathy, I straightened up and pirouetted, arms outstretched.

'Son,' he said finally, 'you was robbed. Why, you could buy that same suit in Albuquerque for a hunnerd-eighty-fi'.'

But he did pass a handful of newspapers through the bars to us before he left, shaking his head. He was one of Nature's gentlemen, I daresay.

We spread the papers on the least squamous section of the floor and lay down; the smell was not so bad at ground level. Sleep coshed me mercifully before I could even begin to dread the morrow.

16

My first thought was, he lied in every word.

Childe Roland

The sun rose like a great, boozy, red face staring into mine. On closer inspection it proved to be a great, boozy, red face staring into mine. It was also smiling stickily.

'Wake up, son,' the night deputy was saying, 'you got a visitor – and you got bail!'

I sprang to my feet and sat down again promptly, squealing at the pain in my kidneys. I let him help me up but Jock managed by himself – he wouldn't take the time of day from a policeman. Behind the deputy there gangled a long, sad man trying hard to smile out of a mouth designed only for refusing credit. He paid out a few yards of arm with a knobbly hand on the end of it which shook mine unconvincingly. For a moment I thought I recognized him.

'Krampf,' he said.

I studied the word but could make nothing of it as a conversational opening. In the end I said, 'Krampf?'

'Dr Milton Krampf III,' he agreed.

'Oh, sorry. C. Mortdecai.'

We let go of each other's hands but went on mumbling civilities. Meanwhile the night deputy lumbered round me, brushing off bits of nastiness from my suit.

'Piss off,' I hissed at him finally – a phrase well-adapted to hissing.

Jock and I needed to wash; Krampf said he would complete the formalities of bail and collect our belongings while we did so. In the washroom I asked Jock whether he had yet recovered the key to the suitcase.

'Christ, Mr Charlie, I only swallowed it dinnertime, di'n't I, and I haven't *been* since then.'

'No, that's right. I say, you couldn't sort of try now, could you?'

'No, I couldn't. I just been thinking about whether I could and I can't. I expect it's the change of water, always binds me.'

'Rubbish, Jock, you know you don't drink water. Did you have much chilli sauce with your hamburgers?'

'What, that hot stuff? Yeah.'

'Oh good.'

The night deputy was dancing about in agony of apology: it appeared that one of the deputies had taken my pistol with him, so as to drop it off at the forensic laboratory in the morning. This was bad news, for our only other weapon was Jock's Luger in the suitcase, whose key was, as it were, *in petto*. He offered to telephone for it but I had no wish to tarry: there was a teleprinter in the outer office and at any moment the British Embassy would be replying to the inquiries which someone must have put in train. The Ambassador had made it clear, you will recall, that the protection of the grand old British flag was not for me and, once repudiated, my diplomatic passport was about as valid as a nine-shilling note.

Outside, the night was as black as Newgate's knocker and the rain was crashing down; when it rains in those parts it really puts its heart into the job. We dived into Krampf's big pale car – with a nice social sense he shunted Jock into the back seat with suitcase. I asked him civilly where he was thinking of taking us.

'Why, I thought you might care to come visit with me a little,' he said easily. 'We have this kind of very private summer residence on the Gulf Coast – mine now, I guess – and that's where the pictures are. Especially the special ones, you know? You'll want to see them.'

'Oh Christ,' I thought, 'that's all I need. The mad millionaire's secret hideaway full of hot old masters and cool young mistresses.'

'That will be delightful,' I said. Then, 'May I ask you how you contrived to rescue us so opportunely, Dr Krampf?'

'Surely, it was easy. Yesterday I was a pretentious *kunstkenner* with a rich daddy – in my whole life I have earned maybe a hundred dollars by art history. Today I am a hundred million dollars – give or take a few million which Johanna gets – and that sort of money gets anybody out of jail here. I don't mean you bribe with it or anything like that, you just have to have it. Oh, I guess you mean how did I come to be *here*? That's easy, too; I flew in about noon to the ranch to arrange about shipping the body, it'll be on its way as soon as the police are finished with it. Family mausoleum is up in Vermont; good thing it's summer – in winter the ground gets so hard up there they just sharpen one end and hammer you into the ground, ha, ha.'

'Ha ha,' I agreed. I never liked my father, either, but I wouldn't have spoken of him as 'it' the day after his death.

'The police at the rancho heard about the Rolls and, uh, the other auto piling up and later they heard you'd been apprehended. Two guys from the FBI or some other Federal setup were there by then and they left soon after, said they were coming on here. I followed as soon as I'd sorted things out, in case they were being stupid. I mean, I knew that a man with your views on Giorgione couldn't be all bad, ha ha. Yeah, *sure* I know your work, I read *Burlington Magazine* every month, it's essential reading. I mean, for instance, you can't fully understand the achievement of Mondrian until you understand how Mantegna paved the way for him.'

I gagged quietly.

'Which reminds me,' he went on, 'I believe you were bringing my father a certain canvas; would you like to tell me where it is? I guess it's mine now?'

I said I guessed it was. The Spanish Government, of course, probably held a different view, but then they think they own Gibraltar too, don't they?

'It's in the Rolls, lined into the soft-top. I'm afraid you'll have a little difficulty retrieving it but at least it's safe for the time being, what? Oh, by the way, there's a little formality at the box office which your father didn't live to complete.'

'Oh?'

'Yes. Sort of, fifty thousand pounds, really.'

'Isn't that rather cheap, Mr Mortdecai?'

'Ah, well, you see the chap who actually swiped it has already been paid; the fifty thou is just my own little sort of *pourboire*.'

'I get it. Well, how and where do you want it? Swiss bank, numbered account, I guess?'

'Goodness, no, I should hate to think of it lying there in amongst all that chocolate and horid Gruyère cheese and Alps. Do you think you could get it to Japan for me?'

'Surely. We have this development firm in Nagasaki; we'll retain you as, oh, aesthetic consultant on a five-year contract at, say, £11,000 a year. O.K.?'

'Six years at £10,000 would suit me just as well.'

'You have a deal.'

'Thank you very much.'

He shot me such an honest glance that I almost believed he meant it. He didn't, naturally. I don't mean that he begrudged me the fifty thousand – he hadn't been rich long enough to start being stingy about money. No, what I mean is that, quite clearly, I was now surplus to his requirements in all sorts of ways and allowing me to live much longer could form no part of his programme. Having sound views on Giorgione didn't carry with it the privilege of staying alive; why, I might linger on for years, a misery to myself and a burden to others.

We chatted on.

He didn't seem to know much about the relining process – surprising, really, in an authority on the Moderns, when you consider that the average modern picture is in need of attention within five years of the paint drying; indeed, many of them are cracking or flaking off the canvas long before that.

It's not that they couldn't learn proper techniques if they wanted to; I think it's because they're sort of subconsciously *shy* about posterity seeing their work.

'Are you sure,' Krampf kept saying, 'that this, uh, process will not have damaged the picture?'

'Look,' I said at last, 'pictures aren't damaged that way. To damage a picture thoroughly you need a stupid housewife with a rag and some ammonia, or methylated spirits, or a good proprietary picture-cleaning fluid. You can slash a picture to ribbons and a good liner and restorer will have it back as good as new before you can cough – remember the Rokeby Venus?'

'Yes,' he said. 'Suffragette with an axe, wasn't it?'

'And you can paint another picture over it and the restorer – perhaps centuries later – will clean back to the original – no bother. Remember your father's Crivelli?'

His ears pricked up and the car wobbled.

'Crivelli? No. What Crivelli? Did he have a Crivelli? A good one?'

'It was a very good one, Bernardo Tatti said so. Your father bought it somewhere in the Veneto in 1949 or '50. You know how they sell Old Masters in Italy – the important ones hardly ever go through commercial galleries. As soon as someone with serious money makes it known that he's in the market for serious works of art he will find himself invited to a palazzo for the week-end. His titled host will very delicately indicate that he has to pay a lot of taxes in the near future – and *that's* a joke in Italy – and may be forced, even, to sell an Old Master or two.

'Your father bought the Crivelli like that. It bore certificates by the greatest experts: they always do, of course. *You* know. The subject was the Virgin and Child with a bare bottom and lots of pears and pomegranates and melons – quite lovely. Like the Frick Crivelli, but smaller.

'The Duke or Count hinted that he wasn't *quite* certain of his title to the picture but he could see that your father wasn't a man to fuss about such trifles – it had to be smuggled out in any case, because of the law against export of works of art. Your father took it to an artist friend in Rome who gave it a coat of size then daubed a piece of Futurist-Vorticist rubbish on top. (Sorry, forgot that was your field.) Boldly signed and dated 1949, it went through the customs with no more than a pitying glance.

'Back in the States, he sent it to the best restorer in New York with a note saying, "Clean off modern overpaint; restore and expose original." After a few weeks he sent the restorer one of his cables – you know – "REPORT IMMEDIATELY PROGRESS ON QUOTE MODERN UNQUOTE PAINTING."

'The restorer cabled back, "HAVE REMOVED QUOTE MODERN UNQUOTE PAINTING STOP HAVE REMOVED QUOTE CRIVELLI UNQUOTE MADONNA STOP AM DOWN TO PORTRAIT OF MUSSOLINI STOP WHERE DO I STOP QUERY."'

Dr Krampf didn't laugh. He looked straight ahead, his knuckles tight on the wheel. After a while I said diffidently, 'Well, your father came to think it very funny indeed after the first shock. And your father was not easily amused.'

'My father was a simple-minded, sex-crazed jerk,' he said evenly. 'What had he given for the picture?' I told him and he winced. Conversation flagged. The car went a little faster.

After a while Jock cleared his throat sheepishly.

'Excuse me, Mr Charlie, could you ask Dr Crump to stop somewhere soon? I got to go to the bog. Call of nature,' he added, by way of a grace note.

'Really, Jock,' I said sternly, to conceal my pleasure, 'you should have thought of that before you came out. It's all that chilli sauce, I expect.'

We stopped at an all-night diner attached to a motel. Twenty minutes later, crammed with distressful fried eggs, we decided that we might as well spend what was left of the night there. Jock passed me the suitcase key, as good as new: I had expected to see it pitted and corroded by his powerful digestive juices.

I locked my door although I was pretty sure Krampf would bide his time until he had us in his kind-of-very-private summer residence. As I climbed into bed I decided that I must make a careful, objective analysis of my situation in the light of facts alone. 'If hopes were dupes,' I told myself, 'fears may be liars.' Surely the razor-keen Mortdecai brain could think its way out of this nasty, but after all primitive, mess.

Unfortunately the razor-keen brain fell asleep as soon as its container hit the pillow. *Most* unfortunately, really, as it turned out.

17

And, thus we half-men struggle. At the end,
God, I conclude, compensates, punishes.

Andrea del Sarto

How sharper than a serpent's tooth is an awakening without tea!
Jock, honest fellow, brought me all sorts of motel provender
but tea was not amongst those present. If Paris, as Galiani says,
is the café of Europe, then the US of A must be the hot-dog
stand of the world. 'Faugh!' I said, but I ate some to please
Jock.

It was nearly noon; I had slept a solid eight hours. Bathed,
shaved and dressed in my nattiest, I sallied out into the morning
sunshine, full of the spirit of Sir Percy Blakeney-Mortdecai, *le
Bouton Ecarlate.* '*A la lanterne* with Citoyen de Krampf', I murmured, flicking a speck of snot from the irreproachable Méchlin
lace of my jabot.

There was a powder-blue Buick outside.

A.L. Rowse once said that making a really important historical
discovery is very like sitting, inadvertently, on a cat. I felt, at that
moment, like just such an historian – and, indeed, like just such
a cat. Dr Krampf, who was in the driving seat, cannot have failed
to notice my standing high jump and my strangled squeal, but he
elaborately gave no sign of surprise. Jock and I got in, for it was
evidently the car we had arrived in, and after a certain amount of
good-morning swapping we set off.

This way and that, like Odysseus on so many occasions, I divided my swift mind. The suitcase key, the fruit of Jock's honest labours, was twice blessed: it had furnished me with clean underwear and Jock with his friendly neighbourhood Luger – a pretty strong partnership. My diplomatic passport would probably pass muster in most smaller airports for perhaps another twenty-four hours, though hardly longer. We were two, Krampf at present but one. I was pretty certain that he was thinking of abolishing me – owners of powder-blue Buicks could be no friends of mine and I knew far too much about the provenance of his newly inherited collection and little things like who-killed-daddy – but he cannot have known for certain that we knew this. He, it was clear, had to get us to ground of his own choosing before he could fit us for cement overcoats – if that's the phrase I want – but we were now in a position to dissuade him.

We drove on, south and east, stopping for a horrid lunch at a place called Fort Stockton, where I surreptitiously bought a map and studied it, locked in the used-beer department. Then we drove some more, across the Pecos river toward Sonora. (Just place names now, all magic gone.) Just before Sonora I said to Krampf, 'I'm sorry, my dear chap, but we can't after all stay with you this weekend.' He kept his hands on the wheel but boggled at me sideways.

'How d'you mean?'

'Something came up, you see.'

'I don't get it – what could have come up?'

'Well, as a matter of fact, I've just received a cable.'

'You've just receive a c . . .?'

'Yes, reminding me of a subsequent engagement. So perhaps you'd be awfully kind and turn north at Sonora?'

'Mr Mortdecai, I know this is some kind of a joke so I'm just going to keep right on for the Gulf, heh heh. Mind you,' he chuckled, 'if I didn't know your pistol was back in the forensic laboratory I'd be tempted to take you seriously, heh heh.'

'Jock, show Dr Krampf the Luger.' Jock showed him, leaning over from the back seat. Krampf looked at it carefully; he saw, if he knew about Lugers, the little *Geladen* indicator sticking up above the breech; then he accelerated, a sensible thing to do, for no one gives the *gesnickschuss* to a chap driving at seventy m.p.h.

'Jock, the point of the left shoulder, please.' Jock's great fist, brass-shod, came down like a steam hammer and I steadied the wheel as Krampf's arm went dead.

He slowed down and stopped: you can't drive properly when you're crying. I changed places with him rapidly and we continued – I had a feeling you're not allowed to loiter on Interstate Highway 10. He just sat there beside me nursing his arm, saying nothing, looking straight ahead through his tears. A sure confirmation of naughty intent, for an honest man would be protesting volubly, wouldn't he?

Abilene is a hundred and fifty miles north of Sonora; we did a lot of those miles in the next two hours and Krampf still just sat there, apparently unafraid; his faith in the power of a hundred million dollars still unshaken. After San Angelo – I sang '*E lucevan le stelle*' as we passed through: opera lovers will know why – I started looking about for likely spots, for the evenings were drawing in, and soon after crossing the Colorado I found one, an unnumbered dirt road which followed the bed of a dry river. Satisfied that we could not be overlooked, I got out, urging Krampf before me.

'Krampf,' I said, 'I fear you wish me ill. At present it is no part of my plans to have Krampfs after my blood as well as everyone else, so I must thwart your designs on my person. Do I make myself clear? I propose to leave you here, securely bound, warmly clad but without any money. At the airport I shall write to the police telling them where to look for you and enclosing your money, for I am not that kind of a thief. You are unlikely to die before they find you. Any questions?'

He looked at me levelly, wondering whether he could get my liver out with his fingernails. He didn't say anything, nor did he spit.

'Wallet,' I said, snapping my fingers. He brought out a slim snakeskin job and tossed it rudely at my feet. I picked it up, I'm not proud. It contained a driving licence, several of the better sort of credit cards, photographs of some hideous children and a portrait of Madison. The portrait, of course, was on a thousand dollar bill.

'No small money?' I asked. 'No, I suppose not. You wouldn't like handling it, you'd know where it had been. And you don't look like a heavy tipper.'

'Mr Charlie,' said Jock, 'rich blokes over here don't keep ordinary money in their wallets, they have it in their trousers in a sort of clip made out of a gold coin.'

'You're right, Jock, full marks. Krampf, the bill-clip, please.'

He reached grudgingly for his hip pocket, too grudgingly, and suddenly I realized what else was there: I aimed a swift kick at his goolies, he stepped back, stumbled and dragged out the Lilliput pistol as he fell. I didn't hear the shot but my left arm seemed to be torn out by the roots and as I fell I saw Jock's boot connecting with Krampf's head.

I must have faded out for a few moments; the pain was excruciating. When I came to, Jock was dabbing at my armpit with a dressing from the car's first-aid kit; the little bullet had passed along my armpit, shredding it horridly but missing the axillary artery by enough millimetres for safety. It was a very good first-aid box: when we had stanched the bleeding and done an adequate bandage job we turned our attention to the motionless Krampf.

'Tie him up now, Jock, while he's still out.'

A long pause.

'Uh, Mr Charlie, uh, would you have a look at him?'

I looked. The side of his head felt like a bag of Smith's Potato Crisps. Another generation of Krampfs had carried its bat to the Eternal Pavilion to have a word with the Great Scorer.

'Really, Jock, you are too bad,' I snapped. 'That's twice in two days. If I've told you once I've told you a dozen times, I *will* not have you killing chaps all the time.'

'Sorry, Mr Charlie,' he said sulkily. 'But I di'n't mean to, did I? I mean, I was saving your life, wasn't I?'

'Yes, Jock, I suppose you were. I'm sorry if I spoke hastily – I am in some pain, you realize.'

We buried him darkly at dead of night, the sods with our bayonets turning, as you might say. Then we listened for a long time, drove quietly back to the main road and on to Abilene.

There were planes from Abilene that night to Denver and to Kansas City; Jock and I took one each.

'See you in Quebec, then, Jock,' I said.

'O.K., Mr Charlie.'

18

> The Bactrian was but a wild, childish man,
> And could not write nor speak, but only loved:
> So, lest the memory of this go quite,
> Seeing that I to-morrow fight the beasts,
> I tell the same to Phoebas, whom believe!
>
> *A Death in the Desert*

You must have noticed that until now my tangled tale has observed at least some of the unities proper to tragedy: I have not tried to relate what other people thought or did when this was outside my knowledge; I have not whisked you hither and yon without suitable transport and I have never started a sentence with the words 'some days later'. Each morning has witnessed the little death of a heavy drinker's awakening and 'each slow dusk a drawing down of blind'. The English, as Raymond Chandler has pointed out, may not always be the best writers in the world but they are incomparably the best dull writers.

If I have not always made clear the *rationale* of these events, it is partly because you are probably better at that sort of thing than I am and partly because I confess myself quite bemused by finding that the events which I thought I was controlling were in fact controlling me.

It has amused me, these last few weeks, to cast my recollections into some sort of disciplined mould but this foolishness must now cease, for the days are drawing in and time's helicopter beats the air furiously over my head. Events have overtaken literature: there is time for a few more leisured pages and then perhaps for some journal jottings; after that, I suspect, no time at all, ever.

It looks as though, by a piece of vulgar irony, I have come home to die within sight of the scenes of my hated childhood: the ways of Providence are indeed unscrupulous, as Pat once said to Mike as they were walking down Broadway – or was it O'Connell Street?

Getting here was easy. We flew from Quebec to Eire in the same aircraft but not together. At Shannon, Jock walked straight through Immigration waving his Tourist Passport, they didn't even look at it. He was carrying the suitcase. He took a domestic flight to Collinstown Airport, Dublin, and waited for me at a nice pub called Jury's in College Green.

For my part, I spent a quiet hour in the lavatory at Shannon with half a bottle of whisky, mingled with various groups of travellers, told all and sundry that my wife, children and luggage were in planes headed for Dublin, Belfast and Cork, and wept myself tiresomely and bibulously out and into a taxi without anyone asking for a passport. I think perhaps they were rather glad to get rid of me. The taxi driver milked me systematically of currency all the way to Mullingar, where I shaved, changed clothes and accent, and took another taxi to Dublin.

Jock was at Jury's as arranged, but only barely; in another few minutes he would have been ejected for he was pissed as a pudding and someone had taught him a naughty phrase in Erse which he kept singing to the tune of 'The Wearing of the Boyne' or whatever they call it.

We took a cheap night flight to Blackpool, and only acted drunk enough to fit in with the rest of the passengers. The airport staff were waiting to go to bed or wherever people go in Blackpool: they turned their backs on the whole lot of us. We took separate taxis to separate small and hateful hotels. I had potato pie for supper, I don't know what Jock had.

In the morning we took separate trains and met, by arrangement, in the buffet on Carnforth Station. You may never have heard of Carnforth but you must have seen the station, especially the buffet, for it was there that they made *Brief Encounter* and it is sacred to the memory of Celia Johnson. Nowadays Carnforth has no other claim to fame: once a thriving steel town with an important railway junction, today it is distinguished only by the singular, and clearly *intentional*, ugliness of every building and by the extraordinary niceness of the people who inhabit them – even the bank managers. I was born five miles away, at a place called Silverdale.

Carnforth is in the extreme northwest corner of Lancashire and has sometimes called itself the Gateway to the Lake District. It is not quite on the coast, it is not quite anything, really. There are some good pubs. There used to be a cinema when I was a boy but I was never allowed to go, and it's closed now. Except for Bingo, naturally.

One of the hotels is kept by a nice fat old Italian called Dino something; he's known me since I was a *bambino*. I told him that I was just back from America where I had made some enemies and that I had to lie low.

'Donter worry Mr Charlie, thoser bloddy Sicilian bosstuds donter find you here. If I see them hang around I get the police bloddy quick – are good boys here, not afraid ofer stinking Mafiosi.'

'It's no really quite like that, Dino. I think if you see anyone you'd better just let me know quietly.'

'O.K., Mr Charlie.'

'Thank you, Dino. *Evviva Napoli!*'

'*Abassa Milano!*'

'*Cazzone pendente!*' we cried in chorus – our old slogan from years ago.

Jock and I stayed there in close retirement for perhaps five weeks until my armpit was healed and I had grown a more or less plausible beard. (I want to make it quite clear that Dino had no idea that we had done anything wrong.) I stopped dyeing my hair and eating starchy foods and soon I looked a well-preserved seventy. Finally, before venturing out, I removed both my upper canine teeth, which are attached to a wire clip: with my upper incisors resting lightly on the lower lip I look the picture of senile idiocy, it always makes Mrs Spon *shriek*. I let my now grizzled hair grow long and fluffy, bought a pair of good field-glasses and mingled with the bird watchers. It's astonishing how many there are nowadays: ornithology used to be an arcane hobby for embittered schoolmasters, dotty spinsters and lonely little boys but now it is as normal a weekend occupation as rug-making or wife-swapping. I was terribly keen on it when I was at school, so I knew the right cries and, as a matter of fact, I became rather keen again and thoroughly enjoyed my outings.

This part of Lancashire contains some of the best bird-watching terrain in England: sea and shore birds in their millions haunt the vast salt-marshes and tidal flats of Morecambe Bay, and the reeds of Leighton Moss – an RSPB sanctuary – are alive with duck, swans, gulls and even the bittern.

I gave Dino three hundred pounds and he bought me a second-hand dark-green Mini, registered in his name. I plastered on a few stickers – SAVE LEVENS HALL, VOTE CONSERVATIVE, VISIT STEAM-TOWN – and dumped a Karri-Kot in the back seat: an inspired piece of camouflage, you must admit. We contrived to get a pair of tinted contact lenses for Jock, changing his startling blue eyes to a dirty brown. He liked them very much, called them 'me shades'.

Meanwhile, since Carnforth is on STD now, it was safe to dial a number of guarded calls to London, where various naughty friends, in exchange for a lot of money, set to work creating new identities for Jock and me, so that we could get to Australia and start a new life amongst the Sheilas and Cobbers. New identities are very expensive and take a long time, but the process of obtaining them is so much easier now that there are all these drugs about. You simply find a chap who's on the big H-for-heroin and not long for this world, preferably a chap with at least some points of resemblance to you. You take him under your wing – or rather your naughty friends do – lodge him, supply him with H and feed him whenever he can gag anything down. You get his National Insurance Card paid up to date, buy him a passport, open a Post Office Savings Account in his name, pass the driving test for him and fix him up with an imaginary job at a real place. (The 'employer' gets his wages back in cash, doubled.) Then you pay a very expensive craftsman to substitute your photograph in the new passport and you're a new man.

(The drug addict, of course, now becomes a bit superfluous: you can have him knocked off professionally but that's an extra, and awfully expensive nowadays. The best and cheapest course is to deprive him of his medicine for three days or so until he's quite beside himself, then leave him in a busy public lavatory – Piccadilly Underground is much favoured in the trade – with a syringe containing a heavy overdose, and let Nature take its kindly course. The coroner will scarcely glance at him: he's probably better off where he is; why, he might have lingered on for years, etc.)

In short, all seemed well except that William Hickey or one of those columnists had once or twice dropped delicate hints that certain People in High Places had been receiving certain photographs, which might or might not have referred to the Hockbottle art work. If so, I couldn't really see who could be doing it – surely not Johanna? One of Hockbottle's horrid friends? *Martland*? I didn't let it worry me.

Last night, when I walked into the bar of Dino's hotel, full of fresh air and nursing a splendid appetite, I would have told anyone that things were going uncommonly well. I had spent the afternoon on the Moss and had been fortunate enough to have had a pair of Bearded Tits in my field-glasses for several minutes – and if you think there's no such bird you can jolly well look it up in the nearest bird book. That was last night, only.

Last night when I walked into the bar

The barman should have smiled and said, 'Evening, Mr Jackson, what do you fancy?' I mean, that's what he'd said to me every evening for weeks.

Instead he gave me a hostile stare and said, 'Well, Paddy, usual I suppose?' I was completely taken aback.

'Come on,' said the barman disagreeably, 'make your mind up. There's other people want serving, you know.'

Two strangers at the end of the bar studied me casually in the mirror behind the display bottle. I twigged.

'Arl roight arl roight,' I growled thickly, 'av coorse Oi'll have me usual, ye cross-grained little sod.'

He pushed a double Jameson's Irish whisky across the bar at me.

'And watch your language,' he said, 'or you can get out.'

'Bollocks,' I said and tossed the whisky back messily. I wiped my mouth with the back of my hand, belched and lurched out. It is a good thing that a serious ornithologist's field clothes are more or less the same as an Irish navvy's drinking kit. I fled upstairs and found Jock sitting on the bed, reading the *Beano*.

'Come on,' I said, 'they're on to us.'

We had kept in a state of readiness for any emergency so we were out of the hotel by the kitchen entrance some ninety seconds after I had left the bar, heading for the station yard where I had parked the Mini. I started the engine and backed out of the slot; I was quite calm, there was no reason for them to have suspected me.

Then I cursed, stalling the engine, paralysed with dismay.

'Smatter, Mr Charlie, forgotten something?'

'No, Jock. Remembered something.'

I had remembered that I had not paid for my whisky – and that the barman had not asked me to do so. Drunken Irish navvies hardly ever have charge accounts at respectable provincial hotels.

I got the engine started again, jammed the gears cruelly into mesh and swung out of the yard into the street. A man standing at the corner turned and raced back towards the hotel. I prayed that their car was pointing in the wrong direction.

I rammed the unprotesting little Mini out of town to the north on the Millhead Road; just before the second railway bridge I doused the lights and whisked it off to the left, towards Hagg House and the marsh. The road dwindled to a footpath and then to a wet track; we squashed barbed wire, nosed our way down banks, half-lifted the Mini across the impossibly soft parts, cursed and prayed and listened for the sounds of pursuit. To our left some three-headed spawn of Cerberus started to yelp and yap dementedly. We continued west, hating the dog with a deep, rich hatred, and found the River Keer by pitching into it. To be exact, the Mini had pitched down its bank and come to rest, nose downward, in the squishy sand beside the channel, for the tide was far out. I grabbed the almost empty suitcase, Jock grabbed the knapsack and we scrambled into the stream, gasping with shock as the cold water reached groin level. At the far side we stopped before scaling the bank and showing ourselves on the skyline; half a mile behind us an engine raced in a low gear; two cones of light from headlamps waved about in the sky, then suddenly went out.

The stars were bright but we were too far away to be seen by our pursuers; we scrambled up the bank – how I blessed my new-found physical fitness – and made off northwestwards, heading towards the lights of Grange-Over-Sands, six miles away across the glistening mud flats.

It was quite unlike anything that has ever happened to me, it was the strangest journey I have ever made. The darkness, the unheard, nearby sea, the whistle and bleat of the wings of flocks of bewildered birds, the slap of our feet on the wet sand and the *fear* that drove us on towards the wriggling lights so far across the bay.

But I had this much going for me: I was on familiar ground. My plan was to strike Quicksand Pool – a two-mile treacherous lagoon – at its most dangerous point, then turn northeastwards and follow it to its narrowest part and cross there. At that point, the friendly shore of Silverdale would bear due north at two miles' distance. This depended on our having crossed the Keer at the right spot, and on the tide being where I believed it to be – I had no choice but to assume that I was right about both.

That was where the nightmare began.

Jock was loping a few yards to my left when we both found ourselves on quaking ground. I did what you should do in such a case – keep moving fast but circle back sharply to your starting point. Jock didn't. He stopped, grunted, tried to pull back, splashed about, stuck fast. I dropped the suitcase and hunted for him in the dark while he called to me, his voice high with panic as I had never heard it before. I got hold of his hand and started to sink also; I threw myself down, only my elbows now on the quagmire. It was like pulling at an oak tree. I knelt to get better purchase but my knees sank straight in, terrifyingly.

'Lie forward,' I snarled at him.

'Can't, Mr Charlie – I'm up to me belly.'

'Wait, I'll get the suitcase.'

I had to strike a match to find the suitcase, then another to find Jock again in the tantalizing shimmer of wet sand and starshine. I thrust the suitcase forward and he laid his arms on it, hugging it to his chest, driving it into the mud as he bore down on it.

'No good, Mr Charlie,' he said at last. 'I'm up to me armpits and I can't breathe much any more.' His voice was a horrid travesty.

Behind us – not nearly far enough behind us – I heard the rhythmic patter of feet on wet sand.

'Go on, Mr Charlie, scarper!'

'Christ, Jock, what do you think I am?'

'Don't be stupid,' he gasped. 'Piss off. But do me a favour first. You know. I don't want it like this. Might take half an hour. Go on, *do* it.'

'Christ, Jock,' I said again, appalled.

'Go on, me old mate. Quick. Put the leather in.'

I scrambled to my feet, aghast. Then I couldn't bear the noises he was making any more and I stepped on to the suitcase with my left foot and trod on his head with my right foot, grinding at it. He made dreadful noises but his head wouldn't go under. I kicked at it frantically again and again, until the noises stopped, then I clawed up the suitcase and ran blindly, weeping with horror and terror and love.

When I heard the water chuckling below me I guessed my position and threw myself at the channel, not caring whether it was the crossing place or not. I got over, leaving my right shoe in the mud – *that* shoe, thank God – and ran north, each breath tearing at my windpipe. Once I fell and couldn't get up; behind me and to the left I saw torches flickering: perhaps one of them had gone to join Jock – I don't know, it's not important. I kicked the other shoe off and got up and ran again, cursing and weeping, falling into gullies, tearing my feet on stones and shells, the suitcase battering at my knees, until at last I crashed into the remains of the breakwater at Jenny Brown's Point.

There I pulled myself together a little, sitting on the suitcase, trying to think calmly, starting to learn to live with what had happened. No, with what I had done. With what I *have* done. A soft rain began to fall and I turned my face up to it, letting it rinse away some of the heat and the evil.

The knapsack was back at Quicksand Pool; all the necessities of life were in it. The suitcase was almost empty except for some packets of currency. I needed a weapon, shoes, dry clothes, food, a drink, shelter and – above all – a friendly word from someone, anyone.

Keeping the low limestone cliffs on my right hand I stumbled along the shore for almost a mile to Know End Point, where the saltmarsh proper begins – that strange landscape of sea-washed turf and gutters and flashes where the finest lambs in England graze.

Above me and to my right shone the lights of the honest bungalow dwellers of Silverdale: I found myself envying them bitterly. It is chaps like them who have the secret of happiness, they know the art of it, they always knew it. Happiness is an annuity, or it's shares in a Building Society; it's a pension and blue hydrangeas, and wonderfully clever grandchildren, and being on the Committee, and just-a-few-earlies in the vegetable garden, and being alive and wonderful-for-his-age when old so-and-so is under the sod, and it's double-glazing and sitting by the electric fire remembering that time when you told the Area Manager where he got off and that other time when that Doris . . .

Happiness is easy: I don't know why more people don't go in for it.

I stole along the road leading up from the shore. My watch said 11.40. It was Friday, so licensing hours would have ended at eleven, plus ten minutes drinking-up time plus, say, another ten minutes getting rid of the nuisances. My soaked and ragged socks made wet whispers on the pavement. There were no cars outside the hotel, no lights on in front. I was starting to shake with cold and reaction and the hope of succour as I hobbled through the darkened car park and round to the kitchen window.

I could see the landlord, or joint proprietor as he prefers to be called, standing quite near the kitchen door; he was wearing the disgraceful old hat which he always puts on for cellar work and his face, as ever, was that of a hanging judge. He has watched my career with a jaundiced eye for some five and twenty years, on and off, and he has not been impressed.

He opened the kitchen door and looked me up and down impassively.

'Good evening, Mr Mortdecai,' he said, 'you've lost a bit of weight.'

'Harry,' I gabbled, 'you've got to help me. Please.'

'Mr Mortdecai, the last time you asked me for drinks after hours was in nineteen hundred and fifty-six. The answer is still no.'

'No, Harry, really. I'm in serious trouble.'

'That's right, Sir.'

'Eh?'

'I said – "that's right, Sir."'

'How d'you mean?'

'I mean two gentlemen were here inquiring after your whereabouts last evening, stating that they were from the Special Branch.

They were most affable but they displayed great reluctance to produce their credentials when requested to do so.' He always talks like that.

I didn't say anything more, I just looked at him beseechingly. He didn't actually smile but his glare softened a little, perhaps.

'You'd better be off now, Mr Mortdecai, or you'll be disturbing my routine and I'll be forgetting to bolt the garden door or something.'

'Yes. Well, thanks, Harry. Goodnight.'

'Goodnight, Charlie.'

I slunk back into the shadow of the squash court and crouched there in the rain with my thoughts. He had called me *Charlie*, he never had before. That was one for the book: that was the friendly word. Jock, at the end, had called me his old mate.

One by one the lights in the hotel went out. The church clock had struck half-past midnight with the familiar flatness before I crept round the building, through the rock terrace, and tied the garden door. Sure enough, someone had carelessly forgotten to bolt it. It gives on to a little sun-parlour with two sun-faded settees. I peeled off my drenched clothes, draped them on one settee and my wracked body on the other, with a grunt. As my eyes grew used to the dimness I discerned a group of objects on the table between the settees. Someone had carelessly left a warm old topcoat there, and some woollen underclothes and a towel: also a loaf of bread, three quarters of a cold chicken, forty Embassy tipped cigarettes, a bottle of Teacher's whisky and a pair of tennis shoes. It's astonishing how careless some of these hoteliers are, no wonder they're always complaining.

It must have been four o'clock in the morning when I let myself out of the little sun-parlour. The moon had risen and luminous clouds were scudding across it at a great pace. I skirted the hotel and found the footpath behind it which goes across the Lots, those strangely contoured limestone downs clad with springy turf. I gave the Burrows' heifers the surprise of their lives as I jogged between them in the dark. It is only a few hundred yards to the Cove, where once the sailing ships from Furness unloaded ore for the furnace at Leighton Beck. Now, since the channels shifted, it is close-nibbled turf, covered with a few inches of sea-water two or three times a month.

What is more to the point, there is a cave in the cliff, below the inexplicable ivy-gnawed battlements which surmount it. It is an uninviting cave, even the children do not care to explore it, and there is reputed to be a sudden drop at the end of it, to an unplumbed pit. Dawn was making its first faint innuendos in the East as I clambered in.

I slept until noon out of sheer exhaustion, then ate some more of the bread and chicken and drank more of the Scotch. Then I went to sleep again: dreams would be bad, I knew, but waking thoughts for once were worse. I awoke in the late afternoon.

The light is fading rapidly now. Later tonight I shall call on my brother.

To be exact, it was in the early hours of this Sunday morning that I stole out of the cave and drifted up into the village through the dark. The last television set had been reluctantly switched off, the last poodle had been out for its last piddle, the last cup of Bournvita had been brewed. Cove Road was like a well-kept grave: husbands and wives lay dreaming of past excesses and future coffee-mornings; they gave out no vibrations, it was hard to believe they were there. A motor car approached, driven with the careful sedateness of a consciously drunk driver; I stepped into the shadows until it had passed. A cat rubbed itself against my right foot; a few days ago I would have kicked it without compunction but now I could not even kick my own brother. Not with that foot.

The cat followed me up the slope of Walling's Lane, mewing inquisitively, but it turned tail at the sight of the big white tom who crouched under the hedge like a phantom Dick Turpin. Lights were burning up at Yewbarrow and a strain of New Orleans jazz filtered down through the trees – old Bon would be settling down to an all-night poker and whisky session. As I turned right at Silver Ridge there was one brief deep bay from the St. Bernard, then no more sounds save for the whisper of my own feet along Elmslack. Someone had been burning garden rubbish and a ghost of the smell lingered – one of the most poignant scents in the world, at once wild and homely.

Off the lane I picked my way along the just discernible footpath which drops down to the back wall of Woodfields Hall, the seat of Robin, Second Baron Mortdecai, etc. Golly, what a name.

He was born shortly before the Great War, as you can tell: it was *de rigueur* to call your son Robin in that decade and my mother was remorselessly *de rigueur*, as anyone could tell you, if nothing else.

You'd never guess where I am writing this. I'm sitting, knees doubled up to my chin, on my childhood's lavatory in the nursery wing of my brother's house. It has happier memories for me than most of the rest of the house, which is haunted by my father's cupidity and chronic envy, my mother's febrile regret at having married an impossible cad and now by my brother's crawling disgust at everything and everyone. Including himself. And especially me – he wouldn't spit in my face if it were on fire, unless he could spit petrol.

Beside me on the wall there is a roll of soft, pink lavatory paper: our nurse would never have allowed that, she believed in Spartan bums for the children of the upper classes and we had to use the old-fashioned, crackling, broken-glass variety.

I have just been in my old bedroom which is always kept ready for me, never altered or disturbed; just the kind of false note my brother loves sardonically to strike. He often says, 'Do remember that you always have a home here, Charlie,' then waits for me to look sick. Under a floorboard in my room I groped for and found a large oilskin package containing my first and favourite handgun, a 1920 Police and Military Model Smith and Wesson .455, the most beautiful heavy revolver ever designed. A few years ago, before I took up whisky as an indoor sport, I could do impressive things to a playing card with this pistol at twenty paces, and I am confident that I could still hit a larger target in a good light. Like, say, Martland.

There is one box of military ammunition for it – nickel jacketed and very noisy – and most of a box of plain lead target stuff, hand-loaded with a low powder charge, much more useful for what I have in mind. You wouldn't be allowed to use it in war, of course, that soft lead ball can do dreadful things to anything it hits, I'm happy to say.

I shall finish my bottle of Teacher's, with a wary eye on the door lest a long-dead Nanny should catch me, then go downstairs and visit my brother. I shall not tell him how I got into the house. I shall just let him worry about it, it's the sort of thing he does worry about. I have no intention of shooting him, it would be an inexcusable self-indulgence at this time. In any case, it would probably be doing him a favour and I owe him a lot of things but no favours.

I called him brother, Englishman and friend!

As I let myself quietly into the library, my brother Robin was sitting with his back to me, writing his memoirs with a scratchy noise. Without turning round or ceasing to scratch at the paper he said,

'Hullo, Charlie, I didn't hear anyone let you in?'

'Expecting me, Robin?'

'Everyone else knocks.' Pause. 'Didn't you have any trouble with the dogs as you came through the kitchen garden?'

'Look, those dogs of yours are as much use as tits on a warthog. If I'd been a burglar they'd have offered to hold my torch.'

'You'll be wanting a drink,' he said, flatly, insultingly.

'I've given it up, thanks.'

He stopped scribbling and turned round. Looked me up and down, slowly, caressingly.

'Going ratting?' he asked at last.

'No, you needn't worry tonight.'

'Would you like something to eat?'

'Yes, please. Not now,' I added as his hand went to the bell. 'I'll help myself later. Tell me who has been asking for me lately.'

'No village drabs with babies in their arms this year. Just a couple of comedians from some obscure branch of the Foreign Office, I didn't ask what they wanted. Oh, and a hard-faced bitch who said you'd been heard of in Silverdale and wanted to ask you to address the Lakeland Ladies' Etching Society or something of that sort.'

'I see. What did you tell them?'

'Said I thought you were in America, was that right?'

'Quite right, Robin. Thanks.' I didn't ask him how he knew I had been in America; he wouldn't have told me and I didn't really care. He sets aside a certain portion of his valuable time to following my doings, in the hopes that one day I'll give him an opening. He's like that.

'Robin, I'm on a Government assignment which I can't tell you about but it does involve getting quietly up into the Lake District and living rough for a few days – I need some stuff. A sleeping bag, some tinned food, a bicycle, torch, batteries, that sort of thing.' I watched him thinking how many of the items he could plausibly pretend not to have. I unbuttoned my coat, which fell open: the handle of the Smith and Wesson stuck up out of my waistband like a dog's leg.

'Come along,' he said cordially, 'let's see what we can rustle up.'

We rustled up everything in the end, although I had to remind him where some of the things were kept. I also took the Lake District sheet of the one-inch Ordnance Survey map to add colour to my fibs and two bottles of Black Label whisky.

'Thought you'd given it up, dear boy?'

'This is just for washing wounds out with,' I explained courteously.

I also took a bottle of turpentine. You, shrewd reader, will have guessed why, but he was mystified.

'Look,' I said as he let me out, 'please don't tell anyone, *anyone*, that I've been here, or where I'm going, will you?'

'Of course not,' he said warmly, looking me straight in the eye to show me his falseness. I waited.

'And Charlie . . .'

'Yes,' I said, face blank.

'Do remember, you always have a home here.'

'Thanks, old chap,' I replied gruffly.

As Hemingway says somewhere: even when you have learned not to answer letters, families have many ways of being dangerous.

Topheavy with my load of Boy-Scout dunnage, I pedalled erratically to the cemetery, then down Bottom's Lane, turned left at the Green and skirted Leighton Moss until I came to Crag Foot. I pushed the machine very quietly past the farm for fear of dogs and threaded my way up the broken road to the Crag.

The Crag is a sort of crag-shaped feature of limestone, rich in minerals and seamed with crevasses or 'grikes' as they call them hereabouts. It is a mile square on the map (SD 47:49,73) but it seems a great deal larger when you are trying to pick your way over it. Here, two hundred years ago, hoved the dreaded Three Fingered Jack, conning the Marsh with his spy-glass for unprotected travellers whose bones now lie full fathom five, enriching the greedy sands of Morecambe Bay. (Oh Jock – 'never shake thy gory locks at me!')

The Crag is riddled and pitted with holes of every sort, the Dog Hole, Fairy Hole, Badger Hole – all of which have given up ancient bones and implements – and forgotten shafts where minerals were dug in the vague past, and the foundations of immeasurably old stone huts and, highest of all, defence works made by the Ancient Britons themselves. It's a wonderful place for breaking a leg, even the poachers won't risk it at night. In front are the salt marshes and the sea, behind stands the Gothick beauty of Leighton Hall. To the right you can look down over the reedy haven of Leighton Moss and to your left there is the desolation of Carnforth.

Copper was the great thing to mine for here, long ago, but what I was aiming for was a certain paint mine. A red-oxide working, to be exact. Red-oxide or ruddle-mining was a thriving industry on the Crag once upon a time and the deserted shafts still weep a messy redness, the colour of a really vulgar Swiss sunset. It took me an hour to find the shaft I remembered best; it goes down steeply for ten feet, looking very wet and red, but then flattens out, turns right at an acute angle and becomes quite dry and airy. A friendly bramble now cloaks its entrance, I had the devil of a job fighting my way in.

19

So, I soberly laid my last plan
To extinguish the man.
Round his creep-hole, with never a break
Ran my fires for his sake;
Over-head, did my thunder combine
With my under-ground mine:
Till I looked from my labour content
To enjoy the event.

Instans Tyrannus

Happiness is pear-shaped

'Playing it pear-shaped' was a favourite expression of Jock's; it seemed to mean deftly turning a situation to one's own advantage; seizing a favorable opportunity: Boxing Clever.

So the new, resourceful, *pear-shaped* Mortdecai arose at noon and brewed his own tea today over a little butane camping stove. Quite successfully. How about that, Kit Carson? Move over, Jim Bridger!

As I sipped it I tried to think the situation over carefully, examining it for neglected apertures, but to little avail – noon on Sunday has a special significance for some of us, you know; it is the time when the pubs open. The thought of all those happy drinkers bellying up to the bar counters in Silverdale and Warton kept driving all pear-shaped considerations out of my head. True, there was whisky, but noon on the Sabbath is sacred to bottled beer. I *wanted* some.

There hasn't been a soul on the Crag all day; I can't understand how people can frowst in public houses drinking bottled beer when there's all this splendid fresh air and scenery to be had for nothing. Even the campers, whose lurid tents and tasteful pastel caravans pimple the landscape here and there like dragon's teeth, are not in evidence: they're probably leading the simple life in front of their portable tellies, watching a nature programme, bless them. Most of them will be back in Bradford tomorrow, glowing with virtue and comparing mosquito bites.

I have taken the bicycle to pieces and wangled it all down into the cave. I've also been down to the icy spring which runs in a miniature canyon between two huge slabs of limestone; I washed myself all over, squeaking with the cold, and even drank a little of the water. It was delicious but I had to drink some Black Label when I got back up here, to take the taste away. It would never do to take up hydropathy at my age. Hydrophobia, yes, perhaps.

There is a most inaccessible spot above the mine where no one can creep up on you and I have built a small, discreet camp fire on which a can of baked beans is warming. From where I sit I can see the long necklace of Morecambe's lights – 'the bright boroughs, the circle-citadels there'.

Later

I like the 'wet and wilderness, weeds' of this place very much. It is quiet and no one has been near. I have been sleeping very happily, dreaming innocent dreams, listening to the sweet wild call of the redshanks whenever I wake. Now more than ever seems it sweet to die; the grave cannot be darker nor more solitary than this: nor stiller except when the wind, stirring the brambles at the entrance furtively, tries to frighten me. I recall the only really poignant ghost story –

(*Sexton:* 'What are you a-sniggering at?'
Ghost: 'It's not funny enough for two.')

Another day – I'm not sure which, now

I saw a marsh-harrier this morning; it quartered the reed beds of the Moss for a time, then flew strongly across Slackwood Farm to vanish in Fleagarth Wood. There's a new tent in Fleagarth, the first I've seen there; it's the usual awful fluorescent orange – when I was a boy tents were of proper colours, khaki or white or green. I studied the unsuspecting simple-lifers through my bird-watching binoculars – 8.5×44 Audubons – they seem to be a fat-bummed father, a rangy, muscular mum and a long, lean, grown-up son. I wish them joy of their late holiday, for it has started to rain in a subdued, determined sort of way. Lord Alvanley used to say that his greatest pleasure was to sit in the window of his club and 'watch it rain on the damned people'.

I am simmering a tin of frankfurter sausages on my little butane stove. I have some sliced plastic bread to clothe them in but I wish I had thought to bring mustard and bottled beer. Still, appetite and fresh air make a fine relish: I shall eat like a Boy Scout. 'Palate, the hutch of tasty lust, Desire not to be rinsed with wine.'

The same day, I think

I have been very abstemious with the whisky: I still have one and a quarter bottles of the lovely bully; when these are gone I shall have to sally forth and restock. Food is running short: I have two large cans of beans, one ditto of corned beef, a third of a sliced loaf and five rashers of bacon. (I must eat those raw: the smell of frying bacon carries for miles, did you know?) The local magnates, I fear, are going to lose a pheasant or two in the near future; they are still quite tame for they have not been shot at yet. The pheasants, I mean, not the magnates. I dread the thought of plucking and dressing them – again I mean the pheasants – I used not to mind but my stomach is more tremulous nowadays. Perhaps I shall simply emulate Nebuchadnezzar, that princely poephage, and *graze*. (Now, here's the *good* news: there's plenty of it.)

It feels like Tuesday, but I could be wrong

After my icy morning wash I have climbed circuitously to the highest point of the Crag, marked FORT on the map. Far below me I can see the gamekeeper's Landrover bouncing and splashing along the half-flooded causeway towards his release pens on the near side of the Moss, and the RSPB warden pottering about usefully in a boat on the Scrape. People often marvel at the existence of a successful bird sanctuary in a shooting preserve but there is no real paradox: what better place for a shy bird to breed than a well-keepered shoot? Shooting only takes place long after the breeding season, after all, and serious sportsmen – nearly all good naturalists – would no more shoot a rare bird than their own wives. All right, perhaps they do sometimes shoot a rarity by accident, but then we sometimes shoot our own wives, on purpose, don't we?

I am looking on this skulking period as a kind of holiday and I'm sure it's doing me a power of good. With any luck my ill-wishers are miles away, combing the Lake District for me and terrorizing the campers there. Indeed, they may have decided that I died with Jock; they may all have gone home. If I only had a few bottles of beer I would be feeling positively serene.

Noon

I have been *lulling* myself again.

I made my usual binocular survey ten minutes ago, before venturing forth to the little deserted vertical shaft which I have been using as a lavatory. The Fleagarth tent was apparently deserted; probably, I thought, they were all inside playing cosy games. (Incest – The Game That All the Family Enjoys?) I had crept to within thirty yards of the natural latrine before I smelled the sweet, chocolatey smell of American pipe tobacco. Parting the brambles I saw, standing with his back to me, the form of a long, lean young man, apparently using *my* privy. He was not in fact using it; just looking. He went on looking. He had an American haircut and wore those unbecoming Bermuda shorts. I didn't wait for him to turn around – I never could tell one young American from another – I just eased gently backwards and stole silently back here to my paint mine.

I am sure he is one of the Fleagarth campers: what can he have been doing? Perhaps he is a geologist, perhaps an inefficient badger-watcher, perhaps just an idiot; but the deep, sickening sensation in my belly will not be assuaged by these hypotheses. My belly is convinced that Fleagarth holds an anti-Mortdecai squad. Idle to wonder which lot they are – I can think of very few people who are not anti-Mortdecai this week.

Later

> 'Finish, good lady, the bright day is done
> And we are for the dark.'

This is it, or that is that; slice it where you will, the game's up. For several minutes just now I had the whole Fleagarth Mob in my field-glasses through a gap in the bramble defences. The thin American – whose shoulders are broader every time I study him – is perhaps one of the Smith and Jones comedy act I met in the sheriff's office in New Mexico; perhaps he is Colonel Blucher; it doesn't matter, probably their own mummies couldn't tell them apart. The burly female part of the sketch I seem to know, I fancy I last saw her fuming in a Triumph Herald at Piccadilly Circus, *you* remember. From the way she handles herself I'd say she was past child bearing but not past entering Judoka contests at Black Belt level.

Grow old along with me – if you're quick – for the best is yet to be. The *tertium quid*, the fat-bummed daddy-figure is – oh, you've guessed it – yes; Martland. Excepting myself, I've never seen anyone more ripe for death. Why I should hate him so much I cannot understand, he has never done me any serious harm; yet.

My recce this afternoon didn't get very far; before I parted my *porte-cochère* of bramble I heard the sound of water buffaloes tromping through a swamp: it was Martland himself, on all fours, being a Woodcraft Indian, looking for *spoor*. Back I slunk, mustering a faint giggle. I could have shot him there and then, I nearly did. I could scarcely have missed the pungent, powdered division of his suety nates as he bent over – he's going to get it in the end, why not that end? Take, oh take those hips away, that so sweetly were forsworn at Hailsham College for the Sons of Officers, and elsewhere.

But I am saving powder and shot for when – if – they find my creep-hole; this Smith and Wesson discharged in a narrow mine-shaft will sound enough like a poacher's twelve-bore to bring the keeper and his two-fisted mates running: I wouldn't give anything for Martland & Co's chances against a determined keeper at this time of the year. Poor Martland, he hasn't tackled anything rougher than a traffic warden since the War.

They are all supping cocoa or something around a wet and smokey woodfire outside their tent in Fleagarth: I have studied them carefully through the glasses and there is positively no deception.

What, still alive at forty-two – a fine upstanding chap like you?

Well, yes.

Just.

My manuscript, interlarded with useful currency notes, lies in the bowels of a Warton pillar box, en route for La Maison Spon. I wonder whose eyes will read these last jottings, whose scissors trim away which indiscretions, whose hand strike the match to burn them? Perhaps only your eyes, Blucher. Not yours, I hope, Martland, for I intend that you shall accompany me down to wherever naughty art dealers go when they die. And I shall not let you hold my hand.

They were all out on the Crag in the dark when I returned from Warton; it was a nightmare. For them too, I imagine. I have only a confused memory of creeping and quaking, stalking and counter-stalking, straining aching ears into the blackness and hearing more sounds than there were; finally, the mindless panic of knowing that I was lost.

I regrouped my mental forces – sadly depleted – and forced myself to crouch in a hole until I could orient myself and calm the jam session of my nerves. I had almost succeeded in becoming Major the Honble Dashwood 'Mad Jack' Mortdecai, V.D. and Scar, the ice-cool toast of the Ypres Salient, when a voice close beside me said,

'Charlie?'

I vomited up my heart, bit it savagely and swallowed it again. My eyes were shut fast, waiting for the shot.

'No,' came a whisper from behind me, 'it's me.' My heart shook itself, tried a tentative beat or two, settled into some sort of ragged rhythm. Martland and the woman rustled about a bit then floundered quietly down the slope.

Where was the American? He was at my lavatory again, that's where he was. Probably booby-trapping it. I think he heard me coming, for all movement stopped. I lowered myself to the ground with infinite caution and could see him, eight feet tall against the sky. He took a noiseless step toward me, then another. To my surprise I was now quite calm, the wanky old avenger preparing to kill his man. My pistol was in the paint mine – just as well, perhaps. First, kick in the family jewels, I decided; second, leg-sweep behind knees; third, bounce rock on head until tender. If no rock, drop knee on face, break hyoid bone in throat with side of hand. Should serve. I began positively to look forward to his next step, although I am not a violent man by nature.

He took the next step – a cock pheasant exploded from under his feet with all the racket and drama of, well, of a rocketing cock pheasant. Now, one of the few things which do not startle old country-bred Mortdecai is a rocketing pheasant, but it was not so with the American; he squeaked, jumped, ducked, crouched and dragged out a great long thing which can only have been an automatic with a silencer fitted. As the shards of silence reassembled themselves I could hear him panting painfully in the dark. At last he rose, tucked the pistol away and drifted off down the slope, thoroughly ashamed of himself, I hope.

I had to come back here to the mine; pistol, food, suitcase and bicycle were and are all here: I need them all except, perhaps, the bicycle.

There is a safe and smelly snugness about this little grave already: I can scarcely hope that they will not nose me out but they cannot, after all, put me further underground than this. There's a Stalingrad for all of us somewhere.

> 'Ici gît qui, pour avoir trop aimer les gaupes,
> Descendit, jeune encore, au royaume des taupes.'

In any case, to run now would be to die sooner, in some spot of their choosing and in some way I might not much like. I prefer it here, where I dreamed the dreams of youth and, later, lifted many a lawless leg – to use the words of R. Burns (1759–96).

You will not find it hard to believe that, since returning to this, my oubliette, I have had more than one suck at my brother's delicious whisky. I intend to have a couple more, then to consult sagacious sleep.

Only a little later

Why we so used to relish the life stories of condemned men, and why so many of us mourn the passing of capital punishment, is because ordinary decent chaps like us have a fine feeling for the dramatic proprieties: we know that tragedy cannot properly end in nine years' comfy incarceration and useful, satisfying work in the prison bakery. We know that death is the only end of art. A chap who has gone to all the trouble of strangling his wife is *entitled* to his moment of splendour on the gallows – it is a crime to make him sew mailbags like a common thief.

We loved those tales told at the gallows-foot because they freed us from the tyranny and vulgarity of the happy ending; the long, idiot senescence, the wonderful grandchildren, the tactful inquiries about the life-insurance premiums.

Positively the last day – booking for smoking-concerts now

Since there's no help, come then, let's kiss and part. Something has gone wrong. I shall attract no help by firing my pistol, for today is evidently the first of September: duck shooting has begun and since before dawn the Moss and the shore have echoed with sporting musketry.

Martland has found me; I suppose I always knew he would. He came to the mouth of the mine and called down to me. I didn't answer.

'Charlie, we know you're down there, we can *smell* you, for God's sake! Look, Charlie, the others can't hear me, I'm willing to give you a break. Tell me where the bloody picture is, get me off the hook, and I'll give you a night's start; you might get clear away.'

He *can't* have thought I'd believe that, can he?

'Charlie, we've got Jock, he's alive . . .'

I knew that was a lie and suddenly I was filled with rage at his shabbiness. Without exposing myself I aimed the .455 at a knob of rock near the entrance and loosed off a round. The noise deafened me momentarily but I could still hear the snarl of the big distorted bullet ricocheting toward Martland. When he spoke again, from another spot, his voice was tight with fear and hatred.

'All right, Mortdecai. Here's another deal. Tell me where the bloody picture is and where the other photographs are and I promise I'll shoot you cleanly. That's the most you can hope for now – and you'll have to trust me even for that.' He enjoyed that bit. I fired again, praying that the mangled lead would take his face off. He spoke again, explaining how void my chances were, not understanding that I had written off my life and wanted only his. He listed lovingly the people who wanted me dead, from the Spanish Government to the Lord's Day Observance Society – I was positively flattered at the extent of the mess I had made. Then he went away.

Later they shot at me with a silenced pistol for half an hour, listening between shots for a cry of pain or surrender. The slugs, screaming and buzzing as they tore from wall to wall, nearly drove me insane but only one touched me; they didn't know whether the shaft turned left or right. The one lucky shot laid my scalp open and it is bleeding into my eyes – I must look a *sight*.

The American tried coaxing me next but he, too, had nothing to offer but a quick death in exchange for information and a written confession. They must have raised the Rolls from its grave in the canyon, for he knows the Goya wasn't in the soft-top. Spain, it seems, is due to renew a treaty with the USA about Strategic Air Force bases on her territory, but every time the US reminds them about it, the Spaniards change the subject to the Goya. 'Duchess of Wellington' – 'known to have been stolen on behalf of an American and to have entered the US.' He wouldn't have told me about the bases if he thought I had any chance of surviving, would he?

I didn't bother to reply, I was busy with the turpentine.

Then he told me the alternative, the *dirty* death: they have sent for a canister of cyanide, the stuff they use on rabbits here and on people over there. So evidently I cannot hope for Martland to come down and fetch me. I shall have to go out to him. It's of no importance.

I have finished with the turpentine; mixed with whisky it has served beautifully to dissolve the lining of my suitcase and now the

Goya smiles at me from the wall, fresh and lovely as the day she was painted, the incomparable, naked 'Duquesa de Wellington,' mine to keep for the rest of my life. '*Donc, Dieu existe.*'

There is enough whisky to last me until the light fades and then – who could be afraid? – I shall emerge with my six-gun blazing, like some shaggy hero of the Old West. I know that I shall be able to kill Martland; then one of the others will kill me and I shall fall like a bright exhalation in the evening down to hell where there is no art and no alcohol, for this is, after all, quite a moral tale. You see that, don't you?

After you with the pistol

All the characters in this book are fictitious: any similarity to real people or corpses is both accidental and disgusting.

The epigraphs are all by Alfred, Lord Tennyson except one which is a palpable forgery. The forgery is signed, after a fashion.

Disclaimer

There is not a word of truth in this book. I have neither met nor heard of anyone who resembles any character in it, I am glad to say. They are all figments of my heated imagination, every one of them. This is particularly true of the fictional narrator, whose only resemblance to me is around the waist-line.

I apologize for what he says about the art-trade. Why, some of my best friends, etc.

There is, I believe, a very sophisticated cop-shop South of the Thames but I have never seen it except in the mind's eye, which is where I should like to keep it. The only pub I know called The Bunch of Grapes is in Gracie Fields' deathless aspidistra song. I believe that there was once a shop in the East End called Mycock's Electrical but I know of no pig-abattoirs of that name.

The lavatory inspection-panel ruse for smuggling heroin was, indeed, once used but it has long been 'blown' or I would not have related it. It is almost as old-fashioned as using motor-car tyres, cameras from Kowloon, hollowed-out boomerangs from Bendigo (New South Wales), 'pregnant' ladies from Amsterdam, long-playing records pressed out of ganja resin, or even dusty carpets from Kashmir which need a little attention from a certain dry-cleaner in London's dockland before they are delivered to the consignee. The same is true of other naughty techniques described: pray do not let them tempt you to embark upon a life of crime. You may be a hare but 'Old Bill' is a most capable tortoise.

I apologize to Air France: its hostesses are all excellent linguists. Many of them can even understand my French.

1 Mortdecai prepares to meet his Maker

Come into the garden, Maud,
I am here at the gate alone . . .

Maud

Yes, well, there it was. That was that. I'd had my life.

So I drank the last of the whisky, looked a loving last once more on the naked Duchess and shed perhaps – I forget – a tear of self-pity, that last of luxuries, before climbing stiffly to my feet. The heavy, friendly old Smith & Wesson pistol was loaded in all chambers with the murderous soft lead target ammunition. I pulled the hammer back a little, which allows the cylinder to spin. I span it, listening to the quick, fat chuckle of the ratchet.

Then I sat down again.

I had left it just that few minutes too late and there had been just too small a jolt of Scotch in the tail of the bottle. Had there been even one more fluid ounce, I could have gone roaring out of my smelly cavern like some old grizzly bear, but now sobriety had me by the throat. You see, I had begun to consider just where the bullets would smash into my well-nourished body; what bones would be shattered, what spillikins of the said bones would be sent splintering through which of my delicate organs, how *long* this mangling would last before generous Death brushed pain aside and passed his hand over my eyelids, closing them forever.

No, wait, sorry. Hang about a bit. It has just occurred to me that you might be a trifle puzzled as to why Charlie Mortdecai – I – should have been preparing for death in a smelly cavern, chaperoned only by a naked Duchess, a large revolver and an empty whisky-bottle. I realize that some might find these circumstances unusual, perhaps even bizarre.

This, then, is what happened before you came in. Nude readers begin here. There's this chap Me, you see – the Hon. Charlie Mortdecai – I was actually christened Charlie – who is, or rather am, a nice, rich, cowardly, fun-loving art-dealer who dabbles in crime to take his mind off his haemorrhoids. Then there's this fantastic painting by Goya of 'The Duchess of Wellington' who, at the time of being painted, had absent-mindedly forgotten to put her knickers back on. Or, indeed, anything else. Having so much respect for other people's property that I sometimes feel bound to care for it myself, I had nicked the painting from the Prado, Madrid, and exported it personally to a millionaire art-lover in New Mexico. I found the art-lover freshly murdered, and his randy-eyed young widow casting about for a replacement. All went wrong, as all these things do, and, as my sense of fun started to fray at the cuffs, I shortened my lines of communication – as the generals used to say – and made tracks for England, home and beauty, in the order named.

All sorts of people were by that time disliking Mortdecai warmly, and in an almost-final hot pursuit I was obliged to kick in the head of my trusty thug Jock, who was about to die even more unpleasantly in the quicksands of Morecambe Bay, Lancashire. I – Mortdecai – holed up in a disused red-oxide mine on Warton Crag (still in Lancashire), found that my enemies had traced me thither, and realized that my life was over. I was in a pretty shabby mental and physical state by then and resolved to get as drunk as I could, then to come roaring out of my stinking lair and kill at least Martland, chief of my persecutors.

Right? Any questions? There I was, then, preparing to go out and meet the kind of messy death I had too often seen happen to other people. I couldn't see myself in the rôle at all.

Ah, yes, *but*. What else? Where was your actual alternative?

I upturned the bottle and collected three more drops, or it may have been four.

'Pull yourself together, Mortdecai,' I told myself sternly. 'Nothing in life became you like the leaving of it. It is a far, far better thing that you do now. You are ready and ripe for death. You'll *like* it up there.'

'Up?' I thought. '*Up* there? Must you joke at a time like this?'

Then I looked again at the painted Duchess, her canvas propped against the wall of the mine-shaft, smiling like a whole choir of Mona Lisas, voluptuously sexless, erotic only on a level that I could never reach. Although God knows I have tried.

'Oh, very well,' I told her.

I crawled to the entrance of the little mine. There was no sound outside, no movement, but they were there, all right. There was nowhere else they would be.

I emerged.

An enormous light burst out but, unaccountably, it was pointed not at me but in the opposite direction. It illumined not me but a pallid, startled Martland. Well, at least I could fulfil that part of my programme. He peered down the beam at me, making urgent little movements with his hands.

'Martland,' I said. I had never heard myself use that voice before but I knew that there was no need for more than the one word.

He opened his mouth. It seemed difficult for him. Perhaps he was going to remind me that we had been at school together. I couldn't find it in my heart to shoot anyone looking as soppy as he did, but my trigger-finger had a life of its own. The pistol jumped hard in my hand and a puff of dust bounced out of his trousers just below the belt-buckle.

I gazed at the spot, entranced. There wasn't any blood; you couldn't even see a hole. Martland looked puzzled, vexed even. He sat down hard on his bottom and looked at me, cross and disappointed. Then he started dying and it was rather dreadful and went on and on and made me feel even more ill than I was and I couldn't bear it and I shot him again and again but I couldn't seem to make him stop dying.

Whoever was working the searchlight finally tore himself away from the spectacle and nailed me with the beam. I clicked the revolver three or four times – empty as Mortdecai now – three or four times up into the glaring eye of the light, threw it as hard as I could, missed again.

'Mr Mortdecai,' said a polite American voice.

I whipped around, eyes tearing at the darkness, my gut hungry for the coming of the bullets.

'No, Mr Mortdecai,' the voice went on, 'please compose yourself. Nobody's killing anyone else tonight. Everything's going to be all right. I mean, *really* all right.'

You cannot imagine how disappointing it is to be all braced for death and then to find, at the very moment of truth, that they're not frying tonight. I sort of suddenly found myself sitting down and weeping noisily; the sobs tore through my breast like the bullets that hadn't.

They gave me a flask of whisky and I was sick again and again but at last I kept some down and then there was a dull, silencer *plop* from Martland's direction and the noises of his dying stopped and then the woman got me to my feet and helped me down the slope and across the road and up into Fleagarth Wood and to their tent. She was very strong and smelled of old fur coats. I was asleep as I hit the groundsheet.

2 Mortdecai finds that his Maker does not want to meet him

> . . . when the steam
> Floats up from those dim fields about the homes
> Of happy men that have the power to die . . .
>
> *Tithonus*

The woman woke me up a few moments later. The moments must have been hours, actually, for a dank and dirty dawn was oozing into the tent. I squealed angrily and burrowed back down into the sleeping-bag: it smelled of nasty policewomen but I loved it – there were no people there. She coaxed me awake with a finger-and-thumb-nail in the ear-lobe: she must have found that in the works of Lord Baden-Powell. (Don't you often wonder what B.P. would have done for a living if he had lived in these times? *Oxfam?* Peace Corps?)

She had won her Camp Cookery Badge, that was clear, for the mug of tea wheedled into my quaking fingers was of no tenderfoot quality. I, personally, have no quarrel with Evaporated Milk: it lends a heartening, lusty thickness to cheap tea which, once in a while, I find most gratifying.

Then she made me wash and shave (she lent me a tiny razor with a pink plastic handle: it was called 'Miaouw' – why?) and then she showed me where the Elsan was and then we went, *hand in hand*, down through the wood to where a huge American camper-van was parked just off the road. We climbed in. Two other people were there already. One was on a stretcher, covered all over with a blanket. Well, Martland, obviously. I didn't have any feelings about that. Not then. Later, perhaps. The other was the American, gabbling gibberish into a wireless set which was quacking back at him. He was, it fuzzily seemed to me, patiently telling someone to get into touch with someone else who would authorize yet another someone to blah-blah. He was very polite to the quacker. At last he went through the 'Roger and out' nonsense, switched off all the little knobs and turned around, giving me a smile which was quite unwarranted, considering how early in the day it was. He proved to be a man called Colonel Blucher, whom I had met before. We had never actually hit each other.

'Good morning, Mr Mortdecai,' he said, still smiling in that unwarranted way.

'Oink,' I said. There was, clearly, something pretty wrong with me still, for I had meant to be a trifle civiller than that, but 'Oink' was what came out.

He blinked a little but took no offence.

'I'm very, very sorry to have to rouse you so early, Mr Mortdecai, for I recall that you are not an early riser. You must be very tired still?'

I was more articulate this time.

'Oinkle oink,' I said courteously. It was the strangest feeling: the words were perfectly clear in my head but all I could produce were these farmyard imitations. Distraught, I sat down heavily and put my head in my hands. A sort of juicy noise underneath me and a sort of knobbly softness made me realize that I was sitting on Martland. I jumped up again, squeaking. Blucher was looking worried so, naturally, I tried to hit him, didn't I? I mean, it seemed a sensible thing to do at the time. But my wild swing only threw me flat on my face and I started to cry again. I wanted my mummy badly, but I knew she wouldn't be coming: she never did, you know, even when she was alive. She was one of those Mums who believe that Christopher Robin kills all known germs. A kind of literary Harpic.

Blucher came and put his arm around me and helped me to my feet and I fancy I probably started to scream a bit – for I thought it was Jock come back from his grave in the quagmire – so he took something out of his hip-pocket and, with a look of infinite compassion on his face, slugged me carefully behind the ear. This was much better.

'Roger and out,' I thought gratefully as the lovely blackness encompassed me.

3   Mortdecai regains consciousness, if you can properly call it that

All things are taken from us, and become
Portions and parcels of the dreadful Past.

The Lotus-Eaters

To this day I still do not know where it was that I awoke nor, indeed, how long I had been separated from my cogitative faculties, bless them. But I think it must have been somewhere awful in the North-West of England, like Preston or Wigan or even Chorley, God forbid. The lapse of time must have been quite three or four weeks: I could tell by my toenails, which no one had thought to cut. They felt horrid. I felt cross.

'I have had a Nervous Breakdown,' I told myself crossly, 'the sort of thing that one's aunts have for Christmas.' I lay motionless for what seemed a long time. This was to deceive *them*, you see, whoever they were, and to give me time to think about it all. I soon became aware that there were no *them* in the room and that what I wanted was a great, burly drink to help me think. I decided, too, that since they had kept me alive they must want something from me and that a drink would not be an unreasonable *quid pro quo* for whatever it was, if you follow me. (You will observe that the very recollection of that time interferes with my well-known lucidity.)

Another thinking-bout persuaded me that the way to get such a drink was to summon whatever chalk-faced, black-uniformed,

Kafkaesque she-policewoman was standing guard over me. I could find no bell to ring so I heaved myself out of bed and sat down absurdly on the floor, weeping with puny rage.

My getting out of bed must have triggered some sort of alarum, for the swing-doors swung or swang and an apparition appeared. I examined it narrowly. It was clearly the photographic negative of a chalk-faced, black-uniformed police-woman.

'You are clearly a photographic negative,' I cried accusingly. 'Be off with you!' Her face, you see, was of the deepest black and her uniform of the brightest white: all wrong. She giggled, showing, paradoxically, about forty-eight large *white* teeth.

'No, mahn,' she retorted, 'negative. Ah'm not under-developed, jest underprivileged.' I looked again; she spoke truth. As she scooped me up and lifted me into bed (oh the shame of it) I was even more convinced, for my nose was flattened by one of her magnificent 100-Watt headlamps. Despite my effete condition (oh, all right, I know that's not the right word but you know perfectly well what I mean) I felt the old Adam surging about freely in my loins – and I don't mean the gardener. I desired more than anything else in the world to go out and slay a dragon or two for her: the thought was so beautiful that I began to weep again.

She brought me a drink; rather a thin one but undeniably alcoholic. Enoch Powell had lost my vote for good. I cried a little more, rather relishing it. The tears, I mean, not the drink, which tasted like milk from a dead sow. It was probably Bourbon or something of that sort.

Much later she came in again, smiling enormously, and stood with her back to the open door.

'Now – here's Doctor Farbstein to see you,' she chortled richly, as though it was all a huge joke. A great, jolly, bearded chap brushed past her splendid bosom (I swear they *twanged*) and came and sat on my bed. He was full of fun.

'Go away,' I piped feebly, 'I am an anti-Semite.'

'You should have thought of that before they circumcised you,' he roared merrily. A stray beam of sunshine (perhaps we weren't in North-West England after all) struck splinters of gold from his brave Assyrian beard; Kingsley Amis would have recognized them instantly for beads of breakfast egg but I am a romantic, as you must have realized by now, even if you have still not read my previous adventures.

'You have been quite ill, you know,' he said, keeping his face straight and trying to sound grave and concerned.

'I am *still* quite ill,' I retorted with dignity, 'and my toenails are a disgrace to the National Health Service. How long have I been in this pre-Lysol *guet-apens*, this quasi-medical Lubyanka?'

'Oh, ages and ages it seems,' he replied cheerily. 'Every now and then they tell me you're stirring and I pop in and shoot you full of paraldehyde to stop you chasing the nurses and then I forget you for days on end. "Letting Nature take its kindly course" is what we call it.'

'And what have I been eating, pray?'

'Well, nothing much, really, I fancy. Nurse Quickly tells me that the dust lies thick on your bed-pan.'

'Faugh!' I said. I realized then that I was indeed on the mend, for it takes a strong man to say 'faugh' properly and with the proper curl of the upper lip.

But I realized, too, that this was a man who was a match for me unless I could soon put him down. I summoned up my most aristocratic glare.

'If you are indeed a doctor, as your ah sunburned accomplice claims,' I grated, 'perhaps you will have the goodness to tell me who your employers are.'

He leaned low over my bed and smiled seraphically, his beard splitting to disclose a row of teeth which seemed to be a random selection from Bassett's celebrated Liquorice Allsorts.

'*SMERSH!*' he whispered. The garlic on his breath was like acetylene.

'Where have you been lunching?' I croaked.

'In Manchester,' he murmured happily. 'In one of the only two fine Armenian restaurants in Western Europe. The other, I am happy to say, is also in Manchester.'

'I shall have some Armenian food sent in,' I said, 'and with no further delay or shilly-shallying. See to it that there is lots of *houmous*. And whom do you really work for?'

'You would be horribly sick. And I work for the Professor of Psychiatry in the University Hospital of North-East Manchester, if you want to know.'

'I don't care how sick I would be – it would provide employment for these nurses, who seem to be disgracefully underworked. And I don't believe a word of this North-East Manchester nonsense: only London is allowed to have points of the compass, everyone knows that. You are clearly one of these impostors, probably struck off the register for using an unsterilized button-hook.'

He leaned close to me again.

'Arseholes,' he murmured.

'That too, probably,' I rejoined.

We became rather friends at that point – was it what he would have called aversion-therapy? – and he agreed that he might see his way to sending in a little *houmous* and hot Armenian bread and perhaps a touch of that lovely sour-bean salad with a chick-pea or two sculling about in it. He also said that I might be allowed a visitor.

'Who would visit me?' I asked, shedding another ready tear.

'There's droves of them,' he leered, 'queues of juicy little *shicksas* wanking in the waiting-room; it's becoming quite a health-hazard.'

'Oh, bollocks,' I said.

'Suck 'em,' he replied. Salt of the earth, some of these doctors.

Having settled the amenities he became less human and got down to business.

'I won't bother to tell you what's the matter with you,' he said crisply, 'because you'd only ask me to spell it and I can't. You might call it traumatic massive neurasthenia if you were a country GP thirty years out of date. Someone of your age might well call it a nervous breakdown, which is how mentally inadequate people describe a syndrome of boring signs and symptoms exhibited by people who find that they have bitten off more than they can emotionally chew.'

I thought about that.

'The answer to that,' I said at last, 'is in the plural again.'

He thought about that.

'Now I come to think of it,' he said judicially, 'you could just be right. However, what matters is that I've had you under heavy sedation for a good long time and I think you're now pretty well all right – at any rate, as all right as you were before, ha ha. You may find yourself crying a little from time to time but it'll pass. I'm going to give you stimulants now – one of the methedrines – they'll soon sort you out. In the meantime, just go on using the Kleenex, ha ha, and cry as much as you like.'

My lower lip trembled.

'No, no!' he shouted, 'not now! Because here' – and with this he flung open the door like an exhibitionist's mackintosh – 'here is your visitor!'

It was Jock who stood in the doorway.

I felt the blood draining out of my brain; I think I may have shrieked. I know I fainted. When consciousness came back there was still Jock in the doorway, although I clearly – all too clearly – remembered having kicked his head in, weeks before, as he lay in the grip of that quagmire.

He was grinning uncertainly, as though unsure of his welcome; his head was bandaged, there was a black patch over one of his eyes and new gaps in his few, strong, yellow teeth.

'You all right, Mr Charlie?' he asked.

'Thanks Jock, yes.' Then I turned to Dr Farbstein.

'You disgusting bastard,' I snarled, 'you call yourself a doctor and spring things like this on your patients? What are you trying to do, kill me?'

He chuckled happily, making a noise like a cow defecating.

'Psychotherapy,' he said. 'Shock, terror, rage. Probably done you a power of good.'

'Hit him, Jock,' I pleaded. 'Hard.' Jock's face fell.

'He's all right, Mr Charlie. Honest. I been playing gin rummy with him every day. Won *pounds*.'

Farbstein slid out, doubtless on his way to spread a little more sunshine elsewhere. He was probably a very good doctor, if you like that kind of doctor. When I felt a little better I said 'Look, Jock . . .'

'Forget it Mr Charlie. You only done it because I asked you to. My mum would have done the same if she'd been there. Lucky you wasn't wearing boots, reely.'

I was a bit startled: I mean, I suppose Jock must have had a mummy at some stage but I couldn't quite visualize her, least of all in boots. I suddenly felt desperately tired and fell asleep.

When I awoke, Jock was perched decorously on the end of my bed, looking hungrily out of the window at what can only have been a giggle of passing nurses.

'Jock,' I said, 'how on earth did they . . .'

'Range Rover. They got a sort of winch on the axle; wound me out with it. Didn't half hurt. Dislocated me shoulder, cracked a couple of ribs and give me a double rupture in me actual groin. All sorted out now.'

'Is your eye, er, badly hurt?'

'It's gorn,' he said cheerfully. 'You put the leather smack into it and I was wearing me contact lenses. The nurses like me patch, romantic they call it. I'm not having no glass eye, bugger that, me uncle had one and swallowed it, never got it back.'

'Goodness,' I said feebly, 'how was that?'

'He put it in his mouth, see, to warm it up and make it so it would slip in the socket easy, then he hiccupped, having been on the piss the night before. Down it went. Cured the hiccups but he never saw the eye again.'

'I see.' How the other half lives; to be sure. There was a long and happy silence.

'*Never* got it back?' I wondered aloud.

'Nah. Me uncle even got the croaker to have a look up his bum but he said he couldn't see nothink. "Funny," says me uncle, "I can see you as clear as anythink, doctor." '

'Jock, you're a bloody liar,' I said.

'Mr Charlie?'

'Speaking.'

'You don't half owe me a lot of wages.'

'Sorry, Jock. You shall have them as soon as I am strong enough to lift a cheque-book. And, now I come to think of it, I've got a hefty Employer's Liability insurance policy on you; I think you get two thousand pounds for an eye. Out of my own pocket I shall buy you the finest glass eye that money can buy, even if I have to pay cash. Please wear it in the house; you can save the romantic black patch for your wenching expeditions.'

Jock lapsed into an awed silence: in his world people only get two thousand pounds by doing highly illegal things which earn you five years in the nick. I fell asleep again.

'Mr Charlie?' I opened a petulant eyelid
'Yes,' I said, 'this is still I.'

'You remember when you went to see that Colonel Blucher geezer at the American Embassy?'

'I remember vividly.'

'Well, he's here. Well, any road, he comes here every day almost. He's got them all jumping except Doctor Farbstein; I reckon Doctor Farbstein reckons he's a Kraut.'

'That figures.'

'Funny thing is,' he went on, 'he never asks me nothing – Blucher I mean – just asks are they looking after me and would I like a Monopoly set to play with the nurses with.'

I waited while he subsided into helpless giggles.

'Jock,' I said gently when he had finished. 'I know Colonel Blucher's here. As a matter of fact, he's right behind you, standing in the doorway.'

He was. So was a huge, black, automatic pistol, which was pointing unerringly at Jock's pelvis. (Very nice, very professional: the pelvic region doesn't move around nearly as much as the head and the thorax. A bullet there, smashing through bladder and privates and all the other butcher's offal we keep in our pelvic girdles, is just as certain as one between the eyes and, I'm told, a great deal more painful.)

Blucher ostentatiously flicked on the safety-catch and magicked the pistol away into the waistband of his trousers. That is a very good place to carry a pistol while you still have a waist-line; afterwards the bulge becomes a little ambiguous.

'Sorry about the dramatics, gentlemen,' he said, 'but I thought this might just be a good time to remind you that you are alive right now because I put in a request for you. I can change my mind at any time I feel I have to.'

Well, *really*! I cringed of course, but it was only partly funk: the rest was embarrassment at his lamentable bad taste.

'Are you aware,' I asked bravely, 'that you are occupying space which I have other uses for? Or rather, for which I have other uses?'

'I like P.G. Wodehouse too, sir,' he rejoined, 'but I would hesitate to use any kind of flippancy in the situation you find yourself in. Or rather, in which you find yourself.'

I gaped at the man. Perhaps he was human after all.

'What exactly do you want me to do?' I asked.

'Well, it's more *who*, really. Think of someone young and beautiful and fabulously rich.'

I thought. I thought briefly because I am not wholly stupid.

'Mrs Krampf,' I said.

'Right,' he said. 'Marry her. That's all.'

'All?'

'Well, practically all.'

'I need to go back to sleep,' I said. Back to sleep is where I went.

4 Mortdecai applies his razor-keen brain to the proposition

O Sorrow, wilt thou live with me
No casual mistress, but a wife.

In Memoriam

To tell the truth, that was not one of the times when I enjoyed a long and untroubled repose. Well, look, do you remember the last time *you* were told that you could continue living on the condition that you married a madly beautiful, sex-happy she-millionaire whom you were pretty sure had murdered her last husband in an almost undetectable way? Did *you* get in the wholesome eight hours of sleep?

The actual sequence of events was that I awoke, sat up and chewed fingernails, cigarettes and Scotch whisky – not necessarily in that order – for an hour or two. (I need scarcely tell you that Jock had smuggled me in a bottle of Messrs Haig and Haig's best and brightest.)

Those secret agents and chaps that you read about in the story-books would have had it all figured out to the last bloodstain in a moment, I don't doubt, but I had not their resilience, nor their youth. Perhaps, too, I was not, in those days, quite as clever as I am now. After a while I said 'bollox' and 'I dunno' and 'soddem' – in that order, this time – and went back to sleep after all. I don't really know why I troubled to wake up in the first place, for it was evident to the most casual eye that the old anti-Mortdecai conspiracy still had its hand on the wheel, its finger on the pulse and its thumb up to the knuckle-joint. 'Soddem' was without doubt the best phrase I had coined that day. I said it again. It seemed to help.

'I gotta get me bottle back,' mumbled Jock the next day, sitting on my bed and watching Nurse Quickly deal with my neglected toenails.

'Oh, I'd not worry about that, Jock. They're sending us off on a convalescent holiday to the Lake District tomorrow – a couple of lungfuls of mountain air and you'll be as full of fight as a lion. It's all these nurses that have been sapping your strength.' He shifted uneasily.

'I don't reckon you quite got the idea about "bottle", Mr Charlie. It isn't just guts, it's more like sort of relishing using your guts. You know, like sort of having a bit of a laugh when you're duffing someone up.'

'I think I see,' I said, shuddering thoughtfully and strumming one of Nurse Quickly's gorgeous breasts with a newly trimmed great toe. Without a flicker of expression she drove half an inch of scissor-point into my other foot. I didn't scream; I have a bit of bottle myself, you know.

A moment later, when she had completed my pedicure, Jock took the scissors gently from her and with one hand crumpled them up. Then he held out his spade-like hand, cupped. Nurse Quickly leaned forward until the breast previously referred to rested in his hand. He growled quietly; she made a sort of throaty noise as he started to squeeze. Disgusted, I dragged my foot with some difficulty out from between them and sulkily turned my back.

They left the room together, without a word, headed for the linen-cupboard if I know anything about hospitals.

'Youth, flaming youth,' I thought bitterly.

5   Mortdecai decides that there are plenty of fates nicer than death

'Tirra lirra' by the river
Sang Sir Lancelot.

The Lady of Shalott

Well, there we were, Blucher and Jock and me, sitting around a table on the terrace of an hotel under one of those Lake District mountains that people send you postcards of, sipping tea (!) and watching a party of idiots getting ready to walk up the mountain. It was a fine day for early November in Lakeland – in fact it was a fine day for anywhere in England, any time – but it was only about five hours before dusk and the climb they were planning takes a smart three hours each way. A Mountain Rescue Warden was pleading with them, almost tearfully, but they just looked at him with amused contempt, the way a female learner-driver looks at her instructor. (She *knows* that hand-signals are a lot of nonsense invented by men to baffle women; why, her mother has been driving for years and has never used a hand-signal and she's never been hurt. A few other people, yes, perhaps, but not her.)

The mountain-rescue chap finally raised both hands and dropped them in a gesture of finality. He turned away from the group and walked towards us, grinding his teeth audibly. Then he stopped, whirled around and *counted* them ostentatiously. That would have frightened me. They just giggled. As he walked towards us I made a sympathetic grimace and he paused at our table.

'Look at the buggers,' he grated. 'Wearing *sandals*! Just a lot of nasty accidents looking for somewhere to happen. Coom nine o'clock, me and my mates'll be scouring t'bloody mountain for the twist in t'dark, brecking wor necks. And I'll miss t'Midnight Movie, like as not.'

'Too bad,' I said, keeping my face straight.

'Why do you do it?' Blucher asked him.

'For *foon*,' he growled, and stalked away.

'Going to overhaul his equipment,' said Blucher wisely.

'Or beat his wife,' I said.

We went on sipping tea; that is to say, Blucher and I sipped while Jock sort of hoovered his up with a lovely, wristy motion of the upper lip. I don't much care about tea-drinking in the afternoon; in the morning the stuff Jock brings to me in bed is like that Nepenthe which the wife of Thone gave to Jove-born Helena, but in the p.m. it always makes me think of Ganges mud in which crocodiles have been coupling.

'Well, now,' said Blucher.

I put on my intelligent, receptive face, the one I wear when a heavy customer, pen poised over cheque-book, starts to tell me about his philosophy of art-collecting.

'Mr Mortdecai, why do you suppose I and my superiors have uh preserved you from uh death at very very great trouble and expense?'

'You told me: you want me to marry Johanna Krampf. I cannot begin to understand why. By the way, what did you do with Martland's er cadaver or mortal coil?'

'I understand it was fished out of the Thames at Wapping Old Stairs. The uh marine organisms had done a good job and the cause of death is recorded as "uncertain". Police suspect a vengeance homicide.'

'Goodness,' I said, 'their *minds*!'

He fidgeted fretfully. I was not asking the right questions. Chaps like him do not like to volunteer information, they like it to be wheedled out. I sighed.

'All right,' I said, 'why must I marry Mrs Krampf? Is she planning to overthrow the Constitution of the United States?'

'Charlie,' he said heavily.

'Please don't be formal,' I interrupted. 'My acquaintances call me Mr Mortdecai.'

'Mortdecai,' he compromised, 'if you have a fault it is a regrettable tendency towards flippancy. I am a humourless man and I recognize it – few humourless people can – I do ask you to bear this in mind and to remember that I hold the strings of your life in my hand.'

'Like the Blind Fury with the Abhorrèd Shears,' I chirrupped. It was his turn to sigh.

'Ah, *shit*,' is what he sighed. 'Look, I perfectly realize that you are not afraid of death; in your own kooky way I believe you to be a pretty brave man. But death as an inevitability-concept-situation is very very far removed from the slow infliction of death by means of PAIN.' He sort of barked that last word. Then he collected himself, leaned over the table towards me and spoke gently, reasonably.

'Mortdecai, my Agency is concerned only with winning. We are not regular guys in any sense of the word; we have no code of behaviour which would stand the light of day, still less an in-depth investigation by the *Washington Post*. What we do have is a number of specialized operatives who are skilled in inflicting PAIN. Many of them have been doing it for years, they think about it all the time. I'm afraid that some of them kind of like it. Do I have to go on?'

I straightened up in my chair, looked bright, helpful, unflippant.

'You have my undivided attention,' I assured him. He looked meaningfully at Jock. I took the hint, suggested to Jock that we must be boring him and that the hotel swarmed with chambermaids whose bottoms needed pinching. He ambled off.

'Right,' said Blucher. 'Now. Mrs Krampf seems to be kind of crazy about you. I won't say I find that easy to understand, I guess it's a case of whatever turns you on. I don't have any clearcut idea right now of why we want you around her except that we know there must be something. Something big. A few months before her husband uh died, our uh accountancy branch, as we call it, had detected the clandestine movement of very large amounts of currency into and out of the Krampf empire. After his demise we looked for these movements to cease. They did not. In fact they increased. Understand, we're not talking about low-grade, bush-league money-shifting – that's for the IRS or Currency Control guys. We're talking about sums of money which could buy a Central

American republic – or two African ones – overnight and still leave you a little walking-about money. We don't have any idea what it's all about. So go marry Mrs Krampf and find out.'

'Okay,' I said briskly, colloquially, 'I'll cable her first thing tomorrow and slip her the good news.'

'You don't have to do that, Mortdecai. She's already here.'

'Here?' I squeaked, looking about me wildly, like any pregnant nun. 'What do you mean "here"?'

'I mean right here in this hotel. In your room, I guess. Try looking in your bed.'

I made a sort of imploring noise. He patted me on the shoulder in a scoutmasterly way.

'You ate a dozen and a half oysters at luncheon, Mortdecai. I *believe* in you. Go in there and win, boy.' I gave him a look of pure hatred and crept whimpering into the hotel and up to my room.

She was there all right but she wasn't in bed, thank goodness, nor even naked: she was wearing a thing which looked like a cream silk pillowcase with three holes cut in it – cost hundreds of pounds, probably – Mrs Spon would have priced it at a glance. It made her look a great deal more than naked. I fancy I blushed. She paused, poised, for a second or two, drinking me in like Wordsworth devouring a field of yellow – yes, yellow – daffodils. Then she rushed forward and into my arms with an impact which would have felled a lesser man.

'Oh, Charlie Charlie Charlie,' she cried, 'Charlie Charlie Charlie!'

'Yes yes yes,' I countered, 'there there there,' patting her awkwardly on her charming left buttock. (That is not to say that the other, or right, buttock was not equally delectable, I only single out the left for praise because it was the one under advisement at the time, you understand.)

She squirmed ecstatically in my arms and, to my great relief, I felt the dozen and a half oysters getting down to their task in the dormant Mortdecai glands. (Wonderfully selfless little chaps, oysters, I always think; they let you swallow them alive without a murmur of protest and then, instead of wreaking revenge like the surly radish, they issue this splendid aphrodisiac dividend. What beautiful lives they must lead, to be sure.)

'Well,' I thought, 'here goes,' and made an unequivocal move towards what J. Donne (1573–1631) calls 'the right true end of love' but to my amazement she pushed me away firmly and sort of wiggled her frock back into position.

'No, Charlie, not until we are married. What would you think of me?' I gaped in a disappointed way but I must admit to having felt a bit *reprieved*, if you take my meaning. You see, this gave me time to put myself into the hands of a capable trainer: a canter round the paddock every morning and a diet of beefsteak, oysters and Guinness would soon lift me out of the selling-plate class and put me into good, mid-season form.

'Charlie, dear, you are going to marry me, aren't you, hunh? Your lovely doctor said marriage would be very therapeutic for you.'

'Farbstein said that, did he?' I asked nastily.

'No, darling, who's Farbstein? I mean the cute American doctor who's here looking after you – Dr Blücher?' She pronounced it beautifully, in the accents of old Vienna.

'Ah, yes, Blücher. *Doctor* Blücher, yes, of course. "Cute" is the very word for him. But I think he'd not much like you to pronounce it that way, he'd think it sounded kind of Kraut: he likes to say it "Bloocher". To rhyme with "butcher",' I added thoughtfully.

'Thank you, dear. But you didn't answer my question,' she said, pouting prettily. (Pouting is one of those dying arts; Mrs Spon can do it, so can the boy who creates my shirts, but it's almost as rare nowadays as tittering and sniggering. There are, I believe, a few portly old gentlemen who can still *chuckle*.)

'Dearest Johanna, of *course* I mean to marry you and as soon as possible. Let us say next month. People will talk, of course . . .'

'Charlie, dear, I was thinking more of tomorrow, really. I have this crazy British Special Licence for it. No, it was easy; I just got the Chancellor from the US Embassy to take me to see one of your Archbishops, such a sweet, silly old guy. I said I guessed your religion was "atheist" and he said, well, so were most of his bishops so he wrote "Church of England" on the form. Was that all right, Charlie?'

'Fine.' I kept my face straight.

'And Charlie, I have a surprise for you, I hope you'll be pleased; I called up the Vicar in your own village – well, it's only maybe forty miles from here – and he was, well sort of hesitant at first about your church-attendance record, he said he couldn't recollect seeing you there since he confirmed you thirty years ago, but I told him how the Archbishop had officially written you down as a Church of Englander and anyway he finally came around and said, Okay, he'd stick his neck out.'

'He said *that*?'

'Well, no, what he said was something kind of sad and resigned in Latin or maybe Greek but you could tell that was what he meant.'

'Quite so.' I'd have given a lot to have heard that bit of Latin or maybe Greek, for our Vicar has a pretty wit.

'Oh, yes, and he said how about a best man and I said "Oh Golly" and he said he'd round up your brother Lord Mortdecai to do it. Isn't that lovely?'

'*Quite* lovely,' I said heavily.

'You're not cross, are you, Charlie? Are you? Oh, and he can't get the choir together on a weekday morning, he's real sorry about that; do you mind terribly?'

'I can bear it with fortitude.'

'Ah, but his wife has a gang of ladies who sing Bach and I told him yes, great.'

'Splendid,' I said, sincere at last.

'And the organist is going to play "Sheep May Safely Graze" before the ceremony and "*Amanti Costanti*" from *Le Nozze de Figaro* as we go out: how *about* that?'

'Johanna, you are brilliant, I love you excessively, I should have married you years ago.' I almost meant it.

Then she came and sat on my knee and we nuzzled and chewed each other's faces a goodish bit and murmured sweet nothings and so forth. Pleasant for a while but it becomes a trifle painful for the male half of the sketch, doesn't it?

Johanna said she wanted an early night and would have sandwiches sent up to her room, and as soon as I could stand up I escorted her thither.

'Not before time,' said the look on the face of a passing chambermaid.

Back in my room I sank wearily into a chair and lifted the telephone.

'Room service?' I said. 'How many oysters have you in the hotel?'

6 Mortdecai reaps his reward and gets reaped a bit himself

You must wake and call me early, call me early, mother dear;
. . . It seemed so hard at first, mother . . .
But still I think it can't be long before I find release;
And that good man, the clergyman, has told me words of peace.

The May Queen

The marriage which had been arranged, as the newspapers say, took place, as the newspapers say, the next day at noon. The Vicar preached ripely and briefly, the ladies' Bach Group sang like little cock-angels, the organist made his organ peal like Kraft-Ebbing's onion (sorry) and, of course, my brother almost made me puke. The fact that his morning clothes were clearly the work of that genius in Cork Street, whereas mine had been hired in Kendal from a firm which had once made a pair of spats for the Duke of Cambridge, had nothing to do with my disgust. It was his *unction*.

After the ceremony, to make quite sure that he had spoiled my day, he drew me aside and asked me, infinitely tactfully, whether I was quite sure that I could really afford to support a wife who dressed so well, and could he help. While asking this he flicked compassionate glances at the set of my alleged coat around the shoulders.

'Oh yes, I think I can manage, Robin, but thanks for the offer.'

'Then she must be the relict of Milton Q. Krampf, who died the other month in odd circumstances, hmh?'

'I fancy that was his name – why?'

'Nothing at all, dear boy, nothing at all. But do always remember that you have a home here, won't you.'

'Thank you, Robin,' I said, gnashing mentally. How can a chap as nice as me have a brother like that?

Then he wanted us all to go up to the Hall for champagne and things but I put my foot down; I had taken enough stick for one day and I certainly was not going to bare my buttocks for more. Why, he might even have unlocked his wife from wherever he keeps her, like something from *Jane Eyre*. 'Brrrr,' I thought.

So we went to the pub across the road and ordered an Old-Fashioned (Johanna), a split of Roederer (Robin), a Bourbon on the rocks (Blucher), a glass of milk (me) and a half of bitter (the Vicar). The congregation behind us – retired chaps, unemployed chaps and a few idle window-cleaners and coffin-makers – murmured 'rhubarb, rhubarb' while the landlady told us that she hadn't got any of that except the half of bitter. In the end we settled for brandy and soda all round except for the Vicar and the unemployed chaps. (Goodness, have you ever tasted cheap brandy? Don't, don't.) Robin insisted on paying, he loves to do things like that and he loves to count the change, it makes him happy.

Then I went to the lav and changed my clothes and gave the hireling garments to Blucher to return to the honest artisan in Kendal – I enjoyed making him do that. Soon afterwards we parted in a spaghetti-like tangle of insincere matiness – except for the Vicar, who was doing his Christian best to believe that we were all nice chaps – and went our separate ways.

My separate way was to be driven two-hundred-odd miles to London in what Johanna called 'a cute little British auto' – a Jensen Interceptor. She had no patience with the absurd British affectation of using the left-hand side of the road; I probably secreted more adrenalin in those four hours than Niki Lauda uses in a whole Grand Prix season.

White and quaking, I was decanted at Brown's Hotel, London, W1, where Johanna firmly sent me to bed for a nap with a huge pottle of brandy and soda. It was, of course, good brandy this time. Sleep, Nature's kindly nurse, ravelled up the sleeve of care until dinner-time, when I arose with my nerve-endings more or less adequately darned. We dined in the hotel, which spares me the trouble of saying how good the dinner was. The waiter, who to my certain knowledge has been there since 1938, murmured into my ear that he could recommend the mustard: a statement that has never failed to charm me. Indeed, those were the very words, spoken by that very waiter, which first opened my youthful eyes on the enchanted landscape of gastronomy, long, long ago. (Few men and almost no women understand about mustard, you must have noticed that. They think that mustard-powder and water mixed five minutes before dinner makes a condiment; you and I know that this is merely a poultice for sore feet.)

Then we went to the River Room or the Saddle Room or whichever night-club it was that year; my heart was not really in it. I moodily ordered a plate of radishes to throw at passing dancers of my acquaintance but my aim was poor and I desisted after a professional wrestler offered to tear my leg off and beat me with the wet end. Johanna was in tearing high spirits and laughed merrily; she almost charmed away my sense of doom and inadequacy.

Back at the hotel, she showed no signs of fatigue; what she did show me was a nightdress which could have gone through the mail as a postcard if there had been enough space on it to accommodate a postage-stamp.

Only a few of the oysters seemed to be pulling their weight but I was pretty good the first time.

My mental clock is amazingly good: at 10.31 I opened a petulant eye and croaked a complaint to Jock. Where, where, was the life-giving cup of tea, the balm which, at 10.30 precisely, brings the Mortdecais of this world back to some kind of membership of the human race? 'Jock!' I croaked again, desperately. A throaty, girlish voice beside me murmured that Jock wasn't around. I swivelled a bloodshot eyeball and focused it on my bride. She was wearing that absurd nightdress again – it seemed to have lost its shoulder-straps. She was sitting up, toying with *The Times* crossword; the garment in question only afforded modesty because her nipples were supporting it like a pair of chapel hat-pegs. I shut my eyes firmly.

'Charlie darling?'

'Grmblumblegroink,' I said, unconvincingly.

'Charlie dearest, can you think of a word of seven letters beginning with "m" and ending with a double "e" and meaning "an extra performance in the afternoon"?'

'Matinée,' I mumbled.

'But doesn't "*matin*" mean morning, Charlie?'

'Yes, well, the original meaning of matinée was "a way of amusing oneself in the morning",' I said learnedly. A moment later I could have bitten off my tongue.

Luckily, one intelligent, public-spirited oyster had been holding itself in reserve against just such a contingency.

It really is quite astonishing how sex affects the sexes. I mean, it usually leaves the chap tottering about and feeling like a disposable dish-rag in search of an incinerator, whereas the female half of the sketch tends to skip about uttering glad cries and exhibiting only those delightful smudges under the eyes which head-waiters would notice. Another by-product of the primal act in women is that they exhibit a frenetic desire to go shopping.

'Charlie, dear,' said Johanna, 'I think I shall go shopping. I hear you have a cute little street right here in London called Bond Street, right? Kind of a poor man's Rue de Rivoli?'

'More of a rich man's *Marché des Puces*,' I said, 'but you have the general idea. Almost any taxi-driver will know the way there; it's almost a furlong. Don't overtip. Have fun. I'll go to my bank, I think.'

That was where I went, on foot, for the good of my health. This journey involved passing through the more Chinese parts of Soho – for reasons which I shall presently make clear – and I chanced to glance through the window of a particularly well-set-up-looking restaurant. To my amazement, there sat Johanna, deep in conversation with a portly person who looked like an owner of such a place. She did not see me.

Now, you do not have to be a natural worrier to worry a little at the sight of your bride deep in conversation with Soho restaurant-owners when she has assured you that she is shopping in Bond Street, nor do you have to be a jealous or suspicious man to feel a stirring of curiosity as to what such a bride could possibly have to discuss with such a restaurant-owner. I mean, I had papers to prove that Johanna was my ever-loving wife; I had her word for it that she was in Bond Street, snapping up bargains in wild mink and such, and the restaurant-owner's best friend would have felt bound to admit that he, the restaurant-manager, was as Chinese as a restaurant-owner can be, even in Soho.

Pray do not for a moment think that I dislike Chinese chaps; some of my best friends are those who make life beautiful with spare-ribs cooked in oyster sauce, not to mention pieces of duck swaddled in pancakes. No, what disturbed me was a certain wrongness about this situation, a wrongness which imparted an all-too-familiar twitching pang in the soles of my feet. Johanna, you see, was not a liar in the way that ordinary wives are liars. Although my acquaintance with her so far had been brief and torrid, I had formed the opinion that she was too rich, too self-confident, too *clever* to resort to lying in day-to-day matters.

Why, then, was she not in Bond Street, as advertised, scribbling her signature on Travellers' Cheques and scooping up emerald parures and things?

What I did was what I always do when in doubt: I telephoned Jock.

'Jock,' I said, for this was his name, you see, 'Jock, are you still friends with that rough, ugly, deaf-and-dumb night watchman at those publishers in Soho Square?'

'Yeah,' he said succinctly.

'Then straddle your great motor-bike, Jock, scoop up this sturdy, deaf-and-dumb friend and drop him in Gerrard Street. He is to enter a restaurant called the No Tin Fuk and order a simple, nourishing repast. Give him some money for this because I am sure those publishers he works for keep him short of the readies. When in the restaurant he is to watch, guardedly, a beautiful blonde lady called Mrs M. – yes, the one I married the other day – and to use his skill at lip-reading. She will be talking to a portly Chinese gentleman; I long to know what she is saying.'

'Right, Mr Charlie.'

'Make all haste, Jock, please.'

'That's us you hear coming round the corner,' he said.

I replaced the receiver in a courteous position then trotted puzzledly off to my bank. This was not my real bank, where I keep my overdraft, it's what I call my Savings Bank. It isn't even a Savings Bank in any ordinary sense of the word: it is the long-established premises of the most learned print-seller in London, an ancient person who does not approve of me for reasons which I do not understand. Why I call him my Savings Bank is as follows: I have a large and lavishly-produced book called *The Complete Etchings of Rembrandt van Rijn*. Every etching R. van R. ever etched is reproduced in its exact size and so exquisitely that it is hard to believe that they are not the originals. Moreover, these illustrations are 'tipped in', which means that they are printed separately and just lightly gummed to the pages by one edge. Whenever I have a few pennies to spare in my pocket, pennies which I might not want to confuse the nice tax-man with, I trundle round to the said print-dealer and buy a Rembrandt etching from him. A real one, of course, for he sells no others. This purchase takes some little while because he is an honest man, you see, and honest men can afford to stick out for the real price. Unlike some I could name.

When I have bought such an etching I toddle home, rip out the appropriate illustration in the *Complete Etchings*, and lovingly replace it with the real one I have just bought. Your common burglar would not dream of nicking such a book but, as it stands today, it's worth about a quarter of a million in any large city in the world. Decent chaps like me scarcely ever have to flee for our lives but, if we must, it's nice to have our savings with us unobtrusively. Your common Customs Officer, bless him, is unlikely to spare a glance for a fat, dull art-book with little or no pornographic content, carried by a fat, dull art-dealer.

The ancient dealer, on this occasion, grudgingly admitted that he had a pretty fine second-state impression of 'The Three Trees' with thread margins, and gave me the sort of look which art-dealers give you when they are pretty sure that you cannot afford the work of art in question. I, however, was embarrassingly flush with money from my American caper and said disdainfully that what I really had in mind was an impression of the first state of that etching, on vellum. He reminded me that there was only one such example, which happens to be in Samuel Pepys's scrapbook in the Library of a place called Magdalene College, which is in a town called Cambridge, famed for its unsound scholarship and web-footed peasantry. Forty minutes later he handed over the etching and gave me a glass of better sherry than you would think, while I parted with a sheaf of great, vulgar currency-notes. Over his largest print-cabinet he has a mahogany tablet inscribed with the words of one of my favourite authors, Psalms xx, 14: '*It is naught, it is naught, sayeth the buyer: but when he is gone his way, then he boasteth.*' As I lurched out, grumbling, he directed my attention to this.

'There's an even better writer,' I snarled, 'called Psalms xxviii, 20, and *he* says *He that maketh haste to be rich shall not be innocent!*' I thought I had him there but he blandly asked me which of us I was referring to. You can't win, you see, you can't win. Ordinary art-dealers are human beings in their spare time but honest print-sellers are a race apart.

Here is what us scholars call an excursus. If you are an honest man the following page or two can be of no possible interest to you. You are an honest man? You are sure of that? Very well, turn to page 214, because this part is only about how people deploy sums of money which used to belong to other people.

Taking large slabs of money away from other people is, I am told, a simple action for anyone who is strong and brave and doesn't lose any sleep after hitting people on the head or breaking the law in other ways. Getting it into the fiscal system again in one's own favour is a different matter altogether. Take a few examples, starting from the bottom.

(A) Your simple villain whose only task in the caper was nicking a get-away car just before the event and wiping the fingerprints or 'dabs' off it afterwards. He gets perhaps £500 in used one-pound notes and, regardless of his superiors' warnings, splashes them about in his local pub, buying drinks for one and all. The boys in blue pick him up within 72 hours and kindly ask him to tell them the names of his superiors. He does not tell them, not out of honour-amongst-thieves but because his superiors have been too smart to let him know their names. This is unfortunate for the simple villain because the fuzz has to make quite sure that he does not know. He is often *tired* when he finally comes up before the magistrate.

(B) The slightly less simple villain with a sensible streak of cowardice who learns of the capture of villain (A) and, at dead of night, takes his £1000 in used notes, dumps them in the nearest public lavatory, telephone-kiosk or other evil-smelling place and, in the morning, resumes his honest trade of scrap-metal merchant or whatever.

(C) The mealy-mouthed person who did nothing but 'finger' the caper slits open his Softa-Slumba mattress and tucks his £25,000 therein while his wife is getting her blue-rinse at the hairdressers. After eight or nine months, when he thinks all is safe, he buys a bungalow and pays the deposit in cash. Two nice gentlemen from the Inland Revenue call in for a chat; they go away quite satisfied. While he is heaving sigh of relief, two other nice gentlemen in blue uniforms call in for a chat and suggest that he pack a toothbrush and a pair of pyjamas.

(D) Now we are among the Brass, the higher echelons of the piece of villainy under discussion. This villain, called (D), is old-fashioned; he believes that a numbered account in a Swiss bank is as safe as the Houses of Parliament. He hasn't heard about Guy Fawkes. He has heard about Interpol but he believes it is designed to protect chaps like him – chaps who have numbered accounts in Swiss banks. His trial is long, expensive and complicated. He gets a nice job in the prison library but *horrid* things happen to him in the showers.

(E) He thinks that he can run for it; he has two passports. His share is, perhaps, £150,000. His arithmetic is not good: that kind of money is very nice in, say, South Norwood, but it sort of dwindles as you scoot around the world at today's prices, especially if you feel bound to arrange for your ever-loving wife to meet you in Peru or places like that.

(F) Yes, well, (F) is nearly the smartest of the bunch. First he tucks away a handy little sum like £20,000 in a safe place in case he gets nicked. (£20,000 will get you out of any prison in the world, everyone knows that.) Then he takes the rest of his ill-gotten g's and, having bought a dinner-jacket far above his station in life, he joins one of those gaming-clubs where they sneer at you if you are seen with anything so plebeian as a £10 note. He buys a couple of hundred poundsworth of chips; plays at this table and that and, in the small hours of the morning, gives the lovely cashier-lady a handful of chips and bank-notes, say, £2000, telling her to credit his account. He gives her a tenner for herself and she assumes that he has won. He does this discreetly for months, sometimes seeming to lose but usually winning. Every once in a while the lovely cashier-lady tells him that he has an awful lot of money in his account and he lets a big cheque which he can prove to be gambling-winnings slide into his account at the bank. You can legalize about a hundred thousand a year in this way if you are careful.

(G) He is the man who organized the whole thing. (G) is very rich already. There are no problems for him; his holding-companies can make his one-third of a million vanish like a snowflake on a frying-pan. I'm sure there's a moral there somewhere.

If it comes to that, I daresay there's a better moral in my book of Rembrandt etchings.

Back in my slum on the fourth floor in Upper Brook Street (W1) (I know it's a duplex, but I still think it's robbery at £275 a week) I was happily tipping-in my new purchase into the *Complete Etchings* when Jock sidled in.

'Jock,' I said severely, 'I have repeatedly asked you not to sidle. I will not have this sidling. It smacks of the criminal classes. If you wish to better yourself you must learn to shimmer. What's the name of those naval-outfitter chaps at the Piccadilly end of Bond Street?'

'Gieves?'

'That's it. There you are, you see,' I said, completely vindicated. Jock is not good at these things. He waited until I had fully relished my vindication; then he uttered.

'I got what rows 'e wrote.' I stared at the fellow. He showed none of the outward signs of brain-disease but these signs would not necessarily have been apparent, you see, for it is well known in art-dealing circles that you could stuff Jock's brain into any hedgehog's navel without causing the little creature more than a moment's passing discomfort, while Jock, on his part, would not notice the loss until the next time he played dominoes.

'What rows who wrote?' I asked at length.

'Nah, *Rosie*,' he said, 'me deaf-and-dumb mate. It's his monniker.'

'Goodness, is he one of *those*? How awkward for him, with his disabilities. I mean, however does he lisp and titter in sign-language?'

'Nah. His whole monniker is Rosenstein or Rosinbloom or one of them Eyetalian names but he doesn't like you to use it because he hates foreigners.'

'I see. Well, let's have it.' He handed me a newspaper folded open at the Sports Page, around the margins of which Rosie had done his dictation. I gave him marks for camouflage: the only way a ruffianly publisher's nark can be seen reading or writing without arousing suspicion is when he is at work picking his daily loser, and figuring out what a pound each way at nine to four will bring in after tax.

This is what he had written. 'I cooden get sat were I cood see the Chink's moosh but I cood see the lady ok she has lovly lips –' I frowned here '– I cood read ever word she said.' I unfrowned. 'She said No Mr Lee i have explained befor I don't want a million pounds. I already have a million pounds. I want the use of your organization. I have the women and you have the organization. I want to sell no part of my end. You will do very well out of your part of the operation. I can finance my self. Now for the last time is it a deal or not. Good. Now I must go shopping. I hav to buy my husband a present to put him in a good mood for what I am goin to ask him to do about the womin.'

I read it again and again. Aghast is the only word for what I was. Of course I had no illusion about Johanna's saintliness – she was very rich, wasn't she? – but the White Slave Trade! The sheer brilliance and audacity of reviving that wonderfully old-fashioned way of turning an honest million dazzled me. Johanna was, clearly, even cleverer than I had thought. The only bit that gnawed at my conscience was the suggestion that I was to be involved. It has always been my policy that wives should be free, nay, encouraged to do their own things but that spouses should not be conscripted. Let wives give cocktail parties until the distillery runs dry, but do not ask me to be polite to their awful friends. Let them take up knitting or some such wholesome exercise, but do not expect me to hold the wool. Above all, let them dabble in a little lucrative illegality – but on no account ask C. Mortdecai to participate except in helping to spend the proceeds with his well-known good taste.

White-slaving, you see, is strictly against the law. That is well-known. I might get *caught*; think how my friends would chuckle. Goodness, how they would chuckle if, after all the dubious capers I have survived, I were to be 'sent up the stairs' for living off the immoral earnings of naughty ladies.

I don't know how the ordinary man in the street reacts to musing furiously for a few hours at having learned that his newly wedded wife is a big wheel in the white-slaving trade. Some would doubtless fish out a little pocket calculator and start figuring percentages. Others would pack a bag and run for their lives. I would have telephoned Col. Blucher and told him all, but he had refused to give me any procedure for getting in touch with him for the nonce; this would come later, he promised me, but in the meantime I was to 'play it by ear'. (He had translated this for me as: 'Feel for your own handholds, Mortdecai; it's only a very small mountain you have to climb. Just *kid* yourself that there's a guy above you with a rope. You'll make out. I guess.')

Since that telephone call was denied me I adopted Alternative Plan B, which involves taking a firm handhold upon a bottle of Scotch and reading a few pages of the adventures of people called Mulliner, as related by the late P.G. Wodehouse. It was, after a while, difficult to concentrate because the doorbell rang and rang as obsequious chaps delivered huge cardboard boxes full of Johanna's shopping-loot, but when she at last arrived in person I was mellowed by Mulliner tales and, I suppose, not a little soothed by the healing Scotch whisky. What I was not in was a honeymoon frame of mind.

She embraced me with all the innocent fervour of a bride who has never said anything to a Chinese restaurant-proprietor more compromising than a shy request for a doggy-bag. She ran in and out of the bedroom, ripping open valuable cardboard boxes and parading before me wearing their contents. I made suitable noises but my heart was not in it. To tell the truth, my conscience, with whom I had not been on speaking terms for twenty years, was murmuring that the boxes alone would have kept a starving stockbroker in cigars for a week. For her last trick she appeared in a piece of night-wear which made her previous night's garment look like something a retired headmistress might wear in the Arctic Circle. I cringed.

'Johanna,' I said as she sat on my knee.

'Mhm?'

I cleared my throat. 'Johanna darling, is there anything good on the television tonight?'

'No.'

'How can you be so sure?'

'There never is.'

'But shall we just look at the newspaper to make sure? I mean, we might be missing an old Gary Cooper or Humphrey Bogart or . . .'

'Tonight,' she said in a firm but loving voice, 'there is nothing whatever on the television. Unless . . .' she cast an appraising eye on the large, solidly-built television set '. . . well, I guess I could sort of lean over it? I mean, if you *really* want something on the TV?'

'Try not to be immodest, I beg of you,' I said in a distant, British sort of voice. 'What you are trying to say, evidently, is that since there is nothing on the television you would prefer to spend the evening at the cinema.'

'The movie-houses are all closed.' I couldn't tell her that she lied, could I? Nor could I explain, in so many words, that an hour or so watching *Naughty Knickers* or *Adventures of a Teenage Window-cleaner* might inflame me to the point where I could forget the terrifying wench-mongering trade in which she was about to involve me and summon up enough of the Old Adam to play the part of the lust-crazed bridegroom.

I made her two, or it might have been three, strong – hopefully soporific – drinks, then followed her to bed.

7   Mortdecai is given an order which no decent man would even consider for a moment

It was my duty to have loved the highest:
It surely was my profit had I known:
It would have been my pleasure had I seen.

Guinevere

Later that night, my confidence in the invigorating powers of the vitamins E and B12 once again ratified, I was sinking into a well-earned hoggish slumber when Johanna prodded me and said:

'Charlie, little stallion, I want you to do something . . .'

'Darling, we've only just . . . I mean, I'm not a young man, I've explained that before . . . perhaps in the morning, eh?'

'Silly, I didn't mean that; what do you think I am, a nymphomaniac or something?'

I mumbled something sort of reprieved and perhaps ungallant, nuzzling back sleepily between her warm, damp breasts.

'What I want you to do is something *quite* different.' I stirred; the words strained and sifted through the well-earned slumbrousness already referred to. Misgiving took me by the throat; I could almost feel my teeth rattle.

'Darling Johanna,' I said in as reasonable a voice as I could muster, 'wouldn't *tomorrow* night be a better time for anything, ah, *far-out* that you have in mind? I mean . . .' she giggled.

'Yes, Charlie dear, I know that you are no longer a young man – although you could fool most people.' I smirked. 'In the dark, of course,' she continued, spoiling it for me. 'No, I don't want you to tax your beautiful glands. Well, just the adrenalin ones maybe. I just want you to kill someone for me. OK.?'

'Kill someone?' I burbled sleepily. 'Certainly. Any time. Slay a dragon or two with pleasure, any time. Any time after breakfast, that is. Got to get my sleep now, d'you see.'

She shook my shoulder, which only made me nuzzle more firmly, more determined to sleep. Then she shook a much more vulnerable limb and I awoke indignantly.

'I say,' I said, 'don't do that! Might damage a chap. And where would you be then, eh? Make a nonsense of your honeymoon, you can see that, I'm sure. G'night.'

She sat up in bed in a peremptory fashion, taking most of the bedclothes with her. There was nothing to do but awake. I awoke. I shall not pretend that my mood was mild.

'My dear Johanna, this is neither the time nor the occasion for tantrums. All the world over, chaps and their charming bedmates are zizzing away for all they are worth, irrespective of colour or creed, coiling in the tissue-restoring eight or nine hours. You asked something of me which I agreed to accomplish tomorrow. Can't recall what it was but I'm delighted to fall in with your lightest wish. Tomorrow. Whatever it is.'

'Oh, Charlie, have you forgotten already? I simply asked you to kill someone for me. It doesn't seem much to ask one's bridegroom on one's honeymoon. However, if it's too much trouble . . .'

'Not at all; don't be petulant, darling. It'll be the work of a moment, work of a moment. Just give Jock the feller's name and address and he'll see to it the day after tomorrow. Goodnight again, sweetheart.'

'Charlie!'

'Oh well, all right, I suppose he could manage it *tomorrow* night but he'll have to scout about for a pistol with no history, you understand. I mean, I couldn't ask him to use his own Luger on this feller, could I? You see that, surely?'

'Charlie, the person to be killed isn't a, uh, feller. In fact you'd probably think it improper to call her a person, even.'

'You speak in riddles, Johanna of my heart,' I sighed. 'Who is this august "she" – the Queen of bloody England?'

She clapped her hands together, as pleased as a little girl.

'Oh Charlie, you guessed, you guessed!'

I distinctly remember saying 'good-morning' to Jock next morning.

'Good morning, Jock' were the words I selected, for they never fail to please.

'Morning, Mr Charlie,' he rejoined, setting the tea-tray down within reach of my quaking hand. 'Breakfast?' he asked.

'Buttered eggs, I think, please.'

'Right, Mr Charlie. Scrambled eggs.'

'Buttered eggs,' I repeated (but Jock will not yield on this point of language) 'and very runny. Do not agitate them too much, I detest the gravelly appearance: a well-buttered egg should appear as large, soft, creamy clots. Like Roedean schoolgirls, *you* know.'

'Toast?' was all the reaction I got out of him.

'Well, of course toast. Toast-making is one of your few talents; I may as well get the good of it while you still have possession of your faculties.'

You can't get through Jock's guard – his riposte was like a flash of lightning. 'And an Alka-Seltzer, I reckon?' he said. Game, set and match to him, as ever.

'Please salt the eggs for me,' I said by way of conceding defeat, 'I always overdo it and spoil them. And do please remember, the fine, white pepper for eggs, not the coarse-ground stuff from the Rubi.' (Cipriani of Harry's Bar in Venice once told me why waiters of the better sort call that huge pepper-grinder a 'Rubi': it is in honour of the late, celebrated Brazilian playboy Porfirio Rubirosa. I don't understand it myself because my mind is pure.)

Jock pretended not to be listening; this is an easy trick if you happen not to be listening and one quite unfair to an employer who is in the throes of struggling to the surface of wakefulness.

'Sod him,' I thought bitterly. Then I remembered.

'By the way, Jock,' I said casually . . . (If you happen to be a physician in General Practice, God forbid, you will be all too familiar with the 'By the way, Doctor' gambit. It works like this: a chap is concerned because his left testicle has turned bright green, so he goes to his croaker or physician and complains of headaches and constipation. Having collected his prescriptions he starts to exit and then, his hand on the doorknob, turns back and casually mumbles 'By the way, Doctor, it's probably nothing of interest but . . .')

'By the way, Jock,' I said casually, 'Mrs Mortdecai wants the Queen shot.'

'Awright, Mr Charlie. Did you say two eggs or three?'

'The *Queen*,' I insisted.

'Yeah, I heard you. You mean the old ponce what runs the drag-club down Twickenham way. I'll do him tomorrow night, no sweat. You'll have to give me a score to buy an old throwaway shooter, though, I'm not using me good Luger.'

'No, no, Jock. I refer to Her Majesty Queen Elizabeth the II, whom God preserve and upon whom the sun never sets, etcetera.' He fell silent; anyone who didn't know him might well have thought that he was thinking.

'Jock,' I said sternly after a while, 'your glass eye is leaking. Pray take it out and wipe it.'

' 'Tisn't watering. It's crying,' he said in an ashamed but defiant voice.

'Eh?'

'Yeah, well, she's a lovely lady, isn't she? She never bought me no beer but she never did no one no harm, did she?'

I know how to deal with rhetorical questions; you don't answer them.

'Couldn't we just do the Earl of —'

'*No!*'

'— or Princess — I mean no one would . . .'

'The *Queen*,' I said firmly. 'For personal reasons, such as fear, cowardice, patriotism etcetera, I am as reluctant as you to perform this dastardly act but international politics says the deed must be done. So does my wife. Two eggs, please.'

'Two eggs,' he muttered, shambling out of the room.

How dearly I would have loved to sink back into innocent sleep but matters of great moment had me by the lug-hole and furthermore Jock sulks if I let my eggs grow cold. I ate them up, every scrap, although they were far from perfect. As I ate, I planned.

An hour later, carelessly clad and deliberately unshaven, I went off to consult my gunsmith. I don't mean my real gunsmith, of course; he is a bishop-like personage who presides over dim, hushed premises near St James's Palace and knows the difference between a gentleman and a person. The chap I was going to see is what you might call my other gunsmith, a chap of great dishonesty who sells illegal firearms to *persons* and whose only work-bench skills are fitting new barrels to pistols which have been in a little trouble and sawing off a few inches from shotgun barrels. He believes me to be a sort of Gentleman Jim The Country House Jewel Thief and I have not thought fit to correct this belief. He does not know my name, naturally. His only points of principle are to refuse credit, to refuse cheques and to refuse to sell firearms to Irishmen. This last is not because he dislikes the Irish or their politics, but for their own good. He is not convinced that they will hold the weapon the right way round, you see, and he likes his customers to come back.

He greeted me with his usual surliness: dealers in illegal firearms almost never smile, you must have noticed that. He was discreetly clad in a filthy singlet and underpants and the carrotty hair with which he is matted was dark with sweat. He had been making toffee-apples, you see, for this is his 'front', and the darkened, poky room into which he admitted me was fiercely hot and heavy with the stench of boiling sugar, rotten fruit and gun-oil. The murmur of wasps and blow-flies in the immemorial toffee-vats was quite terrifying to me. (As a child I once swallowed a wasp in a glass of lemonade; it stung me on the left tonsil and my mother feared – in a half-hearted but well-bred way – for my life. Nowadays I *stamp* on wasps when the conservation chaps aren't looking.)

'Hello, Ginge!' I cried.

'Oy, mate,' he replied.

'Look, Ginge, do you think we could go into another room? I'm wearing silk underclothes, you see, and they're horrid when one sweats.'

With ill grace he led me into a little, overstuffed back-parlour which was as icy as the workshop had been tropical. With unconscious grace he threw a stolen mink bolero around his shoulders and squatted on a horsehair-covered tuffet. I must say he did look droll but I didn't dare to snigger; he is very strong and rough and famous throughout the Borough of Poplar for hitting people in vulnerable parts on the smallest provocation.

'A friend of mine . . .' I began.

'Oh, ah,' he sneered.

'A friend of mine,' I repeated firmly, 'does a little commercial poaching – or culling – of deer in the Highlands of Scotland the Brave. He has a large standing order for venison from an hotel whose name I seem to forget. The police have taken his rifle away and are being stuffy about giving it back. He needs another. What have you got, Ginge?'

'Nuffink,' he said.

'He's a bit particular about his guns,' I went on. 'He likes something with a bit of class. And it's got to be a stopper, a high-velocity job, something with real clout.'

'I got nuffink like that.'

'And the ammunition must be fresh; no stale old ex-army rubbish.'

'I gotter go now, mate.'

'And, of course, a good telescopic sight.'

'Fuck off.'

So far, the dialogue was going well, the protocol was in the best tradition. Dealing with chaps like Ginge is extraordinarily like negotiating with a Soviet Trade Delegation. I fished out the flat half-bottle of whisky and tossed it to him. He drank from the bottle, dirty dog, and didn't pass it back. He belched, thrust a hand into his underpants and scratched thoughtfully.

'Got a Mannlicher,' he grunted after another swig. I made a sympathetic face and suggested a course of penicillin. He ignored that.

'Pre-war.'

'No.'

'Clip holds three.'

'Useless.'

'Belonged to a Count.'

'A *what*?'

'Count. What they call a Graf. Got a coat of arms on the lock-plate, all in gold and stuff.'

'Worse and worse.'

'And it ain't never been in no trouble. Guarantee.'

'You begin to half-interest me, Ginge.'

'Two hundred and eighty quid. Cash.'

I stood up. 'Next millionaire I meet I'll tell him about it. Cheers, Ginge.'

'Lovely Zeiss 'scope on it, × 2½.'

'× 2½!' I squeaked (you try squeaking the phrase '× 2½'). 'That's no use, is it?'

'Look,' he said, 'if you need more than that on 'scope you don't want a rifle, you want a bleeding anti-aircraft gun.'

I began to sulk in good earnest and he sensed it instantly; he has that sixth sense which stands Armenian carpet-dealers in such good stead. He stole out and returned with a slim, elegant leather case which he dumped into what I still like to call my lap. It contained the Mannlicher in three easily assembled parts; the sniperscope, a fitted torch for shooting crocodiles or mistresses by night, and two hundred pounds of pretty fresh 7.65 mm ammunition, not to mention a rosewood cleaning-rod, a silver oil-bottle, a crested silver sandwich-box, a roll of 4″ × 2″ flannelette and a tool-kit complete with the thing for picking Boy Scouts out of Girl Guides' knickers. It was quite beautiful; I longed to own it.

'You could get a fortune for this from an antique-dealer,' I yawned, 'but my friend wants something to shoot things with. No one has used a toy like this since Goering roamed the primeval swamps.'

'Two hundred and seventy-five quid,' he said, 'that's me last word.'

Twenty minutes, two bursts of ill temper and half a bottle of Scotch later, I left owning the rifle and having paid two hundred pounds, which we had both known all along was what I was going to pay.

'What's that old load of rubbish for then?' asked Jock surlily when I brought it home.

'It's what we're going to do that job with.'

'You can. I'm not,' he said.

'Jock!'

'I'm British. By the way, it's me night off, innit, and I'm off playing dominoes. There's some cold pork in the fridge. Madam's out, gorn to some pub called the Clarence House.'

I waved an icy, dismissive hand. Things were bad enough without having to bandy words with uppity servants who couldn't muster up enough loyalty to join their indulgent masters in so traditional an old English practice as a spot of regicide.

The cold pork in the fridge was wilting at the edges; it and I exchanged looks of mutual contempt, like two women wearing the same hat in the Royal Enclosure at Ascot. I changed into a slightly nattier suit and went off to Isow's, where I ate more than was good for me. One always does at Isow's, but it's worth it.

I retired early to the narrow bed in my dressing-room, for I needed to digest and furiously to muse and plan. I heard Johanna open the door a fraction – I made convincing zizzing-noises and she crept away. I heard the merest rattle and clink as she dropped her tiara into the jewel-box, then all was silence.

I continued to muse and plan. By the time I fell asleep I had formulated a tripartite plan:

(1) Obtain an impenetrable disguise.

(2) Select a sniper's post.

(3) Arrange an escape-route.

Something attempted, something done had earned a night's repose and a night's repose was what I got, broken only by those contented noises from the digestive tract familiar to all who have dined at Isow's. Well, I had some nasty dreams, too, but I have always maintained that relating one's dreams is the third most boring a man can do. I need not tell you what the other two are.

8   Mortdecai dips a terrified toe into the shark-infested waters of regicide

O purblind race of miserable men,
How many among us at this very hour
Do forge a lifelong trouble for ourselves,
By taking true for false, or false for true!

Geraint and Enid

The suit was dreadful, quite dreadful. Clearly, it had been made for a colour-blind Roumanian pimp or perhaps ponce in the 1940s. The checks of the blue-and-orange pattern were, it must be admitted, not much larger than an ordinary packet of cigarettes: perhaps the pimp or ponce had been aiming at an inconspicuous effect. There were no dirty postcards in the pockets, nor any factory-reject french letters: this reassured me that it had at least been to the dry-cleaners. I bought it in a shop called GENTS' WARDROBES PURCHASED and indeed its folds draped themselves from my shoulders in just the manner of a plywood wardrobe. GENTS' WARDROBES PURCHASED also sold me a pair of shoes to match, although these, in their brown-and-white splendour, seemed to date from an even earlier day – a fortune-hunting petty nobleman might well have sported them in the *Salon Privé* at Monte in, say, 1936.

I glanced just once at myself in their fitting-room mirror: under the bludgeonings of suit I may have winced but I swear I did not cry aloud.

There seemed to be no end to the resources of GENTS' W.P. 'Vere,' I asked in my best Mittel-Europ accent, 'Vere could I buy a goot, strong, musical-instrument case for my musical instrument? I vould need vun of about *so* big' – even as I gestured, the hateful suit sliced cruelly into my armpits – 'ze kind dot ze Shicago gangsters used to carry dere sob-moshine gons in, ha ha!'

'Have you come to the right place!' cried Mr G.W.P. merrily. 'Step this way, sir, mind the step; we make a little speciality of musical-instrument cases. There now, I'm sure you'll find the box of your dreams amongst this little lot!' I gave him a suspicious squint, for everyone knows that 'box' has another and naughtier meaning, but he did not seem to be pulling my plonker. There was in truth great store of stoutly-constructed musical-instrument kennels; it was a rare and bizarre sight. I had the measurements of the Mannlicher in my mind's eye (any art-dealer worth his salt can glance at a frame and tell whether it will fit any picture in his stock or whether it can or cannot be cut down to size without altering the sweep of the carving) and I soon selected a perversely-shaped box or case designed, I don't doubt, for a baritone saxophone and haggled over it just long enough to avoid arousing suspicion in G.W.P.'s breast.

I stuffed my execrable gents' natty suiting and co-respondent shoes into the instrument-case and homeward plodded my moody way, as weary as any Stoke Poges ploughman, pausing only at Lillywhite's to buy a checkered golfing-cap of the sort which I had until then believed only to exist in the works of P.G. Wodehouse. I used my Yorkshire accent in Lillywhite's, to throw them off the scent, d'you see. The secret-agent cloak was by now falling across my shoulders so snugly that I felt like an ivy-mantled tower. I aroused, I believe, no suspicion; even without the accent they would have taken me for a North-Country man, no other would buy such a cap.

Jock flicked a baleful eye on the instrument-case when I arrived at the flat. The other, non-baleful eye, the glass one, was pointed at the empyrean or ceiling in a way which suggested that, could it speak, it would have said, 'Oh my Gawd.'

'Pray put this banjo-coffin into the wardrobe in my dressing-room,' I said in dignified, masterly tones, 'and I beg you not to glance inside, for the contents shock even me: the effect of them upon an honest ton of soil like yourself . . .'

'You mean "son of toil", Mr Charlie.'

'Perhaps I do, perhaps I do. Be that as it may, tell me now, without evasion and in your own words, omitting no detail however slight, what is for dinner tonight?'

'Madam is out,' he said smugly. 'Playing bridge.'

'So?' I said haughtily. 'Are you trying to tell me that I must send out or, God forbid, *go* out for dinner? Is there nothing in the pantry? Are you, Jock, supping off bread and cheese? I find this hard to believe, for you were ever one to eat above your station in life.' His eyes glowered, one at the floor, the other at the cornice, above his station in life.

'I was just going to have a bit of a snack,' he mumbled in as civil a voice as he could muster.

'Yes?' I prompted gently.

'Yeah, well, a coupla *blintzes* with caviar inside and some sour cream what I found left over, didn't I, and a few kipper fillets soused with wine I bought out of my own pocket and I can prove it; then nothink but a Minute Steak what was going to waste, wrapped round a liddle concodgion of me own made out of chicken-livers and that.'

'Are you trying to tell me,' I said levelly, 'that there is only enough for you?' He pondered loyally awhile.

'Bit short on the caviar side,' he said at last. I handed him my keys.

'Ten minutes OK, Mr Charlie?'

'You mean ten minutes after you have produced the drinks tray?'

' 'Course.'

'Then; right, Jock.'

'Right, Mr Charlie.'

When Johanna returned I was in bed with an improving book by St Francis de Sales or perhaps Le Marquis de Sade, I forget which, and was not quick enough to snap out the bedside light. She had won at bridge, she always does; this elates her. She was radiant. She sang as she danced about the room, scattering garments both here and there.

We cannot all afford oysters and Guinness's stout but I promise you that there are times when a little £20 jar of Beluga caviar will fill the gap admirably.

The next day, sure that Jock was in his pantry doing useful things and that Johanna was in the shower, I huddled on my new 'clothes' and was about to slink out of the flat unobserved. Johanna caught me in the very act of slinking and staggered about laughing like a little mad thing at the sight of my rainbow garb. She has one of those rippling, silvery laughs which are quite enchanting when they are directed at anyone but oneself.

'Hush!' I commanded. 'If Jock sees me in this suit he will give in his notice. He has his pride, you see.'

'But, Charlie, dearest,' she murmured between one silvery ripple and another, 'why are you dressed as an undertaker? And does the black, important box contain your embalming equipment?'

'I see nothing to laugh at,' I replied stiffly, 'in the sight of a Briton true preparing to assassinate his Sovereign against his better judgment.'

'I am sorry, Charlie,' she said soberly. 'I didn't realize that you were in *disguise.*'

'Well, I jolly well am,' I said.

As I passed the kitchen there was a muffled, flatulent sound, too treble to be one of Jock's.

'Jock,' I said sternly, 'the canary is constipated again. I have no faith in the new vet. Pray telephone the Zoo and ask their advice.'

'Right, Mr Charlie,' he said – and then, *sotto voce*, he said something which sounded like, 'Give him a look at your new suit.'

I walked – nay, slunk – for what seemed miles until I was well away from those parts of London where any friends of mine might live, then I hailed a taxi and directed it to the City, where there was only an outside chance that I might encounter my stockbroker or the chief of my Lloyds' syndicate. In my pocket I had a map of the Royal Route which I had torn out of Jock's newspaper, which is the kind of newspaper which Jock reads. (Fleet Street calls them 'tit-and-bum rags' but Jock is ever faithful to Shirley Temple; what he dearly loves, true-born Briton though he be, is those candid snapshots of junior royals taking an 'arser' from a horse in a *puissance* trial. Perhaps he sometimes also spots the stick of type in the corner which tells of 15,000,000 homeless in West Bengal. Perhaps. His social conscience is a couple of notches higher than the World Council of Churches, but that's about it.) In my pocket, as I was saying before you interrupted me, I had a map of the Royal Route. My *Times* had not specified in the 'Court Circular' – and probably would not say until after the event – which kind of vehicle Her M. would be travelling in but, since this was a State Occasion (a Reception and Luncheon at the Cordwanglers' Hall with foreign royals present), I was hoping that the Royal Party would be in one of the State Landaus – open tops, you see – rather than in one of those great, weighty Daimlers or Rolls-Royces which every amateur assassin knows to be bullet-proof.

My newspaper route-map showed that the Royal Progress was to pass briefly through a grotty little City street on its way to Cordwanglers' Hall and it was to that very street that I directed my cab, and there that I had the cabbie decant me, over-tipping him just enough to give him the impression that I was not a native son of London, but not enough to make him remember me. Those of you who have ever been unlucky enough to be a secret agent or hired assassin will understand how my mind was working.

Up and down the grotty street I toddled, the instrument-case bumping cruelly against my thigh, but not a single BED AND BREAKFAST sign could I descry. What I did descry on my third toddle was a tall, narrow-shouldered, grubby building with the name of a firm of solicitors on the ground-floor windows and an assortment of dirty lace curtains in the windows of the upper floors. A skinny slattern in curlers slouched in the basement area, listlessly pushing dirt about with what had once been a broom.

'Goot mornink!' I said, raising my golfing-cap in a Continental sort of way and smirking amiably. She looked up at me from the 'area'; her eyes were those of a long-retired whore who had never really enjoyed her work.

''E's out,' she said, dismissively.

'I voz wonderink –'

'*Out*,' she repeated. The atmosphere was heavy with the scent of overdue hire-purchase payments.

'I voz wonderink vedder you might haff a small room I could use in ze evenings . . .'

'Yer what?'

'Ya, to play wiz my instroment, you onderstand.'

'Yer *what*?' I realized that, from her position down in the 'area', she could not see my saxophone-case and might have misconstrued me a bit. I raised the case and waggled it.

'My vife,' I explained, 'doz not vish me to play wiz it at home any more. It makes her ongry wiz me.'

' 'Ungry?'

'Ya,' I said, inspired, 'hongry. Then she eat too much, you understand, and become fat an dis spoil our loff-life pecoss I cannot stand fat vomen.' I eyed her with undisguised admiration; she smoothed the ratty house-coat over her skinniness.

Ten minutes later I was the tenant of a second-floor room overlooking the street, having paid a modest rental one month in advance and having agreed that I should only practise my instrument during those hours when the solicitor downstairs was not practising law, that I should not entertain *friends* in the room and that I should not use the bathroom. There was a wash-hand basin in the room, you see, to receive any peremptory calls of nature.

At home that night I passed a hateful couple of hours with my tape-recorder and an album of some overpaid saxophonist of the early 1940s, recording bits and pieces of the fellow's beastly art and repeating phrases again and again as though striving to achieve what a saxophonist would probably call perfection. I shall not name the musician for, who knows, he may well be alive to this day (there is no justice, none) and, to my certain knowledge, the Performing Rights Society is very much alive and poised like a pussy-cat at a mousehole.

For the next few days I played the part. The Great Game. Wore the mask. Worse, I wore the suit and, dear God, the very shoes. Each evening I would creep to that narrow house in that shabby street in the City, clad in the shameful attire, and mount the stairs after fluttering a lecherous eyelash or two at the landlady. Ensconced in the mean room, smelling of undernourished mice (yes, the *room*) I would play over the tape of the nameless saxophonist, occasionally varying the volume, stopping and starting and so forth, while I peered through the window, measuring angles and distances and fields-of-fire until I could stand the bloody saxophone no more, whereupon I would shuffle downstairs, side-step the now clean and lipsticked but still skinny landlady, and pace moodily down the street towards a taxi-point. The moodiness of the pacing, I need hardly say, was because I was pacing out distances in the street and relating them to my field-of-fire. I reckoned that the State Landau would be clocking up a brisk 12 mph on the day. Trigonometry was the only thing I was good at when I was at school. Well, it was the only thing the masters *knew* about that I was good at.

Look, let me make it quite clear that I liked none of this at all, not any of it. I don't speak of wearing clothes which George Melly would scorn, nor of the shoes, the 'banana specials' which still visit me in my dreams. I am speaking, seriously for once, of the basic rottenness of it all. This country had accepted my family, had been good to us, had allowed us to become moderately rich and had never pointed the finger of scorn. Why then was I using all my wits to send its Sovereign to a premature grave? Well, yes, my wife had told me to do it, which is a pretty good reason for most chaps to do most things, especially if, as in this case, there was a strong hint that I might find myself slightly dead if the product did not please. There was also the dread Colonel Blucher, who had made it clear that I was to play along with Johanna until otherwise instructed. None of this made me feel any better about my activities; I was sharply aware that Jock's sense of values was better than mine.

However, in those days I was a man of iron, and was dedicated to the ideal of staying alive – an ideal which seems paltry in retrospect but seemed sensible at the time. Staying alive has a kind of immediacy about it: ask anyone who has been confronted with the choice between life and death.

So I oiled the rifle, visited the horrid house, smirked at the landlady, played the saxophone-tapes, wore the suit, the shoes; nay, even the golfing-cap itself. You have read about the Spartan boy with the fox in his bosom gnawing at his vitals but making no murmur? Very well, I have made myself clear.

'Jock,' I said one morning, to Jock, 'Jock, I need a little help.'

'Mr Charlie,' he said heavily, 'if it's about the matter what we discussed a few days ago, then before you say another word the answer is "no". I wouldn't shop you, not even if it was ever so, you know that, but I carn 'elp. Not with that.'

'Not even a touch of driving after the event?' I wheedled.

'Sorry, Mr Charlie, I coulden turn a wheel of a jam-jar in such circombstations.'

'Very well, Jock, I daresay I shall manage single-handed. I respect your principles and attach no blame to you. But if I should be, ah, *nicked*, may I depend upon you to visit me in the condemned cell?'

' 'Course.'

'And perhaps bring me in a pot or two of caviar? The real Grosrybriest, I mean, not the stuff we put out at parties.'

' 'Course.'

'And perhaps,' I added wistfully, 'a jar or two of those partridge-breasts in jelly, eh? I mean, I hear frightful tales of what prison governors consider "a hearty breakfast" for the chap about to do his hundred-yards dash to the gallows. Greasy mutton chops with chips and beans and, and . . . *things*.'

'Don't you worry your head about none of that, Mr Charlie, I'll see you right, I got friends in them places. Anyway, they done away with capital punishment, didn't they? You won't draw much more than, ooh, say twenty-five years. A doddle. Do it standing on your head. Only thing to remember is, don't let them big black queers catch you in the showers.' I did not shudder for I wished to retain Jock's respect, but the effort cost me a few hundred calories.

'Look, Jock,' I said gently, 'you are right about the abolition of capital punishment but there is one thing they can still top you for.'

'Reely?'

'Yes.'

'Like what?'

'Like High Treason.'

9 Mortdecai prepares to put himself beyond the pale but wishes that he had a better class of landlady

Her manners had not that repose
Which stamps the caste of Vere de Vere.

Lady Clara Vere de Vere

The dreaded day came. As I left the flat Jock wordlessly handed me my hat and umbrella. I refused the latter; it takes more than a mere umbrella to make an assassin feel like a gentleman. Nevertheless, as I waited for the lift, I found myself humming a stave from the National Anthem, the bit about 'Long may she reign'. Clearly, some Freudian bits in the back of my brain were longing for *rain*, you see, so that the Royal party would be travelling in a nice bullet-proof limousine rather than in the open State Landau. London weather let me down, as it always does: the sun shone as mercilessly as a bank-manager's smile.

I travelled by tube – subway? – to the nearest station to my City lodgings and entered the Public Lavatory. (It was early in the day, you see, the Stock Exchange was busy and Parliament was in session so there was little danger of being accosted.) I changed into the suit, the shoes, the cap.

A few minutes later; well, there I was at the window, sliding the telescopic sight onto the Mannlicher, my fingers twitching with trepidation about the abominable act I was about to perform – twitching, too, with fury and revulsion at the way my skinny landlady had unequivocally brushed herself against me on the stairs and suggested that I might join her for 'a glass of summink' in her boudoir.

'Oftervords, oftervords,' I had mumbled, trying to muster a leer although well knowing – nay, hoping – that there would be no oftervords.

So there I was, the lovely Spanish mahogany stock of the rifle becoming more and more slippery with sweat, no matter how often I wiped my guilty hands on the trouser-legs of the hated suit. My wristlet-watch, although a creation of Patek Philippe himself, ticked ever more slowly, as though it had been dipped in the very best butter.

At last there was to be heard a distant sound of hooraying, then a sort of galumphing noise which betokened the advent of horse-drawn carriages full of Royals and their Head of State guests. I wiped the hands once more, allowed the rifle-muzzle to protrude a further inch or two (for I could descry no security-idiots on the rooftops across the street) and cuddled the butt to my shoulder, telescopic eye-piece to watery eye. Here they came – in the bloody State Landau, sure enough – all of them doing that wonderful, inimitable Royal wave of the hand which only Queen Elizabeth the Queen Mother can do properly. Obviously, I couldn't do it: the murder, I mean, not the wave. I must have been mad to have thought that I could. (When St Peter, at the Pearly Gates, gives me that form to fill in, the only claim I shall be able to make in mitigation is that I never shot at a sitter in my life.) (Naturally, I don't count rats, carrion-crows, ex-presidents of Uganda and that sort of thing.)

Nevertheless, my cowardly, regicide right hand seemed to have a life of its own; it drew back the bolt of the Mannlicher and shoved it forward to usher a cartridge into the breech. It jammed. The bolt, I mean – or rather the cartridge. I wrenched the bolt back fiercely until the distorted cartridge sprang free and whirred past my ear to strike a tasteful colour-print of Van Gogh's 'Two Pansies Sharing a Pot'. I crammed the bolt forward again and it jammed again. The cavalcade was about to pass the point where my field-of-fire would be ineffective. I cursed Jock with love and respect (I had checked those cartridges that very morning – who else could have nobbled them?) but, with thoughts of survival in my mind, wrestled with the bolt-action so that I could loose off just one shot to show that I had tried. It was just as I had cleared the third cartridge and clunked in a fresh clip that I found out why there had been no security-idiots lumbering about on the rooftops across the street. It was because they were kicking in the door of my squalid room. Just behind me.

Now there are two ways of kicking in doors. The first, which I was taught by a gentleman in Philadelphia, is quick, neat and almost soundless. These chaps used the other method. Had I been a dedicated villain I could have shot them into bite-sized helpings before they delivered the third kick, but my heart was not in it. When they at length tumbled in through the wreckage of the door I lifted them to their great feet and dusted them off courteously. The door had not been locked but I did not tell them this, I didn't want to spoil their day. Each of them arrested me again and again, urging me to say things which might be used in evidence against me and sticking evidence-tabs on everything in sight, while the skinny landlady gibbered and squawked behind them, averring that she had suspected all along that I was not a true-born Englishman.

The copper's voices were fierce, grave and *proud*. This was a Tower of London job, you see; your true regicide is not submitted to the squalor of Wormwood Scrubs where he might have to rub shoulders with muggers, wife-bashers, child-rapists and common property-developers. I was special. (My only regret, as they snucked the handcuffs about my wrists, was that I had not made it perfectly clear to Jock that the little jars of partridge-breasts in jelly are quite useless without fresh brown bread and butter.) The coppers scarcely hit me at all but they searched me thoroughly for incriminating documents such as five-pound notes, gold cigarette-cases and so forth but all they found was the receipted bill for the suit I was wearing. I hope they did not give GENTS' WARDROBES PURCHASED a bad time.

The frisking was disgracefully inefficient – I had to remind them about the small of my back, where evil men often tape a 'shiv' or ground-down razor. While I giggled three tall men loomed in the doorway, brushing aside the debris with fastidious feet. No common British coppers, these, the very feet told one that. They were in fact Colonel Blucher and a brace of his myrmidons.

Blucher brandished a plastic triptych bespattered with the marks of important rubber stamps. The coppers stopped arresting me and started calling Blucher 'Sir'. Someone told the landlady to shut up, for which relief much thanks, and there was a sort of tableau. Then Blucher thanked the bobbies civilly but in the flat sort of voice which means 'fuck off'.

I do not know who reimbursed the landlady for her burst door and shattered dreams but it was not I. As we left she made a gesture which she should not have known how to make, for she was clearly not a showjumper.

'In Ongary,' I told her, ''ve make zat sign like zis' – and I demonstrated, using fewer fingers.

Inexplicably, Blucher seemed pleased with me. Inexplicably, too, he seemed incurious about my regicidal ploy but I told him all about it nevertheless, for attempted assassination always makes one babble; everyone knows that.

'And I suppose it was your lot who jimmied the cartridges,' I ended, gratefully.

'Why, no, Mr Mortdecai; it wasn't us at all.'

'Ah, then Jock is as patriotic as I suspected all along.'

'Well, no, I wouldn't say it was Jock, either.'

'Who then?'

'I really couldn't say.' I knew what that meant. I *thought* I knew what that meant.

They dropped me off at the wrong end of Brook Street, for security reasons I daresay. The walk did me good. Jock opened the door with an expressionless face and, as I passed through the kitchen, thrust a lusty drink into my hand with a similar lack of emotion. The first sip told me that he had understood that this was no time for such niceties as soda-water.

Johanna was in the drawing-room, her lovely eyes gummed to the television set, whereon there was a chap playing something wonderfully tedious on a tin-whistle made of solid platinum.

'Look, Johanna,' I said apologetically . . .

'SSHHHH!' she said. (There are certain instruments which seem to exercise an unaccountable fascination on female human beings. Did you know, for instance, that in ancient Athens there was a law against chaps playing flutes under girls' windows? There was nothing about giving them bunches of flowers, boxes of chocolates or mink coats, but playing the flute was reckoned to be taking an unfair advantage; even *clever* girls succumbed to it. I'm not making that up, I'm really not; ask any Greek Historian. Ask him in that lucid interval between the after-luncheon nap and the cocktail hour.)

When the chap had finished his tootling and was shaking the spit out of his valuable whistle, I moistened my own whistle with what was left of the valuable Scotch and said –

'Look, Johanna, I'm awfully sorry but . . .'

'It's all right, Charlie dear, please don't go on. I couldn't bear to hear you explaining how you failed me. Even the best men can break under stress.' I thought about that one, for I knew that she was not a woman to use words carelessly. Many a bitter rejoinder and witty retort sprang to mind.

'Ah, well, yes,' was what I decided to say. Even she could not think of a riposte to that one. We dined early, later, because this was the night when our lovely Italian cook comes and 'obliges' and she likes to get away early because of what she calls 'Binko'. (You probably won't have heard of 'Bingo', it's a game where the odds are slightly worse against the player than at the 'fruit-machine' but you don't have to wear your palm out pulling the handle. It's jolly good for the economy too, they tell me; you see, if a chap earning £80 a week is giving his wife £20 of that for Bingo and encouraging greyhounds himself with a similar amount, well, he's not going to settle for any lousy, vile-capitalistic differential of bloody 5%, is he?)

We dined early, off a simple *bollito misto* and in a flurry of sparkling conversation like, 'Pass the salt, please, dear,' and 'Oh, dear, I'm sorry about this wine.' My final *jeu d'esprit* was, 'Johanna, darling, I think I'm going to get an early night, d'you mind?' She was ready for that punch; she gave me her sweetest smile and said that she didn't mind a bit; there was a horror movie on TV starting right now.

It must have been two hours later when she crept into my dressing-room and said that the horror-movie had frightened her dreadfully.

'There, there,' I mumbled sleepily, patting her where her night-dress should have been. Then she asked me what had gone wrong in the assassination ploy and I told her that the cartridge just wouldn't slide into the breech. She couldn't seem to comprehend at first, so

I sort of demonstrated. A few minutes later she said that she almost understood except the bit about the bolt-action. I went downstairs and made a couple of drinks. Playing for time, you understand.

She fell asleep perhaps half an hour later; ballistics is a very boring subject.

A little before dawn she shook me awake again. I was surly; I always am at that hour.

'Charlie, dear,' she said, 'there's one thing I don't understand.' I made unconvincing sleep-noises but to no avail. 'You see, Charlie, there were supposed to be *three* cartridges in the clip, weren't there?'

'Oh, very well,' I said.

10 Mortdecai is given a perfectly simple, nay, delightful task and makes a dog's breakfast of it

. . . And the thicket closed
Behind her and the forest echo'd 'fool'.

Merlyn and Vivien

'All the same, Charlie dear,' she said as I pushed a listless rasher around my breakfast-plate, 'all the same, you didn't do awfully well, did you? With the *assassination*, I mean? I bet a CIA man would have checked every cartridge; the CIA brass accepts no excuses, they say.' The only retort I could think of was one such as I could never think of using a gently-nurtured millionairess, so I held my tongue and stabbed spitefully at a fried egg. 'Maybe,' she went on, 'that assignment was a little tough for you – as you often say, you are no longer a young man, are you?' Employing a strength of wrist and hand which I did not know I still possessed, I divided a slice of crisp fried bread with one stroke of the knife, sending half of it skimming across the room like a clay pigeon. 'So,' she said, 'I have thought of a little task for you which you will find simple and delightful.'

I made guarded, mistrustful noises which may or may not have been audible over the munching of fried bread.

'All you have to do is to make friends – make *great* friends – with a beautiful young woman. She is a sort of business-associate of mine in a confidential enterprise and I have a feeling that she is leaking. Oh do stop raising your eyebrows in that silly way, dear; you know I mean that she has been chatting a bit too freely with our uh competitors. I want you to get close to her, spend freely as though you were tired of carrying all that money around; this will make her gaze at you lovingly. Then start to wheedle; see if she is as careless a talker as I suspect. You might hint that you are a researcher journalist for one of the English Sunday papers, hunh?'

My knife and fork crashed down on my plate – a lesser plate would have cracked from side to side – and I stood up, giving an Arctic glare which would have withered a lesser woman.

'There are some things,' I said stiffly, 'which a chap simply cannot be asked to do. Assassination, yes. Impersonating a Sunday journalist, no.'

'Forgive me, dear,' she said hastily, 'I was perhaps lacking in, uh, insight when I suggested that. Just hint, then, that you are a heavy investor and that you have heard that she might be on the inside of some nice little deal such as you love to buy a piece of and that you have a wallet to prove it. But get close to her first, win her confidence; I'm sure she will find you adorable. Well, gosh, *I* do, don't I?'

I sat down again but my breakfast no longer held any charms for me; it looked like a cruel parody of a painting by Kandinsky.

'Very well,' I said at last, 'how and where do I make pals with this lady?'

'Tonight, darling. It's all arranged. Her name is Loretta. You are to be her partner at a reception: it's only at one of those Gulf Arab Embassies so you don't have to hunt for a white tie and tails, a simple tuxedo will do. Sorry, I mean dinner-jacket.'

Loretta proved to have one of those wonderfully flower-like, vulnerable faces; her eyes seemed always to be on the point of brimming with happy tears and her generous lips seemed to have been bruised with a thousand savage kisses. I found myself longing to protect her, which is what it's all about really, isn't it? Bridegroom though I was, I became painfully desirous of finding whether the rest of her bore out the promise of that lovely face.

After the reception and after what passes as a buffet in that class of Embassy she shuddered delicately at my suggestion of a visit to a night-club. (I, too, shuddered a little but mine was a shudder of relief at not having to spend a great deal of money. I mean, I'm not *mean*, I'm really not, but fifty pounds for cheap champagne and a surplus of decibels has never struck me as good value. '*Quantum meruit*,' is what I say.)

'Take me home,' she murmured. Her murmur was of the brand which sends the familiar tingle galloping up from the base of the spine to the dorsal region. I took her. Home, I mean. 'Home' proved to be an apartment in a discreetly splendid block of flats off Curzon Street. The porter discreetly failed to see us but his back was benign. If ever a porter's back registered the words 'Bless you, my children,' that porter's back did so.

At the door of her apartment she handed me the key – I cannot bear bossy women who pretend to be able to open a door unaided – and stood facing me in such a position that I would have to stand very close to her indeed in order to reach the keyhole. Her great, violet-coloured eyes gazed up at me, swimming with the aforesaid unshed tears, her lips trembled tremulously and, in short, she was exuding all those infinitesimal signals which are supposed to tell a chap that a girl expects to be kissed, and that right speedily. I fell to the task with a will. She was very good at it. When her breathing quickened I found the keyhole and, still locked in each other's arms, we fox-trotted into her apartment. It was a lavish sort of pad, full of flowers and dominated by a monstrous sofa drawn up in front of a blazing fire of genuine logs. She vanished for a moment and returned bare-footed with a bottle of Armagnac and two glasses. I forget what the Armagnac was like, I was spellbound by the sight of her perfectly-shaped little toes as she twiddled them in front of the blaze.

As a conversational opener I lamely pointed out that this was well-known to be a sure way of catching chilblains and, inexplicably, she burst into laughter. Then she fell upon me frantically. Our mouths met and clamped together with all the mindless determination of a pair of bar-magnets. For a minute or two, or it may have been three, nothing was to be heard but the succulent sounds of face-chewing, the crackle of the logs and the bee-loud noise of certain zip-fasteners. (If ever I am forced by the soaring price of blackmail to write my memoirs, I have determined to entitle them *The Zip is my Undoing*.)

Suddenly, when it became abundantly clear that Loretta complaisantly expected me to work my wicked will on her, I unstuck myself from her embrace with a guilty start. Was I not a bridegroom? Was I not in love with my bride Johanna? The answers were 'Definitely' and 'Yes, I suppose so,' in that order. I had been told to 'get close' to Loretta – was I, perhaps, exceeding my brief? Loretta was languorously making it clear that I was certainly exceeding my briefs, if you will forgive a little vulgarity just this once.

'Look, ah, darling,' I gabbled, 'I've just had the most awful thought.'

'It's all right,' she murmured, 'I took my pill this morning.'

'No no no, I didn't mean that; I meant that I absolutely promised to telephone my, ah, business manager before –' I stole a glance at my watch '– before midnight. He flies to Frankfurt or one of those places at crack of dawn. Could I possibly . . .?'

'*Hurry*,' she said, handing me the telephone. I dialled. Johanna's cool and lovely voice answered. Summoning up what rusty remains of the German language I could recall, I addressed her throatily.

'*Ah, Herr, er, Johann! Hier ist Charlie Mortdecai!*'

'Darling, are you drunk already?'

'No, no,' I cried, still employing the German tongue, 'canst thou German understand?'

'Well, sure, Charlie dear; your German is a little different from mine but I think I can make out.'

'Good. Understanding is what I need shall. There is here something of a small difficulty. To retain the confidence of our friend it seems necessary that I to bed take her must. What shall I do? Hullo? Hullo? Canst thou me hear?'

'Yes, dear. You mean you want a "Green Card", hunh?'

'What is that? Ah, yes, now I understand.'

'Well, OK, just this once. But Charlie . . .'

'*Ja, Herr Johann?*'

'You are not to *enjoy* it.'

'No, Herr Johann. Goodnight.'

'Oh, and Charlie?'

'*Ja?*'

'Save some, hunh?'

'*Zu befehl, Herr Johann*,' I said. I wiped a furtive bead of sweat from the brow and hung up. Turning back to Loretta I said,

'Sorry about that, darling. Frantically important business. Sure you understand.'

'*Naturlich*,' she said in tones of frosty sweetness. '*Es scheint mir dass du versucht hast von deiner Frau eine Freischute zu bekommen, und ich kann mir auch denken für was.*'

'What what what?' I asked reasonably.

'I mean, does she say it's OK to screw?'

'Oh dear, oh God,' I thought, 'I used my real name on the bloody telephone.'

'Ho ho,' I said aloud, archly, and for want of anything more sensible to do or say I enfolded her in my arms and kissed her passionately. She had re-zipped herself – all the weary work to do again – but as my fingers tugged at the rip-cord she stood up.

'Goodnight, darling,' she said.

'How do you mean, "goodnight"?'

'Well, I suppose I mean sort of "goodnight".'

'But but but . . .'

'Yes, it would have been such fun but I mean to go on living.'

'Eh?'

'I mean I don't want to get killed this week. Or any week. Here is your hat and umbrella. Please do not think hardly of me; I think you are cute, I have always loved stupid men. Oh and darling, do button yourself up in front – the nights are cold, you might catch chilblains.'

The porter was reading behind his desk in the foyer. His face was benignly blank but it seemed to me that his eyebrows rose a fraction as I shambled past him.

'Goodnight,' I mumbled.

'Good*night*, sir,' he answered puzzledly and went back to his copy of *Forum*. He had probably been reading about premature ejaculation.

At home, Johanna, too, raised an eyebrow, far lovelier and more damaging than that of the porter.

'Home so soon, Charlie dear?'

I snarled in a muffled sort of way and poured myself one of the largest whiskies-and-soda of my career. I did not punish the soda-water syphon too hard. Wordlessly, Johanna handed me two

E capsules from a little gold *drageoir*. I swallowed them sulkily.

'I'm blown,' I said at length.

'*Blown*, Charlie? You mean Loretta . . .?'

'No, no; I mean my *cover* is blown – don't you ever read spy-stories? Loretta knows who I am, the bitch speaks German. Better than I do, in fact.' She seemed to smother a smile.

'But of course she does, dearest; she *is* German, you see.'

'You should have told me.'

'You should have asked.' I restrained the words which sprang to my lips for I was not one to use vile language in front of women, never having been married before, you understand.

'Anyway,' I said, when the blessed whisky had got a firm foot-hold on my bloodstream, 'the operation failed. I got nothing out of her.'

'Nor, uh, into . . .?'

'I cannot bear coarseness in women.'

'Don't be so stuffy, Charlie; I didn't for one moment expect her to prattle. She is very highly-trained indeed. As a matter of fact it was you I was checking out, not her. A kind of initiative test, you know?' I digested this, along with another whisky and s., which might have been the big brother of the previous one. My blood boiled with chagrin and frustration while many a bitter reflection on the nature of womankind occurred to me. It seemed to me that the only way to retain my tatters of self-respect was to stalk off to my bed in a marked manner.

'I think I shall go to bed,' I said in the distant tones of a man who has drunk both Armagnac and Scotch whisky and who has, moreover, been thwarted in the very act of a passionate encounter.

'Bed?' she said. 'Great! Can I come?' I studied her with a slight stirring of grudged admiration. She stood up with a little movement, shrugging off her *peignoir* to reveal a shameless little creation in black lace which seemed to be precariously supported only by her out-thrust breasts. The black lace ended just where her long and lovely legs began; had she not been a natural blonde one might have been at a loss to detect the hem-line. My look of admiration changed subtly into one of affection – I was reminded of my earlier rôle of 'heavy investor'.

'Can I?' she repeated meekly.

'I don't know,' I said, 'but I'm pretty certain that I could.'

She trotted towards the bedroom. I am not a lustful man but there is something about the sight of a beautiful woman trotting upstairs before me, clad in that kind of night-attire, which arouses the beast in me, I know not why.

'Charlie?' she said, a few moments later, 'Charlie?'

'Mm-hmm?' I panted, engrossed.

'Charlie, are you pretending that I am Loretta?'

'Certainly not,' I lied. 'I am thinking of my fag at school, if you want to know.'

'You are vile and base,' she murmured happily.

'Charlie,' she said the next morning.

'Oink.'

Firmly extricating my face from between her breasts she repeated the name.

'Yes yes,' I said petulantly, 'this is still I. Whom did you expect it to be? Onassis?'

'Listen, Charlie – no, stop that – just for a moment anyway; I have to talk to you. Your date with Loretta last night was only your second assignment but you must admit you made a bit of a cock-up of it, didn't you?'

'Don't admire your turn of phrase,' I grumbled sleepily.

'You know quite well what I mean. Now, if you are to be really useful to me – no, *stop* it, I didn't mean that – you must be trained.'

'Rubbish. I am trained. By experts. In the War.'

'Yes, I know; I have your War Office dossier in the desk downstairs. It cost me two hundred pounds.' (I awoke at this point.) 'You scored very high in unarmed combat and sabotage and shooting people but that was twenty-five years ago, right? And you never took the subversion course, did you?'

'Forget,' I said, feigning a sleepiness which I no longer felt.

'Well, you didn't. They tried to get you into that scene just after the War and you gave them some flippant reply about flat feet and cowardice.'

'The cowardice bit was true.'

'Well, dear, you are booked in this very evening to start a course at our very own Training College.'

'Oh no I'm not and anyway, what do you mean "our"? Who is this "we"?'

'Yes you are, darling. And "we" is me and some girl-friends of mine; I'll tell you all about it one day soon. You'll love the College, Charlie.'

'Oh no I shan't, because I'm not bloody going.'

'Lovely old house near Leighton Buzzard.'

'I'm going back to sleep.'

'Are you sure, darling? About going back to sleep?' I did not, as it turned out, go back to sleep until some eight minutes later, after she had wrung from me my slow consent, to name but one.

Since I am incapable of telling falsehoods I must confess that, when I married Johanna, I had been keenly relishing the prospect of a great battle for power between her and Jock. Alas, Jock had fallen under Johanna's spell and was by now a mere pawn, anticipating her lightest wish. Had I, in my bachelor days, requested breakfast at half-past noon, which was when it was requested that day, Jock would have summoned a cab and sent me off to the nearest Lyons Corner House. Today, his only comment as he brought on the corn-flakes, the kippers, the kidneys and the kedgeree was a genteel request about when Madam would require luncheon.

'Why are you making those weird, growling noises, Charlie?' asked Johanna. 'You sound like the Big-Cat House in the Zoo!'

'It is the smell of these kippers which makes you think of that zoological enclave,' I said, hoping that Jock would hear me and suffer a little. In a little while, crammed with kedgeree and strong, sweet coffee, I felt emboldened to reopen the subject of the Training College for Young Ladies, making it clear that any assent wrung from me while under the influence of natural blondes was inadmissible under English law. In short, I was not going there.

'Look,' I explained in a reasonable voice, 'all that rubbishy, reach-me-down judo and karate that they teach silly women at night-classes is junk. The women believe they are achieving results because, while they are striking absurd Kung-fu attitudes, waving their podgy hands about in absurder ways and making ultimately absurd noises with their mouths, the well-paid instructor is not about to step forward and deliver a round-house left into her belly while he delivers an old-fashioned right hand into her lipstick, is he? Although I bet he would often like to do so. But he is held back by the gentlemanly instincts which say that you do not strike ladies in vulnerable places, which is most places in ladies. I have never quite understood these prejudices myself because I am not a true-born Englishman, but they exist nonetheless.

'Your common rapist or mugger,' I went on, 'has no such compunction. He does not wait politely while the lady waves her hands at him in minatory ways, nor is he daunted by any Oriental noises she may emit. He simply steps forward and gives the object of his desire a bunch of fives in the moosh – regardless of the valuable crockery implanted there by her dentist – and follows it up by a similar punch just below her cross-my-heart living-bra. This never fails. (Policewomen, of course, know a trick or two; this means that they stay conscious maybe thirty seconds longer and spend maybe thirty days longer in hospital.)

'My advice,' I went on didactically, 'to any woman assailed by rapist or mugger would be as follows. In the case of a rapist: instantly lie on your back, raise your heels in the air and cry, "Take me, take me, I *want* you." This will disconcert almost all rapists, especially if the lady happens to be the kind of lady that only a rapist would look at twice. If he is so intent upon his purpose as not to be cowed by this simple ploy but persists in his purpose, why there is little harm done; lie quite still, try to enjoy it. The choice is a simple one: a brief and possibly not unpleasant invasion of one's physical privacy – or a painful bashing causing the loss of one's good looks and perhaps one's life. Who, after all, misses a slice from a cut cake, eh? In any event, on no account endeavour to have the rapist apprehended, for his lawyer will certainly convince many of the jury that you led him on and the trial will be more painful than the ravishment itself.

'In the case of a mugger, instantly hand him your purse – for you will scarcely be so stupid as to be carrying anything valuable in it – kick off your shoes and *run*. Run like the wind, screaming loudly. Scream like a steam-whistle; such chaps are most averse to noise when about their chosen trade. My life-long study of the art of warfare has taught me that running away is certainly the most cost-effective type of fighting. It doesn't win many battles but it saves you a lot of troops. Ask any Italian general if you catch him out of his hair-net. Or, indeed, if you can catch him at all.'

Having delivered those few, well-chosen words I reached for a kipper in the manner of a lecturer about to take a sip of water.

'Charlie,' she said mildly, 'our College isn't really much like those night-classes in judo. You'll find out when you get there.'

'But my dear, haven't I just made it clear that I am not going to your beastly College? Must I say it again? *I am not going to the College.*'

That evening, on my way to the College, I stopped at St Alban's to drink a little beer and purchase a couple of flat half-bottles of Scotch, in case the College should prove to be teetotal. I also made a telephone call to Blucher – after that assassination fiasco, he had conceded it might be more 'secure' to give me a number and 'procedure' for getting in touch with him in emergencies. I dialled the memorized number, let it ring the prescribed twelve times, hung up, counted out thirty seconds then dialled again. A warm voice answered instantly, saying that it was the Home and Colonial Stores – a likely story, I must say.

'Please may I speak to Daddy,' I asked, gagging over the childish mumbo-jumbo, 'Mummy's very poorly.'

'Oh dear, what a shame. Are you far away?' I gave her the number of the call-box; hung up; lit a cigarette. A fat harridan loomed outside the kiosk, glaring at me and pointing at her wristwatch. I recked not of her. She rapped on the glass, displaying a fistful of coppers and mouthing at me. I leered at the money and commenced to unbutton my top-coat. She went away. The telephone rang.

'Hullo,' said Blucher's voice, 'this is Daddy. Who is this?'

'Willy here,' I said from between clenched teeth.

'Why, hi, Willy. Are you at a secure telephone?'

'Oh, for Christ's sake. Look, I'm on my way to some kind of a Training College, it's called Dingley Dell if you'll believe that. It's near . . .'

'I know where it's near. Say, what's that dingus you Britishers wear when you're playing cricket?'

'I don't understand. We wear lots of things when we play cricket.'

'I mean the thing you wear under your pants, to kind of protect your family jewels, you know?'

'You mean a "box", I suppose. But what the hell . . .?' Had I not known him to be a humourless man I might have supposed him to be amused.

'Is there a sports store there in St Alban's?'

'I could not say. But if there is one it will certainly be closed by this time of the evening.'

'Gosh, that's tough. Oh well, good luck, Willy. Keep in touch.' He hung up. I drove off, musing furiously. My breast was seething with many an emotion but jollity was not among those present.

11   Mortdecai takes a bit of stick and drops the phrase 'gentler sex' from his vocabulary

I read, before my eyelids dropt their shade,
'The Legend of Good Women', long ago
Sung by the morning star of song, who made
His music heard below.

A Dream of Fair Women

Dingley Dell, for all its preposterous name, was indeed a stately pile so far as I could see in the dusk. As I navigated the stately drive an inordinate number of stately floodlights bathed both it and me in the radiance of some half a million Watts. A chunky girl in breeches met me at the foot of the steps.

'Mr Mortdecai? Oh, super. Now I can let the dogs out as soon as you're safely indoors. My name's Fiona, by the way. Just leave your keys in the car, I'll put it away.'

I carried my own bags up the steps to where a plumpish butler was silhouetted against the light.

'Welcome to College, Mr Mortdecai,' said the silhouette in what I took to be effeminate tones.

'Yes,' I said.

'You have just time to bathe, sir. We do not change for dinner. Allow me to take your hat and coat.' He took them, also my umbrella. As I advanced gratefully to the great log-fire blazing in the fireplace of the hall I saw the butler leap at me, whirling my umbrella in the general direction of my lower jawbone. I ducked, of course, for ducking is one of my more polished skills, and took the umbrella away from him by rolling it over his thumb, then I dropped (but stay, let me explain: experts never *whack* at people with sticks, umbrellas and things, for the movement is a clumsy one, easily out-manoeuvred and incapable of doing any damage unless the stick be a right heavy one, which makes the manoeuvre even clumsier. No, the use of such a makeshift weapon is to lunge, stiff-armed, at the midriff: even if the ferrule does not pierce the skin it can be relied upon to smarten up the liver, spleen or diaphragm in an agonizing and often lethal way.) I dropped, as I was about to say, into a stiff-armed lunge at the midriff, calculated to do great harm to the sturdiest butler, but at the very latest split-second I perceived to my dismay that he, the butler, was in fact a she-butler and my point wavered, passing over her hip. She snatched it *en passant* and twitched it further, so that I staggered towards her in time to receive a raised knee. The knee was clumsily timed, I was able to take it harmlessly on my chest and, as I stumbled past, seized the ankle and threw her. Keeping my grip on the ankle I twirled it vigorously so that she rolled over and over and pitched up with a satisfying noise against the wainscot. Face down. I placed a foot in the small of her back.

'Freeze,' I snarled angrily, for I was angry. 'Freeze or I'll stamp on your kidneys until they pop like rotten tomatoes.'

'Oh well *done*, Mortdecai, awf'lly well done!' boomed a voice from the minstrel's gallery. 'Ethel, you may get up now – but extra combat-classes for you all this week, I'm afraid, dear. You made an awful nonsense of that attack, didn't you?'

By now the owner of the voice was descending the great staircase; she was a massive creature, all beef down to the ankles, just like a Mullingar heifer. She advanced towards me, hand outstretched in a jovial way. I made to take the hand but hers slipped upwards and caught my thumb in an iron grip, bending it cruelly backwards. Well, I remembered how to deal with that, of course: you sit down, roll backwards and kick the offending hand away with the flat of both feet.

'Capital, capital!' she boomed. 'Shan't have much to teach *you* in the dirty-fighting class. Now, you see, we run a taut ship here and you must be on the *qui vive* at all times. For your own good, you know. But since this is your first night there'll be no more surprises until after breakfast tomorrow. Honour bright.' I relaxed. She smashed a great fist into the pit of my stomach and I subsided, whooping for breath, onto the carpet.

'Subversion Lesson Number One,' she said amiably, 'don't trust anyone. Ever. No, please, no lower-deck language; some of the girls are *prudes*.' I stood up warily, planning a move. 'No, Mr Mortdecai, you are not allowed to strike me, I am the Commandant. You call me Madam. Have you a gun?'

I pretended, snobbishly, to misunderstand. 'A shot-gun?' I said heavily, 'No, I did not bring one. I was not told that you would be offering me any shooting.'

'I mean, as you well know, a side-arm – a pistol if you prefer.'

'No. I do not commonly come armed when invited to country houses.' I spoke as stiffly as I could.

'Then we must fit you up. What do you fancy? I always use this' – and she plucked out a horrid old cannon – 'but then I'm old-fashioned, you see.' I sneered at the weapon.

'Service Webley .38 on a .45 frame,' I sneered. 'Should be in a museum. Kicks like – like a female butler.'

'Perhaps,' she said placidly. 'But it suits me.' She absently loosed off a round which whirred past my ear and caused a log in the fireplace to leap pyrotechnically. My ears sang with the roar and adrenalin squirted from my every pore. 'What weapon would you prefer, Mr Mortdecai?' I pulled myself together.

'Smith & Wesson,' I said, '.38 Special Airweight.'

She nodded approvingly, strode to the house-telephone.

'Armourer? Ah, Nancy; one Airweight, one box of graphite cartridges, one of solid, four spare clips, cleaning kit and a Thurston pocket holster.'

'*Shoulder*-holster, please,' I said defiantly, for my figure does not lend itself to the trousering of pistols.

'No, Mortdecai, you'll be wearing combat clothes, no time to unzip your blouse, you know.' A chubby little matron bustled up with two cardboard boxes. The pistol was still in its original grease. I handed it back in a lordly way.

'Pray clean it,' I said lordlily, 'and while you're about it, file off that silly foresight.'

'We look after our own pieces here,' she snapped. 'And you can have the foresight off in the morning when you report to the armoury. That's *if* I decide you don't need it.'

'Clean it now, Mortdecai,' said the Commandant, 'and load it with the graphite rounds. They pulverize on contact, you know, quite harmless unless you get one in the eye. You'll just have time before dinner.'

The butler, Ethel, showed me to my room and, as I lowered my suitcase to the ground, planted a succulent kiss on the top of my head, just where the hair is thinning a bit. I stared at her. She stuck out her tongue. 'You didn't hurt me a bit,' she pouted.

'Sorry about that,' I said ambiguously.

The room was Spartan: an iron cot, hard mattress, no sheets, no heating, two rough blankets, a deal table and a kitchen chair. I have been in cosier prison cells. I broke out one of my half-bottles and sucked at it vigorously while I cleaned the pistol. Soon both it and I were 'clean, bright and slightly oiled' as we used to say in the Army. I loaded a clip with the graphite rounds but thoughtfully introduced, first of all, one solid cartridge into the bottom of the clip. Emerging from the shower I heard a rasping boom from some hidden loud-speaker: 'Mortdecai – moving target outside your window – SHOOT!' Shrugging a shoulder, I scooped up the Airweight from under my pillow, flung back the curtains, flung back the casement window, all in jig-time. I could just see a shadowy man-size target trundling jerkily across the lawn. Flipping off the safety-catch I squeezed the trigger. There was a resounding click.

'Lesson Two, Mortdecai,' said the loudspeaker, 'always keep your pistol loaded and within reach.'

'It *was* bloody loaded,' I snarled.

'I know. I took the clip out while you were under the shower. Careless, very.'

'How the hell am I supposed to shower with a pistol about me?' I yelled.

'Sponge-bag,' said the loudspeaker succinctly.

When the dinner-gong roared I strolled warily downstairs, happy in the awareness of my pistol-heavy trousers pocket. There's nothing like a nice new pistol to dispel a feeling of castration. Not a soul struck at me. Taking a line from the grimness of my quarters, I had been dreading dinner but I was agreeably surprised. Hare soup, a casserole of pheasant with apples *à la Normande*, a soufflé and one of those savouries that women make, all washed down with a couple of decilitres of something which tasted quite like Burgundy.

'Excellent,' I said at length, 'quite delicious,' and beamed amiably down the huge refectory-table. There were two or three silent men present but most of the staff and students were women, some six or eight of whom were undeniably nubile. Following my gaze, the Commandant said off-handedly, 'Would you care for a girl to keep you warm tonight?' I gulped, which is not a thing one should do when drinking brandy, it makes it go down the wrong way. Much of mine went down my shirt-front. 'I daresay,' she went on absently, 'that one or two of them will be feeling randy – it's all that violence on television, you know. No? Well, perhaps you're wise. Need all your strength tomorrow.'

I turned my attention frantically upon the middle-aged woman on my right. She proved to be one of those astrology-bores that you meet everywhere nowadays and promptly asked me under which Sign I had been born.

Haven't the least idea,' I said, pishing and tushing freely.

'Oh, but you *must* know! What is your birth-date?' It seemed only civil to tell her, especially since she did not ask the *year*, but I took the opportunity to deliver my set-piece lecture about the stultifying folly of those who believe, in the third quarter of the Twentieth Century, that being born at one particular time and place will govern the whole of one's character and future. 'Why,' I perorated, 'this would mean that every triplet would be run over by a 'bus at the same time as his two siblings! Robert Louis Stevenson once wrote a sentence which has been the guiding-star of my life: "Children dear, never believe anything which insults your intelligence." Reading that at an impressionable age has, I am confident, formed my nature much more positively than the moment, some er, *chrm*, forty years ago when a fashionable *accoucheur* glanced at an unreliable time-piece and, realizing that he had another appointment, decided to spare my mother any further vexation by calling for the high forceps. Surely you can see that?'

She, the astrology-bore, was wearing that rapt, attentive look which women use when wishing to flatter pompous idiots. Being an experienced pompous idiot, I know that this look means that the woman is not listening at all but is merely waiting for you to stop making noises with your mouth so that she can do a spot of uttering herself.

(As it happens, and if you must know, I was born on the last day of September, because my father begat me on the Christmas night of a year which I do not propose to divulge; I know this to be true because my father told me so in front of my mother and several of her friends – he was like that. When he saw my face fall he quite misconstrued my feelings and explained apologetically that he had been drunk at the time. My mother did not speak to him for weeks afterwards but few people noticed this because, by then, she was not speaking to him much at all, anyway. She was a woman of great beauty and dignity, although unpleasing in almost every other way you could imagine and a good few which you could not.)

When I had drawn to a close and had vouchsafed my birth-date the astrology lady seemed thrilled. 'You're a Libra, then, how wonderful! Guess what my sign is. Oh, do!' I ransacked my mind for zodiacal signs. 'Virgo?' I said.

'*Silly*,' she said, lightly slapping my wrist. 'I'm a ram – Aries. We rams are made *for* Libras.' Well, I couldn't correct her Latin, could I, so I just eyed her guardedly. Her face would have passed for an old but once expensive handbag and the crocodile-hide of her neck and bosom would have attracted a snappy bid from Gucci's luggage-factory. 'Not Wanted On Voyage' was the phrase which sprang to mind.

'Oh, come, come,' I said diffidently.

'No, no – I must go, mustn't I, Commandant? Goodnight, dear Libra. My name is Kitty, by the way . . . if you care to know.' With that she left the table, smiling at me. People with teeth like hers should not smile. For a sickening moment I feared that she might be off to my bedroom, to await me there like a sacrificial ram.

'Do please stop grinding your teeth, Mr Mortdecai,' said the Commandant as soon as Kitty was out of earshot. 'She is really a most capable person except for the astrology nonsense.' I could not quite stop grinding the teeth.

'If only,' I grated, 'if *only* such capable people would spare a moment to apply a dab of logic onto what they call their thinking; if only . . .'

'If only,' mocked the Commandant. 'If only! Paah! That is a phrase for kiddies to say to their teddy-bears. If only your uncle had wheels he'd be a tea-trolley. Come to that, if only your aunt had balls she'd be your uncle.' I glowered at her, for this was, after all, not the Australian Embassy.

'*My* aunts,' I said in a rebuking sort of voice, 'all possess balls. Indeed, I can call to mind few aunts who do not sport a cluster of such things. I cannot claim ever to have *rummaged* an aunt but I'm prepared to offer any amount of seven-to-three that . . .'

'Enough!' said the Commandant, raising a commanding hand. 'No wagers are permitted here, pray remember that you are not in a WRNS mess.' I would not have minded offering five-to-two against that proposition also, but took the coward's way out and said that I was awfully sorry. Then I said that I was awfully tired, too, and asked permission to leave the festive board. (The stopper, I noticed, was firmly in the neck of the brandy-decanter.)

I pined to clock up a few sleeping-hours but it seemed that I must first collect my 'lessons' from the Commandant's Office; these proved to be an arm-aching load of Xeroxed brochures about how to Kill/Maim/Cheat/Lie/Deceive/Subvert/Communicate/Bewilder/Terrorize/Persuade/Forge/Impersonate/Evade/Explode/Compromise and do all sorts of other horrid things to other people. A second stack was about how to recognize Aircraft/Weapons/Ships/Missiles/CIA Agents/Narcotics and Counterfeit Currency while at the same time Living in Rough Country/Surviving at Sea/Confuting Interrogative Techniques and Mastering Five Simple Ways of Suicide (three of them almost painless).

Under my breath I muttered a short word concerning the hidden attributes of aunts.

'Cheer up, Mortdecai,' roared the Commandant, 'you're only here for three weeks and – only the first twenty days are painful!' She must have got that one out of the *Beano* comic.

'Ha ha,' I said politely. 'Goodnight, er, Madam.'

'Goodnight . . . oh, wait a sec – *catch!*' and with this she threw a blotting-pad towards me. Well, I wasn't born yesterday, as I have often freely admitted. I let it fall at my feet, making no attempt to catch it, and I had the Airweight out and pointing at her equator before she had even begun to haul out her old Webley.

'Oh, jolly good, Mortdecai,' she crowed, 'oh full marks!'

'Old stuff,' I said, closing the door behind me.

The only nice thing that happened to me that day was two minutes later, that night. No one was in my bedroom: no sacrificial rams, no half-assed Amazons hoping to sublimate their castration-complexes by boffing me on the head or other soft, vulnerable parts. Someone had been there, all right, because my suitcase had been unlocked – I had expected that, for any school-boy, indeed, any airport luggage-handler can open the ordinary suitcase in a trice, using only a set of those feeler-gauges which you can buy at any garage. I was unconcerned, for the smaller suitcase is made of sterner stuff: it has a combination lock with three cylinders, each bearing ten numbers. I cannot say off-hand how many permutations this affords but I would guess that it would take the average chambermaid something like a million years to hit upon the right one. Even your average chamber maid does not have that kind of time to spare unless she is exceptionally ugly and there are no tired business-men in the hotel.

'BAD, Mortdecai,' quacked the loudspeaker as I drew a pair of pyjamas from the larger suitcase, '*bad*. Lesson Four.'

'*Three*,' I snapped.

'No, four. Never leave incriminating matter in easily-opened luggage.' I allowed myself a smug smirk.

'Anything incrim . . ., that is to say, *private*, is in the other, smaller suitcase.'

'The other, smaller suitcase was the suitcase I meant,' said the loudspeaker. I tried the smaller, unopenable suitcase. It, too, was unlocked. As I gaped the hated voice squawked out again.

'Our research has shown us that people in middle life find it difficult to memorize random numbers; they tend to utilize numbers which they are unlikely to forget. If you must set your lock to the numbers of your birthday – 30th of the 9th, right? –

then never tell the date of your birthday to people like Kitty. *That* was Lesson Three.'

I muttered something obscure.

'What you suggest, Mortdecai, I have tried once or twice. It gave me little or no pleasure.'

'I'm leaving,' I said flatly. 'Now.'

'Ah, yes, well, that's not really awfully easy: all students' bedrooms are automatically time-locked and cannot possibly be re-opened until *reveille*. No, please don't look at the window, don't; the grounds are full of Fiona's Dobermann Pinschers and the Dobermanns are full of blood-lust. You'd have to shoot an awful lot of them before you even got near the electrified fence and Fiona would be *cross* if you hurt even one of them. She lives for those doggies. She's a sweet child but her temper is ungovernable and she will insist on carrying that silly old sawn-off shotgun.'

I began to understand that the loudspeaker was trying to tell me something. I sat on the edge of the bed, for I always fume better in a seated posture. How, I asked myself, had the old she-butch known that I had been casting wistful looks at the window? My eye fell upon the big looking-glass which commanded both my bed and the entrance to the bathroom. I snapped out the light, stole to the mirror, flattened my nose against it. Sure enough, there was a faint glow to be discerned; the unmistakable glow of a cigarette being puffed upon by an ageing Girl Guide. It was the work of a moment to find my First Aid Kit, to tape a First Field Dressing across the mirror and to switch the light on again.

'Oh, *well* done, Mortdecai, there's good stuff in you after all.' said the loudspeaker. 'That was going to be Lesson Five, after the girls had watched you get into your sleeping-suit, ho ho.'

I did not deign to answer but marched into the bathroom to ply an angry toothbrush and conceal one or two trifling matters which had not been in either suitcase. On the bathroom mirror a message was scrawled in lipstick: 'PLEASE DO NOT HIDE THINGS IN THE LAVATORY CISTERN: IT ONLY MAKES WORK FOR THE PLUMBER.'

Huddled in my comfortless bed, I made shift to study the thinnest of my lesson-brochures: the one entitled *Mastering Five*

Simple Ways of Suicide, for this seemed to fall in with my mood at the time. I was shuddering my way through the passage about how to bite through the large blood-vessel at the base of the tongue and breathe in the resultant blood until asphyxia supervened, when the lights went out.

'Soddem,' I said to myself, composing myself to sleep.

12 Mortdecai finally realizes that he is not attending a night-class in self-defence for old ladies

Comrades, leave me here a little, while as yet 'tis early morn:
Leave me here, and when you want me, sound upon your bugle horn.
Locksley Hall

Towards morning, in that half-awakened state when the worst and best dreams come, my repose was marred by hideous visions of female dominators: Catherine the Great, Mrs Bandaranaike, the Erinyes, Mrs Indira Gandhi, Leila Khaled, Ulrike Meinhof, Marion Coyle, Fusako Shigenobu, the Valkyries, Eleanor Roosevelt, Ermyntrude of the Bloody Sword, Mrs Golda Meir, Carrie Nation, the Empress Livia . . . all trooped before my inward eye, gibbering and cursing and waving their blood-boltered hands, red to the elbows. I was bracing myself to receive comfort from the vision of Mrs Margaret Thatcher, for I have ever been a staunch Tory, when to my delighted relief I was aroused into full wakefulness by a whirr and a clunk from the time-lock on my door.

'Wakey wakey, Mortdecai,' cackled the hateful loud-speaker. 'Three minutes for a shower, one for brushing teeth, two for shaving. Draw a tracksuit from the Quartermaster in eight minutes, be at the Gym in ten. Any questions?'

'Tea?' I questioned feebly.

'No, Mortdecai; PT. Do you a power of good. You can skip it if you like but the only entrance to the breakfast-hall is through the Gym.'

PT was hell. People made me prance absurdly, climb up and down wall-bars, hurl myself at hateful vaulting-horses and try to do press-ups. Then they threw monstrous medicine-balls at me. I panted and groaned my way through it until a bell rang and we all trooped into the showers. They were communal, unsegregated showers. Kitty twinkled at me as she soaped her luggage-like carcass and the younger girls played *pranks* on me.

Breakfast, on the other hand, was unrivalled. It was one of those lovely country-house breakfasts where you lift the lids off silver dishes on the sideboard and find eggs and kidneys and chops and bacon and kippers and haddock and kedgeree and fried ham and devilled turkey and scrambled eggs and grilled tomatoes and, when you sit down, there are two sorts of tea as well as coffee and jam and three sorts of marmalade and people keep bringing you more and more hot toast. I ate heartily for, although I do not love such things, I knew that I must keep my strength up, you see.

'This is your last time to sit at the head of the table beside me,' said the Commandant. I made rueful noises, muffled by the piece of toast (laden with that black, chunky marmalade which Oxford makes so well) which I was gnashing. 'Yes,' she went on, 'another guest will arrive before luncheon and it is the privilege of the latest-arrived to sit on my right hand, naturally.' I opened my mouth to make the kind of joke that chaps like me make but closed it again.

'Quite understand,' I gurgled, sluicing a recalcitrant shard of toast down with another cup of capital coffee.

'Ladies!' she suddenly bellowed – ignoring the weedy males at the table – 'Ladies. Captain Mortdecai will be reporting to the Armoury in five minutes to shoot-in his new pistol. According to the custom of the College, when he emerges he will be Fair Game for 24 hours.' People laughed and said 'hooray' and things like that, but the piece of toast jolted to a halt on its way down the Mortdecai gizzard.

'?'I asked courteously.

'It means,' she explained courteously, 'that from 1010 hours you are Fair Game. It is the custom here with new students, whatever their age, sex or weight. Let me put it like this: it will be open season on C. Mortdecai from the hour stated. Your fellow students will take all reasonable care to avoid maiming you seriously, for it is all in fun, you see. Some of your predecessors have survived their Fair Game Day with little more than the loss of a tooth or two.' She gazed at the butter melting into her toast and heaved what might well have been a sigh of regret for happier days, days when no pat of butter durst slink into a piece of toast without written orders signed by herself.

'Good luck, Mortdecai,' she said dismissively.

No retort sprang to my lips.

It was a bad day; a rotten day. (It was like a compressed version of that hateful first term at a fourth-rate Public School when you are hounded and persecuted and you can't lock yourself into the lavatory to cry because the lavatories have no locks and you spend all your private-study time writing frantic, tear-spattered letters to your parents, imploring them to take you away although you know they will only reply in a jocose way, using phrases like 'forming your character' and so forth.) When I say that the pleasantest two hours of this first day at the Terror College of Dingley Dell were spent high up in the fork of a Douglas Fir or some other hateful fourth-rate conifer, being shot at with graphite bullets, I think I have said all.

I lost not a single tooth, but the black eye I sported at dinner excited some tasteless ribaldry. I recked not of it, for dinner was, once again, superb; it seemed to heal all wounds. They tried to spoil the *Navarin d'Agneau* for me by saying that it was my turn to wash up but at this point I dug in my heels. There are some things a white man simply does not do. Yell for mercy from armed lesbians when halfway up a Douglas Fir or other conifer, yes. Wash up after them, no.

The place of honour beside the Commandant was empty throughout dinner; the new guest or victim had clearly not yet reported aboard. I was glad not to be sitting there bandying polite remarks with Madam, nor having to avert my gaze from Kitty's appalling and treacherous bosom. In my new place, halfway down the table, I was flanked on the one hand by an amusing, scholarly American who told me that he guessed I could call him a kind of Sinologist, and on the other by quite the nubilest girl on the premises. She had an engaging giggle and a blouseful of the most ravishing tits you can imagine. She promised that she would take over my washing-up chores for me and then confided that I had hit her with a graphite bullet that afternoon and raised a *drettful* bruise which she couldn't show me just then because she was sitting on it.

So soon as the stopper clunked into the neck of the brandy-decanter I pleaded fatigue – which was no less than the truth – and chugged up to my bedroom. Tomorrow morning was to be devoted to Theory, which meant that I must master an instructional brochure or two before folding the hands to zizz. First I mastered a generous slug out of one of my half-bottles, then selected the *Racial Impersonation* booklet to take to bed with me. The chapter entitled 'Somato-Ethnic Ambience-Values' seemed just the thing to induce a wholesome slumber but I was wrong – for the eleventh time that day. 'Somato-Ethnic Ambience-Values' proved to be about all kinds of fascinating things; I read avidly. It seems that these S-E-A-Values are all about what ethologists call the *Umwelt* – the area of alarm around members of the brute creation, such as human beings. It seems that we are all born with, or acquire, a racial sense of personal territory around our bodies and that outside this inner periphery of 'privacy' there lies an outer sphere of 'friendliness' which may be penetrated by permission or mutual agreement. Thus, if you are interviewing someone whom you wish to humiliate without actually saying so, you seat him just far enough away from yourself to make him feel vaguely ill at ease, to make him speak just a little louder than he cares to – and to enable you to raise your voice in a minatory way. Most tycoons learn this dodge when they are mere suckling managing directors – and it was not the least of Hitler's secret weapons. On the other hand, ask the bloke to come behind your desk and sit a couple of feet from you and he feels admitted to your ring of dentifrice confidence.

Similarly, if you are impersonating an Arab or Levantine, you must chat with other Arabs or Levantines belly to belly: if you step back from the dread gush of garlic and dental caries you will cause raised eyebrows, be your disguise and your mastery of the language never so perfect.

There were lots more fascinating nuggets, some of which I knew already. I knew, for instance, that you don't touch people's turbans but then I have never desired to. I knew that amongst Muslims you don't touch food with your left hand but I didn't know that to touch almost anything with it can be construed as a deadly insult in certain circumstances. (Muslims, you see, only use the left hand for one purpose. Shortage of water in the desert, you understand.) I knew, too, that a closed-lips smile from certain kinds of Chinese means 'I don't understand,' but I had not known that a broader smile means 'You are embarrassing me,' and that a smile revealing the teeth means something quite else again. Chinese restaurants, I felt, after reading the brochure, would never be quite the same for me again. (I was comparatively innocent at the time; had I been given a glimpse into the future I would have been through the window in a flash, prepared to take my chances with the Dobermanns and the electric fence.)

I was still poring over these gobbets of useful lore when the lights went out and, thirty seconds later, the dyke-like voice of the loudspeaker told me that the lights were about to go out.

I composed myself to sleep by trying to visualize just where the bruise on my charming dinner-partner was situated. Had I been younger and less fatigued, such thoughts would have kept me awake.

13 Mortdecai is dismayed to find that this game is not being played for bobby-pins, nor even for money

With prudes for proctors, dowagers for deans
And sweet girl graduates in their golden hair.

The Princess

The Theory Morning went well; when it came to my turn I was able to do a pretty convincing imitation of a Levantine, for I had begged a clove of garlic from the kitchen; the Instructress fell back in disorder when I came bellying up to her, whining and waving my hands and gurking out great poisonous gusts of that prince of vegetables.

My pretty table-mate at luncheon also reeled back aghast but I had saved a snippet of the garlic against this very contingency and she chewed it obediently. 'Why,' she cried a moment later, 'I can't smell you at all any more!' I enquired courteously after her bruise and learnt that it was still quite drettful and that she had meant to wub arnica into it but couldn't quite weach it herself. We looked at each other speculatively.

This did not prevent her, later that afternoon, from doing her best to smarten me up painfully during the 'Seek and Destroy' exercise in the extensive shrubbery and plantation: indeed, she playfully planted, from quite twenty feet away, a graphite bullet squarely into the rolled-up pair of woollen socks which I had prudently placed where a cricketer keeps his box.

'You shall pay for this,' I muttered, gazing at the scarlet stain with which the crotch of my combat-trousers was splashed. (I was on the White side of this particular ploy or *Kriegspiel*, you see, while she was Red and our bullets were appropriately tinted.) I dutifully reported myself dead to the nearest Umpire, who tittered, sprayed an aerosol detergent on my red badge of honour and sent me back into the fray blushing. Craftily, I slithered across the lawn to the ditch or ha-ha, wormed along it until I was past the shrubbery, slithered out again and took up my position in a small, unkempt patch of scrub on the fringe of the plantation. (I was taught, long ago, always to choose the smallest piece of cover which will hold you; if you are behind the most barely adequate of the hummocks or bushes you will be the last to be rushed and may well be able to rake the other chaps with flank-fire while they are rushing the bigger ones. I don't know what they teach soldiers in these days of neutron-bombs. Prayer, perhaps.)

I had chosen my spot well; not a single sinner passed within range for the best part of an hour and I almost think I was beginning to doze off, lulled by the fragrance of myrtle, pine-needles and many another pleasing pong such as botanists relish on a warm afternoon. I was aroused from my musings by the faintest of scraping sounds from, of all places, the direction of ha-ha. 'Har har!' I thought, 'Gotcher!' for I was confident that this scraping sound was from my nubile friend; confident, too, that she would either surrender and offer to show me her bruise or, failing that, give me a sight of her on the skyline so that I could match up the bruise with another.

Nothing of the sort. The student who emerged from the ha-ha was small and skinny and, against all the rules, not wearing the College combat dress. What she was wearing was a sort of hooded track-suit of dull sky-blue – rather like the old French Army field-colour – but striped and slashed diagonally with dark green, as was her face. But I am no milliner; I simply shot her in the chest.

It was a lovely shot. Have you ever swung to a really fast pheasant and known, even as you pulled the trigger, that you could not possibly have missed, that the bird will drop tidily, quite dead, so close to your feet that your dog will have nothing to do but thump his tail approvingly? No? Oh. Well then, have you ever, at the poker-table, drawn a card to a 7, 8, 9, 10 straight with the absolute certainty that the card will be a 6 or a knave? No? *Really* not? Then, clearly, you are a golfer and will know the feeling that golfers never tire of describing: the feeling just as you finish your swing that this is a really meaty one which will send your ball right onto the green and make you wish that you weren't just playing for a lousy fiver.

This was, as I say, a lovely shot at that distance; it hit the girl on the central vertical axis, exactly half-way between the navel and the clavicle. Had it been a real bullet it would have collected a goodly chunk of her sternum and shredded it through the aorta, not killing her quite instantly but giving her perhaps a second and a half in which to regret that she had not chosen some other career.

Her reactions were slow, or perhaps she was simply a dullard; she checked in her stride and looked down stupidly at the 'wound', touched the splash of white powder in a puzzled sort of way, raised her fingers to her lips and tasted them. I raised my head from behind the hummock and cheerily told her that she was dead. She shot at me, which was against the rules. I wasted no time in protesting, for her bullet struck a stone in the hummock and screamed away *en ricochet* – no graphite bullet that. 'Bitch!' I thought angrily and squeezed off a couple of rounds at her camouflaged face – this, too, was against the rules. One of them must have connected for she screamed and clutched at her eyes. The odd thing was that she was screaming in no European language that I had ever heard and the screams were delivered in a round tenor voice. A *man*'s voice.

As I stood up a shot came from another direction and I felt a strong snatch at the waist of my combat-blouse: another camouflaged Oriental was emerging from the ha-ha. I knew I was down to the last round in the clip – the solid, cupro-nickel coated round – but I have always set my personal safety before that of people who are trying to kill me. I shot him in the head. He died uncomplainingly, passing no remarks.

A third man clambered out of the ditch, similarly camouflaged. This was a bad thing, because my pistol was empty and the spare clip was filled with graphite only. As I scrabbled in my pocket a genteel sort of sound, like a bank manager's fingers drumming on his desk-top, was to be heard from the plantation behind me. The man rose to his full height, stared down at his chest as puzzledly as the first chap had stared, then dropped dead. I swung around, still trying to drag the clip from my pocket.

Johanna emerged from the trees, holding a curious kind of machine-pistol of a brand I had never seen before.

'What's new, pussy-cat?' I quavered valiantly. She planted a wifely but perfunctory kiss on my cheek before trotting over to the ha-ha to seek out any further fiends in human shape. She found none. We took the chap with the sore eye back to the College with us.

Over a cup of tea in the Commandant's office, or 'den' as she chose to call it, we chatted of this and that. Johanna's cup of tea was what she calls a 'General Montgomery', which is a fearful kind of dry Martini and so called because the proportion of gin to vermouth is twelve to one. Mine was a richly-deserved Red Hackle De Luxe – a fluid expressly designed to twitch people back from the very edge of the grave – while the Commandant was demurely sipping neat Navy rum. The actual teapot seethed unloved upon its tray.

'Look,' I said. They looked, politely.

'Look, why were those awful people trying to kill me, eh? Eh?'

'They weren't,' said the Commandant crisply.

'Well, you would certainly have had me fooled.'

'Charlie dear, they were not trying to kill you *in particular* is what Sibyl means. Yes, dear, this is Sibyl but you must continue to call her Madam while you're here. (Oh Charlie, dear, please don't let your mouth hang open like that.) They were infiltrating the Command Post, you see.' I didn't see.

'Where's that?' I asked.

'Why, here, dear.'

'No no no, quite wrong, this is Dingley Dell College, ask anyone.'

'Well, yes, dear, but it's a few other things as well. All sorts of things, in fact.'

I had a nasty feeling that someone would soon say that I should not trouble my pretty head with such things, so I shut up.

'In fact,' Johanna said with becoming modesty, 'it was probably me they were hoping to kill. I was kind of expecting it, you know? That's why I wasn't at dinner last night, sitting on – OK, *at* – Sibyl's right hand. I arrived here just after dawn, when Fiona would have locked her doggies up, and spent the day in the plantation or whatever you call it in Britain and there I was, just in time to save your life, wasn't I, darling?'

'Indeed you were,' I said bitterly. 'Indeed you were. Forgive me for not having thanked you at the time. Let's see, how many times does that make?'

She gave me a long, level look which should have stuck out between my shoulder-blades but I was not abashed for I have received many such looks in my career. It takes a very long and level look indeed to abash a dealer in Old Master paintings.

'Who, then,' I asked curtly, 'were these avenging angels? Mere fortune-hunters? Cast-off lovers? I feel I have a right to know, you know.'

This time she raised an eyebrow. Long, level looks I can cope with, but when Johanna raises an eyebrow strong men have been known to rend their garments. I quailed. My question had been in bad taste.

'Sorry,' I said.

'They were from 14K.'

'That's 14, Quai d'Orsay?' I asked brightly. 'Assassination rules; *Au Quai?*' They looked at me. I fancy I did a spot more quailing.

'No, Charlie dear, it means Number 14, Po Wah Road, Canton, China. That used to be the headquarters of a sort of Tong – they call them Triads now in the newspapers – formed by the old Nationalist Government or, to be exact, by Madam Chiang, Sun Yat Sen's grand-daughter, which amounts to the same thing – in 1945 as a "bulwark against Communism". They're still anti-Communist but they have kind of diversified their operations in the last twenty years or so. They're into the Golden Triangle in a big way now.'

I both boggled and blushed, as any chap would who has shared many a loving jest with his bride about her being a natural blonde. She gave me another of the looks; there was little kindness in it.

'Charlie, even you must have heard of the Golden Triangle; it is the opium-growing area bounded by the hill-country of Burma, Laos and Thailand. You must have realized what all those nasty little wars are about. Well, 14K desperately needs acetic anhydride and they can only get it from us. *Now* do you see?'

'No,' I said frankly.

'Oh, golly. Acetic anhydride is for refining morphine. It's essential. Refining opium into morphine reduces its bulk and increases its value; refining morphine into heroin does the same – in spades. You can buy a kilo of Number Three in Bangkok for a couple of hundred pounds; as heroin in Hong Kong it's worth maybe £6000 wholesale, which means, say £30,000 on the streets. If you can get it to Amsterdam you can triple that, even after paying off the narcotics-gendarmes who have starving mistresses and a mortgage to support. In New York . . .'

'Yes, yes,' I said, 'I know all that, although the prices seem to rise every week. And I know about the Police Sergeant in Hong Kong who has fifty-six bank accounts, too. But when I said "No" I meant "No, I don't know who this '*us*' is – I mean this 'us' who has a half-Nelson on the acetic what-d'ye-call-it." Who, in fact, is this "us?" ' I asked with a fine disregard for the niceties of the English tongue. She exchanged a quick glance with the Commandant.

'Oh, I see,' she said. 'Yes, well, I guess you might as well know. "Us" are – oh, hell, you've got me doing it now – *we* are – or rather we're friends with – the Woh Singh Wo, probably the most ancient Tong in China.'

'Oh, ah,' I said feebly.

'Yes. We're in a sort of league with them. It's a little complicated to explain just now . . .'

'White slaves?' I asked curtly. She stared at me, then giggled in that annoying silvery-tinkle way.

'No, Charlie, you have it upside down, dear.'

'Sometimes, yes,' I said stiffly, for I do not care to have my bedroom fads spoken of in public, 'but what do you mean? Are you – we – *against* white slaving?'

'Well, yes, you might say that. Yes, that's very good, Charlie.' She went off into the silvery laugh again.

'Now look here,' I said, trying to control the Mortdecai temper, 'I'm not an inquisitive man but would you mind telling me, just between the three of us . . .'

'Four,' she said. I counted us. We were three.

'Eh?' I said.

'No, Ho,' said a voice behind me. I laid an egg as I whirled round. There, behind me, bulked a massive Chinese gentleman in a silk suit. I still don't know how he got there.

'Charlie, this is my friend Mr Ho. Mr Ho, this is my husband.' The Chinese chap made noises both respectful and disbelieving.

I pulled myself together and ransacked my mind for a telling remark.

'How do you do,' is what came out.

'I manage,' he said. I smiled, not showing the teeth.

There fell a sort of silence. Mr Ho did not sit down. Johanna and the Commandant – I would never learn to call her Sibyl – looked at their laps as though they had embroidery there. It fell to me to biff the ball of conversation about.

'Mr ah, Ho,' I began, in the jovial, over-civil way in which one addresses chaps whose skins aren't quite the same colour as one's own.

'No, *Ho*,' he said.

'Eh?'

'No, not eh, not ah ho: *Ho*,' he insisted. I began to feel like the straight man on a Linguaphone record; decided to assert myself.

'What's your line of business then, Mr Ho?' I asked jovially.

'Hut,' he said. There was little in that remark for me so I let it fall to the floor, hoping that the maid would brush it under the chair next morning.

'Charlie dear, Mr Ho is saying that he *hurts* people. He does it for a living, you see.'

'Oh, ah,' I said.

'Charlie dear, the phrase "oh ah" is very rude in Cantonese.'

I said a very rude word in English, then subsided into a sulky silence.

'Mr Ho, would you like to bring the prisoner in, please?' said the Commandant. He did not reply. I glanced at him: he was not there. I reckon that I can shift the Mortdecai carcass around fairly noiselessly but this man was quite uncanny; he was even better than old Wooster's manservant who, as is well known, used to shimmer for England.

'Mr Ho is the Red Stick for the Woh Singh Wo in England,' said Johanna hurriedly. 'That's sort of, uh, *enforcer*.' He was back in a twinkling, carrying the prisoner over his shoulder as casually as you or I might carry a beach-bag, if we were the kind of person who carries beach-bags.

'Interrogate him,' said the Commandant, 'but please don't make a mess. The carpet is a costly one.' Mr Ho dumped the man on the floor, took a plastic Pak-a-Mak out of his pocket and threw it at him. The man unrolled it, lay down tidily on it. He was quite naked except for a bandage on his face where my bullet had hit him but his other eye was open and alert. He showed no signs of fear except that his penis had sort of shrivelled up as though he had just come out of a cold bath.

'If you're going to torture him,' I said, 'I'm leaving.'

'Probabry not necessary,' said Mr Ho. 'If he is professional, will know I can make him talk, will not waste our time. Most torture is crap; it amuses torturer onry; makes innocent man confess to anything, makes guilty man rie, makes stupid man dead too soon. Gestapo rubbish.

'Professional torture simple.

'First, hut very much at beginning. Most peopre do not rearise how much pain huts.

'Second, remove male members. Most peopre talk before this.

'Third, remove eyesight.

'Fourth, promise quick death. That is all. Watch.'

He produced a black doctor's bag. I trembled at the thought of the dreadful instruments he would take out of it but the contents were positively homely. One ordinary electric iron, which he placed tidily at the soles of the prisoner's feet. He did not plug it in. The prisoner raised himself on one elbow and watched dispassionately. Then Ho laid a coil of thin wire with wooden handles at each and – such as grocers use for cutting cheese – on the man's genitals. The man's face did not display any emotion but his penis seemed to shrivel a little more. Then Ho produced a teaspoon and laid it on the carpet at the level of the man's remaining eyeball and a long, tenpenny nail which he laid on the man's left breast.

The man seemed to appraise these ordinary, workaday objects – how sensible of Mr Ho to carry nothing incriminating – and came to a decision. He uttered a series of polite, deprecating quacks in what was probably Cantonese.

'There!' said Mr Ho kindly. 'He is professional. Says he knows one thing. Only one. Will say it, if kill quick; now. OK?'

Mr Ho cleared away everything except the long, tenpenny nail, which he left over the man's heart. The man rattled off a string of syllables in the same polite and unemotional tones he had used before. Mr Ho wrote things on a piece of paper and handed it to the Commandant.

'And what the hell is that supposed to mean?' she bellowed. Johanna took the slip of paper and shook her head, passed it to me.

'It's a map-reference,' I said in my cold, war-experienced, adjutant's voice. 'LSE64 is the sheet number, Ordnance Survey. H6 is the kilometre square. 625975 is the ground reference.' The Commandant snatched it and pressed a tit on her buzzer-console, asked for 'Library' and told someone called Annie to find sheet LSE6$_4$ and that right speedily. We waited, in silence and various degrees of fraughtness. Apart from Mr Ho, the least agitated member of our tea-party was the Chinese prisoner, who was gazing absorbedly up the Commandant's skirt. I was glad to note that his penis had unshrivelled itself a goodish bit. Ah well, whatever turns you on. For my part, I'd hate to go to eternal bliss with the memory of an old bull-dyke's directoire knickers imprinted on my retina for all eternity but that's what makes horse-races, isn't it?

Annie the Librarian brought in the map. Johanna and the Commandant looked at it. Rather in the way they had looked at me.

'Oh, dear,' said Johanna.

'Oh, shit,' said the Commandant in her coarse way. 'They know where, er, our man er *you-know-who* is.' She tried to work out the six-figure reference and snarled. I explained that the first figures go laterally, the others vertically. 'You must put it across a woman before you can get it up her,' I explained, quoting an old Army mnemonic. They glared at me but let me find the spot. It was an **ANCIENT FORT** overlooking a main road in a featureless waste of Yorkshire moorland.

'Mortdecai must go,' said the Commandant briskly. 'He's expendable.'

'Hoy!' I protested.

'Sibyl didn't mean it like that, Charlie dear,' said Johanna worriedly.

'Also he's crafty; a survivor; can shoot a bit,' added the Commandant, hoping to mollify me. She addressed herself to her buzzer-console again: 'Sandwiches for two days please, kitchen: high-protein ones, none of your fancy egg-and-salad; one litre flask of strong black coffee, no sugar; one litre bottle of Scotch whisky. To be in Mr Mortdecai's car, which will be at the door in five minutes exactly.'

'How do you know I don't take sugar?' I asked rebelliously.

'*No* gentleman takes sugar in black coffee. Besides, it's bad for you. No, I'm not talking about your disgraceful waistline. Sugar and alcohol together trigger off your insulin and give you hypoglycaemia – symptoms are faulty judgment, undue fatigue, anxiety, inner trembling.'

'I get the last two when ordered to go and find people called *you-know-who* on lonely Yorkshire moors at five minutes notice,' I retorted. 'Anyhow, how do I recognize this chap, how will he recognize me and what do I do if I find him?'

'He will be on foot, if we're lucky,' she said cryptically. 'He answers to the name of Freddie. Just tell him what has happened and he'll know you're genuine.'

'Thank God I don't have to approach a complete stranger and whisper to him that the moon is shining brightly and wait for him to say that the price of fish and chips is going up,' I quipped.

'Try not to babble, Charlie dear.'

'If possible, get him out of there fast, and back here in one piece. If he can't come, take a message. If he's, ah, unable to speak, search him.'

'For what?'

'I don't know,' she said simply.

'I see.'

'Now, pop upstairs, get warm clothes, stout shoes and a couple of clips of cartridges. The real ones.'

'What about him?' I asked, indicating the patient prisoner. 'He's heard all this; probably understands English. And shouldn't someone see to his poor eye?'

'Irrelevant,' she said absently, 'he's been promised a quick death – a kindness really, because if we were to let him go his friends would give him a slow and exceedingly nasty one. Mr Ho?'

She gave Ho a half-tumbler of raw vodka which he handed to the naked chap. The chap tossed it off in one gulp, nodded appreciatively. Mr Ho gave him a lighted cigarette. He took two deep and happy drags then ground it out on the carpet (in his place I'd have said I was trying to give them up, of course; I couldn't have wasted such an opportunity). Then he lay down again on the Pak-a-Mak and made not a tremor as Ho knelt beside him, measured off one hand's-breadth below the left nipple and, finding the space between the appropriate ribs, positioned the point of the six-inch nail, holding it in place with an index finger on its head. Then Ho turned to me and politely said, 'Prease, he try to kill you – you wanna kill him?'

'Goodness, no,' I gabbled, 'I mean thanks awfully, kind of you, very, but I've already killed one chap today and I'm trying to . . .'

'Mr Ho,' said the Commandant, 'I think it might be better if you did it outside. You'll find a girl called Fiona at the kennels, she'll show you where the graves are.'

Mr Ho left the room in a marked manner – a little hurt, I fancy – the prisoner folded the Pak-a-Mak neatly, bobbed politely to the company and trotted off behind him.

I hope that, when my own three oranges turn up on the Celestial fruit-machine, I shall accept the jackpot of mortality with as much dignity.

'Goodbye, Charlie dear,' said Johanna. 'Drive carefully.'

'Good luck, Mortdecai,' said the Commandant gruffly.

'Yes,' is what I said.

14   Mortdecai's interest in bird-watching falters

What does little birdie say
In her nest at peep of day?

Sea Dreams

I must say I do approve of seagulls. Most petty criminals nowadays are so bad at their jobs – don't you agree? – while gulls are as dedicated as traffic-wardens and a great deal cheerier about their chosen vocation. They (the seagulls) gather in the grey light of dawn, shouting dirty jokes at each other and screaming with ribald laughter, waking up slug-a-beds like you and me, then when they have decided what to do that day, off they fly – and how good they are at flying, not an erg of energy wasted – scrounging, stealing, murdering and generally fulfilling their slots in the ecology. At lunchtime, when we are munching our first brandy-and-soda of the day, they congregate again in some spacious field, their bellies full for the nonce, and stand there in silence, sensibly digesting and *loafing* until it is time for another worm or two (in the case of the little Black-headed sort) or a tasty dead dog (in the case of the Greater Black-backed buggers). How wonderfully uplifting it is to watch them wheeling and swooping in the wake of a car-ferry, waiting for idiots to purchase British Rail sandwiches and throw them overboard after one disgustful bite! The very poetry of motion!

When all the world and I were young and people still knew their proper stations in life, seagulls were something that happened at sea, only occasionally calling in at the shore to defecate on your nice new sun-hat so that Nursey could give you a bad time. Nowadays you see them everywhere, raiding dustbins and queueing up outside fish-and-chip shops instead of swimming in their nice oil-slicks and eating up their nice, freshly polluted herring-guts.

The assorted seagulls who were grouped at the foot of the **ANCIENT FORT** were not exhibiting the poetry of motion, nor where they loafing, nor yelling like spoiled brats as seagulls should. *Waiting* is what they were doing. Waiting around a bundle of old rags. As I drew nearer they all rose into the air in a sulky fashion, except for a Greater Black-backed (*Larus Marinus*), big as a Michaelmas goose, who remained perched on the bundle of rags. Foraging for something. I broke into a run. The gull's beak emerged from the raggedy man's face, gulping something white and glistening from which scarlet ribbons hung. The bird gave me a murderous, yellow-rimmed glance from one of its eyeballs then flapped insolently away. I had nothing to throw at it.

When I had finished vomiting, I turned the raggedy man over onto his face and ran down the fell-side to the road. I should of course have searched him as ordered but, to tell the truth, I was filled with horror at the thought that he might still be alive. That may sound strange to you but you weren't there, were you? I had, of course, left my car some miles away and had walked across the moors to the map-reference and the **ANCIENT FORT** and the raggedy man. I waved down a passing car and had great trouble persuading the television-sodden driver that he was not on 'Candid Camera' and that no, I really wasn't Robert Morley, before he became grudgingly convinced that a man was actually dying or dead and that he must take me to the nearest telephone. From there I telephoned Blucher's secretary and gave her all the *nu*'s that were fit to print.

'Wait there,' she ordered. Since I still had one and one-half sandwiches and an almost-full pocket flask I fell in with her wishes. Night, too, fell. One hundred years and one almost-full pocket-flask later a Cocteau-like motor-bicycle policeman came roaring out of the gloaming, followed in a few moments by a 'bad-news wagon' (that means a police-car, *hypocrite lecteur*) and an ambulance. I led them all up to the **ANCIENT FORT** breaking each of my legs several times en route. There were several brief altercations: when the Sergeant berated me for having turned the raggedy chap over onto his face 'thus possibly destroying evidence'. I explained that certain feathered friends had been destroying evidence even more effectively. He did not believe me until they turned the chap over onto his back again, whereupon the dashing, fearless motor-bike copper was ill all over the Sergeant's brand-new shoes, starting another altercation which, conjoined with the ambulance-men's bitter discussion about overtime, fairly made the welkin ring. I found it all a bit sordid.

'Trotskyist pig!'

'They cost me nineteen pounds ninety-five only last week!'

'Get no bloody home-life in this job, do we?'

'Filthy Maoist revisionary!'

'I should afford such shoes on my pay.'

'Got the shop-steward in your pockets, haven't you, eh?'

'They're supposed to have the rubbed-off wet-look and look at the buggers now!'

'Well, at least I'm not in the bosses' pockets, I can say that . . .'

'Drop of turps will have 'em good as new in no time . . .'

'No, it's not the bosses' *pockets* you're in, comrade . . .'

'You calling me a brown-nose, brother?'

I stole away, murmuring 'Oh dear, oh dear' and musing on dialectical materialism and the Majesty of the Law. I was quite right: I had indeed left almost half a sandwich in the telephone-box. It occurred to me to telephone Blucher again, hoping to get him in person this time. He was not in the least amused. Had I searched the man? Why not? Was the chap dead? What did I mean I wasn't sure? Why wasn't I there beside him, watching every move of every copper? I began to feel like Macbeth in Act II, Scene 2, where his wife says 'Infirm of purpose; give me the daggers,' when the door of the booth or kiosk was flung open and the Sergeant demanded to be told who it was that I was telephoning.

'Sweet, cuddlesome dreams, my own dearest little fluffy-puss,' I said into the receiver as I replaced it in a dignified fashion, before turning upon the fellow and raising a brace of icy eyebrows. (I yield to none when it comes to eyebrow-raising; I was taught by my father himself, who could have eyebrow-raised for Great Britain had he not been so haughty.) The Sergeant cringed a little, as I had been cringing under the lash of Blucher's ice-maiden voice. This cringing of his gave me time to wonder what kind of pressure Blucher could have applied – and to whom – and what I was supposed to do – or be.

The necessary, hasty trip to the mortuary over, we all pitched up at the cop-shop of the county town – I cannot remember its name but I shall always think of it as Heckmondwyke – where I was given great mugs of tea and met an Inspector of Detectives who positively bulged with intelligence and well-feigned friendliness. He asked me only the most natural and obvious questions then told me courteously that a room was booked for me at the cleaner of the two local hostelries and that the Detective Sergeant would take me there. Oh yes, and would pick me up in the morning, so that we could foregather at the morgue.

'Didn't seem awfully interested, did he?' I said nonchalantly as the Sergeant decanted me in front of what I suppose I must call the hotel.

'Well, only an old tramp,' said the Sergeant.

'Ah,' I said.

Dinner was 'off', of course, for it was by now quite eight o'clock, but an embittered crone, after I had bribed her richly, made me a bowl of soup and something called am-an-eggs. The soup was not good but she had at least taken the packet off before adding the warm water. I prefer not to discuss the am-an-eggs.

It would be idle to pretend that I slept well.

Well, there we were next morning, all well-washed, shaven, after-shave fragrant; costly our habits as our purse could buy. (Indeed, rather costlier in the case of the Detective Constable: policemen in expensive suits *worry* me.) It was shaming to look at the dirty old corpse on the mortuary slab. Refrigeration had only a little abated the richness of his bodily odours. His mouth gaped open in a derisive way; the teeth in his mouth were few – and few of them could have met. The Inspector took his time looking at the teeth.

'Even a tramp,' I said crossly, from my guilty heart and from between well-dentifriced ivory-castles, 'even a tramp could have got himself a set of gnashers from the National Health. I mean, dammit.'

'That's right,' said the Inspector as he rose from peering into the carrion old mouth.

We trooped into the room where the tramp's pitiful clothes and other gear were laid out on a trestle-table, together with the prescribed three copies of the list of these possessions. Our nostrils were assailed with the cloying horror of a lavender-flavoured aerosol 'air-freshener' and the Inspector snarled at the uniformed bloke in charge.

'I might have wanted to *smell* these things,' is what he snarled.

'Sorry, sir.'

'Anything that turns you on . . .' murmured the Detective Constable by the door. The Inspector pretended not to have heard – help is hard to come by these days and, in any case, he had noticed the Detective Sergeant's deadly glance at the DC: the glance which says that certain DC's are going to find themselves lumbered with a nasty little bit of extra duty tomorrow.

The objects laid out on the trestle-table were not a suitable sight for the squeamish. In the matter of underclothes the deceased's policy seemed to have been 'live and let live', not to mention 'increase and multiply'. There were several layers of these intimate garments and its was apparent that the local police had not found a volunteer to separate them. The Inspector braced himself and went about the task himself: he was a man of iron. Then he checked, against the list, the pitiful, trumpery possessions from the corpse's pockets and haversack. He checked them as minutely as a prosecuting attorney might scan President Nixon's Christmas-present list.

There were ancient, nameless scraps of what might once have been food. There was a retired baked-beans tin with two holes in the edges to take a loop of wire; the inside was caked with tea, the outside with soot. There was a twist of plug-tobacco engraved with tooth-marks: whether by man or beast it would be hard to say. There was a cheap, blunt, celluloid-handled penknife of the sort which is made to sell. To schoolboys. Something stirred in my mind. There was a piece of soap, gnarled and grime-fissured. A tin box containing a dozen red-top matches and half an inch of candle. A coloured photograph from a 'girlie' magazine – a 'beaver-shot' as they call it, much creased and be-thumbed. An onion, the sweating heel of a piece of cheese and some cold fried potatoes, neatly packed in one of those foil-lined cartons they use in Chinese take-away restaurants. Grubby twists of paper containing sugar, tea, salt . . . ah, well, you know the sort of thing. Or perhaps you don't; lucky you.

Oh yes, and there was a nice, clean £10 note.

The Inspector at last rose from his absurdly detailed inspection of the chattels, blew his nose and shook himself like a dog.

'Not a tramp,' he said. His voice was flat; he was not accusing anyone.

'Not?' I asked after a pause.

'But . . .' said the Sergeant after a longer pause.

'Sir!' huffed the DC.

'Use your eyes, lad,' said the Inspector. 'The facts are as plain as the nose on your face.' The DC, being well-gifted in the nose-department, fell silent. This was the point at which I began to take the Inspector seriously.

After he had signed receipts and things and had shrugged off his subordinates he carried me off to the cop-shop canteen, where he regaled me with delectable tea and the finest and crispest ham-rolls I have ever sunk tooth into.

'Well,' I said, when the crust-munching noises had died down, 'are you going to tell me or not?'

'Teeth and toenails,' he answered cryptically.

'Eh?'

'Aye. No blame to you for not noticing, but those twits out there are supposed to have been taught to use their eyes.'

I kept my mouth shut. I, too, had been taught things of that kind long ago, but there was no profit in telling him the story of my life and I hoped, in any case, to hear him spell out his thoughts as to an innocent bystander, for there is no more rewarding experience than to listen to a man who is really good at his job. This man was very good.

'First,' he said, licking a trace of mustard from a capable thumb, 'when did you last see a genuine old-fashioned foot-tramp in England?'

'Why, now I come to think of it, not for a hell of a long time. Used to be part of the landscape, didn't they, but I can't say that I –'

'Right. I said *foot*-tramp to rule out Romanies and didicoys and such. I don't reckon there's six real tramps walking the roads of

England today and there haven't been since, oh, about 1960. The casual-wards are all closed down, so are the pay-flops; and the Rowton Houses are all turning into Commercial Hotels. They say there's a few old stagers still trudging Wild Wales, but that's it.

'Moreover, your real old tramp used to have a regular beat of about two hundred miles, so he'd pass through any given "manor" maybe once in a good summer and three times in winter. Even those morons out there who call themselves detectives would certainly know any walking-gent who went through the manor regular.'

'Meths-drinker?' I asked.

'No. None of the signs. And meths-drinkers haven't the strength to walk any distance. And they usually have a flat half-bottle of the rubbish taped to the small of their back in case they get nicked. And they don't eat. Our man liked his food – if you can call it food.'

'So?'

'So, second,' he said, examining his forefinger for any lingering mustard, 'you were dead right when you worried that he'd not got himself a set of dining-snappers off the National Health. In fact, as a glance at his gums and canines would have told any *real* policeman, he had once owned a costly set of bridgework – not your National Health sort – and had only parted with them a few months ago. Say, about the time he took his last bath.'

'And third?' I prompted.

'Third,' he said, holding up his middle finger in a gesture which would be considered vulgar in Italy, 'third, no scissors.'

'No scissors,' I repeated in an intelligent sort of voice.

'No scissors. In me early days I've looked over the belongings of many a tramp found dead in a ditch. Some of them had pictures of the lass that drove them onto the road, some of them had rosaries, some had a little bag of golden sovereigns and I remember one that had a New Testament in Greek. But the one thing that they all had was a good, strong pair of scissors. You wouldn't last long walking the road if you couldn't cut your toenails. A tramp's toenails are his bread and butter, you might say. Our man here didn't even have a strong sharp knife, did he? No; not a tramp, definitely.'

I made the sort of admiring noises you used to make when your geometry-master triumphantly said 'QED'.

'I don't mind telling you,' he went on, 'that I regret saying that bit about him not being a tramp in front of the Sergeant and the DC. But I know that you can be relied on to keep your mouth shut, sir' – I jumped a little at the 'sir' – 'because obviously neither of us wants idiots like them wondering why someone would be wanting to pass himself off as a tramp in *this particular* part of the country.' He looked narrowly at me as he said that last bit: I did my best to look inscrutable, hoping to give the impression that I well knew the special fact about 'this particular part of the country' and that I might well have, tucked into my left boot, a very special kind of identity-credential too grand to be shown to common coppers.

'Funny about that nice new tenner he had on him,' mused the Inspector. 'Looked to be fresh from the mint, didn't it?'

'Yes.'

Not even folded, was it?'

'No.'

'What was the number on it again, did you happen to notice?'

'Yes,' I said absently – *stupidly* – 'JZ9833672, wasn't it?'

'Ah, yes, that was it. Funny, that.'

'How d'you mean, "funny"?' I asked. 'Funny that I should remember it? I have an eidetic memory for numbers, can't help it. Born with it.' He did not take the trouble to check my statement – he was good at his job, he knew I was lying.

'No,' he said, 'I meant funny that it's from the same series as a large number of perfectly genuine tenners that the London lads reckon have come into the country not a month ago. From Singapore or one of those places. You must admit that's funny.'

'Hilarious,' I said.

'Yes, well, goodbye now, sir, we really can't detain you any longer.'

'Oh, but if I can be of any further help . . .'

'No, sir; what I meant to say was that I'm sorry we can't *detain* you. In custody, as they say. Like, for instance, dropping you in the Quiet Room for a couple of days and then having two or three of the lads beat the shit out of you until you told us what this caper is all about. Would have been nice,' he added thoughtfully. 'You know, interesting. We jacks are an inquisitive lot, see?' I may have gulped a little at this point.

'But you seem to have some very heavy friends, sir, so I will just bid you a friendly farewell. For now.' He shook me warmly by the hand.

Outside, waiting for me, there was one of those lovely black cars which only police-forces can afford. The uniformed driver opened the door for me. 'Where to, sir?' he asked in a uniformed sort of voice.

'Well,' I said, 'as a matter of fact I have a car of my own which I sort of left just off the road about, let's see, about twenty miles away; it's a . . .'

'We know where your car is, sir,' he said.

15 Mortdecai loses faith in matrimony, takes holy orders *pro tem* and sees a dentist more frightened than a dentist's client

But the jingling of the guinea helps the hurt that Honour feels
Locksley Hall

When your kitchen sink is blocked and you have to summon a plumber because both it and the maid are making threatening noises, he – the plumber – unscrews the thingummy at the bottom of the wonderfully aptly-named U-trap and shows you triumphantly the mass of detritus that he has liberated from it, with all the pride of a young mother exhibiting the malevolent squashed-tomato which she assures you is a baby. This great, greasy gobbet of nastiness (I refer, of course, to the sink-occlusion, not to the family-planning error) proves to be a closely-matted cupful of vegetable-peelings, pubic hair and nameless, grey, fatty matter.

What I am trying to describe is the condition of the enfeebled Mortdecai brain on its – my – return to the Training College or Command Post or whatever.

'Ah, Mortdecai,' growled the Commandant gruffly.

'Charlie, dear!' cried Johanna.

'Drink?' I muttered, subsiding into an armchair.

'Drink!' snapped Johanna absently. The Commandant leapt to the booze-cupboard and made me a drink with surprising alacrity and rather too much soda-water. I filed the surprising-alacrity bit away into that part of my mind where I file things which I must think about when I feel stronger. Then I filed the whisky and s. into the most confidential part of the Mortdecai system and called for another.

'So you found him, Charlie dear?'

'Yes.' A thought squirmed in my brain. 'How did you know?' (I had, you see, telephoned no one but Colonel Blucher.)

'Just guessed, darling. And you wouldn't be back so soon if you were still looking for him, would you?'

'Glib,' I thought bitterly. 'Glib, *glib*.' I often bitterly think words like 'glib, *glib*' after listening to things which women have said; I'm sure I'm not alone in this.

'And how are you, Charlie? I hope it wasn't a horrid experience?'

'Not at all,' I replied bitterly. 'Wonderful shake-up. As good as a week at the seaside. Stimulating. Refreshing.' I gargled a little more.

'Do tell us all about it,' she murmured when the noises had died down. I told her almost all about it. From A to, let us say, W – omitting X, you see.

'And of course you wrote down the number of the nice, new, fresh ten-pound note, Charlie?'

'Naturally,' I said. Two panic-stricken glares focused upon me.

'But only,' I added smugly, 'upon the tablets of my memory.' Two batches of panic-stricken female breath were exhaled. I raised an eyebrow of the kind my mother used to raise when parsons preached unsound doctrine at Mattins. They gazed at me expectantly while I pretended to ransack my memory; then the Commandant took the hint and refilled my glass. I delivered the serial-number of the note in a gift-wrapped sort of way. They wrote it down, then the Commandant went to her desk and fiddled with absurd secret drawers (look, there are only just so many places in a bureau where a secret drawer can lurk – ask any antique-dealer) and produced a slim little book. They compared the number I had given them with the nonsense in the slim little book, looking cross, grave and worried in that order until I lost patience and rose to my feet. Secret Service games are boring even when played by men.

'Off to bed,' I said. 'Tired, you see. Must go to bed.'

'No, Charlie dear.'

'Eh?'

'I mean, you must be off to China; not bed.' I did not even try to absorb such nonsense. 'Rubbish!' I cried manfully, snaring the whisky-decanter as I swept out of the room. I did not sweep far, for Johanna called me back in masterful tones quite unbecoming in a bride.

'You will like it in China, Charlie.'

'Oh no I bloody won't, they'll take one look at me and send me off to be politically re-educated on some co-operative farm in Hunan. *I* know.'

'Well, no dear, I didn't mean Red China – not this time anyway – more Macao, really. It's independent or Portuguese or something – I guess it amounts to the same thing. A great gambling centre, you'll love it.'

'No,' I said firmly.

'Flying First Class in a Jumbo. With a bar.'

'No,' I said, but she could see that I was weakening.

'A suite in the best hotel and a bankroll to gamble with. Say a thousand.'

'Dollars or pounds?'

'Pounds.'

'Oh, very well. But I must go to bed first.'

'OK. In fact, goody.'

'I'm sorry I cannot invite you to share a nuptial couch,' I added stiffly, 'my bed is some two feet six inches wide and there are enough electronic bugs in the room to start an epidemic.'

'Yes,' she said obscurely.

When I emerged from the shower, briskly towelling the Mortdecai tum, Johanna was in the said 2′ 6″ bed.

'I've had the bugs turned off, Charlie.'

'Oh yeah?' I said in American.

'Yeah. I kinda own this joint, you know?' I winced.

'I didn't know,' I said stuffily, 'and there still isn't enough room in that bed for two.'

'You wanna bet, buster?'

There was enough room. And I mean that most sincerely.

'I think that, on the whole, I'd better take Jock with me,' I said later, during the interval for refreshments. 'After all, three eyes are better than two, eh?'

'No, Charlie. He is too conspicuous, people would remember him, whereas you're kind of unremarkable, you sort of melt into the background, you know?'

'No, I didn't know that,' I said stiffly, for that is the kind of remark which stings.

'Anyway, dear, he's a xenophobe, isn't he – he'd probably hit all sorts of people and attract attention.'

'Oh, very well,' I said. 'Back to the grind,' I added, but not out loud of course.

Johanna drove me to London the next morning. She is a wonderful driver but I used the passenger's brake a goodish number of times; the journey was, in fact, one long cringe for me. We finally pitched up unscathed at Upper Brook Street, W1, having stopped briefly at one of those places where they make passport photographs of you while you wait.

'But I already *have* a passport,' I said.

'Well, dear, I thought you'd like a nice new one.'

From the flat she made a number of guarded telephone calls to all sorts of people; the upshot was that by late afternoon I was the proud possessor of First Class tickets on a Boeing 747 and a Vatican City passport, complete with all necessary visas and made out in the name of Fr Thomas Rosenthal, SJ; occupation: Curial Secretary. I didn't think that was very funny and said so, huffedly.

'Darling,' she said, 'I do realize that at your age you wouldn't be just a Fr still, but if we'd made you a Monsignore or Bp or something the airline people would make a *fuss* of you and that wouldn't be secure, right? Tell you what, I'll send the passport back and have them promote you Canon. Hunh? Would you settle for Canon?'

'Oh, leave it alone, Johanna; I'm truly not sulking. The Church wouldn't be the first career I've muffed. Anyway, I'm not at all sure they have Canons in Rome and Monsignores have to wear puce breeches, I think.'

'Oh, good. I knew you wouldn't mind being a simple Fr. You have a kind of wonderful modesty . . .' I raised a deprecatory hand.

'I shall of course need a few strings of rosary-beads and a Breviary or two – I'm sure you've thought of that.'

'Charlie, darling, you're supposed to be a *Jesuit*, remember? They're not into all that stuff.'

'Of course not; silly of me.'

I don't mind admitting that I enjoyed the flight; I was the only First Class passenger and the stewardess was most attentive. Most attentive. I began to understand why Johanna had taken such pains over me the previous night, if you see what I mean. (If you don't see what I mean, congratulations on a clean mind.)

My hotel was of a *luxe* which surprised me: *tout confort moderne* would be understating by a bushel and a peck. It was not quite like that one in Bangkok where you have to shake the sheets each night to rid your bed-clothes of little golden girls, though the management of this one was certainly doing its best. But you don't want to hear about that sort of thing, do you?

In the morning I sprang out of bed with a glad cry and promptly sprang into it again with a whimper. I was never strong, even as a boy, and on that morning I felt so enfeebled both in body and mind that I doubt whether I could have hit the ground with my hat. Certainly, I was in no state to play at Secret Agents with Sinister Orientals. Jet-lag and other factors had me by the throat, to name only one organ; I built up my strength by having first one delicious breakfast and then, after a two-hour digestive nap, just such another, washing them down with nutritive glasses of brandy and soda which, in that sort of hotel, you can summon up without the aid of floor-waiters: you simply press the appropriate tit on a 'Refreshments Console' which looks for all the world like a miniature cinema-organ.

By lunch-time I felt able to totter down to the restaurant and recruit my strength properly; I had something green and crisp and tasty which was evidently the pubic hair of mermaidens but which the waiter assured me was fried seaweed. Then there were slivers of duck cooked in a sort of jam; a delicious goo made of the swim-bladders of some improbable fish; deep-fried dumpling-like things each containing a huge and succulent prawn, and so on and so forth: there was no limit to their inventiveness.

There was also something to drink which they said was distilled from rice. It had the deceptively innocent taste which made Pimm's No. 1 such a handy drink for seducing girls when I was at University. I went gratefully back towards my room, smiling at one and all. I was in that delightful stage of not-quite-drunkenness when one overtips happily and there was no lack of minions to overtip. I even pressed a sheaf of currency into the hand of someone who proved to be an American guest; he said, 'OK, Father, whaddya fancy?' Realizing my mistake, and remembering my clerical kit or garb, I waved an airy hand and told him to play it for me on anything he fancied: it would all go to the poor. Then I found my room, crashed the Mortdecai turnip onto the pillow and completed the cure with a couple of hours of the dreamless.

By late afternoon the cure was completed and I felt strong enough to open the sealed envelope of instructions which Johanna had given me at Heathrow Airport.

'Lo Fang Hi,' it read, 'Doctor of Dentistry and Orthodontics.' Clearly a poor joke but nevertheless I looked him up in the telephone-book (even if you do know that the Chinese keep their surnames where we keep our Christian ones, a Chinese telephone directory is a skull-popper) and found him. I telephoned him. A shrill and agitated voice admitted to being Dr Lo. I resisted the temptation to say 'Hi' and said, instead, that I was a toothpaste-salesman – for that was what I had been told to say. What he said was that I might come around as soon as I liked, indeed, he suggested I came very soon. Yes, very soon *indeed*, prease. I hung up, musingly. The Roman collar had been tormenting my neck and I recalled that I had rarely seen a toothpaste-salesman in a cassock, so I changed into an inconspicuous little burnt-orange lightweight which that chap in the Rue de Rivoli ran up for me in the day when £300 would still buy a casual suit.

The address, to my surprise, was not 'In the Street of the Thousand Baseballs, 'Neath the sign of the Swinging Tit' as the old ballad has it, but in Nathan Street, Kowloon, which proved to be a dull, respectable sort of boulevard, reminiscent of Wigmore St, London W1. (I do not know who Mr Nathan was nor why he should have such a street named after him; indeed I know nothing of Mr Wimpole, no, nor even Wigmore, although I could tell you a thing or two about Harley.)

The cab-driver spoke American with a pronounced Chinese accent. He was also the proud owner of a sense of humour: he had evidently taken Buster Keaton's correspondence-course. When I told him to take to No. 18, Lancaster Buildings, Nathan Road, Kowloon, he leaned over his seat and eyed me in a tiresome, inscrutable way.

'Cannot take you there, buddy.'

'Oh? And why not, pray?'

'Can take you to Rancaster Birradings, Nathan Rod, but not Number 18.'

'Why not?' I asked, a tremor in my voice this time.

'Number 18 on third floor; taxi does not fit into erevator.'

'Ha ha,' I said stiffly, 'but I notice that your meter is running; laugh on your own time, or while driving me capably to Lancaster Buildings, Nathan Road.'

'You a poreeseman?'

'Certainly not. I happen to be a toothpaste-salesman, if you must know.'

He wagged his head respectfully, as though I had said something impressive, or perhaps funny. He took me to Lancaster Buildings in an expert and blessedly silent fashion. On arrival I under-tipped him by precisely $2\frac{1}{2}\%$ – not enough to cause a scene but just enough to make it clear that taxi-drivers should not jest with sahibs.

Number 18 was indeed on the third floor of Lancaster Buildings and the door to Dr Lo's consulting-room was clearly inscribed RING AND ENTER. I rang, but could not enter, for the door was locked. Hearing sounds within I rapped irritably on the frosted glass, then louder and still louder, crying words such as 'Hoy!' All of a sudden, the door opened, a large, tan-coloured hand reached out, grabbed the front of my lightweight Paris suit and whisked me inside, depositing me upon an uncomfortable armchair. The owner of the tan-coloured hand was grasping a large, crude Stechkin automatic pistol in his other tan-coloured hand and waving it in an admonitory sort of way. I understood his desires instantly, for the Stechkin is by no means a lady's handbag-gun, and sat in my nice chair as quiet as any little mouse.

There was a patient in the dentist's operating-chair, being attended to by a brace of dentists. At first it seemed odd to me that the dentists were wearing dark-blue mackintoshes, just like the chap with the Stechkin, while the patient was wearing a white dentist's smock. (Sorry, a dentist's white smock.) I began to believe that the patient was, in fact, Dr Lo and that the dentists were quite unqualified in dentistry, especially when I noticed that they were using the drill on him although he refused to open his mouth. When Dr Lo – for it must have been he – passed out for the third or fourth time, his assailants were unable to bring him round. He had not uttered a word through his clenched teeth, although he had squealed through his nose a little, from time to time. I remember thinking that Mr Ho would have done much better, making much less mess.

The chaps in blue mackintoshes conversed in quacking tones together for a while, then turned on me.

'Who you?' asked one of them. I clapped my hand against my jaw in a piteous way and mimed the miseries of a tooth-ache sufferer. The man took my hand away from my jaw and slammed it with the side of his heavy pistol. Then he picked me up from the floor, sat me back in the chair.

'Tooth-ache better now?' I nodded vigorously. 'You recognize our faces again maybe?' There was no longer any need to mime suffering.

'Goodness, no; you chaps all look the same to . . . I mean, *no*, I have a terrible head for figures, that's to say faces or . . .'

He shifted the big pistol to his right hand and slammed me with it again. Now I really did need a dentist. He had not, in fact, rendered me unconscious but I decided to be so for all practical purposes. I let my head loll. He did not hit me again.

Through half-closed eyes I watched the three mackintoshed persons take off the clothes of the unconscious Dr Lo. He was a well-nourished dentist, as dentists go. One of the nasties took something out of his coat-pocket and threw the cardboard outer wrapping over his shoulder. It landed at my feet: the brand-name was 'Bull-Stik' – one of those terrifying new cyanoacrylic adhesives for which there is no known solvent. If you get it on your fingers, don't touch them, it will mean surgery. One of the three men spread it all over the seat of the dentist's chair and sat the naked Dr Lo down upon it, legs well apart. Then they played other pranks with the stuff which you will not wish to read about and which I would gladly forget. To tell the truth, I passed out in good earnest. Delayed shock, that sort of thing.

When I came to my senses I found my mouth full of little hard, pebbly scraps which I spat out onto my hand. Well, yes, assorted fillings, of course.

The three mackintosh-men had left so I tottered over to where Dr Lo was sitting. His eyes were more or less open.

'Police?' I asked. He made no sign. 'Look,' I said, 'you've got to have an ambulance and they'll call the police anyway; it will look odd if we don't call them straightaway.'

He nodded his head slowly and carefully, as though he had just come to realize that he was a very old man. He was, in fact, in his forties – or had been that morning. I, too, felt that I had aged.

'First,' I said (I couldn't talk very well because of the damage to my teeth; he couldn't talk at all for reasons which will occur to you), 'first, what have you got for me that I must take away?' His head rotated slowly and his gaze fastened on the wall beside the door. I went over to the wall. 'This?' I asked, pointing to a rather bad scroll painting. He shook his head. I pointed in turn to several framed diplomas designed to reassure the customer that Lo Fang Hi was licensed to yank teeth within reason. He went on shaking his head and staring mutely at the wall. There was nothing else on the wall except some fly-dirt and a vulgar toothpaste-advertisement featuring a foot-high Mr Toothpaste Tube with arms and legs, surrounded by a score or so of actual tubes of the said dentifrice. That is to say, it had once been surrounded by such tubes but these were now scattered on the floor, each one burst open and squeezed-out by the nasties. I prised Mr T. Tube himself off the wall. He was filled with a fine white powder.

I have no idea what heroin and cocaine are supposed to taste like, so I didn't do the fingertip-tasting thing that they do on television if you're still awake at that time of the night, but I had little doubt about its not being baby-powder.

I was never a star pupil at mental arithmetic but a quick and terrified calculation taught me that I had become the proud but shy possessor of something more than half a kilogramme of highly illegal white powder. Say, eighty thousand pounds in Amsterdam. More to the point, say fifty years in nick. I cannot say that I was much gratified; I am as fond of eighty thousand pounds as the next man – for I am not haughty like my brother – but I do prefer to have it quietly dumped for me in the Union des Banques Suisses, rather than carrying it around in an improbable toothpaste-tube full of prison-sentences.

Dr Lo started to make alarming noises. I have always been a charitable man but this was the first time that I had ever blown a Chinese dentist's nose for him. He could not, of course, breathe through his mouth. Then I telephoned for an ambulance and policemen and scrammed, for I am a survivor.

Back at the hotel I telephone Johanna – did you know that you can *dial* London from China? – and told her, guardedly that all was not well with her toothsome friend and that her husband, too, had known better days. She told me to get some change, walk down the street to a telephone kiosk and ring again. This I did, for I am ever anxious to please. Soon we were in touch again, on a wonderfully clear line.

'It's really easy, Charlie dear,' she said when I had unrolled the tapestry of my dismay. 'Do you have a pencil or pen?'

'Of course I have,' I snapped 'but what the hell –'

'Then write this down. Secrete the uh dentifrice about your person. Take an early flight tomorrow from Hong Kong to Delhi. Then Delhi to Paris. Then take Air France Flight ZZ 690 to J.F. Kennedy Airport, New York. Can you spell that? OK. Now, in flight, go to the toilet – sorry, dear, I'll never get used to saying "lavatory" – and unscrew the inspection plate behind the pan. Hide the stuff in there. At Kennedy, walk through customs and book on Flight ZZ 887 to Chicago: this is the same aircraft but it's now a domestic flight – no customs, get it? In flight, retrieve the dentifrice. Call me from Chicago and I'll tell you what to do next. OK?'

'No,' I said.

'How do you mean, "no", dear?'

'I mean, sort of "no". It means, no, I won't do it. I have seen a film about San Quentin penitentiary and I hate every stone of it. I shall not do it. I shall flush that stuff down what you call the toilet as soon as I get back to the hotel. Please do not try to persuade me for my mind is made up.'

'Charlie.'

'Yes?'

'Remember when I coaxed you to have that vasectomy done just after we were married?'

'Yes.'

'In that cute little clinic?'

'Yes.'

They did not perform a vasectomy.'

'Good God!' I cried, appalled. 'Why, I might have had a baby!'

'I don't think so, dear. What they did do was implant in your, uh, groin a tiny explosive capsule with a quartz-decay time-system. It explodes in, let's see, ten days time. Only the guy who put it in can take it out without activating a kind of fail-safe mechanism, so please don't let anyone meddle with it: I kind of like you as you are, you know? Hey, Charlie, are you still there?'

'Yes,' I said heavily. 'Very well. Just give me those flight numbers again. And Johanna?'

'Yes dear?'

'Tell the chap who knows how to take the gadget out of me to be very, very careful crossing the road, eh?'

16 Mortdecai takes a little more drink than is good for him and is frightened by a competent frightener

> Being of noble fostering, I glance
> Lightly into old Laggan's ingle-nook . . .
> Rabbits or snipe-fowl – even nicer things:
> Has any longer title – God-remitted?
>
> *The Old Poacher*

I stayed not upon the order of my going, nor even to lose my £1000 at the tables in far-famed Macao, but crammed everything – well, almost everything – into my suitcase and went down to the desk to pay my bill and book a ticket on the night-flight. The desk-clerk – how is it that they all contrive to look the same? – said that he had something in the safe for me. Had there been anywhere to run to I daresay I would have run. As it was, I made a nonchalant 'Oh, ah?' The desk-chap twiddled the safe and fished out a stout envelope; it was addressed in a scrawly hand to 'The Friend of the Poor' and the clerk had omitted to remove the clipped-on piece of paper which read 'For the overweight, Jewish-looking guy who wears his collar back to front and drinks too much.' I am not proud, I opened the envelope: it contained a note saying 'Dear Father, I played your dough at the craps table and made five straight passes and then faded a couple other shooters taking the odds and got lucky and I taken 5% for my time and trouble and I hope the poor will offer up a prayer for yours truly . . .' The other contents of the envelope were a quite improbable wodge of currency notes of all nations. Hotels like the one I had been staying at have, of course, all-night banking facilities: I bought a cashier's cheque for my winnings (and most of my £1000 walking-about money) and sent it to the poor, as my conscience dictated. The only poor I could think of at the time was C. Mortdecai in Upper Brook Street, London, W1. I shall always remember that nice American as the only honest man I have ever met.

Painlessly gaining the price of another Rembrandt etching for the rainy-day scrap-book usually has a soothing effect on the nerve-endings but, long before my taxi-cab dumped me at the airport, I was quaking again. This was not necessarily a bad thing; had I been able to put a bold front on I would certainly have been apprehended as an obvious malefactor but, twitching with terror as I was, the customs chaps and security thugs wafted me through as a clear case of St Vitus' Dance or Parkinson's Disease – well-known occupational hazards among Curial Secretaries.

All went as merrily as a wedding-bell until the penultimate leg of the journey: Paris to New York, via Air France. A little too merrily, indeed, for by then I was a bit biffed – you know, a little the worse for my dinner, which had been several courses of Scotch whisky – and on my journey to the lavatory or toilet I sat, quite inadvertently, on the laps of several of my fellow-passengers. Their reactions varied from 'Ooh, aren't you *bold!*' via '*Ach, du lieber Augustin*' to '*Pas gentil, ça!*', while one impassive Chinese gentleman ignored me completely, pretending that his lap was quite free of any Mortdecai. Having at last locked myself in the loo or bog, I found that I had failed to arm myself with the necessary screwdriver with which to unscrewdrive the inspection-plate.

Back to my seat I teetered, watched narrowly now by the stewardess. When she came to enquire after my well-being I had decided upon a *ruse*: I would tell her that the zip of my trousers was jammed and that she must find me a screwdriver so that I could free the Mortdecai plumbing system. Alas, my usual fluent French deserted me – look, can *you* remember the French for 'screwdriver' when you're biffed? – and I had to resort to a certain amount of sign-language, pointing vigorously at my fly while vociferating the word 'screwdriver' again and again. Her English was little better than my French.

' "Screw" I onderstand,' she said demurely 'but what is zis "draivaire", hein?'

' "Draivaire",' I said wildly, ' "drivaire" is like, yes, *conducteur*!' and again I frantically pointed at that area of my trousers where my personal lightning-conductor is housed. She clapped her hands gleefully as understanding came to her.

'Ah! Now I onderstand! You weesh me to tell the *conducteur* – the pilot – that you weesh to do to him what Général de Gaulle has done to the whole French nation, not so?'

'Oh, sweet Christ and chips and tomato sauce,' I sighed, subsiding into my seat. This baffled the stewardess; she went away and brought another stewardess, a polyglot of dusky hue and tenor-baritone voice.

'I doth spake English a few better what she,' growled this new one, 'exprime what be this thou askings?' But she knew what a screwdriver was (it's *tournevis* in French, as any sober man can tell you). Five minutes later the perilous powder was safely screwed up behind the lavatory pan and I was pulling myself together on the lavatory floor.

'Pull yourself together,' I told myself sternly. 'You must excite no suspicion. You cannot afford to be lodged in some foreign nick with a quartz-decay timing-system nestling beside your *vas deferens*. A low profile is what you must keep.' So I strolled down the aisle to my seat, twirling the screwdriver and whistling a nonchalant bar or two from *Cosi Fan Tutte*, having craftily left my trouser-fly agape to encourage onlookers to understand the object of my mission. I don't suppose anyone gave me a second glance.

Everything continued to go wonderfully smoothly and soon, soon I was in wondrous Chicago and little the worse for my journey. (I suspect that the much-vaunted 'jet-lag syndrome' is nothing more than the common hangover of commerce. Certainly, I felt no worse than I would normally expect to feel at that time of day.)

The windiness of Chicago is grossly over-described: I was much windier myself. On the journey to my hotel I strained my eyes out of the taxi's windows, hoping to catch a glimpse of some mobsters cutting-down dirty, double-crossing rats with 'type-writers' or blasting their molls with 'pineapples' but none was to be seen. When I complained of this to the cabbie he chuckled fatly.

'Nixon we got,' he said over his shoulder, 'who needs Capone?' I pretended to understand. Well, I'd heard of Capone of course: he'll have a place in history, won't he?

My hotel was really just the same hotel that I've stayed in all over the world except that it was a bit taller than most. They'll never take the place of Claridge's or the Connaught; still less the duplex penthouse suite in the Bristol (that's in Paris, France) but at least you know where you are in these new ones. You know exactly the size and springiness of your bed, exactly what the room-service will be like if you can get them to answer the phone – and you know better than to put your shoes outside the door.

I visited the loo or toilet – who would not? – and found the porcelain pan protected by the usual strip of 'sanitized' paper. (This reassures Americans that they may sit safely, for Americans are terrified of germs, everyone knows that. Hotel-managers love it for its 'cost-effectiveness': whipping a piece of paper around the receiver and giving a blast of aerosol takes far less time than actually cleaning it. Only Arabs are not fooled: they stand on the seat.) Then I had a brisk shower (the shower was programmed to scald you or freeze you; you didn't stay under it long – 'cost-effectiveness' again, you see) and, having put on a fresh clothe or two, I had a brisk debate with myself. The upshot was that I telephoned Blucher before Johanna, for reasons which will occur to you. Blucher seemed full of merriment.

'How full of merriment you seem, to be sure,' I said sourly.

'Well, Mr Mortdecai, to tell the truth I just took a call from a Chinese gentleman – he doesn't exactly work for me but he sometimes throws me a bit of news just for laughs, you know? – and he tells me that you sat on his lap when you were about forty minutes out from Paris, France.'

'An unexpected air-pocket. I rebuked the *conducteur* – sorry, the pilot – for his clumsy driving.'

'An air-pocket at 30,000 feet? Yeah, of course. And the screw-driver bit – don't tell me you tried the old toilet-inspection-panel routine? You did? You really did?' Had I not known him for a humourless man I might almost have thought that he was stifling a laugh.

'Hey,' he went on, 'did you taste the stuff since you retrieved it? I mean, it may really *be* tooth-powder now, huh?'

'It may very well have been that in the first place, for all I know.'

'Hunh? Oh. Yes, that's good thinking. Well, I'd say you should just call your lady now and do exactly what she tells you. Some of our fellows will be sort of close at hand with fresh diapers for you but you won't see them. And don't call me again until you get back to the UK unless something comes up that you really can't handle. OK?'

'You mean, like death?'

'Oh, golly, *no*,' he said seriously. 'If you get dead do not on any account call us; we'd have to disown you, that's the ground-rules, right?'

'Right,' I said with equal seriousness. Then I said, 'I suppose you wouldn't care to tell me what this is all about?'

'Right,' he said. I hung up. Then I called Johanna.

'Darling!' she cried when I told her the news. 'Wonderful! Now, just you sit there by the telephone with a drink and I'll have someone come and see you.'

'Do you know what time it is here?' I squeaked, outraged.

'I know what time it is here, Charlie; what time do you have there in Chicago?'

'*Dinner*-time,' I snarled, for the Spartan boy's fox was indeed gnawing at my very vitals.

'Well, just sit there with *two* drinks, dear; the person who's coming to see you will give you a lovely dinner, I promise.'

'Oh, very well,' I said, as I have so often said before. Another revolt quelled, another outpost surrendered. Why do nations pay great salaries to Generals when women can do the job just as well without even using an army? I decided on a spot of toothbrushing – as well as the drink, of course, not instead of.

'Why, why, why Mortdecai?' I asked myself as I burnished the teeth still extant (my initials are, in fact, C.S.v.C. Mortdecai, but let it pass, let it pass), 'why are you suffering these slings and arrows?'

The answer was simple, for the question was merely rhetorical: suffer these slings and arrows or lose my end of the life-death trade-in I had agreed to with Blucher. I have no particular objection to death as such; it pays all bills and lays on others the chore of hiding the pornograms, the illegal firearms, the incriminating letters: all these things become of little importance when you have six feet of sod o'er you. On the other hand – I distinctly remember saying 'on the other hand' gravely to my toothbrush as I rinsed it – on the other hand, d'you see, death was not something I was actually craving just then. For one thing, I was not in a state of grace and, more to the point, I was burning with desire for revenge upon the perfidious Johanna who had played that horrid prank with the quartz-decay capsule implant. (On the 'plane I had thought of asking the stewardess to listen to my *vesiculae seminales* and tell me if she could hear anything ticking, but once again my command of French had failed me. In any case, it is possible that she might have thought it an odd request.)

'Heigh-ho!' I thought, then trotted briefly down to the hotel's drug-store where I made a purchase or two. I don't think they had ever before been asked for half a kilo of baby-powder. I also bought some stout envelopes and stamps. Lots of stamps. A brief trip back to my room, another to the post office and soon I was relaxing in an arm-chair, my jet-lag symptoms reacting well to the treatment I was pouring into them but my hunger unabated. Only such a man of iron as I could have resisted the temptation to ring for a sandwich or two but I placed my trust in Johanna: if she says there is a good dinner in the offing, then the offing is what the said dinner is in.

Not that I didn't feel a twinge of trepidation as I awaited my host. By the time the door-bell rang I had arranged the odds in my mind: seven to three said a Mafioso with padded shoulders who would *frisk* me before treating me to *spaghetti coi vongole* plus deep-fried baby *zucchini* with the flowers still attached and lots of fried *piperoni* on the side, while ten would get you seven that it would be a slinky she-sadist who would frisk me only with contemptuous eyes before making me take her to Sardi's or somewhere like that and buy her pheasant under glass – the most boring grocery in the world.

I was wrong, not for the first time. Who oozed into my suite when I answered the bell was none other than the portly Chinese gentleman upon whose lap I had roosted for a while in the Boeing 747.

'Harrow,' he said civilly. I glanced at his tie.

'Surely you mean Clifton? Oh, yes, sorry, I see; harro to you, too. Have a drink?'

'Thankyou, no. I bereave you are hungry? Come.'

I came. Went, rather.

You will hardly be surprised to learn that it was a Chinese meal with which I was regaled, but in a Chinese restaurant of no common sort, nor of the nastiness I would have expected from my first impressions of Chicago – a city which seemed intent upon finding how low a lowest common denominator can be. (I hasten to say that some of my best friends may well be Chicagoans – without actually advertising the fact – but have you ever snuffed the scent of the Chicago River as it slides greasily under the nine bridges in the centre of the Windy City? Alligators have been known to flee, holding perfumed handkerchiefs to their noses. As for the carrion gusts from Lake Michigan itself, 'Faugh!' is too mild a word by half.)

This restaurant, as I was saying before I caught ecology, was not one of those where oafs stir three or four dishes together and eat the resultant mess with chips and soy sauce, while the waiters watch inscrutably, thinking their own thoughts. No, it was one of those rare ones which has no menu – people just bring you a succession of tiny dishes of nameless things to be eaten one at a time and without soy sauce. I tried not to disappoint these dedicated waiters and gifted cooks; tried, too, to earn a reputation for being the fastest chopstick in the Northern Mid-West.

My host's name proved to be either Ree or Lee: my uncertainty about this is perfectly genuine. At Oxford we had a Korean professor who trilled his name unmistakably as 'Ree' but insisted on writing 'Lee'. He saw no anomaly in this.

As we dabbled in the finger-bowls, my courteous host murmured courteously that he bereaved I had a package for him. I dabbled thoughtfully.

'That may well be,' I said guardedly, 'or, perhaps, not. What?'

He gazed at me civilly. I replied with equal civility.

'You see, I have no instructions about lashing out samples of toothpowder or dentifrice to one and all, however delectable the dinner they give.'

'Mr Mortdecai,' he said heavily, or as heavily as chaps like that can, 'you are surely experienced enough to know that in this particurar rine of business it is not considered porite, or even safe, to pray, ah, sirry buggers. We have, you understand, certain resources, ah?'

'Oh, goodness, yes,' I hastened to say, 'goodness yes. Indeed, I've had the pleasure and privilege of meeting your Mr Ho. Ah? That's really why I've sort of taken out insurance. I mean, I've a simple-minded sort of mind, you understand, no trace of a death-wish or any of that rubbish: self-preservation is so much more fun than self-destructiveness, don't you agree? Eh? Or rather, "Ah", eh?'

'What sort of precautions have you taken, Mr Mortdecai?'

'Oh, well, I've sort of entrusted the toothpowder to the US Mails: an incorruptible lot, I'm told. Neither frost nor sleet nor trade unions prevents these messengers from etc. And it's gone to a safe address. Old-fashioned, I know, but the best I could think of at the time. I'm sure you understand.'

'Mr Mortdecai,' he murmured suavely, pouring me another cup of delicious tea, 'if you have met my subordinate, Mr Ho, you must surely rearize that this safe address can be ericited from you in ress time than it takes to say what I am saying.'

'Oh, my word, yes; I quite understand that, but the address is no secret at all, you may have it for the asking. It's the Commercial Attaché at the British Embassy in Washington – he doubles in security co-ordination or whatever they call it now, as I'm sure you know. Old school-friend of mine; knows my face, you see. I sort of worked for him in the 1940s if you know what I mean. He's quite potty about security, wouldn't dream of handing the package to anyone but me. And I mean, me *unaccompanied*, of course. And if I didn't say the right sort of words he'd give me a cosy bedroom in the Embassy for as long as I needed it. You see?'

He thought a while but without ostentation.

'I see,' he said. (An English chap would have said 'Yes, I see, I *see*,' but your actual Oriental is economical with words.)

'How much do you want?' he asked.

'Money?' I asked disdainfully. 'Nothing at all. Still less, God forbid, any part of that costly tooth-powder, for I fancy I know what happens to people who own such things when other people wish to own them. No, all I wish is a little information. I have become tired and vexed, you see, at being used as a cat's-paw in matters about which I know nothing. This prodding from random directions insults my intelligence. I am prepared to fight under almost any flag if the money is good, but I do need to have a squint at the flag first. I am too overweight to play, ah, silly buggers.'

I could tell by the way he mused over this that he was a clever man. How much cleverer than me he was, of course, remained an open question.

'That is quite understandable, Mr Mortdecai,' he said at last, 'and it seems to me that your case-officer has been running you without a proper regard for your interrigence and, ah, other quarities. I agree that you should be given a view of the frag under which you are fighting – but you rearise that I must first get a little crearance. Ah?'

'Ah,' I agreed. He invited me to his office. We entered. That sounds easy, but entering the office of a clandestine Chinese gentleman seems to involve being goggled at through peepholes, scanned by metal-detectors and listening to the office-owner murmur into voice-sensitive locks – all that stuff which so destroys the quality of life nowadays. Death, too, now I come to think of it. He gave me a glass of the actual John Smith's Glenlivet to sip while he dialled a number so prodigal in digits that it had to be somewhere far, far away. His polite stare at me while he waited for his connection bore no trace of hostility but it had the effect of making me feel far, far away from home and loved ones; one would have thought that he was costing me out in terms of coffin-wood – or perhaps concrete and baling-wire. I let my tummy sag out fully, hoping to make myself look less cost-effective. The telephone crackled at last.

'Harro!' he said. '. . . may make more noise,' I murmured, for I can never resist finishing a quotation. His stare at me sharpened and he switched into a language which sounded like a malicious send-up of a Welsh newsreader but was, I suppose, one of the many brands of Chinese. He clacked and grunted and fluted awhile then listened intently while similar noises from his interlocutor made the instrument positively vibrate in his hand. This went on for a time then, in beautifully-modulated but outdated French, he said, '*D'accord. Au'voir, re copain.*' Showing off, I suppose. Having replaced the receiver he said to me, 'Would you rike to wash your hands, Mr Mortdecai?' I inspected said members: they were indeed sweating profusely. How had he *known*?

Returning from his richly but curiously appointed lavatory, I moved into the attack.

'Well, Mr Ree?' were the stormtrooper words which spear-headed my attack.

'Thankyou, yes,' he replied. My attack was wiped out. I felt just like an infantry subaltern who has thrown away a platoon against a machine-gun emplacement he forgot to mark on his map. (Listening to the Colonel's remarks afterwards is not nearly so unpleasant as sitting down to write twenty letters to next-of-kin while the people in the Orderly Room pretend you're not there. The worst bit is when your batman brings you your dinner to the foxhole or bivvy-tent, saying 'Thought you might be too tired to dine in Mess tonight. Sir.' But I reminisce.)

Having delivered the devastating 'thankyou, yes,' Mr Lee or Ree fell silent, studying me again. I did not break this silence; I felt that it was his move.

'Mr Mortdecai,' he said after a demoralizing interval, 'are you a discreet man? No, prease do not repry, that was not a question but a warning. A rittre more Grenrivet? Good. I keep it for speciah occasions.' Those words 'speciah occasions' hung delicately in the air between us.

'Now,' he went on, 'my friend has agreed that I should tell you enough to exprain a rittle of our work – just enough to encourage you not to pray any more games with goods worth a great sum of money. The conditions are that you do not mention this conversation to your derightful rady wife; that you do not speak of it to any American Coroners you may happen to know (yes, we know about that but we bereave your rady wife does not) and, of course, you make no expranations to your Embassy friend in Washington, who is, forgive me, prease, a fool. In any case, his office is bugged.'

'Tut!' I said, frowningly. He raised a hand.

'We did not bug it' he said reprovingly. 'The Americans did. They are even sirrier than the Engrish. We bug their bugs after they have instorred them. Much cheaper.

'Now, prease pay attention more crosery. If you were to tell any of these people what I shall now tell you, three very powerful organizations would be offended with you. *Offended*.'

I sighed. How life repeats itself, to be sure. *

'Do go on,' I murmured nonchalantly. My hands were sticky with sweat again.

'First, your rady wife is very fond of you but in such circumstances she would have to rate you "insecure" and pass you over to her people for disposah. Fiona, the dog-girl at the Correge, would bury you. Probabry your wife has enough infruence to ensure that you would be dead before buriah; I do not know.'

I did not shudder, I never let foreigners see me shudder, but he must have seen that the beads of sweat were popping out of my forehead like ping-pong balls.

'Next, once you had given this information to a certain American Coroner, you would now be expendabah and he could prease many of his superiors – who have never approved of his keeping you arive – by "terminating you with extreme prejudice" as he would say. Naturarry, you would be interrogated first and this would hurt.'

'Quite,' I quavered. I don't mind telling you that I detest being hurt.

'Last, you would now be an enemy, in the third crass, of my own organization.'

'Only *third* class?' I asked in the indignant tones which Queen Victoria surely used when she received the Abyssinian Order of Chastity, Second Class; 'What is that supposed to mean?'

'It means we would not kill you.'

'Oh, good.'

A muscle in his face twitched, almost as though he were a British cavalry officer who is trying to puzzle out whether someone has made a joke and, if so, whether or not it would be good form to smile.

'No,' he went on, having clearly dismissed any intention of smiling, 'We would not kill you. We do not kill enemies of the third crass. But after a rittle time you would be asking us most poritery for death. We would not feel able to obrige. After another two or three days – this would depend on your stamina and vitarity – let us say two days – we would rerease you conveniently crose to a rairway-bridge. With a white walking-stick – you would of course by then have lost your sight – which would be taped to

*See *Don't Point That Thing at Me*, last chapters.

what would remain of your hand, and a tendorrar note between your teeth. Sorry, yes, gums – you would no ronger have any teeth, naturarry.'

'Naturarry,' I said bravely.

'The ten dorrars would be for you to give to some indigent passer-by who would help you to a convenient part of the rairway-bridge: you would be anxious for such help by then, you understand.'

I pulled myself together, remembering that I was, after all, partly British. We British do not cringe in the presence of the heathen, nor are we daunted by foreign threats. (Well, all right, Suez was a special case, wasn't it?)

'Mr Ree,' I said, as crisply as the words allowed, 'pray tell me something. Is it true that Chinese, ah, persons, consider themselves to be constipated if they do not achieve at least two motions of the bowels each weekday? I have read this somewhere and I long to know whether it be true.' He considered this for quite half a minute, looking as nonplussed as his inscrutability would permit.

'Yes,' he said after the stated half-minute, 'yes, this is true. But I cannot see why you should ask such a thing. Are there not matters of almost equal importance . . .?'

'I ask,' I said, maintaining the British crispness, 'because I fear for your health. It seems to me that a good deal of surplus, ah, effluent has been escaping from your mouth during the past few minutes. Your digestive tract seems to have lost all sense of direction. In short, if you will forgive me, I begin to find your talk tedious.'

'Ah,' he said.

'On the other hand,' I continued, 'your points are well taken; indeed I have been in accord with you for some ten minutes. If you will now tell me, in your own words, as much of the truth as your masters have empowered you to tell, then you may depend upon it that I shall impart it to no one. First, I am a man of my word. Second, I am not brave.'

'Ah,' he said again. 'But, Mr Mortdecai, our dossier on you must be at fault, for it states that you can lie like a prostitute and are capable of quite absurd bravery on occasion. But it also says that you are sensible, a virtue often mistaken for cowardice.'

I looked at my watch and stifled a well-bred yawn.

'Mr Ree,' I said, 'you have frightened me, as you intended. This was unnecessary for I was already frightened. Your dossier is right in one respect: I am sensible. Tell me some of the truth. We both know that you can and will kill me later if you decide to do so – and unless I contrive to kill you first, which has no part in my plans at present. Meanwhile, perhaps I might have just a touch more of that delicious malt whisky? And enough plausible facts to persuade me to part with the toothpowder, eh?'

How brave I was, to be sure. Mr Ree passed me a Kleenex. I mopped the sweat off my forehead. He began to utter.

'Your wife is Johanna Mortdecai,' he told me. Well, I knew that, of course, but I wasn't about to walk into any straight-line situations; I didn't even nod.

'She is the chief financier – forgive me, financière? – of the Women's Domination Society; arso, Deputy Head of it.'

'You mean Women's *Liberation*, don't you?' I said in the embarrassed tones one uses to foreigners who get words wrong.

'No, Mr Mortdecai. Women's Riberation is a piece of sirriness which was froated to, ah, test the temperature of the water and to mask the rear movement. It was instructive to see how many sirry women were prepared to, shall we say, cut off their bras to spite their breasts.' He had made a joke. I smiled, not showing the teeth. 'Quite agree,' I said. 'I mean, if God hadn't meant us to wear trusses, he wouldn't have given us ruptures, would he?' He didn't smile.

'The Women's Domination Society is very serious. It is probabry the richest private organization in the world; even richer than the Parestinian Popurar Front – with whom they happen to be friends.' I was about to say something valiant about how little I cared for the riches and murderous capacity of the PFLP when I recalled that, some forty years ago, I had promised an aged aunt never to tell a lie. (This was in exchange for a tin of Mackintosh's Quality Street Toffee Selection. Those toffees are long gone – nor would I find them toothsome in this my middle age – but a Mortdecai's promise, even to an aunt, is not to be paltered with.) So I held my tongue.

'They intend,' continued Mr Lee, 'to assume controh of the world.' I gave him that look – often practised before the mirror – which I give to players at stud poker who back into the betting on the fourth card. He was unimpressed.

'How can they *not* win?' he asked. 'First, the terrifying American middre-aged woman controhs quite three-fifths of the wealth of the richest country in the world. Second, the women "behind the curtain" – in the harems of the Musrim world – controh wealth which even Zurich could not count. Third, the female interrectuals of Israel and India have their poriticah worlds by the, ah, borrocks. Fourth, women have the insensate drive of the castration comprex; the same knowledge of inferiority which makes rittre men into tyrants. Arexander the Great was incapable with women; Attira the Hun died trying to achieve an erection; Naporeon had an absurdry small penis (36mm – it was sold at Sotheby's a few years ago) and Adorf Hitrer, as all the world knows, had onry one testicre.'

I shifted uneasily in my chair; he was talking the kind of lunacy which often makes better sense than sense does. Also, I was frantically trying to convert mirrimetres into inches – feet? – in my head.

'Fifth,' he said, spreading his beautifully-tapered fingers on the desk, 'who is to oppose them? Is there one state – other than China – which is not rotten from top to bottom? Can you name one poritician in office who is a strong man – a statesman?'

This was not a rhetorical question; he paused to give me time to answer. I took that time.

'No,' is what I finally said. He nodded a few mirrimetres.

'Sixth and last, they have friends, as I have said. Most of all, they have us.'

'Who are "us"?'

'Issyvoo.'

I boggled as I had never boggled in my life before. 'Issyvoo,' surely, was what the Berliners used to call Christopher Isherwood, the man who will go down to fame as the chap who made the joke about 'the last of the small Spenders'. I allowed myself to raise an eyebrow. He spelled it out for me.

'ICWU. The International Chinese Waiters Union. No, prease do not raugh. Our union – we do not call it that but you would not be interested in its reah name – is the only trury internationah organization in the world. Arso, it is the only Union with no absurd poritical affiriations. Arso, it is the onry Union where the emproyers are equah members with the emproyees. They have to be. Most important of all, it is the only union which has no trouble with brackregs. Such people are given one hour in which to understand that the union is their mother and father. The crever ones understand this in much ress than one hour. The stupid ones; we send a present of money to their families – and a souvenir.'

'Like, say, an ear?' I ventured.

'Something of that sort, yes. But annoyances of that kind do not often happen nowadays. We Chinese, as the world knows, are inveterate gambrers; when you go to your favourite Chinese restaurant and find that it has changed hands it arways means that the owner has lost it at the gaining table.'

'I knew that,' I said.

'The new owner is onry a manager, you understand. He now owes the union a great deah of money, as do all the waiters, according to their station in rife. You understand that all this calls for heavy financing, far more than the union dues can suppry. Your charming rady wife supprives this through her organization. Partry by supporting our cash-flow, partry through making avairable her capable young radies as couriers so that we can, ah, adjust the supply of *medicines* internationarry. I think that is all you need to know, ah?'

'Beauty is truth, truth beauty – that is all . . . ye need to know,,' I said, dipping deep into the Grecian Urn.

'Sorry?'

'Keats.'

'Kits?'

'Yes – it means little pussies.'

'Ah. I can arrange . . .'

'Please do not go to any such trouble; I was simply accepting that I had been given what information you were permitted to give me.'

'I have been frank with you, Mr Mortdecai. You bereave that, I hope.'

'Of course. Santa Claus lives. You shall have your icing sugar. Meet me in Washington tomorrow?'

17 Charlie passes on some perilous groceries and receives a zonk with less than his habitual meekness

Man with the head and woman with the heart:
Man to command and woman to obey;
All else confusion.

The Princess

'What-ho, Charlie!' cried Humphrey as I was ushered in to his tastefully-decorated sanctum or office in the Embassy next day.

'What-ho, what-ho, Humpers!' I retorted courteously. We swapped a few more civilities, freely using the useful phrase 'what-ho'. It saves one thinking, you see, and saves one the chore of trying to remember whether the other chap is married, divorced, queer or whatever. Best of all, it saves one from the peril of asking after the chap's parents. Humphrey, you see, is the scion of a pretty antique Irish family, which means that at least one of his nearest and dearest is chained up in a cellar, living on dry bread and biting the heads off rats for pastime.

Moreover, this what-hoing gave Humphrey the opportunity to draw from his pocket a calling-card upon which, neatly typed, were the words THIS PLACE IS BUGGED. I nodded vigorously in what he probably thought was comprehension but which I intended as agreement; guilty knowledge if you like.

'Too early for a drink, I suppose?' he asked, glancing at his watch.

'On the contrary, damn' nearly too late,' I said, glancing needlessly at mine. 'Wheel on the life-giving fluids without delay.' He went to a cupboard, unlocked it and drew out the two fat envelopes I had sent him, raising his eyebrows and saying, 'Scotch or Bourbon?'

'Both,' I quipped merrily.

'Greedy sod,' he laughed, handing me both packages, followed by a huge brandy and soda which was, in fact, what he knew I would be needing at that time of day. (These chaps don't get into Intelligence merely on charm; never mind what the after-shave manufacturers say.)

We Woostered away for a while, giggling silently at the thought of grim-jawed FBI men and beetle-browed CIA men frantically sending out 'Code Orange-Five Trace Orders' on such ornaments of the Drones Club as Ooffy Prosser and Barmy Fotheringay-Phipps. (Indeed, one hopes that they took 'Drones Club' to be the code name for 'The Firm's' new London 'safe-house' – and, who knows, it may well be for all I know.)

While we idly bandied these Woosterisms – and he and I are confirmed bandiers of such things – he slid a scribbling-pad across the desk and I scribbled on it enough news to pay him richly for his kindness. To be exact, I wrote down everything I knew that I knew Colonel Blucher knew, if I make myself clear, together with a couple of other snippets which would put him ahead of the game and give him something to trade with Blucher. I selected with care a few bits to omit: he wouldn't have believed them and, in any case, they concerned my personal safety. ('Idle, intelligent, devious; a survivor,' read the summary of my character on my last school report and I have not changed; I am no butterfly.)

After another invigorating suck at the brandy-tit we parted with many a friendly message to Freddie Widgeon and Honoria Glossop. As he courteously ushered me to the door he paused beside what he no doubt knew to be a well-bugged standard lamp and whispered hoarsely, 'Charlie, *don't believe a word old Mulliner says*.' I gasped but mumbled assent, grinning inaudibly.

Mr Ree was waiting at the rendezvous as advertised, staring politely into space like a man doing long-division sums in his head.

Or working out a fool-proof way of murdering his wife. He offered me a drink but his heart was evidently not in the offer and I, too, was more anxious to do business than to quaff. Frankly, I would rather carry an Irish-made time-bomb around the streets than a package of heroin. If that's what it was.

We walked around the block to a spot chosen by Mr Ree where he was sure that we could not be overseen by stupid, bumbling, British Intelligence blokes. (It will be a sad day for the world when the Oriental gent realizes that Western bumbling is only Eastern guile in a different idiom. Well, a lot of it, anyway.) We sidled into an entry. He opened a capacious briefcase. I slipped a fat envelope into it. He gave me a fraction of a bow and a long, steady look before popping into a large, vulgar, black limousine which had been idling beside a fire-plug under the indulgent eye of a well-paid policeman. I did not much relish the long, steady look from Mr Ree; it was the sort of look which seems to say, 'Mortdecai, this stuff had better be what it's supposed to be: we have ways of making you scream.' I waved a nonchalant hand, confident that the churning acid in my stomach could not be seen by the naked eye. Then I studied the scrap of paper he had pressed into my hand. It was not, as I hoped, a munificent piece of walking-about money: it was better, much better. It read 'MESSAGE FROM WIFE BEGINS QUARTZ-DECAY IMPLANT JUST A JOKE COMMA FEAR NOT COMMA PLEASE DONT BE CROSS LOVE HANNA STOP ENDS.'

'Stop ends indeed,' I snarled.

Before the limousine was out of eyeshot another, even more vulgar black limousine swept up to the kerb – just like they do in the story-books. I gave it no more than a brief and haughty glance whilst I made taxi-attracting gestures to passing taxis. The taxi-drivers did not seem to understand my British gestures. Just as my fears were changing into honest British annoyance, I became aware that respectable-looking chaps were issuing from the limousine – the second, longer, more vulgar limousine, you understand. I recked not of them but continued to beckon imperiously at passing taxi-cabs. It was at that point that I was zonked on the back of the head.

Now you who – forgive me – have nothing better to do than read such tales of daring and true love as this which I now relate, must have read many a description of what it feels like to be zonked on the occiput. Stars burst wondrously, blue-birds twitter, fireworks effulge, bells chime and so forth. None of this is true; none has been written by chaps who have actually experienced such a zonk.

Speaking as one who has in his time received not one or two but several such cowardly buffets, I am in a position to record the resultant phenomena in scientific form, such as any serious medical journal would gladly accept for publication.

(A) The subject feels a distinct zonking sensation at the rear of he bonce or cranium. A momentary agony is experienced.

(B) This causes the novice to say '*Aaargh!*' or words to that effect, according to his ethnic group. The seasoned chap, who is no stranger to zonks, subsides quietly, lest he receive just such another.

(C) The subject then sinks into an untroubled sleep, more dreamless than he has known since puberty.

(D) He awakes, reluctantly, to find himself infested with a shattering headache and a great thirst. Moreover, he is surrounded by large, ugly men who view his awakening coldly, for they are engrossed in a game called three-handed pinochle. He goes back to sleep. It is now but a fitful sleep.

(E) He is awakened again, this time by one of the coarse, ugly men and in a fashion so coarse that I cannot describe it in a narrative intended for family reading.

(F) Full, now, of indignation, piss-and-vinegar, etc, he launches a death-dealing karate-chop at his tormentor, not realizing how enervating have been the effects of the professional zonk. The d.-dealing k.-chop misses by several feeble inches. The ugly chap does not even smile: he *smacks* the patient across the chops with a spade-like hand, back and forth and to and fro. In Brooklyn I understand this is rendered as 'whackity-whap, biff, zap'.

(G) Weeping bitterly with shame and rage, the subject collapses onto the carpet. The ugly chap raises him compassionately to his feet by grabbing a handful of hair.

All these things happened to me in the order named and I have a couple of neuroses to prove it. I was taken to a lavatory or toilet – no wait, it's called a bathroom in the USA – and was allowed to be sick, wash my face and, as my grandmother would say, 'straighten my veil'. (In my will I have bequeathed my collection of euphemisms to the National Trust.)

I felt a little better but my indignation was lessened by no whit. I am assured that there is many a chap who accepts a slosh on the brain-pan with equanimity. Some, I daresay, positively welcome such wallops as aids to meditation; others reproach themselves for not having loved their fellow-men enough. I was never such a one. Being coshed or sapped never fails to fill me with a quite irrational annoyance. We overweight cowards in early middle age have few inexpensive recreations left to us: indignant rage – so long as one's blood-pressure is no worse than 120/80 – is both cheap and satisfying.

It was, then, a furious and unforgiving Mortdecai whose face was wiped and whose trousers were adjusted by large, ugly men and who was half-carried into a darkened room and dumped into a wonderfully comfortable chair. He – I – raged vaguely and luxuriously for a minute or two until sleep slunk up like a black panther and sank its kindly fangs into what remained of the Mortdecai brain. Curiously delicious dreams involving over-ripe schoolgirls ensued – quite unsuitable for these chaste pages. (It has often been remarked that men about to face death on the field of battle or, indeed, the very gallows itself, frantically seek solace in the sexual act. The same is true of the common hangover: a raw egg beaten up in Worcester Sauce or Tabasco is a useful placebo for the hung-over novice; a pint of flat and tepid ale is a kill-or-cure specific/emetic for those with leathern stomachs, while a brace of large brandies marks out your seasoned boozer who knows that he needs an empiric to get him back into the human race as quickly as may be. You may depend upon it, however, that the only sovereign cure for us men of iron is a brisk five minutes of what Jock coarsely calls 'rumpy-pumpy'. It is positively warranted to scour the cobwebs from the most infested skull; no home should be without it. Try some tomorrow. I shan't pretend that you can buy it at all reputable chemists but you will find a registry office in most large towns. I digress, I know, but usefully: these words of mine alone are worth the price of admission.)

The curiously delicious dreams of which I speak were snapped off short by a flood of blinding light and a gentle shake or two at my shoulder. I opened reluctant eyes, sat up, turned my gaze first upon the shoulder-shaker, who proved to be the smallest and fattest of the ugly persecutors. He looked unhappy. I eyed him dangerously, then stared to my front across about an acre of black-glass desk towards a set of apologetic features flickering in the mid-distance.

When my eyes could focus I recognized the apologetic features as those of Col. Blucher.

'Hey, Mr Mortdecai, are you OK?' he asked with what seemed to be anxiety.

'Grrr,' I growled, for neither 'yes' nor 'no' seemed to fill the bill.

'Look, Mr Mortdecai, I'm really very very sorry you were kind of uh roughed up a little . . .'

'*Grrr*,' I reiterated, putting a little more venom into the word this time.

'. . . but you see I had to get you off the street fast and I had to make it look like it wasn't *friends* picking you up and I didn't have any skilled help this side of town and I guess these fellers uh kind of got their orders at second-hand and they're well kind of hostility-situation-orientated . . .'

'Again?'

'. . . hostility-situation-orientated and, well, when guys like these snatch a guy they snatch him real good, hunh?'

'Are you trying to say, Colonel, that these men exceeded their orders?'

'Well, I'd say so.'

'And you will, of course, be rebuking them?'

'Why yes, I guess I shall. Hey, Elmer' – this was to the ugly chap beside my chair – 'Elmer, why don't you go get yourself some chow?' As Elmer turned towards the door I rose to my feet and, in the nasty, rasping voice I developed years ago when I was an adjutant in the Guards, I rasped the word '*Elmer?*'

He span around in a clockwise direction, thus meeting my left hook to the liver and, indeed, aiding it. How it sank in, to be sure. We have all heard of those miraculous punches which 'travelled no more than four inches', have we not? Well, this one must have travelled quite twenty inches and had some 180 pounds of Mortdecai muscle, fat and spite behind it. The ugly chap went '*Urrrgghhh*', or something which sounded uncommonly like it, and folded up like an ill-made Venetian blind. (Jock, you see, had long ago told me that 'when you give a geezer a bunch of fives in the gut, don't think about the gut, nor the abominal wall; just make out that you're hitting his bleeding back-bone – from the front; see?' Jock *knows* about these things, you understand.)

Blucher pressed a buzzer, I suppose, for the other two ugly men entered and, at a gesture from Blucher's pinkie, hauled out their stricken comrade before he could damage the carpet beyond repair.

I sank back into my chair, feeling a trifle more in tune with the infinite. Blucher registered neither approval nor mild reproof although I fancy a corner of his mouth twitched in what might have been amusement in another man.

'Well, now, where were we?' I asked comfortably.

18 Mortdecai does not get the right vibrations

That a lie which all a lie may be met and fought with outright.
But a lie which is part a truth is a harder matter to fight.

The Grandmother

Blucher made a courteous gesture, indicating that he was all ears and was prepared to lend me them unreservedly. I glanced around the office; it was clearly not his own but on loan from some Midas-like business-man, for the walls were bespattered with exceedingly costly graphics by Münch, Braque, Picasso, Léger and all those chaps – beyond the dreams of avarice if that's the kind of thing one likes; certainly beyond the reach of Blucher's salary and outside his Agency's Scale of Office Furnishings. Nevertheless, in Washington most places are bugged, everyone knows that, don't they? I skated the other heavy package of powder across the frozen black lake of the desk; it landed on his lap with a satisfying thump followed by a manly grunt of discomfort from Col. Blucher.

'I am prepared to tell all,' I murmured to him, 'but not between these walls. I am a survivor, you see, and I have a certificate from my old headmaster to prove it. Let us go for a stroll: a little fresh air will be jolly good for us both.'

He looked at me incuriously, which meant, of course, that he was thinking furiously; I could almost hear his synapses crackling and popping like breakfast cereal. 'Would the lies he could have his lads beat out of me be more valuable than the half-truths I was prepared to volunteer?' was evidently the question which he had fed into his crew-cut nut. He came to the right decision: after all, coming to decisions is what such chaps are paid for – like 'one who gathers samphire, dreadful trade'.

'Hey, that's a great idea, Charlie!' he said. 'Let's go.'

In the outer office the two larger ugly chaps were still playing pinochle, but two-handed now because from the open door of the lavatory or bathroom came a rhythmical '*Urrgh, urrgh*' from Elmer. I paused by their table and cleared my throat. Neither of them looked up. 'Tell Elmer,' I said in the voice of an overpaid physician, 'that he should take more exercise and drink less. The only hard thing about him is his liver.' One ugly chap kept his eyes on his cards (and who shall blame him, because a quick kibitz had shown me that he only needed the last queen to perfect what pinochle-players call a 'round-house') but the other slowly raised his eyes to mine and gave me his best and coldest Edward G. Robinson stare – the one that is supposed to make you think of *gats*, concrete overcoats and paving-slabs dropped into the Potomac River with your ankles wired to them. I have seen such looks done better.

'Well, so long, youse guys,' I said, courteously using their dialect. Neither of the pinochle-players responded but Elmer said '*Urrrghh*' from the lavatory or bathroom.

The way to take a stroll for fresh air in Washington, DC, is to hail an air-conditioned taxi-cab. This I did. I entered the first which offered itself, drawing a vexed look from Blucher. Well, obviously, he must have thought me too half-smart to take the first cab; it would have been the second which would have been in his pay, which is why I took the first, you see. Goodness, how clever I was in those days – barely a year ago!

The driver squinted at us from his little air-conditioned womb of armoured glass and steel-mesh (being zonked is an occupational hazard which even cab-drivers dislike) and asked us courteously how he could earn the pleasure of being of service to us. Well, what he actually said was 'Yeah?' but one could tell that it was a civil 'yeah'.

'Just drive around the sights, OK?' said Blucher. 'You know, Grant's tomb, places like that?'

'And the National Gallery, please,' I chirped up, 'in fact, the National Gallery first. Oh, and could you stop at a shop where I could buy a torch?'

'He means, like a flashlight, from a drug-store,' explained Blucher. The driver did not even shrug his shoulders; he had been driving idiots around all day, we would not even figure in the bleary reminiscences with which he would regale his wife that night as she bathed his bunions.

'Do you care to start telling now?' Blucher asked me. I shot him a glance fraught with caution and cowardice, flicking an eye at the driver. 'Well, hell, why the National Gallery, hunh?' I began to feel a little in command of the situation: I can cower with the best but, given a fraction of an edge, I am happier in the dominant rôle.

'First,' I said, 'I wish to go there. Second, I earnestly wish to rinse my eyes out with some good art after seeing those frightful graphics in your office. Third, the NG, that stately pleasure-dome, is probably the only unbugged place in this fair city. Fourth, I have a long-standing appointment with a chap called Giorgio del Castelfranco, who has a picture in the Gallery which I both covet and suspect. OK?'

'Sure,' he said with policeman-like innocence, 'you mean the guy who was Bellini's pupil in Venice – around about when Columbus was discovering America? Hunh? The guy we jerks call Giorgione?'

'That would be he,' I said bitterly. 'And you can cut out the dialect.'

'Gosh, I really enjoyed your piece about him in the *Giornale delle Belle Arte* last year; you really made that Berenson guy look a right Charlie – gosh, sorry, Charlie . . .'

'That's all right,' I said. 'I have been called worse.' But I sulked all the way to the National Gallery and insisted on paying off the cabbie myself. He examined my tip carefully, interestedly, then handed it back with a charitable sort of look.

Inside the Gallery, I stalked unswervingly past all the lovely art that Lord Duveen had sold to Kress and Widener and fellows like that in the palmy, piping days when Lord Mortdecai (yes, my papa) was peddling piddling pastiches to minor European royalty whose cheques were as good as their word. I halted in an important way in front of the Giorgione and played my torch or flashlight upon it. In a trice a wardress had pounced on me and wrested it out of my hand, making noises like a she-vulture laying its first egg. I handed her my wallet, open at the place which displays my art-historian credentials, and bade her show it to a curator. She was back in another trice or two, spraying apologies and calling me 'Dr Mortdecai' and telling me that I might shine my flashlight at anything. Anything I liked.

'Thank you,' I said, ignoring the explicitness. I shone the torch on this part and that of the painting, making art-historical noises such as 'ah' and 'hum' and 'oh dear', while Blucher fretted, shifting from foot to foot.

'Look, Mr Mortdecai,' he said at last, 'would you care to tell me what it is you're looking for? I mean, we do have to . . .' I shot him a patronizing glance over my shoulder.

'I am looking,' I said pompously, 'for the brushwork of the young Titian in or about the year 1510. I do not see it. It occurs to me that I just may have been wrong about this picture.'

'But gosh,' he said, 'it says right here on the tablet that this art-work is by Giorgione . . .'

'And it may now continue to say so for the time being,' I said with more than usual pomposity, tossing the torch or flashlight petulantly into the nearest litter-bin. (In the US of A they call waste-paper baskets 'newspaper-baskets', which shows a fine sense of values. I like American realists. American *idealists*, of course, are like all idealists: they are people who kill people.)

'But here,' I said, 'is what we have been waiting for.' Blucher stared. A titter of thirteen-year-old schoolgirls was swarming into the shrine of art, frantically shepherded by one of those women who are born to be schoolmarms – you know the species well, I'm sure; some of them have quite nice legs but the thick ankles, the slack bust and the calm panic peering from behind the contact-lenses give them away every time. I know a chap who nearly married one of them: he gave me all the field-identification tips. I cannot remember just what it was that Blucher said but, had he been an Englishman he would have said 'Eh?'

I took his arm and steered him into the formicating mass. The girls tittered, and even *groped* us while their teacher prated, but I, at last, felt safe: there is no directional microphone which can sort out the words of devious Mortdecais from the prattle of pubescence. Blucher twigged, although it was clear that he thought my precaution a bit far-fetched. (He is – I must be careful not to say 'was' – one of those who would be glad to die for the Pentagon's idea of democracy whereas I am a simple man who believes in the survival of the fittest. Since I have no sons it is clear that the fittest Mordecai to survive is me: I'm sure you see that.)

'Well,' he growled into my ear, just loudly enough to overcome the roosting-starlings noise of next year's gang-bang material, 'Well, give me the dirt, Mr Mortdecai.'

'You're going to think I'm an idiot,' I began.

He looked at me strangely. 'I wouldn't touch a straight line like that to save my soul,' he said.

I pretended not to have heard. 'You see, that package of powder, the one I collected from the aircraft; well, I sort of took out a little life insurance. I made up a duplicate package full of baby-powder – how they stared in the drug-store! – and put them both into envelopes and posted them by special delivery to a safe place. When I was satisfied that the chap who contacted me was the right chap I got them out of the safe place and gave one to the chap in question as arranged.' I wasn't watching Blucher's face but I swear I could hear his eyes narrowing. 'Which package?' he asked in a narrow-eyed sort of voice.

'That's the *trouble*,' I wailed convincingly, 'I don't *know*. You see, I marked them "A" and "B" – respectively – but when it came to the crunch I simply couldn't remember which was "A". Nor, if it comes to that, which was "B".' We fell silent. The schoolmarm was droning on usefully about Palma Vecchio although the picture she was discussing was clearly labelled Palma Giovane. It didn't matter: no one was listening. The nymphets were ganging up on us quite terrifyingly, I began to realize what hell it must be to be a pop-singer. Blucher had one hand pressed to his jacket, where the shoulder-holster lives, another on the zip of his trousers or pants.

'The awful thing is,' I went on, 'that the original package, as I think you pointed out, may well only have been tooth-powder in the first place, so there is a fair chance that my er contact . . .'

'Mr Lee,' he interjected helpfully.

'Or Ree,' I agreed, 'is going to be very very cross with me and that you too are going to suspect that I have not played a straight bat.'

'Yes,' he said. That was all he said.

The teacher moved on to another work of some choice and master spirit, shooting hateful glances at us and a few despairing ones at her pupils. We followed. I murmured into Blucher's ear almost all of what Mr Ree had told me. He turned and stared.

'And you *believe* that?' he asked in an incredulous voice.

'Well, it fits all the facts so far,' I said, swatting behind me at a gently-nurtured teenager who was being *impertinent* to me with an electrical vibrator, 'but if you have a more plausible scenario I shall be delighted to hear it.' He thought, then started – nay leapt into the air as though a great insight had come to him.

'An insight?' I asked in my polite voice.

'No, a schoolgirl. Let's please get to hell out of this place, please, *please*? I never knew that schoolgirls could be like this, did you?'

'Well, yes, I did; but then I read dirty books, you see, Colonel.'

There's nothing in a remark like that for chaps like Blucher. He boggled a moment then reiterated his request that we should get out. I fell in with his wishes. We got. We also took a taxi-cab – I let him choose it this time – to an eating-place where they solds us things to eat which tasted like dead policemen on toast. Blucher, clearly, was musing as he ingested his share of the garbage (the coffee in such places is often good; drink lots of it with your food; it's hell on the ulcers but it takes away the taste). I, too, was musing as frantically as a man can muse, for it was evident to my trained mind that the Blind Fury with the Abhorrèd Shears was sharpening them up for a snip at the Mortdecai life-span. I say again that I am not especially afraid of death, for the best authorities tell us that it is no more painful and undignified than birth, but I do feel that I'd like to have a say in the when and where and how. Particularly the 'how'.

'Blucher,' I said, pushing away my tepid and scarcely-touched platter, 'Blucher, it seems to me that there are few, if any, chaps with an interest in keeping me alive. I *wish* to stay alive, for reasons which I shall not trouble you with at present. Your suggestions would be welcome.' He turned his face to me, gave one last chew at whatever was in his mouth and looked at me gravely. There was a trickle of greasy gravy on his chin.

'There is a trickle of greasy gravy on your chin,' I murmured. He wiped it off. 'What was that again?' he asked.

'I said,' I said, 'that it would be nice to stay alive and could you perhaps give me a few ideas.' This time he looked blank, then almost friendly. He turned to the short-order cook or assistant-poisoner and called for more coffee and a toothpick. Then he turned back to me. His face was now benign – I'd never have dreamed that he could command so many expressions in so short a time. 'You know, Mr Mortdecai, I like you, I really do. We could use a few hundred guys like you in this country.' With that, he reached out and kneaded my shoulder in a brotherly sort of a way. His hand was large and hard but I did not wince nor cry aloud.

'About the staying-alive thing . . .?' I asked. His face went grave again and he shook his head slowly and compassionately.

'No way,' he said.

19 Mortdecai finds himself in possession of some art-work which he could well do without and learns about policemen's widows and fishcakes

Gigantic daughter of the West,
We drink to thee across the flood . . .

Hands All Round

I am not one to whimper, for I have found that it does one no good. I did not even wet myself, although the provocation was intense. I lit a nonchalant cigarette, using only four matches and only slightly burning my valuable Sulka necktie. Blucher, clearly impressed by my British *sang-froid*, offered a sturdy word or two of comfort.

'Until I contact the Controller of my Agency,' he said, 'I have no orders to, uh, effect termination on.you. Like I said, I kind of like you. I'd say you had maybe eighty or ninety minutes before any such orders reach me. Until then, you can reckon that anyone shooting at you is on the side of the bamboo-shoot and water-chestnut princes.'

'Goodbye,' I said, rising.

'Good luck,' he said.

Outside on the pavement I felt curiously naked; I had never before felt so keen a desire for a pair of blue spectacles, a false nose and a large ginger beard, but it was now too late to regret such elementary precautions. A courteous cab sped me to the airport in something less than a hundred years. By the time I had retrieved my suitcase and booked into a London flight my hair had, I was sure, whitened noticeably around the roots.

So far as I could see there was not a single Chinese person on the aircraft. It was not until just before take-off that Mr Lee and a young compatriot boarded. Neither of them looked at me. If it comes to that, I didn't look at them after the first time, I glared straight ahead like a driver who has been stopped for speeding and doesn't much want the policeman to get a sniff of his breath.

I offered myself all sorts of explanations. They can't have known that I'd be on that particular flight, could they? Could they? Or perhaps Johanna had asked them to be my bodyguard, how about that? Perhaps Mr Lee took that flight every day or perhaps he was hastening back to Soho for the Chinese New Year, his bag stuffed with goodies for his grandchildren. He was clearly the kind of chap who would have any number of grandchildren, all of whom he would dote on. Perhaps it wasn't Mr Lee at all: it is well known that all these chaps look alike. My fevered imagination fantasized away until we were thoroughly airborne and the Captain's voice came crackling out of the public address system with the usual wonderfully sincere wishes for an enjoyable flight. 'Ha ha,' I said bitterly, drawing a nasty look from the obviously teetotal lady sitting next to me. The loudspeaker went on to tell us that we would be cruising at large numbers of thousands of feet (aircraft drivers are the last bastion against metrication) and that our air-speed would be an immense number of mph. I felt like complaining at this excessive speed for I was in no great hurry to reach the end of the journey – it is better to travel hopelessly than to arrive.

When the stewardess arrived to take our orders for drinks my neighbour asked for a glass of iced water; I confirmed her worst suspicions by ordering two large brandies, one bottle of dry ginger ale and no ice. I was proud to note that there was scarcely a quaver in my voice. When the wench brought the life-giving potations I heard myself asking her whether she happened to know the date of Chinese New Year's Day.

'Why, no sir, I guess I don't, I'm sorry. But hey, there's two Chinese gentlemen sitting right there in front; just let me finish with the drinks and I'll go ask them.'

'No no no no,' I squeaked, 'I wouldn't dream of –'

'It's no trouble, sir. You're very welcome.'

Soon I saw her leaning over the seats of the two Chinese gentlemen, brightly pointing back to where I sat quaking. They did not look around. She tripped back and said, 'You're out of luck, sir, they say it was three weeks ago. Oh, and they said they were real sorry you missed out.'

'Thank you. How kind.'

'You're welcome.' Officious bitch. I unfolded my *Times* with studied nonchalance, laid it on my briefcase and applied myself to the crossword. I am not one who completes this crossword while his breakfast egg boils to medium-soft but on a good day a medium-hard puzzle lies stricken at my feet in half an hour or so. This was one of the other days. I readily solved 'One who uses public transport – a target, exterminated (9,6)' and wrote in 'passenger pigeon' with a hollow laugh, but after that I seemed unable to concentrate. I blamed this on my briefcase, which did not seem to be affording the usual flat surface. Indeed, it did not seem to be flat at all. I gave it a petulant palpation: sure enough, there seemed to be a fat, cylindrical bulge lying diagonally inside it. Distraught as I was, I was nevertheless certain that I owned no object of that shape and dimensions, or, if I did, it certainly could not be in my briefcase. I undid the catch of the flap and had a cautious grope inside; sure enough, my questing fingers found a stiff cardboard cylinder, measuring some eighteen inches in length and four inches in diameter. I closed the flap and – quaking now as I had never quaked before – reached for the unexpended portion of the brandy. It dashed past my uvula, tonsils, larynx and pharynx without touching the sides. Then I lay back in my reclining seat, regulated my breathing and applied myself to frenzied thought. A bomb or similar anti-Mortdecai device? Surely not: Mr Lee was on that very aircraft. Moreover, the metal-detectors of the security men at the airport would have detected anything of the kind. A monstrous tube of Smarties' chocolate beans from a well-wisher? But I could think of no well-wisher.

Consumed now with vulgar curiosity and death-wish, I opened the bag again and drew out the cylinder. It was light. It was made of cardboard and looked exactly like the cylinders in which people store and dispatch prints and drawings, things like that. I raised one end to my eye and, pointing it at the window or porthole, peered through it. I found myself gazing at the left-hand unit of the bust of my teetotal neighbour. She cuffed it aside and made a noise like an expiring soda-water syphon. I think I said 'Whoops!' but I cannot be sure.

Nothing seemed to be in the cylinder except a roll of heavy paper so I inserted a couple of fingers, gave a skilful twirl and extracted it like a well-buttered *escargot*. Unrolled, it seemed to be a good colour-reproduction of a Rouault gouache painting; closer inspection proved it be a clever *copy* in gouache, all done by hand. I say 'copy' because the original happens to be a rather famous Rouault called *Après-midi d'un Clown* and it is in the Peggy Guggenheim collection or one of those places. It really was beautifully executed, more like a forgery than a copy, for the copyist had laid it down on a jaconet backing and had even added a *cachet de vente*, a couple of collectors' marks and a museum reference number. I tut-tutted or tsk-tsked a bit, because it had been rolled the wrong way, with the paint side inside, a practice which any art-dealer knows better than. My portly she-neighbour was making her soda-syphon noises again and I realized that the painting was perhaps a little *explicit*: in Rouault's day, you see, clowns seemed to spend their *après-midis* in the most bizarre fashion. (For my part, I have never taken much interest in modern art; I feel that it is a subject which calls for a good deal less research.) As I rolled up the gouache and twiddled it back into the cylinder a scrap of paper fell out of the opposite end. It was typewritten and said YOU MAY WELL FIND THIS USEFUL AT HEATHROW. I tore the scrap of paper into as many pieces as it had room for, musing anguishedly the while. I mean, it is not often that copies of famous Rouault gouaches creep unobserved into your briefcase and it is still rarer to be told that they will prove useful at airports. I would have liked to go to the lavatory but that would have meant passing Mr Lee and his friend and, on the way back, they might have *looked* at me. I was in no shape to cope with that sort of thing. I took the coward's way out, I stabbed the appropriate bell-push and asked the stewardess for 'some more of that ginger ale and, yes, perhaps a spot more of that brandy'. My neighbour – I shall always think of her as Carrie Nation – whispered to the stewardess urgently. The stewardess looked at me puzzledly. I looked at the stewardess smilingly but I fancy the smile came out as more of a lopsided leer, really. In a few moments Carrie Nation had been moved to another seat and, more to the point, my brandy had been delivered at the pit-head.

I supped, mused, supped again. Nothing made sense. I made another attack on the virtue of the crossword; it was by the compiler who always tries to work in the word 'tedding' – I suspect Adrian Bell – so I had no difficulty with 'Currying favour with Tory bandleader; making hay while the sun never sets', but the rest defeated me. I gave myself up to thoughts about survival, staying alive, things like that. One good result of this thought or thinking was engendered by the fact that the airport security people with their metal-detectors had not detected the Rouault copy in my briefcase but had pin-pointed my silver pocket-flask in a trice. This had to mean that the two Chinese gentlemen could scarcely be carrying anything more lethal than a cardboard dagger. Their gats, shivs and other bits of mayhem equipment must be in their suitcases, in the hold of the aircraft. Clearly, then, when I arrived at Heathrow, London, all I had to do was *not* to wait for my own suitcase to creak out of the constipated luggage-delivery system but to abandon it, flee through Customs with nothing but my briefcase and take a speedy taxi to Walthamstow or some other improbable place where I might have a friend. Meanwhile, the Chinese gentlemen would be fretting and fuming at the luggage-carousel, impatient for their murder-tackle to appear.

How lucidly one thinks, to be sure, when one has taken just a suspicion of brandy more than one should. I folded my hands smugly across that part of the torso which lies a little south of the liver and had a little zizz. When I awoke, the smugness was still there; I seized the *Times* crossword, gave it a masterful glare and had it whining for mercy in twenty minutes.

I have always sneered in a well-bred way at those idiots who, as soon as the aircraft's engines have been switched off, stand up, clutching their brats and other hand-luggage for quite ten minutes until the surly cabin-crew deign to open the doors, but on this occasion I was well to the fore and sped down the ramp far ahead of the field. Had this been Newmarket, a casual observer equipped with field-glasses and a stop-watch would have hastened to the nearest telephone and had a chat with his bookie.

Ignoring all signs telling people where they might wait for their luggage I galloped straight to the Customs Area and towards the blessed sign which said TAXIS, waving my innocent briefcase at the customs chap. He crooked an authoritative finger at me; I skidded to a halt. 'Nothing to declare, officer,' I cried merrily, 'just the old briefcase full of the old paper-work, eh? Mustn't detain you, sure you're a busy man yourself –'

'Open it,' he said. 'Sir.'

'Certainly, certainly, certainly,' I quipped, 'but do be quick, there's a good chap, or all the taxis will be taken. Nothing in there, I assure you.'

Every once in a while I encounter people who don't like me. This customs chap was one of those. He dwelt upon every least object in the briefcase as though he were an aged *courreur* pawing over his collection of pubic hairs. He left the cardboard cylinder to the last. 'What's this then, sir?' he asked.

'A picture or painting,' I said impatiently, glancing ever and again at the baggage-hall where my fellow-travellers (if I may coin a phrase) awaited their luggage. 'A mere copy. No Commercial Value and Not For Re-sale.'

'Reelly,' he said. 'Let's just have a look, please.' Fretfully, I extracted and unrolled the said art-work. 'There,' I said, 'it's the *Après-midi d'un Clown* by Rouault. It's in the Guggenheim or one of those places.'

'The Weltschmerzer Foundation?' he prompted.

'That's it, that's it; jolly good. It's in the Weltschmerzer, of course. Chicago.'

'Oh no it's not, sir.'

'?'

'It *was* there until last Wensdee; then some villains bust into the place, got away with a million quidsworth of this old rubbish.'

My mouth opened and shut, opened and shut, miming those soundless 'oh's' that goldfish make when they want their water changed. I was spared the effort of saying something useful by a civil cough which seemed to come from behind my left shoulder.

A glance in that direction showed me a large, civil chap wearing a mackintosh or raincoat. A rapid swivel of some 270 degrees showed a similar chap, wearing a benign look, behind my right shoulder.

Permit me to digress for a moment. Every sound, professional team of thieves has a 'brain' who plans the villainy; a 'manager' who puts up the working capital; a 'fence' who will buy and sell the loot before it is even separated from its owners; a 'toolman' who knows how to neutralize burglar-alarm systems and to open locks, be they ever so sophisticated; a 'peterman' who can use a thermic lance on a safe or perhaps inject a fluid ounce of liquid explosive and detonate it with no more noise than a sparrow farting in its sleep; a 'hooligan' – regrettably – who will, at need, hit inquisitive passers-by with an iron bar; a 'bent' night-watchman or security-firm employee who is prepared to be concussed for £500 and a small percentage of the take; and – this is the chap you *didn't* know about – a 'lighthouse'. Your 'lighthouse' takes no active part in the actual breaking-and-entering; he simply strolls about with his hands in his pockets. He has but one simple, God-given skill: he can recognize 'fuzz', 'filth', 'Old Bill' or any other form of copper, however plainly-clothed, at two hundred metres on a dark night. No one – least of all the 'lighthouse' himself – knows how he does it, but there it is. There are only three reliable ones in the whole of London and they are paid the same as the hooligan.

What I am trying to say is that, had I been born into a different social stratum, I would have made a handsome living as a 'lighthouse'. The two chaps looming behind my shoulders were unmistakably 'fuzz'.

'Hello,' I said.

'I am Detective Inspector Jaggard,' said the chap on my left, 'and this is Detective Sergeant Blackwell. We are from the Fine Art Squad.' I shot another glance into the baggage hall; the carousel was beginning to rotate and my fellow-passengers were thronging around it. Suddenly I realized why my anonymous benefactor had assured me cryptically that the Rouault might well be of use to me at Heathrow.

'Flash the tin,' I said in my Bogart voice.

'I beg your pardon?' said the DI.

'Let's see the potsy.' They looked at each other, smiling thin smiles.

'Detectives here do not carry gilt shield-badges,' explained the DI, 'but here is my warrant-card, which is almost as impressive and, unlike the "potsy" you speak of, cannot be bought in toy-shops.' It seemed to be a very valid sort of warrant-card. 'It's a fair cop,' I said happily. 'Lead me to the nearest dungeon. Oh yes, and perhaps Sergeant Blackwell might be kind enough to collect my suitcase while you and I go to the Black Maria. It's a sort of pigskin job by Gucci, has my initials on it, can't mistake it.'

'That'll be "C.M." for Charlie Mortdecai, right, sir?' said the sergeant.

'Right,' I said, giving him a nod of approval.

'Then why,' asked the DI, 'does your passport say that you are Fr T. Rosenthal, SJ?'

Like any jesting Pilate, he did not stay for an answer but steered me courteously to one of those large black motor-cars which the better class of policeman has the use of. In a minute or two we were joined by the DS, who had found my suitcase. He did not give it to me. Nor did he drive to what you call Scotland Yard and what coppers call 'Headquarters' – he drove us over Battersea Bridge to that new place on the South Bank which they set up for the Serious Crimes Squad after that train-robbery (remember?) and which now houses all sorts of esoteric arms of the law. Such as, for instance, CII, which thinks up crimes before the villains do and has people sitting on the steps waiting for them. Such as, too, CI, which polices naughty policemen and is known affectionately as Rubber Heels; the late Martland's Special Power Group or SOGPU, and, of course, the Fine Art Squad which is so highly trained that its members can tell which way up a Picasso should hang. (Picasso, of course, is no longer in a position to contradict them.) The whole place is most secure and secret, except that any taxi-driver in London will take you there unerringly.

In a cosy room on the ground floor they formally charged me with illegal entry or something vague like that so that they could get me remanded in the morning, then we ascended three floors in a large lift, passed through a heavy iron door watched over by closed-circuit television, crowded into a much smaller lift and went down eight floors. I am no great lover of the bowels of the earth but the said bowels were just what I craved at the time. They were peopled by large, *English* male policemen: not an American, a Chinese waiter nor a militant woman was to be seen. They ushered me into a simply-furnished, well-lit room, stuck a telephone into a jack-plug, attached a tape-recorder to it and invited me to make my 'privilege phone-call'. I was in no two minds about whom I should call: I dialled Mrs Spon, the best interior decorator in London and the only thoroughly capable person I know. I sketched in the outlines of my plight, asked her to get in touch with my 'brief' (as we rats of the underworld call our lawyers) and with Johanna, and to tell Jock to stand by the telephone around the clock. 'Tell him,' I urged, 'that he is not to go out except on spoken instructions by you or me. If he must play dominoes he may have his friends in and they may drink my beer within reason. Oh, and Mrs Spon, you might make it clear to the brief that I am in no pressing hurry to be sprung – no writs of *habeas corpus* – I wish to clear my name of this foul imputation before breathing free air again.'

'I twig,' she said. I replaced the receiver with a certain smugness: when Mrs Spon says that she has twigged then twig is what she has done. I'd back her to take the Grand Fleet into action after ten minutes of instruction from a Petty Officer, she's like that. She wears wonderfully expensive clothes and has a face like a disused quarry.

'Well now,' I said to my two captors, 'I daresay you'll be wanting to, ah, grill me a bit, eh?' They looked at each other, then back at me, then shook their heads in unison.

'I think you'd better wait for your lawyer, sir,' said Inspector Jaggard.

'For your own sake, sir,' said Sergeant Blackwell. They didn't frighten me. On the floor stood my suitcase, briefcase and the plastic bag containing my duty-free allowance of brandy and cigarettes. I reached for the plastic bag. They didn't hit me. I toddled into the adjoining lavatory and found two plastic tooth-glasses. I gave myself a jolt of the brandy, then poured two drinks for them.

'I think we're on duty, aren't we, Sergeant?' Blackwell consulted his watch. 'Hard to say, sir.' I put three packets of duty-free cigarettes beside Jaggard's glass and two beside Blackwell's, then tactfully visited the lavatory again. When I returned the glasses were empty, the cigarettes pocketed, but I was under no illusions. Policemen like them are not hungry for a free swig of brandy and a packet of king-size gaspers; they had only taken them to lull me into the belief that they were easy-going chaps. But I had observed their eyes, you see; they were the eyes of career-policemen, quite different from the fierce eye of a copper who can be bought. I offered them the key to my suitcase, saying that if they cared to rummage it now I could enjoy the creature comforts it contained, such as soap, clean underwear and so forth. Blackwell gave it a perfunctory rummage; Jaggard didn't even bother to watch, we all knew that there would be nothing illegal in it. Then I indicated that I would quite like a little lie-down and they said that they were, in fact, going off duty themselves and that their guvnor, the Detective Chief Inspector, might be down for a chat when my lawyer arrived. Then they locked me in. I didn't mind a bit – there are times when being locked in is comforting. After a quick scrub at the depleted ivory castles with Mr Eucryl's justly-celebrated Smoker's Dentifrice, I threw myself on the cot and sank into the arms of Morpheus. My last waking thought was one of pleasure that they had not ripped open the lining of my suitcase; it is a very expensive suitcase. Moreover, I tend to keep a few large, vulgar currency notes under the lining in case I ever need to buy a steam-yacht in a hurry.

I cannot have slept for more than an hour or so when the door made unlocking noises and I sprang to my feet – trouserless as I was – prepared to sell my life dearly. It was only a uniformed, fatherly 'Old Bill' who wanted to know what I would like for supper.

'There's a very good Chinese take-away just down the road – hoy, are you all right, sir?'

'Fine, thank you, fine, fine. It's just that I have an allergy to Chinese food. I'll just have whatever's going in the canteen.'

'It's rissoles tonight,' he warned me.

'Capital, capital. Nothing nicer. Wheel them on, do. And, ah, I daresay there'll be a touch of HP sauce or something of that sort, eh?'

'That *and* tomato sauce, sir.'

'Oh, Sergeant,' I said as he began to exit. 'Yessir?' replied the constable.

'Do you have *many* Chinese chaps working in the canteen?'

'Lord love you, no, sir. All the staff is widows of officers of the Force. Their attitude is a bit Bolshie sometimes but when they set their minds to it they make the finest fishcakes South of the Thames. It's fishcakes tomorrow night, sir, will you be here?'

'I hope so,' I said sincerely. 'Wild horses have often tried to drag me away from a well-made fishcake, with little or no success.'

The rissoles were all that a rissole-lover could wish for; they were accompanied by frozen french beans and faultless mashed potatoes, not to mention a full bottle each of HP sauce and tomato ditto, also bread and butter in abundance and a huge tin mug of strong orange-coloured tea such as I had thought only Jock could make. Tears sprang to my eyes as I slipped a packet of duty-free king-sized into 'Old Bill's' kindly pocket.

Stomach assuaged for the nonce, I was about to fling myself once more onto the cot when my eye fell upon the telephone, which Jaggard and Blackwell had carelessly left in my room or cell. I lifted the receiver and applied it to my ear. It was giving off a dialling-tone which meant that they had left it through to an open line.

'Oh, *really*,' I thought. I mean, people don't achieve the rank of DI, or even DS, if they inadvertently leave live telephones about in the cells of International Art Thieves. I applied myself to the problem of how best to squeeze a little gravy out of the situation. At last I decided to muddy the wells of investigatory technique by telephoning Pete the Welshman – a person who often works for me. I should explain that all those people who work for art-dealers – re-liners, restorers, mount-cutters, frame-makers, etc. – are congenital liars and thieves: they observe that their masters sometimes depart from the truth and soon come to believe that mendacity and peculation are all that is required to make a fortune in the fine art trade. How wrong they are, to be sure. Pete is also a Welshman and a fervent chapel-goer, which puts him well ahead of the game. I dialled his number.

'Hello, Pete,' I said. 'You know who this is, don't you?'

'Do you know what fucking time of night it is?' he snarled.

'Look, Pete, let's save the social amenities; this is business. You know that big job . . .?'

'Ah,' he lied unhesitatingly.

'Dump it,' I said. 'Forget it. You never saw it. Right?'

'Right,' he said. A casual listener – and I knew that there would be several – would believe that Pete knew what I was talking about. They would have been wrong. I hung up.

I reckoned that that little chat should guarantee me at least another twenty-four hours in the security of that stoutly-constructed nick. I decided on a digestive nap; fell asleep to dream of fishcakes on the morrow.

20 Mortdecai, crazed by the thought of fishcakes and terrified by the thought of liberty, is held in contempt of court, to name but one.

This madness has come on us for our sins

The Holy Grail

My lawyer woke me up to tell me that no one, after all, wanted to interrogate me that night and was there anything else I wanted. Half-awake, I imprudently told him that what I wanted more than anything was to spend a lengthy sojourn in this very room or cell, for fate's fickle finger was feeling for my fundament and I had to find out, somehow, before I was released, who was on whose side, the only certainty being that no one was on mine. When I say that I said this imprudently, I mean that, had I been fully in my senses, I'd have realized that the place probably boasted more bugs than a Sailors' Mission Refuge. He semaphored meaningfully with his eyebrows – only lawyers nowadays seem to be able to grow eyebrows, even bank managers seem to have lost the art – and I shut up. He said that he would be in court in the morning and warned me sadly, but with a huge wink, that I must prepare myself to be remanded in custody for weeks and weeks. Then he goodnighted me, I changed into pyjamas and in a trice was sleeping the sleep of the unjust, which is quite as dreamless as the sleep of the just if the unjust sleeper has a litre of Red Hackle on his bedside table.

I was awakened by the arrival of another great mug of orange-hued tea and a dish of eggs and bacon. Dawn's left hand was in the sky. The e's and b would not have brought a smile to the face of Egon Ronay but I plied a lusty knife and fork, knowing that I must keep my strength up. The journey to the magistrate's court was on my mind, of course: the route thereto was doubtless thick with Chinese snipers *faisant la haie*.

As it turned out, those fears were groundless, for this de-luxe cop-shop had its own magistrate and mini-court on the premises. It was a cosy little gathering: one ill-shaven Mortdecai escorted by one kindly turnkey, one magistrate who exhibited all the signs of a magistrate who has not had enough sleep, one lawyer giving me the blank sort of look which means 'keep your mouth shut and leave this to me', one haggard Detective Inspector Jaggard glaring at his notebook as though it had said something rude to him; one world-weary clerk and – to my dismay – one Johanna looking quite ravishing in an oxlip-yellow suit and hat.

The clerk droned legally for a while; Jaggard put on a joke-policeman voice while he read bits from his notebook about how he had proceeded from here to there on information received . . . but I must not trouble you with such minutiae: I am sure that you have been in magistrates' courts yourselves. Just as I was expecting the blessed words which would remand the prisoner, C. Mortdecai, in custody for weeks and weeks, revelling in fishcakes far from the madding Triads, the blow fell. My treacherous lawyer rose and submitted that the prisoner's wife, Mrs C. Mortdecai, had received a visit, late the previous night, from a Fr T. Rosenthal, SJ, who had explained how – after some muddle at Immigration – he had found himself in possession of a passport in the name of Mortdecai. And could he have his own passport back, please. And, no, he couldn't be produced in court because he had gone into Retreat at Heythrop and the Preliminary Confession alone would take some twelve hours, not to mention the penance after. 'Just an absurd muddle,' said my brief, avoiding my glance, 'great credit to the vigilance of the police etc. etc.'

I opened my mouth to claim that I was clearly an International Art Thief and deserved more courtesy than this but then I remembered that I had only been charged with Illegal Entry into Her Majesty's Domains. No word of Rouault or his gouaches had passed anyone's lips.

The magistrate apologized to me, hoped that I had not been too much inconvenienced, dismissed me without a stain on my character. I was free to go.

I looked around me frantically: the turnkey was giving a friendly nod, Jaggard was sneering, Johanna was irradiating the most wifely smile you can imagine. I knew that the instant I stepped into the freedom of the street I was a dead man – curiously, too, the thought of those incomparable fishcakes surged into my mind. My best friends would not claim that I am a fast thinker; I like to mull these things over for a day or two, but it was clear that there was no time for mulling. I did a Fred Astaire double-shuffle around the turnkey or gaoler, strode up the steps to the magistrate, right hand outstretched. The beak's expression made it clear that he didn't have a lot of time for these Continental expressions of emotion but, after an inward struggle, held out his hand. I seized it, whisked his frail body from the bench and gave him the heel of my hand in the hooter. Sleepy before, he now became a sleeper in earnest. Hordes of capable people sprang out of the woodwork and restrained me (restrained means 'hit') but I recked little of their blows for, in the twinkling of an eye, I was once again in my comfy cell, secure in the knowledge that bail is rarely allowed to chaps who wantonly alter the appearance of Stipendiary Magistrates. I allowed myself a snort of whisky and poured the rest into the plastic duty-free bag, lest any vengeful copper should try to take it away from me.

I am not one of those who, in times of stress, sits on the edge of a bed gnashing his nails and cursing whichever fool or blackguard made this world: I am more one of those who lies down on the bed in question and snatches a nap. When the door opened at lunch-time I kept the eyes firmly closed. A voice which could only have emanated from one of those fierce young policemen said 'Lunch.' I remained tacit and mute. I heard him lift the empty whisky-bottle, shake it and replace it onto the table with a disgusted slam. He went out, locking the door. After counting from one to ten I opened an eye. The luncheon he had brought was in three of those little white cartons with tin-foil tops such as Chinese take-away places sell. I coaxed a little Scotch out of the plastic shopping bag, mingled it with water and went back to sleep. A dead rat might have coaxed a reaction from my salivary glands sooner than anything with bean-shoots and soy-sauce.

Sergeant Blackwell came to see me soon afterwards; he looked at my untouched lunch and said '*Waste!*'

'Thirty-nine inches,' I quipped, 'bust, forty-two.'

'Neither funny nor plausible,' he said. Both true, of course. Then he took me upstairs to the charge-room and charged me with common assault, actual bodily harm, contempt of court and many another thing including, I fancy, unimaginative potty-training in early childhood, while I hung my head in a suitable fashion.

Back in my cell I asked for something to read; he was back in ten minutes with a tattered Bible.

'I think I've read this,' I said.

'It's all we've got,' he retorted, 'Enid Blyton is only for trusties.'

The Good Book was printed upon fine India paper and the first few pages had been used by sacreligious chaps for rolling fags with (that's *cigarettes*), so that *Genesis* began at the bit where Cain says 'My punishment is more than I can bear. Behold, thou hast driven me out this day from the face of the earth; . . . and I shall be a fugitive and a vagabond in the earth; and it shall come to pass that every one that findeth me shall slay me.' I never did find out what happened to Cain except that he went to the land of Nod which is to the East of Eden; I joined him there.

It was one of those days when a chap simply cannot get a good day's sleep; it seemed I had scarcely closed my eyes before last night's 'Old Bill' was warning me to get shaved for Six o'Clock Court. He watched me with something of admiration in his eye as I plied the disposable razor; many a villain, he told me, had sworn to give that particular magistrate a knuckle-sandwich but none had hitherto made good the threat. I could see that he found it hard to believe that my only motive was a determination to graze upon the fabled fishcakes.

Back in the intimate court-room, the cast was almost the same as it had been that morning, except that my custodian was now the 'Old Bill', the magistrate was one of those soppy, earnest chaps who long to hear of broken homes and deprived childhoods and Johanna was looking esculent in a cinnamon sheath such as you could not buy with a lifetime's trading-stamps. Yes, and there was a flaccid man with a big face whom I had never seen before but who was clearly one of those Harley Street chaps who charge you fifty guineas for telling you to take a long sea voyage and more exercise.

Detective Inspector Jaggard flatly recited the facts about my disgraceful behaviour that morning. It seemed to me that the magistrate permitted a thin smile to cross his face as Jaggard related how his brother of the bench would never again be quite the same around the nose. My brief called Johanna to the witness-box. She dabbed a tearful eye with a couple of square inches of cambric as she told how valiantly I had fought against my, uh, terrible, uh, disability and how she was ready to stand by me until I had conquered it. For my part I gaped. Probably I was meant to gape. Then the flaccid chap was called: I had been wrong about him, his address was not Harley Street but Wigmore Street.

He had, it seemed, been treating me for more than a year and was getting some pretty good results; all sorts of mental diseases with names I cannot remember had succumbed to his therapy and the slight, residual hostility-issue-orientation towards legal authority was fast vanishing and he would stake his reputation that this morning's little outburst was just a preter-ultimate orgasmic sublimation which was, not to put too fine a point on it, a jolly good thing and meant that I was now cured. He also had my wife's assurance that I was very sorry and that I would pay for the nose.

I wagged my head with admiration; so fine a liar was wasted in Wigmore Street. There had been times in his declaration when I had been on the point of believing him myself.

You must have noticed that most magistrates, when looking wise, peer over the tops of their spectacles. This one was trendy: he prodded the gig-lamps up to his forehead and peered under them. He asked the mendacious medico if he could advance any other extenuating circs., had the prisoner been the product of a broken home, a deprived childhood, that sort of thing?

'Oh dear, yes, *very*,' said the liar, speaking more truthfully than he realized, 'but, er*chrmmm*, you understand, at this stage, sure you follow me . . .' and he jerked his head a couple of millimetres in my direction.

'Just so, just so,' said the kindly stipendiary. Beaming at me, he hit me with a hundred quid for his fellow-magistrate's conk

– well, that was the least he could do, I realized that – added a few more bobs for contempt of court, bound me over in my own recognizances to keep the peace and begged me, like any father, to listen to my doctor and loved ones who knew what was best for me. He didn't tell me to give up smoking cigarettes.

Going down the stairs, free as a bird and terrified as a clay pigeon, I accosted Jaggard. 'Charge me with pinching the Rouault,' I whined; 'I'll plead guilty, it's a fair cop.' He stared at me bleakly as only Detective-Inspectors can.

'Unfortunately, sir,' he said (the 'sir' stuck in his throat a bit), 'it seems that just before the robbery your lady wife had agreed to buy that Rouault from Miss Gertrude Weltschmerzer for you. As a wedding-present. I have spoken to Miss Weltschmerzer on the international telephone. She confirms this.' He spoke in the bitter tones of a policeman who has to live and work in a world where 'law and order' has become a dirty phrase. I truly felt sorry for him.

'Well, well,' I babbled, 'that was nice of her, wasn't it. Matter of fact, I'm thinking of buying her an antique pendant.'

'You mean, like a spare?' he said.

I stopped feeling sorry for him.

Downstairs, I collected my possessions, gave the plastic bag of whisky to the kindly Old Bill, along with the remainder of the duty-free cigarettes – who knows when you may need a friend in the Force? – and joined Johanna in her cute little Jensen Interceptor. Not a shot was fired as she drove us to Upper Brook Street. She looked beautiful behind the wheel, as all lovely women do behind the wheels of sports cars. All she said was 'Oh, Charlie, Charlie, Charlie.'

All I said was, 'Yes.'

Jock was at home, looking useful. I had forgotten to bring him any American comic-books but he didn't sulk. I took him aside and murmured an instruction or two about dinner. My conversation with Johanna was desultory.

'Charlie dear, don't tire yourself telling me all about your adventures. I know most of it and can guess the rest.'

'Darling Charlie, why are you keeping away from the windows in that kind of furtive way?'

'Charlie, what on earth are those *strange* brown things you are eating?'

'Fishcakes,' I mumbled from a full mouth and a fuller heart. 'Made by policemen's widows.'

'I see . . .'

'Charlie, I expect you're very tired?'

'Very.'

'*Too* tired?'

'I didn't say that, did I?'

21 Mortdecai takes an educational tour around a food-processing plant and improves his mind no end.

The dirty nurse, Experience, in her kind
Hath fouled me.

The Last Tournament

I awoke the next morning at an earlier hour than usual.

'Johanna,' I said, 'could you please stop doing that for a moment?'

'Shchroombleshly,' she said, indistinctly.

'How much did that Wigmore Street wank-shrink cost you?'

'A thousand,' she said, clearing her throat.

'And the Rouault?'

'Nothing. No, really, nothing – I just happened to have heard that Gertie Weltschmerzer was having to find a really serious sum of money to pay her last-husband-but-one not to publish his memoirs, so I called her and congratulated her on the *convenient* burglary and sort of dropped the name of the president of her insurance firm who happens to be an old buddy of mine and she made the sort of noises that rich women make – you know, like this . . .'

'Later,' I said. 'First the narrative.'

'Where was I? Oh yes, when she stopped making noises like a gobbler – that's what we call a turkey in the States – I sort of reminded her that the Rouault couldn't have been burgled because she'd sold it to me just a couple of days before. She had to think about that for a while because she's a little dumb, you know? and then she said why, *sure* she remembered and she hoped my husband would enjoy it. That's all, except that I feel I ought to check that my husband does enjoy it.'

I managed to enjoy it although it was, as I have said, quite indecently early in the morning.

Jock, announcing his imminent appearance by a polite cough which almost took the door off its hinges (I have taught him that good servants never knock), brought in a tray for Johanna laden with the sort of coffee which you and I drink after dinner but which Daughters of the Revolution pour into their stomachs at crack of dawn. Small wonder that the American Colonies were the first to win their independence – if that's what they still call it. Before I could doze off again my own tray arrived, just a few eggs, a half-dozen slices of toast and a steaming pot of well-judged tea. Jock, you see, although not bred to service, has a heaven-sent knowledge of what the young master will require in the way of tea. I would pit him against any Wigmore Street physician when it comes to prescribing tea: there are times, as I'm sure you know, when these things *matter*. I mean, an art-dealer who has nothing to face that day but a brisk flurry of bidding at Sotheby's needs naught but the soothing Oolong. A morning at Christie's indicates the Lapsang Souchong. A battle-royal at Bonham's over, say, a Pater which only one other dealer has spotted, calls for the Broken Orange Pekoe Tips – nay, even the Earl Grey itself. For an art-dealer in terror of his life, however, and one who has valiantly embarked on Part Two of his honeymoon in early middle age, only two specifics are in the field: Twining's Queen Mary's Blend or Fortnum's Royal. What I'd call a two-horse race. I forget which it was; I only remember that I slunk out of bed before its fortifying effect made me forget that I am no longer a youngster. (That's all right about the 'size of the dog in the fight and the size of the fight in the dog' but art-dealers in their late forties have *livers* to consider; other organs have to take their place in the queue.)

Jock really is a compassionate man when he sets his mind to it: it was not until I was under the shower that he slipped me the bad news.

'Mr Charlie,' was how he phrased it, 'Mr Charlie, there's two gemmun downstairs waiting to see you.'

'*Two* gentlemen?' I said, soaping freely the parts which I can still reach, 'Two? Nonsense, Jock, I only know three gentlemen altogether; one of them is serving a life-sentence for murdering an unwanted mistress, another deals in rare books in Oxford and the third has gone to the bad . . . publishing, something like that.' He heard me out patiently; he knows the difference between prattle and orders; then he said, 'I di'n't mean *gemmun* when I said gemmun, Mr Charlie, I only said gemmun because you don't like me to say –'

'Quite right, Jock,' I said, raising a soapy hand. 'Are you trying to say that they are art-dealers?' He wagged a regretful head.

'Nar. They're fuzz. Big Brass Fuzz.' I turned the shower to cold; this never fails to make the intellect surge around.

'Have we any tea-bags in the kitchen? We have? *Really?* Well, make them some tea and tell them that I shall be down presently.'

'Ah, Jaggard, Blackwell!' I cried as I bounced into the drawing-room a few moments later, 'Got some tea, eh?' The two men turned and looked at me. They had no tea, nor were they Jaggard and Blackwell. Nor did they get up. They were large, blank-faced, empty-eyed coppers, but for some reason my 'lighthouse' started to flicker a bit. They were almost like coppers but not quite.

'Mr Mortdecai?' asked one of them.

'True,' I said.

'Interpol. Robinson, London.' He pointed to the other chap. 'Hommel, Amsterdam.' That made sense; the lighthouse ceased to flash. Interpol are not like other boys and Dutch fuzz does not look like English fuzz.

'How can I help you?' I asked.

'Get your hat, please.' I thought about that.

'Warrant cards?' I said diffidently. They gave me the world-weary look which policemen give to clients who have read too many thrillers. I strolled about aimlessly until I could get a squint down the Dutchman's jacket. Sure enough, he was wearing a shoulder-holster bursting with what looked like the good old Browning HPM 1935 – a pistol which contains 14 rounds of 9mm Parabellum and weighs a couple of pounds unloaded, a splendid weapon for slapping people on the side of the head with but nevertheless an odd choice of ironmongery for anyone who isn't expecting an invasion.

'I've got one, too,' said the English jack.

'Am I under arrest,' I asked, 'and if so, what for?' The Dutchman allowed himself a sigh, or it may have been a yawn.

'Yost get the hat, Mr Mortdecai,' he said. 'Please.' At that point Johanna entered the room and gave a startled glance at our visitors – a glance of recognition, I'd have said.

'Don't go with these men, Charlie,' she said sharply.

'They are armed,' I explained.

'So am I,' growled Jock from the other doorway, his beefy hand full of Luger.

'Thank you, Jock, but please put it down *now*. The gentleman on the sofa is holding a gun under his mackintosh and I fancy it's pointing at my gut. Also, Mrs Mortdecai is present.' I watched Jock slowly figuring out the odds, praying that he would make the right decision. I often boast that I am not especially afraid of dying but on the other hand I have this heavy addiction to life and I'm told that the withdrawal symptoms are shocking. Finally he placed the Luger on the floor – you do not *drop* automatic pistols – and, at a gesture from the Dutch chap, kicked it across the carpet. He kicked it in such fashion that it slid far under the big break-front bookcase: he is not just an ugly face, you know.

One of them ushered Johanna and Jock into the kitchen and locked them in; the other didn't rip out the telephone cord, he unscrewed the mouthpiece, took out the diaphragm and put it in his pocket.

'Extension?' he asked.

'No.'

'Where is it?'

'In the bedroom.' He walked me there and repeated the procedure. He was *good*. Then we went. Their motor-car was a sensible, Rover-like vehicle and I was made to sit in the front, beside the Dutchman who was driving. The English copper – well, I was still not sure that he wasn't – leaned forward and said that I must not do anything foolish because his pistol was pointed at my left kidney. Now, every schoolboy knows that if a man means to shoot you he does so there and then, without shilly-shallying. Clearly, they wanted me alive, so the threat was idle. I hoped it was idle. I craned over my shoulder for a glimpse of the sidearm in question: he snarled at me to face the front. The pistol was there all right and I had had just enough time to see that it was one of those monstrous US Government Colt.45 automatics which can blow a hole through a brick wall. What was nice about this particular weapon was that it was not wearing a silencer; to let off such a thing in a car would stop the traffic for miles. That was the third mistake they had made. I applied myself to thought.

'Where are you taking me?' I asked idly.

'Home,' said the Dutchman. This was probably meant to be a joke. We sped eastward. As we passed St Paul's I courteously pointed out its beauties to the Dutchman.

'Shot op,' he said.

We sped further eastward, now in parts of London quite unfamiliar to me.

'Where is "home", please?' I asked.

The Englishman answered this time. 'Home's where the heart is,' he said with all the jovial smugness of a large man holding a large pistol. 'We're just taking you somewhere nice and quiet where they can ask you a few questions, then if your lady wife delivers Mr Ree to Gerrard Street within twenty-four hours we let you go, don't we?'

'Shot OP!' said the Dutchman. He seemed to be in charge. Those few words had made my day, however, for it was now clear that they were but the minions of another 'they' who needed to know something that I knew and that I was also a valuable hostage. I was more than ever sure that this was not a time for people to blow holes through the Mortdecai kidneys.

When we came to a complicated road-junction, crammed with traffic and well-populated with uniformed policemen, I murmured to the Dutch chap that we drove on the left in England. He was, as a matter of fact, doing so but it gave him pause and the wheel wobbled. I snatched the ignition keys; the car stalled in the midst of a welter of furious traffic and I sprang out. Sure enough, they didn't shoot at me. I ran over to the nearest 'Old Bill', gabbled that the driver was having a heart attack and where was the nearest telephone. He pointed to a kiosk then stamped majestically towards the car, which was now the centre of a tumult of block traffic.

In the kiosk I frantically dialled my own number and rammed in a wasteful 10p piece. Johanna answered from the dressing-room extension which had not been noticed.

'Look,' I said, 'I'm in a phone-box, corner of . . .' I read off what it said on the instrument '. . . and I've got away from them but not for long. I'll be . . .' I frantically looked out of the kiosk, saw a great, grubby, warehouse-like building opposite with a name on it '. . . Mycock's Farm-cured Bacon,' I read out.

'This is no time for jokes, Charlie dear.'

'Just get Jock here; fast.' I replaced the receiver, did not even spare the time to check the returned coins box. I ran towards the excellent Mr Mycock. Inside the door an elderly slattern, redolent of Jeyes' Fluid, pointed to where the guvnor would be. 'He's probably having his dinner,' she added. 'Out of a bottle.' As soon as she was out of sight I changed direction again and again, diving into the abattoir's labyrinth. The pong of scorched pig became excruciating; I longed for that Jeyes' Fluid. The air was split by an appalling shriek – it was the dinner-time whistle but it gave me a bad moment. I pulled myself together, affecting the arrogant stroll of a Ministry of Health official looking for the germ *Clostridium Botulinum*. The workers who thronged out past me did not even spare me a glance, they were off to chance paratyphoid from beef pies at The Bunch of Grapes; they wouldn't eat *pork* pies, they'd seen them being made. As I stalked proudly through the corridors, turning randomly every now and again in a purposeful sort of way, I was doing feverish sums in mental arithmetic concerned with how quickly Jock could possibly get here. It's all very well being clever and devious, you see, but when you are eyeball-deep in lethal shit you need a thug – a thug who has coped with such situations since his first term in Borstal. Jock is just such a thug – few art-dealers could afford him – and I was confident that he would make all speed to the Mycock *cochonnerie* and would be properly equipped with one pair of brass knuckles, one Luger and, if he had been able to find the key, one Banker's Special Revolver such as I keep in my bedside table. Twenty minutes was how I had the race handicapped. I had to survive for just twenty minutes.

I squeezed past a cluster of bins marked PET-FOOD ONLY: WASH HANDS AFTER HANDLING and was about to thread my way through another lot marked IRELAND AND BELGIUM ONLY when I saw a large chap about thirty feet away, holding a pistol with two hands. He was the Dutchman. The pistol was pointed at me. The two-handed grip was perfectly good procedure according to the book they teach policemen with, but it seemed to me that if he was any good with that thing he would, at that range, have been holding it in one hand, pointing it at the ground a couple of yards in front of his feet. All the same, I froze, as any sensible chap would.

'Comm, Mr Mortdecai,' he said persuasively, 'comm; you have donn the teatricals. Yost comm with the honds behind the head and no one will hort you.' I started to breathe deeply; in, count ten, out – this is supposed to hyperoxygenate the system. Added to the adrenalin which was sloshing around in my blood-vessels, it had a salutary effect: I felt convinced that I could have held Cassius Clay for quite two rounds. Unless he got me against the ropes, of course.

I went on hyperoxygenating; the Dutchman's pistol roved up and down from my privates to my forehead. He was the first to become bored.

'Mr Mortdecai,' he said in a dangerous voice, 'are you comming now?' Well, I couldn't resist a straight line like that, could I?

'No,' I said, 'just breathing hard.' While he was thinking about that I feinted a dive to the left, then, for my life, plunged to the right, behind the friendly bins of pig-pieces. 'Rooty-toot-toot-toot' went his shooter. One round went howling off the wall, the others pierced the bins. He was not quite as bad as I had thought but he was not as good as he thought. That two-handed grip, you see, gives you a grand one-off first shot but when you swing to another target you invariably loose off too soon. The good pistol-shooter always lowers his weapon when tracking the second target and only raises it again when he has it cold. Ask anyone. Wyatt Earp, for instance.

I durst not give him time to change his magazine so I shed my jacket and slung it over the bins. 'Rooty-toot-toot' went the Browning. That made seven rounds expended, seven to go; even I could tell that. The floor sloped down in a gentle ramp towards him. I kicked over a couple of bins which rolled down the slope, dripping pig's blood and goodness knows what else. He shot at them, for the Dutch are cleanly folk. Ten rounds gone, four to go. I raised an unoccupied bin-lid and slammed it onto the floor; he fired two more rounds, quite wildly.

Where I had kicked the bins away I saw that there was a monstrous iron door with a lever instead of a handle. It looked like an excellent door to be behind.

'Jackson!' I bellowed – it seemed a plausible sort of name – 'JACKSON! Don't use the bombs: I'm coming out to take him myself.' Hommel can scarcely have believed that, but he must have dithered a bit because I got that great iron door open and scrambled through it without a shot being fired at me. The room inside the door was cold as the tip of an Eskimo's tool: it was, indeed, what the meat-trade calls a Cold Room. The lever on my side of the door had a position marked SECURE in red paint. I made it so. High up on two walls were those rubber-flap kind of entrances you see in hospitals; between them and through them ran an endless belt with large hooks. (Yes, just like a dirty weekend with a shark-fisher.) A pistol roared outside and a bullet spanged against the splendidly solid iron door. I sat with my back to the door and quaked, partly with cold, for I had discarded my jacket in that little *ruse de guerre*, you remember. The secure lever beside my head wagged and clicked but did not allow admission. Then I heard voices, urgent voices: the Dutchman was no longer alone. An unpleasing sort of whirring, grating noise made itself heard: evidently they had got hold of some kind of electrical tool and were working on the door-handle. Had I been a religious man I should probably have offered up a brisk prayer or two, but I am proud, you see: I mean, I never praised Him when I was knee-deep in gravy so it would have seemed shabby to apply for help from a bacon-factory.

The grating noises on the other side of the door increased: I looked about me desperately. On the wall was one of these huge electrical switches such as American Presidents use for starting World War Last. It might well set off an alarum, I thought; it might turn off all the electrical power in Mr Mycock's bacon-factory – certainly, it couldn't make things worse. I heaved with all my might and closed the contacts.

What happened was that pigs started trundling through the room. They were not exactly navigating under their own power, you understand, for they had all crossed The Great Divide or made the Great Change; they were hanging from the hooks on the endless belt, their contents had been neatly scooped out and were doubtless inhabiting the PET-FOOD ONLY: WASH HANDS AFTER HANDLING bin. They were the first truly happy pigs I had ever seen.

The eighth – or it may have been the ninth – pig wasn't really a pig in the strictest sense of the word; it was a large Dutchman, fully-clothed in what would be called a suit in Amsterdam. He was hanging onto a hook with one hand and seemed to have all his entrails. His other hand brandished the Browning HPM 1935, which he fired at me as he dropped to the floor, making his fourth mistake that day. The shot took a little flesh off the side of my belly – a place where I can well afford to lose a little flesh – then he aimed carefully at the pit of my belly and squeezed the trigger again. Nothing happened. As he looked stupidly down at the empty pistol I kicked it out of his hand.

'That was fourteen,' I said kindly. 'Can't you count? Haven't you a spare magazine?' Dazedly, he patted the pocket where the spare magazine nested. Meanwhile, I had picked up the Browning; I clouted him on the side of the head with it. He passed no remarks, he simply subsided like a chap who has earned a night's repose. I took the spare magazine out of his pocket, removed the empty one from the pistol (using my handkerchief to avoid leaving misleading fingerprints) and popped it into his pocket. I cannot perfectly recall what happened then, nor would you care to know. Suffice it to say that the endless belt was still churning along with its dangling hooks and, well, it seemed a good idea at the time.

It was now becoming colder every moment and I was shaking like any aspen, but even cowards derive a little warmth from a handful of Browning HPM with a full magazine. I awaited what might befall, regretting nothing but having wasted a perfectly good jacket. An indistinct voice shouted through the door.

'Eh?' I shouted valiantly.

'Open up, Mr Charlie,' shouted Jock. I opened up. Had I been one of these emotional Continental chaps, I believe I would have clasped him to my bosom.

'We got to get out, Mr Charlie, the place'll be crawling with Old Bill in about ten seconds flat.' We took off at a dog-trot. To my horror, at the turn of the corridor stood Johanna, holding my Banker's Special like a girl who knows how to use Banker's Specials. She gave me one of those smiles which jellify the knees, but the brain remained in gear. From the direction of the entrance there came a sort of crowd-scene noise and, rising above it, the sound of patient exasperation which only policemen can make. Someone came clumping nigh and we ducked into the nearest room. There were no pigs in it. What was in it was bales and bales of newly-laundered white coats and overalls such as those who work in bacon-factories love to wear.

When the legions had thundered past we emerged, white-clad, and I was snapping orders about stretchers at Jock, calling him 'Orderly' and asking 'Nurse' if she knew how to use portable cyclometric infusion apparatus. She said she did, which was not the first time she had lied to me. The policemen at the entrance paid us no heed, they were busy keeping people out. 'Bart's Hospital,' I snapped at the taxi-driver, 'casualty entrance. Emergency: use your horn.' At Bart's we dispersed, shedding white clothing, found the main entrance and took three separate taxis home. I arrived first – I needed that healing drink.

'Well,' I said curtly when the others had assembled, 'first things first.' I still had a residue of hospital-registrar arrogance in my voice. 'Does either of you know what happened to the other chap – the English one?'

'Yeah,' said Jock. 'He's face down in one of them big bins of pigs' guts.'

'Oh dear,' I said, 'poor fellow, how horrid for him. I mean, I don't actually feel any *affection* for him but he must be hideously uncomfortable.'

'I don't fink he's feeling uncomfortable, Mr Charlie.'

'Oh dear,' I said again. 'I suppose that means I've got to send that Luger of yours to Ginge the Gunsmith again? I don't suppose you had time to pick up the used cartridge-cases? No? Ah well.'

(Perhaps a word of explanation to the innocent is called for here. The ballistics wizards, as everyone knows, can infallibly tell which bullet has been fired from which fire-arm – they use comparison-microscopes – and the cartridge-cases are an even greater give-away. Therefore, anyone who has used a fire-arm for a naughty purpose tends to toss it over London Bridge into the Thames where, I fancy, the accumulation of fire-arms so discarded must by now be constituting a hazard to shipping. Jock, however, will no more be persuaded to discard his Luger than to part with his autographed photograph of Shirley Temple. This means that whenever he has 'used up' someone with it I have to pay Ginge a great deal of money to 'tiddly' it. This involves putting in a new striker-pin, buffing up the face of the breech-block and engraving a few new scratches on it and doing some extremely fancy work with a lathe on the chamber and barrel. After Ginge has finished with a pistol the comparison-microscopes get a fit of the sulks and the ballistics wizards go home and beat their wives.)

'Now, Johanna,' I said in a no-nonsense voice, 'you seemed to know those two chaps: who were they? The Englishman and the Dutchman? Eh?'

'They were both Dutchmen, Charlie dear. Deputy Commissioner Rubinstein likes to call himself Robinson because his English is perfect, isn't it?'

'Yes, wasn't it?' I said.

'And they really were both policemen but very, very bent ones. You see, darling, most of the heroin in the world passes through Amsterdam – or do I mean Rotterdam? – and that amounts to a great many millions of pounds, you understand, and you can't really blame an underpaid policeman for kind of not noticing that someone is absent-mindedly dropping ten thousand pounds a year into a West Indies branch of the Bank of Nova Scotia for him, can you? I mean, when it comes to privacy, the Bank of Nova Scotia makes those Swiss banks look like back-numbers of *Playboy*.'

'No,' I agreed, 'I cannot blame them for this. Indeed, I might well suffer a pang or two of temptation myself in the circumstances. What I can – and do – blame them for is for attempting to blow big, painful holes through essential organs of mine which I have not yet finished with.'

'Yes,' she said, 'there is that. But they *got* their blame all right, didn't they, dear?'

'True, true. And now you will please be kind enough to tell me who was employing these sticky-fingered arms of the law. I mean, at the time when they put the old snatcheroo on me.'

'What beautiful American you speak, Charlie!'

'Never mind about that, just tell me who gave them The Notice about me.'

'Is that the same as a "contract" in the States?'

'Oh, burst a bleeding frog!' I bellowed – I believe this was the first time I ever raised my voice to her – 'Forget the semantics, what I want to know is who they were working for.'

'*Pas devant les doméstiques,*' she murmured. Jock left the room in a marked manner; his intellect is second to, well, almost anyone's, but he does know two French sentences. One of them begins with '*Vooly voo cooshey*' and the other is the one Johanna had used. He can be hurt; he has his pride.

'They were working for Mr Lee, silly,' said Johanna.

'And where is Mr Lee now, would you say?' She lifted the telephone, giving me that smile; dialled a number and said something into it in a language I didn't recognize. She listened for perhaps thirty seconds, then said something which sounded like a number. Then she gave me that smile again, the one that softens every bone in my body except one. Hung up. I mean, she hung up the telephone. 'Mr Lee is at present approaching the John F. Kennedy International Airport, Charlie dear. He should be touching down in about fifty minutes. He is in a big, comfy jet and no one else is aboard except a dozen or so of his, uh, naughty friends, six real Interpol agents, half the staff of the US Narcotics Bureau and your friend the Commandant.'

'You mean the dreaded Commandant of that College of yours?' I squeaked. 'Are you trying to tell me that she was on the side of the angels all the time? Next you'll be telling me that she'll draw an MBE for her part in this nonsense!'

'She got her MBE when you were at school, Charlie. Parachuting into Belgium. Her OBE came through when she snitched a boatload of Hungarian scientists out from a little Yugoslav port called Rijeka in the '50s. The least she can draw from this little caper is a DBE – in fact I'm putting her in for a Life Peerage.'

'*You*'re putting . . .'

'Yes, dear.' That seemed to close that subject. Then I thought of another question.

'Just what do *you* expect to draw from this, Johanna?'

'You, dear.' I looked wildly around; there was no one else in the room.

'Me?' I said.

'Yes.' Oh well, I thought, ask a silly question and you'll get a silly answer. Little did she know that Colonel Blucher had offered me a spot of survival in this vale of tears in exchange for infiltrating whatever organization Johanna thought she was running; little did Blucher know how abject a dog's breakfast

I had made of it all. I rose and made courteous noises to the effect that I had to go and see a chap in Jule's Bar in Jermyn Street.

'Yes, do go and have a little fun, dear; I know you'll forgive me if I don't join you tonight.' Game, set and match against me, as usual.

22 Mordecai learns the truth, kicks the slats out of a kitchen cupboard and finds solace in bread and jam

Oh selfless man and stainless gentleman!

Merlin and Vivien

It's odd how one drinks different things in different places. For instance, although I hate champagne cocktails, I always accept a couple from one particular mistress because a champagne cocktail, as anyone will tell you, gets to you where you live very fast and two such drinks enable me to ignore the grotesque schnozzle with which this particular lady has been endowed and to concentrate upon her other charms, which are of great distinction. To take other examples, there are some pubs where I just naturally order a scoop of Guiness and a 'half 'un' of Paddy on the side; there is one in Jersey where they always put a large whisky into a split of fresh orange-juice, ignoring the raised eyebrows of the other customers; another place where, even if I have been absent for a year, they draw me a pint of the very best bitter and lay beside it a ball-point pen because they know that I have come there to solve a crossword-puzzle. There is an Italian place in Oxford, which I used to pop into of a morning on my way home, where they are too tactful to greet me, they simply mix a massive brandy and soda and compassionately help me to fold my fingers around it. There is even a place, many miles from anywhere, where I drink something which I think is called Margarita; it comes in a filth-encrusted bottle without a label and seems to be 140-proof tomato ketchup. I could multiply examples but what I am driving at is that, for some reason, when I am in Jule's in Jermyn Street, which is arguably the best pub in the world, I always order Canadian rye whisky with ginger ale. Then I send a glass of wine to the pianist with a courteous message and he flicks a courteous glance at me and plays it. Ingrid Bergman never comes in but a man can dream, can't he?

Having gone through the ritual, and having summoned up the second drink, I made my way to the telephone and dialled Blucher's 'secure' number.

'This is the Home and Colonial Stores,' fluted the familiar voice.

'And my prick's a bloater,' I snarled, for I was in no mood to be paltered with.

'Indeed?' said the voice. 'Then I suggest you get in touch with the Royal College of Surgeons, where you may learn something to your advantage.'

'Grrrr,' I said. She replaced the receiver. I found another coin, dialled again.

'Please may I speak to Daddy?' I grated between clenched teeth.

'Why, sir?' I remembered the rest of the absurd password.

'Mummy's poorly.' There were clicks and scrambler-noises and at last Blucher was on the line.

'I want to speak to you,' I said. 'Now. I've had it up to here.'

'Where's here?' I told him. He was there in rather less than five minutes, which indicated that his Agency, whatever it was, was squandering prodigious sums of US tax-payers' money on addresses far above their station in life. Moreover, he was carrying an umbrella, which did not even begin to make him look like an Englishman.

I ordered a drink for him, although it went against the grain. He was, after all, my guest.

'Just two questions,' I murmured thinly. 'Exactly who have I been working for? And has it finished now? And, if so, do I stay alive?'

'That's *three* questions, Mr Mortdecai.' (You may recall that, early in our acquaintanceship, I had rebuked him for using my Christian name.)

'Very well, three,' I snapped. 'So you can count up to three. I know *women* who can count up to nine. Just start at question one and move gently down the list, using your own words.'

'I have an auto – sorry, a car – outside. Let's drive around a little, hunh? Then I'll take you home.' I thought about that a while, then agreed. I had, after all, telephoned him because I felt that extermination by his Agency would at least be efficient and hygienic; infinitely preferable to being made lethal sport of by female terrorists or Chinese gentlemen bearing grudges.

His car was not one of those great, black limousines that people are taken for rides in; it was a little 'topolino' Fiat with nothing sinister about it but a parking-ticket on the windscreen. He drove, as discreetly as a Rural Dean who has had two helpings of sherry-trifle and dreads being asked to puff into a breathalyser, to Grosvenor Square. To No. 24, Grosvenor Square, to be exact. That's the American Embassy, as if you didn't know.

'I'm not going in there,' I said.

'Neither am I. My desk will be chin-high with paper-work, all marked "Urgent". I'm just stopping here because the cops won't give me a bad time; the number of this car is on the privilege list.'

'How the other half lives, to be sure,' I murmured.

'Now, Mr Mortdecai; your questions. First, you have been working for the United Nations. OK, laugh, enjoy, enjoy. But you have. My own Agency co-operates closely with that particular branch of UNO and I can say most sincerely that in the last few weeks we have achieved some very, very spectacular results.' I probably said something feeble like 'Well done' but he ignored whatever it was and continued.

'Your second question – "has it finished now?" – I can only answer with a kind of qualified "yes". Your third question – the one about whether you get to stay alive – is a little tough. So far as my bosses are concerned I think I can say that there is now no problem.' He turned and looked at me as though trying to puzzle out why anyone like me should want to stay alive. I squared my shoulders and looked as haughty as one can in the passenger-seat of a little Fiat. 'But, Mr Mortdecai, I'm sure you understand that in an operation as complex as this there are many, many loose ends which take a while to sort of mop up and winkle out and we could not of course justify in our budget an expense like protecting, say, you, around the clock for the next few months. I'm sure you see that.'

'I quite see that,' I said, ignoring his garish mixture of metaphors.

'Have you ever thought of the Seychelles?' he asked. 'The Antilles? Samoa? The Virgin Islands?' I turned upon him a stony glare which should have made him think of Easter Island.

'Well, how about the Channel Islands? Your wife has a half-share in a really beautiful mansion there.' I hadn't known that, but there were many things I didn't know about Johanna in those days.

'How do you know that?' I demanded.

He fixed me with that pitying look with which people often fix me when they have decided that I am simple-minded. Often, if the circumstances are propitious, I wipe off the pitying look with what Jock calls a 'bunch of fives', but the passenger-seat of a right-hand drive Topolino is not what I would call a propitious circumstance: the only possible blow would be a round-house left – and the driving-mirror was in the way. Moreover, I was giving away fifteen years, not to mention thirty pounds of self-indulgence.

'I have always longed to visit the Isle of Jersey,' is what I said.

You must guard against hating people or even things: it is easy to become like what you hate. Victory at Entebbe destroys us more surely than defeat at Kursk. I did not hate Blucher at all as he drove me home, although I had to work hard at it.

Johanna was not at home but Jock was, of course. His good eye seemed to look at Blucher almost benignly; had I not been preoccupied with other matters – like life and death – I might have thought this strange, for Jock has never been one to betray a liking for the fuzz. I offered Blucher an assortment of chairs, bade Jock supply him with anything he might long for in the way of drinks or eatables, then melted away apologetically as a host melts when he wishes to put the cat out. What I urgently wanted was to get under the shower and refresh the frame with newly-laundred gents' underwear, half-hose and shirtings as now worn.

I indulged myself, as ever; it must have been quite half an hour before I reappeared, sweet-smelling and freshly clad, in the drawing-room, secure in the expectation that Blucher would have taken his leave. I was wrong, of course. What he had taken was the infernal liberty of sitting next to my wife, Johanna, on the little Louis Quinze sofa which is not designed to support two people unless the two people do not happen to mind a certain intimacy, a certain warm proximity of hip and thigh. They were chuckling, I heard them distinctly. I do not often stand aghast but aghast was what I stood then.

'Charlie dear,' cried Johanna, 'we thought you were never coming. Do sit, darling; have something to drink, you must be tired.' I sat in the least comfortable chair in the room and forced a drink between my unwilling lips. (This was, you understand, only to mask or muffle the grinding of my teeth.)

'Ah, well, Blucher,' I said, 'I see that you have made the acquaintance of my wife. Good, splendid, yes.'

'Darling, we've known each other for ages and ages . . .' Blucher looked at her and nodded knowingly, lovingly. I took another gulp of whisky to disguise the gnashing. No conversational gambit offered itself to me; I merely glowered at the few square inches of carpet between my feet.

'Charlie, dear, you're not being the perfect host tonight – couldn't you sort of tell your guest a funny story or something? I mean, he did save your life, huh?' I lost patience at that point. All bets were off.

'Look,' I rasped, 'this guest of mine – perhaps I should say ours – *sold* me my life. The price was that I married you. I liked being married to you until about five minutes ago, I really did, although the, er, extramarital tasks have been a little trying. But he didn't save my life, he bought and sold it.'

Johanna put onto her face that sweet, tolerant look of a Spock-trained mother whose child has just wet the bed for the third time that night.

'You don't have it quite right, Charlie dear. As a matter of fact, our guest figured that it would be tidiest to sort of terminate you long ago. It was I who bought your life.' My brain started to feel like one of those cages where white mice run happily, mindlessly in a wire treadmill.

'Of course,' I said bitterly, 'of course, of course. You bought my life. I must remember to thank you. No use my asking why, I suppose?'

'Because I loved you, you great, stupid, self-satisfied prig!' she blazed. I never know what to say on occasions like that; I usually just shuffle my feet and look silly.

'Er, was that last word "prig" or "pig"?' I asked, for want of anything better to say. She didn't answer, just sat there with a face of thunder, tapping her foot on the carpet as though there were some small pest there. Like, say, a Mortdecai. I distinctly saw Blucher's hand take hers and squeeze it fondly.

'And how much did you pay for this alleged life of mine?' I asked, my worst fears coming to the forefront of my brain and starting to dance a lewd jig. To my astonishment she giggled – and in the most fetching way. I had never heard her giggle before.

'Please make us some drinks first, Charlie dear.' I did so but with an ill grace, although I softened a little when it came to measuring out my own.

'Now,' she said cosily, 'Franzl will tell you all about it.'

'*Franzl!*' I squeaked. 'Franzl?'

'Hey, that's great, Charlie old boy; I knew you and I'd get onto first-name terms in the end. Now, like I said back there at the beginning, the price of you staying alive was marrying Hänschen here.'

'*Hänschen?*' I squawked.

'Why sure, don't you call her that? No? Well, what I didn't make clear was that it was her idea, not mine. See, she had this crazy idea that you were the only man in the world for her; well, she always had these really weird fantasies, you know?'

'No.'

'Well, she does. Anyway, her organization had penetrated about as far as possible and it was pretty clear that the Chinese guys weren't about to show any more of their cards without the pot being sweetened up with some heavy action. My own Agency, which is more clandestine than, uh, subversive, was also up against a stone wall and the lousy CIA were commencing to sniff around at our fire-hydrants. Uh, lamp-posts?'

'Go on.'

'Well, we'd sort of theoretically ageed that a kind of catalyst was needed, like throwing a new face into the game who might blunder about and get the deer moving . . .'

'He means, Charlie dear, someone resourceful like you but who was not familiar with the scenario . . .'

'You mean,' I said, 'that what I didn't know couldn't be tortured out of me?'

'No, dear, just someone with no preconceived notions which might make you follow . . .'

'. . . the kind of pattern that a trained agent would; we had to puzzle them by throwing into the ball-game someone clearly unprofessional, someone half-smart . . .'

'He means, dear, that it was like suddenly putting an English Rugby International into the Yale-Harvard match. I knew it was desperately dangerous for you – Franzl offered me eleven to two against your surviving the first week – but it was better than having all those awful people in Lancashire quite certainly destroying you in your cave. You do see that, don't you darling?' All I could see was Blucher's hand patting hers and, when I tore my glance away, the whitening of my own knuckles. Blucher took up the story again.

'Also, like I said, the bad guys were looking for some heavy action; really heavy, so we dreamed up this attempted assassination of Her Majesty. We never thought you'd get to first base and gosh, we were worried when it started to look like you'd get away with it. We were a little late getting to you that time – the traffice re-routed and all – it surely was lucky that cartridge jammed in the breech. I guess you'd really have done it, hunh?'

'As a matter of fact, I don't believe I would. Jock wouldn't have liked it, you see; he would have handed in his notice.'

'Well, he wouldn't have needed to do that. You see, there was an Oriental guy in the window right across the street from you with a sniper's rifle and he'd have bipped you right between the eyes one fifth of one second after you fired. To save you from interrogation, you understand.'

'You did wonderfully well, Charlie dear. I have been so proud of you.'

'Yes, you really did, Charlie old boy.' He put an arm about my wife's shoulders and kissed her noisily on the cheek. This was too much. My knuckles were now Whiter-Than-White and I'm confident that any trained observer would have observed that the veins in my forehead were bulging out like firemen's hoses. I rose to my feet, eyeing them dangerously. We Mortdecais do not make a practice of tearing our guests limb from limb, especially when there are ladies present, however base and treacherous the lady. I must confess, however, that I came pretty close to breaking this rule, and indeed might well have done so had I not recalled that it simply is not done to strike a guest whose posture, while embracing one's wife, betrays a shameless bulge under the left armpit, where a large, coarse automatic pistol evidently lurks. I stalked out of the room in a marked manner. I did not trip over anything, nor did I slam the door.

Jock, staunch fellow, was in the kitchen, his great boots propped up on the hygienic working-surface. He peered at me over the top edge of his copy of *Film Fun*. I launched a great kick at the nearest pastel-coloured eezi-slide kitchen-fitment and dented it severely. Jock rummaged in a pocket for his glass eye, moistened it in the mug of tea before him and popped it deftly into its socket.

'You all right, Mr Charlie?'

'I am in splendid form, Jock,' I snarled, 'capital, topping, never better. We cuckolds feel no pain, you know.' He gaped as I delivered a truly mighty kick at the same fitment. This time my foot went through it and was trapped in the ruptured plastic and three-ply. Jock helped me get my shoe off with the aid of the kitchen scissors and I was able to free my foot and limp to the kitchen table.

'Reckon that old kick done you a power of good, Mr Charlie, better than a week at the seaside. Anything else you fancy?'

'How is the canary?' I countered. 'Still sulking?'

'Nah, he's back in lovely voice, a fair treat to listen to him, I had to put a clorth over his cage to shut the little bugger up. What I done was, I give him some hard-boiled egg, a pinch of cayenne in his hempseed and a sup of rum in his drinking water and now, bing-bong, he's ready to take on all comers. Booking for smoking-concerts now.'

'Give me that very cure, Jock,' I said moodily, 'but leaving out the hard-boiled egg, the cayenne, the hempseed and the drinking-water.'

'Right, Mr Charlie; one large Navy rum coming up. Er, will Madam be wanting anythink?'

'I could not say. She seems to be in close conference with Colonel Blucher.'

'Yeah, well, she hasn't seen him for munce, has she?'

'I could not say.'

'Well, he is her bruvver, inne?'

'Jock, what the hell are you talking about?'

'Well, I mean, Mrs M is his *sister*, isn't she? Same thing, innit?'

Many things began to become clear; one of the clearest of these things was that for once in my life I had behaved like a twit.

'Oh, ah?' I said.

'Yeah,' said Jock. I re-assembled what I like to think of as my thoughts.

'Jock,' I said, 'unswathe the said canary; I long to hear a few of its dulcet notes. But in doing so pray do not forget the large glass of Navy rum which I ordered quite ninety seconds ago.' As the honest fellow clumped towards the pantry I recalled something which had been simmering in the back of my mind all the live-long day: the very crux or pivot of the whole situation, the pin upon which everything turned.

'Jock!' I cried anguishedly. He stopped in his tracks, span upon his heel.

'Jock, please add one of your extra-special jam-sandwiches to that order, if you will be so kind.'

'Right, Mr Charlie; that's one large rum, one jem semwidge.'

'And one canary.'

'Right, Mr Charlie.'

'Right, Jock,' I said.

Something nasty in the woodshed

Et Amicorum

Because I do not expect to survive to write another novel about Jersey, I must ask, in alphabetical order, Alan, Angela, Barry, Betty, Bobbie, Dick, Gordon, Heather, Hugh, Jean, Joan, John, Mary, Nick, Olive, Paul, Peter, Rosemary, Stanley, Terry, Topper, Vera – and a hundred other kindly Jersey folk to accept this as a trifling repayment for all their kindness and tolerance. I hope, too, that they will not mind if I add the names of a black Labrador named Pompey and a canary called Bert.

The epigraphs are all by Swinburne, except one which is a palpable forgery.

None of the people in this novel bears any intentional resemblance to any real person: real people are far too improbable for use in fiction.

The Honorary Police of Jersey are used to being teased: all those whom I have had the pleasure of meeting are just, honourable, intelligent and can take a joke.

I must not thank by name all the kindly Jersey folk who have answered my countless questions – that would be a poor recompense for their patience.

The fictional narrator is a nasty, waspish man: pray do not confuse him with the author, who is gentle and kind.

The Swinburne forgery is, in a way, signed.

I

Till the slow sea rise and the sheer cliff crumble,
Till terrace and meadow the deep gulfs drink,
Till the strength of the waves of the high tides humble
The fields that lessen, the rocks that shrink,
Here now in his triumph where all things falter,
Stretched out on the spoils that his own hand spread,
As a god self-slain on his own strange altar,
Death lies dead.

A Forsaken Garden

The Islands

Seven thousand years ago – give or take a few months – a great
deal of water left the North Sea for good reasons of its own
which I cannot recall off-hand and poured over the lower parts of
North-West Europe, forming the English Channel and effectively
separating England from France, to the mutual gratification of both
parties (for if it had not happened, you see, we English would
have been foreigners and the French would have had to eat bread
sauce).

Not much later the sea scoured away at some of the craggier
bits of the French coast and separated part of the higher ground
from the mainland. You call the resulting islands the Channel Isles
because you know no better: their true and ancient name is *Les
Iles Normandes*. It has been argued that they do not belong to the

United Kingdom but rather the other way about, for they were part of the Duchy of Normandy long before William did his conquering in England – and they are the only surviving parts of that Duchy. They are fiercely loyal to the Crown and the toast is still 'The Queen – our Duke'. The Isles all have different, ancient and peculiar laws and constitutions, as well as some pretty odd customs. Of which more later.

This Island

It is called Jersey and is constructed of granite, shale, diorite and porphyrite, as every schoolboy knows. The whole thing is sort of tilted so that it faces south, which I'm sure is good for the weather. (I never discuss the weather; that is for resort-owners, the peasantry, and certain gentle maniacs who choose to inhabit the Admiralty roof.) The coastline is wild and lovely past belief.

Tobacco and ardent spirits are cheap and income tax benignly low but I dare say these blessings will vanish, along with the Public Schools, as soon as the Socialists get a real majority and start to feel their oats.

The People

There are many layers of these. First, the holiday-makers, who need no description, bless them. Their name is legion.

Next, the farmers, who are all of old Jersiais stock, and, in an unobtrusive and po-faced way, run the Island to their own quiet satisfaction. They have ugly old names, ugly old faces and *hideous* old wives. Their workers are like them but drunker. Some transient peasants drift in from Normandy, Brittany and even Wales to see to the daffodil, potato and tomato harvests; they are small and squat and sinister, like Italians from the Abruzzi, and they are the drunkest of all and who shall blame them.

Third, and best known, are the rich immigrants who have come to enjoy the Isle's peculiar tax benefits. The modest tax they pay swells the local coffers in a way the Jerseyman finds hard to forgive. Some of them are total abstainers, which I suppose is one way of becoming rich, but most of them are pretty drunk too: whisky is about the same price as cheap wine – and much nicer.

They have brought so much money with them that I sometimes

fear the Isle may one day sink beneath its weight. Their conversation is brilliant so long as you stick to the subject of the length of their drawing-rooms – or 'lounges' as they are called in the local *argot*.

Hordes of bankers and other money-borrowers, of every degree of venality, have followed them here like greedy shite-hawks and each prime site in St Helier is snapped up by these shameless guzzlers as soon as it falls vacant. This is probably a bad thing.

There are several minor categories like nobility and gentry, Portuguese waiters, Indian trumpery-mongers, transient barmaids and drunken novelists but these, although uniformly nice, concern our story but little.

The Fauna

The prop of the economy, and the only large mammal other than the Jersey lady, is the Jersey cow. She is doe-eyed and quite beautiful and secretes wonderfully rich milk. She is usually tethered because pasture is precious and fences are costly; in winter she is 'rugged' with a plastic mackintosh and in summer she sports a sun-bonnet. Yes, truly. There are some pigs but I believe no sheep, which is perhaps why a certain Highland Regiment has never been stationed here. There is a great number of horses and the suburban cavalry may be seen tittuping along the lanes at any hour of the day.

Wild-life is scarce except for sea-birds; the dominant species are the magpie and the sparrow. There is no shooting land and therefore no gamekeepers, so the ubiquitous magpie munches up all the nestlings; only the sparrow, that bird of Venus, can outbreed magpies by diddling his mate all the year round, sturdy little chap. In the late autumn small rare birds may sometimes be seen on passage, resting in the fields of unborn daffodils.

The Flora

This is chiefly grass and gardening, the latter often of an excruciating garishness. There is some bracken and gorse on parcels of land waiting for planning permission but all the rest is luxury crops: early potatoes, daffodils, anemones, tomatoes and the occasional shy cauliflower. Certain cabbages with prodigally long stalks are grown for tourists to photograph: the natives assure them with straight faces that these are grown for walking-sticks but no one in his senses would believe that, would he?

The Buildings

These range from the gloomy to the absurd via the pretentious. St Helier is a positive barrel of architectural fun: even Sir John Betjeman would be unable to keep a straight face. In the countryside the characteristic building is a large, grim farmhouse made of liver-coloured granite, with huge outer walls and a shortage of windows. Rich incomers grab them avidly and modernize them hideously. The finished article is worth ten times the price of a comparable house in England. I don't know whether that's a good thing or not.

The Language

This is rather a difficult bit. Your actual Jerseyman of the artisan classes speaks something which sounds quite like English until you try to understand it, then you realize that it is like an Australian trying to imitate a Liverpudlian. 'His' is pronounced 'ease' and most sentences begin with the phrase 'My Chri' and end with the vocable 'eh?' It is an unlovely tongue and one can readily learn to dislike it.

Laws and other official matter are written in a quaint old Norman-French reminiscent of Domesday-Book Latin. Members of the grand old Jersey families can still speak it, I'm told, but you won't get them to admit it.

The true *patois Jersiais* is something quite different and barbarous beyond belief. (*Guinness es bouan por té.*) When I tell you that the word 'Jersey' represents the Latin 'Caesarea' I think you will take my meaning.

Finally, most tradespeople can produce enough schoolboy French of modern vintage to puzzle the transient workers with, especially since the latter are usually tired and drunk.

The Police

There is a small body of men, based in St Helier, called the Paid Police. I'm sure they love that. They are much like English police but fewer and not so angry. They have uniforms and equipment; they seem honest and amiable; they don't hit people. Unlike some I could name.

Much more important (outside St Helier) are the Honorary Police, who are of course unpaid. They do not wear uniforms – you are supposed to *know* who they are. Each of the twelve Parishes has a Connétable; under him are the Centeniers, each of whom in theory protects and disciplines a hundred families and leads five Vingteniers who guard twenty families each. These are all elective posts but elections rarely afford any surprises, if you see what I mean, and in any case there is little competition for these honours.

No one is legally under arrest in Jersey until a Centenier has tapped him on the shoulder with his absurd, tiny truncheon of office (you can imagine how the Paid Police like *that* rule) and it is said that a Centenier who has mislaid his truncheon wrenches off the handle from the nearest lavatory chain. Luckily, Centeniers do not often feel it necessary to arrest their friends, neighbours and cousins, unless the offence is grave, and thus a great deal of public money is saved and a great many lavatories are left intact. It works quite well, really. The Centenier takes his erring neighbour for a quiet chat and puts the fear of God in him, thus preventing a recurrence of the offence much more effectively than an expensive trial, a suspended sentence and a year of reporting to some mud-brained Probation Officer with a diploma in Social Science from Nersdley Polytechnic.

One of the Houses

It belongs to Sam Davenant and is called La Gouluterie, from a water-meadow which is part of the estate. This probably takes its name from Simon le Goulue who was Connétable of S. Magloire Parish in 1540, but zealous antiquaries suspect that *goulues* – round-bellied pottery crocks for seething beans in – were once potted in this clayey field. I suspect that Simon or one of his forebears was called 'le Goulue' because he was a bit of a bean-crock himself.

The dottier kind of amateur antiquary will, of course, assure you that the name has something to do with fertility-rites, but then they always do, don't they?

Much of the building dates from the sixteenth century and there are traces of earlier work and hints of religious use. It is of a pleasant, pink granite of the sort no longer quarried and it has been tactfully coaxed into a state of comfort and dignity. There are tourelles, rondelines, bénitiers and so forth – I'm sure you know what all those are. For my part, I forget. Most of the front is at the back – doors, terraces and so on – but the front proper faces a sunny, agreeable courtyard on the other side of which lies the Other House, which belongs to Sam's best friend.

The Other House

This belongs to George Breakspear who is Sam's best friend and it is called Les Cherche-fuites – I don't know what that means. It has been extensively dandified in the eighteenth century and its windows, because of the exigencies of the underlying granite, are all slightly out of kilter, which rescues it from the drab symmetry of most houses of that period. Like La Gouluterie, much of its front is at the back (gardens, pool etc.) and at the back, too, there is a curious and engaging porch with concave glazing of the kind associated in Jersey with 'cod houses' – places built in the piping times of the cod industry when dozens of daring Jersey skippers ventured to the Grand Banks and suddenly found themselves rich. At one side there is an ugly Victorian stable of yellow brick with a clock which doesn't go.

Consider, Then,

These two agreeable houses beaming affably at each other across the old stone cider-press in the centre of the courtyard; consider, too, how rare and fortunate it is that the owners should be such firm friends. (The fact that the owners' wives loathe each other's essential tripes is of little importance, one supposes, and indeed it rarely comes to the surface even when they are alone.)

Consider, Too

The proprietors of these houses, starting with George Breakspear of Les Cherche-fuites. George believes in God, but only the C. of E. brand, as advertised on television by virtue of the Equal Time Agreement, although he has an Open Mind because he has seen some Pretty Queer Things in India and places like that. His manners are too good to let his religion show, which is as it should be. He is not a fool. You would guess that he had been a brevet major in the War; in fact he was a full and substantive brigadier and holds the DSO, the MC and many another bauble but, here again, his too stringent manners forbid him to use either the rank or the ribandry in civil life. (This is going a little too far, I think: it is subtly *rude* to keep your honours in your handkerchief drawer along with the french letters. Give me, any day, those jolly European hussar officers who swagger out at night in their splendid comic-opera uniforms, rather than those po-faced English Guardees who change, at the drop of a bowler hat, into sad imitations of solvent stockbrokers. Officers should have dash and debts and drabs and, above all, duns, whom they can horsewhip outside their quarters to give them an appetite for breakfast, don't you agree?)

George is of middle height, average appearance and normal weight. His friends do not always recognize him, which is what it's all about, isn't it. In his favourite armchair in his club they recognize him, of course, because he's *there* you see. The better sort of bartenders recognize him, too, but that's their job.

His clothes are in such quiet good taste that they almost amount to a disguise, a cloak of invisibility, perhaps.

Despite this greyish coloration one somehow knows for certain that, were the Hun or Boche to invade us, George would not only spring capably to arms on the instant but would, without debate or question, assume command by invoking some ancient English password, token or shibboleth which we would all recognize, although hearing it for the first time since King Arthur sank below the waves of that lake near Avalon.

In the meantime, however, here and now in Jersey, one certainly didn't want not to know him, for he listened to one's stories; he poured big (but not vulgarly big) drinks; did not smile too unhappily if one swore in front of his wife and, if the party lasted too long for him, he didn't make going-to-bed noises, he just sort of faded away and re-materialized, one supposes, in his dressing-room.

He drinks quite a lot in a diffident sort of way; there's no shooting in Jersey, you see, and that makes the winter days rather long unless you happen to be over-sexed.

He scraped a sort of degree at Cambridge and won a boxing blue – one almost says 'of course' – and he is knowledgeable about the Napoleonic wars. He is one of those enviable people who – like Balliol men – are serenely certain that what they do and think and are is right. This inability to see any flaws in oneself is a branch of pottiness, of course, but much less harmful than being unable to see any good in oneself.

George cannot quite understand why we gave up India and he is a little puzzled about Suez. He polishes his shoes himself; they are all old, crackled and expensive.

He is, or was, what used to be called a gentleman, or have I said that already?

George's Wife

is called Sonia, although her women-friends say that the name on her birth-certificate was probably Ruby. It is hard to say why she and George married; you sometimes catch them stealing puzzled glances at each other as though they, too, were wondering still.

She is a slut and a bitch, every woman can tell this at a glance, so can most homosexuals. Nice young men can persuade themselves that her languishing glances are for them alone, although they should surely be able to see that her instructions to the gardener about bedding-out are an equally clear invitation to bedding-in. George believes in her, I think, but like Matilda's aunt, the effort sometimes nearly kills him. She is flashy by nature, choice and art: her eyes are deep blue and enormous, her skin is like magnolia petals and her hair is so black that it seems to be Navy-blue. Her breasts, when they are lugged up and squashed together by her valuable brassière, resemble nothing so much as the bum of a beautiful child, but when she is naked they are lax and unpleasing, the muscle tone long gone. I happen to prefer a breast that I can hold in one hand, don't you? – but I know that Americans, for instance, prefer quantity, if you'll forgive the pun.

Under a shellac-layer of cultivation and coffee-table books her manners and morals are those of a skilled whore who has succeeded in retiring early and now dedicates her craft to personal pleasure alone. She is very good at it indeed. I dare say.

While by no means mutton-dressed-as-lamb she is nevertheless subtly wrongly clothed, in that and in one other respect. She wears clothes exactly three years too young for her – never more, never less – and, like those men who contrive always to have two days' growth of beard – never more, never less – just so she is always expensively dressed in the height of last year's fashion: never quite up-to-date nor ever quite out of it.

This of course pleases her women friends mightily, although their menfolk do not twig and are in any case more concerned with admiring Sonia's teats.

She is, of course, an accomplished liar but then they all are, aren't they? (Or aren't you married?) George is quite clever enough to detect her in her falsehoods but both breeding and common-sense forbid this in him.

Sonia and George have two sons. One of them, very clever, is serving out the last of his stretch at a school called Wellington; Sonia does not mind having a son at school – although she manages to give the impression that he is at *prep* school – but she is a little cross at the existence of the other son who is what is called grown-up. He is marvellously stupid and drives a helicopter for the Army or Navy or some such out-dated nonsense. He is always breaking their valuable aircraft but his superiors never seem to mind, they just buy him a new one. They don't pay for it themselves, you see. You do.

Now Sam Davenant

and straight away we detect a falsehood, an affectation, for no one has been christened Sam for a hundred years. His real name is Sacheverell, of course. At school he would have died rather than divulge this but nowadays he quite likes one to find out.

He affects to be affected, which he is otherwise not, if you see what I mean, and hopes that his chief fault, congenital idleness or *accidie*, will pass as an affectation. His infrequent swings to the manic phase, made much of, help him to carry this off.

He would think shame to be seen out of bed before noon – unless he had been up all night – and has eaten no breakfast for twenty years.

He is almost tiresomely well-read. In public he is usually immersed in a trashy paper-back but it is quite certain that in his bedroom he reads Gibbon, Fénelon, Horace and '*tous ces defunts cockolores*'. On the other hand, he stoutly denies that he has ever heard of Marcuse and Borges, whoever they may be. (For my part, I adamantly believe in teaching Fénelon, Racine, Milton and Gibbon to the young as soon as may be; you cannot learn too early in life that most classical literature is both dull and unimportant.)

Sam is absurdly kind, easy-going, tolerant and has a harsh word for no one, but I have long recognized in him an insane iron core which would make him, if ultimately provoked, a very bad enemy indeed. He used to play backgammon uncommonly well until the sparks took it up, whereupon he dropped it; he's like that. I can sometimes beat him at poker.

He seems to be quite rich in a vague sort of way but no one knows how or whence. He hints naughtily at gun-running or worse in his youth – perhaps white-slaving – but I suspect a string of dry-cleaning shops in Northern Ireland: why else should he be so vexed about the news of bomb-outrages in Belfast?

He is tall, pale, curly-haired, thickening a little and a trifle older than me. Let us say fifty.

On the Other Hand

his wife is tiny, sweet, silly and called Violet, if you'll believe it. Sam calls her The Shrinker. She does, indeed, shrink from most things; I've watched her often. Sam treats her with amused tolerance but secretly adores her, if I may quote from the women's weeklies. She is nervously vulnerable and can blush and even faint, just as they used to in the olden days.

On rare occasions she is an inspired cook but most of the time she burns or otherwise ruins food but, luckily, Sam is not greedy and can cook. I must not pretend to any knowledge of their nuptial relationships but I should think on the whole probably not. He treats her with a courtesy so elaborate that you might be forgiven for thinking that he hated her, but you would be wrong.

There is something vaguely mysterious about Violet's mother who is always referred to as 'poor mummy'. She is, I suppose, either potty or an alcoholic or kleptomaniac or some such nonsense and there are times when I wonder a little about Violet herself: her verbal habits are odd and she tends to say things like 'rabbits breed like hot cakes'.

And Now, For My Last Trick

this is the narrator, or, if you'll pardon the accidence, me. My name is Charlie Mortdecai (I was actually *christened* Charlie: I think my mother was subtly getting at my father) and I'm a Honble because my father used to be – and my brother (God rot his soul) is – a Baron, which is a kind of failed Viscount, you might say, if you cared about that sort of nonsense. As my father did.

For the time being I live just a few furlongs across the fields from the two houses in half of a lovely mansion (a mansion, according to estate agents and other housemongers, is a house with two staircases) called Wutherings with my absurdly beautiful new Austrian-Jewish-American wife, Johanna, and my equally unbelievable one-eyed, one-fanged thug, Jock. (I'm by way of being an art-dealer, you see, which is why I have to keep a thug.) I'm not here permanently; I haven't enough money to make it worth while dodging taxes and my wife has too much of it to bother. I really live in London but, although I'm not exactly *persona non grata* there, a particular branch of the police sort of prefers me to live outside the place for a while. You wouldn't be interested in the reason and there's nothing in the fine print that says I can't be a little shady, is there?

Nor would you be interested in my reasons for having married Johanna, suffice it to say that it was not for her money. She loves me fiercely, for reasons which are a mystery to me, and I have come to like her very much. We don't understand each other in the least, which is probably a good thing, but we agree fervently that Mozart is marvellous and Wagner vulgar. She doesn't care to talk very much, which is the prime ingredient for a happy marriage: in Runyon's deathless words – 'Naturally, a doll who is willing to listen instead of wishing to gab herself is bound to be popular because if there is anything most citizens hate and despise it is a gabby doll.'

In any case, we are, in an important sense, worlds apart for she is
devoted to the game of Contract Bridge – a kind of lunatic whist –
whilst I dearly love Gin Rummy which Johanna loathes because it
is too utterly simple-minded and perhaps because I always win. She
really is quite astonishingly beautiful* but too well-bred to flutter
her eyelashes at other men. We never quarrel; the nearest we ever
got to it was once, when I was being intolerable: she quietly said,
'Charlie dear, which of us shall leave the room?'

All three of our houses stand in the parish of S. Magloire, the
smallest parish in Jersey. It is wedged between S. Jean and Trinity
and has a short coastline of its own at Belle Etoile Bay – just East
– or is it West? – of Bonne Nuit Bay. Such pretty names, I always
think.

* See *Don't Point That Thing at Me.*

2

And Pan by noon and Bacchus by night,
Fleeter of foot than the fleet-foot kid,
Follows with dancing and fills with delight
The Mænad and the Bassarid;
And soft as lips that laugh and hide
The laughing leaves of the trees divide,
And screen from seeing and leave in sight
The god pursuing, the maiden hid.

Atalanta in Calydon

It all started – or at any rate the narrative I have to offer all started
– at Easter last year: that season when we remind each other of the
judicial murder of a Jewish revolutionary two thousand years ago
by distributing chocolate eggs to the children of people we dislike.

I had been in a vile temper all day and had cursed Jock roundly.
He knew very well that it was only because there had been no
newspapers and hence no *Times* crossword, but for reasons of his
own he had chosen to sulk. When I asked what was for dinner
he pointed out smugly that gentlemen's menservants always have
the day off on Easter Monday and, indeed, those with thoughtful
masters were often given the whole week-end.

I explained to him kindly that he was not a proper manservant,
trained to gentlemen's service, but only a mere thug and that I
had noticed lately that he was getting notions above his station in
life.

His answer was in the plural – and they bounce.

Shaking with rage at having nursed such a viper in my bosom, I huddled on some clothes and drove off to get dinner in St Helier, my tyres cutting up the gravel savagely and spraying it on to the lawn. (The gardener had, in any case, been making grumbling noises for weeks and I would be well shot of him: his snail-like working pace had earned him the sobriquet 'Flash' from Johanna.)

In St Helier, the restaurant I had readied my gastric juices for was, of course, closed. It wasn't just Easter Bunny time, it was That Kind of Day, too. That did it. Stomach churning with chagrin and thwarted peptins, I went to the Club, determined to spite myself with cold steak-and-kidney pie and spurious new potatoes forced into pallid maturity in Cyprus with doses of chicken-crut and peasants' pee.

On the steps I met George, coming down.

'Eaten already?' I asked.

'No. Looked at the menu. A shop-girl would eat any quantity of it. I'm off. Come back with me and play backgammon. There's half a duck in the fridge if the maid hasn't swiped it. And you could make one of your potato salads. And I'd open a bottle of that Fleurie you like so much.'

It was a deal. Off we sped, he in his Rover, I in my absurd Mini GT which I bought because I can never resist a contradiction in terms.

As we swung into the courtyard and George killed the engine I heard the screams. He didn't hear them until he'd opened the door of his better-insulated car, so I was first at the door, which was locked. He stabbed it with his key and was through the hall and up the stairs before I had recovered from the mighty shove he had given me.

In the bedroom was his wife, quite bare, legs spread wide and shrieking as though she were approaching a grade on the Atcheson, Topeka and Santa Fé Railroad, Inc.

I couldn't help noticing that her bush, contrary to the usual practice, was of a lighter shade than the hair of her head. The window was open wide and a warm wind stirred the curtains but the room was fragrant with sex. George was already out of the window and taking a grip of the creeper on the wall outside. It ripped loose under his weight and he landed on the gravel below with what I suppose I may as well call a sickening thud and an oath more suitable to the Sergeants' Mess than to his own station in life.

Sonia left off shrieking, pulled a rumpled sheet over her rumpled charms and started concentrating on tragic expressions and ugly gulping noises. I studied her curiously. It was an act, but then she was a woman, so she wasn't necessarily acting, if you follow me. I had never before observed the behaviour-pattern of a recent rape-victim (I can't say *rapée*, can I – it reminds one of that delicious Rapée Morvandelle that one puts into *quiches*.) (It's also a kind of snuff, isn't it?) nor had I any preconceptions as to how such a victim would react, but somehow I found the performance unsatisfying; suspension of disbelief wouldn't quite come. However, there was no time to waste. I had no intention, I need scarcely say, of following George and the rapist out of the window: I am a little portly just at present and I was wearing a new and costly mohair suit, but I felt that something should be done and I felt, too, a little *de trop* in that bedroom.

'There, there,' I said, patting what I took to be her shoulder under the sheet but which proved, embarrassingly, to be what pornographers call a *quivering mound* and she began to steam-whistle again.

'Oops, sorry,' I mumbled as I fled, my carefully-built reputation for being *uno di quelli* shattered.

Downstairs and out through the back door, there was nothing to be seen but the ambiguous outlines of costly shrubs, no smell but the drowsy odours of night-scented whatever-they-ares and no sound but the growling of my still unfilled belly.

George might be anywhere, the rapist still more so, if his exploits had left him with any strength.

'Chemise de femme,
Armure ad hoc
Pour la gaie prise
Et la belle choque'

was running through my head. Sonia's nightdress, the short sort, calculated for sea-level, had been on the floor, you see, suggesting a leisurely and fastidious rapist.

There was nothing to be done out there in the garden; dirty fighting is one of my favourite outdoor sports, believe it or not, but

I do like a little advantage – umbrageous shrubberies bulging with mad rapists are not my notion of advantageous ground. I attribute my long life and good health to cowardice.

I went indoors and lifted the telephone. Then I put it down again. Sonia might not *want* a doctor; probably a bidet and a codeine tablet would fill the bill, if I may coin a phrase. George might not *want* the police or any other third party to learn of the invasion of his wife's secret garden.

What I did was, I made a stiff drink of gin and orange juice and tonic, such as I knew Sonia loved, and carried it up to the bedroom, administering it with many a 'there, there, child'. Then I went downstairs and made a similar confection for myself, except that it was made of whisky and soda. Then I had another which tasted even better and gave me enough lightning-like decision to go across the courtyard and find Sam.

'Sam,' I said, when he answered my knock, 'there is trouble across the way.'

'Only trouble?' he said. 'It sounded like a steam traction-engine rally. I nearly went over but I thought it impertinent to interfere in what might be a private argument.'

I outlined the situation to him and he went to fetch Violet from the other end of the house. Her face was red and tear-stained and I cocked an inquiring eyebrow,

'It's all right,' she said, 'it's just the crabs.'

'The *crabs*?' I cried, shocked by such candour. 'My dear, however did you catch *them*?'

'I didn't. The plumber did.'

'You are weeping because the plumber has contracted crabs?'

Sam would ordinarily have let this go on, relishing Violet's tangled thought-patterns, but time pressed.

'The plumber,' he explained, 'is a keen sea-fisher, as they all are here. He has today given us two fine shanker crabs, alive alive-oh. Violet is boiling them and the sound of their knocking on the saucepan-lid fills her with compassion. *Hinc illae lachry-mae.*'

Violet smiled sweetly, vacantly, through her tears.

A minute later we were at Les Cherche-fuites, where all was going as merrily as a wedding-bell. George was covered with mud, bits of wistaria and gravel-rash, and was making grating, brigadier-like noises into the telephone. Sonia was striking well-raped attitudes

reminiscent of Emma Hamilton portraying Lucrece, and was
fetching huge and unbecoming sobs up from deep in her thorax.
Violet rushed to her and went into the 'there, there' and 'now, now'
routine but to no avail, for Sonia merely shifted into the higher
register. Violet steered her firmly off to the bathroom to wash her
face or whatever women do for each other in times of stress.

George subsided into an armchair, glaring at the tumbler of
Scotch I had pressed into his hand.

'Bloody swine,' he growled. 'Raped my wife. Ruined my
wistaria.'

'I'll send my man round first thing in the morning to have a look
at it,' said Sam. 'The wistaria I mean. They're very tenacious things
– soon recover. Wistaria,' he added; gratuitously, it seemed to me.

I started to tiptoe out: I love dramas but I am no sort of
horticulturalist.

'Don't go,' said George.

'No, don't go,' said Sam.

I didn't go, I hadn't really wanted to. I wondered whether George
had forgotten about the half of a cold duck and bottle of Fleurie. I
helped myself to a little more of his Scotch.

'Who were you telephoning, George?' asked Sam.

'Doctor.'

'Wise, d'you think? Bit shaming for Sonia?'

'Irrelevant. Bastard may have damaged her insides, given her
some filthy disease, even a brat . . . God knows . . .' His voice
trailed off into a choking, hate-filled silence.

'What I have to decide,' he went on quietly, 'is police or not.'

That was, indeed, a matter for thought. Even the Paid Police, if
they could eventually be coaxed out from St Helier, could hardly
be expected to make much of a possible footprint or two and a
ravished wife's incoherent babblings, while the Honorary Police, in
the person of the local Vingtenier, pillar of the community though
he might be, could do little more than search his brain for known
or likely rapists in his twenty families (excluding those to whom
he was related, which would rule out most) and then summon his
Centenier. The Centenier, excellent and astute man, could do little
more than search *his* brain: his appointment and specialized training
were approximately those of the Chairman of a Parish Council in
England and he had neither the equipment, the men, nor the

skills necessary to carry out a drag-net operation or house-to-house search. And what to look for in such a search? Someone breathing hard? Worst of all, such a public fuss would stamp Sonia for ever as the 'poor lady what got raped last Easter'.

'On the whole,' said Sam gently, 'I'd think not.'

'Yes,' I said with my customary ambiguity.

'I see all that,' said George, 'and obviously I agree with it. But there is a citizen's duty. Personal embarrassment shouldn't count. It's the law, d'you see. Much more important than us. Even if it is an ass. Otherwise where are we?'

'But if we know it can't help?' (Sam)

'Well, yes, that's the point, isn't it?' He thought for a while, ignoring the drink in his hand.

'Yes, got it,' he said at length, 'I hold the Queen's commission and in any case there's that citizen's arrest law, isn't there. I'll have a private chat with the Centenier tomorrow, explain my position. Then we three form a *posse comitatus*; hound the swine down. Yes, that's it. Good night, you men. Report here at noon tomorrow. Bring your own sandwiches.'

Sam gazed at him aghast: Nature had not formed him to be a posse-member.

I, too, gazed at him aghast: there was clearly not going to be any cold duck that night.

Violet entered, weeping freely again.

'It is really quite dreadful,' she said, 'poor dear girl. He did *very* odd things to her as well as, well, you know, and she is frightened out of her wits. He must have been a maniac, he was wearing a mask and funny-smelling clothes, and, oh yes, he had a sword painted on his tummy.'

George growled and cursed a bit; Sam's eyebrows shot up and I began to muse furiously.

'Bloody bastard,' said George.

'How perfectly extraordinary,' said Sam.

'What kind of a mask?' I asked.

The others looked at me, a touch of rebuke in their eyes, as though I had said 'District Nurse' in front of the children.

'One of those joke-shop rubber masks, she thinks. You know, Dracula or the Beast from 5,000 Fathoms.'

'Just so,' I said. 'The Beast.'

'Aha! said Sam. 'I think I twig. But the sword thing is new, isn't it?'

'Yes, but I think it fits.'

'How?'

'Not sure enough now, tell you some other time.'

'Would somebody mind telling *me*,' snarled George, 'what the f –' he paused, collected himself. 'Sorry,' he resumed, 'I mean, I don't quite follow you men.'

'The Beast of Jersey,' Sam explained. 'You know, the chap who terrorized the Island for a dozen years; used to creep into children's rooms, carry them out of the window, do odd things to them in the fields – not always very nasty – then pop them back into their little beds. The police think that there may have been more than a hundred such assaults but naturally most of them were not reported, for reasons which you will, um, appreciate. He used to wear a rubber mask, most of the victims said that he had an odd smell and he wore bizarre clothes, studded with nails. Just before you moved here they caught a chap called Paisnel, who is now serving thirty years, rightly or wrongly.'

'Shouldn't like to be him,' I interjected, 'convicts are madly sentimental and they do *beastly* things to offenders against children. Make them sing alto, see what I mean.'

'Yes. I dare say they do. No experience in that field myself. Take your word for it.'

That was cheaper than Sam's usual level of badinage; I made a mental note to see that he suffered for it. I'm not a vengeful chap but I can't allow my friends to make cheap witticisms, can I? It's a question of the quality of life.

'What was interesting,' Sam went on as I chewed my spleen, 'was that Paisnel kept on saying that it was "all part of something" but he wouldn't say what and he said that when he was arrested he was on his way to meet "certain people" but he wouldn't say whom.'

'Perfectly obvious,' said George; 'the beggar was one of these witches or witchmasters. It all comes back to me now. The plumber told me all about it when he came in drunk just after Christmas. Seems it wasn't this Paisnel fellow at all, all the locals know who it was, including most of the Honorary Police . . . or did he say that Paisnel was just part of it?'

'That strain again,' murmured Sam, 'it hath a dying fall . . .'

'Quite right. And this Paisnel had a secret room, hadn't he, with a pottery frog or toad in it and *that* was supposed to be "part of it" too. And there was one of these Papist Palm Sunday crosses in the car he was nabbed in and they say he screamed when they asked him to touch it.'

'Codswallop?' I prompted.

'Not necessarily. Seen too many funny things myself to be ready to scoff at, ah, funny things.'

'In India, I dare say?'

He glared at me suspiciously.

'Yes,' curtly. 'There and elsewhere. Well, mustn't keep you chaps any longer. Good of you to help, very.'

Hunger stabbed me as I drove home. There was nothing inviting in the fridge, certainly not the half of a cold duck, but I happen to know where Jock hides his 'perks' and I spitefully wolfed a whole tin of caviare (the real Grosrybrest; Jock steals nothing but the best, he spurns Beluga and Ocietrova) on hot toast and left the kitchen in a horrid mess. On purpose.

Upstairs, Johanna appeared to be asleep and I slunk gratefully into bed like a thief in the night.

'Gotcha!' she yelled triumphantly.

'Have a care, for God's sake, you'll have me singing alto.'

'Where have you been, you naughty little stud?'

I told her the whole story and she listened enthralled.

'Let's play rapists,' she said when I had finished.

'I'm not climbing through any bloody window.'

'I'll let you off that bit.'

'But I haven't a rubber mask.'

'*Extemporize.*'

'Oh, really.'

'I shall pretend to be asleep and you shall *sneak* into the room and *leap* upon me and work your wicked will and I shall scream and scream but very softly so as not to wake our nice landlord.'

'Promise not to scratch?'

'Only gently.'

Much later I crept down to the kitchen to make myself a jam-sandwich. Jock was there, moodily eating baked beans. He bore all the marks of a servant who has lost heavily at dominoes. We did not speak. I, for one, was thinking.

3

Who hath given, who hath sold it thee,
Knowledge of me?
Has the wilderness told it thee?
Hast thou learnt of the sea?
Hast thou communed in spirit with night? have the winds
taken counsel with thee?

Hertha

Johanna and I do not share a bedroom, still less a bed. To sleep in the same bed with a member of the opposite sex is barbarous, unhygienic, unaesthetic and, in these blessed days of the electric blanket, quite unnecessary. It means, too, that wakefulness in one is visited upon the other partner and, worst of all, it is conducive to carnality in the mornings – terribly bad for the heart and makes you eat too large a breakfast. When I find a woman that I want to spend the whole night with – I mean, including sleep – in the same bed, then I shall know that I'm in love – or senile. Probably, by then, both.

It was in my dressing-room, then, that Jock aroused me on Easter Tuesday. His 'good morning' was no gruffer than usual; there was perhaps hope that he had declared a truce. Nevertheless, I tasted my tea guardedly, for the keenest weapon in Jock's arsenal is to make tea with water *which has not quite boiled*: a fearful revenge, but then Jock is a man of violence, this is why I employ him.

The tea was good. Jock had selected the Assam Flowery BOP from Jackson's *atelier* and had made it with his deftest touch. I beamed upon the honest fellow.

'Jock, today I am to be a member of a posse. Pray lay out for me a suit of Levis, a ten-gallon hat, high-heeled boots, a Winchester '73 rifle and a strong, durable horse.'

'We ain't got none of that, Mr Charlie.'

'Then plus-fours, stout boots and a great cudgel.'

'Right. Am I coming?'

'Not at this stage, but please stay near the telephone until I call.'

'Right. 'Course you know you won't catch him, don't you?'

I gaped.

'Catch whom?'

'The bloke who rogered Mrs Breakspear, of course. Silly bugger, he only had to say please, didn't he?'

'Watch your tongue. Mr Breakspear's a friend of mine.'

'Sorry, Mr Charlie. But everybody . . .'

'Shut up. Anyway, how do you come to have heard of the, er, incident?'

'Girl who delivers the newspapers.'

'But the papers come from Grouville and they're here before eight. How can it have got so far overnight?'

'Jersey,' he said enigmatically.

'Yes. Of course. But what's this about never catching him?'

'Use your common-sense, Mr Charlie. Where are you going to *look*, for one thing?'

'I had been asking myself that, I admit. What was the other thing?'

'*They* say you won't. The Jerseys. *They* know.'

'Hm, yes, that is another thing.'

'Yeah.'

At noon, clad in thick Irish thornproof tweeds and brandishing an ashplant, I clumped in my great boots into the drawing-room at Les Cherche-fuites. George was wearing flannels and a white shirt, Sam was wearing Bermuda shorts and a silk Palm Beach shirt. They gazed at me wonderingly.

'This is only a conference,' George explained gently.

'Oh. I see.'

'Have you brought many beaters?' Sam asked.

'No.'

'But a *loader*, perhaps?'

My riposte was swift as light.

'I usually drink a glass of bottled beer at about this time,' I said, and went out to the kitchen to fetch it.

Back in the drawing-room I noticed a large, ill-assembled man in a blue suit fidgeting on the edge of an upright chair. His head was many sizes too small for his great frame but his hands made up for it; they were like shovels. He proved to be the Centenier, one Hyacinthe le Mignone, and he shook hands with great gentleness, like a man who is afraid of breaking things. His voice was just such a melancholy, long, withdrawing roar as Matthew Arnold used to delight in.

The conference had barely begun, only civilities and things had thitherto been exchanged. The Centenier began to utter.

'Well, Mr Breakspear,' he roared, 'I 'aven't yet turned up anything you could call a positive lead. We 'ave only two known sex-offenders worth the name in this Parish and neither of them seems to fit the bill. One of them has a diseased mind all right, eh? but 'is modus operandi is quite unlike that what your lady has related. 'E is chiefly interested in little girls' bicycle-saddles which we reckon a 'armless hobby for an ageing man, though we keep a sharp eye on 'im, eh? 'E did indeed once coax a liddle lass into a daffodil field but as soon as 'e started getting above 'imself she stuck 'er finger in 'is eye and run and told 'er father, who 'appened to be the Vingtenier and 'urt the old man real nasty; I don't reckon 'e'll try that again, eh?'

This was entrancing stuff, it made me wish that I were a novelist.

'The other one is just a kid of fifteen or so. 'E 'as bin blessed with a unusually large member, which 'e cannot resist showing to respectable women once in a while, eh? None of them 'as ever made a complaint but the boy always comes to me and confesses and tries to wag it at me – says 'e wants me to understand!'

'And do you *look*?' I asked, with a straight face.

'My Chri' no. I tell 'im to show it to the College of Surgeons and give 'im a kick up the arse, eh? I probably seen better anyway,' he added with a betraying modesty.

'The only other possibility,' he went on, 'oh, thanks, I shouldn't really, my wife will give me hell if she smells it on me breath; the only other possibility is some person or persons unknown who in the Spring and early Summer months persists in stealing ladies' knickers from washing lines. But this doesn't sound like a desperate bloke who climbs in windows and takes on strong young ladies, does it? It sounds more like someone addicted to what we call the Solitary Vice. What's more, he always pinches these great big old bloomers, eh? what we used to call bumbags, not the sort of pretty frilly things your lady will likely wear.'

He lapsed into a thoughtful silence, his eyes hooded.

'Get on, man,' barked George.

'So we reckon 'e's not likely from our Parish but where is 'e from then? Trinity's the nearest next Parish and they 'aven't anyone there to compare with us.'

There was a pardonable pride in his voice.

'They got two or three poofs like we all 'ave and a couple of little tarts on the game – Dirty Gertie and Cutprice Alice and them – but they stick to St Helier, where the money is, eh? Oh, and there's a geezer who rings up ladies and goes on about what he fancies doing to them but we all know who 'e is and 'e's a well-liked chap and does no harm, 'e's terrified of 'is wife. And that's it.'

'What about St John's?' said George, levelly.

'Don't reelly know. Lot of savages there, but nothing like this that I've heard of. Old La Pouquelaye, of course, but 'e's just disgusting. Calves, 'e does it with.'

We sat silently; dazed at this revelation of how the other half lives. I felt that life had passed me by.

'Have you talked to the Paid Police?' asked George.

'Of course, sir. They said they were always glad to hear about our country goings-on but they didn't see how they could help. Unless me and my Vingteniers could give them something to work on.'

'Such as?'

'Well, footprints first. Any good ones, they said they'd come and take casts of.'

'No luck, I'm afraid. I've already looked. I sort of landed heavily when pursuing the beggar and must have wiped out his traces under the window. After that he seems to have kept to the gravel. No sign at all.'

'You sure, sir?'

'I helped to form the Reconnaissance Corps in 1942.'

'Ah. I was helping to form the Jersey Resistance just about then meself.'

They gave each other keen, soldierly looks, such as strong men exchange in the works of R. Kipling.

'Then they said about fingerprints and other clues.'

'Bad luck there, too. My wife's maid did the room thoroughly before we were up. Officious bitch. Usually can't get her to empty an ashtray.'

'That's unfortunate, eh?'

'Very. But I don't suppose you have much of a fingerprint file on the Island.'

'Not what you'd call an up-to-date one. Well, the other thing is semen stains. It seems they can get them classified now, like blood.'

'No,' said George.

'So if you could let me have the lady's sheets, or any garments –'

'I said no.'

'Perhaps the doctor took some samples –'

'Positively bloody NO!' George bellowed, quite startling us all.

'Yes, of course, sir. There's a sort of delicacy –'

George stood up.

The Centenier shut up.

'You won't stay to luncheon?' asked George in a voice from the nineteenth century. 'No. Well, I must thank you for all your help. Most kind. You hadn't a hat? No. A fine day, is it not. Goodbye.'

He closed the front door, quite gently. When he was back in the room he eyed us, defying us to grin. At last, he grinned himself.

'The phrase you are groping for,' I said carefully, 'is "Fuck an old rat".'

'Fuck an old rat,' he said. 'A good cavalry expression. The cavalry has its rôle, after all, in modern life.'

Sam seemed to awake from a heavy slumber.

'I could *eat* an old rat,' he said.

'There was half a cold duck in the fridge,' George said apologetically, 'but I'm afraid I ate it last night just after you men had left. Sonia is in no shape for cooking and the maid cannot tell an Aga from an autoclave. Let us go to Bonne Nuit Bay and eat lobsters.'

'But will they let Charlie in?' asked Sam sweetly. 'I mean, he does look just a little *farouche* . . .'

I gazed at him thoughtfully. His tongue was ever sharp but lately he seemed to have been gargling with acid.

'I shall go and change,' I said stiffly. 'Please order for me. I shall have a medium-sized hen lobster split and broiled with a great deal of butter, three potato croquettes and a salad made with the hearts of two lettuces. I shall dress the salad myself.'

'Wine?' said Sam.

'Thank you, how kind. I shall drink whatever you offer; your judgement in these matters is famous.'

Over lunch we agreed that very little could be done until we had more information. George set up a fighting-fund of £100: ten £5 bribes to be slipped to gardeners and other venal fellows who might lay their ears to the ground, and five £10 rewards for any of them who brought in concrete information. Larger rewards, he shrewdly pointed out, might well provoke imagination rather than hard news.

We parted at three; I, for one, in that state of tentative eupepsia which only a broiled lobster and a bottle of Gewurtztraminer can bestow, augmented by the fact that Sam had, indeed, paid for the wine.

I drove to St Helier and the Library of the Museum of the *Société Jersiaise*. They said it was private but I murmured the name of a learned Rector and, instantly, red carpets blossomed beneath my feet.

The material I wanted was dispersed and hard to find, for I particularly did not want to enlist the librarian's help, and, when I found it, a great deal was in *Patois Jersiais* and the rest in antique Norman-French. A sample of *Patois* will, I think, give you an idea of the horrors of that tongue: '*S'lou iou que l'vent est quand l'soleit s'couoche la séthée d'la S. Miché, ché s'la qu'nous etha l'vent pour l'hivé.*' This is supposed to mean that the direction of the wind at sunset on Michaelmas Day will be the prevailing wind throughout the following winter – a likely story, I must say.

I staggered out into the evening sunshine and the monstrous regiment of tourists with my head buzzing-full of recondite information. It was clear that scholarship of that kind was not for Mortdecai: a specialist was called for. Nevertheless, I now knew a few things about Paisnel which the police didn't. For instance, both he and his china toad had indeed been 'part of something'; something which is supposed to have died three hundred years ago, something almost as nasty as the people who stamped it out – or thought they had.

Johanna was out when I arrived at the flat; she would be playing bridge, the least strenuous of her vices, bless her. With luck she would get home very late and too tired for romps.

I wrote to Hatchards for a copy of *Malleus Maleficarum*, that great compendium of medieval horrors, and begged them, with many an underlining, to see that it was in *English*.

Jock and I, on friendly terms again, feasted in the kitchen on pork chops, fried peas and mashed potatoes, capping them with a *croque-monsieur* in case of night starvation.

Then, aiding digestion with a bottle of Mr Teacher's best and brightest, we watched Bogart and Bergman in *Casablanca*, that flawless pearl of a film. There wasn't a dry eye in the house. If television didn't exist, someone would have to invent it, is what I say.

I was in hoggish slumber when Johanna climbed into my bed, she was glowing with the radiance of a woman who has just won more than eighty pounds from a close friend. She spends at least that sum each month on her breakfast champagne but her pleasure was intense and she tried to communicate it to me in her own special way.

'No, please,' I protested, 'it's very late and I am suffering from Excess at Table.'

'Well at least tell me what happened today,'she pouted. 'Did you catch the Fiend in Human Shape?'

'We didn't look. We've decided that all we can do for the present is lay our ears to the ground and hope for gossip. But we did meet a lovely Centenier who told us all about the local sex-maniacs.'

She listened, saucer-eyed, as I related all I could remember about the neighbourhood satyrs.

'And in St John's,' I ended, 'there's a well-respected man who does it with *calves*: what do you say to that?'

She rolled over on to all fours, her delightful bottom coquettishly raised.

'Mooo?' she asked hopefully.

'Oh, very well.'

4

His speech is a burning fire;
With his lips he travaileth;
In his heart is a blind desire,
In his eyes foreknowledge of death;
He weaves, and is clothed with derision;
Sows, and he shall not reap;
His life is a watch or a vision
Between a sleep and a sleep.

Atalanta

'Jock,' I said to Jock as I sipped the blessed second cup of the true Earl Grey's Blend on the morning of Easter Wednesday. (I suppose there *is* an Easter Wednesday? For my part the only moveable feast which has any charms is the saddle-of-mutton trolley at Simpson's.)

'Jock,' I said, 'although you are but a rough, untutored fellow I have observed in you certain qualities which I prize. For once I do not refer to your heaven-sent gifts with the teapot and the frying-pan but to another, rarer talent.'

He moved his head slightly, so that his glass eye could give me a non-committal look.

'I refer, on this occasion, to your innate ability to get into conversations, eternal friendships and fights with chaps in pubs.'

'Hunh. You gave me a right bad time when I had me last little punch-up, didn't you?'

'Yes, well, but that was because you *killed* the chap, wasn't it, and I've told you and told you not to, and you know what it does to my digestion, and I had to tell *fibs* to the police about you having been with me all evening watching Molière on the television and they didn't believe a word of it, did they?'

He gave me his juiciest smile, the one that still frightens even me, the one which exposes a single, long, yellow fang nestling on his liver-hued nether lip.

Be that as it may,' I went on, 'this gift or knack of yours shall now be usefully employed. Here are ten pounds, the finest that the Bailiwick of Jersey can print. You are to lay them out on beer, cider, rum or whatever pleases your actual rebarbative Jerseyman. Do not buy drinks for any but true-born Jerseymen. They are the ones who will know.'

'Know what, Mr Charlie?'

'Know who was where on Easter Monday. Know who is the sort of chap who would climb up a perilous wistaria to slake his lawless lust; know who still takes part in very old-fashioned and naughty revels – and know, perhaps, who keeps a china toad on his, ah, mantelpiece.'

He thought for a minute or two, or at any rate, he frowned and chewed his lip as he has seen other people do when they were thinking.

'I can't ask these Jerseys that sort of stuff. They'd shut up like bloody clams.'

'Don't ask them. Tell them. Tell them what *you* think it's all about. Talk rubbish while you fill their ale-pots. Then watch: see who smiles. Listen: and see who calls you an idiot. Do not hit them; play the mug, let them pull your plonker. Someone will walk into the trap.'

'You mean, do a Les Kellet?'

'Exactly.'

(Les Kellet is a superb wrestler and consummate clown: he seems to stumble about in a happy daze but his stumbles usually occur just when his opponent leaps on him for the *coup de grâce*. He is puzzled and sorry when the opponent shoots through the ropes and lands on his bonce outside the ring. Sometimes he helps the other chap back into the ring, dusts him down, then administers a fearsome forearm smash and the winning pinfall. Sometimes, too, he picks up the referee absent-mindedly and hits the other chap with him. He is very brave and strong and amusing.)

I briefed Jock a little more from the depths of my ignorance and waved him away in the general direction of the tavern doors.

Soon I heard his great motor-bike start up and burble down the lane. I say 'burble' because it's one of those lovely old pre-war Ariel 1,000c.c. machines with four cylinders and Brooklands fishtail exhausts. It is Jock's pride and joy and I find it utterly terrifying.

The pubs would be open and thronged already, they never seem to close in Jersey. (There are frequent flights from Heathrow; book now to avoid disappointment.) I went back to sleep, secure in the knowledge that the matter of liquoring-up the peasantry was in the hands of a mastercraftsman. Going back to sleep is infinitely sweeter than going to sleep in the first place.

I had scarcely closed my eyes, it seemed, before Johanna aroused me – and I use the word 'aroused' with precision. I opened an eye.

'Have you brought tea?' I asked.

'Of course not. You *are* funny, Charlie.'

'In that case, NO, and let me remind you of Uncle Fred and Auntie Mabel who fainted at the breakfast-table.'

'Charlie, it is not the morning, it is past one o'clock. And you don't eat breakfast, you know you don't.'

I fled to the shower but I was too slow, she got in as well. We re-enacted the battle of Custer's Last Stand. Later, I found that it had been only half-past eleven in the morning after all; it's a poor thing if a chap's own wife lies to him, don't you think?

Then she drove us over to Gorey in the East of the Island for a surprise luncheon at 'The Moorings' where the shellfish are very good. Johanna kept on looking at me anxiously as though she feared I might faint at table. On the way home, for some obscure, American reason, she stopped to buy me a huge bottle of multi-vitamin pills.

Jock was still out. Johanna and I sat on the lawn in the sun and drank hock and seltzer. She will not usually drink in the afternoons but I explained that it was Oscar Wilde's birthday and, who knows, it may well have been.

In the evening we went to a dinner-party on the Isle of Alderney, which has been aptly described as 1,500 alcoholics clinging to a rock. It was a delicious dinner but the flight home in Sam's little Piper was terrifying: he smelled of *drink*.

Jock was in the kitchen when we returned. He was by no means drunk by his standards but there was a betraying woodenness about his face and gait which suggested that his Jersey chums had not drunk the ten pounds unassisted.

Johanna, who was 'excused games' as we used to say at Roedean, went to bed.

'Well, Jock, any news?'

'Not really Mr Charlie, but I got a few night-lines laid, you might say. Wasted a bit of time on a bloke who turned out to be a Guernsey: well, I didn't know, did I?'

'I believe they wear a different sort of pullover.'

'Well I'm not a bloody milliner, am I?'

'No, Jock. Press on.'

'Well, some of the Jerseys seemed sort of interested and I reckon one or two of them would have opened up a bit if their mates hadn't bin there. Anyway, I got one of them coming here tomorrow night to play dominoes; I pretended I'd pinched a bottle of your Scotch.'

'*Pretended?*'

'Yeah. Oh, and I took on an old geezer to come and help out in the garden a few hours a week, hope that's all right. He seemed a right old character, met 'im in the pub at Carrefour Selous, the governor there says the old geezer knows every inch of Jersey and never had a bath in 'is life.'

'What a splendid chap he must be, I long to meet him. What is that you are eating?'

'Cormbeef samwidge.'

'With lots of mustard?'

' 'Course.'

'And thickly-sliced onions, I daresay?'

'Right.'

'The bread sounds fresh and crusty.'

'Oh, all right, let me finish this and I'll make you one.'

'How you read my mind!' I marvelled.

'Mr Charlie?'

'Yes, Jock?'

'What's a crappo?'

'I've no idea. Why?'

'Well this Guernsey said it was a matey thing to say to the Jerseys and he put me on to saying it to one of them and the Jersey tried to hit me.'

'*Tried?* Jock, have you been fighting?'

'Nah. I caught his fist and sort of squeezed till he said it was all a mistake and the landlord told him I didn't mean no harm, but when I asked what it meant they got nasty again so I left it alone and bought another round and there was no hard feelings except I think they kicked the Guernsey man up the bum when they got him outside. Funny you don't know what crappo means, I've heard you talk French lovely.'

'*Crapaud*!' I cried.

'Yeah, that's it. Crappo.'

'It's a French word; it means a toad.'

'A toad, eh?'

'Yes. And you say the Jerseys don't like it?'

'They '*ate* it. They reckon it's a diabolical liberty.'

'And "diabolical" may be a better word than you think.'

'Eh?'

'Never mind. Where's that sandwich?'

'Coming. Oh, one other thing I nearly forgot. When I was going on about this raper bloke having a sword painted on his belly, one or two of them sort of nudged each other and the old geezer who's coming to do the garden had a bit of a chuckle too. I didn't ask, I could see they weren't going to let on. Private joke, I reckon. Or p'raps it means something dirty.'

'Perhaps both. I think I detect the distant clash of phallic cymbals.'

'Eh?'

'Yes. Ah, the sandwich. How delicious. I shall take it to bed with me. Good night, Jock.'

'Goo' night, Mr Charlie.'

I know I meant to go and say good night to Johanna, for I realize how much these little civilities mean to the frailer sex, but I dare say I forgot. Even men aren't perfect.

5

Yea, he is strong, thou say'st,
A mystery many-faced,
The wild beasts know him and the wild birds flee;
The blind night sees him, death
Shrinks beaten at his breath,
And his right hand is heavy on the sea:
We know he hath made us, and is king;
We know not if he care for anything.

To Victor Hugo

Nothing really happened the following day except that, in the morning, my liver and I could by no means seem to get along together. I drank Milk of Magnesia, Alka-Seltzer and Eno's Fruit Salts, in that order, until my stomach was a mere cave of the winds and the waters, but to no avail.

'You need a drink, Mr Charlie,' said Jock, with rough compassion.

'Do you really think that might help?'

'Bloody sure it would.'

I had one, just to please Jock and, do you know, he was perfectly right. He *knows*, you see.

Nothing really had happened in the newspapers that day, either, except that some Arabs had murdered some Jews, some Jews had retaliated on some Arabs, some Indians had perfected an atomic bomb for dropping on Pakistanis and various assorted Irishmen had murdered each other in unpleasant ways. You really have to hand it to God, you know, he has terrific staying-power. Jehovah against Mohammed, Brahma against Allah, Catholic against Protestant: religion really keeps the fun going, doesn't it. If God didn't exist the professional soldiers would have to invent him, wouldn't they?

Nothing nearly so warlike had happened in Jersey, except that an old lady had found a neighbour lifting potatoes which he had inadvertently planted in land which had since been adjudged hers, so she had raised the ancient *Clameur de Haro*, which dates back to Rollo, the first Norman Lord of the Island. What you have to do to raise the *Clameur* is to collect a witness or two, drop on your knees and shout '*Haro! Haro! Haro! A l'aide, mon prince! On me fait tort!*' Whereupon the wrongdoer has to stop whatever wrong he is doing and the whole situation freezes until it can be sorted out at a high level. You have to be pretty sure of yourself to raise the *Clameur*; they take it seriously in Jersey and, even if you are technically in the right, you can find yourself 'amerced' for a good round fine if you have been wasting the court's time on spite or trivialities – or if your plea doesn't fit the conditions for proper clamouring.

Nothing happened chez Mortdecai, either, except that the new gardener appeared. His name may well have been something like Henri Le Pieton Gastineau, but his native wood-notes wild were blemished by a complete absence of teeth and, even when he took them out of his pocket and burnished them on the seat of his trousers before popping them into his mouth, it was hard to achieve a real communion of souls. What I did establish was that he wanted '*quat' louis les sept heures*' which my razor-like brain converted into 57 pence per hour – a fair rate if he happened to be capable of toil. As it turned out he was a positive dynamo. 'Flash', our tame slug, tried playing head-gardener and bullying him, but got nowhere: he then played his last card and offered his notice – which to his intense chagrin we accepted.

Nothing was new except that it was the First of May, which was Pinch-Bum Day when I was at my dame-school but is now known as Labour Day, when portly, well-paid Trades Union officials persuade lean, ill-paid Trades Union dues-payers to march about the streets saying 'hooray' for excellent reasons of their own. They carry beautiful woven banners each of which would keep a starving docker's wife in Bingo cards for a week. But I digress.

Nothing happened personally to me except that a funny thing happened to me at the Pistol and Rifle Club which I always attend on the first Thursday of the month.

I had decided to give my old and beautiful .455 Smith and Wesson Military and Police Model of 1902 an airing. The men there teased me about it as ever; most of them have amazing small-bore weapons with tailored handles and changeable sights, but they know that I can still make the pop-up man-sized target look pretty sick at standard Olympic range. Although I say it as shouldn't. It weighs 2¾ pounds fully loaded and the barrel is 6 inches long; using the high-load, nickel-jacketed military ammunition it can punch holes in a brick wall and it makes a deafening and highly satisfying noise. Everyone with an organ-inferiority should have one. (Like, say, Bach?)

A nice police-sergeant made his usual joke about it, saying that if I bought it a pair of wheels I could get a commission in the Royal Artillery, and then the funny thing that happened to me was that he asked me if I had my bullets specially cast.

'Yes, a nice chap in London,' I said.

'Lead?' he asked. I was puzzled.

'Of course, lead, what else?'

'No, nothing, just asking. There's a bloke here on the Island who'll cast them in *anything*, if ever you need it.'

'Well, thanks,' I said, still puzzled.

That was the funny thing that happened.

I didn't give it any more thought. I was too preoccupied with what always preoccupies me on the First of May: the essential *swindle* of all English months and May in particular. Why have we let the poets and, no doubt, politicians, sell us all this rubbish about the months? I mean, May conjures up the vision of happy, sun-burned maidens prancing on the village green and retiring at dusk to the nearest hedgerow to be turned into happy, sunburned, unmarried mothers-to-be; but the truth is that the pallid and pimply village maiden of today is waving her lumpish hips in a discotheque in the nearby town, munching a contraceptive pill while the rain roars down outside and the Babycham fizzes in its glass. Anyone braving a hedgerow in an English May, even in full oilskins, courts both pneumonia and insecticide-poisoning. Perhaps the only month which one can depend on is January, when the cold is always as promised and one can still sometimes hear the ring of skates on the frozen tarn and, if one is lucky, the shriek of a drowning skater.

When I say that nothing happened that day, I did not mean to suggest that nothing happened that night. Much did.

Johanna was watching lovingly as I mopped up the gravy of one of the finest coq-au-vins (coqs au vin?) of my life with a huge crust of crusty bread when the telephone rang.

'Tell them I'm out,' I snarled, 'or dead, or bankrupt, I don't care; but I'm not answering that machine, tell the Post Office to take it away in the morning, we'll be better without it.'

'It's for you, Mr Charlie,' said Jock a moment later.

'Look, are you incapable of . . .' I started, but then I saw Jock's expression. I went to the telephone, wiping my lips. Sam was on the line. It was a Sam I had never heard.

'Get round here, Charlie, fast. It's Violet.'

'You mean . . .?'

'Yes. Get here.'

I got. To be exact, I told Jock to get there on his motor-bike, carrying his low friend (perhaps glad to be free from the domino-lesson) on the pillion; while I bundled Johanna into the Mini. I knew she was probably safe from rapists (they rarely have the stamina to strike twice in one night) but I knew, too, that all women love to comfort their frailer sisters in adversity.

At La Gouluterie, Sam was in the courtyard, giving Jock and his domino-friend orders in the ugliest voice I have ever heard. He sent them off and turned to me.

'Charlie, send Johanna up to Violet; the doctor and police are coming. Jock is patrolling on his motor-bike towards Belle Etoile Bay and back via Wutherings; his friend is working the fields – don't shoot him by accident. You will drive me to Sion and I'll work back from there. Then you will drive like hell to St John's Church and come slowly back without lights. Are you armed?'

'Naturally.'

'Then grab anyone in trousers; if they can't give a wholly satisfactory account of themselves force them into the car. I'll pay any fines for wrongful arrest. Got all that? Then let's go.'

'What's George doing?'

'Nothing. They're out.'

With that he opened a gun-case and assembled his beautiful Churchill XXV shotgun with a brutality which made me wince. Off we sped. We saw no one. I left him at Sion, drove fast to St John's, crawled back, stopping to look and listen from time to time. One party of drunks arguing bitterly about football. One burly she-hitch-hiker from Wigan: she hadn't seen anyone. One sinister chap who was a rapist if ever I saw one but he already had a local maiden with him: the dirty look she gave me indicated that she was actually *hoping* to lose her maiden status even if it meant braving a hedgerow and that I was delaying things. Her swain claimed to have heard, ten minutes earlier, a large motor-bike driving towards the *Route Militaire* very fast, then stopping. A few minutes later it had started up again and gone North, much more slowly. That had evidently been Jock: this lad, for all his saucy looks, was a good witness. His restless sacrifice was tugging at his sleeve, saying –

'Ow, come on Norman, it's none of our business,' and so forth, so I attracted his interest by taking out the fat little Banker's Special revolver and spinning the cylinder, as though to check the load. This fascinated him, it was the Wild West come true.

'You the police, then, eh?'

I chuckled fatly.

'No, no. It's a little more important than that,' I said, in what he may well have taken for a Secret Service voice. 'Have you seen or heard anyone else – on foot perhaps?'

'No.'

'Would you have noticed, do you think?'

'Bloody right. I'm keeping me ear open for the young lady's dad, ain't I?'

'Yes, of course. Quite right. Well, thanks for your help.'

I was almost at the car when he made a chirruping noise and beckoned me. I went back to him.

'Funny you should ask that, mister. There's a bugger in the field of taters behind us, just come in through the hedge. I can't see him but I can hear him.'

'Ow, Norman, it's none of our business, etc.'

'Belt up, daft cow.' (How courtship has changed since our days, has it not?)

Norman and I stole into the field and, sure enough, a bugger was, indeed, tip-toeing through the taters. When the time and place were ripe I swept his feet from under him and Norman dived. The man squealed, cursed foully, kicked and clawed. When we had subdued him he proved to be Jock's domino-pupil, much chagrined: about five pounds' worth as it turned out. I gave Norman a sweetener too, and he eagerly proffered his name and address in case I ever needed any more deeds of derring-do.

The domino-man and I arrived at La Gouluterie at the very moment when George's Rover arrived with George and Sam, who had been picked up on the *Route Militaire*. Jock swept up on his Ariel before we had entered the house. Nothing to report, from anyone.

Except the doctor. He didn't like any part of this; he was a measles-and-mumps man and his mask of professional confidence was slipping. Much of what he said was for Sam's ear alone but we others could see Sam's face twist and darken as he listened. The professional murmuring went on, while Sam ground his teeth. George looked detachedly into space and I fidgeted. It was not, as the children say nowadays, my scene at all.

The situation was so fraught that Sam almost forgot to give the doctor his ritual glass of brown sherry before speeding him off on some other errand of mercy. (He was probably an excellent chap, a credit to Apothecaries' Hall, but I find it hard to trust doctors with large, unhygienic moustaches. 'He that sinneth, let him fall into the hands of the Physician', I always say.)

Johanna came downstairs looking troubled: Violet had at last succumbed to the massive dose of sedative that the doctor had hosed into her (would you believe 15 millilitres of paraldehyde?) but she was in a pretty sorry state. We all went into conference and the story-until-now emerged as follows.

The assailant had apparently entered the house through the pantry window. Violet had been in her bedroom, taking off her make-up before showering. She had been clad only in those sensible woolly knickers which girls like Violet always wear. Suddenly a hideous shape had appeared in her dressing-table mirror – only for a second, because the light went out an instant later.

Sam had been in his study, which is lined with books, even the doors, which make it virtually sound-proof; but in any case Johanna doesn't think Violet would have screamed, she would have been petrified with terror.

The rapist had been rough, to put it mildly, and had savaged Violet both here and there. The Marquis de Sade could have taken his correspondence course profitably. He seemed to have been motivated more by hatred than lust. Violet had babbled incoherently to Johanna for a few minutes before lapsing into a clenched sort of silence and the few cogent bits which Johanna could remember were:

'He stank horridly, like a goat.'

'He smelt of grease, but nasty.'

'He was wearing a horrid mask, it smelt of rubber.'

'He hated me.'

'He had a sword painted on his tummy.' (In Violet's Noddy-world, even mad rapists have tummies, not bellies. Enid Blyton, Enid Blyton, how much we all owe you!)

'He had spikes on his arms.' (George and I looked at each other, this was straight from the Beast of Jersey case-book.) 'He kept on saying beastly things, they were in a weird language – no, not patois – but I could tell they were beastly things.'

'His hands were all covered with earth, they *hurt* me.'

The really nasty thing, however, the thing that had made her at last scream, was that, after the fiend had slid out of the window, she had felt something cold and wet, high up between her thighs.

It had wriggled.

'It was a frog, for Christ's sake,' said Sam disgustedly, 'the man is clearly insane.'

'A *frog?*' I asked.

'That's what I said.'

'Sam, was it sort of greeny yellow with long hind-legs?'

'God blast it, Charlie, you do try a man's patience. I was in no mood to look at the thing's legs. I just snatched it up and threw it.'

'Where?'

He half rose, murder in his eyes, then thought better of it.

'I think I threw it into the waste-paper basket,' he said, in the strangled sort of voice you use when you want people to know that no further questions will be answered.

'Johanna,' I said, 'will you please go and find it?'

She went. She found it. It wasn't greenish-yellow with long legs, it was brown and naevous and squat.

'It's a *toad*,' I said.

'So?'

'Nothing.'

'Sod you too.'

'I think there is no one here,' I said gently, 'who would not be the better for a drink.'

Sam got up in a robotical sort of way and started to dish out the liquor; courteously assisted by me, for I feared that, in his distress, I might receive the wrong brand of Scotch, which would have quite spoiled my evening.

We guzzled our drinks silently, respectfully, like distant cousins helping themselves to baked ham after the funeral.

'Oh, one other thing Violet said,' said Johanna. We stopped guzzling: Johanna can make most people stop doing most things when she chooses, without even raising her voice. I wonder why that is.

'Yes, that's it,' she went on, 'she said she recognized the man's voice.'

'What?' shouted two of the three of us.

'Yes.' Her lovely eyes danced innocently, aimlessly around the room, alighting on everything and everyone except Sam. 'Well, to be exact, in the midst of some alarming chatter about her mother and so on she suddenly said, "I could tell that voice anywhere, *anywhere*; I couldn't be wrong" or something like that.' She paused; too long.

'Well, who, for God's sake?' George growled at last.

'She didn't say. Perhaps she only meant that she would know it again.'

My ensuing silence was puzzled; George's and Sam's silences appeared to be merely disgusted, but you never can tell.

Why I was puzzled was because Johanna was using the warm, true, *real* voice which she only uses when she is lying. Which isn't often, naturally; with all those looks and all that money, why should she bother?

I had the feeling, intensely, that a lot of complicated reactions were taking place in the room which I wasn't quite following because I didn't know what I was looking for. I'm not at all sure that Johanna knew, either, but it was clear to me that she was less at sea than I was. I gave up after a while with a mental 'heigh-ho' or two and applied myself to Sam's Scotch.

Like a good guest, I saw to it that Sam, too, ingested enough of the delicious fluid to ensure him a good night's rest in spite of everything; then we slunk away.

Johanna went to bed; kissing me but not fondly.

Jock was up, brewing 'Sergeant-Major's' which is the sort of tea you used to relish when coming off guard-duty in a January dawn: it is the cheapest Indian tea *boiled-up* with sugar and condensed milk. It is not at all like tea as you and I know it but it is very good indeed. I gazed at it longingly.

'You don't want none of that, Mr Charlie,' said Jock, 'you'll be wanting to get off to boo-boo's.' I glared.

'Have you been listening at keyholes?' I demanded.

' 'Course not. I've heard Madam use the phrase in public, frequently.'

'Ugh.'

'Yeah.'

I turned away.

'Mr Charlie,' he said.

'Yes?'

'That mate of mine I was teaching dominoes – the one you scragged.'

'Yeah.'

'He was going on about toads. He reckons the Jerseys think a lot of them, which is why they don't like being called them.'

'You put that beautifully, Jock.'

'Yeah. He got on about it because the old geezer who's come to do the garden just buried one alive in a pickle-jar to make the flowers grow.'

'To make the flowers grow? Do go on.'

'They all do it here, he reckons. It doesn't seem to bother the toads, they're nearly always alive when they dig them up in the autumn. Funny, innit? You'd think they'd get hungry.'

'Or thirsty?'

'Yeah. Anyway, a lot of the Jerseys, specially the old ones, reckon a toad's sort of holy and they don't like people taking the mickey about it.'

I took a gulp of his tea.

'You should put a little rum in this,' I advised.

'Well, I haven't got any rum, have I?'

'Do you mean you have forgotten how to pick the lock of the drinks cupboard?'

He maintained an injured silence. I went to fetch the rum, while he made some more Sergeant-Major's.

When we were firmly seated astride the tea and certain Welsh Rabbits which Jock had conjured up to help it down, I waxed informative, a vice of mine which I can by no means cure.

'Jock,' I said, 'did you know that for fifteen centuries people believed that the toad had a precious jewel inside its skull?'

'Reelly?' he said. 'What give them that idea, then?'

'Pliny or Aristotle or one of those chaps who wrote it in a book.'

Jock munched and golluped awhile.

'Well, didn't nobody think to chop one open and take a look?'

'Not as far as I know.'

'Fucking ignorant, all them wops, aren't they,' he said, obscurely.

I couldn't find it in my heart to contradict him.

'He went on about hares, too,' Jock went on. 'Seems there aren't supposed to be any hares on the Island but a few years back there was a right big bugger seen and the farmers reckoned it sucked all the milk out of them funny little cows they have here. So they laid up for it and shot it and better-shot it but it wasn't no use, so one of them put a silver button in his gun and shot it in the bum and the hare goes off limping and the next day this creepy old tart who lives nearby has a bandage on her leg.'

'That is probably one of the oldest stories in the world,' I told him, for indeed it is.

I was too tired to take a shower that night: all I wanted was to go to boo-boo's. I brushed my teeth, of course. As I did so I realized why the nice chap at the Pistol and Rifle Club had been so keen on introducing me to the chap who would cast bullets in anything.

Silver was what he had had in mind.

6

I said 'she must be swift and white,
And subtly warm, and half perverse,
And sweet, like sharp soft fruit to bite,
And like a snake's love lithe and fierce.'
Men have guessed worse.

Felise

We had another conference the next morning. Sonia, it seemed, was bearing up and getting about a little, but Violet's case was worse: she had quite stopped speaking and, although she followed you with her eyes, she moved no other part of herself. Sam had got one spoonful of Brand's celebrated Calves' Foot Jelly into her; the second time she had bitten the spoon. After that she wouldn't open her mouth at all. The doctor had mumbled about some sort of psychotic withdrawal which he himself clearly wasn't on very good terms with, and had given her another generous needleful of sedative.

'He didn't quite say "go on taking the tablets",' said Sam, 'but you could see the words on the tip of his tongue. If she hasn't snapped out of it tomorrow I'm getting a second opinion.'

We all nodded and made kindly murmuring sounds, except George who said 'bloody swine' several times.

Sam asked me if I could recommend a good pistol and how should he go about getting one. I told him, and advised a good vintage piece which would be an investment. He didn't seem too interested in that aspect, he wanted something which could be depended upon to punch large and painful holes into rapists.

'Calm yourself,' I urged. 'The best and most modern pistol won't make even a tiny hole in anyone at whom it is not accurately pointed. Most pistols are only for frightening people and making loud noises. The thing is to have it *handy*. Chaps like you and me only need a pistol perhaps once in our lives' – I wasn't being quite truthful there – 'but then we want it in a great hurry indeed. Take my advice and buy a capable, vintage one which you can make a profit on when all this has died down. There is, for instance, a very splendid old Mauser 7.65 mm not five miles away, which can be bought for £150; it's the sort with a wooden scabbard which clips onto the pistol-butt to form a stock and transforms it into a small carbine. It is a most reliable pistol and if you can point it straight it will knock an ox over at half a mile. It is also rather a beautiful object in an ugly sort of way.' He grumbled a bit but took my advice and the Mauserchap's telephone number.

'Yes, yes,' said George, 'that's all very well about the small-arms issue but this is supposed to be an O-Group and we should be doing an Appreciation of the Situation.'

(Those of you who haven't had the luck to serve in the Army should be told that an O-Group is a conference called by an infantry leader below field rank who is finally facing the fact that he is lost and wants his junior officers and senior NCOs to admit that they, too, are lost. An O-Group is always held out of ear-shot of the men, naturally, although the men have known that their officers were lost *hours* before the O-Group is summoned; their idea of a good officer is simply one who calls an O-Group at a time when they want *tea*. Soldiers, up to and, sometimes, including the rank of major, are capital chaps: join *now* – you're too late to have a crack at the Japs but the Irish are good for years yet.)

'I have here,' said George in an efficient sort of voice, 'a list of all nubile women within a mile's radius of this house. I propose we lie out at night, turn and turn about, watching their houses and ready to blow the arse off the filthy hog when he next tries to, er, strike.'

'George,' I said gently. 'George? Who furnished you with this list?'

'The Centenier – he spent hours with his Vingteniers drawing it up.' I let one of those long silences develop, so that all of us could see the daftness of that. Then I said:

'Good. Yes. But we are only three, you know, and have premises and wives of our own to guard – and we don't really know the terrain awfully intimately. More to the point, if you kill a chap even in your own *house* nowadays, with one of his fists in your safe and the other in your wife, you're facing a murder charge and the court will be told by hired psychiatrists that the offender is a poor, disturbed lad who has been upset by a nasty film he saw at the Odeon last week but he's a lovely son to his old mother. Old mothers are marvellous in the witness box, born actors every one, they can even make policemen weep, I've seen it, it's as good as the television. They would give you a very bad time.'

George snarled and gargled a while; he wasn't very cogent but we got the impression that, if he were let loose for a few hours with a Vickers Medium Machine-Gun, the world would be a better place and all potential rapists would be queuing up in Cathedral Closes, applying for jobs as counter-tenors.

Sam and I watched him curiously: I think we both felt that this was not the quiet, capable George we both knew and, in some sort, respected – the George whose most interesting feature was his dullness. We put it down, I suppose, to his recent ordeal and Sam doubtless, although he was showing a surprisingly better front to the world, had a fellow-feeling for him. (I myself gave up having fellow-feelings in my last term at school because I was working hard for University entrance; I like to think that I am a *prude* at heart.)

'I think,' I said, when the noise had died down, 'that I'd better go to Oxford.'

Sam mustered a flash of his old spirit.

'Is this really the best time to consider completing your education, Charlie? Is the call of the cloisters suddenly so strong? What will you read – Divinity?'

'Tush,' I replied. 'I shall go and see my old tutor, who knows more about witchcraft, demonology and kindred nonsense than any man living. It is perfectly clear that we have a disgusting situation here where some vile sub-human is committing outrages for ancient and nasty reasons which we do not comprehend. We cannot stamp him out until we know what he thinks he is doing, and why. I shall go to ask my old tutor. Has anyone any better suggestions?'

No one had any better suggestions.

'My own wife,' I went on, 'has not yet, to my best knowledge, been ravished, so you will see that my mission is pretty disinterested. In the circumstances, and since giving hospitality to dons in Oxford comes wickedly dear, I fancy you may care to split my expenses with me.'

They made fumbling gestures in the direction of their cheque-book pockets but I waved them away.

'Payment by results,' I said. 'If we get any good of my trip I shall submit an expense-sheet.'

'But what about Johanna?' came a tragic voice from half-way up the stairs. It was Sonia: pallid, voluminously wrappered, with just a tactful hint of make-up here and there which most chaps – *nice* chaps – would not have noticed. We all leaped to our feet and surged about getting her chairs, cushions, foot-stools and assorted restoratives. (I made a slight restorative for myself while I was about it, for George did not seem to be on form as a host that night.)

'What about Johanna?' she asked again, 'hadn't she better stay here while you're away so that I can protect her?'

I looked at her kindly.

'You're very kind,' I said, 'but Jock, too, is no slouch in the art of defence. They call it Martial Arts nowadays but when Jock was at Borstal it was known, quite simply, as a "flying drop-kick at the wedding-tackle". I'd back Jock against the finest Kung-fu artist ever groomed by Mr Metro-Goldwyn. He has a gift for it, you see.'

She nodded wisely. She knows she's not clever but she thinks I am, poor deluded bitch.

'Yes, but d'you trust the chap?' asked George.

This annoyed me but I decided I should give a civil answer.

'Jock is true as steel,' I said carefully. 'He has been in love with Shirley Temple since he was fourteen and will not lightly change. He is no butterfly. Second, he owes me a favour or perhaps two and crooks like Jock hold that sort of thing much more sacred than honest men do. Third – and I know this sounds absurd – I am the only man that Jock is afraid of.'

Sam and George shifted uneasily in their seats, they didn't know how to cope with rubbish like that. Sonia said:

'Oh, I think that's absolutely beautiful. I mean, to have a relationship like that, I mean, based on wonderful mutual um . . .'

I looked at her kindly again. Perhaps a little kindlier than last time. You see, we anti-feminists don't dislike women in the least; we prize, cherish, and pity them. We are compassionate. Goodness, to think of the poor wretches having to waddle through life with all those absurd fatty appendages sticking out of them; to have all the useful part of their lives made miserable by the triple plague of constipation, menstruation and parturition; worst of all, to have to cope with these handicaps with only a kind of fuzzy half-brain – a pretty head randomly filled, like a tiddly-winks cup, with brightly-coloured scraps of rubbish – why, it wrings the very heart with pity. You know how your dog sometimes gazes anguishedly at you, its almost human eyes yearning to understand, longing to communicate? You remember how often you have felt that it was on the very brink of breaking through the barrier and joining you? I think that's why you and I are so kind to women, bless 'em. (Moreover, you scarcely ever see them chasing cats or fouling the footpaths.)

'Yes,' I answered her.

Just as we were leaving, Sonia rushed out to the door, still playing the mobled queen.

'Charlie,' she cried, 'will someone look after your dear little canary while you're away?'

'Probably,' I said, vaguely.

'What my old nanny used to say,' grumbled George, 'was that people shouldn't have pets if they weren't prepared to look after them properly.'

'Just what I always say about wives,' I answered brightly. Well, perhaps it wasn't in the best of taste. I never signed any promises about good taste, I'd as soon join the Temperance League.

Johanna went to bed without saying good night. Jock was out, probably hitting people, he never tires of it. I didn't worry about that, he's careful now: people he quarrels with usually walk away – carrying their teeth in their hat. I made some telephone calls to travel-agents and old Oxford tutors then went sulkily to bed, taking with me a volume of Beatrix Potter to comfort my sad heart; it was *The Tale of Mrs Tiggywinkle*, it never fails to please.

7

God is buried and dead to us,
Even the spirit of earth,
Freedom; so have they said to us,
Some with mocking and mirth,
Some with heartbreak and tears;
And a God without eyes, without ears,
Who shall sing of him, dead in the birth?

To Walt Whitman in America

I took the noon flight for Heathrow the next day. I'm not one of the jet-set, more of the biplane set, Johanna says, but I don't at all mind flying except in those terrifying little planes where you sit in the open behind the driver and have to rap on his helmet if you want to tell him to slow down a bit. This was a large, experienced-looking craft and it said on the side that its engines came from the Rolls-Royce stable, most reassuring. Two Jersey worthies whom I know slightly took the seats beside me and, when we were air-borne, I ordered three large gins-and-tonic with my customary munificence. The hostess asked me if I wanted them all in one glass; I believe she was being *pert*.

You don't have to go right into London nowadays if you're headed West: an airlines bus takes you from Heathrow to Reading quite painlessly and trains thence to Oxford, where Dryden, my old tutor, hoves, are plentiful.

Goodness, have you *seen* Oxford Station since they did it up? It's quite amazingly smart and modern and not much more than twice as inconvenient as it was before.

Something quite dreadful happened to me as I stood outside the station waiting for Dryden: a leprous creature, clad in filthy tatters, beard matted and barbaric necklaces jingling, shambled up to me, mopping and mowing, his demeanour both piteous and threatening.

'Be off with you!' I quavered valiantly, brandishing my umbrella. 'I shall not submit to your mugging; I happen to be a personal friend of the station-master, aye, and of the Warden of All Souls, too!'

'Mr Mortdecai?' he fluted in the purest Wykehamist tones. 'My name's Francis, I'm a pupil of Dr Dryden, he's asked me to pick you up, he can't come himself, he's got the squitters. *I've* got the crabs, if you want to know,' he added gloomily. 'And a tutorial and two demos tomorrow.'

I fumbled around in my word-bag for a while.

'How do you do?' I said at length.

He took charge of my suitcase and led me to about five thousand pounds' worth of Italian GT motor-car in which we vroomed painlessly towards the dreaming-spires section of the city. I didn't know quite what to chat about, it's the generation gap I suppose. He was extraordinarily civil and, on closer inspection, as clean as can be. I think he was just boasting about the crabs.

Scone College, my *alma mater*, hadn't changed a bit except that the outside was richly adorned with huge painted words such as 'PEACE', 'SHIT', 'TROTSKY LIVES' and similar sentiments. I thought it something of an improvement, for it took one's eyes off the architecture. Fred was on duty in the Porter's Lodge as he had been when I was there last: he remembered me well and said that I owed him half a sovereign in connection with some long-forgotten horse-race. I wasn't taken in, but I coughed up.

My rooms were ready for me and quite habitable, except that the undergraduate incumbent (this was in the vacation, you see) had pinned up a poster of a little fat black chap called Maharaj ji Guru in such a position that it smirked at the bed. I couldn't move the chap's poster, naturally, so I moved the bed. Bathed and changed, I still had half an hour to spend before I could report at the Senior Common Room where Dryden would, if recovered, meet me and take me to dinner at High Table, so

I strolled over to the Buttery. On the lawn where, in the brave days, we used to play croquet some forty tatterdemalions were squatting silently – a sorry sight. No doubt they were meditating or protesting; they certainly weren't having any fun. As I strolled past them in my exceedingly beautiful dinner jacket I raised a hand in benediction.

'Peace!' I said.

'Shit!' said a spokesman.

'Trotsky lives!' I answered stoutly. You see, you *can* communicate with young people if you take the trouble to learn their lingo.

'Hallo, Mr Mortdecai,' said Henry, the buttery steward, 'have you been away?'

'No, no, no,' I said, 'I was here only seven years ago.'

'So you were, sir. End of a Trinity term it was, I fancy, and you were rude to one of those Hungarian persons that are all over the place now – I can't ever say their names, they always seem to come out rude-sounding when I try.'

'I know just what you mean, Henry. And I'm dying of thirst.'

He really did remember me, for he reached down one of the battered pewter quarts from which we giants used to sup our ale in the olden days. I strolled outside with my tankard so that I could pour half its contents surreptitiously onto the lawn, for I am not the man I was.

'I suppose you find that sort of thing a bit galling, don't you, Henry?' I said, waving my hand towards the solemn sit-in on the lawn.

'Oh, I dunno. I've been here all my life, as well you know. They're not much different from your year, or any year. When I first come here it was top hats and frock-coats on Sunday and parading up and down the Broad Walk; then it was riding-breeches and fox-terriers; then it was Oxford bags and *bull*-terriers. After the war it was them blue demob suits, then tweed jackets and flannels; then straw bashers and blazers come back in and then it was jeans and bare feet and now it's beards and beads and probably tomorrow it'll be top hats again. Only thing I got against this lot is they will eat chocolate-bars with their little gills of beer, and they spend half their money on the french-letter machine in the Junior Common Room. They should be drinking their beer and rowing their boats and learning their books; there's plenty of time for all that sex when they've got their degrees.'

'Just so,' I said. I bade him good night, donned my gown and set sail for the SCR.

Dryden was profuse in his apologies for not having met me at the station.

'I do hope Margate found you without difficulty?'

'Margate? No, it was a rum chap called Francis.'

'Yes, that's right, Francis Margate. A *very* nice boy. Brightest Viscount I've taught for years.'

'I hope your, ah, squitters are better, John? Your pupil seemed to be concerned about you.'

'Oh, goodness, they don't trouble me, I've had them for years, it's the port here, d'you see, worst port in Oxford, don't know why I stay. I've had splendid offers from all sorts of places, Sussex, Lancaster, Uganda – all sorts of places.'

'They all sound much the same to me. What, in fact, did prevent you from meeting me?'

'Oh, I had luncheon at one of those women's colleges, can't recall the name, they get you frightfully drunk, you probably know, shocking lot, boozers every one. So I felt a little *tired* after luncheon and Francis hadn't his essay ready so I offered to let him meet you instead.'

'Just so,' I said. (I find that I say 'just so' often in Oxford, I wonder why that is?)

He then gave me a *filthy* glass of sherry without a word of apology and led me up to the Warden so that I might pay my respects. I paid them.

'How nice,' the Warden said with apparent civility, 'to see an old member.'

To this day I cannot be sure whether it was a gibe or simply an unfortunate turn of phrase.

I strayed around the Common Room until I found a hideous pot-plant which seemed to deserve my sherry. A moment later, we formed the usual sort of procession and shuffled off to Hall, High Table and dinner. High Table was much as it has always been, except for the cut of the dinner-jackets and the absurd youthfulness of the dons, but a glance over my shoulder into the bear-pit of Hall made me shudder. Two hundred shaggy Tom-a-Bedlams with their

molls and doxies were scrambling and squabbling around a row of
stainless-steel soup-kitchen counters, snapping and snarling like
Welsh Nationalists in committee, or Italian press-photographers
in pursuit of an adulterous Royal. Every few moments one of them
would break out of the *mêlée*, guarding a plate heaped with nameless
things and chips, which he would savage at the table, cursing and
belching the while. The long oak tables bore none of the ancient
silver of my youth – they have to keep it locked up nowadays –
but there were long, proud lines of bottles of Daddie's Favourite
Sauce – and jolly nice it is too, I dare say. But I turned away with a
shudder and dipped a reluctant spoon into the Mock Turtle before
me. (You can tell how even the memory of it all upsets me if you
note that I started the last sentence with a conjunction, a thing I
never do.)

You must not think that I am carping when I say that dinner
was five courses of poisonous ordure: I expected it and would
have been disturbed if it had been good. High Table dinner in
Oxford, as perhaps you know, is always in inverse ratio to the
brains-content of the College which offers it. Scone is a very brainy
College indeed. If you want a good tuck-in in Oxford you have to
go to places like Pembroke, Trinity or St Edmund Hall, where
they play rugger and hockey and things like that and, if you're
spotted reading a book, someone takes you aside and has a chat
with you.

No, what really spoiled my evening was that Scone had gone in
for the ultimate gimmick and acquired a she-don. She resembled
nothing so much as a badly-tied bundle of old bits of string; her
smile was the bitter, clenched rictus of a woman pretending to
enjoy natural childbirth and we disliked each other on sight to our
mutual satisfaction. She was not wearing a bust-bodice or 'bra',
that was clear; her blouse was gallantly taking the strain at about
the level of her navel.

I couldn't say anything, could I – as a mere Old Member I was
only a guest and she was listening intently – but I met the Warden's
eye and gave him a long, level look. He smiled sheepishly, a sort of
qualified apology.

After dinner, in the Common Room, Dryden mischievously
introduced us.

'Gwladys,' he said with relish. 'Charlie Mortdecai has been dying to meet you.'

'*Bronwen*,' she said curtly. Clearly, Dryden had used that gambit before.

'Enchanted,' I exclaimed in the *galant* voice which I hoped would most enrage her, 'it's high time this stuffy old place had a few pretty faces to brighten it up.'

She turned on me that particularly nasty look which your breakfast kipper gives you when you have a hang-over.

'And what's your field?' I asked.

'Sexual Sociometrics.'

'I might have guessed,' I replied archly. She turned away. Never let a day go by without making an enemy, is what I say, even if it's only a woman.

'You have made a conquest,' murmured Dryden in my ear.

'Have you any whisky in your rooms?'

'Only Chivas Regal.'

'Then let us go there.'

His room are the best set in Scone: there are *boiseries* and a pair of bookcases only rivalled by those in the Pepysian Library in Cambridge and a certain house in Sussex, whose name escapes me. Moreover, he has a bathroom of his own, an unheard-of luxury in Scone, where the *corpus sanum* – or *vile* – runs a very bad second to the *mens sana*. (The story goes that, long ago, when it was first proposed in the College *concilium* that bathrooms should be provided for undergraduates, an ancient life-fellow protested in piping tones that the lads couldn't possibly need such things: 'Why, they're only here for eight weeks at a time!' But then came the strange late-Victorian epoch, shot through with obscure guilts, when the English – whom Erasmus had named as the grubbiest race in Europe – found that nothing would do but that they must scrub themselves from head to foot whenever they could spare a moment from smartening up Fuzzy-Wuzzy and other Breeds Without The Law. There are three times as many undergraduates in Scone now, and the bathrooms are just as few, but now no one seems to mind any more.)

'Well now,' said Dryden, when the beaded bubbles of Chivas Regal were winking at the brim, 'I gather that you have taken up the worship of Wicca and find that it compels you to range around the countryside stealing ducks.'

'No, no, *no*, John, you must have mis-heard me on the telephone: duck was not the word I used and it's not me at all, it's some other chap.'

'That's what they all say,' kindly, sadly, 'but tell me all about your, ah, *friend*.'

He was, of course, teasing me, and he knew very well that I knew that he knew that I knew he was, if I make myself clear. I started from the beginning, for I am not skilled in narrative, and went on to the end. It electrified him; he sat up straight and poured profligate drinks for both of us.

'Well, I do call that splendid,' he chortled, rubbing his big, pink hands together. (Can you chortle, by the way? I can giggle and snigger but chortling and chuckling are quite out of my range. It's a dying art, some modern Cecil Sharp should go around recording the last few practitioners.)

'How do you mean, *splendid?*' I asked when the chortling was over. 'My friends and their wives don't think it's a bit splendid, I can tell you.'

'Of course, of course. Forgive me. My heart goes out to them. What I meant was that in the midst of all this bogus satanist revival that's going on it's rather gratifying to a scholar that a serious recrudescence of the real tradition is taking place in just the sort of base and backward community where one had hoped the last embers of the Old Religion might, indeed, still be glowing.' (What lovely sentences he constructs. I wish I could write one half so well as he talks.)

'Yes,' he went on, 'it's all there: the desecration of Easter for a start. It probably starts at Easter every year, you know, but few victims of ravishment ever complain to the police for reasons which doubtless spring to your mind; the counter-accusations and cross-examinations at the trial can be most shaming in cases of this kind. Moreover, the sturdy native Jersey women would, for the most part, appreciate that they had been singled out for what amounts to a religious rite – it is just as if an Englishwoman were told by the Vicar that it was her turn to do the flowers in Church for Easter: a nuisance but an honour. Do you follow me?'

'So far I'm abreast of you.'

'Then there's the inverted cross –'

'What inverted cross?' I interrupted.

'Why the one on the witchmaster's belly, to be sure; hadn't you twigged? The ladies would naturally have thought it to be a sword and it may well have been pointed at the top to represent the woven crosses they give out in churches on Palm Sunday, this combining an insult to Christianity and an ancient sex-symbol. Do you happen to know what colour it was?'

'I'm afraid not.'

'Try and find out, there's a dear boy. And find out whether it left any paint marks: it would be quite splendid – that is to say, very interesting – if it proved not to be painted at all but pyschosomatically produced. The body can do wonderful things, as I'm sure you know, under hypnosis or auto-induced hysteria. The stigmata, of course, springs to mind, and levitation: there's far too much evidence to dismiss.'

I shot him a furtive look. He was displaying just a little too much zeal for his hobby-horse; committedness is next to pottiness, especially in elderly dons.

'You are thinking that I am riding my hobby-horse a little hard,' he said – beaming at my guilty start – 'and I confess to finding the subject almost unwholesomely engaging.'

I mumbled a few disclaimers which he waved aside.

'The words "hobby-horse" and "levitation",' he resumed, 'bring us to the next point, the riding-jollop.'

'How's that again?'

'Riding-jollop. There are many names for it but the formulae are all very similar. It is the pungent mixture a witch smears on his or her body before going to the Sabbat. The greasy base stops up the pores and thus subtly alters the body's chemistry, another ingredient reddens and excites the skin, while the bizarre stench – added to the guilty knowledge of what the jollop is made of – heightens the witch's impure excitement to the point where he *knows* that he can fly. In the case of she-witches, a canter round the kitchen with the broom-stick between her legs adds a little extra elation, no doubt.'

'No doubt,' I agreed.

'Whether any of them succeeds in flying is an open question: it is their certain conviction that they *can* that is important. Do you care to know the ingredients of the jollop?'

'No thanks. My dinner sits a little queasily on my stomach as it is.'

'You are probably wise. By the bye, did you happen to notice in your local paper that any new-born babies had been missing shortly before Easter?'

'Whatever has that –?' I said. 'Oh, yes, I see; how very nasty. Do they really? No, I wouldn't have noticed that sort of thing. People shouldn't have babies if they're not prepared to look after them is what *my* old nanny used to say.'

'You might just check, dear boy. It would have been in the dark of the moon before Easter. But of course it might have been the sort of baby which doesn't get recorded. You know, "ditch-delivered of a drab".'

'Just so. "Eye of newt and blood of bat".'

'Precisely. But *try*. Now we come to the toads. I've always felt that Jersey's particular fondness for toads might indicate that it was perhaps the last outpost of the Old Religion, for the toad was easily the most popular Familiar for witches. The warts on its skin, you see, remind one of the extra nipples which every she-witch was supposed to have and that goes back (am I boring you, dear boy? How is your glass?) that goes back to the polymastia or superfluity of breasts of the ancients. I need not remind you of Diana of the Ephesians, who must have looked like a fir-cone, as dear Jim Cabell pointed out.'

'But I thought that the cat was the favourite familiar? I mean, Grimalkin and all that?'

'A wide-spread and pardonable error, Mortdecai. First, you see, by the time of the great witch-hunts of the seventeenth century – best-known because they were politically inspired you see, for there was a sort of suggestion of confrontation between the High Church and Papist Cavaliers, who, oddly, were supposed to more or less tolerate the Old Religion (perhaps they knew how to use it?) and the Puritans, who chose to see witchcraft as an extension of Rome; by this time, I say, the serious witches had gone very thoroughly underground and the only ones left on the surface were a few old crones practising a little Goëtic magic to help their friendly neighbours and to smarten up their petty persecutors.

'Now, the rules of witch-finding were that a witch always had a devil's nipple, by which she could give suck to her Familiar. They used to tie the poor old biddies up and watch them, certain that when the Familiar became hungry it would come around for its rations. Most old ladies, to this day, own a pussy-cat – and most old ladies tend to have a wart or a mole or two, this is common knowledge. You see? Moreover, there is an ancient confusion here, for the word "cat" used also to mean a stick, such as witches might ride on. (Perhaps you played "tip-cat" as a child? No?) In short, you may be sure that the toad, not the cat, is the most popular and effective familiar. "Was" perhaps I should say. Or rather "was deemed to be",' he ended lamely. The warmth of his defence of the toad led me to suspect uneasily that a close search of his quarters would pretty certainly reveal a comfortable vivarium somewhere, bursting with the little batrachians.

'Well, John,' I said heavily, 'that's all quite riveting and I'm more than grateful for the insight you have supplied into the way this awful chap's mind works and so forth, but now I feel we should be thinking about remedies and things, don't you? I mean, to you it's an entrancing piece of living folk-lore, no doubt, but over there in Jersey two of my good friends' wives have been horribly assaulted and one of them, if I'm not mistaken, is in jeopardy of grave mental illness. I mean, conversation of old customs and so on I'm all for, and I'd be the first to join a society for preserving the Piddle-Hinton Cruddy Dance etc., but you wouldn't actually subscribe to a fund for the preservation of the practice of *thuggee*, would you? To my mind, this Johnny should be stopped. Or am I being old-fashioned?'

'Oh Mortdecai, Mortdecai,' he said – how funny it sounded, sort of hyphenated – 'you were always impatient with things of the spirit. I remember you were rusticated in your second year, were you not, for –'

'Yes.'

'And again in your last year for –'

'Yes, John, but is this to the point?'

'Yes, of course, *no*, you're quite right. Remedies are what you must have, I see that, I really do. Now, let me think. We shall assume that the violator is (and I have not a scrap of *doubt* that he is), properly versed in all the side-knowledge of his dread religion. Therefore, he can be daunted in several ways. First and easiest, common salt (rock-salt is better) sprinkled liberally on all entrances into the room; door-sills, window-sills, hearth-stones and even transoms and ventilation-louvres. Second, garlands of wild garlic festooned around those same apertures are reckoned sovereign, but you would be hard put to find wild garlic in Jersey, or anywhere, at this time of the year and its smell is really quite beastly.'

'I know. I have tried to eat wild duck which have been feeding off it. The very dustbin rejects them.'

'Just so. Third, and this has not been known to fail, the person fearful of visitations from a witch or warlock should go to bed clutching a crucifix made either of wood, or, much better, of either or both of the two noble metals – gold and silver: the very best of all is a cross made of one of the hardest woods such as ebony or lignum vitae and inlaid with silver and gold. He or she should memorize a simple cantrip to recite to the emissary of the Desired – chrm – that is to say, the *Evil* One, which I shall now dictate to you.'

'Look John, forgive me, but I don't think we are approaching this on the right lines. For one thing, I've no intention of distributing cantrips and costly crucifixes to every rapable woman in the Parish of St Magloire. For another, we don't want just to keep the beggar out of our bedrooms, we want to catch him if possible – kill him if that becomes necessary – but at all costs to stop him for good.'

'Oh dear, that is a very different matter indeed. You really mustn't kill him if you can help it, you know; he may very well be the last living receptacle of some extremely ancient knowledge, we have no way of guessing whether he has yet initiated a successor to the Black Goatskin. No, no, you must try not to kill him. You might, in any case, find it a little difficult, heh, heh.'

'I know; I'm thinking of ordering a box of silver bullets.'

'My word, Mortdecai,' he cried, clapping his hands merrily, 'you always were a resourceful fellow, even the Dean said as much when you almost won the Newdigate with a thousand lines lifted from Shelley's *Cenci*. Did you get rusticated that time?'

'No, I played the "youthful prank" gambit. The Proctors hit me for fifty pounds. My father paid. I threatened to marry a barmaid if he didn't.'

'There you are again, you see. *Resourceful*. But no, try to avoid killing him. As to capturing him, I really cannot offer any suggestions. He will be endued with Fiendish cunning, you understand, and will have all sorts of other resources which we cannot gauge, it really depends on whether he's been to Chorazin or not.' He seemed to be addressing himself.

'Chorazin?'

'Ah, yes, well, just a scholarly aside, not to the point really. It's a place mentioned in the Bible, just a few mounds today – or so they tell me – and one goes there, or rather chaps like your witchmaster go there, to complete their education, so to speak.'

'A sort of Sabbatical?' I prompted.

'Just so, ha ha. Very good. Yes, they went there to, as it were, pay their respects to Someone; it was called the *Peregrinatio Nigra*, the Black Pilgrimage, you know.'

'Thank you,' I said.

'I'm sorry, dear boy, I had forgotten that undergraduates used once to have a little Latin. Now; catching this chap; I honestly cannot think of a method which would have much hope of success. I suppose one could leave an attractive young woman unguarded in a spinney or copse – but who would volunteer to be the bait? One could hardly *tether* her, could one, it would look suspicious. No, I think your best plan is to fight him on his own terms and bar him from your neighbourhood for good – make him cry *vicisti*, which –'

'Thank you,' I said.

'Oh dear, I'm sorry. Yes; you must give him a whiff of grape-shot and let him know that he's outgunned; he will give you best, I'm sure, and turn his talents elsewhere. In short; you must have a Mass said.'

'A *Mass*?'

'A Satanic Mass, naturally. One of the real, juicy ones. You will then be, as it were, under the protection of his, ah, Supervisor, and he'll have no choice but to leave you and yours alone. You might say it will put the fear of the Devil into him, heh heh.'

I found myself in a quandary. How real was the witchcraft element in our rapist? Dryden, the top scholar in the field, clearly was satisfied that the man was a dangerous adept – but then, how potty was Dryden? Could I go back to Jersey and tell George and Sam that what we needed was a Black Mass? On the other hand, what was on the other hand? Lying out night after night in damp potato fields, hoping that the chap would blunder into one's arms? And what would that prove? Or lie in wait in the wardrobes of likely victims' bedrooms? Quite absurd; moreover, if the Beast of Jersey was any guide, our man would have been watching the chosen house for hours, perhaps days, and rapable women abound in Jersey – if you don't object to legs like bedroom jugs.

'Very well,' I said at length. 'We'll give the Satanic Mass a crack of the whip; I'm sure you know best.'

'Capital, capital; I always said that you were a capable man. I remember saying so to the Dean when –'

'*Yes*, John. Now, how does one go about arranging that sort of beano?'

'Of course, let us be practical. First, we must select a suitable Mass. What? Oh, goodness, yes, there are many. Many. By far the best is the Medici Mass, it never fails, it is positively and finally lethal, but there are no reliable texts of its *Graduale* to be had – all corrupt, every one of them, such a shame. In any case, the *Missa Mediciensis* involves the dismemberment of a beautiful young boy, which I fancy you might think a horrid *waste* – or am I thinking of a chap with a name like yours who came up in the same year as you?'

'Bonfiglioli?' I asked.

'Yes, that was he. Sorry, Mortdecai. And in any case, unless your Jersey witchmaster is uncommonly learned he may not have heard of that particular ritual and it is of the greatest importance that he should *know* what forces you are throwing against him. You see that, don't you?'

'It makes sense, certainly.'

'Ah. Yes. Now I have it: the very one, the *Messe de Saint Sécaire*.'

'And who, pray, was Saint Sécaire?'

'Well, he probably wasn't a saint; in fact he may never have been what you or I would call a *person* even, but his name is known everywhere from the Basque country to the Lowlands-Low amongst the sort of people who know about that sort of thing.'

'You speak in riddles, John.'

'Naturally. Now, you will need only three things: first, an unfrocked priest, for the ritual demands it. I know the very chap: he teaches in a prep-school in Eastbourne and is both reliable and cheap. It will only cost you his steamer-fare – chaps like that never travel by *air* for obvious reasons – and a few bottles of Pastis; some clean straw to sleep-it-off on and perhaps a couple of fivers as a going-away present.'

'I have a servant called Jock who will anticipate his every need.'

'Splendid. Then, you will need a text of the Ritual. There is only one sound copy in existence: it is in the incomparable library of a ridiculous old lecher called Lord Dunromin. I shall give you a letter to him: if you grovel a bit and pretend to believe that he is – as he loves to think – the wickedest man in England, he may be persuaded to let you have a sight of the manuscript and copy out such parts as differ most grossly from the *Ordinale*. Pay particular attention to the peculiarities of the *Introit*, the *Kyrie* and the, well, the *equivalent* of the *Agnus Dei*.'

I scribbled some notes on my shirt-cuff, for I knew that such an anachronism would please him.

'Finally,' he went on, 'and this may be a trifle difficult, you will need a ruined church which has been deconsecrated – preferably one with a toad dwelling beneath the altar. Do you suppose you could manage that, eh?'

'As a matter of fact there is just such a place in Jersey; it's called La Hougue Bie. An abandoned sixteenth-century chapel stands on a mound which contains one of the finest megalithic pre-Christian tombs in Europe. I am sure toads abound there but, should they be absent, it would be the work of a moment – and indeed a kindness – to introduce them to such a haven.'

'Excellent! You are sure that the chapel has been deconsecrated? No? Then you must make sure. You could, of course, *desecrate* it yourself, but it's not really the same thing and you might find the process a little *trying*. There would be, perhaps *annoyances*, in a place of such antiquity. I'm sure you understand me.'

'Only too well.'

'Then I think we have covered everything and you, no doubt, will be eager to get to bed.'

I didn't sleep awfully well, perhaps I'd eaten something which disagreed with me. Once I awoke in a panic: some frightful cantrip had been chanting itself inside my head, but it was only an innocent verse from *The Wind in the Willows*:

'The clever men at Oxford
Know all that there is to be knowed.
But they none of them know one half as much
As intelligent Mr Toad!'

I couldn't understand why it had frightened me so much.

8

By the One who may don the black raiment
Of the Goat which was never a goat
Now come I to exact the dread payment
For the lie that was born in the throat.

In a High Place, to decent men nameless,
Guarding ever the Branchless Rod,
Lies a thing which is pallid and shameless,
Ill with lust for a frightful god.

O, Ashtaroth, darling of Sidon,
Loathly Chemosh, who raves in the night,
I bring the red kiss which shall widen,
For thy servant, a way to thy sight.

Asmodeus

Dryden was kind enough to take me to my train in the morning.
He drives fast and decisively but he has his own little theories about
how to deal with other road-users and the drive was not enjoyable. I
once diffidently pointed out to him that we were entering a one-way
street: he beamed at me, an index finger laid against his nose, and
cried:

'Ah, but *which* way? We are not *told*, you see!' This savouring
of his triumph led him to mount the pavement, so I let the rest
of the trip unwind itself without further comment – and with my

eyes closed. I remember wishing that I knew a cantrip or two to recite.

How Dryden puts you on a train is as follows. He stalls his elderly Wolseley on the 'TAXIS ONLY' sign, leaps out, pops the jack under the sill and gives it a couple of turns. This, he finds, gives him some twenty minutes' grace. Then he strikes a Joan of Arc stance, umbrella pointing to the empyrean, and cries 'Porter!' again and again, in tones of increasing pitch and theatricality, until every sensate being within earshot is frantically seeking porters for the poor gentleman and you, his passenger, are quite magenta-hued with shame and chagrin.

When a porter is at last thrust forward by the compassionate throng, rubbing his red eyes and peering about him in the unaccustomed daylight like a spider evicted from a Scotchman's purse, Dryden takes him firmly by the arm.

'This gentleman,' he explains, laying a forefinger on your waistcoat, 'has to travel to London. It is most important.' He gently turns the porter to the East and points along the up-line. '*London*,' he repeats. 'Pray see to it, and you are to keep this for yourself.' With this he turns away, his duty done, he has *looked after you*. The porter gapes at the tiny coin pressed into his palm, but his sense of humour prevails and he takes your bag with a half-bow and offers to carry your umbrella, too. He leads you to the ticket-office and explains to the clerk just what it is you need. When he has got you into a corner-seat-facing-the-engine in a first-class compartment and has straightened the anti-macassar, he looks around as though seeking a travelling-rug to tuck about your knees. You over-tip him grossly, I need scarcely say. You know that later you may find it all most amusing, but just now you want to spit.

As the train gave a preliminary lurch I rose and looked out of the window. Dryden was on the platform – perhaps he had been asking the guard to *look after* me. But no, he was hurrying along, bobbing up and down to scan first-class compartments.

'Hoy!' I cried, waving. He broke into a canter, but the train was a match for him.

'Turnips!' he seemed to cry as he lost ground. '*Turnips!*'

'Turnips?' I roared, but by then we were out of earshot.

'What the devil does he mean, "turnips"?' I mused aloud as I sat down. Unnoticed by me, the compartment had filled. Opposite me, a respectable old woman, who in the ordinary way would have offered me a religious tract or two, was offering me the nastiest look you can imagine. I played the only possible counter-move: I fished out my silver pocket-flask and took a swig. It did her a power of good. In the diagonally opposite corner sat an albino priest, who looked up from his Breviary to give me a saintly, sloppy smile, as much to say that, if my DTs became intolerable, he would wrestle in prayer with me. The fourth corner was occupied by an obvious merchant-banker – try as they will, they cannot disguise those shifty eyes, that rat-trap mouth. He was working on *The Times* crossword, but to the exclusion of turnips, pocket-flasks and everything else: it is this power of concentration which singles out a man for the merchant-banking trade.

The old lady continued to stare fixedly at the tasteful sepia view of Tewkesbury Abbey, above my head, perhaps willing it to fall on me. I must say I rather liked the cut of her jib, while her clear distaste for the Mortdecais of this world did her credit. I have often thought of acquiring an old lady to keep as a pet. They'd be of little use for a shooting man, of course – no nose, d'you see, and useless over marshy ground – but for the town-dweller they are incomparable. I cannot understand why people pay fortunes for nasty cats and dogs who leave puddles and puppies and kittens all over the place when, for nothing but the cost of her keep, one can have an old lady, clean as a new pin and warranted past child-bearing. Old ladies can help one, too, in countless little ways such as marking shirts and arranging flowers: tricks which few dogs and no cats can be taught. True, they can be noisy, but I imagine that a few cuts of the whip would break them of this – or I dare say they could be surgically muted for a trifling sum. True, too, they are a wasting asset and, if you had the bad luck to pick a poor doer, she might become bed-ridden and linger on for years; a misery to herself and a burden to others. I suppose the thing to do would be to leave, pointedly, a bottle of brandy and a loaded revolver on her commode, as one used to do with a Guards Officer who'd been caught with his fingers in the tambourine.

People shouldn't keep people if they're not prepared to look after them, don't you agree?

London, of course, was hell: it gets worse every day. I pine for the slow, placid, pastoral way of life they still enjoy in New York. Leaving my bag at the Connaught I pottered about until luncheon, having a chat with a shirt-maker here, a haberdasher there and a boot-maker in t'other place. Then I refreshed myself with oysters at a place whose name I shall not tell you, for I do not wish you to go there: you would not like it and there is barely enough room for me.

When it was time to call on Lord Dunromin I made my way to his club, which is one of those ancient, hateful clubs called Bogg's or Crutt's or Frigg's – you know the sort of thing. This particular sink, known to other clubmen as the 'Senior Lechers', is a *bad* place. Members must be old, contemptuous, well-born but spurned by decent society, and expensively dressed in quiet bad taste.

The club porter flicked an eye over my clothes, glanced at the label inside my hat and admitted that the Earl was in the Smoking Room and might well be expecting me. Did I know where the Smoking Room was? I looked at him stonily – I've been squashed by experts. He led me to the Smoking Room.

The Earl didn't get up. He has been the wickedest man in England for years: he now hopes to be the rudest, too. The All-England selectors have long had their corporate eye on him. He looked at my clothes. The two-second glance contrived to embody genuine embarrassment, suppressed amusement and feigned compassion. It was well done; he was in a different league from the hall-porter. I didn't wait to be asked, I sat down.

'How do you do?' I said.

'Oink,' he replied

This brought a waiter. Lord Dunromin loudly ordered 'a glass of the cheese port' for me, while pouring himself something from a decanter at his elbow.

He turned to the window to sneer at a passing omnibus. I studied him. His face was a shade or two darker than my port, a shade or two paler than his. Viewed through my glass, his features became quite black, only the eyes gleaming redly.

'Well,' he said at last, rounding on me, 'are you going to interview me or not?'

This threw me somewhat, but it seemed a small thing to do if it would give him pleasure.

'Of course. Sorry. Now, how long have you considered yourself to be the wickedest man in England?' I asked.

'*Europe*. And I don't like that word "considered". And, since I was fifteen. Sacked from all three Public Schools, both Universities, four clubs and the Foreign Office.'

'My word. And to what do you attribute your success?'

'Lust. What they call sex nowadays. Workin' me wicked will on school matrons, housemaids, chaps' wives, daughters; that sort of thing.'

'Have you enjoyed it all, and have you given it up now?'

'Enjoyed, yes, every minute. And given up now, yes again. Too easy, too tiring, interferes with the television. Watching it, I mean, not the reception, har har.'

I gave him a perfunctory smile.

'Too *easy*?' I asked, as rudely as I could.

'Nowadays, yes, definitely. Look at the way these young fellers with the awful hair get away with it: all pursued by *herds* of young women, lowing with lust, *beggin'* for it. Why, when I was a boy we were proud to get even an ugly bit of crumpet, but look at 'em now – have to fight the gels off. *Pretty* gels, too, ugly ones seem all to have vanished. It's like the policemen, I suppose,' he added cryptically.

'But since those early days, Lord Dunromin, you've never found it difficult, have you?'

'Certainly not. Certainly not. Just the reverse. Indeed, I've never understood why men of our generation' – I started: surely he didn't mean to include *me*? – 'ever found seducin' difficult. I mean, we few really competent seducers can never feel vain about our prowess for we know how absurdly, how *insultingly* simple the whole thing is. I mean, to start with, women are nearly all astonishingly stupid – you must know that – it's hard to believe, sometimes, that they belong to the same *species* as you and me. Do you know that nine out of ten of 'em cannot tell margarine from butter? It's a fact, I promise you, I've seen it proved again and again on the television.

'Then there's another thing in the seducer's favour: almost all women, whether they know it or not, are actually dyin' to be seduced – it's important to them, d'you see? Some want it because they're not married, some because they are; some because they're really too old for it and some because they're too young, heh heh; beautiful women need it to flatter their vanity and ugly ones need reassurance; a very few need it because they're over-sexed but these are the exceptions – most of them are really quite frigid but they go on assuming the horizontal in the hope that their next mount will be Mr Right himself, who will at last waken them and induce in their absurd insides the magical moment they have all read so much about in the garbage they all read. In short, I doubt whether there's such a thing as an unseducible woman in the world. Tragic thing is, not one in a thousand is worth your powder and shot. *Experto crede*. Older ones, by and large, are the best value: they always think it might be their last time, d'you see.'

I'd had quite enough of this, it sounded like an editorial in the *Boy's Own Paper* or an epilogue by a YMCA Warden, but, just as I was about to break in, the Earl was back in his stride, his pink and bulging eyes fixed on the ceiling, his voice sonorous.

'Any man armed with this simple knowledge is invincible: he can cut a great swathe through the female ranks like an Attila as long as his glands hold out. He need not be handsome, glib or rich (although, a motor-car is considered pretty essential these days), indeed, it often rather helps to be poor, scrawny and tongue-tied. Even the portly need not despair, for experienced gels dread the assault of a bony pelvis and many of them associate us chubbier chaps with their fathers, for whom they have usually nurtured a furtive, pubescent passion.

'As I say, the mere knowledge that it's a bowler's wicket should be enough to give the would-be stud all the advantage he needs, but while I'm on the subject I might as well dish out a few practical tips for which I have no further use. Are you taking notes?'

'Well, no,' I said, 'as a matter of fact I –'

'Then do so. Hey, waiter, bring a glass of brandy for my er, for this er, gentleman. No, no, *you* know, that *other* brandy. Now, listen attentively.

'(A),' he said, pronouncing the brackets perfectly, 'you must flatter the target continuously and as grossly as you can without actually giving yourself the giggles – you simply cannot spread the butter on too thick. Never mind if they don't believe it, the subject will nonetheless fascinate them.

'(B); Remember that women *feel the cold*: I cannot stress this too strongly. A woman sitting in a draught is a mere inanimate lump, while a woman with warm hands and feet is an army with its flank turned – a battle half-won. See to it.

'(C); Generations of readers of *Peg's Paper* have been taught that the way to win a man's heart is to encourage him to talk about himself. So *never* talk about yourself at all; this restraint will so craze them with curiosity that they will often surrender their chaste treasure in an effort to win your confidence.

'(D); Fill them to the brim with hot, rich, *food* at frequent intervals, this is both cheaper and better than alcohol, which makes them weep or vomit or behave in other dreary ways. Food induces in them a delicious languor, most conducive to venery. Try some today – you can get it at Fortnum's, of course, and Paxton and Whitfields and, er, Fortnum's . . . places like that.

'(E); Before making the final assault on a woman's virtue, at all costs persuade her to remove her shoes. This can easily be achieved without any appearance of impropriety, yet she will instantly feel pleasantly undressed and vaguely surrendered. (She will also feel *happier*, for her shoes are almost certainly a size too small.) Encourage her to remove the rest of her clothes herself, a little at a time; this puts you in a very strong position indeed.

'(F); Calm her fears continually during the penultimate stage; speak soothing, meaningless words to her as you would to a spirited horse, particularly if she is at all religious. If necessary, you can explain to her that you are not really doing it to her at all: she will believe this against the evidence of her senses if it is put to her reasonably. Indeed, this is sometimes the only way with the very devout ones.

'(G); Take particular care not to ladder stockings, tear shoulder-straps or disarrange hair-styles, particularly if the target is a *poor* gel. Virginities are for giving away, after all, but a good hair-do can cost as much as two or three guineas, did you know that?

' "All this is all very well" I hear you say' – I opened my mouth and then shut it resignedly – ' "and we're damned grateful and so forth, but what about getting rid of them when we've lost interest and have our eyes on a bit of fresh? How about a few tips on that, eh?" "Ah," I reply,' he boomed on, ' "there you have me", for a woman scorned is a pretty adhesive thing and a serious threat to the environment, as they say nowadays. There's no fixed rule. Sometimes you can, so to speak, recycle her by fobbing her off on a less gifted friend but I usually find that the best thing is to be frank and manly about it: explain to the subject in kindly words that she has been but the plaything of an idle hour and that now you propose to cast her aside like a soiled glove. Some will acidly reply that "there's plenty of fresh further up" but most will be so furiously vexed that their love for you will vanish like a rat up a gutter, and they will make their own way to the soiled-glove bin at high speed.'

He chuckled fatly, wheezed, started to cough alarmingly. When he had learned to breathe again I thanked him for his lecturette and reminded him that the subject of my call was yet to be broached.

'How d'you mean?' he snorted. 'Given you enough for a dozen articles.'

'You have indeed, but I'm not a writer, you know, although I may turn to it if I should ever fall on evil times.'

'But you *are* the young feller from the *Gazette* Diary, aren't you?' He was glaring at me with deep suspicion.

'Good God, no!' I cried, shocked for the first time today. 'What a dreadful . . .! I've never been so . . .!'

'Well, who the devil are you, then, and how did you get in here?'

We sorted it out after a while and soon I had wrung from him his slow consent to my having a sight of the abominable Mass.

As I left the Club, I remarked an inky wretch, shaking with alcohol, whining and carneying to the Hall Porter: I wished him joy of his interview.

The Earl's house was but a step away. It was one of those Belgravian massifs with fronts like old Euston Station. The servants in such houses are still English (where do they *find* them?) and the step at the front door is so designed that the butler, when he opens the door, looms over you dauntingly. The one who loomed in answer to my ring was a fine, well-grown specimen who had clearly eaten up every scrap of his gruel when he was a nursling butler. His manner was civil, if condescending, but his eye said that he knew all about gents who wanted to read in the master's library. He stripped me of hat, coat, and umbrella with the ease of a skilled craftsman and led me along a gallery of statuary towards the library. The sculpture was astonishingly fine and of a fruitiness not usually seen outside the rare Supplement to the *Museo Borbonico*. I could not resist pausing in front of an unusually explicit 'Leda and the Swan': I understood at last how the swan had managed the trick. You'd never believe it.

At the end of the gallery there was a sort of vestibule lit only by a concealed ray of light playing on a terminal figure of Pan – the Tree with one Branch – which, as we passed, suddenly became a drinking-fountain in the most dramatic and peculiar way. The butler shunted me into the library, indicated the librarian's desk and left me to my own devices – or solitary vices, as I dare say he thought. I ambled down an alley of shelves crammed with a bewildering accumulation of priceless, richly-bound filth and rubbish. Nerciat rubbed shoulders with D.H. Lawrence, the Large Paper set of de Sade (Illustrated by Austin Osman Spare) jostled an incunable *Hermes Trismegistus*, and ten different editions of *L'Histoire d'O* were piquant bedfellows to De la Bodin's *Démonomanie des Sorciers*.

The Earl's librarian was a pretty slip of a girl with circles under her eyes. She didn't look as though she got much time for reading.

'Are you *Green Girls in Paris*?' she asked. I thought about it.

'No, I'm more the Mass of S. Sécaire, really.'

'Ah, yes. I've put it out for you. It's in a nice plain seventeenth-century cursive without contractions, so you shouldn't have much trouble. I've also put out a plain Latin Missal; it'll save you a lot of time, you need only copy out the variant passages.'

'Thanks, you're very kind.'

'Not at all. That will be fifty pounds, please.'

'Fifty pounds? But surely, that's unheard of between fellow scholars. I mean, common courtesy . . .'

'The Earl is not a scholar and common courtesy is outside his sphere of interest. He has just instructed me on the telephone that the fee is fifty pounds and that you have already had – I think he said racing tips – worth more than that.'

I reflected that George and Sam were sharing out-of-pocket expenses so I coughed up, although with ill grace. She wouldn't accept a Diner's Club card, she wouldn't take a cheque, but she would send a footman round to Carlos Place, where squat the proprietors of my overdraft, buttock-deep in pieces-of-eight. The box-office formalities over, I spent a long and disgusting hour or two copying out the relevant passages of the Mass in a silence broken only by the fidgeting and snickering of the man who had arrived to read *Green Girls in Paris* – an aged person whose thoughts should have been on higher things.

'Faugh,' I thought.

Then I had a bath and a few drinks and things at my own club – a temple of light compared with Dunromin's hell-hole – and flew back to Jersey.

Jock met me at the airport in the 'Big Jam-Jar' as he calls the Rolls. The news was not good. Johanna had not been raped but the wife of a friendly doctor, living a mile from us, had. A bogus call to a road-accident had lured her husband away. The rapist had unscrewed the bulb from the light over the porch and rung the door-bell. The other details were as before.

'And I found out from the new gardener, the old geezer, what this sword on the belly means,' said Jock.

'So have I,' I said. 'Did he seem to connect it with Easter at all?'

'Nah. He kept on saying it was because of the Pakis, which is daft, innit, 'cos there's no Pakis on the Island except them shops in St Helier, where they sell the duty-free watches.'

'Jock, the French word for Easter is *Pâques*: in the toothless mouth of an ancient Jerseyman it would, indeed, sound just like "Pakis".'

'Well, there you are, aren't you?'

'Yes. What's the word on Mrs Sam?'

'Well, not great. I hear she got worse and they took her off to the mainland 'smorning. Mr Davenant's been ringing up to find when you're expected back; he sounds in a bit of a mess.'

'Oh dear, do you think he'll be round this evening?'

'No, he was ringing up from England. He'll be back tomorrow morning, wants to come to lunch.'

'So he shall,' I said. 'So he shall. But, more to the point, is there anything for my supper tonight?'

'Yeah, I got you a nice little treat of kidneys done in wine and mustard on fried bread with a few sauté potatoes all garlicky.'

'The very thing!' I cried. 'I trust you will join me, Jock?'

'Too bloody right I will, Mr Charlie.'

9

What adders came to shed their coats?
What coiled obscene
Small serpents with soft stretching throats
Caressed Faustine?

Faustine

Spring was infesting the air in no uncertain fashion the next day and I awoke, for once, with a feeling of well-being and an urge to go for long country walks. Needing to share this feeling I marched into Johanna's room and flung the curtains wide.

'How can you *lie* there,' I cried, 'with the sun streaming in and all the world going a-Maying?'

I didn't quite catch the two words she mumbled in reply, but they were not 'good morning'.

Soon I was downstairs, stamping about and disrupting the household by demanding a proper breakfast instead of my usual alka-seltzer and dexedrin. It was all quite delicious – porridge and kippers and bacon and eggs and toast and marmalade except that the last mouthful of bacon turned to ashes in my mouth when Jock dumped the mail beside my plate, for on top of the pile lay one of those dread, buff-coloured envelopes marked OHMS. I quaked as I read. Her Majesty's Inspector of Taxes noted with feigned puzzlement that, according to my Tax Return for the previous year, my expenditure had exceeded my income; what, then, he asked with concern, had I been living on? He managed to suggest, although not in so many words, that he was *worried* about me. Was I *eating* properly?

I wrote him a cheque for an entirely irrelevant £111.99 which would fox the computer for a month or two, then I spent a happy ten minutes erasing the name and address on the letter and typing in a fresh one, re-directing it to my new-found friend, the lady-don of Scone College. *Share* the good things of life is what I always say. We shall pass this way but once, you know.

George arrived before Sam and told me about the rapist's latest exploit. He had telephoned the victim's husband that morning for they were friends and had confirmed the gossip that all the nasty magical trappings had been in evidence. There was still no description worth the name: the doctor's wife had tried, sturdy lass, to snatch the man's mask off while he was most deeply preoccupied with his task but he had immediately stunned her with a blow to the temple with the side of his clenched fist – a surprisingly kind blow and, it seemed to me, rather a knowledgeable one. All she could say with certainty was that he was strong, well-built and perhaps in early middle age.

'It seems she's not too shaken up,' George went on, 'been a nurse, you see, in the Army. Hard to shock those lassies. She's more furious than anything else, I gather.'

'And how's Sonia?'

'Oh, well, she still plays up a bit when she remembers to, but on the whole I'd say she was pretty well recovered. Not like poor Vi, she seems to have been knocked for six. By the way, be careful what you say to Sam, he's taking it very hard. Quite murderous.'

Sam entered as though on cue; paler than usual, less kempt, a humourless look on his face. He swallowed half the drink I gave him before sitting down.

'Well?' was what he snapped when he did sit down.

'No, Sam,' I said, 'nothing is well and I should prefer to discuss things after we have all refreshed ourselves a little, don't you agree?' He only glared, not agreeing at all, so I went about on the other tack.

'But first,' I said, 'if you feel like talking about it, we are anxious to know how things are with Violet. Where is she, for instance?'

He finished his drink with a second swallow. It had been really quite a stiff drink for lunch-time. I made him another, giving myself a touch more freedom with the soda-water this time.

'Awful bloody place near Virginia Water,' he said at last. 'Not the big Virginia Water place but one of the other nursing homes round there which specialize in what they like to call Nervous Disorders. Frightful Victorian barracks in Revived Lombardic Gothic; rather like Manchester Town Hall but with rhododendrons and monkey-puzzle trees all around it. Pink, portly consultants flouncing down the corridors, each with comet's tail of adoring matrons and sisters and nurses and lavatory attendants trailing behind them, like little boys following a horse with a shovel and bucket for the good of their father's roses. Foul bitch of a receptionist broke it to me gently that the charges were £60 a day then watched me narrowly to see if I winced. "Payable fortnightly in advance," she went on. I gave her a cheque for eight hundred and forty pounds and she said that "doctor" would probably see Violet that night. I said that for eight hundred and forty pounds "doctor" would bloody well see her there and then. She looked at me as though I'd farted in church. We had *words* then, and I won, although I had to apologize for saying "bloody".'

'I pity the prawn which pits its feeble wits against you,' I quoted. His glare told me that flippancy was not suited to the mood of the moment. (I can't help it you know: some unkind friend once showed me a passage in a Medical Encyclopedia.

'MORIA:' it said – '*A morbid determination to make supposedly witty remarks. Sometimes occurring in people with frontal growths of the brain.*')

' "Doctor",' he went on, 'proved to be a Viennese Jewess –'

'Just like Johanna,' I reminded him brightly, before he could put his foot in it.

'Not at all like Johanna. This was Baudelaire's original "*affreuse juive*", she looked like a malevolent sack of potatoes. But surprisingly civilized and clearly on top of her job. She listened to the receptionist's account of things with her hands folded in her lap, she didn't look at her once but the receptionist was choking back tears in no time. Amazing old bitch. She had that kind of cheerful callousness you only find in the very best doctors: I've no faith in the grave, considerate ones: I knew too many medical students at Oxford. Then she took me up to her office and asked about Violet's people and of course I had to tell her about "Lucia di Lammermoor".'

I made tactful noises. 'Lucia di Lammermoor' is what Sam calls his mother-in-law, who is about as *affreuse* as any mother-in-law can aspire to be. She dresses like a sixteen-year-old in dirndl skirts and little socks, her hair is long and gold and false and her face looks like an accident in a paint-factory. She is always in and out of expensive nursing homes for the nervously afflicted but whether this is just a rich woman's hobby or whether she is a boozer who has to be dried out periodically or whether she really is barmy none of her family has ever decided – or much cared. When last heard-of she had taken wing to North Africa with an eighteen-year-old faith-healer who also happened to be a lift-attendant.

'I gave Dr Wankel – yes, Golda Wankel – the names of the last two loony-bins she's patronized and she rang them up straight away – said it could be important – but neither of them could find the case-history or whatever it's called. Odd, that, don't you think?'

'Only fairly odd.'

'Eh? Oh. I see. Well, then, she asked me all sorts of peculiar things about Violet – does she sort of tend to misinterpret things, does she muddle common turns of phrase – well, you know how we all tease her about saying things like "crafty as a door-nail" and "dead as a wagon-load of monkeys" – and I had to answer "yes" to an awful lot of them, which really made me quite worried.'

His speech was getting a little wobbly: I have a horror of seeing my fellow-men weep. I made him a monstrous drink and tried to change the subject. He took the drink and rallied, but he would not wear the change of subject.

'The next bit was rather awful,' he went on steadily. 'We went up to where Violet had been put – nice enough room – and Dr Wankel squirted some sodium amytal into her. It stopped her staring at one in that awful way but it didn't make her utter at all. La Wankel lifted her arm up (Violet's, I mean) and it just stayed there. Then she bent it and it stayed there, too. She said that's called "*flexibilitas cereas*", which is typical of something or other, it seems. Then she shoved her arms down again and tapped it gently and every time it was tapped it rose a little – like an Anglepoise lamp. That's called "*mitgehen*" apparently. Rather beastly to watch. Then I was chucked out so that Wankel could give her a thorough physical examination and I had to wait outside for about a hundred years. Afterwards I was too knocked-out to pay much attention but I gathered that it was a toss-up whether Violet's trance was depressive or catatonic and that the difference was important. Either way there seems to be a good chance that Violet might suddenly rouse and dive out of the window – the catatonics seem to get the idea that they're angels – and that turns out to mean an agency nurse all round the clock at another huge sum per diem. Then the kindly Wankel gave me a bed – free! – and a pill, and I slept until 'plane-time this morning and that's all.'

I made him another drink, it was easier than saying anything.

Jock, his timing as perfect as ever, announced luncheon and we sat down to gulls' eggs, terrine of rabbit and cold curry puffs. I defy anyone to dwell on private miseries with one of Jock's cold curry puffs melting on his tongue, they stand alone, they really do. We drank bottled beer, for I disapprove of wine at luncheon: it either promotes drowsiness or inflames the animal spirits – either way it wastes the afternoon. Sam was a trifle less jumpy when victualled; George seemed somnolent, unwilling to join in.

'Now,' Sam said, 'tell us about the Oxford venture, Charlie. What did your emeritus Magus suggest?'

I told them, trying to keep the apologetic tone from my voice, doing my best to offer blasphemous folly as the only kind of reason which could prevail. What had seemed to make sense in Oxford sounded merely crack-pot over a Jersey luncheon-table and their blank stares, their shared sidelong glances, did not much help me toward persuasiveness. I ended lamely.

'And if you fellows can offer anything better,' I ended lamely, 'I'd be delighted to hear it.'

There was a long, treacly silence. George ran an exploratory index finger over each hair in his eyebrows, then checked the lobes of his ears and the cleft in his chin before starting to remind himself of the contours of his thumb-shaped nose.

Sam, on the other hand, was motionless, seeming rapt in the study of a curry-stain on the tablecloth.

Jock came in and cleared things away while George and Sam maintained their silences. I was damned if I was going to help them start the ball rolling; indeed, it occurred to me that many worthy people would say that I was damned already.

'All right,' said Sam at last. 'I'm prepared to give it a crack of the whip. If the swine's as demented as he seems to be, then I suppose we can best fight him with this insane garbage.'

George nodded slowly.

'Probably the only language he understands,' he said in a sort of gritty, country-magistrate's voice. 'Distasteful. Probably useless. Certainly expensive. But, as Charlie says, what else comes to mind? Seen stranger things than this taking effect, now I come to think of it. Yes; in India, places like that.'

'You men do realize,' I said, 'that you'll have to sort of participate, don't you? I mean, there's one or two rather dreary things that have to be done during the Mass, you see, and the unfrocked priest will, so to speak, have his hands full for much of the time.'

'Yes,' said Sam.

'Yes, I suppose so,' said George. 'But I'm damned if I'm memorizing any Black Paternosters backwards or any of that rot.'

'Black Paternosters?' I asked. 'Have you been studying the subject a bit, George?'

'We've all read our Dennis Wheatley at some time or another, Charlie,' said Sam.

'Speak for yourself!' I said sharply.

'Let me get it clear in my head,' George said. 'This mummery is supposed to discourage the witch-chap and make him feel that we're as well in with demons and things as he is, so he'd better lay off, is that it?'

'More or less, but there's a bit more to it than that. You see, it embodies a fairly hefty curse which is supposed to make the object of our attentions waste away and die nastily, so if our man really believes in what he's doing and is familiar with this particular ritual – and Dryden is pretty sure he does and is – he ought to be thoroughly scared and might well give up his activities altogether.'

'West African witch-doctors can still do it,' said George. 'Thousands of well-documented cases. If the victim really believes he's going to die on a certain day he just jolly well lies down and dies.'

'Do you mean to say,' Sam asked slowly, 'that there's a chance that this thing might actually kill our man?'

'Well, yes, I'm afraid it seems quite possible.'

'Excellent. When do we start?'

'Just one moment,' said George, 'it's occurred to me – how does the fellow know that this Mass has been performed and what Mass it is and who's on the receiving end and so on?'

'I'm glad you asked that,' I said. 'There's only one way and it will cost us all a certain amount of embarrassment but it will work.'

I then told them the method. After a noisy and acrimonious ten minutes they agreed to it, but our friendship did not come unscathed out of the discussion.

Jock came in at that point with a telegram *on a salver*: he loves to show off in front of what he calls Company. I suspect that he'd really love to be a proper manservant; perhaps I'll buy him a striped waistcoat for Christmas.

The wire was from Dryden. Its wording made me boggle for a moment: 'DESHABILLE ARRIVES FALAISEWISE TOMORROW TURNIP PASTIES ESSENTIAL'.

If Dryden has fault it is that he fancies himself a master of telegraphese; it grieves his friends mightily. There was a time when he could take it or leave it alone but now, I fear, he is 'medically dependent' as the booze-doctors say. The *déshabille* clearly meant 'the unfrocked one', the *Falaise* is one of the Weymouth-to-Jersey mail-packets, 'pasties' was obviously a textual emendation of 'Pastis' by some officious Post Office worker but 'turnip' remained as obscure as it had been on Oxford Station.

'Jock,' I said, 'is there any Pastis in the house?'

'There's a bottle of Pernod, same thing innit?'

'Lay in half a case of Pastis today, please. How are we off for turnips?'

'Funny you should ask that, Mr Charlie; the old geezer in the garden just planted a row 'smorning. Planted another toad, too. But they won't be ready for a couple of munce yet.'

'There should be some of the little French ones in the shops by now. Try the covered market in St Helier, or French Lane. If not, perhaps they can be bought tinned or frozen or dried – I leave it up to you, you understand these back-alleys of the world of retailing – "*nourri dans le sérail, tu en connais les détours*" – but get some by tomorrow night, even if you have to pay cash.'

'Right. How many?'

'How do they sell them, do you know? I mean, by weight, d'you suppose, or by the yard or what? What?'

'By the pound, I reckon.'

'Well, would you say that a couple of pounds would be a good stiff dose for a consenting adult?'

'Plenty.'

'Right, then.'

'Right, Mr Charlie.'

'Fascinating though it is,' said Sam heavily, 'to see you in your rôle of pantry-man, are you certain that there are not subjects of almost equal importance to be discussed?'

I explained all, but neither he nor George was much mollified. Their earlier doubts about our project were renewed by this talk of 'leguminous mystification' (Sam) and 'awful Romish fellows soaked in absinthe' (George). I soothed them a bit but they were still restive. Moreover, they had a scheme of their own up their sleeves which they now insisted we should carry into effect concurrently with the Satanic Mass ploy.

'You see,' said Sam, 'we've been thinking about the victims as distinct from the witchcraft aspect – in case the latter is by any chance a red herring – and, although three victims is not a very useful number to generalize from, one can draw a few tentative conclusions. First, all three families who've suffered are English. This could suggest a hatred for English people generally.'

'It could also suggest,' I put in, 'an *Englishman* who doesn't fancy Jersey women.'

'An *Englishman*?' scoffed George, 'with all that witch nonsense? Tommyrot.'

'I thought we were leaving out the witchcraft aspect for the moment.'

'So we are,' said Sam, 'and your point is well taken, if we are to be logical. But to proceed. George and I are both tolerably well off – though not in the class of the millionaire immigrants who seem so to excite the Jersiais' dislike – but the husband of the last victim, the doctor, is only as rich as a thriving general practice can make him and he has been in Jersey for twenty years, well liked by one and all. However, we are all three in what's called the middle class so it could be a class-hatred or/and an anti-English thing. Notice I say anti-English not anti-British, because Jersey is probably the loyalest of the Crown's appanages. Then there's the age of the victims: they're all in their thirties. This could well be because we all happen to have wives in their thirties or it could indicate that the rapist simply likes women of that age. This could suggest again' – it was choking him to say this, for he was evidently more in the mood for murder than reason – 'that he actually *likes* a good-looking woman in her prime, in what I shall have to call a fairly normal way; I mean, if he was an assaulter of little girls or old ladies we could be sure that he was really vilely mad, couldn't we? The last point is that the three victims are all closely grouped on the map, which suggests a pedestrian, don't you think, or someone who doesn't dare to use a motor-car – unlike the Beast of Jersey, of course, who is supposed to have driven all over the Island to his, ah, targets.'

'Or again, a comparative stranger,' I put in gently, 'like an Englishman who wasn't familiar with all the "back doubles"?'

'Yes,' Sam said patiently, 'it could, indeed, suggest that, too.'

George made that noise, usually rendered as 'Pshaw', which only those who have served in the Indian Army can make.

'So George and I, while you were away, drew up a list, as best we could, of good-looking English women, in their thirties, wives of substantial English *rentiers* or professional men, and living within a mile of here. We believe that the total of probable targets comes to no more than seventeen and that we four (I'm including Jock) could set ambushes which would give us almost a twenty-five per cent chance, each night, of being in the right place.'

'Yes, but how would you convince the rapist, supposing that he is watching the house, that he had a clear field?'

'Easily,' said George, the military man taking over from the back-room boffins, 'so long as we have the cooperation of the, ah, householders.' (One felt that he had almost said 'of the civilian population'.) 'Each of us enters a selected house at the sort of hour when most people are working: say, just before noon – lots of these Jersey workmen spend half the afternoon in pubs, better avoid afternoons. Early in the evening, the husband goes off ostentatiously in his car, loudly saying that he won't be much later than midnight, while wife waves goodbye at door. Then whichever one of us is on guard continues to lie low in the house or, if there's good cover outside commanding all entrances, makes his way to the cover. The wife in question potters about downstairs for a bit then goes upstairs, puts light on in bedroom, perhaps shows herself for a moment at bedroom window, then puts out main bedroom lights, leaving bedside one on, and creeps off to some other room; locks herself in. We lie in wait. Armed.'

'That sounds perfect,' I said cautiously. 'Perfect. Except for a couple of things, if you'll bear with me.'

Sam sighed boredly; George grunted guardedly.

'As follows,' I went on. 'First, just supposing my half-serious theory that it is an Englishman were right, how could one tell that one was not tipping him one's hand and, indeed, guarding his very own homestead?'

'Well, if one must take that seriously, we simply take care not to let any householder under guard on a given evening know which other houses are being guarded.'

'Good,' I said, 'but, better still, let him not know that *any* other houses are under surveillance.'

'Well, all right, that makes sense, come to think of it.'

'Second,' I went on remorselessly, 'what about our wives while we are out boy-scouting? Johanna is a pretty hand with a pistol but even so, without Jock's presence, she might be a bit vulnerable, and she's a natural next target. Sonia may or may not be off the fellow's list now but, after her horrid experience, she probably wouldn't much care to be left alone.'

'Perfectly simple,' George said impatiently, 'Sonia gives a bridge party, invites Johanna, couple of extra men, no one leaves until we return.'

I gaped, horror-stricken. I knew not what to say; I could only shoot a piteous glance at Sam.

'What is uppermost in Charlie's mind, I fancy,' said Sam, 'is that Johanna is really rather in the international league at Bridge – she has partnered Omar Sharif – while Sonia, although she plays with gusto and brio, has this trifling inability to remember what are trumps, and, worse for some reason known only to bridge-players, persists in recanting.'

'Revoking,' I said.

'I dare say you're right, Charlie.'

George assumed his brigadier-voice; just like Matthew Arnold donning his singing-robe.

'Look here, Mortdecai, I'd hate to think that you were making difficulties for the *fun* of it but I must say you're not being exactly constructive in your criticism.'

I cringed a bit; I felt that I had failed the Staff Course at Camberley. Mortdecai would never wear the coveted red tabs on his khaki. 'RTU' (Returned to Unit) would follow his name for ever – never 'psc' (passed staff-college).

'Ah, *shit*!' I thought, as better men have, I'm sure, thought before me, at similar crises in their lives.

'Well,' I said aloud, 'no doubt some other sort of party could be arranged; it's not something to fuss about, is it?'

'That's better.' George was prepared to give the weedy subaltern another chance. 'Of *course* there are other kinds of party: there are whist-drives, are there not, and beetle-drives and canasta-evenings; all sorts of things. One can deal with that sort of detail at, ah, the time.' (Once again, I heard him, almost, say 'at platoon level'. 'After all,' he seemed to be saying 'what are sergeants *for*?')

'Yes, George,' I said, restraining my impulse to call him 'Sir'. 'But my last objection is one that I have raised before. The question of fire-arms. You simple cannot go popping off at people just because they're rapists.'

'I can,' said Sam.

'So can I,' said George.

'Well, I can't. My .455 has to live chained up in the Pistol Club Armoury; my Banker's Special and Johanna's little Savage .28 have to be locked up in bed-side table drawers when we are in and in the safe when we're out. I'd risk *flourishing* a pistol at a miscreant out-of-doors, I suppose, but if I shot someone, except in clear self-defence against an *armed* miscreant, I'd be in line for a long prison sentence. You men would, probably, be in a slightly better position because you've actually suffered from this chap and you'd get the benefit of the "no-jury-would-convict" convention, but I'd look pretty feeble up against a smart barrister explaining that I'd killed a chap because I'd thought he was a chap who'd ravished the wife of a chap I knew, wouldn't I?'

'All right,' said Sam, 'just don't shoot to kill. You're meant to be a first-class pistol-shot, aren't you? Aim at his legs.'

'First-class pistol-shots,' I said, 'know that to hit a human leg in motion with a pistol is a matter of the merest chance. Moreover, the human frame is extraordinarily perverse about dying. You can plant a bullet in the head and the subject walks away – witness that South African premier a few years ago. You can empty a magazine of ammunition into his left breast and he spends a few weeks in hospital, inconvenienced only by saw-edged bed-pans. Yet, pop a small-calibre bullet into the fleshy part of his leg and it nicks the femoral artery and he bleeds to death before the ambulance arrives. You get away with manslaughter and count yourself lucky.'

There was a long and sulky silence. Finally Sam said:

'Argh, go piss up your kilt, Mortdecai.'

'Certainly,' I replied stiffly, 'but I shall require a certain amount of privacy for that. Must you go? Can't you stay?'

'Oh, now, look here chaps,' said George, 'come *on*. Let's not get excited about trifles. It's quite simple and Charlie's talking perfectly good sense. There's no reason why he should risk a prison sentence just to oblige his friends.'

His tone made it clear that *he* would do just that, but that he was a true-born Englishman, unlike certain Mortdecais he could name.

'It's quite simple,' he repeated, 'we all go armed but Charlie carries an empty gun. And a stout stick, or something of that sort. All agreed?'

Sam made the kind of noise you make when you don't mean 'no' but you're too miffed to say 'yes'.

I said, 'Well, now, I'm afraid there's just one more thing.'

'Oh, sweet Christ crucified!' roared Sam. 'What now?'

I didn't take offence this time. He had, after all, been through a bad time. But I had to make the point.

'I'm afraid Jock mustn't carry his pistol at all. His Lüger is highly illegal and moreover he has *form*.'

'?' said George.

'Done some *porridge*,' I explained.

'?'

' "Porridge" is a term used by rats of the underworld,' I said patiently, 'and it means penal servitude. There is a legend, you see, that if, when eating the wholesome breakfast provided on the last morning of your "stretch", you do not eat up all your nice porridge, you will be back in durance vile within the year. Any warder will tell you that. Jock has partly-eaten several plates of such porridge at Her Majesty's expense and if he were to be caught with any kind of firearm at all it would go very hard with him. If he actually shot someone he'd get approximately ninety-nine years: with maximum remission for good behaviour, call it sixty-six. He'd be a hundred and ten when he got out and would expect me to give him his job back, although he'd almost certainly have forgotten how to make decent tea.'

'Oh, stop drivelling, Charlie, your point is taken. Jock will be armed with a stout stick. All right?'

'He has, I believe, a length of lead piping, covered with soft leather.'

'Or a length of lead piping covered with soft leather. Is that all? Then I suggest we start tonight. Here are four sets of names and addresses. Any preferences?'

Quick as a flash I laid claim to Brisbane House, for Lady Quinn-Philpott has the finest cellar in the North of the Island, and no rapist in his senses would tackle her, for her strength is as the strength of ten, because her soul is pure, you see. Moreover, she has a Dobermann Pinscher. The others made their dispositions, leaving Jock, by default, in charge of a tomato-grower's bungalow, inhabited by the most rapable wife you can imagine. Indeed, if Johanna ever left me any time for private study I could quite fancy her myself. I suspected that, if the rapist appeared at that bungalow on that night, he would have to ask Jock to move over.

George telephoned hither and thither arranging for our vigils. Sam seemed to be trying to win a wager as to how rapidly he could empty my whisky decanter. I explained to Jock exactly how my sandwich-case was to be filled. Johanna threw one of her rare tantrums when told that she was to spend the evening playing cards with Sonia. Jock had a shower and overhauled, I daresay, his stock of the products of the London Rubber Company – that excellent condominium. At last they all went away and I was free to do some serious thinking on the sofa, with my shoes off and my eyes closed. A heavy luncheon always brings out the philosopher in me.

The evening's ambuscades were, of course, a complete washout as far as raper-catching was concerned.

I caught an excellent dinner and a splendid bottle of Chateau Léoville Poyferré '61.

Sam caught a strayed Jersey cow in the udders with the unchoked barrel of his shotgun.

George caught a nasty cold from crouching under a hydrangea.

I hate to think what Jock caught but I'm sure it was worth it.

When I collected Johanna from the card-party at George's house she wasn't speaking to anyone, least of all to me. I told her about George's ordeal under the dripping hydrangea and all she said was 'lucky George'.

'Good night,' I said as we parted in the hall.

'Good night, Clausewitz,' she replied.

Jock was already abed, sure of a good night's sleep, bless him, so I had to make my own sandwich.

As I stole upstairs with it I felt a sort of strange feeling about Johanna. Had I been twenty – or even fifteen – years younger I would probably have mistaken it for being in love. Perhaps it was a trace of regret for having, so long ago and so rightly, decided that emotion was not for me, that I was better without it. As I hesitated on the landing, the half-gnawed sandwich in my treacherous hand, I had an absurd compulsion to go into her room, to see her honey-coloured hair spread over the pillows and to say soppy, apologetic, *affectionate* things. Make her smile, perhaps. She might have been crying, you see; even women cry sometimes. But I have a fixed rule: whenever you feel like holding someone's hand, have a drink instead – it's better for all concerned in the long run.

I compromised by finishing the sandwich and shuffled off to my lonely bed in a miasma of spring-onions and self-pity: who could ask for more? Borges remarks that there is no more skilful consolation than that we have chosen our own misfortunes. 'Thus,' he explains, 'every negligence is deliberate . . . every humiliation a penitence . . . every death a suicide.'

I brushed my teeth with especial care in case Johanna should take it into her head to come and say good night to me but she didn't of course; they never do.

10

Thou hast conquered, O pale Galilean; the world has grown gray from thy breath;
We have drunken of things Lethean, and fed on the fullness of death.

Hymn to Proserpine

Kicking and screaming, then whining and sulking, I was wrenched out of bed and sent off to meet the Weymouth packet-boat and Father Tichborne, the practitioner recommended by John Dryden. I call him *Father* Tichborne, unfrocked though he had been, on the same reasoning that my grandmama would have called a '£50 cook', however virginal, 'Mrs' out of courtesy. (Mind you, that was £50 a year *and all found*, which meant four or five gross meals a day washed down with ale and stout; bones-and-dripping money, back-handers from all the tradesmen, the privilege of offering hot mutton sandwiches to Police Constables; the right to persecute everyone below the rank of butler or governess: licence to get hopelessly pissed every six weeks (except in Methodist households of course); at least one kitchen-maid to do all the real work (£50 cooks *never* peeled potatoes) and often as much as seven days holiday a year if you could prove that at least one of your parents was dying. Today, no doubt, they would expect the use of a wireless set, too. You know, those people were *happier* before we started spoiling them.)

Yes, well, there I was on Albert Quay, awaiting the M.V. *Falaise* and Father Tichborne. (*Albert* Quay, imagine! Did you know that both Edward VII and George VI were really called Albert but the

Family wouldn't let them use it on the throne out of reverence for Queen Victoria's Consort and the Privy Council wouldn't, either, because it sounded so common. 'Albert' I mean, not the Privy Council. Both right, of course.) ('This is the last and greatest treason: To do the wrong thing for the right reason' sings Alfred Prufrock, if that's the right way round. And if it matters.)

Yes, well, there on Albert Quay I stood, snuffing the sea breezes until the smell of used beer and vomit and package-tour operators presaged the advent of the *Falaise*.

I spotted him at once, a great rangy buck-priest in a silk soutane. Evil eyes burned from an ascetic face oddly marred by soft and sensual lips, which were just then snarling at the Customs man.

'Hello,' I said, offering a hand, 'my name's Mortdecai.'

He gave me a slow leer, disclosing an assortment of teeth which, had they been cleaner, would have done credit to an alligator.

'And I suppose your friends call you "cheeky",' he retorted, sweeping past me to where a group of saucy-looking lads awaited him. He whispered to them and they all eyed me.

'Isn't he *bold*?' one of them tittered.

Sweating with shame I moved off in quest of the true Fr Tichborne, who proved, when I found him, to be a well-washed, shiny little chap with a face just like that of a Volkswagen. He was sitting on a bench leafing through the latest copy of *Playgirl* with an air of studious detachment and wearing a snappy, dark-green mohair suit which he shouldn't have been able to afford on a prep-school master's salary. Exchanging humdrum civilities, we entered my Mini, where I noticed that he exuded a faint but agreeable smell of seed-cake, which I supposed was really the Pastis escaping from his well-opened pores. As we moved off, he let out a shrill cry of dismay. I clapped the brakes on.

'My corporal!' he squeaked, 'I've forgotten my corporal!' I was alarmed: Johanna is broad-minded about that sort of thing but Jock is not: he would make *remarks*.

'Do you mean,' I asked, 'that you have brought a, er, Non-Commissioned *friend* with you?'

'No no no,' he said testily, 'it's the special *altar* corporal for the Mass we're going to celebrate.'

Mystified, I helped him to search and we found, in the Customs shed, a string shopping-bag containing a lot of folded cloth.

'Do show,' I said.

'Well, not here, I think. The embroidery on it might seem a little, well, surprising, to the casual bystander. And that Customs officer is observing us narrowly.'

On the way home we paused at the 'Carrefour Selous' for refreshment, early though it was.

'This is a very characteristic local inn,' I explained. 'They drink something here called Pastis, I think, and speak highly of it. Would you care to try?'

'I have heard of it,' he said gravely, 'and I long to try it.'

'What do you think?' I asked diffidently a little later.

'Mmm. Quite delicious. Stronger than sherry, I fancy. I say, it won't make me *tight*, will it?'

'I shouldn't think so.'

'But what is that that you are drinking, Mr Mortdecai?'

'It is called whisky. It is a malt liquor distilled in the highlands of Scotland. I believe they sell quite a lot of it in Jersey.'

We gazed at each other with straight faces. He was the first to laugh – after that there was no embarrassment. It takes one to know one, they say; whatever that means.

Johanna took to him on sight, which was reassuring for she is never wrong about people, whilst I almost always am. She was fussing over him and telling him how tired he must be and what could she offer him to drink (ha ha) when Jock loomed in the doorway and announced luncheon in the doom-laden voice of a servant who is in the mood to give in his notice at the drop of a hat.

'This is Fr Tichborne, Jock,' I said brightly.

'Reelly,' he said.

'Yes. His bags are in the car – perhaps you would bring them in presently.'

Jock turned on his heel and clumped towards the door.

'Oh, and you could bring his corporal in, too?'

Jock ground to a halt and looked over his shoulder in a dangerous sort of way.

' 'Is *wot?*'

'It's in a string bag,' I explained blandly. It made my day, it really did, although I knew I'd pay for it.

Johanna insisted on seeing the corporal and although Tichborne blushed and demurred she got her way. She usually does.

'You see,' said Tichborne anxiously as he unrolled the cloth, 'one can't use the consecrated corporal – for one thing it might put off the sort of person we're hoping to, er, invoke, and for another it would be *rude*, simply; I mean, I always believe in extending common courtesy to what I might call the Other Side, even though one has to be a bit horrid about Them during the actual ceremony. Do you follow me?'

We made guarded noises.

'Moreover, this sort of Mass used to be performed on the, er, person of a young *person*, so to speak, but we've found that using a corporal depicting such a young person in the appropriate attitude serves just as well. I mean, I do speak from some experience.'

The cloth was now unfurled and spread out on the sofa-table. I must say that even I found it a little startling: the appropriate attitude of the young person certainly seemed to speak from experience, to use Tichborne's phrase, and the embroidress had been explicit to the last prick of her needle, if I may coin another. Both Tichborne and I cast worried glances at the gently-nurtured Johanna.

'Wow!' she exclaimed politely, 'that is really out of sight!' (She only uses Americanisms defensively.) For my part, I wished heartily that the thing *were* out of sight, lest Jock should come in. (Most brutal criminals are *prudes*, did you know? Of course you did, forgive me.)

'You can say that again, sister,' I growled, falling into her vernacular. She looked at me strangely, perhaps admiring my gift of tongues.

'You mean the "Wow",' she asked, 'or the other bit?'

'Never mind.'

'But this lovely needlework must have cost a fortune, Father Tichborne,' she resumed, 'wherever did you get it made?'

'As a matter of fact I did it myself,' he said, crimson with shame and vanity. 'It took ages, I don't mind telling you.'

'Working from life, evidently?' I put in.

'Well, no, more from memory, really.'

It seemed a good point at which to end that conversation. As we rolled the corporal up George arrived to inspect Fr Tichborne.

Introduced, he made the civilizedest noises he could muster, giving the impression that, in his view, the only good Papist was an unfrocked Papist.

Tichborne gained a little ground by asking him about his regiment but lost it all again by saying that he himself had been a chaplain with the Free French.

'I'll just bet you were,' said Johanna brightly.

George's face turned a sort of pale shade of black; he took it rather hard.

'The French were on our side, George,' I reminded him. 'This last time, I mean.'

'You will stay to lunch, won't you, George?' said Johanna.

He couldn't, he had another appointment, he'd already had luncheon, he never ate luncheon, Sonia was expecting him for luncheon, he had a train to catch. There are no trains on Jersey, of course: I think he just wanted to go and kick something. It's all to do with a place called Dakar, for some reason.

Luncheon was rather awful at first: it was the cook's day off and therefore Jock had the duty and you could see that he didn't much relish waiting on Fr Tichborne. He served soup to Johanna, then, despite my coughs and glares, to me. I gave Tichborne an apologetic grimace. His plate of soup arrived quite three minutes later.

'Dash it, Jock,' I snapped, 'your thumb is in Fr Tichborne's soup!'

' 'S all right, Mr Charlie, it ain't hot.' Tichborne frowned at me and shook his head, so I let it pass.

The next thing was kidneys wrapped in bacon and stuffed into baked potatoes. Quite delicious, except for Tichborne's, which was small, late and badly burned.

Really angry now, I opened my mouth to admonish Jock severely, but Tichborne raised his hand.

'Jock,' he said in a quiet, gentle voice, 'once is happen-stance, twice is coincidence, three times is enemy action. By that I mean that if you once more disgrace Mrs Mortdecai in this shabby way I shall take you out into the garden and punch your nose quite flat.'

An awful silence fell. Johanna's eyes were wide open, as was my mouth. Jock started to swell like a bull-frog. Fr Tichborne poured himself a glass of water.

'Gaw blimey!' said Jock at last.

'Guard your tongue!' commanded the little priest in a voice of thunder. 'The words you have just uttered mean "God blind me" – you have already lost the sight of one eye: be very careful Whom you invoke to pluck out its fellow.'

I glanced up: no plaster was falling from the ceiling.

The awful silence went on.

Finally Jock nodded and vanished into the kitchen. He emerged and laid a large and beautiful kidney in front of Fr Tichborne.

'You better have mine,' he said. 'Sir.'

When the green baize door had closed behind him, Johanna said, 'Golly.'

Fr Tichborne said, 'I believe I've made a friend.'

I said, 'You must come and stay *often*.'

Later, as we mumbled a little cheese – Brie, I think it was – mounted (the cheese, not us, of course – I *must* learn to be lucid) – the cheese, I say, mounted on Mr Carr's incomparable Table Water Biscuits – goodness, what a muddle this sentence is in, as dear Judge Jeffreys said at the Bloody Assize; let me start again. During the cheese-eating period I apologized to Fr Tichborne that I had not been able to offer him any turnips with his luncheon but that I was having the market scoured and hoped to be able to make those sapid roots manifest at dinner.

'Turnips?' he said, faintly. '*Turnips?* This is uncommonly thoughtful of you but, to be frank, it would be disingenuous of me to pretend that I was a *leading* turnip-eater.'

'Not?' I said puzzledly. 'But Dr Dryden assured me, albeit cryptically, that turnips were of the very essence.'

He cogitated puzzledly awhile.

'Hah!' he cried at last. 'Hah! Of course!'

'Yes, yes,' we agreed, 'of course . . .?'

'No no,' he went on, 'I see, I see; he knew I would need a slice or two of turnip for our ritual. You see, at the, ah, *equivalent* of the Elevation of the Host one must either use a consecrated Wafer which has been desecrated – and I've told you how I hate to be rude to the Other Side – or one must bake a travesty of it oneself (naughty old Sir Francis Dashwood and his Hell-fire Club chums used to call it a "Holy Ghost Pye") or, best of all, one uses what one might call a caricature of the Host: in fact, one makes it out of a slice of turnip. Stained black, you know, and cut into, well, a sort of curious shape, if you follow me.' He looked at us worriedly. 'It gives less offence, you see,' he went on, 'and it seems to work quite as well. *Quite* as well. Really.'

'Would you like some coffee?' said Johanna.

That afternoon, all friends now and all full of luncheon – for I fancy Jock had scoffed a moody tin of caviare – we set off for a reconnaissance of the chapels, furnished with a capable picnic hamper in case the sun shone.

I'm sorry, but I shall have to explain about these chapels. There is a place in Grouville Parish, in the East of the Island, called La Hougue Bie. I believe no one is certain what the name means. It is a monstrous, man-made mound inside which, only excavated fifty years ago, there is a dolmen: a tomb made some five thousand years ago of great slabs of stone. To reach the main tomb-chamber you have to creep, bent double, for what seems a very long way indeed along a stone tunnel. If you are claustrophobic, or superstitious or simply a coward, then you will find it a dismal and grimly place indeed. I hate it for all three reasons and I hate, too, the thought of the brutish folk who built it; I loathe to speculate on what disgusting compulsion made them drag and raise those monstrous stones and then spade over them those countless tons of earth, all to encyst some frightful little prehistoric Hitler.

Nevertheless, I believe that we should all visit such a place from time to time, in order to remind ourselves how recently we sprang from the brutes.

Crowning the great mound and, curiously, exactly above the main tomb-chamber, someone in the twelfth century raised a decent little chapel dedicated to *Notre Dame de la Clarté*. A few centuries later another decent chap dug himself out a crypt in the pious – if mistaken – belief that it was a replica of the Holy Sepulchre itself, and then tacked another chapel onto the first. This latter is called the Jerusalem Chapel.

I didn't go into the dolmen myself; once had been enough for me – I just don't enjoy feeling my flesh crawl. Jock was prowling about the surrounding area looking absurdly like a professional crook but the nice tourists paid him no heed: they probably assumed he was a security-firm guard, there's no telling the two apart, is there? Fr Tichborne, on the other hand, dived into the dank darkness of the tunnel with every sign of relish and emerged looking flushed and excited, like a young bishop with his first actress.

'Do you have a portable tape-recorder?' were his first words.

'Of course I have, who hasn't? But whatever for?'

'Tell you tonight. After dinner.' And with that he dived back into the hell-hole. I spent five instructive minutes in the excellent little Agricultural Museum near the mound, marvelling at the monstrous tools the tillers toiled with in the olden days. How they must have sweated, to be sure; it made me feel quite faint.

When Tichborne re-emerged we rounded up Jock and 'cased' the chapels. ('Cased', you understand, is a piece of thieves' cant meaning 'surveyed with intent to commit a felony' – but I dare say that you, who must be the sort of person who reads this sort of story, would know that sort of thing already.)

The earlier chapel – *Notre Dame de la Clarté* – exhibited a notice saying that it had been 'recoiled' by some meddlesome bishop with too much time on his hands. Tichborne explained that this meant sort of re-consecrated and de-Romanized.

'Drat it,' he added petulantly.

The Jerusalem Chapel, however, displayed no such advertising matter and Tichborne said that it would do beautifully – almost certainly disused since they closed all the chantry-chapels after the Reformation thing in 1548, he told us.

'Reelly?' said Jock.

In the car going home we asked Jock whether it would be practicable to gain access to the chapel and dolmen by night in a clandestine fashion.

'A doddle,' he replied. 'Just a doddle. The gate into the grounds isn't worth opening, you can nip over it easy if your piles are better this week. Sorry, sir.' (I was startled until I realized that 'sir' was meant for Tichborne – then I was a little *piqued*.) 'That underground tomb,' he went on, 'has got a first-class padlock but the chain to it is no better than the common shit-house variety (beg pardon, sir) and a liddle old pair of wire-cutters will soon sort that out.'

'Ah,' said Tichborne, 'but what about that formidable great iron lock to the chapel?'

Jock made a coarse noise by expelling air from between his closed lips.

'That ain't a formigal lock,' he said contemptuously, ' 't'ain't even a Yale; it's just *big*. I could open that bugger with me old . . . er, I could open that lock with any old bit of wire. No sweat.'

'Jock,' I said, 'pray stop the car at the next decent inn or hostelry so that I may buy you a large and toothsome drink. "Thou shalt not muzzle the ox when he stampeth out the corn" is what I say. So did Deuteronomy.'

'XXV; 4,' agreed Tichborne.

'Reelly,' said Jock.

That night, after dinner (I think it was *Médaillons de Chevreuil S. Hubert au Purée de Marrons* with a saucy little Chambertin on the side, unless it was a Friday, in which case Jock would have gone out to fetch fish and chips) that night, I say, I reminded Fr Tichborne about his interest in portable tape-recorders.

'You were going to explain about portable tape-recorders,' is how I put it to him.

'Yes, yes,' he said, 'I believe I was. Yes, so I was.'

His childlike eyes flitted about wildly as he sipped at Johanna's incomparable, inherited brandy: one got the impression that it was not quite his *bag*, as the children say nowadays.

'I must apologize for this brandy,' I said, flicking a glance at Johanna. 'For my part I believe I'd rather have some of that Pastis stuff: could you face it? I daresay there's some in the house . . .?'

A few gollups of Pastis later (it's really just absinthe without the wormwood) he was relaxed and expansive.

'Do you promise not to laugh?' were his first words.

We crossed our hearts.

'Well, two years ago I read a book by a man called Konstantin Raudive. It's a perfectly respectable book and endorsed by respectable scientists. Raudive claims, indeed proves, that he heard gentle chattering and muttering coming from the unused intervals of tape from his recorder. I had had the same experience but had put it down to the random wireless reception . . . er, *radio?*'

'Wireless is fine with me,' I said.

'Oh, good. Well, as I say, I had thought it was the sort of stray reception that people get from hearing-aids and things but after reading Raudive I naturally tested it and found that even on virgin tape I still got the gentle muttering if it was played through on "record" in silence and at a nil recording level. Like Raudive, I found that if I boosted the gain when playing-back it sounded uncommonly like speech, but with quite strange intonations, odd grammatical sequences, random relevance.'

Johanna rose, excused herself gracefully and said that she really had to go to bed. She hates long words, although she is very clever. (Why do I persist in entangling myself with clever women when the only ones I find truly adorable are the transcendentally stupid, the ones whose intellects are bounded on the North by the ability to count to nine? Alas, the latter get rarer every day. '*Il y a des gens qui rougissent d'avoir aimé une femme, le jour qu'ils aperçoivent qu'elle est bête. Ceux-la sont des aliborons vaniteux, faits pour brouter les chardons les plus impurs de la création, ou les faveurs d'un bas-bleu. La bêtise est souvent l'ornement de la beauté; c'est elle qui donne aux yeux cette limpidité morne des étangs noirâtres et ce calme huileux des mers tropicales.*' I forget who wrote that. Probably not Simone Weil.)

'Do go on, Fr Tichborne,' I said when the good nights were over.

'I say, would you care to drop the "Fr" now?' he asked. 'The boys at school call me "Eric" – I can't imagine why, for it's not my name, but I quite like it.'

'Please go on, Eric. And pray call me "Charlie".'

'Thank you. Well, once I got the hang of these odd attempts at communication, I found them quite, well . . .'

'Mm?'

'Interesting,' he said defiantly. 'Interesting!'

Trying, as ever, like Caesar's wife, to be all things to all men, I tried to help.

'But disturbing?' I guessed.

'Yes, that too. Certainly that. Disturbing is a *good* word. You see, I began to recognize voices and to unscramble them and they were all from dead chaps, you see, like my old headmaster and the Principal of my Seminary and people whose books I had read – well, of course I couldn't recognize their voices but if you hear a chap talking really barbarous Latin with a strong Slav accent and telling you not to wash because it's a sin of fleshly luxury and then he says his name is Jerome, what can you think?'

'What indeed?'

'Quite. But I felt that I had to go on taping and listening and trying to hear and understand and it got worse.'

I slid some more Pastis into his glass, added a little water and helped him aim it at his mouth. He wasn't drunk, I think he was in some sort of private ecstasy, like a menopausal woman thinking about Cassius Clay.

'It got worse?' I prompted.

'Much worse. Cardinal Manning shouted and *shouted* at me and seemed to know all about my, er, case; and then someone calling himself Pio Nono kept on saying that he would pray for me but that he couldn't promise anything and then, worst of all . . .' His voice broke.

'Your mother?' I asked gently.

'Oh, no, she's always very understanding. It was St Francis. At first I hoped it was Francis of Assisi but he soon put me right: it was St Francis *Xavier*. He was horrid to me. Horrid. You can have no idea what that old bastard can be like.'

His eyes were full of tears. Well, of course, I know what to do with drunken nut-cases. You humour them, listen to them, get them really pissed, then put them to bed, first loosening their collars and removing their boots. My only pre-occupation was how to loosen a Roman collar and how to prevent Eric from moistening my landlord's rather good Empire sofa.

'Look,' he said suddenly and articulating clearly, 'would you like to hear? Please?'

'Certainly, certainly; I'll go and fetch the tape-recorder. Tell you what, let me just freshen up your glass first.'

I fetched my rather good tape-recorder, broke open a new sixty-minute blank tape, fed it deftly into the machine and set it ready for action at $3\frac{3}{4}''$ per second. Eric gazed at the machine in an ambivalent sort of way, as you or I might gaze at the dentist's drill, which both giveth and taketh away pain. He went on gazing until I sort of shuffled and fidgeted. He looked up at me with a startling, seraphic smile.

'Forgive me,' he said, 'I should have told you. All these phenomena seem to be linked to an alpha-rhythm in the brain of around eight to twelve cycles. It seems that people who can do telepathy and telekinesis and thing like that are people who can more or less organize their alpha-waves. Sometimes it can be induced by hypnosis, sometimes it just occurs naturally when one is falling asleep or in a half-aware condition when awakened from sleep too soon; adolescents and menopausal women can often induce it by thinking unclean thoughts with their eyes shut. Mediums who insist on half-darkness and silence and so forth during their parlour-séances are usually, if they're at all genuine, fumbling for conditions in which they can depress their alpha-waves to the required level, whether they know it or not. I suspect that many "fake" mediums are women who are genuinely receptive at times but do not understand how to set up the conditions properly and so fudge the results when it doesn't really work.'

I was a little taken aback. Not much of this made a great deal of sense to me, but it certainly didn't sound like the ramblings of a drunkard.

'They've done a lot of work on this in the Soviet Union,' he went on, 'and I must say that it does rather look as though their approach has been rather more intelligent than the Americans. I mean, they feel that things which are clearly outside the laws of science as at present understood cannot be examined by standard scientific methodology. Like trying to weigh neutrons on a grocer's scales, do you see.'

'That seems reasonable to me,' I said. 'I remember saying to one of those psychic/psychologic researchers from a comic new University – Lancaster? – that most poker-players are familiar with that rare and wonderful feeling which occurs perhaps once in a thousand hands, when they *know* they cannot lose: I told him that I'd had it twice and so strongly that I hadn't looked at my hand, hadn't drawn to it, had betted it to the hilt and had not been in the least surprised when I'd won. The researcher-twit's reaction was to deal me singles from a cold pack of cards, inviting me to guess the colours. My results were nine per cent below random probability, or whatever they call it. That made me a liar in his eyes and him an idiot in mine. I could have told him, had he had the wit to ask, that the necessary conditions were that we should have been playing a real game for several hours, that I should have ingested perhaps a third of a bottle of brandy, that I should have been slightly ahead of my table-stakes by virtue of the ordinary run of cards and that, in short, I should have been in that state of drowsy euphoria where I was effectively asleep in all bodily departments except my card-sense.'

'You couldn't have put it better!' cried Eric. 'All the conditions were there, you see: mild fatigue, mild euphoria, mild depression from the brandy – I'll bet your alpha-waves were at something very like ten cycles per second.'

'No takers,' I said.

'Quite. By the way, I'm sorry to say "quite" all the time but much of my work lies amongst Americans and they *expect* Englishmen to say it.'

'Just so,' I said.

'Whether these receptions, if that is a useful word, come because of me, or through me, or merely *from* me, I cannot say,' he went on. 'So far, however, like Raudive, I must admit that I have not encountered any words which were in a language I did not know, nor from any sources with which I was not familiar. This might seem to suggest that I am, as it were, the prime mover; but it could just be a communication-problem, don't you think?'

I didn't mean to say 'quite' but it seemed to slip out. I poured him some more Pastis and gave him a friendly grin, which probably looked more like a rictus.

'Well,' I boomed uncertainly, 'let's have a shot, shall we?' He did his gazing act again for a minute or two, then put an arm protectively around the machine and sort of nestled against it as he switched on. He gazed moonily at the revolving tape for five long minutes, then shook his head violently and rewound the tape to the beginning.

'No good?' I asked cheerfully.

'Can't say.' He turned the gain up to about half-strength and pressed the 'play' key. The machine began to emit the usual 'white noise' and machine noises and the gentle susurrus of his breathing; nothing else. I was embarrassed for him, wished he hadn't started this nonsense, wondered how I could help him talk his way out of the let-down.

'D'you hear it?' he asked suddenly.

'Oh, Christ, he really is barmy,' I thought, making an apologetic grimace at him, as one does to chaps who point out pink elephants in the corners of a room. He turned up the gain – and I heard it. A soft, infinitely distant twittering, then a chuckie and a protracted cackle which rose and fell in an oddly odious way.

He tinkered with the volume and speed-controls here and there and played with the 'cue' and 'review' keys until suddenly, rising clear and sweet over a tangle of gibberish, a laughing voice quite clearly said:

'FILTH! Filthy sot! Filthy sot? Filthyfilthy filthyfilthy *filthy-filthy*,' on a rising scale which ended with a bat-like shrill which hurt the ears. Eric pressed the 'pause' key and looked at me, his eyes brimming with happy tears.

'That's my mummy,' he said. 'She worries about me a lot.'

There was a time when a remark like that would have given me no trouble: I would have tossed off a rejoinder both witty and respectful, but I am no longer the man I once was. All I could find to say was, 'Really?'

'Oh, yes,' he said, 'she usually comes on before the others start and says something playful.'

'Others?'

'Oh, lots of others. Let's try.'

He fiddled with the knobs and things again and, in a little while, isolated a hoarse, gin-soaked voice, choking with passion, which said *'De profundis clamavt ad te, Domine'* again and again in tones of bitter reproach.

'Not anyone from antiquity,' said Eric. 'That's the sort of Latin that Irish priests still learn in their seminaries today. The speed's not quite right; he sounds lighter than that if one can hit the exact speed.'

'Oscar Wilde on his death-bed?' I couldn't help asking.

'Do you know, you might be right, I really think you might.'

We did not have much more luck, if that's a suitable word, from then on. Someone did some peculiarly unpleasant laughing, Eric's mother came through again in a flurry of animal noises and seemed to accuse him of having practised something which would have brought a blush to the hairy cheeks of old Krafft-Ebing himself ('She will have her little joke,' Eric murmured uneasily) and, near the end, a still, small voice delivered a message plainly intended for me, concerning a matter which Eric could not possibly have known about, and with which I do not propose to trouble the reader at this point. Or ever.

Oh, yes, and whenever we hit one particular speed/volume combination an urbane and friendly voice repeatedly said, 'No, don't. Don't. Not tomorrow. No, I really wouldn't. Not tomorrow. Don't, please.'

'All quite fascinating,' I said heavily when Eric had at last switched everything off. 'Fascinating. It seems to me, though, that it might not be a good idea to let every Tom, Dick and Harry share this sort of, ah, recondite harmony, perhaps?'

'Goodness, no. I only do it when I'm alone or with people of quite exceptional emotional stability – like yourself, if I may say so.'

I didn't – couldn't – comment on this astonishing assessment of me: I keep my emotional stability and things like that at the bottom of my handkerchief drawer, along with the vibrator and the naughty photographs, as W.H. Auden has probably already said. It was the other part of what he said that drew my fire.

'Do you mean to say that you sometimes do this sort of thing *alone*?' I asked, wonderingly. 'At *night*?'

'Goodness, yes. Often. What have I to be afraid of?'

I didn't answer that. If he, with his qualifications, didn't know, it wasn't my place to tell him. I mean, I wasn't his bloody *Bishop*, was I?

He was smart enough, however, to notice that I was becoming moody and he set himself to the task of amusing me, with some success. I yield to few when it comes to telling dirty jokes but it takes a seminary priest to tell a true Catholic story with the right admixture of shyness and authority. He had this art to such a state of perfection that I recall falling about a good deal.

Later, he taught me how to make and drink a 'nose-dive' – an art little known outside the campus of the University of Southern California, where Eric had once spent a happy semester teaching the well-nourished undergraduate girls there the full inwardness of Verlaine's *Chansons Pour Elle*.

How you drink a 'nose-dive' is as follows – you ought to know because it is the only way of gagging down the nastier forms of alcohol, like tequila, pulque, Polish vodka at 149° of proof, paraldehyde and aircraft de-icing fluid. You fill the shot-glass with the desired but normally undrinkable fluid and place the shot-glass inside a high-ball glass, which you then fill, to the level of the shot-glass, with iced orange-juice or some other sharply nourishing fluid. Then you drink it all down as one. The juice, unpolluted with whatever lunatic-soup happens to be in the shot-glass, nevertheless marks its horrors during the progress over your palate. As a bonus, at the end, the adhesion of the inner glass fails and it slides down and bumps you gently on the nose – hence the name of the game. The nose-bumping, I may say, in my experience compels you irresistibly to repeat the process. I have no knowledge of other mixtures but I don't mind telling you that, practised with Pastis and pineapple-juice, you soon find yourself sitting on the carpet, singing songs you didn't think you knew the words of.

It seems to me, but I cannot be sure, that Jock entered the room in the small hours and, with many a kindly word, showed Eric where his room was; returning later to take me out to the shrubbery and hold my head, then to the shower-bath. And so, I dare say, to bed.

Anyone will tell you that there's nothing like Pastis to take one's mind off the things tape-recorders say to you.

I I

Now all strange hours and all strange loves are over,
Dreams and desires and sombre songs and sweet,
Hast thou found place at the great knees and feet
Of some pale Titan-woman like a lover,
Such as thy vision here solicited,
Under the shadow of her fair vast head,
The deep division of prodigious breasts,
The solemn slope of mighty limbs asleep,
The weight of awful tresses that still keep
The savour and shade of old-world pine-forests
Where the wet hill-winds weep?

Ave Atque Vale

For years I had believed that these lines:

'Shot? So quick, so clean an ending?
Oh that was right, lad, that was brave;
Yours was not an ill for mending,
'Twas best to take it to the grave'

were about a horrified young Edwardian who had discovered that
he was a homosexual. I am in a position to correct literary history
in this matter. The lines are about a horrified chap in early middle
age who has discovered, one morning, that he has no head for Pastis.
This, you see, was not the common hangover of commerce, it was

a Plague of Egypt with a top-dressing of the Black Death. Quite clearly incurable. I touched the bell.

'Jock,' I said hollowly, 'pray bring me a pot of tea – the Lapsang Souchong Tips I think – and a loaded revolver. Mine is not an ill for mending: I propose to take it to the grave but I wish to blow the top of my head off first. I have no intention of spending eternity with the top of my head in its present condition.'

He started to steal away.

'Oh, and Jock,' I added, 'when you bring the tea-tray I implore you not to let the spoon or other cutlery rattle against the revolver.'

'Yes, Mr Charlie.' Was there a tinge of contempt in his voice?

I lay there listening to the surly, ragged beating of my heart, the tidal noises my liver was emitting and the figured-bass in the back of my skull. A silvery laugh floated up to me from the kitchen: how could Johanna be *laughing* at a time like this – she should have been on her knees beside my bed, promising to hold my memory sacred forever.

A few feet from where I lay there was a window: a small, diligent spider was spinning a web in one of its corners. He was spinning it *inside* the double-glazing, I have never seen anything more piteous in my life, it made me think of me. I dare say I shed a tear or two. Had a capable Jesuit entered at that moment he could have bagged my soul without firing a shot.

What in fact entered was my tea, borne by Jock with a minimum of clamour. I had some difficulty getting into a position where I could sip it; my bottom kept on sliding down the silk sheets. (How I have longed to have been born of common stock so that I could sleep on kindly Irish linen, but, alas, rank has its obligations as well as its privileges.)

I shall not say that the first sips revived me, for I have ever loved the truth, but it is a fact that they allowed me to contemplate the bare possibility of continuing awhile in this vale of tears.

'Jock,' I said sternly, 'I can distinctly hear Mrs Mortdecai laughing. Explain this as best you can.'

'Couldn't say, Mr Charlie. She's having breakfast with Farver Tichborne and they seem to be relishing it no end.'

'Breakfast!' I squeaked. 'Breakfast? Tichborne is eating *breakfast?*'

'Too right he is. He's had a plate of porridge with cream and sugar, then another plate Scotch-style with salt and dripping and pepper, then two eggs boiled very soft and runny, with richly-buttered toast, and now they're starting on a pound of devilled kidneys with smoked salty bacon. I better run down and see if they'd fancy a bloater or two, I got some lovely ripe ones in the market yesterday.'

'Get out,' I said.

'You fancy anythink?' he asked.

'*Out!*' I cried.

'You ought to try and get something down you, Mr Charlie, you look a bit rotten. Eyes like piss-holes in snow, if you'll pardon the expression.'

I turned my face to the wall, feeling like a collection of passages deleted from the Book of Job.

Even the Job's comforters were not wanting, for, half an hour later, some traitor downstairs allowed my kindly extrovert landlord to invade my death-chamber.

'Hullo hullo hullo!' he boomed. 'What, still slugging abed? You're missing the best part of the day!'

'I'm poorly,' I muttered.

'Rubbish!' he bellowed. 'Nothing a breath of fresh air wouldn't drive away in a trice. It's a *splendid* morning!'

Now, the first thing to remember about landlords is that you cannot tell them to fuck off.

'It's raining,' I said sullenly.

'Certainly not. Not a bit. A fine, brisk morning; clear and cold. Not a spot of rain.'

'It is raining in my heart,' I said coldly. '*Il pleut dans mon coeur comme il pleut sur la ville.*'

'Ah, well, yes, I daresay, but mark my words . . .'

'When you go down,' I said, 'would you be kind enough to ask someone to bring me up a basin to be sick in?'

'Right, well, that's me, I'm off; lots to do. Look after yourself, won't you.'

'Thank you,' I said.

There was nothing for it but to get up, so up was what I got. My symptoms started to sagashuate again but Jock blocked my every move to slink back into bed and, as a reward for shaving myself, he allowed me one of his Salvation Specials, which have been known to twitch a man back from the very brink of the grave. No Jeevesian Worcester sauce and raw eggs for Jock: his potion is simply a dexedrin dissolved in gin and tonic to which he adds a spoonful of Mr Andrew's noted Liver Salts, two effervescing Vitamin C tablets and two ditto Alka-Seltzer. I have little time for foreigners but I must say that Drs Alka and Seltzer should have won the Nobel Prize years ago; my only quarrel with their brain-child is its *noise*.

I was just in time for luncheon, where Eric's shining morning face was much to the fore and Johanna . . . well, smiled at me politely. In the ordinary way I can do great damage to a plate of Jersey *Pais de Mai*, which is a sort of bubble-and-squeak made of potatoes, French beans and onions, fried into a cake and served with little pork sausages, but today the gastric juices simply would not flow and I could only wincingly watch the others eating great store of it while I worked out problems in topology with a hot roll.

Eric took me aside afterwards.

'If you should be feeling a little *effete*,' he said carefully, 'after our sing-song last night . . .?'

'You have a gift for words, Eric. I have never felt effeter. Say on.'

'I have heard it said that a little Pastis is sovereign in these cases. Drives away the evil humours.'

My better judgement rebelled but, as ever, my better judgement received what Jock calls a 'root up the sump' and soon the Pastis was smoothing out the wrinkles in my spleen in cavalry style. When the door-bell rang, two drinks later, I hardly jumped at all. George and Sam entered, snuffing the air curiously.

'Takin' up chemistry?' asked George.

'I have been gargling,' I said stiffly. 'I have a sore throat.'

'To name but a few, I'd say,' said Sam.

'Shall we go?' I said. 'Eric, you'll be able to amuse yourself, won't you? Jock will show you where everything is. Ask for a map if you want to go for a stroll; a man can get lost for months in these Jersey lanes.'

We drove towards St Helier. Where we were going was to the Headquarters of the Paid Police, situated in a street called, bafflingly, *Rouge Bouillon*. Our purpose was to do a delicate deal with a senior officer recommended for his discretion by our sturdy Centenier.

My conscience had been clear for nearly eighteen months, but still I felt a certain unease at entering this Cop-shop; an unease, I must say, soon dispelled by the friendly courtesy extended to us on every hand, with scarcely a chink from a hip-pocketed handcuff. Courteously refusing many an offer of cups of tea, we found ourselves presently in the office of the senior officer in question. I knew him at once for an honest man: my trained eye priced his suit at £40 and dated it as five years old. Bent policemen the world over may hide their guilty gains in the very vaults of Zurich itself, but they cannot resist the mohair suitings, the hand-made shoes. *Experto crede.*

His nostrils twitched delicately.

'My friend has been gargling,' said Sam. 'He has a sore throat.'

'Bad luck,' he said to George.

'Not me; him,' said George, pointing rudely.

'Oh. Well. Now, what can I do to help? It's about these rapes, I understand.'

With a glance at the others, I took it upon myself to be spokesman. He quite liked our reasoning about the rapist's motivation and selectiveness and made a few notes. He explained how his activities were curtailed by the protocol between the Paid and Honorary police – whom he seemed rather to approve of.

'Obviously,' he said, 'there's a bit of friction and frustration; it's natural between professionals and amateurs, but we could never police the country areas in the way that they do – they've got what amounts to a complete Secret Service out there in the *cotils* – and their, ah, summary way of sorting out minor felonies saves us an enormous amount of time and trouble. Every time one of my officers has to testify in court I have to change the whole bloody duty-roster, do you realize that? But I can't interfere in Parish affairs without being asked, any more than Scotland Yard can send men down to a country murder until the local flatfoots admit they're baffled. Having trodden all over the evidence first,' he added bitterly.

Then I told him about our proposed vigilante scheme, carefully omitting to mention our first, abortive try. His brow darkened a bit but he admitted that, there again, it wasn't his business.

'Unless, of course,' he said distinctly, 'anyone was foolish enough to carry weapons on such an expedition.'

We raised hands in horror at the very thought.

Then I broached the real subject of our visit: what we were going to do that night – and what we wanted him to do about it. He laughed at first, then he scowled, then he went a bit purple and raised his voice. I cannot truthfully say that he raved, but he certainly threw himself about a goodish bit. I just went on remorselessly reiterating the logic of the plan, the trifling harm it could do, the possible prophylactic effect, the willingness of the Honorary Police to cooperate if he would join in, the credit which would redound to his Force. He began to see reason; he was not really an unimaginative man. He stuck at one thing, however; he had to have a better indemnity for himself. It was, after all, his career, you understand.

That was when George surprised me – not for the first time.

'Use your phone?' he asked. 'Thanks. Hullo? No, not his secretary, thanks. No, nor his aide-de-camp. Just say it's George Breakspear and that it's urgent. What? Ah, hello, Porky, sorry to wake you up, ha ha; look, you remember that nonsense I told you we were thinking of trying on? Well, Mortdecai's got a man over who understands all about such rubbish and we're all set but the Commander of Detectives here quite naturally feels he needs a bit of higher clearance. Would you have a word with him?'

He had a word with him. The Commander did not actually stand to attention but one felt that, had he been alone, he might have done so. His end of the conversation consisted of seventeen 'yessirs', eight 'of course, sirs' and three 'thank you, sirs'. Then he hung up the telephone and looked at us sternly.

'Well,' he said, 'your friend seems to agree with me that perhaps something might be arranged on the lines you suggest.' We kept our faces solemn. Then we got down to battle-orders, liaised with Connétables and people on the telephone, arranged time-schedules.

'Above all,' I said as we were leaving, 'see that your men do not attempt to arrest the large, ugly man called Jock. First, he would hurt them badly and second, he is not in on the deal.'

'Did I agree to that?'

'Surely it was understood. He's only my servant, you see.'

'Has he any record on the Island?'

'None whatever, I promise you. Just hates having his fingerprints taken.'

'Hmph. All right.'

As we were leaving the main entrance a uniformed sergeant neatly cut me out of the mob and asked whether I could give the Commander a few minutes more of my time – alone. Quaking with guilt and terror I told the others that I would take a taxi home, then I followed the broad-based sergeant back to the C of D's office.

'It's all right, Mr Mortdecai,' he said, 'sit down. You needn't worry. I won't pretend I don't know who you are but I have no quarrel with you. That I know of.' He let that sink in a little.

'What I wanted was to ask you a couple of questions that I couldn't very well ask your friends, since their wives were victims, you understand.'

I didn't understand.

'Well, I'm not too happy about saying positively that all these offences are by the same artist. There's been another one, by the way, here in St Helier, but we've kept it out of the papers and the victim passed out: no description at all. But you know, these things catch on, they sort of become a fashion. It's like little boys setting old ladies on fire in dark alleys – one of them does it and they all think they've got to.'

I shuddered. Some of my best friends have been old ladies – not to mention little boys.

'Now,' he went on, 'we got a semen smear from the doctor's wife and your Centenier contrived to get one from Mrs Davenant's sheets – oh aye, your Centenier isn't half as thick as he likes to pretend – and they're both from the same class of secretor. But that's like saying that they're both blood-group "O". And, as you know, Mr Breakspear was adamant about that sort of thing with regard to Mrs Breakspear, and we couldn't get one from the new victim for reasons I needn't go into. So we haven't even got a third vector.'

I knew what he was going to ask, of course, but I wasn't going to help him, was I?

'I don't understand how I can help you,' I said.

'Well, put it like this. Your lady-wife knows both of the ladies violated in your neighbourhood, right? Well, do you think they might have mentioned anything to her about the assailant's er, personal details, which they might not have cared to tell their husbands?'

'I quite fail to follow you,' I lied.

'Oh yes you bloody do,' he snarled. 'I mean size of male member, whether circumcized, any little peculiarities; things like that.'

'Oh, I see. Oh dear. Use your phone? Hullo, Johanna? Look . . .'

'All right,' she said after a while, 'but "yech".'

'We don't say "yech" in the United Kingdom,' I said, 'we say "faugh".'

'We only say that on the golf-course, but O.K. And I'll try to do the other thing. It may take some time; I'll have to have a Cosy Chat with the cow Sonia.'

'Girl talk,' I said whimsically.

'Faugh!' she said, pronouncing it perfectly.

'This may take a few minutes,' I said to the Commander, looking at him meaningfully. He knew what I meant, he hoisted a great 40-oz bottle of some nameless Scotch on to his desk and raised his eyebrows. I inclined a gracious head. He found two tooth-glasses; they looked a little insanitary but Scotch whisky kills all known germs, as every housewife knows.

Johanna rang back about eight fluid ounces later and rattled off her news in a distant and faintly amused voice.

'That all?' I asked.

'What do you want – blue movies?'

'Good-bye,' I said.

'Good-bye,' she said, 'and Charlie, remember to brush your teeth tonight, huh?'

I hung up and collected my thoughts.

'My wife has recollected things that Mrs Davenant said to her shortly after the assault,' I told the Commander. 'She has also spoken to Mrs Breakspear and to the doctor's wife. The evidence appears, on the face of it, to be conflicting. Violet Davenant said "he was huge, like a horse, he hurt me terribly". Sonia Breakspear describes her assailant as "nothing to write to mother about" and the doctor's wife says, "I don't know – do you mean they come in different sizes?" She's lying, of course; she was a nurse, you see, and all nurses who marry doctors instantly become virgins *ex officio*, it's an understood thing.'

'I have heard that,' he said.

'But Johanna thinks that if he had been something out of the ordinary in any way she would have said something.'

'Yes.'

'As to circumcision, Violet wouldn't have known what one was talking about, Sonia says it wasn't relevant, whatever that means, and the doctor's wife says she thinks "yes". Doesn't help us much, does it?'

'No, not really. Tells us more about the ladies than the rapist, if you follow me, sir.'

We gazed at each other.

'Just so,' is what I said in the end. When I left, shortly afterwards, he behaved as though he felt he had made a friend. For my part, I had reservations.

I didn't have to take a taxi home after all, they lent me a police-car complete with driver. On arrival I offered him a pound note, which he sturdily refused. He wouldn't take a drink, either; he must have thought that I was a spy from the Promotions Board, bless him. What he would accept, to give to the Police Sports Fund, was a bottle of Cyprus sherry which one of us had inadvertently won in a 'raffle' if you know what that is. I felt a pang for whichever athlete won the noxious pottle, but after all, they know the risks when they join the Force, don't they?

How you deal with the tongue of an ox is as follows: you bid the butcher keep it in his pickle-tub for a fortnight, brushing aside his tearful pleas that it should be taken out after eight days. Then you rinse it lovingly and thrust it into the very smallest casserole that will contain it, packing the interstices with many an onion, carrot and other pot-herb. Cover it with heel-taps of wine, beer, cider and, if your cook will let you, the ripe, rich jelly from the bottom of the dripping-pot. Let it ruminate in the back of your oven until you can bear it no longer; whip it out, transfix it to a chopping-board with a brace of forks and – offer up grateful prayers to Whomever gave tongues to the speechless ox. (You can, of course, let it grow cold, when it will slice more delicately, but you will find that you can eat less of it.)

What I am trying to suggest, in my clumsy way, is that we had hot tongue for dinner, along with deliciously bitter turnip-tops and a *Pomme Duchesse* or two for the look of the thing. Eric and Johanna acquitted themselves nobly but I fancy I was well up amongst the leaders.

Later, sinking back amongst the cushions and the apricot brandy, I detected a jarring note. Jock, clearing away the broken meats, was now wearing a black Jersey or Guernsey, a pair of black slacks, black running-shoes and all the signs of a man who might well be carrying a deadly weapon.

'What's this?' I cried. 'What's this? Have you been watching the television again? I've told you and *told* you . . .'

'We're going out tonight, Mr Charlie, aren't we? Going to *chapel*, remember?'

In truth I had quite forgotten. I shall not pretend that the ox-tongue turned to ashes in my belly but it certainly started to give signs of discontent with its lot.

'We'll have to put it off, Jock; I forgot to get the cockerel.'

'Me and Farver Eric collected it 's'afternoon. Lovely bird it is, too, black as your hat.'

I drank all the coffee that was left and bolted the pill which Jock slipped me. Then, as is my wont when attending Satanic Masses in draughty medieval chapels, I packed a few iron rations such as liqueur Scotch, a paper of pheasant sandwiches and a small jar of *Pâté de Lièvre* into a briefcase; adding, after reflection, a pair of coarse warm pyjamas – who knew where I might spend the night? – and, mindful of Johanna's admonition, a toothbrush and tooth-powder.

We drove to George's house and collected Sam and him, both of them grumbling and sulking, then off we all sped on a total of eight wheels: Jock and Eric in my Mini, which was to be their get-away vehicle, and the rest of us in George's large, capable, boring Rover. Just before we left I was kind enough to ask George whether his Rover was licensed, taxed, oiled and possessed of a Roadworthiness Certificate. He looked at me pityingly, of course, but I'm used to that. People are always looking at me pityingly; it's because they think I'm potty, you see. Off, as I say, we sped through the night towards La Hougue Bie and were soon elaborately lost, which is a surprisingly easy thing to do in Jersey because all the country roads, thanks to something called *La Visite du Branquage*, look exactly the same. Indeed, getting lost in Jersey is one of the few outdoor sports one can enjoy in the colder evenings: it's tough on petrol but it saves you a fortune in other ways. None of us got very cross except, of course, George. When we finally pitched up at the site we parked the Rover at a discreet distance; Jock, it seemed, had already secreted the Mini in some furtive backwater which he had previously reconnoitred. We foregathered at the main gate. It really wasn't worth diddling the padlock: George did a splendid Army-style gate-vault and I, full of stinking pride, followed suit and bruised my belly badly. Sam and Eric, long purged of any competitive spirit, simply crept between the bars. I didn't see what Jock did, he's a professional – he simply materialized beside us in the dark.

We huddled together glumly, just inside the gate, while Jock loped off soundlessly into the night, feather-footed as any questing vole, to ascertain that the honest proprietaries of the ossuaries were abed. It seemed a very long time before he reappeared.

'Sorry, Mr Charlie, but there was this courting couple, see, and I had to put the fear into them, didn't I? See them off, see?'

'And are they quite gone now?'

He looked at me miffedly. When Jock sees people off, they stay seen off.

'Yes, Mr Charlie. Off like bleeding rabbits, him still holding his trousers up, her leaving certain garments behind in a wasteful fashion which I happen to have in my pocket this moment if you wish to check.'

I shuddered delicately, told him I would take his word for it.

Urged by a now surly George and Sam, we made our way over to the great mound itself, that horrid pile of the guts of ages long-gone and never to be one-half comprehended. Jock busied himself briefly with the padlock and chain which guarded the entrance to the underground passage leading to the grave-chamber and disappeared with Eric, my tape-recorder and a plastic bag full of the best toads available. When they emerged we all made our way up the winding path which leads to the chapels crowning the mound. Jock was as good as his word: the lock of the Jerusalem Chapel fell to his bow and spear with no more protest than a subdued clunk.

Eric bustled into the chapel in a business-like way, as one to the manner born. George, Sam and I followed him with different degrees of reticence. The rooster had been fed with raisins soaked in rum by Jock: I wish to make it clear that it was not I who carried it. Eric wasted no time; he dabbed little bits of this and that on the remains of the ancient altar and then spread over it his splendid corporal. The rest of us huddled, a little sheepishly perhaps, at the back of the tiny chancel – no larger than a bathroom in the better kind of country house. When I say 'the rest of us' I exclude Jock, of course, who was lurking somewhere in the shadows of the porch – his favourite place in times of turpitude and quite right too.

Strong though we were of purpose, I suspect that a show of hands, had it been taken at that moment, would have indicated a pretty *nem. con.* desire to return home and forget the whole thing. Except for Eric. He was growing almost visibly, taking on the stature of the craftsman who knows that what he is doing is not a thing that anyone else could do better; the dignity, if you like, of a scientist devising a hydrogen bomb, torn by the knowledge of evil but driven by the compulsion of research and the jackboot of human history.

'You will now be silent!' he suddenly said in a voice of such authority that we all stood up straight. He was wearing a long, white *soutane* sort of thing made of heavy silk; the only illumination came from the single candle he had placed on the altar: an ordinary white one, I noticed, and the right way up. Any mumbo-jumbo, it was evident, was not likely to embody the word 'abracadabra'. The candle lit up only the text of the travesty of the Mass before him and a small but startling patch of the embroidery on the corporal.

He said, or seemed to say, a few sentences under his breath. I did not try to hear, I have troubles of my own. Then, in a high, clear voice, he began to patter out the Introit, with the canting, carneying kind of intonation that old-fashioned Irish priests used to use – and still do for all I know. I dare say Sam may have picked up some of the Latin nastinesses that started to creep into the Ritual but I'm sure they were all Greek to George. I, who had both copied and, later, typed out, the Ritual, was expecting these passages, but nevertheless, on Eric's lips they seemed to sound nastier every minute. When he came to the part which, in Lord Dunromin's MS, had been filled only with a rectangle of red ink containing the words *Secrets Infâmes*, his voice, startlingly, dropped quite two octaves and in a horrid, bass grunt he began rhythmically to intone a number of names beginning with Ashtaroth, Astarte, Baal, Chemoz – people like that. I am happy to say that I do not remember more than a few of them – and if I did I certainly should not write them down here: I am not a superstitious man but I do not believe in poking sleeping gods in the eye with a sharp stick. I'm sure you understand me.

We three others had all, I suppose, been prepared for a mixture of tedium and embarrassment but it was quite extraordinary how little Eric Tichborne exuded a sort of aura of command – extraordinary, too, how he changed in stature. When his voice returned to the canting, seminary-priest's whine the inflections seemed to rise and fall in an almost inhuman way which I seemed to have heard before. On the previous night. Coming from my own tape-recorder. I did not like it a bit.

During the particularly tasteless mockery of the *Kyrie Eleison* his voice seemed to be shaking with an emotion which could have been suppressed laughter or, indeed, suppressed tears. Certainly not Pastis. But the strangest thing came afterwards, for his speech seemed to accelerate to a point where he was rattling off words at a speed which one would not have thought the human voice-box capable of. It went on accelerating until it had become the unnerving twitter of – yes – of a tape-recorder played at too fast a speed. This suddenly, inexplicably, broke off and we could hear the agonized rasp of his breathing. This, too, changed, as we watched and listened, and as he bowed and cramped into a spasm apparently asthmatic: wrenching coughs and retchings racked his little frame and, in between, he yelled out bits of Ezekiel: ' . . . *young men riding upon horses . . . there were her breasts pressed . . . there she bruised the teats of her virginity . . .* '

George half-rose and looked at me with a question. I shook my head. This was not something to interfere with. Bit by bit the little broken priest re-assembled himself, leaned upon the altar and pursued the increasingly filthy Ritual but more and more as though the words hurt him physically. It was probably an illusion caused by the candle-flame, but it seemed to me that he was being buffeted about by something that could not have been a wind. I stole a glance at the others: George's face was a mask of disapproval and disgust, his mouth not quite closed. Sam, to my astonishment, displayed a face crumpled up with compassion and, if I was not mistaken, traced with tears.

I don't know what my own face looked like.

Up at the altar, only his hands clearly visible in the pool of candlelight, Fr Tichborne jerked and swayed as his voice grew ever shriller, more frantic. I did not ask the others, afterwards, what they saw but to my mind the light seemed to thicken. I became acutely conscious, all of a sudden, of being exactly above the grave-chamber of the dolmen. Through the soles of my feet I seemed to feel a grinding crepitation as though the great slabs of the roof underground were shifting against the slabs of the side-walls. I am very much grown up, mature and not in the least superstitious, but I don't mind admitting that I wished, just then, that I were young enough to wish that my mother were there, if you take my meaning. Not that she would have helped, of course; she wasn't that kind of mother.

Something was being burned on the altar now, something which gave off a thick, delicious smoke that muddled our thoughts. The rooster was produced and displayed and then certain beastly things happened to it which, in an ordinary time and place, I dare say we should have prevented. The priest turned round to us, arms raised, his gown now kilted up above his navel to keep it clear of the blood-stains. George turned completely around, his face sunk in his hands. Sam did not move but I could hear him whimpering very quietly, piteously. I am, as I have often pointed out, a mature and sensible man; moreover I had personally copied out the Ritual and knew what was coming – I was a little surprised, therefore, to find that I had crossed the fingers of both my hands.

It cannot have been Eric's voice which began to bellow Great Salute and Imprecation of *S. Sécaire*: so little a man could never have whooped and bayed in so disgusting a fashion, nor can I believe that the rocks beneath the chapel could have shifted and groaned so hideously as they seemed to. In that thick, stupefying atmosphere, amidst those atavistic animal noises, nothing was real and when Eric seemed to rise some eight inches from the floor my fuddled surprise was only that I had not seen that he was barefooted and had not known that his right foot was horribly deformed. He was stuttering out the list of things which *S. Sécaire* offers to those against whom he is invoked when I saw his face blacken. He fell towards us on his face. His face, when it struck the stone floor, made a sound which I have been trying to forget ever since. It was inches from my shoe. The silk robe was almost up to his armpits; his body was not good to look at. He went on making odd noises – how was I to know that he was dead?

In any case, it was just then that the door burst open and all sorts of Centeniers, Vingteniers, Connétable's officers, aye and even members of the dread Paid Police themselves, thronged in and arrested every one of us again and again.

Now, according to my plans, you see, we should have been neatly arrested, charged with breaking and entering, and fined some five bob each the next day, giving enough details to enable the *Jersey Evening Post* to make it known to one and all – and particularly, of course, to the witchmaster rapist chap – that the Mass of St Sécaire had in fact been held, with him as the objective. I had, perhaps rather coyly, not made it perfectly clear to George and Sam that we should probably all have to spend the night in durance vile: that is to say, what you and I call 'the nick' – I don't like to cause people premonitory pain, do you? – and of course they would not, in any case, have agreed to the notion.

As it turned out, neither Sam nor George had really pulled himself together before we arrived at the Cop-shop in Rouge Bouillon, nor did they fully understand that they were to be the involuntary guests of the Deputy Lieutenant and Commander-in-Chief of Jersey until they – we – were issued with two blankets apiece, a cup of cocoa and a capital piece of bread and dripping, which I for one was ready for. Luckily, there were plenty of cells – the tourist season had scarcely begun – so that I had one all to myself and was spared any recriminations which my friends might otherwise, in the heat of the moment, have thought fit to heap upon me. The infinitely kindly policeman-gaoler permitted me to keep my briefcase of pyjamas, sandwiches and Scotch, exacting only a token tribute from the last. I shall not pretend that I slept well but at least I brushed my teeth, unlike some I could name.

12

Where the dead red leaves of the years lie rotten,
The cold old crimes and the deeds thrown by,
The misconceived and the misbegotten,
I would find a sin to do ere I die,
Sure to dissolve and destroy me all through . . .

The Triumph of Time

We who assembled in the Commander's office at half-past eight the next morning were but a moody crew. George and Sam seemed to be harbouring some petty resentment about the fact that I had had the simple foresight to pack my toothbrush and things. Perhaps, too, they just didn't like being locked up: there are people like that.

George was stalking up and down, four paces to the left, four to the right, like the captain of a very small ship pacing whatever it is that master-mariners pace. He was snarling a string of names of influential people, all of whom, he made it clear, he was about to telephone, and in the order named. Sam sat in a sort of collapsed lump: like me, he is a lovely talker when he has had his pre-luncheon drinks, but not before, really.

When George had exhausted his mental address-book, the Commander of Detectives cleared his throat in a way that gave the merest hint of smugness.

'Grave charges,' he said. 'Graver, perhaps, than you realize. Certainly graver than we had anticipated. Serious view they'll take of it. Serious. Unacceptable, you see.'

Sam made a brief reference to the Southern end of the digestive tract, in the plural, then relapsed into his lump.

'No, no, sir,' said the C of D, 'that doesn't help a bit, not that attitude doesn't. Constructive is the word. Let's be constructive. See what we can work out. Least harmful, least publicity, least cost to the taxpayer, eh?'

Sam made a suggestion which might or might not have given pleasure to the average taxpayer.

'There you are again, you see, sir. Interesting biologically but not what you'd call constructive. Lucky we haven't got a police stenographer in here, eh?' The gentle threat floated gently to the ground. Sam grumbled, 'Sorry', and George said, 'Hrrmph'. I said that I wasn't used to drinking cocoa for breakfast. The C of D produced his whisky bottle in an insulting fashion.

Then he explained to us, with thinly-disguised relish, that we were up an improbably-named creek in a concrete canoe without a paddle and that the kindest thing he could do, before clapping us into his deepest dungeon, was to allow us to make one telephone call each. George's advocate, the grandest imaginable, kept on saying 'oh dear, oh dear', until George slammed the instrument down. Sam's advocate seemed to be saying 'oy oy, oy oy' until Sam told him curtly that he wanted no moaning at the bar.

My own chap is but a mere solicitor and his reaction was crisp. 'Put the copper on,' he said, crisply.

Two minutes later the C of D told us, crisply, that it had just occurred to him that he couldn't hold us until he could think of some better charges and that, if we were prepared to go through a trifling formality at the box-office, we were free to go for the time being.

We went. I was prepared to chat freely on the way home but the others seemed both tacit and mute. I shall never understand people.

At home, Johanna greeted me with her cryptic smile, the one that makes her look like a rich man's Mona Lisa, and the sisterly sort of kiss with which a wife tells you that she loves you; but. Scorning explanations, I swept off to my dressing-room, leaving instructions that I should be called at twenty minutes before luncheon.

'Yes, dear,' she said. She has a gift for words.

In the event it was Jock who aroused me from a hoggish slumber, which had been intermingled with fearful dreams.

'Chops, Mr Charlie,' he said, 'and chips and them little French beans.'

'You interest me strangely. By the way, Jock, did you make good your escape last night without any, ah, friction?'

'Escape?' he sneered. 'That lot couldn't catch VD in Port Said.'

'*Please*, Jock. I wish to enjoy my luncheon.'

'Yeah. Well, cook's just turned the chops over so you got about four minutes to get downstairs, I reckon.'

I made it. I remember the chops vividly, they were delicious; so were them little French beans.

The afternoon hummed with telephone calls; I felt like W. B. Yeats in his bee-loud glade. First George, who upbraided me sternly, saying that Sonia had been quite frantic at being left alone all night. ('Pooh' is what I mentally said to that.) He was full of plans to import the flower of the English Bar to cow the Royal Court of Jersey.

'Don't be so damn silly,' I said; 'for one thing, they'd probably have no standing here; for another it would take them years to learn the quirks and quiddities of Jersey law. Leave it alone. Trust your Uncle Charlie.'

'Now, look here, Mortdecai,' he began. I explained courteously that I never listened to sentences beginning with those words. He started again, and again I had to interrupt him to explain that, although no great churchgoer, I found blasphemy distasteful. He breathed heavily into the instrument for perhaps half a minute. I felt that I should help him.

'The weather, I believe, is fine for the time of the year, is it not?'

He hung up. I started the *Times* crossword.

Sam was the next to telephone.

'Charlie, are you quite insane or do you really know what you're about? George says you're talking like a lunatic.'

'Have I ever let you down?' I asked simply.

'Have I ever given you the chance before?'

'How is Violet?'

'In complete withdrawal. Diagnosis: not sure. Prognosis: can't say. Being fed intravenously. Change the subject.'

'All right. We had chops for luncheon. Come to dinner: Jock is making Aloo Ghosht Bangalore with his own hands.'

'Charlie, I suppose you realize that if you haven't got this thing right I may have to disembowel you with my own hands?'

'Of course. But if I haven't got it right you may not need to, you see. Come to dinner?'

'Oh, all right. Eight o'clock?'

'Come earlier. Let's get sloshed.'

'All right.'

Johanna, who had wandered in, said, 'How nice to have one's friends in so often.'

'Tell Jock to put some more potatoes in the curry,' I said. 'Dear.'

The next call was the one I was dreading: it was from Jolly Solly my Wonder Solicitor.

'Ho ho ho!' he cried happily, rubbing his hands. (He has one of those loudspeaker telephones which leave both hands free – indispensable for confirmed hand-rubbers.) 'Ho ho! Such an interesting mess as you're in I never hoped to live to see. Legal history we shall make!'

'Less chortling and more news,' I demanded sourly.

'Ah, yes, well, you're naturally anxious. By the way, you've no aged parents whose grey hairs you might bring down in sorrow to the grave? No? Well, that's good news, I suppose. The rest is mostly bad. They're not yet sure how many charges they'll bring against you, half the clerks in the Attorney-General's office are working day and night on it, smacking their lips over the dripping roast. The preliminary list of choices is as follows:

'Breaking and Entering.

'Acting in a manner likely to cause a breach of the peace.

'Foul and disgusting language.

'Obstructing a Police Officer in the execution of his duty.

'Sacrilege under Section 24 of the Larceny Act of 1914: that carries a maximum sentence of life imprisonment, bet you didn't know that, ha ha.

'Sedition, well, yes, arguable.

'*Art. I de la Loi pour Empêcher le Mauvais Traitement des Animaux* – that only carries three months. Oh yes, and a £200 fine.

'*Art. I de la Loi Modifiant le Droit Criminel (Sodomie & Bestialité) confirmée par Ordre de Sa Majesté en Conseil*, I really do hope they don't fix you up for that one: ~~the maximum is~~ life but the *minimum* is three years. Last chap was only deported, but he was potty.

'Theft of one rooster or cockerel – no, the farmer swears Jock didn't pay him for it. You might get that reduced to "Taking and Driving Away without Owner's Permission", ha ha.

'Vagrancy. You didn't have any cash on you, you see.

'Failure to sign a driving licence.

'Breach of the Drugs (Prevention of Misuse) (Jersey) Law of 1964 – that depends on what the stuff Fr Tichborne was burning turns out to be.

'Breach – possibly – of *La Loi sur L'Exercise de la Médecine et Chirurgerie Vétérinaire.*'

I had no time to seek out a looking-glass, nor did I need to: I can say without hesitation that my face was white as any sheet – probably whiter than most.

'That all?' I quavered manfully.

'By no means, Charlie, by no means. I'm afraid that all those can be doubled and redoubled in spades by repeating them with the words "conspiring to" in front of them. Then a number of civil actions would probably lie:

'Trespass to the chapel and damage thereto.

'Trespass to the dolmen and damage thereto.

'Trespass to the Hougue Bie site generally and failure to pay the admission charge.

'Damages in respect of the rooster or cockerel.

'They'll probably think of some more, they've hardly started. Then I'm afraid there's all sorts of sticky possibilities under Ecclesiastical Law – and if that lot brings charges I'd plead guilty outright if I were you: cases in their courts drag out for years and the costs would break you.

'Just for example, if the Bishopric of Coutances hears about it you could be in bad trouble; the Bishop has something called a Right of Interference in anything concerning a priest criminally.

'Then there's a particularly horrid Papal Bull of 1483 which is still in force wherein Pope Sixtus IV protects Jersey churches against all sorts of things with an automatic sentence of "excommunication, anathema, eternal malediction and confiscation of property". Shouldn't worry too much about that unless you happen to be a

Papist – the confiscation of property bit wouldn't hold much water today.'

'Oh good,' I said heavily. 'And *now* have you exhausted all the possibilities? I mean, I've heard about the man in New Orleans who's serving 999 years, but I am no longer a young man, you know.'

'Well, as a matter of fact, I'm afraid there could be quite a lot more. You see, there's practically no codified statutory criminal law in Jersey; virtually all offences are Common Law ones. What that means, to the ordinary customer, is that the Attorney–General can prosecute you for anything deemed offensive or anti-social simply by sticking the word "unlawfully" in front of a description of whatever it was that you did and was objected to. Do you follow me?'

I whimpered assent.

'But let me bring a little sunshine into your life. All domestic motor insurance policies are automatically invalidated when the vehicle is used for an illegal purpose, so they'll certainly nab George Breakspear for driving uninsured. Yes, I thought that might cheer you up a bit. Oh, and by the way, you're lucky that your nasty little ceremony didn't actually succeed in raising up the Devil in person: there's a foot-and-mouth restriction in force at the moment and they would have got you under the Diseases of Animals Act for transporting a cloven-footed beast without a licence, ha ha.'

'Yes, ha ha indeed. In the meantime, what do I do?'

'Wait,' he said, 'and pray.'

I hung up.

Neither waiting nor praying is a skill I can boast of. Thinking was what was required – but thinking requires Scotch whisky, as all great thinkers agree and I had, in an idle moment, made an absurd promise to Johanna. The clock stood at ten to three. I turned the hands on to five-past six and rang the bell for Jock. He brought in the life-giving drinks-tray in what I can only call an insubordinate manner and wordlessly corrected the clock.

'Jock,' I said as the decanter gurgled, 'I rather fancy I am in the shit. It's because of Fr Tichborne dying, you see. Difficult to control the thing now.'

'Wasn't his fault, was it?' said Jock sulkily.

'Of course not, he was an excellent chap, the soul of courtesy; wouldn't have dreamed of embarrassing us on purpose. But the fact remains that it's made everything very difficult. What's to be done?'

'Well, kissing goes by favour, dunnit? Specially in Jersey.'

'I've never really known what that means. What do you take it to mean?'

'Well, say, if the filth' (by which he meant the CID), 'is getting a bit too close to you, you ring up one of your mates who was at Borstal with you and he fits the copper up with a corruption rap. Doesn't matter if it don't stick: they have to suspend him till it's investigated and the new bloke they put on your case hasn't got his contacks, has he, and most of what the first bloke had he kept in his head, didn't he, so you got a couple of munce to sort things out, see?'

'I think I see. Goodness. But I suppose it's the way of the world. I certainly can't think of anything else. Thank you, Jock.'

I rang up George.

'George,' I said in dulcet tones, 'I really must apologize for my incivility just now. Heat of the moment, you understand. Not myself, eh?'

I accepted his grunt as an acceptance of my apology.

'It seems to me,' I went on, 'that our watchword must be "kissing goes by favour" – we must use our *influence*, bring gentle pressure to bear, don't you think? For instance, how well do you know the more august chaps in Jersey; were you at Borst . . . I mean Harrow with any of them? I mean chaps like the chap you rang up from the Police Station yesterday?'

'Very well indeed, some of them.'

'Well, there you are then. Ask them to tea, fill them up with *tuck* – hot buttered crumpets, little meat pies, cherry brandy – all the nice things they won't be allowed to have at home – then remind them of your schooldays together, all those innocent pranks, you know the sort of thing.'

'I am doing precisely that at this moment. Is there anything else?'

'No, not really.'

'Good-bye, then.'

'Good-bye, George.'

The thought of hot buttered crumpets took me by the throat like a tigress: I was racked with desire for them. I strolled into the kitchen, where I found Jock sticking photographs of Shirley Temple into his scrap-book.

'Jock,' I said casually, 'do you suppose there are any hot buttered crumpets in the house?' He glowered at me.

'You know perfickly well what Mrs Mortdecai said about hot buttered crumpets, Mr Charlie. "Better without them" is what she said you was.'

'But this is a special case,' I whined. 'I *need* those crumpets, can't you see that?'

His face remained stony.

'Tell you what, Jock; you forget to mention hot buttered crumpets to Mrs Mortdecai and I'll forget to mention about you pinching her caviare. Kissing goes by favour, you know.' He sighed.

'You catch on quick, Mr Charlie.'

I drew up a chair, rubbing my hands like any lawyer.

For some arcane reason the crumpets they sell in Jersey tend to come in packets of seven, which means that when two crumpet-eaters are gathered together there is a rather sordid gobbling-race for he who finishes his third crumpet before his contender has a natural right to the fourth. We were both well into our third – it looked like being a photo-finish – when the door-bell rang and Jock arose, glumly wiping the melted butter off his chin. It is at times like these that breeding shows. After a rapid mental battle I divided the remaining crumpet into two almost equal halves.

Jock returned, flashed a glance at the muffineer, and announced that some gentlemen from the Press were in the lobby and should he show them into the drawing-room.

The gentlemen of the Press proved to be one personable young woman from the *Jersey Evening Post*, clearly bursting with intelligence, one world-weary young photographer and one large, sad, well-bred chap representing wireless and television. I dealt out glasses of ardent spirits with the deftness of a Mississippi steamboat gambler, then made a deal with them.

'Keep the national press off our backs,' was the burden of my song, 'and you shall have, exclusively, all the information and photographs you can reasonably expect. Fail me in this and

I shall close my doors upon you and Tell All to the *Sunday People*.'

Three shudders followed this, then three fervent nods.

In carefully rehearsed words I told them quite a lot of the truth, bearing down heavily on the fact that the offender was clearly a witchmaster and that it was well known that the *Messe de S. Sécaire* could not fail to draw his teeth and rob him of his mystic powers if he were a true witch and that, if he persisted in his evil-doing, certain of his physical powers would also be grievously afflicted.

Then I darted over to the other half of the house and borrowed from my landlord a large, smelly pipe and a small, smelly poodle. With the one clenched between my teeth (yes, the pipe) and the other snuggled in my arms, I allowed them to take photographs of benign old Mortdecai in his favourite armchair and benigner old Mortdecai pottering about in the garden. They went away quite satisfied. I fled to the bathroom and got rid of the taste of the pipe with mouthwash, changed my clothes and told Jock to send the poodle-polluted suit to the cleaners or, if beyond redemption, to the poor.

Nothing else of any note happened that day except the exquisite curry, throughout which I played records of Wagner: he goes beautifully with curry, the only use I've ever found for him. Sam left early and I too was ready for my bed, as I always am after a night in the cells. I heard Johanna come in from her bridge-party but she went straight to her room, so I suppose she had lost. I lay awake for a long time, thinking of poor little Eric Tichborne and feeling like a pagan suckled in a creed outworn. I dare say you know the feeling, especially if your wife sometimes goes to bed without saying good night.

13

Seven sorrows the priests give their Virgin;
But thy sins, which are seventy times seven,
Seven ages would fail thee to purge in,
And then they would haunt thee in heaven:
Fierce midnights and famishing morrows,
And the loves that complete and control
All the joys of the flesh, all the sorrows
That wear out the soul.

Dolores

I spend the morning and much of the afternoon in bed, moping and pretending to be poorly. Jock brought me no less than three successive cups of his delicious beef-tea, not to mention a sandwich or two from time to time. Johanna tried to take my temperature.

'Oh no you don't!' I cried.

'But we always take it like that in the States.'

I was saved by the bell of the telephone: the Attorney-General's staff wanted to know about my citizenship status. Then it rang again: it was George, whose advocate had been terrifying him. I told him that my solicitor was a much better terrifier and a faster – he had done all his terrifying the previous day. Then it rang again and I told the Chief Superintendent's clerk that, no I couldn't pop down to the Station, I was suffering from a tertiary ague.

This sort of thing went on. There will, I think, be telephones in Hell.

What I was waiting for was the *Jersey Evening Post*, for a good press was essential to the efficacy of our scheme and might well be useful when things came to be considered in Court.

Our copy of the newspaper is delivered at six o'clock but, evidently, other people get theirs earlier, for the telephone calls started again with redoubled vigour at half-past four. Set out in rough order they comprised:

One learned Rector of my acquaintance who wished, sadly and probably sensibly, that we had tried the Church's resources first, instead of imperilling our souls by flirting with the Opposition.

One Christian Scientist – I thought they had all died out – who explained that rape was all in the mind and merely a manifestation of Mortal Error. She was still talking when I hung up on her, but I don't suppose she noticed.

Three separate and distinct Jehovah's Witnesses who told me that Armageddon was scheduled for 1975 and that there would be no place for me among the 50,000 survivors unless I did something about the state of my soul pretty smartly. I didn't try to explain that the thought of surviving in a world populated only by Witnesses horrified me: I just gave them each a telephone number of one boring friend or another who would, I assured them, relish a visit from one of their sect.

Two respectable acquaintances who each had found that they had invited us to dinner on the wrong day and would ring us back in due course.

Three ditto who had accepted invitations from us but now found they had previous – or more likely subsequent – engagements.

One engaging re-incarnation buff who had been the Great Beast of Revelation the last time around.

One quite frantic chap who said I had got it all wrong about the Devil: 'She's a coloured person,' he explained.

Several alleged and assorted witches, some of whom sneered and some of whom offered alibis.

One drunken Irishman who asked for precise directions to my house so that he could call and bash my bloody brains in.

One chap called Smith who said that he was going to church to pray for my soul but with no very lively expectation of success.

One prominent member of the Pressure Group for the Reform of the Cruelty to Animals Law, who proposed to take the poodle away from me and find it a good home. (I told her that I, too, was keen on cruelty to animals but that the poodle was a stuffed one, alas, having died last year in a nameless fashion.)

Clearly, the *Jersey Evening Post* must have done me proud and, indeed, when my copy at last arrived, so it proved. Bannered and splashed across the front page was all the Mortdecai that was fit to print. The photograph sent Johanna and Jock lurching and staggering across the floor in ribald mirth: senile, scholarly old Mortdecai, be-poodled and be-piped, beamed pottily out at one in the most *diverting* way. Miss H. Glossop, the young lady reportress, had evidently done her homework, for her facts were clear and well-researched. Erudite, unworldly old Mortdecai, it appeared, anxious to help friends in distress, had fought fire with fire to such effect that the very celebrant of the rites had dropped dead – to everyone's regret – at the climax of the performance. 'What,' the story implied, 'would the harvest be for the guilty target, when even the innocent gunner, so to speak, couldn't take the recoil?' Miss Glossop went on in an exceedingly well-informed way to recount the marvellous powers attributed to the Mass of *S. Sécaire*, and to pity the witch who pitted his paltry powers against it. No literate diabolist could possibly have missed the point. Moreover, apart from a slight tendency to freely split infinitives, her style evidently derived from the best models: not a single 'subsequently transpired' marred her pellucid prose. I was well pleased. Indeed, I got up in time for dinner and made a few telephone calls myself. Sam was out – no one knew where – but George grudgingly admitted that the ploy seemed to be going well. Solly, his mouth full (solicitors dine much earlier than barristers), admitted that my image might well be a little better for the publicity, and let me know that one or two of the charges had been dropped and only four or five fresh ones had been thought of.

I began to feel positively chipper. Apart from the prospect of a few score years in prison the horizon was pretty clear. Peals of laughter wafted through from the kitchen, where Jock, I suppose, was showing my photograph to his dominoes-friend and the cook. I beamed indulgently.

Dinner was announced.

I need hardly say that I am not one of those whose minds dwell continually on foodstuffs: but when I do, once in a while, turn my mind in that direction it is with a certain single-mindedness; particularly when, as in this case, the grocery under advisement proves to be a guinea-fowl, that triumph of the poulterer's art. This particular feathered friend was an uncommonly well-poultered example: it must have led a beautiful and sheltered life. Hand-in-hand tripped a bottle of Barolo, singing wistful lays of the gravel slopes of the Piedmont. Seldom have I spent a happier and more innocent hour but, as the Master himself tells us, it is at times like these that Fate creeps out of a dark alley, fingering a stuffed eel-skin destined for the back of one's neck.

I threw the end of my *Romeo y Julieta* into the embers of the fire and cast a sort of husbandly look at Johanna. She raised an eyebrow shaped like a seagull's wing. I winked. The telephone rang.

It was the Centenier. He thought I might like to know that there had been another rape. The wife of the tomato grower. Satanic trapping as before but with an addition: having knocked her unconscious with the same gentle punch, he had scribbled the word 'secretary' in greasepaint in a semi-circle on her bare belly, well below the navel.

'Have you read the paper tonight?' I asked.

'I seen the photo of you, sir, but I 'aven't what you might call perused the entire article, 'aving been called out on this case, eh?'

'Take another look at the lady's tummy,' I said, 'I think you'll find the word is *Sécaire*.'

I rose wearily, feeling as old as sin.

'Ah well,' I sighed, 'back to the grind.'

'Oh *good*,' said Johanna. 'Race you to bed?'

'I did not mean that.'

'You were meaning it just now.'

'Just now I was in early middle age. At this moment I feel ready for the Tom and Geriatric ward.'

'All right, we'll play patients and nurses: you shall chase me upstairs, but very slowly; to husband your strength.'

'Oh, very well,' I said.

My heart was not really in it but I appreciated the fact that she wanted to help. For some reason, you see, we can't talk to each other properly.

14

Not utterly struck spiritless
For shame's sake and unworthiness
Of these poor forceless hands that come
Empty, these lips that should be dumb,
This love whose seal can but impress
These weak word-offerings wearisome
Whose blessings have not strength to bless
Nor lightnings fire to burn up aught
Nor smite with thunders of their thought.

Epilogue

A hideous wailing penetrated my grimly dreams: I awoke shuddering. It was only Jock mounting the stairs with my tea-tray, singing 'On the Good Ship Lollipop' in his best falsetto. He does it rather well but there is a time and place for Shirley Temple.

'This *aubade* or *mattinata* must not occur again, Jock. It hurts me in the liver. "Cursed is he who greets his brother with a loud voice in the morning" as Deuteronomy was so fond of pointing out.'

Vengefully, he allowed some tea to slop into my saucer as he handed it to me, then deliberately mopped it up with a well-ripened pocket-handkerchief. Game, set and match to him. The tea, when I could bring myself to sample it, tasted like waters of Babylon which had been too freely wept in.

'How is the canary this morning?'

'Got a bad leg.'

'Then summon the best vet money can buy, spare no expense. A Mr Blampied is well spoken of.'

'He's bin. Said the leg'll 'ave to come orf.'

'Nonsense. I am not a rich man, I cannot afford to keep wooden-legged canaries in idle luxury.'

'He's a singer, Mr Charlie, not a bleedin' dancer. Oh, yeah, and Mr Davenant and Mr Breakspear are waiting for you downstairs.'

'Oh dear, oh Christ, are they really? Er, they seem in a jolly sort of mood, I dare say?'

'Bloody diabolical.'

'Oh. They'll have heard about the new incident, then?'

'Yeah.'

Jock's gift for language had not failed him: 'diabolical' was the only word to express the moods of George and Sam. They stared at me, as I good-morninged them, as though they were a brace of Lady Macbeths confronted with one of the less acceptable kinds of damned spot. I crinkled my mouth into a wry smile. Their mouths stayed grim. I toyed with the idea of telling them a funny story, then discarded it.

'Drinks?' I asked. 'Scotch? Gin and tonic? Bottled beer?'

'Mortdecai,' said George, 'you are a four-letter man.'

'D'you know, I've never quite known what that meant.'

Sam told me; in four letters. I allow no one to speak to me like that.

'Sam,' I began heavily.

He repeated the word.

'Well,' I conceded, 'there may be something in what you suggest. But consider: the rapist – if this incident *is* his work – may not have had time to read yesterday's *Jersey Evening Post*; it had not been long on the streets.'

'Then how do you account for the word *Sécaire*?'

'Oh. You heard about that bit.'

'Yes, we heard. And it seems to us that your perverse and crack-brained scheme has not only disgraced us and put us in jeopardy of gaol but, worst of all, it has not worked. The man is clearly laughing at us.'

'Early days to be certain of that, surely? I mean, it's just possible that it might *really* work, you know. In his subconscious or something . . .' I tailed off lamely.

'Rubbish. We must simply resume the ambushes – every night from now on. The new incident confirms our view that the targets are always likely to be Englishwomen in their thirties and living in this neighbourhood. It's just a matter of time now, and vigilance.'

'And staff-work,' grunted George.

'And loyalty.'

'I see. Very well. We start tonight, I take it? Or do we leave it a night to let the chap re-charge his, ah, batteries?'

'Tonight,' they said with one voice.

'I suppose you're right; chap like that probably doesn't run off batteries – glands like nuclear reactors, I should think.'

'Unfunny. And I suppose you know that we're all due at the Police Station in forty minutes: I dare say you might care to offer us a drink before we leave.'

I opened my mouth and shut it again. It was clear that I could do no right that morning.

The Chief Superintendent met us with a stony look. Like all good policemen who have received hints to lay off from people in high places, he was in an ugly mood. He studied us carefully, one by one – the time-honoured technique of policemen who wish you to understand that they will be Keeping an Eye on you in the future and that you'd better not be caught parking on a yellow line.

'For some reason not confided in me,' he began heavily, 'it has been decided that this is to be treated as a silly prank which ended tragically. Most of the gravamen of the many charges will be laid to the account of the deceased Tichborne. I hope that will please you. You are only to be charged with Unlawfully Entering Private Premises, Unlawfully Causing Scandal and Distress, Failing to prevent a Breach of the Law Against Ill-treatment of Animals and you, Mr Breakspear, with Driving an Uninsured Vehicle and Failing to Sign a Driving Licence.'

I broke out in a sweat of relief. George grated his teeth audibly. Sam's eyes seemed to be fixed on some distant and loathsome object.

'I have been in touch informally,' the policeman went on, 'with the *Société Jersaise*. They are, quite rightly, shocked and furious, but you may find that a written apology and an offer to pay for a new padlock-chain and for the removal of the smoke-stains on the walls of the chapel will satisfy them. Say, three hundred pounds.'

Three cheque-books flashed in the dusty sunshine; three fountain pens scratched and squirted in unison.

'The Police Court magistrate has sent up your case directly to the Royal Court. You are to appear before a special session at precisely two-thirty this afternoon, which gives you plenty of time to enjoy a large and expensive lunch. No, please do not ask me to join you. I am feeling a little sick. Good day to you.'

That man was wasted as a policeman: he should have been the headmaster of a High Anglican public school. We slunk out.

The desk sergeant offered no cups of tea this time; he viewed us coldly. He probably knew little of the matter but the scent of opprobrium must have clung to us: we were no longer gents as such but faces to memorize.

He asked me to identify, and sign for, my tape-recorder complete with one cassette. I did so.

'There's nothing on the cassette,' he explained.

'D'you want to bet?' I asked.

My car was triumphantly displaying a parking-ticket, which the others gazed at with moody satisfaction.

'Well, where are we lunching?' asked George.

'At the nearest rookery for me,' I said, 'it is my day for eating crow.'

In the event we were lucky enough to secure a table at the Borsalino, but we could do scant justice to the excellent fare.

'Don't you *like* the Poulet Borsalino?' asked a puzzled proprietor. Sam looked at him with dreary eyes.

'The Poulet Borsalino is excellent. It is *us* we don't like.'

There was nothing in that for the proprietor; he stole away. (When I tell you that Poulet Borsalino is breast of chicken rolled around gobs of Camembert cheese and deep-fried, you will realize what depths of chagrin caused us to spurn it.)

The Royal Court was intimidating beyond belief. George and Sam's Advocates and my jolly Solicitor joined us in the lobby. The Advocates pursed their lips; Solly gave me a wink. Taking his point, I wrenched the knot of my necktie tight and slid it to one side, rumpling the collar; a simple ruse which reduces one's apparent income by several hundred pounds. *Verb. sap.*, not to mention *experto crede*. We mounted flight after flight of linoleumclad stairs, designed, no doubt, in ancient times to ensure that prisoners arrived in Court flushed and sweating with guilt. Solly goosed me on the stairs, no doubt to cheer me up. Outside the court room itself we were surrendered to the *Greffier*: a terrifying personage in a black robe who looked as though he believed in capital punishment for motoring offences. Soon we were joined by the *Vécomte* – pronounced Viscount – another black-robed officer bearing a great mace, and we processed through oaken doors into the Court. It is a tall, airy, well-lit chamber of great beauty, hung with excellent pictures. Before us, in some majesty and under a splendid canopy, sat the arbiters of our fate. In the centre (Solly explained to me in a whisper) the Deputy Bailiff; to his right a lower throne – empty – where Her Majesty's Lieutenant-Governor would have been sitting had he chosen to exercise his right to attend; on the other side a brace of *Jurats*, chosen from the flower of Jersey's ancient aristocracy. They looked wise and useful, which I believe is their function.

The *Vécomte* stood the mace in its socket before the Bench, the *Greffier* took his stall and the Court of the Inferior Number (so called when only two *Jurats* are sitting) was in session.

The public benches were almost empty: the notice had been too short for the mass of sensation-seekers and only the usual handful of ghoulish old ladies sucking peppermints was there – the ones who don't like all that violence on television and prefer to hear it at first hand, hot from the sty. The sole occupant of the Press bench was my friend Miss H. Glossop, radiating intelligence and goodwill. I had the impression that she would have liked to give me a friendly wave.

There was a deathly hush in the Court, then people recited things in ancient Norman-French; lesser officers repeated them in English; policemen, both Paid and Honorary, related how they had proceeded from one place to another in the execution of their duty and acting on information received and what was more they had notebooks to prove it. Sam's advocate rose and moaned piteously; George's man boomed capably; Solly – a Solly I had never seen before – craved the Court's indulgence to explain briefly that I was – although not in just those words – merely a fucking idiot and more to be pitied than censured.

There was another deathly hush, broken only by peppermint noises from the old ladies. The Deputy Bailiff and *Jurats* retired to debate the finer points and I had a quick consultation with my pocket-flask.

Our judges returned after a very few minutes, wearing damned disinheriting countenances. When everyone was seated, we miscreants were bidden to stand up again. The Deputy Bailiff had a fine command of the language; as he summarized our follies we shrank in stature quite visibly.

Five sonorous minutes made it clear to us, and to all beholders, that we were the sort of reprobates without which the fair Isle of Jersey could well do; that much of the hooliganism, drunkenness and general lowering of moral standards on the Island was directly attributable to such as we; that men of our age should be giving an example to the younger generation and that it had better not happen again, or else.

He took a pause for breath.

'Charlie Strafford Van Cleef Mortdecai,' he said in a voice of doom. 'You are deemed guilty on all three counts. What say you in answer?'

I caught the compelling eye of the old lady opposite. She was leaning forward, her mouth ajar, the great striped peppermint inside clearly visible.

'I'm awfully sorry,' I told the peppermint; 'foolish, ill-advised, unforgivable. Yes. Sorry. Very.'

He told me that I was a man of good family; that I had acted in a disinterested way on my friends' behalf, although foolishly; that the Court was satisfied with my expressions of regret, that the disgrace was probably punishment enough and that the Court was therefore disposed to be lenient. I hung my head to hide my smirk.

'You are therefore committed to prison for a total of twenty-seven months.' The old lady's dentures snapped shut on the unlucky peppermint. 'Or to pay an aggregate fine of four hundred and fifty pounds. Give the prisoner a chair, officer. You are also bound over to be of good behaviour for five years in your own recognizance of a further five hundred pounds.'

He slid his spectacles six inches down his splendid nose. 'Can you pay?' he asked in a kinder voice.

Sam drew fifty pounds less in fines but he didn't get the bit about being of good family, which must have stung.

George drew the same as Sam because, as the Deputy Bailiff pointed out, he had a fine military record. He was on the point of sitting down when the Deputy Bailiff, displaying a sense of timing that Mohammed Ali would have envied, hit him with another hundred and fifty quid for the motor-insurance offence.

Outside, in Royal Square, Solly congratulated me.

'You did very well. I was proud of you. And the Deputy Bailiff was very gentle.'

'*Gentle?*'

'Lord, yes. You should hear him telling off one of us lawyers if we put a foot wrong. Makes one feel like a Labour MP caught soliciting in a public lavatory. Which reminds me, what does one do with a toad?'

'A toad?' I squeaked.

'Well, it could be a frog, I suppose. Sort of brown, warty thing.'

'That's a toad.'

'Yes, well, it arrived this morning and my secretary can't get it to eat. Offered it bread and jam, all sorts of things. Fussy little beast.'

'When you say "arrived" . . .?'

'In a cigar-box. Also enclosed was a piece of lavatory paper, inscribed with the word "Mortdecai". Er, it was *used* lavatory paper.'

I became glad that I had eaten so sparingly at luncheon. Pulling myself together, I said:

'A ribald pun, simply, I should think. On the word *crapaud*, you see.'

'I see,' he said; but he gave me an odd look.

Sam and I dined early, at George's house, then made our selection of women to be protected that night and started to place telephone calls. We were quite unprepared for the stiff hostility with which our suggestions were met; we were, it seemed, social lepers. The first two people we spoke to said, with no attempt at plausibility, that they were otherwise engaged; the third put the receiver down in a marked manner as soon as she heard our names; the fourth said that her husband could look after her perfectly adequately, thank you very much; the fifth said that if we telephoned again she would inform the police. Only the last, a gin-sodden, lust-crazed poetess welcomed our proposal – and her tones made it clear that she had it in mind to do a bit of raping on her own account.

We looked at each other blankly. The telephone rang.

'It's for you, Charlie. Johanna.'

'Charlie,' she said in honeyed tones, 'you may care to know that my bridge-party tonight is off. Yes, off. Lady Pickersgill has telephoned to say that she has a bad cold. So has Lady Cortances. So has Mrs ffrench-Partridge. I hope you are proud of yourself.'

'Gosh, Johanna, I can't tell you how sorry . . .'

'I have just telephoned the airport; they tell me that there are no planes leaving for London tonight. Moreover, the cleaning lady has just told me that she can no longer oblige: she must devote herself in future to caring for her old mother. Whose funeral she attended last year. Moreover, there is a television van parked in the road outside. Moreover, have you seen the evening paper?' Without waiting for a Yes, No, or Don't Know, she hung up.

I went out in the rain to the gate and collected the newspaper. (Your free-born Jersey tradesman will do much for you but he scorns the act of putting newspapers into letterboxes, isn't that odd?)

We studied the front page. The *Jersey Evening Post* had been fair, nay, kindly to us in the report of the trial but the photograph taken of us on the pavement outside the Court was unfortunate to say the least. We three shambling offenders huddled guiltily together, surrounded by venal shysters, mopping and mowing. George was glaring at the camera in a way that could only be called homicidal; Sam looked like an expletive deleted from a Watergate tape while I had been caught scratching my behind and sniggering over my shoulder. All most unfortunate.

We looked at each other; or to be exact, they looked at me while I shiftily avoided their eyes.

'I know,' I said brightly, 'let's all get drunk!'

They stopped looking at me and looked at each other. Sonia reappeared, looked at the photograph and promptly got a fit of the giggles. This can be quite becoming in some women but Sonia has never learned the art: her version is too noisy and she tends to fall about on sofas and things, displaying her knickers. Where applicable. George made his displeasure clear to her and she went back to the real love of her life – her washing-up machine; nasty, noisy thing.

Sam and George started to re-enact the 'let's all look at Charlie in a hateful way' scene, so I rose. I can be hurt, you know.

'I am going home to watch the television,' I said stiffly.

'Oh no you're not,' snapped George. 'You're going home to change into dark clothes, soft shoes and a weapon, and you're reporting back here in fifteen minutes with Jock, similarly clad.'

Now, I may choose to make myself seem a bit of a craven at times, when it suits my book, but I don't take crap like that – even from retired brigadiers. *Especially* from retired brigadiers. I turned to him and gave him a slow, insubordinate stare.

'It will take *twenty* minutes at least,' I said insubordinately, 'because, things at home being what they are, I shall have to look out the clothes myself.'

'Do your best,' said George, not unkindly.

In the event, I was back there in twenty-eight minutes.

'Right,' said George. 'Here's the plan. Since these idiots will not let us lie up *in* their houses we shall have to patrol *outside* their houses – from now until midnight. I shall move between Hautes Croix and this house; Jock will drop Sam at La Sergenté from where he will make his way to St Magloire's Manor and so, past Canberra House, back here; Jock himself, since both Sonia and Johanna are alone and unguarded, will work between Wutherings and Les Cherche-fuites; you, Charlie, will cover the lanes between here and Belle Etoile Bay. None of us will use metalled roads. Any questions?'

There weren't any questions.

15

> There the gladiator, pale for thy pleasure,
> Drew bitter and perilous breath;
> There torments laid hold on the treasure
> Of limbs too delicious for death;
> When thy gardens were lit with live torches;
> When the world was a steed for thy rein;
> When the nations lay prone in thy porches,
> Our Lady of Pain.

Dolores

A cold coming I had of it, I don't mind telling you, just the worst time of the year for a vigilante patrol. I believe I've already given you my views about the month of May in the British Isles. This May night, as I picked my glum way down to Belle Etoile Bay, was cold and black as a schoolgirl's heart and the moon – in its last quarter and now quite devoid of the spirit of public service – reminded me only of a Maria Teresa silver dollar which I had once seen clenched between the buttocks of a Somali lady who was, I fancy, no better than she should be. But enough of that.

Down I stole to Belle Etoile Bay. The sea breathed hoarsely, like a rapist out of training. Back I stole, breathing like a middle-aged vigilante who has neither pocket-flask nor sandwich-case about him because his wife isn't speaking to him. As I entered Chestnut Lane (*La Rue des Châtaigniers*), nearing the end of my beat for the first time round, a *châtaignier* or chestnut tree quietly divided itself into two *châtagniers* or chestnut trees and one of the component parts drifted in my direction. I am often asked what to do when things of this kind happen to you and I always divided my advice into several alternative parts; viz, either

a. blubber, or

b. run, or

c. drop on to your marrow-bones and beg for mercy.

If, of course, you belonged, as I did, to an absurd Special Something Unit in the war – yes, that 1939–45 one – then you can do better. What I did was to drop silently to the ground and roll over several times. This accomplished, I plucked out my pistol and waited. The tree-person froze. After a long time he spoke.

'I can't see your face,' he said, 'but I can see your great arse. I'm putting a Lüger bullet into it in about three seconds flat unless you gimme a good reason why not.'

I stood up, coaxing my lungs back into service.

'Jock,' I said, 'I am recommending you for the Woodcraft Medal. Your impersonation of a tree was most plausible.'

' 'Ullo, Mr Charlie.'

'What do you have on your person, apart from that machine-pistol which I have repeatedly told you not to carry?'

'Got a flat half-bottle of brown rum.'

'Faugh,' I said. 'I'm not as thirsty as that. When you are next at the Wutherings end of your beat, be so good as to find and fill my pocket-flask; I shall patrol back to Belle Etoile Bay and meet you here again in, say, thirty minutes.'

'Right, Mr Charlie. I dare say you'd like the sandwich-case, too?'

'Very well, Jock, since you insist. I suppose I should keep my strength up.'

'Right, Mr Charlie.' He started to melt away.

'Jock!'

'Yeah?'

'There should be a few scraps of cold pheasant in the fridge.'

'They're still there; I don't like pheasant, do I?'

'They will do for the sandwiches, but at all costs remember: pheasant sandwiches are made with brown bread.'

'Yeah.'

He went on melting away, as I did.

Melting away from Chestnut Lane to Belle Etoile Bay involves getting lost, muddy and wet; not to mention breaking your shins against nameless bits of farm machinery left around *on purpose* by Jerseymen. When I got to the Bay the sea was making the same sort of hoarse, defeated noise: 'Oh gaw-blimey,' it seemed to be moaning, " 'ow much longer 'ave I gotter go on wiv this meaningless to-ing and fro-ing?'

'I couldn't have put it better myself,' I assured it.

I turned back towards Chestnut Lane: unlike the sea, I could look forward to pocket-flasks and sandwich-cases. That was my error: the gods keep a sharp and jealous eye on chaps who hug themselves in such expectations.

Bursting cheerfully through a hedgerow, I saw a large and tree-like shape in front of me. I thought it was Jock.

'Jock?' I said.

The shape took a tree-like pace towards me and hit me very hard on the temple. I fell, more slowly than you could imagine, to the ground, my face smacking the mud as gratefully as though it were a pillow. I was incapable of movement but not really unconscious. A small flashlight was turned on to me; I shut my tortured eyes against it but not before I had noticed a shoe close to my face. It was a *good* shoe, the sort of heavy, tan walking-shoe that I might have bought from Ducker's of Oxford in the days when my father paid my bills.

The light went out. I felt a hand feeling my temple in a knowledgeable sort of way; it hurt damnably but there was no crepitation – I dared to hope that I might live. Then two strong hands lifted me to a kneeling position and I opened my eyes. Towering above me was a horrendous creature with a face such as hell itself would have rejected. It was near enough for me to receive its stench, which was abominable. Then its knee came up and struck the point of my jaw with a deafening, blinding smash.

Dimly-experienced things happened to me in my stupor; I was rummaged and buffeted, hoisted and wrenched. Wisely, I decided to remain asleep, and sleep I did until an excruciating pain screamed out of my right ear. I jerked wildly from the pain, which redoubled it, so I fainted, only to awake instantly with an even sharper agony. A great explosion happened close to the ear – and more pain. Awake now, in a sort of way, I mustered enough sense to remain motionless while my frightful assailant rustled away. When I was sure that he had gone I delicately explored my situation. I found that I was standing against a tree. My hands and feet were unencumbered. I tried moving my head – and screamed. Infinitely gently I raised my hands to my ear, asking them to tell my scrambled brain what it was all about. When my hands told me, I fainted again – just as you would have – and awoke instantly with another scream of pain.

My ear, you see, had been nailed to the tree.

I stood very still for what seemed an hour. Then I reached behind me and drew out the Banker's Special pistol from my hip-pocket. I filled my lungs and opened my mouth to shout for help but a sharp agony came from my jawbone and a horrid grating noise and my tongue discovered that my teeth were all in the wrong places.

I pointed the pistol into the air and squeezed the trigger but I had not the strength to work the double-action. Using both hands I contrived to cock the hammer, then I fired. Then again. Then, with immense difficulty, once more. Jock had often acted as loader for me in the shooting field and he would recognize the three-shots distress-signal.

I waited for an eternity. I dared not spend any more cartridges on signals: I needed them in case the madman came back. I spent the time trying to keep awake – each time I started to fade out my weight came on the ear with excruciating effect – and in trying to remember whether it was Lobengula or Cetewayo who used to nail minor offenders to trees. They had to tear *themselves* loose, you see, before the hyenas got them.

At last I heard a bellow from Jock, the most welcome bellow of my life. I croaked an answer. The bellow came nearer. When Jock finally loomed up before me I levelled the pistol at his belly. An hour before, I would have trusted him with my life but tonight the world was insane. All I could think of was that I was not going to be hurt any more. He stepped closer. I sniffed hungrily. There was no trace of the loathly stench of the witch.

'You all right, Mr Charlie?' he asked.

'Eye aws ogen,' I explained.

'Eh?'

'Aw ogen,' I explained crossly, pointing to my chin.

'Jaw broken. Lumme, so it is.'

'Ailed oo ee,' I added, pointing to my ear.

He struck a match and hissed with distress when he saw the plight I was in. The nail, it seems, had been driven in to its very head; my ear had puffed up around it and was full of blood.

'I don't reckon I could get a claw-hammer under it, Mr Charlie. Think I'll have to cut it.'

I didn't want to know what he was going to do: I just wanted him to do it, so that I could lie down and get to sleep. I made vigorous motions towards the ear and shut my eyes hard.

I couldn't grit my teeth while he cut a channel from the head of the nail to the edge of my ear, because my teeth wouldn't meet but I remember weeping copiously. He asked me to move my head. No good: the bit of gristle under the head of the nail held fast. There was a long pause then, to my horror, I felt the point of his knife against the corner of my eye. I wrenched away convulsively and screamed as the ear came free.

'Sorry, Mr Charlie,' he said as he gathered me up from the kindly mud.

The next time I woke up, Jock was dragging me out of the car and into the Emergency part of the General Hospital in St Helier. He propped me up against the counter, where a kindly but stern lady was making tut-tutting noises at me. She handed Jock a form to fill in: I snatched it and scrawled 'SEE IF JOHANNA OK'. Jock nodded, lowered me to the floor and vanished.

The time after that, I awoke under a fierce white light and a compassionate black face. The latter seemed to belong to a Pakistani doctor who was doing fine embroidery on my ear. He beamed at me.

'Werry nasty accident,' he assured me. 'You may thank lucky stars you are in land of living.'

I started to open my mouth to say something witty about Peter Sellers but found that I couldn't. Open my mouth, I mean. It was all sort of wired up and my tongue seemed to be trapped in a barbed-wire entanglement.

'Please to keep quite still,' said the nice doctor, 'and you will be as new in twinkling of eye. If not, all my good work is gone for Burton.'

I kept still.

'Nurse,' he called over his shoulder, 'patient is now on surface.'

The stern lady from Casualty Reception appeared, waving forms.

'Just name, address and next of kin will do for now,' she said, not too sternly. I lifted a pen weighing a hundredweight and wrote. She went away. A moment later she was back, whispering to the doctor.

'Mr Mortdecai,' he said to me, 'it seems we have just admitted a lady of the same name: is she with you? Mrs Johanna Mortdecai?'

I started to get up; they held me down. I fought them. Someone put a needle in my arm and told me gently that the doctor seeing to Johanna would come to see me presently. Unwillingly, I passed out.

When next I awoke I was in a warm, tight bed and a warm, scratchy nightshirt which was soaked with sweat. I felt like hell and a thousand hangovers: death seemed infinitely desirable. Then I remembered Johanna and started to get up but a little, thin nurse held me down without effort, as though she were smoothing a sheet. A new face appeared, a large, pale chap.

'Mr Mortdecai?' he said. 'Good morning. I'm the doctor who has been attending to your wife. She's going to be all right but she's rather badly torn and has lost a good deal of blood.'

I made frantic writing gestures and he handed me a pen and a pad.

'Raped?' I wrote.

'To tell the truth, we don't know. There seems to be no damage down there, although there are extensive injuries elsewhere. We can't ask her about the other thing because she is in deep shock: I'm afraid he hurt her rather badly.'

I took up the pen again.

'Is her ear badly disfigured?' I wrote.

He looked at the words for a long time, as though he couldn't understand them. Slowly he met my eyes, with a look so compassionate that I was frightened.

'I'm sorry, Mr Mortdecai, I thought you knew. Her injuries are not the same as yours at all.'

16

Let us rise up and part; she will not know.
Let us go seaward as the great winds go,
Full of blown sand and foam; what help is here?
There is no help, for all these things are so,
And all the world is bitter as a tear.
And how these things are, though ye strove to show,
She would not know.

A Leave-Taking

The next month or so was pretty rotten. If your mouth is all wired together, you see, you can't brush your teeth and if you also catch a cold, as I did, the whole situation becomes squalid beyond belief. Moreover, they had fitted a beastly tube into one nostril and down into my gullet, and it was through this that they fed me nameless, though probably nourishing, pap. Worse, every book I started to read seemed to carry, on the third or fourth page, wonderfully vivid descriptions of gravy soup, oysters, roasted partridges and steak-and-kidney puddings. Whenever I quaked with lust for food, the little thin nurse would clip a bottle on to my nose-tube and fill my poor stomach with the costive pap, at the same time trying to slip an icy bed-pan under my bottom. Naturally, I never put up with this latter indignity: I used to stride – or perhaps totter – to the loo under my own steam, festooned with protesting nurses and with gruel streaming from my nosetube: an awesome sight I dare say.

When I had some strength I found out where Johanna was and used to creep out and visit her. She was pale and looked much older. I couldn't talk and she didn't want to. I would sit on the side of her bed and pat her hand a bit. She would pat mine a bit and we would wink at each other in a wan sort of way. It helped. I arranged through Jock for flowers and grapes and things to be sent to her at frequent intervals and she arranged, through Jock, for me to receive boxes of Sullivan's cigarettes and things like that. The night nurse, who was fat and saucy, contrived to fiddle a straw into my mouth through a gap where a tooth is missing behind my upper left canine; thereafter I was able, each evening, to drink half a bottle of Burgundy, which blunted the edge of misery a little.

The doctors were pleased with my jaw, they said it was mending well but my ear went bad and they had to cut some of it off, and then the rest of it. That was why Johanna was discharged quite a bit earlier than I was.

My homecoming was not jolly; Johanna had known about the ear but she was a bit taken aback when she saw me without it (I'd discharged myself the moment they took the bandages off) and she burst into tears – a thing I'd never seen her do before. I made a few jests about how she had never thought much of my looks anyway and the lop-sided effect might grow on her but she was inconsolable. I shall never understand women. You probably think you do but you're wrong, you know. They're not a bit like us.

In the end I took her gently to bed and we lay there hand in hand in the dark so that she could cry without my seeing her eyes get puffy and we listened to *Le Nozze di Figaro* which turned out to be a bad mistake: one forgets that it's not nearly such a lighthearted piece for people who understand Italian. As Johanna does. When it came to *Dove Sono* she really broke down and wanted to tell me all about what had happened on that dreadful night. This was too much for me, I simply wasn't up to it; I rushed downstairs and fetched a tray of drinks and we both got a little drunk and then it was better, much better; but we both knew that I had let her down. Again. Well, that's the price you pay for being a coward. I only wish one could be told exactly how much the instalments are, and when they are likely to fall due. A moral coward, you see, is simply someone who has read the fine print on the back of his Birth Certificate and seen the little clause which says 'You can't win'. He knows from then on that the smart thing to do is to run away from everything and he does so. But he doesn't have to like it.

'Jock,' I said the next morning. 'Mrs Mortdecai will not be down to breakfast.' I looked at him levelly. He twigged. His good eye crumpled up into a huge wink, which left the glass one – carelessly inserted – leering up at the cornice. Sure enough, he had read my mind and the eggs and bacon, when they arrived, were mounted on delicious fried bread and accompanied by fried potatoes, all quite counter to Johanna's 'Standing Order Concerning Mr Mortdecai's Waistline'. Well, dash it, why should I persecute my waistline; it's never done me any harm. Yet.

The last fried potato had captured the last runlet of egg-yolk and was about to home in on the Mortdecai waistline when George and Sam appeared. They looked grave and friendly for I too, now, had suffered, I was a member of the club – but they both looked askance at the marmalade and richly-buttered toast which Jock brought in at that moment. Sam never breakfasts and George believes that breakfast is something that gentlemen eat at a quarter past dawn, not at half-past noon.

I waved them to chairs and offered them richly-buttered toast and marmalade. They glanced at it with ill-concealed longing but refused: they were strong; *strong*.

I knew most of their news: there had been only two rapes in the intervening period and one of those had been a bit suspect: a young Jersey girl who was already a teeny bit pregnant by a fiancé who had absent-mindedly joined a boat going to Australia. The other incident bore all the marks of being 'one of ours' but the victim was a hopeless witness, even by female standards, and could add nothing to our dossier.

George and Sam had been patrolling in a desultory and half-hearted way but with no results except that Sam said he had chased a mackintoshed suspect for half a mile but had lost him in the outbuildings of one of George's tenant-farmers. A search had produced nothing but a pair of bicycle-clips in a disused cow-stable.

Sonia was quite recovered. Violet was much worse: clearly catatonic now, having to be watched night and day.

George was withdrawn and morose; Sam was in a state of suppressed hysteria which I found disturbing: long silences punctuated by random and bitter witticisms of poor quality. Not at all the Sam I had known and loved.

News exhausted, we looked at one another dully.

'Drinks?' I asked, dully.

George looked at his wristwatch; Sam opened his mouth and shut it again. I poured drinks. We drank three each, although we had had no luncheon. Johanna joined us. By the hard light of noon she looked older by ten years but her air of command was still there.

'Well, have you boys made a plan?' she asked, looking at me, bless her.

We made three apologetic grimaces. Sam started to sketch out a smile but gave up at the attempt. George cleared his throat. We looked at him wearily.

'Let's go fishing,' he said. 'My bass-boat's all new-painted and varnished and they're putting it into the water tomorrow. Do us all good, a bit of a sail. Try for some mackerel, eh?'

Sam and I, by our silences, registered total disapprobation. George on land is merely brigadier-like; at sea his mission seems to be to prove that Captain Bligh was a softy.

'Oh yes, Charlie, do go!' cried Johanna. 'A bit of a sail will do you so much good, and I would adore some fresh mackerels.'

I shifted sulkily in my chair.

'Or pollocks,' she added, 'or basses or breams. *Please*, Charlie?'

'Oh, very well,' I said. 'If Sam's coming.'

'Of course,' said Sam bitterly, 'of course, of *course*.'

'Wonderful!' said Johanna.

'Nine o'clock, then?' said George.

'Dark by that time,' I said.

'Got a dinner engagement at eight,' said Sam.

'I meant nine a.m.' said George.

We stared at him. Finally he settled for immediately after luncheon and, later still, agreed that this should be construed as 2.30 p.m.

By an excess of zeal, I was at Ouaisné Bay at three minutes short of 2.30 p.m. Clearly, the thing to do was look in at the pub on the shore and seek a fortifying drop of this and that. Sam was already there, fortifying himself diligently.

We grunted, then sat for a while in a silence broken only by the steady sip-sipping noise of two born landsmen about to embark on a sixteen-foot boat captained by another landsman with a Nelson-complex. George stamped into the bar and stared rudely at us.

'Hullo, sailor!' we cried in unison. We had not expected him to smile, so we were not disappointed.

'Waiting for you for five minutes,' he said. 'Can you tear yourselves away? Got any dunnage?'

Sam's dunnage consisted of a slim volume of verse wrapped in a plastic bag to keep typhoons out. Mine was a sou-wester and full oilskins (because the meteorologists had predicted calm, sunny weather), one flask each of hot soup, hot coffee and the cheaper sort of Scotch whisky, my sandwich-case and a pot of cold curried potatoes in case of shipwreck or other Acts of God. George carried a battered, professional-looking ditty-bag full, no doubt, of *sensible* things.

The boat, I must say, looked splendid in all its beginning-of-season paint and varnish and carried a huge, new outboard motor. George's ubiquitous Plumber, who also acts as his waterman, helped us to launch; the new motor started without trouble and we sailed away across little dancing blue waves which stirred even my black heart. There was a light haze which was probably thicker further out, for the doomily-named *La Corbière* ('The Place of Ravens' – our friendly neighbourhood lighthouse) was giving out its long, grunting moan every three minutes, like a fat old person straining at the seat. We recked not of it. In no time we were the best part of a mile out and George bade us troll our lines for mackerel. We trolled, if that is the word I want, for half an hour, but to no avail.

Puffins, shags and smews passed overhead, puffing and shagging and doing whatever smews do, but they weren't interested in that bit of water. Moreover, there were no gulls feeding, and no gulls means no fry and no fry means no mackerel.

'There are no mackerel here, George,' I said, 'moreover, we are going too fast for mackerel; two or three knots would be better.'

'Nonsense,' he replied.

I kneaded a piece of Marmite sandwich and a piece of cheese ditto into a lump on a larger hook, added a heavier weight to my line and almost at once boated a fine big pollock. George glared. I slipped Sam a lum of my mixture and soon he, too, had a good pollock.

'Keep it up, George,' I said, 'this is the perfect speed for pollock.'

'Mackerel obviously not in yet,' he grated. 'Going to bear in a bit, find some broken water and try for bass.'

La Corbière groaned, muffling deeper groans from Sam and me. There's nothing we like better than broken water, of course, but we prefer to brave it with a professional boatman at the helm. In we went, though, and found a stretch of the stuff which looked as though it might serve, although it was unpleasantly close to a razor-edged miniature cliff at the shoreline. Worse was to come.

'Going to step the mast,' said George; 'run up a scrap of sail, then we can cut this engine, get a bit of quiet.'

I am nothing of a mariner but this appalled me. I looked at Sam. He looked at me.

'George,' said Sam gently, 'are you certain that's wise? I mean, isn't this a lee-shore or something?'

'Rubbish,' he said. 'A shore is only a lee-shore if there's an on-shore wind. There is no wind at present but at this time of a warm day we can depend upon some light off-shore airs. And I must remind you, Sam, that there can only be one skipper in a boat: disputing an order can *kill* people.'

'Aye, aye,' said Sam, in a puzzled, insubordinate voice.

I started to remember that I hadn't heard *La Corbière* for some minutes, wondered whether a breeze had got up to dissipate the haze, but too late now. George had raised and locked the little mast into its tabernacle and was halfway up it, wrestling with the daft little leg-o'-mutton sail, when the first gust out of the South-East hit us.

Over we went on to our beam-ends, the outboard motor screaming as the screw found no water to bite, George dangling then vanishing overside amidst a raffle of canvas and cordage. In we drove to the murderous rock, beam on, until a fearful gnashing noise told us that the mast had gone and we felt our craft strike – not with a crash but a nasty, mushy sensation. Bubbles came up from where George must be. I seized an oar and fended us off as best I could; Sam grabbed the gutting-knife and slashed and hacked us free from the raffle of wreckage overside. We caught one glimpse of George, face up, an arm flailing, then the undertow seemed to catch him and he vanished under the boat. He reappeared after a minute, twenty feet to seaward, still with one arm thrashing the water; we ground against the rocks again and again. I fended us off with one oar. The motor coughed and died. Like the fools we were, none of us was wearing a life-jacket, nor was there visible a length of casting-line to throw to George. As I battled with the oar Sam crawled to the little forepeak and rummaged frantically, dragging out our dunnage in search of anything useful; then kneeling, frozen, staring at what he had ripped out of George's sea-bag. It was a tight ball of cloth, wrapped about with $\frac{1}{4}''$ line. Sam raised this to his nose and made a face of loathing.

'What the hell are you doing?' I screamed against the rising noise of wind and sea. He didn't answer. He undid the parcel: it was a mackintosh, the cuffs and shoulders studded with nails. From it he drew a hideous rubber mask. He didn't look at me; he wiped his fingers on a thwart and looked to where George had thrashed his way, one-armed, almost to the side of the boat. Sam took the other oar and slowly, as though carrying out some ritual gesture, raised it two-handed high above his head, blade upwards.

George had his good hand on the gunwale now and we could see a great flap of skin hanging from his scalp and the bloody ruin of his crushed arm. He looked at Sam. His hand left the gunwale and his face vanished. Sam threw the oar into the boat, then lurched aft to the motor. I fended off for dear life: our timbers couldn't take much more punishment from those granite daggers. The engine roared into life; Sam revved it until it screamed and then suddenly we were in open water. I started to bail. Once, looking over my shoulder, I thought I saw something half a furlong away with an arm up-raised, but it was probably only a cormorant.

We were in sight of Ouaisné Bay before either of us said a word.

'I suppose he must be dead by now?'

I didn't answer: it hadn't really been a question. And I was thinking.

'Sonia wasn't raped,' I said flatly.

'No. We'd been lovers – if that's a word fit to use – for months. First time was an accident, both drunk at a party. After that she made me do it again and again; swore she'd tell George if I didn't. That first day of all this, when you and George came home unexpectedly, we thought we were caught and I told Sonia to yell "rape" while I got out of the window. She'd been reading all that muck about the Beast of Jersey, that's what put all the witchcraft trimmings into her head.'

'But George worked it out. What he did to Violet was revenge, simply?'

'Yes. Perhaps he was telling us that he knew. I should have realized. Suppose I was too upset to think it through.'

'I see. Then he must have got a sort of taste for it, I suppose. Brought out a streak of insanity in him, perhaps?'

'An officer and gentleman,' said Sam. He made it sound like the punch-line of a vile joke.

I finished bailing and tied George's horrid paraphernalia to the spare anchor and threw it over the side. I didn't care whether someone might fish it up, I just wanted it out of my sight.

The Plumber met us on the beach, helped us haul-up on to the trailer.

'Where's Mr Breakspear, then?'

'Lost overside. We were nearly wrecked. Tell the Coast-guard, would you.'

'My Chri',' said the Plumber. Then, 'Oh, there's a phone call at the pub for Mr Davenant, from England, urgent. You have to ask for the Personal Calls Operator.' Sam started to walk towards the pub, then broke into a shambling run.

'So it was Mr Breakspear all the time,' said the Plumber.

I didn't answer. I was wondering how many people had known all the time. Perhaps I should have asked my gardener. Perhaps he would even have told me.

Sam came out of the pub, bleak-faced.

'Violet has killed herself,' he said carefully. 'Let's go home. Things to do.'

'Have to go to the police first,' I said. 'Report George missing.'

'Yes, of course. I'd forgotten about that.' His voice was gentle now.

'Don't you want your fish?' the Plumber called after us.

'No, thanks,' I said. 'We know where they've been.'

It was dark when we left the Police Station and drove up the *Grande Route de S. Jean* towards our homes.

'Want to talk?' I asked diffidently.

'Vi was left alone for a moment – nurse went to the loo – and she just got out of bed and hurled herself through the closed window. Can't blame the nurse; Vi hadn't stirred for days. They warned me, of course. Catatonics think they can fly, you see. Angels.'

'Sam –' I started.

'Please shut up, Charlie.'

I tried again when we got to his house.

'Look,' I said, 'won't you please stay with us tonight?'

'Good night, Charlie,' he said and shut the door.

At home, I told Johanna about things as briefly as I could, then announced that I wanted to write letters. I went up to my dressing-room and stood at the open window, in the dark. Across the fields Sam's house was a blaze of lights, then, one by one, they started to go out. I gripped the window-sill. It was very cold and a thin rain sifted on to my face.

When the shot came I stayed where I was.

Jock drifted into the room.

'Shot from over Cherche-fuites way,' he said.

'Yes,' I said.

'Heavy-calibre pistol, by the sound of it.'

'That's right.'

'Well, are we going over there?'

'No.'

'You going to phone then, Mr Charlie?'

'Get out, Jock.'

Five minutes later Johanna crept in and took one of my arms in both of hers, pressing it to her poor breast.

'Dear Charlie, why are you standing here in the dark and shivering. And *crying*? All right, I'm sorry, I'm sorry, of course you're not crying, I can see you're not.'

But she closed the window and drew the curtains and led me to my bed, making me lie down, spreading a quilt over me.

'Good night, Charlie,' she said. 'Please sleep now.'

'Oh, very well,' I said. But I would have liked to tell her about it.

'Johanna,' I said, as she opened the door.

'Yes, Charlie?'

'I forgot to ask – how is the canary?'

She didn't answer.

'He's dead, isn't he?'

She closed the door, very gently.